To. Pat
with love

March 2012

CW00802827

Bitter Triangles

Amy Lecouteur

authorHOUSE®

AuthorHouse™ UK Ltd.
500 Avebury Boulevard
Central Milton Keynes, MK9 2BE
www.authorhouse.co.uk
Phone: 08001974150

First published by AuthorHouse 4/5/2010

ISBN: 978-1-4490-4480-0 (sc)

Printed in the United States of America
Bloomington, Indiana

This book is printed on acid-free paper.

I dedicate this novel with thanks to late Nanna Bess and Grand dad Joe. Also Margery, Trevor and to all who gave me support at that difficult time. If it had not been for the love of my children. I would not have survived.

Contents

Chapter One
Hannah Looks Back

Hannah awoke; she was lying on a bed. She sensed that some one was standing near. Where was she? As her eyes began to focus she saw that, the person standing by the bed was a nurse wearing a blue uniform. The nurse was fixing a bag of blood above the bed? Hannah realised that she was in the Oswestry Orthopaedic hospital and as she became more conscious she now knew why she was there. Immediately she tried to wriggle her toes and to her utmost joy and relief she found that she could do so. Relief flooded her body she was not paralysed. Thank goodness for that. She consequently went back to sleep to be woken again by the immense pain that she felt in her back. Three men were standing by the bed.

One of the men was Mr Einenstien the surgeon who Hannah had met when she had been admitted in June for assessment He had seemed such a friendly man. As Hannah' eyes became more focused she had a clearer picture of him. Underneath an open white coat she saw that he was dressed in a navy blue faintly striped suit. He was a man who she had estimated to be about fifty years old; he had brown hair that was starting to go grey. It was cut fairly short but looked tussled as if it needed a comb running through it. He also wore a short greying beard and dark rimmed glasses. One of the other two men, Hannah also recognised; he was a tall man of what had seemed to Hannah to be of Indian Origin. He had been the surgeon who two days previously had spelled out all the risks that she was taking by having this spinal surgery performed.

Mr Einenstine spoke in a low soft voice asking how she felt, Hannah tried to reply and make conversation but she started to be sick. The pain in her back was unbearable a nurse quickly came forward and gave her an injection to stop her being sick. The three men talked with each other for a few moments and then they smiled down at Hannah and left the ward. Hannah was instructed to use the morphine to help the pain and was told to press the green button on the hand control, which was just in front of her on the bed. This was attached to an electric cable. This she pressed immediately and found that it gave instant and great relief. The next few days were very tough; Hannah had been taking morphine for months to help cope with the pain that she had been suffering from the injury to her spine. Now she was given only a tiny amount. With the after effects of taking so much morphine and the amount of anaesthetic that she had been given so that the surgeons could do their work which had taken several hours. Hannah felt so ill all she wanted to do was close her eyes and die. Hannah struggled to cope for the next few days and with the careful nursing that she was given she soon began to make an improvement and begin to walk again.

Two weeks later she was allowed back home and was making good progress no more morphine was taken only mild painkillers, which gradually became unnecessary. The operation had been a success and she was now able to walk unaided. Mr Einenstine had explained to her back in June when she had been admitted for assessment that if she went ahead with the operation and if it turned out to be successful, which of course he hoped that it would, she would be in for a long haul over the next twelve months and he hoped that she would make a full recovery. Hannah had replied that she would be prepared, so consequently she had been placed on the official waiting list. She had first been to her local GP at the beginning of February and it was now the second week in October, at last she was finally admitted for the surgery to take place. Hannah had been through many set backs and struggles in life before and she had survived, she was not going to give in now. To be able to walk with out the use of crutches and have no further need to be pushed in a wheel chair was pure magic. She had convinced her-self that she would have needed those for the rest of her life. Now thanks to the skill of Mr Einenstien the orthopaedic surgeon and his staff and modern technology Hannah was able to walk again unaided.

Hannah was now in her retirement years and as she looked back over the years, she asked herself. "Why, oh why, had every thing been so hard and difficult why had there been so many battles to be fought?

Life had dealt her so many blows and many were the time when she felt that she had only her self to blame. She thought of the time when Timothy Ford had died. She wondered if at the time, she should have spoken out and told how Noel had been chasing him and getting the child so excited. He had taken no notice of her when she had told him to stop. She had felt badly let down by him at the inquest. She also thought about how she had left home. Would she have been better off if she had had listened to her parents and stayed and worked on the farm as Mary had done. Her parents Fred and Dorothy Thomas were now dead and gone. Four of her six sisters were now retired her brother William and her youngest sister Sandra still had a few years to go before they reached retirement. Hannah had asked her self so many times if she could ever forgive her sister Sandra and the first and only love of her life George Fleming. She would argue that if she could finally forgive the two of them she knew that she would never forget the hell and misery that they had put her through so many years ago.

Hannah had found that life had been hard going right from the start when she had stood up to her mother and decided to leave home. Hannah had been thinking and pondering about what she was going to do when she left The Wellington High school for Girls at the end of the summer term She only had three weeks to go before she finished her school days there was no chance what so ever of her being able to go to university and become a school teacher as she had always wanted.

She and Mary were sat on the grass hedge bank soaking up the warmth of summer sun shine. It would be quite hot later in the day they had been along to the spring and taken a long and thirsty drink from the steel bucket Joyce Wilkins had put to fill. The water was clear and cool they were in no hurry to restart working. Fred had asked the two of them to go to the top field and cut unwanted thistles

"Have you decided what you want to do when you leave school?" Asked Mary

"No not as yet. But I think that I had better give it some thought. I don't fancy cutting thistles for a living"

"What about working in an office? I reckon that you could manage that. Mam could not say a lot it would be very little different than going to school and you would get paid for it? Or you could stay at home and work with me. I am sure there will be plenty of work for both of us, especially now that Dad is thinking of sowing sugar beet. If Dad can't find us both enough to do I am damned sure Mam will"

"Sugar beet, no I don't think that I want to stay at home all the time, you could be right about working in an office. I will have a look in the journal tonight and see if anyone is advertising for a junior clerk. I want to be paid a proper wage not like you. Just given pocket money and having to work so hard, I am too small and thin to be able to do farm work all day long. I would like to have a nice new bike like the one Lizzy has and not have to keep using that thing that Mam has bought me for going to school. "

"What is wrong with the bike that you have got? It gets you to where you want to go, does it not? At least you have a bike of your own; I still have to manage with Mam's old one".

Hannah thought it best to drop the subject of bikes it caught a raw nerve with Mary.

She said no more but later that evening she saw that Mam had bought the Wellinton Journal earlier in the day when she had been shopping. Hannah read the vacancies advertised in it and she saw that Turners the corn merchants were advertising for a junior clerk. She told Mary about it

"Well go and see about it if you think that is what you want to do make an appointment to have an interview and see if you are successful, there is no harm in your trying. I should wait before you say anything to Mam about it and then you can say something when you are sure that you have an interview. If you keep quiet and don't say any thing to her at all, she will want to know why you are making a special effort to dress nice just to go to town. I would wear that red dress with the white dots that Grandma gave you, that cast off of Beccy's. I know that is not the colour that you like but it is a very smart frock and it looks as if it cost a lot more than what Mam would pay for a dress for me"

"You are right Mary I don't like the colour red it clashes with my red nose. I hate always having a red nose".

"So what. Dad always has a red nose. You are very much like him. There are worse things than having a red nose When you start to work and earn some money of your own you will be able to buy your self some face powder and a powder puff that would help to tone it down a bit".

The next day Hannah called in Turners on the way home and asked about the vacancy and made arrangements to have an interview on the Saturday morning.

On Friday evening when her mother went outside to see to her chickens Hannah quickly fetched the red and white spotted dress from upstairs and pressed it with the flat iron and a damp teacloth. She hung it over the wooden chair in the bedroom that she shared with Helen and Sandra. She had bought a new pair of white socks using the money she had earned the previous weekend. Her shoes were cleaned until they shone; hoping that tomorrow Saturday would be another dry day. She would be up early and get her jobs done so that she would have plenty of time left to wash all over, including her hair. She would need time to brush it dry so that it would shine.

Just as she was about to go to bed Hannah told her Mother about the interview she had arranged for next morning Hannah thought that if she left it as late as she possibly could, her mother would have less time to put up an argument against the idea. Hannah knew that her mother was secretly hoping that she would stay and work at home, if her mother started shouting Hannah could just go to bed and say no more

"Tell me how long have you known about this? And why have you not said any thing about this before now?" Dorothy raised her voice as she looked up from the newspaper. "I saw the advert in last week's paper so I called after school on Friday. They said that I could go for an interview tomorrow. It will be all right if I get the job. I will still be able to help with the jobs here when I come home at night. It won't be much difference from what I am doing now" Hannah stammered.

"I'll see what your Dad has to say about this, but I suppose that there will be no harm in your going tomorrow and seeing what they have to say. I don't think that office work will be too bad of a job. Turners have been going for a good number of years". She said sarcastically.

Dorothy quickly became annoyed and angry if any one of the girls were planning to do any thing with out first consulting her. She considered that they must have her permission prior to making any firm decisions which they thought might be of benefit to them. She had not really forgiven Grace for leaving and taking the job to live in with out first consulting her and allowing her to go and see for herself if the job and place was suitable.

Dorothy was not going to admit to the rest of the family, that it was a relief in a way, the fact that she no longer had to worry about Grace's fancy ways as she called them. She often spoke to Mrs and Mr Reynolds when she saw them in the market hall but they did not have much time to pass the time of day. They were far too busy selling their fruit and vegetables, but they did assure her that they were extremely pleased with the help that Grace was able to give them. They also said that Grace seemed happy with her work. They were so glad that she was so capable looking after their little girl and that she was good with helping with cooking and general house keeping. Dorothy could not say much, she knew that there was no argument with that.

Hannah was up early on Saturday morning she had fetched the cows ready for milking by the time Fred had finished raking some life into the Rayburn and refuelling it. He had made the first cup of tea of the day. Hannah soon had her other jobs, feeding the poultry and letting them all out and she only had the calves to feed by the time every one else had risen.

"My goodness you are with it this morning" Mary said as she joined Hannah in the cowshed

"Yes I am, will you see to the dairy on your own today? I am going for that interview and I have to wash my hair. Thank goodness that it is not raining or my new socks would be ruined before I got as far as the Glen. There are only the calves to feed in the loose box then all is finished. Helen will be about to give Mam a hand in the kitchen".

"My you have got your self organised this morning have you not "Mary said sarcastically.

"Got to get a move on; Have you forgotten that I am going for that interview at Turners and I have to be there for ten o'clock? My hair is so thick that it takes ages to dry and if I don't brush it good and proper it will look as if I have been through a gorse bush backwards".

"I see what you mean". Mary was looking at Hannah's uncombed thick auburn hair." Be off with you I will finish the dairy and the rest of the jobs". Hannah took no second telling she went back to the kitchen to get her self ready; she was very pleased that it looked like being a really warm summer day. She collected a piece of sunlight soap from the kitchen sink, a towel as well as a clean pair of knickers. A vest and an old summer frock, she went into the dairy closing the door behind her. She knew that it would only be Mary that would need to come in to the dairy bringing the milk from the cow shed. Bernie would be too busy helping Fred. She quickly stripped herself down to her knickers and washed her hair. She wet it through by using the steel pint cup, which was kept, in the dairy for measuring milk. Hannah rubbed her hair all over with the soap as well as the top half of her now very wet body. Taking the cup she took clean water from the tub and rinsed all the soap from her hair, the soapy lather running down the dairy floor to the drain outside. She wrapped a towel around the top half of her body including her dripping hair; she quickly removed her knickers and stood in the tub to wash the rest of her body. The water was not very warm not much milk had gone through the cooler. Hannah did not mind she and her sisters were used to washing in cold water in the dairy, it saved carrying buckets of water up stairs to their bedroom and washing in the old galvanised bath. When finished Hannah put on the old summer frock and ran to the kitchen putting her dirty washing in the basket in the old larder ready for Tuesday's wash.

"I am hungry"; she said to herself. She took the frying pan from under the kitchen sink and some lard from the old brown basin in the larder She soon fried some bacon an egg and a piece of bread. It was just after eight o'clock according to the grandmother clock hanging on the kitchen wall. When the ending of the war was announced Fred had bought the clock for Dorothy, she had been so pleased about it. "Just some thing to celebrate with" Fred had said. Lizzy who was up and getting ready to go to work joined in and they had breakfast together

Her mother was still seeing to her chickens William and Sandra were still asleep in bed giving Hannah plenty of time to finish drying her hair and getting herself dressed. She would have to leave at about a quarter past nine to be in time for the interview at ten. The breakfast tasted good, Hannah had not realised just how hungry that she was. She washed it down with a cup of tea from the teapot left on the Rayburn. The tea tasted a bit revolting but she did not want to wait for the kettle to boil to make a fresh pot. Her mother would have considered that it was a waste of tea. Her mother considered that it was not the thing to do, to make pots of tea at any time of the day. After the early morning pot of tea had been made no more tea was made until every one came in for their breakfast and other meals of the day. The routine was only broken when and if they had visitors.

Upstairs Hannah quietly took her clothes from the bedroom so as not to wake Helen and Sandra. She could not decide if she should wear a brassiere or not. Grace had given her one of hers when she had left home. It was the only one that Hannah had, she had not developed like Grace, Mary and Lizzy she was more like Beccy and had remained very slim. Grace had told her to start wearing a brassiere to keep her self in shape, as this was the in thing to do. Dorothy still wore the old fashioned type of corsets, which were pin 'k and had bones in it for support and was laced together. She would stand at the sink scrubbing them on wash days. They had the suspenders attached to hold up her stockings. Now there were much more modern versions of the corset on the market, one could buy what was called a suspender belt. Or an all- in- one roll-on. Since the war had finished much finer stockings were coming onto the market called nylons. These were made of man made fibres not like the Lyle stockings that were made from wool. Dorothy and most of the older women wore those. Hannah had seen Grace wearing nylons to go to dances. She decided that once she started work she would be able to buy herself both a suspender belt and some decent nylon stockings. She decided against wearing the brassier today. She just wore a clean vest and knickers and a petticoat under the dress. The new white socks and Becky's hand down dress. Hannah thought that it looked good on her when she went to look at her self in the mirror of her mother's wardrobe she would have loved the dress but for the colour there was nothing that she could do about it. She sat on Liz's and Mary's bed and brushed and brushed her hair until it felt quite dry. She went down to the kitchen and was putting on her shoes, just as her mother came in to the kitchen.

"All dressed up I see. You would do far better working here than go looking for work. You're Dad and me can find enough for you to do with out you going working for strangers". She began to poke the Rayburn, which now had burnt low. She gave it more coal, putting the bucket down on the quarry floor with a thud. Fred, Mary and Bernie would soon in for their breakfast.

Hannah was good with animals and like Mary had never shown any fear of them. Dorothy was hoping that Hannah would have chosen to stay at home and not go and get employment elsewhere.

Hannah ignored her mother and went out of the kitchen to the garage to get her bike and made her way carefully to the road. How she enjoyed the ride in the warm morning sunshine, free wheeling down the banks to the Glen and then down the Ercall.

Nerves began to tell as she leant her bike along side of the wall of Turners premises; she walked into the front entrance and had to take a few deep breaths. It was a few minutes before she noticed the brass bell on the counter which had a note glued along side of it saying Ring for Service. Hannah lifted the bell and shook it gently hoping that it would not to ring too loudly. A middle-aged woman came through the door from what looked to be an office. She wore spectacles on the end of her nose.

"Good morning can I help you" Hannah felt the woman's eyes looking at her from head to toe.

"I have an interview arranged for today. "Hannah tried to hide the fact that the other woman scrutinising her so intently made her feel more nervous

"Oh yes you are Hannah Thomas I presume. Come with me into my office, and we will have a little chat".

Hannah followed her into her office, which was out of sight of the general customers. She just looks like Miss Turner a teacher from school thought. Hannah The woman had short cut hair showing signs of grey. She wore a frilly white blouse under her blue two piece suit. Hannah noticed the skirt of the suit was well worn and had lost its shape, probably from being continually sat on.

The woman turned to Hannah and pointed to a wooden chair.

"Please sit down. I am Mrs Jennings and you will be helping me. You will have a little office through there", she nodded towards another door leading from her office. It will be your job to sort invoices for me and make a note of what each customer has purchased. Also if they have paid for what they have had, I will enter the information into the account ledger. That will enable me to work out the monthly accounts, I am sure that you should be able to manage that". She went on to ask Hannah several questions about her schoolwork smiling at Hannah's ability with maths. You will answer to me and only to me, is that under stood? I will not accept mistakes being made in the accounts we do not want customers complaining that they don't owe for this or that. It would make my job far too difficult if I have to recheck through the invoices. I also warn you, that you are not to be seen in the yard where the men are working. Your wages will be one pound a week and you will be expected to work from nine o'clock in the morning until half past five in the evening and on Saturday mornings until one o'clock lunchtime, is, that understood?" Hannah nodded

"Very good, we understand each other. Incidentally I will not tolerate you coming to work late or taking days off unnecessarily. I will now show you the office where you will be working" She rose from her chair, and opened the door leading into another office.

"Now this is where you will be working". Hannah took one look at the small poky dark little room and she was so disappointed. If this was where she would be expected to work. The walls were half panelled with wood and the upper half of the walls had not been decorated for years. The only window was small showing little daylight because it needed a good cleaning both the inside and out. There was a wooden table placed by the one wall and a wooden chair to sit on a tin tray, which was on the table, contained some pens and pencils and a bottle of ink. "Oh Lordy", she thought "Do I have to sit in here all day, it will be worse than being in school". Mrs Jennings broke into her thoughts

"I am offering you the job and if you decide to accept the position, I am sure we will get along very well indeed, you will start work the first week of August. I have other girls to interview so you must confirm that you are accepting the job by Tuesday morning I expect you will want to see what your parents think about you working for us. Good bye "She showed Hannah out to the front of the building. That was the end of the interview

Hannah collected her bike from where she had left it, she had not the heart to get on it to cycle and hurry home. As she pushed the bike up the Ercall Hannah decided that she could not sit in that poky little office all day it would be worse than sitting at a desk in school. How was she going to tell her Mother that she did not want the job? She knew that her mother would argue that a job was a job and if you were suitable you did not turn it down. Hannah decided that she would call at the Glen and tell Lizzy about it and see if she would tell her what to say when she got back home. She put her bike in the back yard and went down the passage to the back door Mrs Green answered the door when she knocked

"Come to see Lizzy or is it the phone you want to use. My you do look smart. Been some where nice have you" She asked.

Hannah avoided answering all the questions.

"Just wanted to see Lizzy if she is not too busy"

"Come on in love I am sure that she can spare a few minutes although we do have a wedding on this afternoon Rushed off our feet we will be" Hannah followed her into the kitchen and sat on one of the stools Mrs Green pointed to.

"I'll go and find her" She disappeared from the kitchen and a few minutes later she came back with Lizzy

"What have you called for?" Lizzy asked. "Why have you not gone back home?" Hannah told Lizzy of the mornings events.

"I don't want to work at Turners

"Well did they offer you the job?" "Oh yes but I don't like it and I have got to tell Mam. You know that she will blow her top if I don't take it. I can't tell her that I am not good enough because I know that she will see Mrs Jennings when she goes into in there to order and pay the bills."

"Here have a cup of tea to give me a chance to think what you can say when you get back There is a fresh pot made and Mrs Podmore will be through in a minute". Lizzy poured the tea "Here drink this" She passed a cup of tea to Hannah and one to Mrs Green keeping one for herself.

Margaret Podmore joined them in the kitchen. Lizzy quickly rose and poured a fresh cup for Margaret Podmore who was quite surprised to see Hannah sitting there.

"My goodness you do look sorry for your self Hannah. Nothing wrong is there?"

Hannah told her of the job interview.

Margaret Podmore finished her cup of tea and then she asked Hannah to follow her into the second kitchen.

"I don't think that you would enjoy that job at all, as far as I can see you have worked out of doors far too much. I do know where there will be a job if you are interested. The daughter of Mr and Mrs Corfield, Pricilla Ford is coming home from London and bringing her two small boys with her. When Mr Corfield brought the milk this morning he was telling me that they would be looking for some one to help with the boys. He says that they will be able to manage the boys at the weekends so the job would be only during weekdays. He was saying that he does not do any veterinary work at the weekends. What do you think? Should I ask him if you could go and see about it? I am sure that you would be most suitable because he has seen you all growing up and knows you very well". She smiled at Hannah

"Give it some thought and if you are interested, Lizzy can tell me first in the morning. I will tell Mr Corfield and see what he has to say. Off you go and put a smile back on your face that is a smart dress that you are wearing". Hannah just smiled back but was reluctant to tell Margaret Podmore that the dress was a hand down of Becky's.

As she went the rest of the way home, Hannah felt relieved. The day was becoming much warmer; it would be a hot afternoon. The sun shone down through the trees as she pushed her bike up the banks and she was thinking how she was going to tell her Mother that she was not going to sit in that dingy office every week day. She put her bike away in the garage, her stomach was churning and she felt sick from nervousness and she was beginning to feel hungry. Hannah went into the kitchen and there was no sign of her mother. She went toward the door leading to the front room and the stairs to get changed into some old clothes and then go and find Mary.

"Well did you get the job". Hannah stopped in her tracks she had not noticed that her mother was seated the other side of the table doing farm accounts.

"Well yes and no" stammered Hannah.

"What do you mean they either offered you the job or they have not" Dorothy sounded angry at the thought of her daughter being turned down for such a menial office job.

"I can have the job but I don't want to take it" Hannah said watching for her mother's re-action.

"Why don't you want to take it? That is what I want to know?

"The place was horrible I don't want to sit in a dingy office all day"

"You would have been paid for sitting there. In that case you can stay at home and work along side of Mary there will be plenty of work for you to do here". Dorothy said very sternly as if the matter was now closed.

"There is another job that I can have. Mr and Mrs Corfield want a daily nanny to look after their two grandsons who are coming from London to live with them."

"When are these grandsons coming to live with them and how do you find out about this job?

"Mrs Podmore told me, I called in the other day when I posted that letter for you." Hannah lied, her face going bright red. Hannah hated having to tell a lie.

"That's why it took you so long was it, go and get out of that frock, it is almost dinner time, see where Mary, is, I am sure that she will give you some thing to do. As for working for the Corfield's we will have to think about that.

Hannah was glad to retreat to the bedroom. Later when she caught up with Mary in the buildings she had Sandra with her, they were sat on a couple of milking stools on the concrete outside the cowshed door. She told Mary of the mornings events.

"If you take my advice you should go for that job at the Corfield's, it will not be hard work and you will be at home in the evenings and at weekends and you will be able to keep your little job up the Wrekin. You will be able to give us a hand when we are busy".

"Where are Helen and William, there was no sign of them in the house?"

"Oh they went to the woods to fetch a bag of sticks"

"Have Mam and Dad not been into town this morning?

"No Dad reckons that there is too much to do. He wants to start the corn harvest soon making the most of Bernie".

Mary's bit of encouragement sounded great to Hannah. She decided that she would tell Lizzy tonight, so that Mrs

Podmore could arrange an interview with Mrs Corfield for her. Mary broke into Hannah's thoughts "Next time you go for an interview wear some stockings it would make you look a bit older, not so much like a school girl.

"Yes you could be right; I will buy some stockings with what I get paid for working at the Cottage to morrow".

Hannah asked Lizzy that night to arrange an interview for her to see Mrs Corfield and she said no more about it to her Mother.

Dorothy did not like Mrs Corfield. The Corfield's farmed a farm at Cluddely about the same size farm as Fred and Dorothy. The farmhouse and land was rented from the Orleton Estate. The house was three stories high, quite big and impressive. Mrs Corfield was the lady of the house and certainly liked to play the part. She was a very keen bridge player and she liked to be involved with different associations, especially the Conservative association. She enjoyed being lady of the manor and liked to do quite a lot of entertaining. There was a part time domestic cleaner, her husband and her son took care of the workmen and the every day running of the farm, Mr Corfield also did his veterinary work as he called it. Their only son Richard farmed another farm at Uppington on the West Side of the Wrekin. This farm was also rented and belonged to the same estate.

Dorothy considered that Ethel Corfield acted the part of being a lady and was far too big for her boots. Dorothy found out that Ethel Corfield had come from a family of no substance and had not had the education that she herself had been fortune enough to have. Dorothy also considered that Bill Corfield charged more than enough for the castrating of the pigs, bullocks and lambs and the colt.

"Just to keep that woman like a lady" Dorothy would complain when Fred received the bill for Bill Corfield's work, she could not really grumble Bill Corfield was still cheaper than having to call the vet to do the job.

On the way home from school on Monday Hannah bought herself a pair of stockings from Mc Clures with the three shillings that she had earned. The stockings that she bought were a mixture of Lyle and nylon; they were the only ones that she could afford. When she showed them to Mary she realised that she needed a suspender belt to keep them up or she would have to use home made elastic garters which were horrible to wear. Elastic garters were not too bad to use on three -quarter length socks, which came to just below the knee. To have to keep stockings up they were very uncomfortable to wear; they practically stopped ones circulation in the legs. The red rings after the garters were removed would itch for hours. Hannah had no more money and when she told Mary of her plight Mary offered to lend her a belt

"Oh thanks Mary, saved my bacon". She was so relieved when Lizzy came home and told her that Mr Corfield had told her that on Mrs Podmore's recommendation Mrs Corfield would like Hannah to go and see her on Saturday afternoon. Hannah washed and dressed putting on Mary's suspender belt and as she did so, one of the rubber buttons broke away. "Oh Lordy" She said to her self, Mary will kill me for this". She quickly went down to the front room and took a linen covered button from the sewing machine drawer and was able to improvise. A button or a sixpenny coin was often used to replace buttons breaking away from corsets or suspender belts. Hannah had ironed the red and white spotted dress using a damp cloth to press the pleats in place. Dorothy and Fred had gone to a farm sale so neither of them was about when Hannah took her bike and rode off down the road to see Mrs Corfield. She propped the bike by the wall leading to the back door and went and pulled the bell rope. She could hear the bell ringing in the passage just inside the door and the echo going far beyond. This Hannah had done many times before when she had taken messages for her father. She waited patiently and after some time she heard footsteps on the quarry floor approaching the door from the other side.

Mrs Corfield answered the door; she was a woman of almost six feet tall; she looked down at Hannah. She was bit awe inspiring.

"Hello" she said and smiled, promptly putting Hannah at ease. "Come in Hannah and we will have a little chat".

Hannah noticed that the paisley summer dress Mrs Corfield was wearing looked very well made and suited her tall slim figure. Her greying hair was cut short and looked as if she had just had it done by a professional hairdresser. It was waved but not too curly, perming was now becoming fashionable but more often than not the result was very frizzy and far too curly.

Hannah followed her as she led the way through the kitchen; she noticed that there was a cream coloured four-oven Aga cooker in the kitchen If only her mother could afford one of those. Mrs Corfield led the way through the dining room and in to what she referred to as the lounge and indicated to one of the armchairs for Hannah to be seated.

"I am sure that you can drink a cup of tea I most certainly can" She said kindly with a smile. "I will not be a moment" She left Hannah and went to the kitchen. Hannah looked about the room. The chairs were covered with pretty chintz material. Dark oak beams formed part of the ceiling just like the front room ceilings at home. A flower-patterned carpet of reds and greens was from wall to wall something that Hannah certainly was not used to. A china cabinet, which stood on what looked, like a writing bureau, displayed a china tea set and china ornaments which looked as if they had cost a considerable amount of money. Hannah had not seen much real china displayed before. She had seen the large selection of Coalport china displayed in the tearooms at the Forest Glen. Heavy velvet curtains draped the window restricting quite a lot the afternoon sun light but at the same time keeping the room cool from the heat of the day. A small highly polished wooden table with place mats was placed in front of the armchairs Hannah was taking it all in when Mrs Corfield returned to the room carrying a polished wooden tray and placed it on the table. She poured tea into two china cups from a decorated china teapot.

"There you are Hannah have a cup of tea" and she passed one of the cups and saucers to Hannah.

"Thank you." Hannah said appreciating the cup of tea. It was a very hot afternoon and she was glad of the tea to calm her nerves

"We know you quite well because of the messages that you have been bringing for your father and I think that you could be just what my daughter and I will be needing. I believe that you leave school in two weeks and that would suit us fine. My daughters marriage has broken down so consequently she is coming home bringing her two sons. One is called Timothy and he is six years old and the other one is called is James who is three years old and they will come here when the school that he is now attending finishes at the end of the summer term. My daughter Pricilla has worked it out that if you came to start work at eight fifteen in the morning, you could then supervise the children's breakfast and see to the cleaning of Timothy's shoes. Dress him ready, for my husband to take him to school it would then be your job to look after James for the rest of the day. Taking him for walks if the weather permits Playing with him in the garden etc. He still needs a rest some times in the afternoons I would like you then to prepare the vegetables for me to cook for the evening meal. Because of my husband's work we do not have our dinner at midday. If however Pricilla and myself have taken James out with us I will expect you to do some light house work to fill in your time all the washing goes to the laundry in Wellington accept for my daughter's finer things, these she will wash herself? This I am quite sure that you are already used to doing. If neither my daughter nor I were available we would like you to answer the telephone in our absence you will be required to write down any messages that are given to you. There will always be a writing pad and pencil on the chest in the hall way where the telephone is situated when you have written any messages down you must bring the piece of paper and put it under paper weight which is on the dresser in the kitchen. When answering the telephone, I would ask you to refer to your self as the maid. We will pay you twenty-five shillings a week and there will be no need to bring any food with you. You can have something to eat at lunchtime and then you will be free to go home at half past five in the evening. You will finish at one o'clock lunchtime on a Saturday. Also you may make use of the downstairs cloakroom. The bathroom upstairs is for our personal use".

Hannah was not used to drinking from china cups and was relieved to see it placed safely on the table, when she finished her tea. The maid indeed, she thought. Well except for that, the job sounded a very easy job to do. Far easier than the work that she had been doing at home. She felt the improvised button holding her stockings up had moved and was pressing into her leg making it uncomfortable to sit still and not wriggle in the chair. Hannah moved her position on the chair, twenty-five shillings a week sounded good. Hannah started to think what she would be able to afford A suspender belt would be the first priority. And perhaps a new bicycle

"I think that you and I will get on fine together unfortunately I suffer from the most dreadful migraine and I can sometimes be indisposed for most of the day. That is why I keep the rooms dim and cool it seems to help me." She smiled "Shall we say that you can start here a week next Monday Morning. Oh by the way the top three rooms have been turned into a self contained flat. It was done for evacuees during the war they are a lovely couple and have stayed with us since the ending of the war. They are no trouble to us; they both go out to work so you will only come into contact with them perhaps on a Saturday morning". Hannah agreed that she would take the job offered and that she would come, as Mrs Corfield has asked of her. She thanked her for the tea then stood up to leave praying and hoping that the button holding her stocking would not fall to the floor. That would be an awful embarrassment. Lucky for her it did not and she was glad to be shown out through the back door and take her bicycle and head for home.

"Well how did you get on "? Mary wanted to know when she saw Hannah already changed and coming into the yard.

"Ok "said Hannah. "How am I going to tell our Mam that I am going to work for Mrs Corfield? Oh Lordy she is not going to like it one little bit".

"Oh I don't know she will come round when she realises that you will be earning some money of your own and that she does not have to clothe you any more. Just keep out of her way as much as possible. When did you say that you start, a week on Monday well that is not long is it? The harvest will be more or less finished by then and you will be at home in the evenings so what more do you think that she will want".

"Heaven and earth if I know her "Hannah laughed.

Hannah told her mother what she had arranged with Mrs Corfield and she could see by the look that was on mother's face that she did not approve.

"Work for that stuck up woman I thought that if you would not work for us you could have chosen some thing better for yourself. Where has the big idea of being a schoolteacher gone to. I did not send you to that fancy school just to be a skivvy to the likes of lady Corfield. You say that you will finish at half past five so I suppose you will be home by six o'clock that will give you a bit of time to give a hand here when we are busy. There will be beet hoeing to do next year as well as hoeing the swedes and mangols"

Hannah hated hoeing it was a back aching job

"A school teacher" Hannah answered back. "The war put an end to that idea. There was too much to do here potato setting potato picking harvesting"

"Don't you go answering me back there was a war on and we had no choice. We had to grow as much as we could". Hannah decided not to continue any further with the conversation.

Chapter Two
Hannah Starts Employment

Hannah started her new job and found that she enjoyed looking after the two boys. There was so much that she was able to do with them. Taking them for walks playing all sorts of games on the lawn at the front of the house, which were cut and well cared for. When it rained there was colouring books and all sorts of toys that that kept them busy while Hannah prepared the vegetables for the evening meal.

Their mother Pricilla was a small petite woman who was about five foot- two more or less the same height as Hannah she had very dark hair and was an extremely beautiful woman. She wore very smart clothes the likes Hannah had not seen before Smart tailored suits and dresses, high heeled shoes that were so dainty they were just straps of leather that fastened over her feet. She had such small feet no more than a size four. She would put her shoes on the dresser in the kitchen and would clean them herself as she wished to use them. Hannah saw very little of her. Pricilla would be in the kitchen when Hannah arrived in the mornings wearing a very flimsy nightgown and dressing gown and the prettiest slippers on her feet. She would be giving the boys their breakfast and cooking some for her father and then she would retire back to bed and only came down stairs again at about eleven o'clock when she knew that her mother would have risen. Ethel Corfield was always very late getting up in the mornings. Unless they needed to go into town to do some shopping they would stay in the lounge until they needed food at what Hannah had always called dinnertime? Mrs Corfield and her family preferred to call this time of the day lunchtime. Pricilla would often disappear for days on end leaving the two boys in the care of her parents. Apparently she was making visits to London. Hannah often accompanied Mrs Corfield when she wished to go shopping so that Hannah could take care of the boys for her and not let them run loose in the shops while their Grandma concentrated on what she wished to purchase.

When Timothy did not have to attend school he and his brother would be downstairs in the kitchen, Grandpa keeping an eye on them. Hannah would feed them breakfast. One of Hannah's duties was to take tea to both their mother and their grandma. One morning Hannah almost dropped the tea tray when she had knocked the bedroom door and was told to enter. Pricilla was in bed with a very good looking man and as she roused from the pillars to make room for the tray on the bedside table Hannah saw that she and the man were naked to the waist. Pricilla rose to sitting position revealing her naked breasts and did not seem to be the slightest embarrassed. Hannah had never seen her mother naked or her older sisters they had always respected each other's privacy when washing and dressing she had only seen her dad naked to the waist when he washed himself and she had assumed every one wore nightwear. Hannah was glad to place the tray on the bedside table and disappear from the room as quickly as she could.

Hannah was really enjoying her job by the second week of September Timothy had started his new school in Wellington; James was a lovely little boy to take care of and to keep amused. She was able to go and help out at the Cottage on a Sunday and was at home in the evenings to give a hand with any of the work that was still to be done.

George and Thomas Fleming teased her dreadfully when she went to the Cottage. They did so whenever they got the opportunity. They knew that Hannah's face would go bright red. Mary and Hannah walked to the bottom of the hill with them most Sunday evenings. Mary enjoyed their company just as much as Hannah in fact Hannah had taken such a liking to older brother George she believed practically every thing he told her. One particular Sunday Mary had been unable to go to the Cottage both Fred and Dorothy had gone to a family do, and Mary had to stay behind and take care of things. Despite protesting that it was not fair that she should loose out. Dorothy offered to give her a bit of extra money if she would stay and keep an eye on things.

Hannah went to the cottage on her own. When Charlie and the boys were ready to leave, Hannah tagged along with them. At the bend by the farm buildings George suggested to Hannah that she could sit on the cross bar of his bike and have a ride to the bottom of the hill. Thomas noticed Hannah's hesitation and offered that she should have a ride with him. Hannah decided that George being the older of the two would be the safest bet,

"Ok then, anything for a laugh, now you go slowly, you know that it is very bumpy towards the bottom of the hill and I don't want to fall off and hurt my self;" she said. She moved toward George and his bike. She sat side-saddle on the cross bar as she had seen others do Hannah held on tightly to the handlebars.

"I will, I will ", George reassured her. Not believing his luck that Hannah had agreed to ride with him, he secretly had a crush for her. He had one hand on the bicycle handle bar and the other around Hannah. Bumpity bump they went down the track.

"Stay where you are "George said when they reached the bottom of the hill "I will give you a ride home". He turned and peddled his way to wards the Willow moors Thomas and Charlie followed.

Hannah felt George's face so close to her own and the closeness sent a tingle down her spine, she had never been so close to a young man before and this was a new sensation, she smiled with pleasure. When George stopped at the farm gate she got off the bike quickly and said good night to all three and thanked them for seeing her safely home.

The look that she saw in George's eyes said far more than just good night. He had Hannah spell bound. "That's all right "said Charlie you never know who hangs around these woods at night time see you next week end".

"You're looking pleased with your self". Dorothy remarked when Hannah went into the Kitchen "What have you been up to?"

"Nothing Mam, just had a good day" Hannah went on to make idle gossip about Mrs Watson and the family up the Wrekin. That night as she lay in bed, Hannah could still feel the warmth of George's face so close to her own. Her imagination ran riot with her. She wondered if ever he would try to kiss her and what would her re-action be if he did. Should she slap his face or allow him to kiss her again. She had always enjoying reading love stories. Jane Eyre, Wuthering Heights and many more. In her imagination she was always the one to be rescued by a handsome man and driven away into the sunset. Dorothy had not given the girls any sort of love she had been always too preoccupied with making money and now her thoughts were only for what could be done for William's future. She had shown so little interest in the girls, so consequently Hannah had received very little love in her life the only male contact that Hannah had known was when she had been a little girl. Sitting on her father's knee, as he rocked to and fro in his rocking chair in front of the kitchen range. Singing songs, which had been famous in the First World War. Such as, Oh, oh, Antonio oh. Roll out the Barrel and Hang out your washing on the Seigfreid line. George's closeness had stirred feelings that Hannah had not felt before.

Hannah and Mary continued to go to the Cottage throughout the winter months as there was always plenty for them to do, cleaning the tearooms ready for the spring trade. There were always a few people about during the winter months, even when the snow was on the ground. Some would have a go at skiing and others dragged sledges up the hill so that they could slide all the way down again. Charlie and the two brothers continued to go every weekend, there was so much for them to do. More firewood was needed during the winter months and it was their job to keep the shed full of logs. George and Thomas would overhaul the swing boats and repaint them

During the winter months George was making it obvious to Hannah that he fancied her His looks and secret smiles when no one else was looking causing Hannah's face to blush bright pink.

Mrs Corfield's son, who came to the farm to do the accounts, asked Hannah if she would be interested in buying a new bicycle he knew some one who ran a cycle factory in Coventry. He was often at the farm He took charge of some of the work for his father when his father was other wise engaged in his veterinary work. "I could bring a bicycle from the factory in bits and assemble it here; it would certainly work out much cheaper for you than if you bought one from the shops. You could then pay my Mother so much a week until you have paid the total amount off, I am going for two others and it would be no more trouble to bring a third. What do you say?" He smiled at Hannah as he drank from the large cup of coffee she had placed in front of him. Richard managed most of the accounts for his father such as the farm workers wages. He would park his car in the yard and being a tall man took long strides and was in the kitchen in no time at all, usually carrying a bundle of paperwork under his arm. He would go straight in to the dining room where he could spread his paperwork on the table and stay there undisturbed.

"I would love to have a new bike, I really, would and as you have suggested I could pay you for it so much every week. That would be a wonderful idea. Thank you for thinking about me"

"Good, so that is settled, I will be going next week and I will see what I can get the factories are certainly getting going again. The war held things up for a while there was no making of such things as cars, bicycles and many other things".

That evening Hannah was smiling all the way home. To think that I would have a new bike of my own and be able to pay so much a week it will be wonderful. She told her Mother of the idea that night and Dorothy was not very pleased.

"What is wrong with the bike that you already have, it cost me enough when you went to school at Wellington. It will last a lot longer with a bit of care. And as for paying so much a week I have never heard of such things. What do the Corfield's think they are doing encouraging you to get into dept and you have hardly been there five minutes? I am not very happy about it I can tell you but I suppose that you will not listen to me now that you are mixing with that fancy lot". She gave the Rayburn fire a good poking with the steel poker, which she always did when she did not approve of any thing.

Hannah went to bed and decided that she would have the bicycle despite her Mother not being in favour of it. Mary was a bit peeved when Hannah told her about having a new bike. She asked Mary why her Mother had such a bad attitude towards the Cornfields. As far as Hannah could see they only wanted to help her to be able to have a new bike a bit cheaper. What was so wrong about that?

"A new bike" Mary raised her voice "I still have to manage with Mam's old one and I would not have that if Grace had not left home"

Hannah decided to say no more about bikes she just let the matter rest. She would wait and see what this bike was like when Richard Corfield collected it from the factory. She knew that her Mother did give Mary a little money but what she had was not like a weekly wage like Hannah was doing. A certain amount every week so that she could choose how to spend it. Dorothy had told Hannah that now that she was earning she should pay some thing towards the cost of sleeping at home at nights.

Hannah had ignored this as she gave a hand with whatever needed doing when she came home in the evening. She did spend some money on little things for her mother such as a box of fancy cakes or a pretty handkerchief. Hannah had very little to eat at home, no breakfast in the mornings and she would only have a sandwich before she went to bed. There was the fastening up of the poultry buckets and buckets of water to be pumped to fill the troughs in the deep litter shed. Hannah felt that she earned what little keep her Mother gave her.

Richard kept his word and Hannah was so proud of her new bike. The frame was painted black but the colour did not matter. The handlebars were chromium plated and so were the wheel rims, they shone with the newness. Hannah was thrilled to bits with it. She vowed that she would give it a good clean every week. Neither Dorothy nor Mary said any thing more about it. There was not much that they could say or do. The bike was Hannah's and she was paying for it, five shillings a week was taken from her wages.

Hannah was often asked to pluck a pheasant for Mr Corfield's evening meal, this job she did not mind where-as Mrs Corfield would not touch them except to cook them once they had been prepared for the oven. Bill Corfield liked the birds to hang before being plucked They were hung on hooks out side the back door for two or three days and some times even longer. Hannah hated plucking them when they had gone quite green and sometimes fly blown. Mr Corfield liked them, the greener the better. He also liked Hannah to come a little earlier when he was able to get hold of some home made black pudding. She would slice it and place it on a baking tray with rashers of bacon then place it on the shelf of the hot oven of the Aga and let it cook until it was just to his liking. He enjoyed it with two fried eggs and a slice of fried bread, washed down with a large cup of tea. He loved to sit at the kitchen table and have his fry up as he called it. His wife did not approve of him eating in the kitchen but she was usually in bed and did not know one half that went on in the kitchen first thing in the mornings.

Christmas time, Hannah bought small presents for all the family some thing that she had not been able to do before. Hannah and Mary went and cut a small fir tree from the plantation at the bottom of the Wrekin They put the tree in a bucket which they covered with pretty Christmas paper and put it in the front room, Hannah had bought some decorations for it.

"Got nothing better to do with your money "her Mother grumbled.

"Well it is Christmas" retorted Hannah. "You should see what Mrs Corfield and Pricilla have done for Christmas. They have a beautiful tree covered with fairy lights and baubles".

"What Mrs Corfield does is all that we hear about" Dorothy scolded. "We have not got money to burn like they have". Hannah decided to say no more about what went on at work if it put her mother in this sort of mood.

Hannah was not too keen cycling home in the dark; she had bought some lights for her bike and was peddling as hard as she could past the Glen towards home when a voice said

"What are in such a hurry for?"

Hannah recognised that it was George's voice; she stopped and got off her bike.

"Oh Lordy you did frighten me". What are you doing here?" Hannah asked.

"Its alright, just thought that I would walk a bit of the way with you I don't like to think of you coming up this road in the dark".

"Don't be so daft, we are used to coming up this road at night Lizzy has done it for years and she has come to no harm". George fell in step with Hannah as they pushed their bikes she did not attempt to ride it again. When they were out side the gates to the farm they sat for a few minutes on the iron milk stand.

"I finish work at the same time as you it is no trouble for me to come this way round; there will be no tea ready for me until half past six when me Dad gets home. Mam can't dish up before he gets in or he will be in a bad mood for the rest of the evening".

Hannah had enjoyed George's company; she had felt so much safer coming up the road through the woods. The woods could be a bit scary at night although Hannah tried to convince herself that she had nothing to fear. There was only the wild life such as rabbits, foxes and the owls to worry about.

"It's not very warm out here tonight is it?" George said putting his arm gently around Hannah's shoulders and drawing her closer to him. Hannah did not move away she had such a crush for George and to be able to be so close to him was something that she had only dreamt about. Hannah liked his closeness but she was confused as to what to reply or what should she do. Stay close or quickly move away.

"I must go "she said "There is always so much to be done when I get in and it is so cold sat on this stand.

Hannah was taken by complete surprise when George gave her a quick kiss on the lips. He waited for her reaction.

Hannah wanted to stay close and be kissed again but she quickly stood up." I must go in George! She moved to open the gate but George stepped in front of her.

"Don't be like that I did not mean to upset you The looks you have been giving me the past few months I did not think that you mind having a little kiss".

"I did not mind at all George it was very nice of you but I must go in or mother will be in a bad mood if the jobs do not get done".

"OK then I will see you again. Good night" He got on to his bike and rode away into the darkness of the woods.

"You're late tonight" Were her mother's first words as Hannah went into the kitchen; her mother looking up at the clock.

"Yes I was a bit late finishing tonight. Mr Corfield wanted some shoes cleaning ready for tomorrow" Hannah lied.

"I've given you a better education than to clean shoes for the likes as the Cornfields".

Hannah did not answer she took a candle and lit it so that she could go and change into an old frock and coat and then go and help Mary finish the work outside.

Hannah thought about George when she went to bed She still could feel his kiss on her lips and knew that it was what she had wanted him to do. She was still confused as to how she should react if he did it again and decided that she would cross that bridge when she came to it and if it happened again.

George had ridden off home with a smile on his face He was not the least bit upset because Hannah had not stayed for another kiss. She will, he thought that could wait. Mary stopped going to the Cottage after the Easter Bank holiday weekend. She had met a young man who she wished to go out with and she could not do both. The cinemas were open again and showing films twice every day including Sundays. The young man would take her to the cinema on Sunday afternoons and then would help her with the farm work before going for a walk in the evenings. George had been waiting for Hannah to finish work and walked home with her many times and would kiss her goodnight. Hannah had not refused George's kisses in fact she had enjoyed them. She continued going on her own to the Cottage on Sundays just so that she could see George. He would give her a smile but nothing more they both got on with their work as though nothing had happened between them. George showed no signs of affection what-so-ever towards her. This certainly bothered Hannah, Why was he so distant towards her and yet he was so keen to hold her and kiss her when he had been walking with her after work during the weekdays. Hannah wanted to be near him whenever she could She considered that he was her boy friend she knew that he was four and a half years older than her but that did not matter; she had fallen for him good and proper. She thought he was quite a man of the world He had passed his driving test so that he could drive a car He was a first class carpenter. He could use a shotgun with expertise. He seemed to have knowledge about most subjects.

Chapter Three
A Coach Trip and Tragedy

Gwen Watson had noticed that Hannah was always smiling at George and had wondered what was going on but she kept her thoughts to her self. Hannah walked to the bottom of the Wrekin with Charlie, George and Thomas, George did not offer her a ride on his cross bar again and often as not he said goodnight as did the others and left Hannah to walk the rest of the way home by her self.

"Why are you so distant toward me when we are at the Cottage?" Hannah asked George when he was waiting for her one evening to walk her home.

George said that it was better that no one suspected that he was seeing her during the week.

"Nosy buggers; we don't want them up there to know all our business especially that Gwen. She will make mountains out of mole hills if she can and another thing you are only fifteen and as you know that it would be frowned on if we were seen together we must keep it quiet as long as we can. When you are sixteen it will not be so bad".

"I see what you mean I will go along with that. I am sixteen next month and then Mam can't tell me what I can and what I can't do quite so much. Some girls are married at the age of eighteen not that I want to marry at that age there is so much I want to do. I have not been to the seaside and seen the sea. I know if Mam knew that you were meeting me she would blow a fuse and that there would be such a row that she would not calm down for days. She has stated firmly that we all have to marry farmer's sons and not to get involved with any one else or she will give us a piece of her mind and probably turn us out onto the road.

" You will not bring disgrace to my doors." Hannah mimicked her mother and George started to laugh.

"Farmers sons it has to be does it, well we will have to wait and see. I can't believe that you have not been to the seaside After all your Dad does have a car does he not. I tell you what Why don't you come on a day trip to see the sea? My Mother often takes Judith on the day trips that are organised. I am sure that you could come with them and if you tell your mother that you are going with my mother and Judith, I don't see how she can object you have a lot of catching up to do. I will let you know when the next trip is. My mother does not go very often because as you know she and Judith help out up at the Cottage. With having those four kids to cope with Gwen needs all the help that she can get. So it is your birthday next month is it what date?"

"June the twenty third" Hannah said quietly

"I will have to remember that, might think about taking you to the pictures"

"That would be nice I have only been once."

"You have not been very far have you?"

"No there has always been too much work to be done at home. The war made every thing so difficult"

Fred sowed the sugar beet seed on the top field at the top of the Willowmoor bank.

"Do you think them lads that help out up at the Cottage would do a bit of beet hoeing". Fred asked Hannah.

"I can ask Dad, they would only be able to come in the evenings because the Watson's want them at week ends".

"Well that would be a bit of help, better than none at all"

"Yes we will come and give a hand". George said when Hannah asked him. "As long as your dad pays the going rate, there is plenty of beet hoeing to be done and farmers are willing to pay the price to get it done quickly before the weeds over take it"

George and Thomas gave Fred a hand with the beet hoeing Hannah also went in to the field after work. Mary, Fred and Bernie did their best but there was so much other work to be done. Hay harvest had to be started as well as all the other daily chores.

George came on his own, the day of Hannah's birthday and as he left the field he slipped a small packet into her hand. Later when Hannah went to bed she opened it and saw that it was a silk headscarf. She had not possessed any thing so nice before, to her it was beautiful. Unfortunately Helen saw it

"What have you got there" Helen wanted to know. "I saw that lad George give you some thing when he left the field."

"It's only a scarf for my birthday.

"Why did he give you that? Is he your boy friend? I will tell Mam that you have a boy friend".

"No you will not tell Mam any such thing it is only a little present for my birthday and no one else has given me any thing".

"I don't have any money to buy presents with".

"I know that you don't so I don't expect one from you. If Mam says any thing about this scarf you are to say that I bought it. Do you hear?" Hannah said very firmly.

"It's all right for you. You are earning money" Helen whimpered.

"So will you when you leave school".

"But that is not for another two years".

"Oh shut up and go to sleep, I have to go to work in the morning. You can ask Mam to give you some pocket money".

"So I can but I know that I will not get any". Helen had the last word.

Hannah enjoyed her job and had never been so happy except for a fellow called Noel, He was Mrs Corfield's nephew, he always came into the kitchen to say goodnight to his aunt before he drove away from the yard. Some times when he knew that his aunt was not at home he would creep into the kitchen so quietly that Hannah did not heard him come in; he would put his hands around her waist and cause her to jump with surprise. She would wriggle to try and get out of his grip but she found that he was much stronger than she was. She hated it when his hands went over her small breasts and the way that he looked at her. "Give me a kiss" he would whisper".

"No I won't, let me go". Hannah pleaded She was infatuated with George and did not like Noel one little bit. If she wanted kisses she had George who was a very gentle caring man. Noel always smelt of the farm of cow dung, rotten mangols and the smell of pigsties. Hannah being no more than eight stone in weight and was no match for him He was well into his thirties and had bad breath. He was still a bachelor Noel did not like taking no for an answer and threatened Hannah Saying "I will get you one of these days you just wait and see".

Hannah wanted to slap his face but she was too scared of him and she could not tell Mrs Corfield she did not think that she would believe her. Hannah knew that Noel would say that she was telling lies about him. She did tell George and he said to try and keep out of his way as much as possible and that he would sort him out for her if he attempted any thing more.

"I am very careful when I know that he is about and I try to keep out of his way" Hannah did not want trouble, Mrs Corfield allowed Hannah to use the down stair cloak room to wash if she wished. Hannah would make use of it at Saturday lunchtime changing into a clean dress to go into town. It was such a treat to turn on the tap and have warm water running into the white china wash basin. The sweet smell of the scented soap; some thing that her mother never bought Oh how she would have loved to use the bath upstairs but that was for the use of the family.

When the sugar beet hoeing was finished Fred was able to offer George several repair jobs about the farm mending doors and windows that had started to rot with age. William Hollis no longer did any repairs for the estate. His health had deteriorated and very few people saw him about. He was living as a recluse with only his wife for company. Joyce Wilkins did some shopping for them, there was very little that they wanted for.

Hannah liked her Dad asking George to do jobs around the place; it gave her a chance to see him.

"I'll not have you going talking to those lads" Dorothy had stated when she had seen Hannah talking to George in the yard. "You keep away from that one. He is just a working lad and I don't want you to have any thing to do with him. Do you hear me?" She shouted. They had only asked George to do the work so that it would be cheaper than having to have a professional from a building firm.

"Yes Mam" Hannah answered not knowing what else to say. If only she knew Hannah thought. She would go spare. Hannah knew that she loved George and she must not let her Mother sense this. Hannah could not understand her mother's attitude. Why was it so dreadful that George went to work to earn a living and a trade? She had not known any thing other than hard work since she had been little.

The winter came and when spring was in the air George took Hannah to the Clifton cinema one Saturday afternoon. She loved it George sat with his arm around her shoulders and she felt so close to him. If her mother could see her now. She thought, she would go mad. A coach trip was arranged to go for a days outing to Blackpool and George asked Hannah if he could book a seat for her.

"I will have to ask Mam." Hannah had answered.

"Have to ask your Mam if you can have a day out." George was gob smacked.

"Tell her that you are going with Judith and my mother, but I will be on the coach. After all you are coming seventeen and you should be able to stand up for yourself a little bit. It does not seem fair to me that you have to work so hard, there is no let up for you If you are not at Corfield's, you are at the Cottage and if not there you are working at home. I think that it is time you went for a day out and saw the seaside. Say that you will come" George pleaded.

"I will do my best; Mary can go to the cottage for one Sunday in my place".

When Hannah asked her mother if she could go for the day trip explaining that it was to keep Judith company. Dorothy showed that she was not very pleased about it.

"Going to throw your money away on coach trips are you? "She shouted at Hannah.

"It's only for one day and I have never seen the sea, I will do my jobs before I go on the Sunday morning."

After a long argument, Dorothy reluctantly agreed that Hannah could go on the trip.

"I just hope none of those lads that work up at that cottage are going" Dorothy had said.

"No I don't think so, they have to go to the cottage on a Sunday or Mr Watson will not be very happy". That seemed to pacify Dorothy much to Hannah's relief.

"I hope that Hannah is not getting as head-strong as our Grace did" Dorothy said to Fred I don't like her going off with that lot from Wrockwardine I really don't. There is plenty that I can find her to do on her day off if she does not want to go to the Watson's."

"Don't fret so Dot, give the lass a bit of a break She can't come to much harm going to the seaside on a coach. "Fred had noticed how hard that Hannah had worked.

"Its all right for you Fred Thomas, It's me that will be blamed if she gets her self into a mess. It will be me who takes the blame "She repeated. She could see that Fred was taking little notice of her

The morning of the coach trip, Hannah was up at half past six she had the cows in and tied up before Mary joined her at seven o'clock. The weather was hot and humid even for that time in the morning it was obvious that there was going to be a thunderstorm later.

"Just my luck "Hannah said to Mary. "Where is Bernie is he not up yet?"

"Where do you think? Still fast asleep".

"Do you think that a storm will come? That stack of hay in the stackyard has not been thatched Do you think that we could pull a tarpaulin sheet over it just in case. Dad said last night that he was going to put the rest of the hay from the bottom field on that before he put a thatch on it. Come on Hannah and let us see if we can cover it up with a sheet".

The two girls unrolled the tarpaulin sheet and between the two of them they managed to lift it as each climbed a ladder and place it over the hay stack tying the corners down in case a wind got up and blew it off. Hannah had to cycle to Wrockwardine for nine o'clock. Thank goodness her mother was up and out side seeing to her chickens when Hannah went in to wash and change. She took her bike from the garage and was gone off down the road just saying to Helen to tell her mother that she had left and did not know what time that she would be back. Hannah had so looked forward to this day that she was not going to give her mother a chance to grumble at her and spoil every thing. At George's house she put her bike outside the back door; she had not been here before Hannah knocked on the door it was answered by Judith

"Hannah I am so glad that you could come, you are going to sit by me. Mum has a friend who she wants to sit by." Judith said excitedly. "Come on in. George will put your bike in the shed it can stay safe there until we come back. Hannah followed Judith through what looked to be the kitchen and into the living room. It all looked neat and tidy she was told to sit down until it was time to go. Hannah noticed that there was a sideboard in the room, a two seater leather settee and two arm chairs to match. The floor was covered with linoleum and was polished so much that the images of the furniture reflected in it. Underneath the sideboard was a row of polished shoes?

Hannah guessed that they must belong to various members of the family. George's mother Ivy came from upstairs and smiled at Hannah "I bet that you can drink a cup of tea there is still some fresh in the pot we have not been up that long" Hannah thought about what early hour that she had risen to be able to get all the jobs done back home and she certainly welcomed the offer of a cup of tea. . It was a very good cup of tea, which she enjoyed, and also the biscuits that were offered. There was no mention of George and after a while Hannah was beginning to feel that he was not coming and she started to feel disappointed but there was no need he appeared as if from nowhere. He had been in the bathroom and he looked so smart in jacket and trousers his hair immaculately combed. He certainly looked a handsome young man.

The toilet is by the back door" Ivy shouted "see you all use it I don't want to stop the coach for any of you.

"Take no notice" said Judith "Mum is like proper old hen".

Hannah used the toilet, it was a water flush one and the quarry floor was so clean so were the white painted walls.

When the coach arrived in the village; they all clamoured on to it selecting a seat, which suited them best. "Come to the back" Judith whispered Hannah followed her to the seats at the back end of the coach. Coaches were a little smarter than the ordinary every day buses, the seats were more comfortable and the floor between the seats were carpeted. Hannah thought how it all looked so smart. George was seated in front of Judith and Hannah. He was with quite a few of other young men from the village He winked his eye at Hannah before he sat down.

They all had a wonderful day Hannah found it all a little awe-inspiring. The sea, the rides on the pleasure beach. She and Judith stayed together letting the lads go off as they pleased.

"I'm not going on that big ride it costs half a crown a ride and it is frightening, I had a go on it the last time we came." Said Judith "I think that we can leave that one for the lads. Come on Hannah there is plenty for us to see. Mum says that we can go to the top of the tower if there is time".

They had things called hot dogs; sausages in bread rolls, they drank lemonade, ate packets Smiths crisps. Oh how Hannah enjoyed the day. To look out over the sea from the top of the tower, she was transfixed with it all. The day went far too quickly for Hannah It was ten o'clock when the coach dropped them off in the village. Hannah had bought four sticks of rock for Mary, Helen, William and Sandra

"I will come with you" George offered "Can't let her cycle home on her own "He said to his mother.

"All right George" But she warned him". You come straight back here as quickly as you can; you have to go to work tomorrow morning",

"Have you got a key"? George asked Hannah when they reached the farm.

"No the door is never locked. Mam some times pulls the mangle across it so that she will hear it move if any one tries to come in."

"Ok off you go" He gave Hannah a firm kiss on the lips as he said goodnight.

"And what time did you come in last night "? Dorothy asked Hannah the next morning as she was getting ready for work,

"Oh about ten o'clock" Hannah replied.

"It was well after that I can tell you". Dorothy shouted "I'll not have you coming in this house at all hours you know that you are to be in this house by nine o'clock".

"I had to come when the coach brought us back "Hannah tried to make an excuse. "I could not come before".

"Well there will be no more of this "

"I don't see why not I did not come to any harm; I was with Ivy and Judith In fact I had a wonderful day out." Hannah stood firm.

"I'll not have any of your back chat. Do you hear me lady?"

Hannah said no more she just went out, took her bike and went to work. Was it going to be like this every time that she had a day off, she wondered?

By the time that September came Hannah had been on two more coach trips to the seaside but she had to cope with her mother's anger each time she had gone anywhere.

Thursday was market day in Wellington, Mrs Corfield and Pricilla took James with them to do the shopping giving Hannah some free time to do some light housework. They always bought fresh cream cakes and bread rolls for their tea and of course some sweets for the children. Hannah gave the boys their tea in the kitchen. They had eaten quickly so that they could go out to play. Bread rolls with meat and cheese fresh cakes for afters; she had laid the dining room table ready for Mrs Corfield's evening meal. It would soon be half past five and time for Hannah to leave she was meeting George and she did not want to be late. Noel came into the kitchen as usual the boys following him. He started to play with the boys. He pretended to be a monster chasing them around the kitchen table. James disappeared he did not like the monster; he went to his mother who was relaxing in the lounge so tired from doing the shopping. Noel continued to play with Timothy he chased him up the back stairs around the bathroom and back down again. The game went on for some time.

"Stop it, Noel you are getting him too excited" Hannah pleaded. But to no avail Noel took no notice of her. Hannah went into the dining room to put the cruet set on the table and the door closed behind her. Before she could open it again she heard the glass in the door break. And Timothy scream. He had followed her so that he could come to hide behind her. He had pushed the door. His hand had gone through the glass panel of the door which had broken and it was now badly cut and was bleeding profusely. Hannah grabbed the kitchen towel and wrapped around his arm. When Noel saw what had happened he quickly disappeared out through the back door. She called for Mrs Corfield who could hear Timothy crying. She was coming to see what had happened. When she saw Timothy's arm so badly cut she shouted for Pricilla.

"He will have to have a stitch in this let us get him to a doctor quickly".

Noel came into the kitchen pretending that he knew nothing. "Just a nasty accident" Mrs Corfield told him we are going to the doctors you go home and you also Hannah. No need for you to stay any longer, there is nothing that you can do here. We should not be too long away."

When Pricilla saw her son's arm she decided that they should take him to Shrewsbury to the Quarry Place Nursing Home. A privately run Hospital.

"What are you looking so worried about" George asked when he caught up with Hannah

"Noel got Timothy so excited, that there has been an accident". She went on to tell George all about it

"Don't worry, he will be all right in a day or two a bit of a shock but he will get over it". Next morning when Hannah arrived at work there was no sign of the boys so she decided to light the dining room fire ready for when the ladies of the house came down for breakfast. It was such a pleasant welcome to the room; Hannah noticed that a thick piece of cardboard had replaced the broken glass. She was kneeling on the hearth when Mr Corfield came into the room.

"Good morning Hannah, Hannah looked up

"No sign of the boys as yet Mr Corfield, how is Timothy's arm not too bad I hope".

"Come and sit down for a minute my dear. Timothy will not be coming down today. Leave the fire we will decide whether to light it or not". Hannah could tell by his voice that some thing was wrong. She sat down on a chair in the kitchen.

"Timothy died at the hospital last night. Every one is very upset".

"Timothy is dead." Hannah's voice seemed to echo around the kitchen. "But how? But why?" She asked.

"Apparently he needed two stitches to his arm and they thought it best to give him an anaesthetic unfortunately they had not taken into consideration that he had previously eaten his tea. He choked to death as he was coming awake. It does not seem to be any ones fault really just one of those things that can go wrong".

"But he only needed a couple of stitches. Why did they give him an anaesthetic it was not that bad was it"? Hannah sputtered so close to tears.

"I believe that his mother had thought that it was the best for him. There will be an inquest to find out exactly happened. Try to keep yourself busy until lunchtime and then go home.

Hannah was so shocked that she went around in a daze for the rest of the morning. She did not see anything of Mrs Corfield or Pricilla. Mrs Corfield was comforting her daughter who had completely gone to pieces and was sedated by her doctor and confined to her bedroom. Little James came to the kitchen for a while and then Mr Corfield said that he would take care of him when Hannah went home.

"What are you doing back so early"? Dorothy wanted to know "Have they all gone shopping and left you with nothing to do"

"No it's not that, Timothy is dead.

"What do you mean Timothy is dead you said that he had only cut his arm".

Hannah told her mother the whole story.

"Well I can see somebody having to be responsible for that. Died you say Oh that poor woman first her marriage breaks up and now she has lost her son. Dear oh dear."

Hannah went up stairs and sat on her bed and started to cry. After a while she changed into some old clothes and went out side to find Mary and told her what had happened.

"Some one should have to pay for that" was all that Mary could say.

There was so much going on at work during the next few days. People were coming and going Hannah was kept very busy she did not see any thing of Pricilla. Mrs Corfield told Hannah that it was better if she looked after her. And that it was better for her to have James with her as much as possible. When the funeral was arranged Mrs Corfield asked Hannah if she would like to attend and if so she would be pleased if she did and she could ride in one of the funeral cars.

Hannah had not been to a funeral before she had been completely overwhelmed by the tragedy of Timothy's death. There were so many questions that had to be answered What if and why would not go away. Hannah still felt partly responsible If only she had stopped Timothy getting so excited or she should have stopped Noel from chasing him around the kitchen. George gave her all the comfort and support that he could and this certainly helped. The funeral was arranged to be at Wrockwardine Parish church and Timothy to be buried in the new cemetery on the outskirts of the village. Hannah was dreading the day she wore a small black hat and did her best to look as smart as she could. She was dreading the walk from the church through the village to the cemetery. She need not have worried there were so many people there that she was not noticed. Pricilla did not feel well enough to attend so her Mother stayed behind to take care of her.

Mr Corfield told Hannah the date of inquest and that she was requested to attend. This put the fear of God into Hannah. "Mr Corfield I will be scared stiff.

"Don't you go worrying your self"? Mr Corfield reassured her. "You were certainly not to blame and no one is thinking that you are. Accidents will happen. We will be taking you with us. All you will be requested to do is to answer the questions that are asked of you."

"But I don't know if I can "Hannah stammered, scared stiff at the very thought of it all.

On the day of the inquest Hannah was very nervous she felt that she had to appear before judge and jury. She felt as if her own life was at stake and so consequently she felt very sick

Hannah sat in the back of Mr Corfield's car alongside Noel. Richard Corfield and his wife had decided to hear what was said at the inquest so followed in their own car; all four remained silent on the way to Shrewsbury. After parking the car, they walked to the Coroner's office and were directed to take their seats. The room that they were shown into was not as big as Hannah had anticipated. There were five men sat in a row all wearing dark suits. There were another two sat behind a large desk and what looked like a woman secretary sat by them with a pen in her hand and quite an amount of paper work in front of her, Mr and Mrs Corfield were shown to seats in front of Hannah and Noel. The whole room gave an air of officialdom. To Hannah it was very awesome. The men who had been sat together gave their evidence first they were medical staff from the hospital. When Hannah was called she did as she was asked and swore on the bible to tell the truth the whole truth and nothing but the truth. She answered the questions as they were asked and she was glad to be told to go back to her seat. The next witness to be called was Noel He took the stand and made his oath to tell the truth. Hannah could not believe her ears. Noel stated that he had not been in the kitchen at the time of the accident. He told a complete fabrication of lies. You lying toad Hannah was thinking and as if reading her thoughts Noel looked directly at her. She had left it up to him to explain how he had been playing with Timothy prior to the accident. Now he was denying all knowledge of seeing anything.

After summing up and having listened to all the statements The Coroner recorded that it was a death by misadventure.

Mr Corfield was very angry at the result and as soon as they left the building he was very quick to say what he thought.

" Misadventure indeed how on earth did that Coroner come to that decision? In my opinion it was nothing but neglect". Hannah stood frozen to the spot. What did he mean neglect. Neglect on her part or the hospital. He noticed her face going very pale. "I certainly don't mean you Hannah Accidents happen in the home every day. No it was the Hospital that I am so angry with. To do no better than to let the little lad choke is in my opinion beyond comprehension. Mr Richard Corfield took his father to the car and left the rest to follow. It was such a relief to Hannah to be back into the fresh air and walk to the car, she was glad to be taken back to work where she just collected her bike and went home. Should she have said that Noel had got Timothy so excited but she had not been asked that question?

Next day she asked Noel why he had lied in the courtroom.

"You keep your mouth shut" He snarled. "Or else."

"Or else what" Hannah asked.

"You will see. I have got to keep my job; I need the money, it is all right for you. I see you with that boy friend of yours. It does not matter if you have no job your family can afford to keep you; mine can't. My Dad can no longer do the work at home so I have to start again when I go back from here".

Hannah did not bother to make any further conversation with him. She did not like the man and she did not trust him; she decided to say nothing to Mr and Mrs Corfield she felt certain that they would most probably believe him to her story of what had really happened, he was part of their family. Noel would have to live with his conscience.

Over the next few months the atmosphere at work was completely changed for Hannah

As soon as Pricilla had recovered sufficient from Timothy's death the man who she had been seeing decided to take both Pricilla and James back to London to live. The change in circumstances left Hannah with out her boys to take care of. She could not trust Noel and had no further wish to work at the same place as he did. Her work now was mostly cleaning which she did not enjoy. There were far too many reminders of Timothy, Hannah decided to look for another job.

When she discussed her thoughts with George he suggested that she should look for a job where she could live in and have more time for herself and not have to do all the work that she did at home. Hannah thought that this was a wonderful idea and she started to look in the paper for job vacancies. She decided that she would say nothing to her Mother because she knew that she would be against the idea.

It was late October Hannah went to the Cottage on the Sunday morning; for ten o'clock as usual. She knocked on the door and when no one asked her to enter, she decided to open the door a little, and she could hear Gwen and George having an almighty row out in the back kitchen. There was no sign of Eric Watson being sat in his usual chair; where he was she did not know. She could not make out what George and Gwen were arguing about when George saw Hannah coming through to the back kitchen He quickly turned and took hold of her arm very firmly. He appeared to be very flustered and angry. Gwen followed close behind him; her face was scarlet with anger.

"You can take her with you" she shouted.

"We're not staying here today "George told Hannah I know when we are not wanted". He steered Hannah back towards the front door and outside.

"What on earth is going on here" Hannah wanted to know.

"Nothing really" said George "I think that she has got out of bed the wrong side this morning. She is in a right mood and we are not stopping to hear any more of her loud mouth. We are off. She can find some one else to be her skivvy"

"She has been funny with me for the last few Sundays" Hannah remarked. "I know that it is not because I don't do my job properly. Right moody she has been with me at times".

"You don't have to put up with her and her moods, now that you are working in the week. If we don't come up here we can have Sundays to ourselves. I have been thinking about buying a motor bike so that I can take you out to places that you have never seen. I can't afford to buy a car but one day we will have one of the best"

This seemed a good idea to Hannah, George was quite right. To Hannah George was right about practically every thing.

"Where was Eric this morning? He is usually sitting in his chair by the range. "

"She", referring to Gwen "said that he was bad in bed this morning and that he would get up later. Come on let's go". The two of them did not go back home, instead they spent the day together walking. George went and bought some sandwiches from the Glen for their lunch, Hannah stayed out of sight, and she did not want Lizzy to see that she was not at work she would tell her mother as soon as she got home. Then there would be another row in the house as soon as Hannah went home.

Chapter Four
George is Mobile

Dorothy had noticed that Hannah was infatuated with this lad George as she referred to him and she was not at all happy about it. She grumbled to Fred that she was having none of it "She can find some one better than that lad."

"Leave her be the more that you go on about him the more she will want to be with him" Fred had been out working hard all day and did not want to hear Dorothy going on and on.

Hannah decided to knit a Fair Isle woollen pullover for George as a Christmas present. It was her first attempt to knit with several different coloured wools. She made a reasonable job of it, Dorothy was absolutely furious

"If you have money and time to knit fancy things for that lad you can do some knitting for me". The more Dorothy grumbled the more Hannah thought about finding a job where she could live in the thought of leaving home seemed a big step for her to make, but then she thought that Grace had done it, so why should she not do the same. There had not been so many rows in the house since Grace had left. Grace did not bother to come home very often. She was far too busy dressing up and going to dances and having a good time. Hannah could not understand why her mother was so against her seeing George. He had a good job they had a modern house with running water electricity a bathroom and Ivy kept it very clean, far cleaner than Dorothy kept her house. If the girls had not done the housework, most of it would never have been done. Dorothy took it for granted that Mary would give the kitchen a good scrub out on a Thursday when she went into town. Hannah gave a hand when she could. Helen saw to all the other cleaning and polishing when she was not at school. William was more spoilt as he became older and so was Sandra. Dorothy would give Sandra anything within reason to keep her quiet so that she did not have to bother with her. Sandra like William was growing up to be a spoilt brat.

William was now becoming nine years old; he did not attend school if he did not want to. He would go with Fred to the auctions and farm sales and any other excuse that there was. Dorothy and Fred were often receiving notes from the village school head mistress complaining about William's lack of attendance

Eventually Dorothy did start to grow concerned about William's education and started to talk to Fred about it.

"I've been thinking Fred that we ought to be considering sending William to a private school. That Mrs Bailey is just picking on him because he has a day off now and again. She has got it in for the lad. She was a nobody until she married that big farmer Bailey. William will soon be ten and we have to decide what will be the best for him. I only want what is best for him, you give it some thought".

"Aye surry Dot just you think what it would cost to send him to one of them schools" Fred got out of his chair quickly and took his cap from of the peg behind the door he did not wish to go any further with that conversation.

It was announced that The Royal wedding of Princess Elizabeth to the Earl of Mountbatten was to take place on November 20th

Mrs Corfield bought a television set so that they would be able to watch it taking place. This was a wonderful thing. She told Hannah that she too could watch it if she wished Hannah was delighted. She had not seen a television before and was simply amazed to think that they could sit in the lounge and see and hear what was going on in London. The television was rather an expensive item to buy. It had cost over three hundred pounds and very few people could afford such a luxury item.

"Another fancy gadget" Dorothy retorted when Hannah told her all about it. "Money to burn they must have" Hannah could never understand why her mother could not be pleased for what other people did. Perhaps it was because she was jealous of them, but until they had the electricity they were denied such things.

After Christmas Hannah could see that her mother was not going to approve of her seeing George and the rows were causing so much bother to the rest of the family. It affected them all.

"What are you going to do about seeing this George?" Mary asked Hannah, when they were checking the sheep.

"Well I don't see what Mother has got against him".

"He is not a farmer's son, idiot".

"Is that all? Most of the farmer's sons that I have met smell just like their jobs. All muck and wellies Anyway I have been thinking about getting a job where I can live in and then that will put an end to her grumbling",

"You have been what?" Mary looked astonished.

"Don't you say any thing as yet or that will cause another row and I can do without any more of Mam's moaning? And another thing all she really cares about is William and she is spoiling that Sandra until she is as daft as a brush. Yes I have decided that I am getting out of here"

Well I suppose that it would be a relief if Hannah did leave, at least there would be some peace in the house Mary thought

Hannah saw a vacancy advertised for someone to give a hand with two children and it was on condition that the person who applied was able to live in, the job was not too far from Wrockwardine. So Hannah made an appointment to be interviewed for the job and was successful. She gave Mrs Corfield the required week's notice she told her mother what she was proposing to do. And as expected Dorothy flew into a rage.

"You can stay and work for us. I will pay you a pound a week and then we will be able to keep an eye on you." Hannah knew exactly what she meant by that statement, she would stop her from seeing George. Hannah did not put up any argument when the day came for her to leave. She was up early and she made sure that her mother was out feeding her chickens. Hannah took her small suitcase, which contained her few things and left the house with out saying goodbye to any one. She arrived at the place that she was to work It was called a Dorma bungalow. She was shown to a room in the roof. She had to climb a ladder to get to it, which was most peculiar to her. That night was the first time that Hannah had not shared a bedroom with anyone else. She felt so lonely and home sick she knew that there was no going back if she still wanted to see George. She idolised him and knew that she could not give him up.

After Hannah had left every thing calmed down at the farm. Mary for some reason or other had finished with the young man that she had been seeing. This had pleased Dorothy she had been thinking that if Mary had decided to marry what would they do without her? They could never replace her for the amount of work that she did, well not until William was old enough to take her place. Lizzy was walking out with a neighbouring farmer who was a brother to Joe Timmins and was well approved of by her Mother.

Fred missed having Hannah around but thought better of it than to voice his thoughts to Dorothy. She was furious and angry for some time She was so annoyed that Hannah as well as Grace had stood up to her and gone their own way.

"Fred" Dorothy said when they had sat down for the evening. "Joyce Wilkins was saying when she came down this after noon that she thinks that Wilf will be giving up their ground and that it will be coming up for rent. Why don't we have a go and see if we can add it to this place?"

"Aye surry Dot you're right I reckon that we could just about manage it. Unless that Miss Stewart puts in for it and then we would not stand an earthly chance."

"We are doing well at the moment as you say we could manage it, you know that it would give you more ground and we now have William growing up. If we did get it I hope you won't be so stupid and spread muck from this farm onto other land, like you did at the Woods eaves and got us turned out.

"Well I did not know that I was breaking the law at the time did you?"

"You know that now Fred Thomas and you will not be making that mistake again will you"?

"Nay lass we learnt our lesson and we have not done so badly since we came here perhaps we will be able to buy this place one day. But that is for the future, in the mean time we just keep the brooks running free" He smiled at Dorothy and she knew exactly what he meant. Hannah settled in her new job and at first she was much happier now that she did not have to listen to her mother grumbling about her getting too fond of George Fleming. She was now able to see George on a regular basis when she had an afternoon off from work. Unfortunately for her, the new employers had only wanted her to help to scrub and clean for them. They had a small business, they ran a garage, which sold petrol and garage accessories. They had a little café, which was the wife's responsibility. Her husband looked after the petrol pumps. Worst of all they had two of the most unruly children Hannah had ever come across. The boy was aged eleven and he was quite a big boy for his age, his sister was six years old. She was quite a pretty child with blonde hair and average build when not at school these two children were allowed to run completely wild. They had no respect for their parents or anyone else and to Hannah the parents seemed to have no time for them whatsoever

Hannah had been there six months and she was growing very nervous of the boy. She told George how he had waited for her hidden behind a door with a sharp knife in his hand threatening to cut her. Hannah had told the boy to put the knife back in the kitchen before he did some harm. He told her to mind her own business and he could do as he pleased. Hannah did not like the evil look that he had on his face. She had seen that sort of look before on Noel Higgins's face when he had tried to grab her and she had given him a telling off for it. George persuaded. Hannah to look for another job before this lad really did her some harm.

Hannah found another job and then she was able to give her employer one weeks notice as required

The next job Hannah had was at Haybridge Hall and she loved the job. She was asked to help take care of a very rich elderly lady. Her duties were to be there for the old lady, to pass this and take that. Hannah was asked to sit and read to her in the afternoons, fetch her afternoon tea tray from the kitchen and take it up to her room and then return the tray to the kitchen; she had no nursing duties to do such as bathing the old lady. Hannah did not take kindly towards the housekeeper Miss Snipe. A spinster of about fifty five years old, who had been at Hall for many years and she did not take to Hannah, she seemed to resent Hannah for some reason or other. Hannah thought that she resented her for being young and having a regular boy friend. She did not say so in as many words but her attitude was very hostile towards Hannah.

After about six months it was Hannah's mother Dorothy who brought the job to an end. Dorothy knew that Hannah was seeing George now on a regular basis and she certainly did not approve.

"He's not good enough for her". She had often complained to Fred.

"We have given her too good an education to be gallivanting around with the likes of him, comes from a Council house that he does. I reckon that she could do much better for herself than a carpenter. I'll put a stop to it that I will. She would be better off working at home where we can keep an eye on her "

"I think that it would be better if you were to leave well alone. I think that if you go interfering where she works, the lass will only dig her heels in and then you will be no better off. She seems quite happy where she is. Leave it be Dot. Now we are getting on so well, we have enough to worry about coping with every thing here on the farm".

Dorothy took no notice of what Fred had advised; instead she went to speak to Miss Snipe the housekeeper at the hall. Dorothy gave the housekeeper the impression that Hannah had ran away from home just so that she could see this most dreadful lad that she and her husband certainly did not approve of him. The housekeeper told Dorothy that "She did not approve of him either, she told her that she could not do with young men coming to the hall, and she referred to George as riff raff. She continued that "She would certainly not welcome any trouble from this young man at the hall and that it was her business to vouch for who came knocking on the back door. Her employers would be most upset; if what they would consider as riff raff were encouraged any where near the hall, even if the person in question was known to her." She said this to Dorothy with great authority.

This was exactly what Dorothy had wanted to hear and hoped that Hannah would be asked to leave and that she would then have to come back home where she her self could do with the extra help not only in the house but also with the poultry.

Miss Snipe had not liked this woman coming complaining about her daughter. Once Hannah had left the hall on her off duty periods she considered that it was not the responsibility of the hall to worry what the staff got up, but at the same time here was an opportunity to get rid of Hannah. The next person that she employed to assist in caring for the old lady upstairs would be someone who like her self was middle-aged and who had no time for the opposite sex.

Hannah could not believe it when she was asked to sit in the kitchen by the housekeeper and told that she was being given two weeks notice to leave. The housekeeper had told her about Dorothy's visit earlier in the day and explained that she would not tolerate trouble at the hall under any circumstances. You will start two weeks notice as from next Monday.

Hannah was very distressed and she told George all about it. George was really angry when she told him that she had once again to look for another job

"That house keeper is a miserable old crow "That she is. So your mother has tried to do her worst has she that's what your Mother thinks about me is it. Riff, raff?"

"I'm afraid so. George I do not want to go home to live. It has been great to be able to see you on my half days. I can't forgive my Mam for this I really can't and what is more I am not going back home to live and work, I am looking for another job straight away".

"Good for you, If you go home you know that you will not be able to see me any more and I don't want that to happen, I think too much of you. Let's look in last week's journal; you never know. Not all vacancies are filled within a week". Hannah agreed and they cycled back to Wrockwardine and studied the vacancy column. Yes there was a young lady wanted help with small children and the job was in town. Hannah went down to the telephone box and arranged to have an interview the following Sunday afternoon

Hannah was accepted and promised to start the following week. She told Hilda Snipe that she would be leaving by the end of the first week of her notice. Hilda Snipe was not at all pleased

"Have I not enough to do with out running up and down stairs all next week before the new woman starts". She said with surprise. Serve you right, thought Hannah but I am off at the end of the week, you can get on with it.

Hannah's new employers Mr and Mrs Pearson they ran a taxi business in Wellington; they had a fleet of cars including a hearse. The hearse and two of the cars were Rolls Royce, very smart. Weddings and funerals were their speciality. They also had other cars of different makes, which were used for taxi service when required by the general public. When Hannah explained why she was looking for employment, that it was because her Mother did not approve of her boyfriend she found her new boss was very sympathetic. Hannah would be working as a nanny to three small children He did a lot of work with George's employers the Cartwright's who were Funeral Undertakers as well as doing all sorts of joinery work such as general building repairs and any other carpentry work that was needed by their customers.

Geoff Pearson had been doing business with the Cartwright's since he had started his taxi business in Wellington some years ago. He had met George on so many occasions. He thought what a nice and obliging young man George was. Geoff decided to make inquiries from one of the Cartwright brothers as to what sort of reputation George had and he found that they could not speak any more highly of him. Geoff could not see what problem Hannah's mother could have and as far as he could see, the girl could do a lot worse. He told Hannah that he would be prepared to have a chat with her Mother if she cared to come and see him and then he could assure her that he did not think that her daughter could come to much harm. He had told Hannah that she seemed to be just the sort of girl that they were looking for. Geoff's wife Charlotte was a good driver and worked alongside her husband to run the business. The busier that they became the less she was at home and she did not have as much time as she would have liked with her three children but she loved driving and felt that the business had to take precedence

They had three small children two little girls aged six and four years old and a baby boy only two months old. They lived in a town house at the top of New Street. Mr Pearson rented a much larger garage in Victoria Street, which was not far away This garaged the Rolls Royce, hearse, and cars. Hannah would not be asked to have any thing to do with the business except for answering the telephone and taking messages. She could have one half day off on a Wednesday and a half-day every other Sunday. She would be paid twenty-five shillings a week and her board and lodgings would be free. Hannah was thrilled to bits with the arrangements. She was told that she could not have her own bedroom and that she would sleep in the same room as the two little girls they would be in a double bed and she Hannah would have a single one. Hannah was quite happy with this arrangement, as she had been used to sharing rooms and beds back at home.

When Hannah visited George's home his mother Ivy made her most welcome. She would cycle to Wrockwardine on a Wednesday afternoon and stay until George came in from work and then after they had eaten their tea. George would have a bath and change then they would cycle back into town to go to the cinema and watch a film.

George was the elder of Ivy's three children. When he had been a small boy he had an infection called mastoiditis of the ear. It had required immediate surgery. And because of this his mother was inclined to be more protective towards him than what she was towards his brother Thomas and Sister Judith. Ivy was George's greatest ally. When his father had been fairly strict with him George knew that if he wanted his own way he only had to use his charm with his mother and she would persuade his father to agree and approve so consequently George usually had his own way in the end.

George was finishing working as an apprentice training to be a carpenter and joiner, he knew that he was good at his job and he certainly enjoyed working with wood. His employers offered him the chance to attend college one day a week during his apprenticeship so that he could obtain his City at Guilds certificate, but George had been very stubborn and he had refused. He considered that just getting a piece of paper was a waste of time. Apparently later on in years George found out that this was much to his disadvantage. Hannah much to her surprise was to learn that George could sometimes be very stubborn and get very moody. Even if he knew that it was not to be to his benefit. .

There had never been a great deal of money in the Fleming family His Mother and father was well respected in the village community of Wrockwardine. Terrence Fleming worked for the Railway Company as a maintenance engineer foreman. He had been born in Lawley by Little Wenlock and at one time his parents had farmed the Wrekin farm. Terry Fleming worked very hard. He would often be asked to work at weekends when there were fewer trains running

Hannah had met George's Mother Ivy and his sister Judith and brother Thomas from when she had worked weekends up at the Wrekin Cottage. The family had kept themselves to themselves for most of the time. Terry Fleming as George's dad was known enjoyed cycling into Wellington to enjoy a pint of beer at the weekend and playing a game of dominoes with others that patronised the Pheasant inn. Terry had been quite happy that his sons had preferred to find themselves weekend work up the Wrekin instead of hanging around the streets getting into trouble. After all they were earning a little extra money to help clothe them selves and George fancied himself as the best looking lad in the village and there was no doubt about it he was not very far wrong. With his smart clothes his black wavy hair always immaculately combed and his pushbike was always clean and shiny. When George had for some unknown reason had the row with Gwen Watson, Hannah and his family stopped going to the Cottage. He had taken to doing extra jobs of woodwork at weekends. There was always some one wanting repairs doing of one sort or another. New windows or doors which needed to be fitted. He found that he was never short of work and when he was asked to do a job that he could not manage on his own he had his brother to fall back on. Thomas would always give him a hand if it meant that there was a bit of money to be earned. When her sons stopped going, Ivy and Judith both gave up. They said that the atmosphere was dreadful at the Cottage, Gwen was as miserable as sin and Eric Watson's health was deteriorating and without the help of young lads like George and Thomas to do all the heavy work the place was going down hill.

Ivy had stated very firmly that she could get plenty of part time work with out having to climb the Wrekin, if I don't go, neither will I let Judith go up there on her own.

George had told Hannah about his intention to buy a motor bike. Hannah had been thrilled to bits with the idea because now that she was going to have a half-day from work off every other Sunday, there were so many places that they would be able to visit but it would have to depend on when George's work allowed him to take the time off.

"Yes". She had said to George "there are so many places that we could to go and see. Hannah had fallen completely in love with George and she worshipped the ground that he walked on. George could do nothing wrong in Hannah's eyes. She thought the idea of buying a motor bike was wonderful. George told his mother of his intentions.

She was so surprised at what her son had suggested that she quickly asked.

"Well how can you afford to buy a motor bike? I think you should ask your Dad for permission before you go buying one, you know how dangerous that they can be. What I know of him he will not be very happy at all about you having one, I will mention it very casually and see how the land lies with him."

"For heavens sake Mother, I am almost twenty-one; I don't see why he should object. I will soon be able to please myself by law without having to please him. I know that there will probably be a row in the house, but I will not answer to him any longer than I have to."

"How do you think that you are going to pay for a motor bike?" Ivy asked him.

"I will put a deposit as a down payment and pay the rest off by instalments"

"You are what?

"Just as I have said I will put a deposit down and pay the rest off afterwards. Since the end of the war there are lots of people buying things this way otherwise they would never have anything that they could not really afford to buy and it takes such a long time to save any amount of money. I am working full time and I am getting plenty of part time work, so you have no need to worry I'll not bring disgrace to you and the old chap"(as he called his father) George said defiantly watching his mother's face. He knew that it was she who took the blunt of his father's anger when he was upset, not that his Dad would ever lay a finger on his mother but his dad could go on a bit when tired and in a bad mood.

"I am sure that your father will not be very pleased with what you have just told me. We may not have much to shout about but we do not owe a penny to any one. That is how your father and I have managed all these years and he will wish you to do the same." Ivy said very sternly."If you go ahead with your big ideas, then on your own head be it. I have now said what I think of your crazy idea."

Ivy Fleming had waited her chance and when her husband Terry had been in an exceptionally good mood, she had casually hinted that George was thinking about buying a motor bike.

"How the hell does he intend paying for one?" Terry demanded to know.

"I don't rightly know" Ivy lied but if you have a word with him I am sure that he will explain how he proposes to do it".

"So you have some idea of what he is up to. I thought as much or you would not be seeing how the land lies for him. I will have a word with him and see what he has to say. Buying a motor bike indeed, he can forget about that".

"Oh dear", Thought Ivy here we go again another argument.

Terry Fleming was a fairly quiet man He did a hard days work for a days pay. He worked as a foreman of a gang of men. He had worked with some of them for quite a few years and over the years he had solved many problems that he come across, He found that it was better to try and solve problems diplomatically. Much easier than bawling and shouting his head off, He found that he had much better co-operation from the men. This way he was able to share a pint of beer with any one of them and they all had respect for him. And this had always been his philosophy at home. He always came straight home in the evenings. He could have called at the pub for a pint of beer on the way home from work like a lot of the men that he worked with. He preferred to go home to his wife and family. He would put his bicycle in the shed and then as he came in to the back kitchen, hang his cap and jacket on the same hook on the back of the door each night. He would wash his hands and rinse his face in the kitchen sink and then he would sit in his wooden armchair at the table to eat his evening meal. It was easy to see where George had got his good looks. His father was a really good-looking fellow despite his age. He had very thick black wavy hair that was now going grey. He was not tall and at the same time neither was not a slim. In fact he had quite a rounded belly around which he wore a leather belt to keep his thick tweed working trousers up around his waist. The belt was fastened with a brass buckle He had only to threaten the boys with his belt when they were younger and they knew exactly how far they dare to push him before he took it off and gave them a spanking with it. They had grown up to have a great deal of respect for their father, if they misbehaved themselves or played their mother up, he had only to threaten to take his belt off to them and peace would be instantly restored. His bark could be bad and neither George, nor Thomas antagonised him enough to feel his bite

Terry decided to wait his time before confronting his oldest son. He saw his chance when he was sat in his wooden armchair by the fireside. He never did use the more comfortable leather armchairs; he much preferred to sit upright. This position seemed to ease the pains in his back which he had endured throughout the day bending and lifting the heavy wooden sleepers, as they laid them ready for the rail track.

George having already having taken a bath and changed into better clothes was taking a pair of polished shoes from under the side board, it was obvious that he was off out for the evening. Thomas and Judith were not in for some reason or other. Judith had probably gone to see her friend down the village and Thomas had not been in for his tea as yet, he could be doing a bit of overtime for his boss. "Your Mother has hinted to me that you are thinking about buying a motor bike, is this true". His Father asked.

His mother rose from the armchair where she was seated and made the excuse that she had some ironing to do she went into the kitchen, if there was going to be a row she was not sitting listening to the two men. Perhaps I should not have mentioned any thing about the bike. Her husband always seemed to be having a go at George these days. The lad was almost twenty-one. She felt that it was such a pity that the two of them did not have more in common like she thought fathers and sons should have.

"Is it true?" Terry said more firmly "What sort of bike are you thinking of buying and if so where do you propose to get the money? I know that you have not saved that sort of money, according to what I have worked out when you have paid your share towards the house keeping and fancy clothes"

"So what?" George retorted getting quite angry as he put the polished shoes on his feet. To think that his father was insinuating that he should not buy what he wished with the money he earned. He had considered what he had left over was his to do what he liked with and as he wished.

George had become much busier at weekends, he had bought more tools such as an electric drill to make the work easier and quicker to complete. His father had a good big shed in the garden and he had allowed his sons to use it as a workshop. As long as they did not interfere with his gardening tools he had been quite happy to let both his sons set it up as a workshop.

"I asked you how you were proposing to pay for this bike that you are thinking of buying." His father raised his voice again. "I want some answers. Your mother and I have never owed money to any one and we do not intend to start now, and neither should you." He had lit a cigarette and was sitting back enjoying smoking it.

"What get no further than what you have, still going to work on a push bike at your age. You will still be going to work on that when you retire and as for smoking a few fags I notice that you smoke plenty. If you must know I will put a deposit on a bike and then pay it off by monthly instalments. I have already looked into it. The boss at work says that he will give me a good reference. It's an AJS that I am having a, 250." Terry was hoping that it would be no bigger than a 50cc.

"That big; I hope you know what you are doing." Terry said again quite sternly. "So you are buying a motor bike. I hope you know what you are doing. Break your bloody neck I shouldn't wonder." His father continued.

"I know how to ride a motor bike" George retorted being as flippant as he could. "What have you got against them?" George was now standing and looking straight at his father accusingly.

"Too bloody fast" snapped his father. "What about Hannah are you intending to take her on the back of this bike?" George felt it best not to give an answer.

"I would not like to see her get killed. Hannah seems quite a decent girl from what I have heard and seen of her. Your mother and I were hoping that you were going to look after her and settle down." He looked at George daring him to answer back.

Since the ending of the war there were bigger and better motor bikes being made. Some had terrific power and could travel at enormous speeds. There were so many youngsters getting killed on motor bikes. Mostly it was because they were inclined to show off and take the bends on the roads at far too great a speed than they could manage and for not wearing safety helmets. So many had died of head injuries. The government was proposing to bring in legislation to make it compulsory for the wearing of safety helmets so that it would soon be made law.

Terry Fleming could see that he was getting nowhere with this argument it was obvious that George had made up his mind. He decided he would have the last word.

"You promised me that you would keep away from that little tart? Next door. I saw you going up the village just after she went out the other night. You think that I don't notice things. You were lucky that kid of hers was not pinned on you. You're bloody lucky that no one could prove it or you would have had to take the consequences. I would bet a pound to a penny that you were responsible. I would like to know what went wrong up at the Wrekin Cottage. Gwen Watson would not have fallen out with you over anything. Bonking in bed with her I should not have wondered. I notice that you do not get all spived up on a Monday night since you finished going up there. Old Eric Watson would not have known who had been at the house. He went home so drunk on a Monday night. I have heard it said that it is a good job that his pony knew every rock on the track. Or the pair of them would have gone over the side. Many were the time that he and the pony could have been killed. There are some sheer drops down the sides from the main track according to what your mother tells me. I don't expect that old Eric Watson is much use to his wife at his age. Drinks himself silly he does on a Monday and that can't be doing his insides much good. I have heard that the drink that he has had over the years is now taking its toll and that his health is beginning to suffer. It's as I said, if it were not for that pony of his knowing its way home He would never have got home, been dead years ago". He started to chuckle at the thought of the pony falling down the side of the Wrekin taking Eric Watson and the trap with it. This was enough for George.

His father was hitting a raw nerve. He had only mentioned that he intended buying a motor bike to his Mother and now he was being interrogated. He went out of the living room and made for the back door. If his father had only known how near the truth he had been he would have had forty fits.

Ivy had been listening to it all from the kitchen and she was beginning to wonder if she was hearing correctly when George pushed past the ironing board and went out through the back door giving it quite a bang as he went. Ivy decided that it would be better to carry on with what she was doing and pretend that she had not heard the last bit of the conversation. That peroxide blonde that lived next door was about nineteen years old and to Ivy she was a pain. She lived in a little cottage with her grandparents. A lane to a field separated their two properties. No one knew anything about her real parents, and the fact that she lived in a village community did give cause for intrigue and gossip. That blonde was out with any man in trousers. Ivy felt that Terry was quite right to have a go at their son but at the same time, she hated rows in the house. She knew what George got up to and she knew that his father was not as daft and indifferent as George thought that he was. Although he was at work for most of the time, he did not miss much that went on in the village and what he did miss the neighbours told him when they came to him for a cheap hair trim in the garden shed. Terry was extremely good at cutting hair and the village men made great use of him. The thought that George might have been going up the Wrekin on a Monday evening had not crossed Ivy's mind until now that Terry had mentioned it. Oh my goodness, whatever if her husband had been right. He could be it did not bear thinking about. Ivy had just thought that her son had a girl friend and that he did not want to bring her home for some reason or other. But when she began to think about it perhaps her Terry could be right. That woman Gwen Watson was married with four children; surely she had not been using George to satisfy her sexual desires behind her husbands back.

Oh yes she had. If they had only known there would have been more rows in the house. The trouble had begun when Gwen Watson had been very observant and she had seen the looks that had passed between George and Hannah and had waited her time to be absolutely sure. She knew that if she said anything to George there was always the danger that he might tell of their secret liaisons. If George had said anything and if it did get back to her husband there would be the most almighty row and all hell would break loose. At the same time if George did tell, it would not do his reputation much good. If it was found out that he had been sneaking up the Wrekin to go to bed with a married woman, mother of four children, it would not look very good for him at all. His friends would shun him and his father would probably turn him out of home and on to the road. Gwen knew that if her husband did find out he would give her hell for a while but he depended on her to do the work, far too much to throw her out. He would see to it that George would pay for it one way or another He had plenty of drinking pals and some could be of very shady character. Gwen had seduced George when he had been a mere lad of seventeen. He had learned quite a lot about girls with general talk and with the lads at school. He had not plucked up courage to have a girl friend of his own. He had never tried even to kiss a girl. There had been one or two girls that he had fancied but had never had the guts to approach a girl in case he had his face slapped. George was far too full of himself to be intimidated by one of the girls at school He did not want to make a proper fool of himself. He had decided that it would be better to wait until after leaving school and then see what happened. He loved the countryside and when Gwen Watson had asked her brother Charlie if he knew of a good lad from the village who would come with him at weekends to look after the swing boats and help out with other mundane jobs. Charlie had asked Terry Fleming if he would let George go with him up to the Cottage at weekends. And so it had been agreed. George had not been going for more than one year when his brother Thomas asked to go with them so that he too could earn some pocket money and so he had gone along with his brother and there had been plenty of work for all three to do. Gwen had watched this lad George with interest, his good looks and his charm fascinated her. It was a pleasure to have him around the place. She first tried to get his attention by praising him for his work and by the time he was seventeen, he was a very virile young man. Gwen had missed out having the love of a young man when she had been in her teens Eric had seen to that. He had crept into her room at night and persuaded her that he loved her and that he had wanted her. She had fallen for it and had not screamed out when he slipped in between the sheets of her bed. This had gone on completely unknown to their employer Miss Birrell. When Gwen became pregnant the cat was let out of the bag so to speak. Miss Birrell called Gwen the most dreadful names. She made out that Gwen had been a cheap hussy and was not fit to live under her roof for encouraging the good and kindly man Eric into such wanton ways. She was now getting an old lady and she knew that she could not now manage with out Eric's help. She decided that the best and only thing for them to do was to marry and to make it as quickly as possible. She gave them no choice. She had maintained that they would otherwise bring disgrace to her good name. She felt that she would be held responsible for allowing such carryings on under her roof. Gwen had tried to tell her employer the truth about Eric creeping into her room at nights and would have his way with her but she would hear none of it. Gwen told her that if she were sent home in disgrace her Mother would turn her out on to the road. She had no choice but to marry Eric and take the consequences. Soon after Miss Birrell had died and Gwen had become her own mistress for the first time in her life Whether she had any feeling of real love for this fat bellied man who had seduced her when she had been so young. She did not care. She had a roof over her head and good food in her belly and that was a lot more than many other girls who had ended up in the same predicament were able to have. She had felt quite good about being mistress of the house despite all the hard work that it involved, as she had become pregnant again and again and was now the mother of three.

Eric had dreamt of being able to make love to a young woman for the last twenty years. He had never had the opportunity until this young girl Gwen had come to live at the Cottage. And he had plucked up his courage to see what her responses would be if he were to try and bed her. He could not believe his luck when he had persuaded Gwen not to scream out when he had first seduced her. Now that he had married the girl she was his and only his. Eric had liked to have a drink of his favourite whisky before retiring to bed and with the amount of alcohol that he consumed on a Monday when he went into town; it was now taking its toll on his liver. Gwen had given birth to a fourth child just when these two young lads had come to help her brother Charlie with the work. Despite getting pregnant for the fourth time Gwen did not enjoy her husband's lovemaking. When George had come on the scene she had found that she was besotted with him.

Here was the handsome lad, the sort that she had always dreamed of meeting when she had been a young girl. He had the looks the charm that only a few girls could dream about. She took her time, she knew exactly what she was doing, just a smile at the right moment a gentle touch when he was pouring a bucket of water into the tank on the range. She had made sure that it was never at a time when anyone else's eyes could witness and jump to conclusions. She had noticed that George had never repelled her, in fact he would return her smile and respond to her touch and closeness as she had hoped that he would this had led them on the path that they had taken. She had been able to teach him the fine arts of lovemaking and what an apt pupil he had been. Before he had realised what had happened he was well and truly under her spell and was certainly enjoying him self. Gwen knew that George could never deny what wonderful hours that they had spent together. Jealousy had got the better of her, when she thought of all the risks that she had taken for him. She did not consider the risks that he had taken, but she was angry now that she could see that he was about to turn his affections elsewhere as soon as a schoolgirl had come along. She was very angry indeed. She had tackled him about it on the Sunday morning when he had brought her a tray of cakes to the kitchen and she had spotted her chance to have it out with him. Eric had gone back up stairs to lie down after eating very little breakfast, which was certainly not like him. He usually enjoyed the fried bacon or ham and eggs with golden fried bread that she daily put before him. He had not felt very well when he had got up earlier and as he usually did each and every morning, He raked and stoked up the fire in the range so that it brought new life into it ready to start a long heavy day's work. It would have cooled down considerably from the night before.

This range was well banked up with coal when they retired to bed they could not afford to let it go completely out. When Gwen had come downstairs that morning she thought that he looked absolutely dreadful that she had persuaded him to go back to bed. It took her some time to convince him that they could all manage with out his help at least for a little while.

She spotted her chance when she was alone in the back kitchen George placed the tray of cakes on the kitchen table that he had brought from the bake house and turned to leave when Gwen's voice full of anger stopped him in his tracks.

"You have a crush on that girl Hannah, I can see it a mile off and don't you try to deny it I have been watching the pair of you." She said accusingly to George who could see that Gwen was angry.

"Now George I am going to give you have an ultimatum. You either forget about that little floozy or there is to be no creeping up here on Monday evenings to have your pleasures with me." She said with vengeance. George was quite taken aback but to Gwen's utter amazement and anger George had just shrugged his shoulders and said calmly.

"So be it I will not be coming up here again on a Monday night". It was then that Gwen had exploded and when she could see that she was not making any headway she calmed down and tried all her powers of persuasion, but to no avail When she realised that their secret rendezvous were about to come to an end. She lost her temper and told him to get off the hill. But she did not expect him to take Hannah with him and that had left her and her husband two helpers short

Eric's health had not been was too good for several weeks and Gwen had sensed that some thing was really concerning him. When she had mentioned this to him all he had done was to snap her head off, telling her to leave him alone as he considered that he was not ready for the cemetery as yet. When he was ready to snuff it he would tell her.

Eric came downstairs just after George and Hannah had left and wanted to know what all the shouting had been about which he had heard from upstairs. Gwen tried to tell him that it was George who was being awkward and that he had walked out taking Hannah with him saying, that he and Hannah were not coming to work again.

"I don't believe it. Why? What has gone wrong? George has been helping us since he left school and we have not had any problems until now."

"Well you can blame it on that Thomas girl, I think that she has persuaded him that she wants taking out and about on Sundays and the silly lad has fallen for her charm"

"I will have a word with her father when I see him in the auction. I will try to find out what is going on. Where are we going to find good help like George I just do not know? He has been with us for so long. I had got to know that I could depend on him. Dear oh dear if only I was a few years younger" He sighed. Gwen shouted at him "Well you are not. You are getting an old man and you expect me to run this place and rear your kids almost single-handed. Well I have had enough. Do you hear me? I have had enough of being stuck up here on this dammed hill day in day out? All that I have known since I was fourteen is work and more work," She waited for her husband's reaction. She thought he would shout at her and probably throw the nearest thing that he could get his hands on. But he was so amazed at her saying anything back to him in retaliation that he just sat back in his chair and said no more. He did not like to tell her how rotten that he had been feeling just lately and that he was too scared to consult a doctor. Like most men he buried his head in the sand (so to speak) hoping that whatever it was causing him so much pain in his stomach would eventually go away.

Ivy folded the ironing board and put it in its usual place and she took the clean freshly ironed shirts through to the living room. She was intending to take them up stairs and hang them up in the appropriate rooms. Terry's voice stopped her as she went though the living room.

"You know love I reckon that was where George was going on a Monday night I could tell by the look on his face that I had hit on a raw nerve the stupid bugger. If I am right and I am pretty sure that I am. He wants his back side kicking and I would like to be the one to do it. It's a pity that he missed out on having to do National Service. A good spell in the Army would have done him the world of good. What do you think? I reckon that you have spoiled him far too much"

"Now just a minute Terry Don't you dare go blaming me if what you think is right. It's that woman up the Wrekin that you should be shouting at. What I saw of things up there. I could see nothing untoward. I don't think that there was anything going on. The pair of them certainly gave nothing away to the rest of us"

"Well you would not be looking because you did not suspect that there was any thing going on".

"Now just a minute Terry you are only guessing. You know that you could be quite wrong I surely hope that you are"

"I reckon that I am not far wrong I have not sat in this chair watching that lad grow up to know when I am right or when I am wrong".

"Well as you say and if you are right, it is all over now the lad does not go up to the cottage at all so I think that it would be best that you forget all about it in case you are guessing wrongly. I really don't think that he would have been so stupid to take such dangerous risks. I really don't. I cannot accept that he would go to bed with a married woman. As for going in the army it was not his fault that he missed it. He was too old when the government started the National Service. Although he did only just miss it by months."

"Trust you to take his part; you have always been the same, ready to make excuses for him when ever I have a go at him"

"Terry, don't start an argument with me especially when you have no proof of what he has been up to. I can't believe that he would be so stupid and I think that you are jumping to conclusions a bit too quick for my liking"

"You only had to see the expression on that lad's face to know that I was right, but as you say it looks as if that is what they fell out about and it is all over now thank goodness. Eric Watson drinks with some shady characters by what I have heard they sit in the pub on Mondays playing cards for most of the time. It is amazing how much money is passed between hands in an evening. "

"Let's drop the subject can we or we shall be at each others throats and I, for one, do not want that. Forget about the Wrekin Cottage now that there are none of us going up there any more".

"Alright as you say, we don't want to be arguing about some thing we are not sure about but I reckon that I hit on a pretty raw nerve to night".

"Well he certainly went out through the door in a right paddy, let's forget about it. I will go and hang these shirts up before they become a mass of creases. Then I will make us a nice cup of tea"

"Aye you do that lass No point in us getting upset about things that we are not certain about".

"No point at all", Ivy said to herself as she went up stairs but if I thought for one moment that Terry was right, I would go up there and give that woman a piece of my mind. Now that George thinks that we know what has been going on he will go out of his way to keep on the right side of us which I don't think will be such a bad thing at all.

George had really fancied Hannah from the first time that she had gone to help out at the Cottage and he wanted to impress her. The thought that buying a motor bike should help and not only that, they would be able to go further a field together and see so many new and different places. George knew that Hannah was very naïve and shy with regards to boys. He put this down to the fact that she had been reared with girls and that she had gone to a girl's school. It was obvious to him that she was still a virgin. This gave George a great deal of satisfaction. He certainly was going to be the first to have a proper relationship with her if he could. Woe be tide any other lad that dared to try and steal her affections.

He had guessed quite rightly that Hannah was so naïve she knew nothing

About sex. Her Mother and older sisters had told her nothing about what to expect. Hannah had heard the other girls at school giggling and making different remarks but because she had missed so much school during the war years they were not inclined to confide in her. Hannah realised that they had each other for pals, she had often wondered why they referred to one girl in particular as Pro Perry but she had not got a clue as to what the girls were on about. She had accepted that kissing and cuddling was all that there was to having a boy friend.

Hannah settled in with her new family and Mr and Mrs Pearson were quite pleased with her. She was nervous that her mother might come causing more trouble and she made one or two mistakes but they were overlooked. She had started in the August and it was in October that Mr Pearson started to feel unwell; his wife advised that he saw his Doctor and has a check up. His Doctor was not too perturbed about his health and his well being. So his health was given no more thought

Mr Pearson was of small stature and much over weight he had short legs and a rounded belly. He had little hair, infact he was quite bald on top. Hannah guessed that he must be at least twelve years older than his wife. During conversation she found that he had been married before and his first wife had died young. There had been one daughter of that marriage and an aunt had taken pity on the child and had agreed to rear her for him. This enabled Geoff Pearson to help his father run a garage at Coalbrookdale.

After a few years for some reason or other father and son had fallen out and Geoff left his father's garage to start his own taxi business in Wellington. He started with just one fairly old car but he had the advantage of being able to do his own repairs and keep it on the road despite the long hours and miles that he was doing. He became quite successful and bought other cars and had part-time drivers to help him soon after he had a fleet of cars, he decided that he would impress the public so he bought a Rolls Royce Hearse and as the business grew he added two Rolls Royce cars. He used the two cars for weddings as well as for funerals. These were always kept immaculately clean and polished and did look grand when they turned out. The drivers always wore uniform and peaked caps. Geoff Pearson took a great pride in the business. He had engaged a local woman Charlotte Rigsby to work as his housekeeper and bookkeeper. She was quite an intelligent woman in her late twenties. Fairly short in height with brown hair cut short and she had very dark brown eyes, He found that she was very keen on driving and that she enjoyed working along side him with the business. She turned out to be an extremely good driver and was able to help him a great deal and they fell in love and they had married.

He and his new wife got on so well together that they quickly built up the business and they were able to take on more drivers. They were able to afford two full time drivers.

They succeeded in making contracts with the County Council to deliver school meals from a school canteen in town to the outlying schools in the country areas. Also they had the contract to take Lay Preachers out to the country Chapels on Sunday evenings, where, the driver would wait at the last one and then make the return journey bringing the preachers back into town. A woman came in to do the washing and the cleaning. As the children two girls and a baby son had arrived Charlotte Pearson found that she missed the driving and they decided to employ some one to live in to help take care of the little ones and this was where Hannah had come to be employed.

Hannah's job was to help take care of the new baby son Oliver and help with the girls Annette who was six years old and she was such a pretty little girl with blonde curly hair and a china doll complexion. She attended the local infant's school. Her sister Kate had dark hair and resembled their mother. She was a much plainer looking child. She was attending a nursery school. It was Hannah's job to give them breakfast. To see that they were properly dressed and to take and meet them from school. She was also given the responsibility of supervising their evening meal, bathing them and putting all three children to bed. She loved reading their storybooks for them at bedtime. She was able to see George when she had her off duty half days and they had a great time, George took her to the cinema and they both started dancing lessons Hannah had never felt so good. George's family made her so welcome and she got on well with both Ivy and her daughter Judith.

As Christmas approached Hannah decided to go back home to take some presents for the family hoping that her mother had forgiven her for leaving home and that she had accepted that she was seeing George but Hannah was in for a shock.

Hannah cycled to the farm one Wednesday afternoon. Her dad Fred was very pleased to see her and he said so. Hannah accepted a cup of tea and sat down the backside of the kitchen table. They made idle conversation about this and that. After Fred had left the kitchen Dorothy wanted to know if Hannah was still seeing George Hannah decided that it was better not to lie so she just kept quiet. Her silence told her Mother just what she wanted to know. She started to shout at her.

"I'll not have you going out with a lad from a council house". She shouted.

She pointed to the Christmas paper wrapped parcels that Hannah had put on the kitchen table. "And what is more, we don't want you bringing your fancy presents here,"

Hannah was quite shocked at her Mother's attitude it sounded to her as if she was no longer part of the family and that it would have been better had she kept away. She quickly picked up her bag from the kitchen table leaving the presents where they were. She went out through the kitchen door her mother's voice still echoing in her ears. Hannah vowed not to go near again for some time to come.

On Christmas Day Geoff Pearson's health really started to deteriorate, his breathing was becoming laboured and much worse. Charlotte was really concerned for him; he did not show any interest in the little ones at all. It was if he just could not be bothered with them, consequently it turned out to be a very miserable Christmas day for every one. Charlotte's mother and Sister Rosie came during the afternoon but did not stay for tea as they had been invited. They left and advised Charlotte to send for Geoff's doctor next day. This Charlotte did and the doctor called the next afternoon and was not a happy man to be called out on Boxing Day. After an examination he made no hesitation in telephoning for an ambulance, he told Charlotte not to worry too much but as Geoff's breathing was becoming much more laboured the hospital would have far better facilities to treat and help him. He did not want Charlotte to see that he was very concerned for Geoff. He had guessed what was wrong with him but he did not want to alarm Charlotte he decided to let the hospital do that. Charlotte rode in the ambulance with him and Rosie followed in one of the cars, Geoffrey was admitted and put into an isolation ward. The doctors at the hospital diagnosed that he had contacted Poliomyelitis and explained to both Charlotte and Rosie that he was seriously ill. They returned home very forlorn and worried. Day by day Geoff's health deteriorated and he became much worse and it was decided that he needed help with his breathing so consequently he was put into what was called an iron lung. An awe inspiring machine that would do his breathing for him. Hannah often accompanied Charlotte when she could get away from the business to visit him. When they were able to, they took the children with them, hoping that seeing the little ones would encourage Geoff to put up an incentive to fight against his illness. Poliomyelitis was a very infectious disease so consequently they were not allowed to enter the room where he lay. They had to stand outside and look in through a window and try to communicate with hand signals. As her husband's health deteriorated Charlotte became really concerned for both her family and the business. At the end of January Geoff Pearson died of his illness. Poliomyelitis was a scourge at the time so many were dying and being crippled from the disease. It was really frightening.

Hannah's help was needed more that ever now. With Charlotte's older sister Elizabeth to advise her, Charlotte carried on running the business. The going was extremely tough for every one

Soon after her husband's death, Charlotte noticed that all was not well with her baby son Oliver. After several tests at Shrewsbury hospital, it was confirmed that he too had contacted a mild attack of poliomyelitis and it was causing him to have difficulties in sitting upright and with his breathing. The Orthopaedic Surgeon who was in charge of Oliver's case instructed Charlotte how to give Oliver some daily exercises which he considered were necessary. These exercises were not pleasant to give a child of that age. Hannah would have to hold him firmly on the kitchen table. Charlotte would grip his little body firmly and stretched and twisted him as she had been instructed. This exercise was to strengthen his chest and other muscles. Apparently it all helped to save his life and get his muscles especially his lungs functioning, as they should be.

George became fixed on the idea of having the A.J.S. motor bike despite what ever his father's objections were. George talked of nothing else but motor bikes. He spoke to his friends who had bikes and the more he talked and the more he saw the more convinced he was that he was doing the right thing. He and Hannah visited all the motor cycle shops that they could. They would catch the train to Wolverhampton and even went as far as Birmingham to take a look at different models and the prices that were being asked.

A few weeks later George had enough money to put the deposit on an A.J.S. 250 bike and was able to take delivery of it.

"You will have to wrap up warm when you come on the back of this and you will certainly have to buy a crash helmet. I suggest that you treat yourself to a good pair of trousers as warm as possible.

"But George; I have never worn a pair of trousers, my mother would never have heard of such a thing unless you were ordered to and that there was no other choice such as serving in the armed services and only then she considered that it was acceptable. "I will not have you dressing like men. That I will not" Hannah mimicked her mother.

"For goodness sake Hannah, try to forget everything that your Mother has said. She is so far behind the times and so old fashioned. You have just got to get with it a bit more, you try riding on the back of this in the winter months in a skirt and you will be frozen". He said pointing to his lovely new machine.

"Yes, you certainly have a point George, I will see what I can do and any way we won't be going to see my mother for some time I still don't like her attitude towards you. I don't see any point in going there just to start an argument. Do you?" Hannah looked at George hoping that he would agree with her but at the same time she knew that George would not hesitate to tell her mother what he thought of her and it would not be very nice. He had certainly resented Dorothy's attitude towards him and the fact that his family lived in a council house made him an undesirable character to be associating with one of her daughters.

"They are still living in the Victorian age. The days are gone when the parents chose who was good enough for their daughters and who was not. The war has changed everything and now that there are cars and ways and means for the working man to better himself. There are people such as your mother who do not like to accept that times are changing. They certainly do not like it. One day I will make you proud of me, just you wait and see. We will show her you see if we don't"

The look of determination on George's face had said it all as far as Hannah was concerned. She could see his point of view. Her mother was being so old fashioned but then Hannah realised that she had been like that as long as she could remember.

Judith had met a young man named Simon Bradbury who was also keen to have a motor bike so he and George became firm friends. Simon decided that he would also buy a motor bike. He chose to buy a Royal Enfield.

"I have been talking to one of my mates Bill Harper. He has a 550 Matchless. A lovely machine" George said with envy. "He is a member of a motor cycle club and he wants us four to join, I think that I could persuade Simon and Judith to come with us. The four of us could go out together". George was so enthusiastic and carried Hannah a way with his dreams.

Charlotte and her sister Elizabeth decided that the two girls could benefit much more if they were sent to a boarding school. They chose one in Wolverhampton. Hannah was so sad about this decision she felt that they would have been far better at home. It was an awful lot for the little girls to cope with so soon after losing their Daddy. It was with a very sad heart that Charlotte and Hannah took them there. They soon settled down, made new friends and enjoyed the new routine of the school The two of them seemed to be quite happy It was a school that were specialists with children who had lost a parent or both. Charlotte was now able to have a much better chance of concentrating on the running of the business.

Chapter Five
Places To See

Judith Fleming had taken after her father's side of the family in looks and stature. She was about the same height as Hannah five- foot- two. Her hair was like that of George very dark almost black which she kept cut short. She was of a much more solid build and seemed quite a plain girl but when she had applied a little make up she became a very attractive young lady.

George and Hannah started to go out with Judith and Simon, much more often. George took up his friend Bill Harper's suggestion and all four joined him at the motor cycle club. Bill was a brick layer with a local firm; he was so pleased that the four of them had joined. He introduced them to his girl friend Brenda. The meetings were held once a month at the pub called The Swan at Crackley Bank on the Staffordshire border. Hannah and Judith went along with the men to the meetings and consequently the four of them made many new friends.

"What do you think about going to the Isle of Man next year so that we could watch the T.T. Races?" George asked Simon "I have always dreamt of being able to see those bikers ride the race track and have a go ourselves. The members of the public are allowed to ride around the track on the Sunday.

"I don't know." replied Simon thoughtfully "I will think about it. What did you have in mind? Were you thinking that we three men should go or were you thinking of asking the girls to go with us? I can't really see that it would be Brenda's cup of tea. On the other hand do you think that she would let Bill go with out her?"

Brenda was very slim and quite tall she was about five feet eleven. She had light brown hair, which she wore, shoulder length and she had the most beautiful baby blue eyes. When she was out with the crowd she wore quite a lot of make up and she certainly looked a stunner. She was the envy of most of Bills friends at the club. One could see that her clothes were of the best quality and had cost quite a pretty penny. Far more than either Judith or Hannah could afford to spend on clothes. Bill was besotted with her and who could blame him, she was the best looking girl of the crowd.

The next time that the four of them met up with Bill and Brenda at the club the men's conversation promptly turned to talking about their bikes. What speed that they were able to do, what was the consumption of petrol? Different engine parts and where would be the best place to purchase this and that so that they could improve the performance of the bikes. Although Hannah did not understand much about motor bike engines, George had opened up a whole new world for her, she did how ever enjoy going out with George on his bike and the atmosphere of the club; Hannah dreamt that perhaps one day perhaps they would be able to afford a motor car but at the moment that was wishful thinking. George had to work extremely hard so that he could afford to pay the instalments on the bike and the extra cost of running it. This was very different from just having a pushbike. There was insurance and road tax to be paid for. New weatherproof clothes to be bought and George was very determined to show his father that he could afford to do it.

"Hannah there is so much that we can do. I have been thinking about us all going to the Isle of Man and watch the

T.T races in June next year. I have suggested it to Simon and Bill and they seem dead keen to go we could take you girls with us. We could all go together and have a proper holiday. I have always dreamed of being able to go and watch the races. Oh, to be able to ride around the famous T T. track on my own bike, it would be fantastic. Say that you will come, Hannah, so that we can get it all arranged in plenty of time. Talk to Charlotte Pearson and ask for the time off, you have not had a proper holiday that I can remember since I have known you." George sounded so enthusiastic; he was hoping that Hannah would be just as keen to have a holiday.

"But George it has been so difficult for Charlotte trying to run the business and cope with the children since she has lost her husband. I could not let her down if she needed me. I will do as you say and ask. We may be able to work something out the girls will be away at school in June and I am sure her Mother and sister will help with looking after Oliver. As you say George, it will only be for one week. There is Sally who comes in to do the washing and cleaning and I am sure that she would only be too willing to earn an extra penny or two. She has to help out with all the finances at home; her father is quite elderly and unable to work. She tries so hard to make ends meet; she told me that when she was younger she was very ill with tuberculosis and all about the sanatorium by Whitchurch where she was sent to, so that she could get plenty of fresh air into her lungs". Hannah tried to visualise Sally trying to keep up with Oliver. He would run rings around her.

Hannah spoke to Charlotte and she agreed that it was OK for her to have that particular week off in June. Hannah was so excited about it; she could hardly wait to tell George but she would not see him again until the following Sunday afternoon. She knew that he would be so pleased

"I will make it a holiday for you to remember," he said when she told him the good news; he was so pleased for her.

"You leave it to me. Judith is very good at organising this sort of thing. She and I will make the arrangements. We will discuss it with Bill and Brenda at the next club meeting.

Both Simon and Bill were very keen to go to the Isle of Man but Brenda was not. Brenda looked at Bill and smiled with her big baby blue eyes.

"Bill I would love to come away with you but if you think that I could go on a boat across water, there is no chance. I can't stand water so I for one can't possibly go by ferry. Darling I should be so seasick I know that I would. Let me think about it. I will see if Mummy would pay for me to go by plane, if I could fly there I could arrange to meet you, any way I am sure that we can work something out". .

Hannah and Judith looked at each other and raised their eyebrows in amazement. They both knew that it would be of no use what so ever for either of them to ask their Mothers to pay for them to go the Isle of Man by plane. They had no choice but to go with the men by ferry. If the weather were bad, they would have a rough crossing and there was not much that they would be able to do about it. Judith was the first to comment.

"Brenda, I am sure that the crossing will not be that bad. After all we are intending to go in the month of June. Why not come with us and try it? We will take care of you won't we Hannah".

Hannah was non-committal. This was to be the first time that she was to have a real holiday and she was already feeling apprehensive about going on a ferry and crossing the sea even if it was only 83 miles to the Isle of Man.

Judith continued. "Brenda this will be the first time that I have had a real holiday and I know that Hannah has not had one before. Forget about flying and come with us it will be great fun and as you know, all the men can talk about is bikes and it gets so boring for us girls. If you and Hannah did not come to these meetings so that we could have a bit of girls talk, I would not come with Simon every month. That would mean that it would be disappointing for them, I think that they like to show us girls off as much as their bikes.

Both Judith and Brenda had a lot more in common. They both worked in offices, and because of that they enjoyed each others company. Where as Hannah being so quiet and naïve did not have many topics of conversation, it was no use trying to talk about her school days all she had known was school and when not at school it had been work. All she could talk about was Charlotte Pearson and her business and that was not very exciting at all. Where as the other two had been going to a mixed school, they had both attended the New Secondary Modern School at Wellington Consequently they had learnt much more about boys and sex than Hannah had. They were able to talk about how they had fancied different boys and that they had kissed them and if they had not fancied them they had just given them the cold shoulder and had nothing more to do with them. They had found that this was great fun and they both had only gone with Simon and Bill since they had left school. Where as Hannah had never been kissed by any other boy than George! Hannah had always been a little chirpy one as a child competing with her sisters but this was very different.

At the high school the other girls would call you names such as a slut if they found out that you had been seeing more than one boy. Times were changing very quickly and much more freedom was being given as to whom a person saw and whom they went out with. The Victorian attitude was becoming very outdated and old fashioned. Since King Edward had abdicated for the love of a divorced woman and the Americans had been staying in the country during the war, things had certainly changed. New dance halls were opening up and rock and roll music was very popular there was the pallyglide, the twist and Jazz was becoming much more popular. More and more people were now buying television sets showing more and more of modern dances and new ways of life and this was the beginning of a new era, and it was frowned upon by many of the older generation.

Hannah was not interested in looking at other boys she had fallen hook line and sinker for George. He had once threatened what he would do to any other lad who tried to take her from him. "Any lad come sniffing around you will regret it". George had convinced Hannah that she was his girl friend and he would not fancy her going out with any one else. Hannah felt so proud of George to think that he thought that much of her and that he would protect her from all harm. This was the first real love that she had known and it was a new experience for her. All that she could remember from when she had been a little one was work or school and there was certainly no love shown what-so-ever at home or school. It was a case of standing up for one self or being bullied. Hannah had to stand up for her self at home and she had a very quick temper so she saw to it that she was not bullied at school.

Both Judith and Brenda thought that Hannah was very old fashioned by the style of the clothes that she wore. Hannah had bought a pair of dark brown trousers for riding on the back of the motor bike where as Judith's were green and Brenda's were red. Hannah had not been able to afford such an expensive crash helmet as the other two. She would have loved to have one like Judith's but it had been much a more expensive one. It was covered with leather and had a peak on the front of it. Both Judith and Brenda had much more money to spend than Hannah did; they did not have to pay any thing for their keep at home whereas Hannah's wage was much less because of her living in.

George had argued that a crash hat was a crash hat what ever it looked like and if it had not been for the ministry making it compulsory for riders and pillion passengers George would certainly not have bothered buying one.

"But George "Hannah had said. "If it will save the lives of many more young people and us surely it is better that we wear them. I am sure that your Dad feels better about the bike now that we wear them".

"I suppose so, you could have a point but I hate being dictated to and that is what the Government seems to be trying to do all the time. If it is not one thing it's another".

Hannah was inclined to listen to George's opinion more and more and agree with him. What she did not realise was that she was becoming completely brain washed by him. There had been so much other warm and water proof clothing that they had needed to buy that Hannah decided not to say any more about the crash helmet. She decided that perhaps one day she would be able to afford what she considered a much nicer one. She tried to save a little from her wages but some how there was always something or other that she had to spend on. Now that George and Hannah were talking about going to the Isle of Man, George pointed out that they must save really hard for the trip; he did not want to be embarrassed about lack of money in front of the others.

George would take Hannah out on the bike on her Sunday afternoon off and this all cost extra money especially if they stayed out to have a meal instead of going home for tea.

They would often pay a visit to George's Grandmother's house at Upton Magna. Hannah loved the old lady and they would sit and talk about so many things Hannah loved her to talk of her past. The old lady had given birth to George's mother Ivy and then she had given birth to triplets, another daughter and two sons who all still lived with her. The triplets were only a few years older than George, so they had a lot in common. Hannah and George would stay for tea and afterwards they all would sit around the table and play cards or have a go at playing darts with the dartboard that hung on the kitchen wall. How the boys teased Hannah when she had a go at throwing the darts and almost missed the board completely. When Hannah had been at home these games would never have been allowed to be played on a Sunday. Her mother had taught them how to play whist and she herself had often gone to the village hall to a whist drive but cards had never been allowed to be brought out on Sundays

"You would be playing with the devil," Dorothy would shout when one of them asked if they could bring out the playing cards.

George and Hannah did not go up the Wrekin again. They did how ever go occasionally to see her mother and dad and George would often be asked to do some repairs around the farm but Dorothy made it quite clear that George would never be accepted as part of the family. She told Hannah that the sooner that she came to her senses, as she put it, the better that it would be for every one.

Lizzy was going out with a neighbouring farmer Frank Timmins. Brother to Joe Timmins the butcher and he was quite acceptable to Dorothy. She was hoping that Lizzy and Frank would marry one day. Mary had had one or two men friends but nothing seemed to come from the relationships. This certainly pleased her mother. She and Fred needed Mary to work on the farm until William was old enough to leave school and drive the tractor. They had both realised what an asset she was and they both dreaded having to contemplate that one-day she could wish to marry and leave them. If she decided to leave them they could not see how they could manage with out her. It would mean having to pay another man full time to do her work and that would cost money. Bernie was working for them full time and they were managing the work well between them.

Dorothy had discussed the idea with Fred about sending William to a boarding school as soon as he became eleven years old. They had Helen who had just left school but she had got herself a daily job working for Mrs Corfield. Her mother was a bit miffed about it. She did not like another daughter deciding to go there to work but Helen like her sisters wanted to earn her own money. Dorothy made as much use of her when she could. When Helen was not at work, there was plenty to do at home. As for Sandra she was only five coming six and to all the other members of the family it looked as if she was allowed to do just as she liked. She would sometimes make an effort to collect a few morning sticks from the woodpile for her mother and some times fill a coal bucket for her but she would leave it for her Mother to carry any full buckets back into the kitchen. If she could get out of doing any other little jobs, she would

Time and time again Mary had complained to her Mother about Sandra's poor eyesight. Dorothy did however, after some time and Mary's complaining, give in and took Sandra to see a doctor. The doctor had confirmed that there was a problem and made an appointment for her to see an eye specialist at the Eye Ear and Throat hospital in Shrewsbury where it was confirmed that Sandra had cataracts growing over her eyes. She was told that there was little that could be done until the child was older. It would then just take a small amount of surgery to correct the fault. Dorothy was a bit peeved that Mary had been right all along and dismissed the problem as trivial._

June 1952 quickly came around and all George, Bill and Simon could talk about was the T.T. races and hoping that they would be able to see Geoff Duke riding and winning both the 250CC and the 500Cc races. Brenda had still refused to travel by ferry so it was agreed that she would go by plane and that she would catch up with the others when they arrived on the island. To fly was something the other girls could only dream about. Since the end of the war the demand to travel by plane had grown immensely. Lots of people were flying out of the country for their holidays. They were now able to go to all sorts of destinations all over the world hoping to enjoy much better weather than what we were having during our English summers. Planes were now bringing all sorts of merchandise from foreign Countries. Travelling by air was still quite expensive for the everyday working class but as the aeroplane industry became more and more competitive as more planes were being built, the cheaper the fares would become but that would be in the distant future. George with Judith's help had booked rooms for the six of them in a boarding house in Douglas. George, Simon, Bill and the two girls set off on the Saturday morning to ride to Liverpool to board the ferry. They saw so many other bikers riding in the same direction. The variety of different bikes was amazing. Some were large powerful machines. Some very old models and some were no more than 50CC. When the five of them arrived at the Liverpool docks to be loaded on to the ferry they could not believe their eyes when they saw how many other bikers were already there waiting to be loaded. There was so much noise, chatter and excitement and with George, Bill and Simon having fairly big bikes all three felt quite at ease amongst the others as they queued up and waited patiently for their turn to go on board.

What the men had not realised was that the port authorities emptied the petrol tanks of the bikes before they could be loaded on the ferry. This really did antagonise George who had made sure that his tank had been full of petrol before setting out and it was still about three-quarters full. There was no reimbursement for any fuel that was drained from the machines as this was considered a necessity as a fire precaution. They were told that there would be facilities to refill when they landed on the island. During the crossing George and Simon had very little to do with the girls. They were far too busy talking bikes with other male passengers. Neither, Hannah nor Judith had minded, they were not bothered. The two of them had heard enough about motor bikes at the club meetings and it was good to be left to their own devises and talk of other things.

Hannah loved the crossing, she was always at peace when she was near water and it only took a couple of hours and they were unloading again. It took longer to get fuel and deal with the administration than it had to cross the water. Bill was very anxious to catch up with Brenda and became very frustrated with the hold up. Brenda had not been too keen on the holiday and had almost pulled out at the last minute but Judith had persuaded her that they could have a good time and that it would be a bit of fun.

The rooms that they had booked were reasonably good, the three girls had to share one room Brenda was quite peeved about this but calmed down when she found that she did not have to share a bed with either of the other two girls. At least they each did have a single bed. She gave Hannah the impression that she would have much preferred to have been booked into single room in one of the much smarter hotels. The men shared a room higher up in the building.

The landlady kindly offered to provide a cooked meal that evening at little extra cost, all six decided to accept and agreed that is was a good idea. They had had enough of travelling for one day and did not feel inclined to have to go and find some where to feed themselves.

George, Bill and Simon could not wait for next morning Sunday, when the members of the public were allowed to ride around the famous racecourse. They were boasting of what speeds they were going to try and do and what speed they would take this famous corner or that one at. Hannah was beginning to feel nervous at the very thought of it all.

Sunday morning after breakfast, all six donned on their motor cycle gear and went to ride the racecourse, as did hundreds of other bikers. As George rounded some of the bends of the famous track Hannah really thought that she was going to fall off the bike She hated it when George leaned right over to the right or left she felt as if their knees were about to scrape the road surface. It was really scary. Once completed, the men seemed to be content to discuss the course and that became the topic of conversation for the rest of the day. After their evening meal they left their bikes and walked to explore the capital Douglas on foot. Having a pint of beer before turning in ready to see the start of the racing, scheduled for the next day. It was the smaller CC bikes, which raced on the Monday and Wednesday. It would be Friday that the race for the bigger bikes took place; this was the one that George, Bill and Simon had come specially to see.

With two clear days they could do what they wanted to do, they could explore the island or go shopping, or do what ever they wanted to do.

On the Monday morning all six were up early, had breakfasted and were out to find a suitable place to their best advantage to watch the day's events. Hannah could not believe her eyes as they watched the machines racing around the track. It was impossible to tell what speed they were travelling at. She could here the sound of the machine approaching but by the time, she had looked through George's camera lens ready to take a snap shot of the rider it was almost too late the machine had passed by. She was able to take some photos but she certainly did not expect very good results. Judith and Brenda were also doing their best to take photographs of the bikes and riders, but like Hannah they had little success by the time they had tried to focus the camera the bike had gone past. The men were far too engrossed watching the bikes pass by to be bothered with what the girls were up to.

Thursday afternoon George and Hannah decided that being as it was such a beautiful afternoon weather wise they would ride off on their own and have a look at Castle town and the far side of the island. They had arranged to meet up with the others back at their digs for about four o'clock. They rode out to what was called the point.

"Let's stay here for a while" said George. He found a very quiet spot near a lovely little cove. The sea stretched out before them. To Hannah it was breathtakingly beautiful and so tranquil George propped the bike on its stand. He made sure that the ground was solid enough to take the weight of the bike. He was so proud of it, he would not have liked it to fall over and be damaged. They sat down in the warm sand dunes and talked about so many subjects, nothing in particular but at the same time covering so much that they wanted to talk to each other about. They were so happy; Hannah felt that nothing could spoil this day. George held Hannah so close to him and told her that he loved her and what about starting to think about their future together.

"I have been thinking that it is about time that we started to make some plans you will soon be eighteen and we must make a start to think about the future if we are to be together for always".

"That's a funny way of proposing". Hannah giggled. "You know that Mam and Dad will never agree to me marrying you. Mother will stand in the way no matter how nicely that we ask them and Dad will just have to do as he is told"

"I don't expect that they will. I know that I am not good enough for the likes of them." George sounded dreadfully hurt about the fact that Hannah's mother would never accept him as a future husband for their daughter. Did she have to remind him right now, he felt that he could do with out thinking about her mother or her father?

"George you are good enough for me. I will have a go at talking to them again and then perhaps they will come around to the idea. Why don't we go and see them together. We could try and make a good impression. We could tell them that we intend staying together despite their objections; after all we have nothing to lose.

"You must be joking, your mother would have the screaming abdabs and your Dad would then order us off the bank. You know I think your mother blames me for your leaving home. She would have preferred you to stay and work on the farm slogging your guts out for them. You only have to look at Mary and you can see for your self that she is still working as hard as ever and you know what I reckon that when William is older enough to take her place, they will not show any appreciation for all that she has done for them. I could be wrong but I guess that they will not show one little bit. Your Dad might, but what I have seen of him if you're Mother says that William can have this or that; it looks as if William must have it. It looks to me as if your Dad dared not put up any argument and so she always has her own way.

"Don't be so cynical darling I will go and see them on my own if that is how you feel. What do you think if I buy mother a present from here and some little thing for Mary and Sandra? It would be nice to have their blessing if we could. Anyway we have a long way to go as yet".

"If you take presents home don't you forget William or you will be in trouble? We will marry one day I know that we will. I really do love you Hannah" George whispered tenderly. He was beginning to feel very aroused by Hannah's closeness.

"Forget about them for the time being. We will worry about them when we get back".

Hannah had sensed what George was thinking, She glanced at his wristwatch and realised that they been talking for much longer than she had realised. She sat up quite quickly and released herself from his grip.

"We must go George. Look at the time. Your watch says that it is a quarter to four and if you remember you promised to meet the others back at the digs at four o'clock. They wanted all of us to go out for a drink tonight before watching the big race tomorrow. We have to get ourselves a meal or something to eat before we go out for a drink tonight, to morrow night we will have to think about packing up, we have to be out of the digs by twelve o'clock on Saturday. I would like to buy a few presents on Saturday morning, and pack them before we have to go to the docks. Hannah started to brush the sand from her hair and clothes.

"Damn, damn". George said to himself. As they had lain in the warm sand dunes completely oblivious to passers by, it had taken him all his self-control not to make love to Hannah and he was pretty sure that she would have responded if he had tried. He had to face facts, perhaps it would not be too bad if he attempted any thing further once Hannah was eighteen but for the time being he dare not take the risk of getting her pregnant. They would have to marry in disgrace and where would they live and besides they had no money saved worth talking about. To even consider such a move at the present time would be foolhardy and unthinkable but he hated having to control himself to this extent.

Since George had bought the bike and now that he had to work that much harder he did not see much of Nell the blonde from next door. They met less frequently the only time that he went out for pleasure was to the club and when Hannah was able to have time off. When he could, he would be doing work in the evenings and at weekends, he had not realised how much part time work was available

Nell had never bothered about taking any precautions that he knew of. He had sometimes used French letters (condoms as they are called today) She had never seemed worried about getting pregnant. For some reason or other she did not seem to get pregnant. She did once when she had a baby boy and as George knew only too well that he could have been the father. He was not going to admit that to any one because he knew that Nell had been with most of the young lads and married men in the village.

George did not mind, if she was quite happy to give a lesson or two to any of the younger village lads. He only used her to satisfy his needs. He did not love her as he loved Hannah so he did not have much respect for her, in fact if he told the truth he had none what-so- ever. He did not see any reason why the other lads should not do the same as he was as long as she was happy to oblige. None of this was ever discussed in public but most of the village knew what went on. But someone must have been paying her a pretty penny. She was always well dressed, her hair bleached blonde and she liked to wear quite a lot of make up. George had insisted that she wiped her lipstick from off her mouth when he had met her he did not want to go home with that all over his shirt collar. His mother would have soon wanted to know whom he had been with

He no longer had Gwen to satisfy his needs even if it had been only once a week. Thank goodness that he had sometimes used some precaution when they were in bed together. The consequences did not bear thinking about because according to Gwen she and Eric had not made love since the last child had been born she had seen to that. If she got pregnant there would have been some very difficult questions to be answered.

"O.K, lets get going". George said his thoughts changing to his present situation. He put on his crash helmet and took the bike from its stand and started the engine. Hannah sat on the pillion holding George around his middle, they rode off towards Douglas; she had enjoyed their time together she had felt so happy.

She idolised George and as far as she could see he could do no wrong. One day she knew that she would marry him. She let her imagination run away with her and to Hannah the future looked so good.

Geoff Duke won the Friday race and it had made everyone happy. The rest of the holiday went so quickly and before they all had realised it they were back queuing to get on to the ferry on the Saturday afternoon. Brenda had flown back earlier in the day The ferry was late starting to sail and it was the early hours of Sunday morning when they arrived back home in Wrockwardine.

Judith and Simon agreed with George and Hannah that it had been a great week and promised that all being well they would do it again next year. Hannah promised George that she would go and talk to her mother but she knew that it would not be a visit to look forward to. She had made up her mind that she was going to stand up for herself, and if her mother insisted that she should stop seeing George. Hannah was going to have to tell her straight, that she had no intentions of doing any such thing, even if she did have to wait until she was legally entitled to and that would be when she became twenty-one.

Chapter Six

What Does The Future Hold

It took a few weeks for Hannah and George to settle down to their usual mundane routine at work. Things had changed between them since they had spent the holiday together. They were much closer now and they started to talk of their future together and what plans that they could make. Neither of them had much money saved. George was committed to paying the instalments on his motorbike and when he went out for an evening he liked to dress as smart as he possibly could. He also enjoyed smoking cigarettes and by the time he had paid his mother for his share of the housekeeping he had very little money left. It would be a long time before they would be able to buy their own house, if ever. Hannah had saved a few pounds, but because she was living in she was only paid twenty-five shillings a week. Most of it was quickly taken up. She liked to pay her share when she and George went out if she could, because she knew that he was doing his bit to save as hard as he could. Since she had left home she had to buy new clothes for herself and she always tried to buy George's mother something for giving her some tea when she had a meal at George's home. A colleague of George's was a good carpenter, had managed to buy a plot of land and with the help of his girl friend they had bought a really good second hand caravan cheaply. They told George and Hannah how they intended to live in the van and build a house for themselves, and that they would do it as they were able to afford to.

"George" Said Hannah "I think that is a good idea, do you think that we could do something similar?"

"I don't know about that. Just think about what your mother and dad would say about you living in a caravan. I can just see them letting you do that. No way; your mother would shout, "That caravans are only for gypsies and you lady had better start thinking again" George was very good at mimicking her mother.

"Why don't we give that idea some thought and before you dismiss the idea completely think what a really good carpenter you are. You know that you are one of the best, you say so yourself. Why not have a go at building our own caravan. You are in the building trade and could probably buy most of the timber and other stuff that would be needed through the trade. I don't think that we need to say any thing to my mother unless we have to. If we were able to buy a house you could always sell the caravan there is a growing market for them now that the war is over and more and more people are able to afford to buy cars. There are lots of sites being opened up at the seaside for caravans. Wages are certainly rising at quite an alarming rate for the factory workers. They are now able to afford holidays, something that used to be only for the rich to contemplate". Hannah paused to see what George's reaction was going to be.

"My goodness you have certainly been doing your homework have you not?"

"Well we could give it some thought; we don't have to rush into anything because the way that I see it my mother is never going to approve of my marrying you. To me it looks as if I will have to wait until when I officially come of age and that will not be until I am twenty one by law, and only then will I be able to please myself".

The next time that Hannah saw George he sounded very excited "That idea of building a caravan is worth considering" George said enthusiastically." I tell you what we could do; we should go and have a look at caravans on your next Sunday afternoon off. We could go to the place where they have them for sale. Yes I will look into it, we could go and see for ourselves and find out what would be involved". The thought of having to wait until Hannah was twenty-one before they could get married did not appeal to George one little bit. But what choice did they have. After giving it some thought George could see that they had none. To him that was going to be purgatory. Still he supposed that he could go on seeing Nell and let her think that he still cared for her and try not to think about how many other lads he knew that she had been associating with.

During the next few months George and Hannah visited caravan show rooms and pretended to be interested in purchasing a caravan big enough to be able to live it. Consequently the sales reps were only too keen to show them what they wanted to see. How this unit worked or how that worked. How to conceal a double bed and all sorts of ideas that George and Hannah would not have dreamed of. Even a bath could be fitted, hot and cold water a small refrigerator. There was no end to what they could do to make a caravan suitable to live in and very homely.

George told Hannah to keep the sales reps interested while he moved away from any one particular van that they were looking at to another about the same size so that he could take out his ruler and quickly take some measurements.

"The first thing that we have to buy is the iron chassis and find somewhere to put it that will be the biggest outlay as far as money is concerned. I have been giving some thought as to where we could put it and I have been thinking of asking my Dad if I could put it on the far end of the garden alongside that pig sty.

The council had built pigsties at the end of all the gardens when these particular houses had first been built. It was so that the tenant could rear a pig and have it slaughtered for their own consumption and at the same time the pig would eat up all the household food scraps that would otherwise be thrown away. I have done some measuring and it could easily fit there without being any trouble to him as he does not do anything with that bit of rough garden and neither does he use the old pigsty I could make that for storing bits and pieces".

"But George if your dad says that you can put it there how would you get a chassis as big as the one that we would need onto the garden? And how are you going to convince him that we are doing the right thing building one so that we can live in it?" Hannah wanted to know because she too was getting carried away with George's enthusiasm. "If you were able to do that it would be grand, you would be so near the shed and you could work on it in the evenings when you have had your tea that is providing that you have no other work that your customers need doing. The parts for this are going to take all our spare money I would think that although we are going to save a lot of money in the long run it is still going to cost quite a bit. Is it not?"

"Putting the chassis there would be no trouble just take the fence down and then put it up again. First I will ask our old chap" (He was referring to his dad.) I know that my Mother will be no trouble but the old chap can be an awkward sod if he wants to. Still there is no harm in asking, he can only bite my head off and it would not be the first time that he has had a go at me. Look at all the fuss that he made about me buying the motorbike and now he says nothing about it. He has changed his tune now that he can see how far that we are able to go and that we can enjoy our selves we go to places that he could only dream about. The farthest that he and mother seem to go is to see their friends at Crewe and then they go by train because they do not have to pay any fare. Because he works on the railway they can travel free. I expect that he will think that our idea is a daft idea but we have to convince him that it is not and that we can do it"

"I should wait until you know that he is in a good mood. But first sound your mother out and see what she thinks of the idea. I am sure she will see it from your point of view".

"You could be right there yes that is what I will do". George said eagerly.

George told his Mother of his plans and she was so amazed at what George and Hannah proposed to do she declined to comment at first but after a couple of days she voiced her opinion.

"I thought that the pair of you were crazy when you first told me but after giving it some thought there is a possibility that it could work. There is always some one here in the village of Wrockwardine willing to sell a plot of ground. Just look at Dr Thompson who I baby-sit for. Who would have thought that they could have had big house built at the end of the village? Yes I think that it could work for you providing that you intend to build a house and that you don't start a family before then. It would be hard going to have to live in a caravan with little ones running around you both must give that a lot of thought. Go ahead and see what your Dad says. He just might let you put the chassis on the garden and then if in the meantime you can get a house you could always sell it. George I am so glad that you are going steady with Hannah and I am so glad that you are no longer chasing after that blonde next door. I was worried to death when she had that child in case she might have pinned it on you. Not that I could have blamed her."

Not seeing her anymore. That's what you think George smiled to himself.

". No I don't see her any more" He lied "I am quite content with what I have got and I am hoping that Hannah's parents come round and give us their blessing."

"You will be so lucky "His Mother answered "I expect that you will have to wait until Hannah is twenty one, if you are thinking of building this caravan that you have told me about you will have plenty to occupy your selves. It will be interesting to hear what your father has to say about your idea. Remember the fuss he made when you bought the motor bike."

"That's just what we have been thinking. I will ask him. He can only say no and if he does we will find somewhere else to put it". George spoke with his usual defiance.

George waited for the right moment to ask his father for the use of the top end of the garden.

"What do you mean build a caravan on the garden Are you out of your mind George Do you intend to live in it when it is ready?"

"Of cause we do. But not on your garden I do not think that the council would let us do that. The idea is to get started on something so that we can be together while we build our own house. If something does come our way like a decent house to rent or buy we can always sell the van and the money would be put to good use. It would be one way of saving."" George had thought things out very carefully so that he had his answers ready for when his Dad started to question him.

"Let me give this some thought. You have certainly got some big ideas. Would it not have been better to put your name down on the council list for a council house? The councils are starting to build a lot more now that the war is over. I have heard that they are proposing to build houses along by the cemetery and bungalows for the elderly. They reckon that the old cottages next to us will have to be pulled down; they say that they are too old and small to do anything with. You might not think that I do not know what is going on because I am not here all day. Things are certainly going to change in this village. I will have to talk this over with your Mother and see what she has to say about it. We do not want to antagonise the council and risk losing our own house. The council can be very funny if they want to. I don't think that they would take very kindly to your idea of building a caravan on our garden, they might be convinced that you in tend to live in it,

That rent man does not miss much when he calls and as you know only too well, he would report back to the council any miserable little thing he sees. I know that he will".

"Well I only propose to build a caravan I certainly don't intend that we should live in it on the back garden. I don't see how they can complain about that and if we don't go telling every one in the village. You know that it will be a bit before any of the neighbours realise what we are doing".

"It's the neighbours that we have to worry about you know how jealous they get over the slightest little thing. A bit of tittle-tattle and the gossip spreads like wild fire" Terry emphasised his concern.

"Oh sod the neighbours what ever we did they would soon talk about it and if it not us they will soon find some one else to talk about." George decided to close the subject.

He told Hannah when he saw her again that he was sure that his Dad would come round to his way of thinking.

The chassis for the proposed caravan was the biggest item of expenditure. It was two months later that George and Hannah had enough money to buy it. His Dad had given him the go ahead and so it was delivered and unloaded in the lane, which went to a field along side his Dad's house. It took George and Thomas all of one Saturday to take the fence down and get the chassis on to the garden and then replace the garden fence

Thomas was a bit put out, but he did not voice his concerns, he was a man of a very quiet nature. A very deep thinker and shared very little of his thoughts or ideas to any one. When he had been helping out at the Wrekin Cottage he had fancied Hannah from the first day that he had seen her. When she had been a mere slip of a girl of thirteen, but it was not him that she had taken a fancy to. She fancied his brother George. Ever since the two boys had been toddlers it had all ways seemed to him that he lost out to George. Thomas felt that George always had the better deal in life. Their Mother had always taken George's side when it came to settling arguments. It had seemed to Thomas that if it was not George or Judith that she was not fussing about it was his Dad Terry. Thomas had always felt that he was left out of most things that went on at home. Now that George and Hannah had decided to build this caravan it was obvious to him that they intended staying together and eventually getting married.

Thomas decided that it would be of no advantage to him or Hannah to tell her that he loved her. He decided not to reveal to Hannah what feelings he had for her and he also decided that he could not tell Hannah what he knew of his brother. Firstly he had doubts that if he were to tell her what he really knew about George. Hannah would not be prepared to believe him and he could see for himself that she idolised his brother. Secondly George would deny every thing if he were to reveal all or he would probably kill him if he told Hannah what he knew about what George got up to. Did George think that he did not know where he had gone to on a Monday evening, How George had got all dressed up left the house and came back just after ten o'clock at night never saying where he had been or who he had been with. This to Thomas's way of thinking appeared to be most unusual. He was convinced that if George was seeing a young lady he would not have been able to resist boasting about it.

Thomas had discreetly followed George several times and could not believe his eyes when he had followed him and saw where he went. At first he thought that his brother was just making a social call but it soon dawned on him that there was far more going on than what George would have liked to admit to or for any one to have found out about his illicit affair.

Thomas would tell his mother that he was working a little late on a Monday evening. That he was putting in a couple of hours of overtime at work and would be late in for his tea. He found that it was a bit difficult because the two brothers worked for the same firm and he had to be careful not to arouse suppositions. Thomas had made sure that he did a bit of overtime every now and then but not on any pacific evening. His staying to work late threw no suspicion as to where he was. This worked quite well George never knew which nights his brother stayed late as he did very little overtime for his boss. He had so much other work to do. People were asking him to do all sorts of jobs from re-hanging doors to making new window frames Thomas would often be late home on most Monday evenings so it was no loss to George if he was not home at the regular tea time. Thomas worked it out that if he stayed until after half past six and George said anything when his mother asked as to where Thomas was? George was able to confirm that Thomas was still working doing a bit of overtime. As both he and George worked for the same firm his staying to do some over time did not give George any cause to be suspicious.

Thomas had cycled to the bottom of the Wrekin and had concealed himself as he watched to see where his brother was going. He noticed that George turned off before getting to the Forest Glen and had gone along the road that went all the way around the bottom of the hill through Uppington and Spout lane He found that George was turning to go up the Wrekin via the Burnt cottage route. After watching this for a few times The mystery was that although George went up towards the Burnt cottage he was all ways clean and tidy when he came back home He could not have been meeting some one in the plantations of fir trees He would have most certainly have got his smart shoes muddy

Thomas decided that he would go up to the Cottage and see if George was coming up the hill this far; not that he was expecting that George could be meeting any one up the hill. What woman would want to climb the Wrekin when there were so many other places that they could arrange to meet? The more George dressed up and went out on a Monday evening, the more Thomas was intrigued.

He was now convinced that George had to be meeting some one.

Having to share the same room and double bed with George, Thomas could not help notice that George did not shed pine needles on the bedroom floor as he hung his trousers in the wardrobe that they both shared. Thomas knew that if he had been courting in the plantations there would have undoubtedly been pine needles in the turn up of his trousers. He was convinced that George had been seeing a woman he had noticed that he came home smelling of women's cheap perfume.

Thomas went to the Forest glen and he put his bike around the back and out of sight, he then climbed up to the Cottage. The evenings were growing darker and it was quite dark by six o'clock. He had taken a short cut up the hill directly opposite the Forest Glen. It was very steep and very few people knew about the track. When out side the Cottage Thomas found that it was very easy to conceal him self in the shrubbery opposite the front door and all he had to do was wait and see if George came up the Hill as far as this. He could not see what possible reason that George would have to come all the way to the Cottage. Thomas decided that he would give it a few minutes and then leave and go back down through the burnt cottage route

To his amazement he saw George come to the Cottage and he had guessed quite rightly that George had not stopped on his way up. The only light inside the house was the paraffin oil lamp that was on the kitchen table. No curtains had been closed across the windows he saw George put his bike around the back of the tearooms. Why? Thought Thomas should he put his bike out of sight could it be put there for quick get away? But why would George want to get away quickly. Thomas could see no reason for this. He had guessed right George was coming all the way up to the house but why? What did he want up here on a Monday evening and why get dressed up to just come here? As far as he knew Gwen and Eric Watson had only seen the two of them in their working clothes so why had George dressed up?

Both Gwen and George knew that it would have been a very remote chance of any one being about out side after dark. The public in general had always left the hill well before darkness in case they fell and were injured... It would have to be some one with a very good knowledge of the tracks leading up and down the hill to be up here after dark, the tracks leading down could be dangerous. Thomas did not have to worry he was like fox when it came to finding his way about. Every track on the hill was familiar to him. When they had been working weekends up here, he and George had often gone up to the Cottage using different tracks, to see which of them could be there first.

Thomas watched George approach the front door and gently tap it three times. When Gwen opened it George had quickly stepped inside closing the door behind him. Thomas moved quickly on to the front porch and as he watched through the window he was astonished how young Gwen looked in the reflection of the oil lamp He worked it out that she looked at least ten years younger than what she was. Infact she looked beautiful. He had not seen her with her hair hanging loose about her shoulders, neither had he seen the pretty dress that she was wearing and he decided it must be one for special occasions. Her face looked different younger and more beautiful. He thought that she must have applied face powder and lipstick. Thomas was quite impressed. What a pity this woman did not make such an effort on Sundays when every one could see how young and beautiful she could look. As soon as George had closed the door Thomas saw that they could not wait to take hold of each other. Thomas had at first been gob smacked and could not believe what he was witnessing. Gwen could not get enough of George, her hands were all over him Thomas could see her stroking him down low in the groin and soon she had the buttons of his trousers undone and her hand was inside. George was trying to release himself of his jacket and at the same time kiss her passionately. After a few moments they both disappeared from the kitchen towards the passage leading to the stairs. Thomas had noticed the glow of candlelight coming from the window half way up the stairs, and a light in the window of the bedroom facing the East. Thomas did not know that Gwen had previously placed lighted candles on the windowsills to let George know that the coast was clear. Eric was not at home the children were asleep.

Thomas did not to wait to see any more, what he had witnessed took some believing, his head was in turmoil. Should he hang around for much longer or make his way home for his tea. He decided the latter there would be nothing to see here for some considerable time and the air was getting quite chilly just standing around. It could even be a couple of hours later before those two came back down stairs. He had seen all he wanted to and had proof of what George was up to.

Thomas had been suspicious when he had followed George as far as the bottom of the burnt cottage track before. Thomas had noticed that George's clothes had not been soiled which they would have been if he had been with a woman in the forestry plantation. The cheap perfume had been the give a way, it was only too obvious that he had been with a lady friend. It could have been Nell but he had seen her going up the village on a Monday evening after George had gone out on his bike, she was obviously meeting some one else

Never in his wildest dreams had he imagined that George would have been stupid enough to go to bed with a married woman. Certainly not one with four kids to look after. The risk that his stupid brother was taking was incomprehensible. "God" he said to him self, that woman must be desperate to take the risk of taking a young man to her bed because of what I know about Eric Watson he would kill her if he found out. "If I am able to come and see what is going on what is to stop others doing the same". But then he supposed that unless any one was interested in what George was up to No one had any reason to suspect that George and Gwen were meeting like this. He had only followed George out of sheer curiosity as to why he had always dressed up on a Monday evening and that he was not prepared to confide in him as to who the lady was that he was going out with.

For months Thomas was in a quandary, he just did not know if he should reveal what he had witnessed at the Cottage to his father and mother. But after giving it a lot of thought he decided that it would be better for every one if he were to keep his mouth shut. George would just deny what ever Thomas said and make out that he was a liar If George had found out that Thomas had been spying on him he would have waylaid him and given him a good hiding. That was something that Thomas did not want to contemplate. If George did not want to do it himself Thomas was sure that he would be able to find some other fellow that would do any thing for a price. . Thomas also knew that George was still seeing Nell from next door. Another thing that he felt was some thing that would be of no benefit to any one if he were to reveal what he knew.

Thomas could not tell any one how much that he felt for Hannah because he now knew that there was nothing that he could do about it. Hannah did not give him a second glance she treated him, as she should just as George's brother she must never know what he felt for her. As long as he felt this way he could not focus his attention on any others girls.

It was after Christmas that George's Mother Ivy started complaining that she was having some bad headaches. No one in the family seemed too bothered Ivy had told them that she had spoken to Dr Thompson whom she baby sat for in the evenings. He had told her just to take some aspirins but when months later she was still complaining about her head aches and that they seemed to be getting worse. He convinced her to see her own Doctor. He did not say anything but he was worried and had some idea of what could be the matter, he had noticed that she had lost weight although she was always on the slim side it was obvious to him that there was something seriously wrong. Ivy saw her own Doctor who prescribed stronger pain killing tablets.

Judith came home from work one evening and found that her Mother had collapsed in a chair and seemed to be very poorly. The doctor was called and Ivy was admitted to the Royal Salop Infirmary where over the next few weeks her condition deteriorated. The doctors had diagnosed that she was suffering from a brain tumour. They told Terry that there was nothing that they could do for her and that it would only be a matter of time before she would die. The family was absolutely devastated. They could not believe that Ivy could die and leave them; she was only forty-four years old. Hannah found that it was pure hell visiting her as she lay on her hospital bed. There was so little that could be said to give any hope and comfort. When George and Hannah had got back from the hospital visits George went into a world of his own and nothing that Hannah could say was of any help to him so she decided the best thing was to keep quiet and just be there for him.

Weeks later when the time came that Ivy passed away George took it the worst Hannah tried to comfort him the best that she knew how but she could see that the loss of his Mother had knocked him completely side ways. It was something that no one could have fore seen. Judith put on a very brave face. It looked as if she would have to take her mother's place and she was only sixteen coming seventeen. Her Father needed her help with the house hold chores, everything in the family changed. Thomas became more withdrawn and said very little to any one. Then one week completely out of the blue he announced that he was joining the army and would be leaving home very soon. He stated that he had been accepted into the Royal Engineers and would continue to be trained as a carpenter. He said that he had signed on for nine years. His Dad did his best to persuade him not to do this but it was of no use Thomas had made up his mind and he had already signed the necessary paper work. He could not go back to the army officials and say that he had changed his mind and in any case he did not intend to change his mind. He had decided that now his Mother was gone he did not have to worry about hurting her feelings. He hoped that leaving home would give him time to get over his feelings for Hannah as he could now see that he did not have a cat in hells chance of ever having her for his own. His brother had won again.

Wednesday afternoons when Hannah had her half day off she would cycle to the village and give the house a dust and polish she would have a meal-cooked ready for when they came in from work any little thing was a help to save Judith.

She would iron George's shirts and any other washing that he had, she felt that Judith had enough to do and her father had persuaded her not to give up her office job. Terry really appreciated this little bit of help. Especially when Hannah had made a pie or some other sweet that he and Judith did not have time to make. After Thomas had left for the army and with Ivy passing away the house was never the same again. .

George and Hannah started to build their caravan it was going to be a long and tedious job they would only be able to do it as they could afford the necessary materials, and continue to save some money. His father took very little interest with any thing that went on around him he could not accept loosing his beloved Ivy. To him she was so young to have her life so cruelly taken from her. He went around like a zombie getting up and going to work and doing the garden when the evenings allowed enough daylight. He would work for the Railway Company practically every weekend and then on a Sunday night if he felt up to it he would cycle down into Wellington for a pint of beer. This enabled him to drown his sorrows with friends that he had known for many years.

One Sunday afternoon George said that he had heard that Eric Watson had been taken seriously ill and he had voiced his concerns to Judith and Hannah as to how Gwen would be coping up the Wrekin with four children. He did not have long to wait, it was later in the year that he heard that Eric had died and Gwen had moved off the hill. The council had given her a house at Burcott. Not far away from Wrockwardine. New people had taken over the running of the Cottage and George had heard that they were having quite a lot of work done to improve the house and its facilities George knew better than to go and see Gwen. The neighbours who also lived in the row of houses where she had moved to would not miss any thing that went on. Who called to see her and who did not? They would miss nothing whether it would be during the daytime or evenings. So he decided that it was better not to try and renew their relationship. But how he longed for those nights of passion that he had shared with her. He had to be content with only going so far with Hannah. The risk of getting her pregnant was far too great at this stage. They had not told her mother about building the caravan that had still to come. If they had to go and tell her that they would have to get married because he had got her daughter pregnant. He dare not think about that. At the same time he did not think that Hannah would need a lot of persuading to go further and make love properly with him. Hannah had also wondered why George had not taken their relationship any further She was now getting her self very well informed as to what went on with couples both married and single. She could only admire George for not wanting to take their relationship any further and put her in a situation that she knew she could well do with out.

Thomas often wrote to Judith keeping her informed about army life and he seemed to be enjoying him self. He seemed to be making a great many new friends and got on well with his army comrades. The discipline of army life did not seem to bother him and he wrote saying that he was soon to be made up to the position of a Corporal. He said that some days the food had a lot to be desired but his logic was that even if the food that was provided did not do one much good neither would it do one any harm. Being as all the rest of his platoon was eating the same food that he was, he did not see that he had any thing to worry about. He had been informed that he and the rest of the company were to be sent abroad but where they were going had not been disclosed as yet. He said that he would write again and let her know if and when this was likely to happen. In his letters he would always ask of the family and enjoyed receiving Judith's replies especially any news of his

Granny at Upton Magna and the triplets with whom he had always got on very well. He had missed the cycle rides he had taken to see them on Sunday afternoons and if he was allowed any leave before going abroad she was to tell them that he would be there to see them all again.

Judith loved having a letter from Thomas although she had not given him much thought when they had been growing up together; she certainly missed him now so very much. It had been bad enough for her to lose her Mother to whom she was so close. She had not imagined that Thomas would leave home. It was then that she could see what a difference that there was between her two brothers. Judith had under estimated Thomas and had always been closer to George. Probably it could have been because she was seeing Simon. George and Simon got on so well because of their interest in motor bikes where as Thomas preferred to cycle every where.

Any free time that they could be together George and Hannah would sit and draw plans for the interior of the caravan, by visiting different caravan outlets they collected all the leaflets and brochures that they could. They would spend hours looking through them trying to decide what would be the best for their own caravan. Should it have this or should it have that. Hannah was so excited about it all. Most of the main structures of the interior had to be fitted before the outer shell of aluminium George covered the framework with a second hand tarpaulin sheet that he had managed to buy fairly cheaply. The caravan was going to be quite a big one over thirty feet long and that was quite a size when compared to what they had seen. It was to have electricity running water and lots of other mod cons.

Hannah did visit her Mother and Dad now and again and George was still asked to do general repairs for them but neither made any mention of their building a Caravan. They decided it was best to keep quiet about it.

"No need to say anything as yet". She said to George. "The balloon will go off with a bang when I tell them so perhaps it is just as well that we wait awhile".

When Hannah had turned eighteen and it was coming up for Christmas George suggested that they should go and see her Mother and Dad and ask for their permission and allow them to get engaged to be married.

"I don't see why not "George had argued when Hannah had suggested that she thought that it would be better to let sleeping dogs lie for a bit longer.

" That was not the real reason that George had this in mind He had thought that if they were engaged to be married and he accidentally got Hannah pregnant it would not look quite so bad. He was getting thoroughly fed up with having to restrain him self.

When both her grandparents had died, Nell from next door had been re-housed somewhere in Wellington The row of little old cottages was to be demolished and where they had stood the council was proposing that bungalows for old age pensioners should be built on the land. George no longer saw Nell she had a man living with her and she had lost all interest in satisfying all and sundry that wanted to use her whenever it suited them. Such as George and the Godfrey boys whom she had taught all that they knew about love making. Perhaps it was that she was now getting older, or that she had now lost the security that her grandparents had given her in the little cottage. Or perhaps it was the fact that she had come to her senses and realised that all the lads had wanted of her was to satisfy their sexual needs when they had no one else who they could go to.

George and Hannah worked hard on the caravan and after eighteen months it was beginning to take shape, they were thrilled to bits with it and were so pleased that they had thought of the idea in the first place. Quite a few of George's friends who were also carpenters gave him great encouragement and one or two of them decided that they too were going to have a go and that they were going to copy what George and Hannah were doing. They were also hoping that George would show them the rudiments and how it was done. Hannah went home occasionally but she sensed that the atmosphere was no better with her Mother.

"Are you still seeing that lad from Wrockwardine" Her Mother asked.

Hannah said nothing. "So that's it is it. You will live to regret it. We have tried to warn you that it will all turn out to be no good in our eyes (Referring to her self and Fred) you need some one who is going to do a bit of farming a small holding perhaps, like Lizzy and -Frank. They have got engaged and are looking for somewhere to make a start. A wedding next year I should not wonder." Frank was a brother of Joe Timmins the butcher and farmed the farm in Huntington with his older brother. Their farm was next one down the lane to Miss Stewart. Quite a well respected family and although Frank was at least ten years older than Lizzy her Mother had approved of the engagement.

"My goodness that will certainly be something to look forward to; where are they looking for a smallholding?" Hannah asked. She would certainly look forward to a wedding if Lizzy married it would be the first one that she had been to. And it would certainly be a change from funerals.

"The other side of Wellington, not that you're Dad and me will be able to give them very much we have got to think about William and his future. I want him to go to a good school as a boarder if possible it might widen his horizons a bit and make him a better farmer. That teacher at Little Wenlock has got it in for him He can't take a day off with out her sending notes home with him Its just not good enough; on at him almost every other day, she is. I reckon a good boarding school would do him that world of good".

"To a boarding School "Hannah said with amazement. Well there was one thing for sure there would be no skiving off when he felt like it Yes she thought it might do him the world of good but she dare not voice her opinion.

"Well what is wrong with that? You were sent to a good enough school were you not and not a lot of good has it done either you or Grace. skivying for others, you could have done that at home and have been more help to us".

Oh dear Hannah thought as she looked at her mother. You have not changed your tune one little bit since I left home. It looks to me as if you are certainly not prepared to give George the benefit of the doubt. Hannah was not going to let her Mother's remarks get to her. She loved George so what did it matter that he was not a farmer He had other skills and as far a she could see he was prepared to work very hard. He had never been in trouble with the police. So what was so wrong with him? Her Mother was glad to have him do the repairs around the farm for nothing or for a pittance. That seemed to be perfectly all right.

Hannah told George about her visit back home and they decided that it would be better not to go and ask if they could get engaged for the time being. They decided to wait until the following year and see if Lizzy was going to get married and then they thought that Dorothy would have other things on her mind to think about. They also thought it would be better not to mention the caravan for the time being if Dorothy and Fred found out about it, it would be just too bad. If that happened, Hannah would have to tell them of the plans that she and George were making for their future.

Lizzy and Frank were successful with being able to purchase the small holding which Dorothy had told Hannah about. They planned to get married the second week of June. Margaret and Percy Podmore were going to be so disappointed at her leaving them. She had been working for them for ten years. She had worked for them from when she had been thirteen and they had grown very fond of Lizzy and now treated her as their own daughter. But in Hannah's view she did not think that they would have liked to see a daughter of their own work as hard as Lizzy had worked over the years. Dorothy was certainly going to miss her help with the weekly washing on a Tuesday and with putting the younger ones to bed for her. Lizzy had done this almost as long as she could remember.

Dorothy was so busy making all the arrangements for the Wedding. She wanted to ask all her relatives and show them that she and Fred could now afford the best. The wedding service was to take place at Little Wenlock Church and of cause the wedding reception would be held at the Forest Glen. Since the war the Forest Glen had got a very good reputation for wedding parties. Dinners and dances and lots of other events, most of the upper class and the elite now held there wedding receptions there. It was decided that Mary and Rebecca would be bride's maids and of course Lizzy would be all in white. Dorothy booked wedding cars from Charlotte Pearson's garage. By trying impress on her relatives that she and Fred were very popular, she invited who ever she could. Hannah could not believe her ears when her Mother said that she could invite George and also Judith.

"Well I suppose the poor girl has lost her mother so it will do her no harm to come along if she would like to." Dorothy actually smiled as she gave the invitation cards to Hannah to give George saying that it would save a bit of postage.

Who paid for what Hannah never knew, neither was she the slightest bothered but it was a beautiful wedding? She knew that Lizzy paid for her own long white wedding dress. The veil and accessories, who paid for the reception no one ever did find out? Some members of the family said that the Podmore's did? Others said that they did not. All the family knew that the Podmore's had given Lizzy a gold wristwatch for her twenty -first birthday, so they did not think that they would have given her the wedding reception as well.

Hannah and Judith had a great time; to be dressed up so smart was some thing that they had not done before. Neither had they been invited to any weddings. Dorothy had warned them that they must wear hats as well as smart frocks. She had chosen a light blue two piece suit for herself with a large blue hat to match. Fred looked so smart in a navy blue suit He had bought himself a pair of black shoes so that he was not wearing his usual best boots. His hair now going quite grey was well groomed and he wore a white carnation in the buttonhole of his jacket. He looked so proud as he walked down the isle with Lizzy gently holding his arm.

Lizzy looked beautiful. Her white net veil hung down to trail on to the floor. It was secured to her hair with a coronet of cream rose buds that looked so good against her dark brown hair. She carried a bouquet of the same flowers, which were arranged with trailing green fronds of fern, and reached half way down the front of her dress. With having been a waitress for so many years Lizzy had witnessed so many weddings and had made sure that hers was as perfect as it could be the top table stretched all the way across the one side of the room. Granddad and Grandma Wainwright had condescended to be present. Dorothy had considered them to be the most important guests so she had arranged that they should be put to sit on the top table along side herself and Fred Mary and Beccy and Frank's brother. Beccy and Mary wore long pink dresses and flowered head -dresses to match they also carried bouquets of pink roses. They were seated either side the bride. How nervous they all looked. Dorothy had said that she did not want to go through all this fuss again for a very long time. She told Hannah and her sisters that they must try to make conversation with their aunts and uncles as well as their Grandparents. Dorothy had emphasised that unless there was to be another wedding in the family to celebrate, the girls would not have a chance to speak to them for quite some time...

Hannah and Grace did their best. Most of the aunts and uncles were only too happy to chat with the girls especially their Aunt Kathleen and Uncle Collin. They seemed very impressed with the way the girls had all grown and they remarked that they did not think that it would be long before they would be coming back to witness another wedding.

Uncle Collin had a lovely smile on his face and he remarked "I can't believe that you have all grown up into such beautiful young ladies. After all, you did work so hard when the war was on" He was eager to hear what each of the girls was doing at present. When Hannah said hello to her Aunt Lucy, Aunt Lucy just replied. "Now which one of them are you I haven't a clue there are so many of you".

"I'm Hannah". Hannah replied and promptly walked away". She was so indignant. "I haven't a clue there are so many of you." Hannah mimicked her aunt to Grace and they both started to giggle. "How many children has she got lets see there is six as far as I know" Grace was still giggling. Grace and Hannah had a little time to exchange stories of what they were doing these days and about their jobs. They had not bothered with each other since Grace had left home she had seen Grace helping out from time to time on her employers market stall. At these times Grace had practically ignored Hannah saying that she was far too busy and must look after the customers. Many were the time that Hannah had wanted some sisterly advice but she quickly got the message that Grace was not interested. Grace was mixing with an entirely different set of people to Hannah. She was going to dances at Sankey's ballroom at Hadley and any other dinner dances such as the young farmers union. Where as Hannah only thought about George and their future together? Hannah had always been given the impression that a girl did not shop around going from one boy to another. Once you had found a steady boy friend you stuck with him otherwise you soon got a bad name and then no lad would be interested in a girl like that. If girls flirted around with different boys they were given all sorts of names and none were to their advantage; besides the risk of getting pregnant was far too great. After the wedding reception, Lizzy and Frank left for their honeymoon in Llandudno and then they were to start farming at a place called Cold Hatton.

Frank would have to have a full time job and it would mean like many other small holders that Lizzy would have to do a lot of the outside work. It was going to be a hard life for them both. The basic pay for a working man was still only around ten pounds a week unless one worked in a factory. Frank had managed to secure a job with the County Council working on road maintenance. This was going to be some thing that was quite different from farming; Farming had been the only work that he had previously known before getting married. He had known no other work than that of working along side his brother at Huntington. Taking orders from others never did go down very well with someone who was used to being their own boss and then coming home to start again milking his own cows and not getting finished until nine o'clock in the evening soon became tough going for the two of them. No way was the income from a small holding going to pay its way for a few years. Coming to the wedding had given Beccy the opportunity to bring her boy friend to meet her parents and Grace and Hannah made a bet that these two would be the next to get married.

George and Hannah settled back into their routine of work and finishing their caravan. They decided that they would go to see her Mother and father and ask if they could be come engaged. They went to see them on a night when Hannah knew that Mary and Helen would have cycled to the village to part take in a whist drive. Sandra was already in bed. Hannah could not see her mother readily agreeing and she some how had expected to have to put a fight once that the word caravan was mentioned and she had been quite right. They parked the motor bike at the back of the garage and entered the kitchen. It appeared to look no different from when Hannah had been a child, little had altered. There was a different cooker a Rayburn stood in the place of the old black lead range and the water was now brought through pipes, no more having to use the pump on the back yard. Fred was sat in his usual old rocking chair and Dorothy was sat in her usual place by the Rayburn cooker. She told George and Hannah to seat them selves down She had already guessed what they had come for and she was ready for an argument. They seated them selves on the same wooden chairs that had been there all Hannah's child hood, When George asked if he and Hannah could get engaged to be married. He found that he could not get a definite answer. Neither a yes nor a no. When Fred asked him what plans he was making for his and Hannah's future. George told them about the caravan that they had been building on the back garden at home. Dorothy and Fred's reaction only made things much worse. Dorothy exploded.

"I'll have no daughter of mine living in a caravan like a gypsy, that I will not." She shouted. "So if you think that you have come here to ask to get married so that you can go and live in a caravan you can think again. The disgrace of it Fred Just think about the disgrace of it". She opened up the front of the cream enamel cooking range and gave the fire inside a good shaking up with the steel poker; the same poker that Hannah had seen her use over many previous years. Hannah had to smile to her self as she watched Dorothy poke the fire, nothing seemed to have changed. George tried to explain that he was already looking for a building plot and that he intended to build a very smart house for both of them. Fred was beginning to warm to the idea and said that if they gave their permission for them to marry would the two of them be prepared to wait until they had actually got a plot of ground. If so, it would give more indication that they did not intend to make the caravan a permanent home. If this was the case he could see no reason why they could not become engaged providing that they did not hurry into marriage. By the time Fred had finished Dorothy had calmed down a bit and offered George and Hannah a cup of tea; which the two of them thought that they had better accept. Hannah offered to pass the cups and saucers from the kitchen cupboard. Dorothy had took up the conversation again

"And another thing don't the pair of you think that it is about time that you sold that motor bike and bought a car. Risking your lives like you do, I reckon that there is no sense in it."

This was about the worst thing that her Mother could have said to antagonise George, considering that no other members of the family owned a motor car never mind a motor bike. They were all still going around on pedal bikes. After all Hannah thought a motor bike was all that her father had when he had moved to the Willowmoor farm. Liz's' husband Frank was still having to go to work on a push bike because he could not drive and Lizzy had to go shopping on the weekly bus. But the fact that they had started farming was quite acceptable in Dorothy's eyes. George agreed to Fred's terms and said that he was only thinking of getting engaged for the time being. They said goodnight, as they left and it was with great relief that Hannah got onto the back of the bike and rode back to Wellington and work. She told Charlotte all about it next day and all that Charlotte said was"

"Now don't you two go thinking of getting married for a long time you are only eighteen and as you know you can't really go ahead with any thing until your are twenty one."

"Don't worry Charlotte we have not got the caravan finished as yet and we have not got enough money to buy the ground that we want and that is going to take some time to save".

"Thank goodness for that I can't do with having to replace you right now. George must have worked hard to have won your Mother around to his way of thinking. Still that man could charm bees from a honey pot". Hannah had to smile to her self; Charlotte was quite right with that remark. Two weeks later George asked Hannah to see if she could change her Sunday after noon off and have Saturday afternoon He said that he wanted to take her to Shrewsbury and buy her an engagement ring. Charlotte reluctantly agreed.

"I hope you are not going to do this too often You know very well that Saturday can be one of our busiest days of the week".

"I don't think so "Hannah replied" It is not going to be that we get engaged that often". Hannah was beginning to think that Charlotte was being a little selfish considering the long hours that she worked. She was on duty from when she got up in the mornings until she went to bed unless it was a day when she had her off duty. Hannah spent most of the Saturday morning dreaming of what sort of ring that George would be buying for her. These were her thoughts as they boarded the Midland red bus at Wellinton to take them to Shrewsbury. George decided that it would be better for them to go by bus than having to carry all their motorbike clobber around with them such as heavy coats and crash hats Etc. They got off the bus at Shrewsbury and walked up the main street and looked in the shop windows. George told Hannah that the most that he could afford was about thirty pounds. She was a little disappointed especially when she saw the plates of rings displayed in Samuel's shop window. How she would have loved to have one with large diamonds glistening in the afternoon sunlight. George must have guessed what she was thinking. This will only for the time being, when I can afford it. I will buy you one of the best, just like that one and he pointed to large single diamond set in a gold band but the price on that one was three hundred pounds, and that was way out of George's reach

"I don't really mind George. As you say, we will have what we can afford. What about that one, Hannah pointed to a display of rings on which was a ring of two small diamonds and a blue sapphire and it was also with in George's price range.

"OK are you sure about that one "

"Quite" Hannah smiled to reassure George that she loved him and as far as she was concerned that was all that really mattered. They went inside Hannah was asked to try it for size

George bought the ring and put the box with the ring in it, in his inside coat pocket and then he suggested that they went down to the river. "Whatever for?"

"So that we can go for a ride on it" "A boat ride down the river this was certainly something new for Hannah and she was very apprehensive about the whole idea "

But we will need a boat".

"Don't worry about that there will surely be one that we can hire". They walked down towards the river and reached the boathouse by the riverbank. They found that they were able to hire a boat quite quickly and when they climbed into the boat George took up the oars and started to row out on to the water. Hannah found this a little scary at first but soon relaxed and enjoyed the boat trip George was really trying to impress her with his rowing skills of which he had none and was finding it very difficult to go down the river reasonably straight. Hannah could not help her self from laughing and soon George could see the funny side of it, as it happened it turned out to be a wonderful half-day off. They had tea at Sidolie's café before going for the bus. Hannah felt that now George had gone to the trouble of buying her an engagement ring and she knew that she was going to accept it, she was really committed to him. Back in Wellington and out side the garage George said" I think that we have just beaten Judith and Simon to it "He kissed her good night," Why are they thinking of getting engaged, Judith has not said any thing to me"." She will when it's official ""George Fleming. You know more than what you are letting on... Just think when we are able to get married I will be Mrs George Fleming." You sure will and I like the sound of that". George took the ring from its little box and put it on her finger. Terry was very pleased for the both of them when Judith and Simon asked for permission to get engaged. Simon told him that if he were in agreement he was invited to a house party, which his Mother and Dad were going to have and that; they would like him to be there for Judith. "I will borrow a car so that you have no need to worry about transport to my house". Simon said hoping to encourage Terry to go to the party. Simon lived with his parents at Oakengates. His Dad Louis worked at Sankey's factory; he was also a keen gardener. He had quite a lot of ground and had put up several Greenhouses. His hobby was growing lots of tomatoes and flowers which all helped to supplement his income. His wife Elsie helped a great deal with the work and the two of them were extremely happy. Elsie made the arrangements for the engagement party. She invited her three sisters and her two brothers. Being as Simon was an only child she wanted to make quite a splash for him. Elsie had been born and bred on the outskirts of Wellington. One of her sister's Molly had married and moved away to Birmingham but her husband had been killed in the war and she had been left to bring up her two daughters on her own. She worked at the Cadbury chocolate factory in Bournville and she often came and spent time with her sister Elsie so that she could enjoy the peace and quiet of the countryside, it reminded her of her younger days. It was arranged that Molly would come and spend the weekend with Elsie for the party; she could be the life and soul of any party. She was so witty and sporty she would have a go at anything and she was so easy to get on with. She had a knack of putting other people at ease. Her family loved her. The night of the engagement party Terry made a special effort to dress smart to please Judith; He wore his best suit. This was to be her night and he did not want to let her down. Simon picked them up as arranged. Terry was amazed to find that he knew most of Simons Uncles and aunts from way back when he had attended an infant's school at Lawley Bank. He had a wonderful time he took a real shine to Molly; her infectious laugh and witty comments had given his morale a really good boost. Judith could not wait to tell George and Hannah how her father had enjoyed him self at the party. She was much more amazed a week later when she saw him sat at the table with the writing pad and packet of envelopes in front of him He appeared to be writing a letter. Some thing that she had not seen him do before. Judith had paid the necessary house hold bills for him so that he had no need to worry about them and it was not his habit to correspond with any one." What's this? You writing letters Dad? I don't believe it. Who is it that you are writing to? Are you going to tell me?" Well it is none of your business, but I will tell you that Molly and I got on so well at your engagement party that she dared me to write to her. She said that she did not expect a letter as she thought that I would not have the guts. So you see I have got to show her that I am not a chicken. I just might have to meet her again if you two decide to get wed. Imagine how embarrassing that would be. No I will show her, she was always a little cocky one at school. Thinks that I have not got the guts" He chuckled. Judith had not seen her Dad like this since before her Mother's death and she was happy for him. That letter which Terry wrote was followed by many more as he and Molly wrote to each other and when Molly could she would come and stay at her sister's and meet Terry and spend as much time as she could with him. They had well and truly fallen for each other. Romance was definitely in the air. Beccy wrote to her Mother and Dad and told them that she and her boyfriend Arthur would like to get married as they like Lizzy and Frank had found a small holding that they would be able to afford. Beccy had stated that she would love to have her Dad to give her away but she and Arthur did not want a big wedding or any fuss as she called it the money that would be spent on a wedding would be more useful to them to start farming. Arthur had done an apprenticeship as an agricultural engineer working in his father's agricultural engineering business. Since his father had died he had taken a job as an engineer at Cadbury's factory. Beccy stated that Arthur would keep his job for the time being until they were in a position to buy a bigger farm Beccy's letter certainly impressed Dorothy and as she told Fred they must try and give the girl a decent wedding, after all she was still their daughter.

"But what if the old chap (referring to her Grandfather Bill Wainwright) wants to see to it all?" "Well he is not going to, Becky is still our daughter and I will write back and tell her to come home for her wedding. She says that she would like it to be. The end of June. I will see what we can afford. I will tell her to give me a definite date and then I can book the Glen for the reception". Dorothy was letting her mind run away with her as she usually did. She was already making arrangements, much to Fred's amusement.

"Steady on a bit Dot wait until you hear from them and what they want us to do. I don't think that Beccy will expect us to foot the bill and besides. I wonder what the old chap will have to say about this. I am sure that he will want to have some say in what goes on. What do you think?"

"I think nothing. I for one can't see him paying for any thing and as Beccy says that they would prefer to have a bit of money than have a fancy do. So as I have been thinking that if we give her the Wedding the old chap might just give them a cheque to help them make a start". Dorothy stated quite firmly." I reckon that he ought to pay them some thing, the way that she worked for them.

"Leave it with you and see how things go" Fred could see that whatever he said Dorothy would take no notice of him if she had already made up her mind." Liz's wedding had turned out a grand do I suppose that we could do it all over again if we have to"

"What do you mean if we have to? The girl has not cost us anything over the last few years I reckon that we should do a little for her now. That is if you think that we can afford it." Dorothy dealt with the accounts and she knew whether they could afford it or not. But she wanted to put the onus on to Fred so that he could not complain about the cost at a later date. Fred wondered if Dorothy had ever regretted letting Beccy go to live with her grandparents and this was her way of clearing her guilty conscience, but he decided that it was best not to say any thing. After all he had really enjoyed all the fuss that had been made for Liz's wedding. The wedding date was fixed for June the 28th and as usual Dorothy took control of all the arrangements insisting that Mary be one of the bridesmaids. Beccy had no objection to this. She wrote and said that she would ask a girl who was Arthur's cousin and whom she had gone to school with to be the other bride's maid. Arthur had no sister's only two brothers. Dorothy would have liked Sandra who was now five years old to have been a small bride's maid but Beccy had stated firmly that she did not want any more money spending and that two brides maids were sufficient and that was to be that.

"I will see that you are the prettiest little girl there," Dorothy said to Sandra when she had to break the promise that she had already made to Sandra saying that she would be a bridesmaid. I will ask Margaret Podmore to ask her niece to come so that you will have some one to play with. That will be nice won't it? Sandra was growing used to having her own way and had already found that she could out manoeuvre her mother although she was still at such and early age. Sandra had started school the previous September and she had not liked it one little bit. Her eyesight was not good and Miss Goodwin, who had replaced retired Mrs Hayward, had noticed this and had decided to put Sandra to sit at the front of the class where she could keep an eye on her and Sandra did not like this at all. Sandra found that she could pull the wool over her mother's eyes by making up all sorts of excuses to get out of going to school. She only had to say that she was feeling sick or had a headache. She would pretend to sneeze and say that she had a cold. Dorothy was far too busy with the rearing of her poultry to bother to find out if Sandra was telling the truth and would send her back to stay in bed out of her way and told her to come back down when she felt better. Dorothy would quickly scribble a letter for William to give the teacher and that was the end of the matter as far as she was concerned. As soon as Dorothy disappeared out through the back door to see to her chickens Sandra would take a handful of biscuits or a piece of cake and go back to bed on the pretext of being ill. She knew even at the age of five that she could get away with it every time. For some reason or other Dorothy was taken in time and time again. It was to be William's last term at Little Wenlock so Sandra knew that from the end of this school term she would be going on her own. Dorothy had managed to talk Fred into agreeing that it would be in William's best interest to be sent to a boarding school. They had booked for him to go to a school called Millichope Hall the other side of Bridgenorth. Apparently this was a school were most of the local farmers sons were sent the fees were quite high but that did not seem to matter the school was recommended throughout the farming community. William had not been at all happy about their decision to send him to a boarding school there would be no more skiving from school to go with his father to the local cattle markets and farm sales and also miss school for any other excuse. William was growing quite tall for his age and was showing signs of taking after his Mother's side of the family. All he concentrated on was tractors and any other mechanical farm machinery. He showed no interest what so ever in the dairy herd or the sheep and would complain bitterly when he found that he was unable to get out of helping with the milking and sheep dipping and shearing.

Beccy's and Arthur's wedding was lovely. Dorothy had again excelled her self. George had been invited but not Judith. Grace had said that she was bringing her new man to meet her parents so he had been invited. Grace had introduced him as a single man Ian Waterford and that he was a very influential farmer. Both Dorothy and Fred were very happy and pleased for her. They made it quite clear that he was more than welcome to join the family. Hannah was a bit envious of Grace's out fit; it stood out, having been a very expensive one indeed. Something that Hannah knew that she could not have afforded. It was perfect for the occasion. Grace wore a large brimmed hat that put the finishing touch to it. Hannah had to smile to her self when she remembered how Grace had complained about the boys shoes that she had to wear for school and how she had said that one day she would meet her prince charming. Well by the look of her out fit at the wedding she had most certainly met the man of her dreams her new man was very handsome He did look a bit like George About the same height and had very dark hair and he wore a very expensive suit. Hannah thought that he looked much older than Grace; she had guessed that he could be at least ten to fifteen years older. Hannah considered that it was none of her business. She wished that her mother and Dad had made such a fuss of George as they did with Grace's man but then of course he was a farmer who on all accounts was doing exceedingly well Becky wore a full-length white wedding gown and a lace veil, which reached, to the floor. She carried a bouquet of lilies amid green fern. Her ginger hair was combed back from her face giving her an air of sophistication. No one attending that wedding seeing a young lady looking so beautiful could have possibly known that this was Beccy who had worked so hard on her Grandfather's farm. Arthur looked so handsome in his dark Grey suit. Hannah could only dream of what her wedding to George would look like, that was if there would ever be a wedding. Hannah could not see her Mother and Dad backing down and giving her permission to go ahead and marry George despite agreeing to their engagement. She would have to wait until she was twenty-one and even then she could not see her self ever having a white wedding like her sisters. She and George would have to go off quietly probably a register office with out any fuss and this made Hannah feel so sad.

Chapter Seven
Weddings In The Air

At the beginning of December Helen realised that she was pregnant and she did not know what on earth she was going to do. She knew that all hell would be let loose if she were to tell her mother about the predicament that she was in. She had left it as long as she had dared and then she confided with Mary.

Mary knew that their Mother would be furious when she found out and that she would probably go berserk and hit the roof. Helen's boy friend worked on Bill Corfield's farm and he had really fancied Helen and like many other couples who were head over heels in love had let things go a little too far. Getting pregnant before marriage was really frowned upon by the older generation. There was a new more modern generation growing up and they took these things in their stride. A baby born out of wedlock was no longer being brought up as a social out cast or referred to as a bastard and was called all sorts of dreadful names

"Helen, I think the best thing that that you should do is to say nothing until you have sorted a few things out for yourself. Do you think that this boy friend Melvin Fryer will marry you if Mam says that you must and if so where will you live? Could he get another job where there would be a cottage to go with the job? Lots of farmers are always looking for men to work for them and a lot of the jobs offer accommodation to go with the job

"Oh my goodness I have not thought of any thing like that as yet" Helen looked completely bewildered at what Mary was suggesting.

"Get married but how? We've no money it would cost so much for a wedding. Oh Mary, will you tell them? I can't, they will turn me out on to road. Mam said that is what she would do, if any of us were to bring disgrace to her door". Helen could not say any thing else because the tears started to run down her face. She sat down onto the bale of hay and Mary had quite a job to try and console her"

"Helen stop this before Dad comes around the corner and wants to know what is going on. How far pregnant do you think that you are? "The Doctor said that I was three months gone and that the baby would come in June and now it is almost Christmas."

"Well its like I have told you, You must find out if Melvin will marry you and that he is prepared to give up his job and find one with a cottage and then you can have all your answers ready when Mam starts to shout. What does his Dad do for a living? Do you know?"

"Of cause I know. His Dad has a sweet and tobacco shop on Tan Bank and has the barber's shop next door His Mother works in the shop; she sells the sweets and tobacco.""Well thank goodness for that at least they are respectable people. Mam can't say much about them if they own their own business. Just think how she goes on about Hannah and George you know she will never accept George and it is only because his folk live in a council house. Let's leave telling Mam until after Christmas. If she does well with the Christmas poultry, she will be in a good mood for a couple of weeks. I will tell Dad and see what he has got to say. What do you think?

"I can't think of anything rational at the moment I am too scared I've heard of other girls getting pregnant even when they were still at school but I never thought that it could happen to me"

"Well it has. I can't believe that Melvin had got no more common sense He could have waited a bit longer until you were a bit older and then perhaps it would have not seemed so bad"

"If only Mam had talked to us about all this and warned us, it might have helped. She has never warned us about anything. I wonder why? Did you know what could happen? Mary, and if you did why did you not warn me. I feel such a fool and as for having a baby I am scared stiff. What if I die while I'm having it?"

"Don't talk so daft; women don't die in this day and age that was in the olden days before you went into hospital to have them."

"Melvin said that there was no danger but I did not know what he was really doing. He just said that it would hurt a bit and he was too strong for me to stop him I had to let him do as he wanted"

"You stupid girl. Did he not take any precautions like wearing one of those rubber things? How stupid could he be? I suppose that you only let him do it the once and now see what has happened. Oh Lord it will interesting to see how our Mam sorts this out."

"She will kill me I know that she will. What am I to do?"

"You say that you have seen the Doctor and the doctor says that you are most certainly Pregnant."

"Yes I went last week and saw that Lady Doctor. Oh lord you don't think that she will tell Mam do you?"

"No of cause not, she would not be allowed to. You are over sixteen and the Government has lowered the age of consent from eighteen to sixteen. So you are all right on that score they can't prosecute Melvin for getting you in this mess. He only has to say that you wanted him to do it and there is nothing more that can be done about it. You say that you are three months gone so that will make it June next year before you have it because if that is what the Doctor told you? It will make it much easier to tell them" Referring to their parents." There is one thing for sure Mam will not let you have a white wedding She believes in the old fashioned idea that only virgins wear white to be married. That is if they agree to you and Melvin getting married and what is more I am pretty sure that they will insist on it."

"Oh Mary; I have always dreamed of having a white wedding. Just like Lizzy and Beccy." Helen started to cry again.

"We will all have to get ready for Mam to blow up for a bit." Mary continued "She will not like this bit of news one little bit"

Helen made a point of telling Melvin that she was pregnant but he was not the slightest bit interested, he just said "Oh leave it until after Christmas" "Well perhaps we can talk about it in the New Year". Helen was really upset by his complacent attitude. But she said no more, she took it for granted that Melvin would solve all her problems when he was ready to and it was not right now. What she did not realise was that Melvin was not the slightest it interested and that he was not going to take the blame for what had happened. Not if he could help it, he had tried it on with other girls who had been only too glad to let him have his own way and they had not come back to him crying that they were pregnant. He decided that he was going to have nothing to do with this if he could help it. Helen could sort it out for herself and as far as he was concerned her parents could take care of her. Nothing more was said about Helen expecting a baby until after Christmas. Mary finished the milking with her Dad and Bernie. She saw her Dad go to the tractor shed he intending lugging some muck out before the weather turned too wet. There had been several frosts in the last two weeks and the ground had dried out quite nicely.

"Dad "said Mary I've got some thing to tell you, some thing that Mam is not going to like. ""Well what is it. Not bad news. Is it?"

"I thought that if I told you then you could wait until she is in a good mood. "It's that bad is it?

"Yes I think that it is. Helen has got herself into a mess. She is pregnant".

"Oh surry Your Mam won't like that, she won't like that not one little bit. Are you sure about this, has she seen a doctor?" Yes I am sure, and yes she has seen the doctor. Helen is too scared to tell her so what are we going to do?"

"You had better leave it to me I think that I had better break it gently. I suppose it's that lad that works for Bill Corfield, the one who gave us a hand with the beet hoeing last summer"."Aye that's the one At least his family are quite respectable I don't think that Mam can say a lot" Mary was trying to soften the blow as much as she could. "Leave it with me let's go and get some muck lugged before it snows". It was two weeks later as Helen was about to leave the kitchen to go to work Her Mother had intended seeing her and letting her know that she knew about the expected baby.

"Just a minute young lady" Dorothy shouted to Helen who thought that she could get off to work before her Mother had chance to stop her. Mary had told Helen that she had already told their father. That was enough for Helen to be going on with.

"What do you want?" asked Helen moving towards the back door.

"What's this Mary has told your Dad is it true?" Dorothy looked absolutely furious.

"Yes" Helen Whispered and waited for a torrent of abuse which Dorothy gave her. "Bring disgrace to my door would you. Well you can get out as fast as you can and you can go and be with this no good lad that has taken advantage of you. And as for you I would have never have thought any thing like this of you. I thought that you had far more common sense and self respect "You will have to marry the lad and as quickly as possible".

Helen could see that her Mother was already getting things organised and under control". Helen decided to put a bit of blame on her mother. "Well you have never told me about such things have you? That letter that I brought home from school was asking for your permission to have lessons about sex. You threw it onto the fire so I was not allowed to join the class and learn any thing for my self.

"I'll not have you blaming me for the mess that you have got your self into. I told the lot of you. If you were to bring disgrace to my door then you would be turned out onto the street".

Helen said no more and went out through the door. Tears ran down her face as she rode her bike to work. She knew that she would have to tell Melvin what her mother had said and she hoped that he would give her a little bit more support and comfort than the last time that she had spoken to him about it. Helen did not see any thing of Melvin during the day she had to wait until it was time to go home from work. She was glad to see that he was waiting for her in the yard near the back door and she hoped that he would cycle home with her.

"Melvin you know that I said that I thought that I was pregnant Well its true I'm over three months gone and My Mam knows now that I am pregnant and she has blown her top I have not seen her so angry since Grace and Hannah left home. She insisted that I told her who it was that I had been with. I did not want to but I had to tell her that it was you. She wants to know if you are going to marry me and save the disgrace to the family, as she called it. She says that you must and is talking about going to see your Mam and Dad".

"Get married, but where would we live and I've got no money saved what on earth does she think that she is talking about. Get married indeed, "

"Melvin, say that you will marry me and help me out of this mess. Well if we don't mother says that she will turn me out on to the street and where could I go. Oh Melvin you did say that if I let you have your own way it would be quite safe and now look what a mess that I am in"." I will give it a bit of thought but no way do I want to get married, certainly not yet or for several years to come". I don't think that you have much choice we have a baby to think about".

"Don't have much choice. What the devil are you talking about Helen? Get Married; your family has been quick to work things out have they not? Get married indeed I would have to give that a lot of thought. After all you were just as keen as I was, now I suppose you are trying to put all the blame on me I am not very happy about that". The two of them argued backward and forth all the way up the road. Neither of them made any attempt to ride their bikes they were too busy arguing about what could be done and what not could be done. Helen was at the depths of despair. What on earth was going to happen to her if Melvin would not marry her? Where could she go? She had only made one close friend called Carol at school so she decided that she would go and see her at the weekend. Carol was a great comfort to her and was able to calm Helen down a bit. She said that no matter how loud her Mother shouted at her she thought that she would do her best for her in the long run. Dorothy told Fred that she was going to have a talk with Melvin's Mother when she went into town to do the shopping on the next Thursday. Fred for once was in complete agreement he just wanted this mess sorted out as quickly as possible so that once again peace could be restored in the household. The following Thursday Dorothy went into town and as soon as she had finished at her market stall she went to see Mrs Fryer at her shop on Mill bank. "Can I help you" Mrs Fryer asked Dorothy as she entered the sweet and tobacco shop.

"I want a word with you. And it is important that you listen to me. That son of yours has got my daughter pregnant and in case you did not know about it. I want to know what he is prepared to do about it. Turn her on the street that I will.

I will not have disgrace brought to my door step that I won't" Dorothy was now sounding quite angry

"Now just a minute, who ever you are. I know nothing about this and what is more I have not heard of you or your daughter and if it is as you say that your daughter is expecting a child well I consider that she is just as much to blame. I will talk to my husband tonight about this and we will ask Melvin what has been going on. If what you say is true I am sure that he will be very sorry for what he has done and will co-operate fully to do all he can to help your daughter."

"True! Be dammed, do you think that I would be standing here if it was not?" Please would you calm down I am sure that this is not the end of the world. Other girls have found them selves in the same predicament"" not one of my daughters" "Mrs? I am sorry that I did not get your name"." Thomas" Dorothy said very firmly." Well Mrs Thomas I will discuss this with my husband and with Melvin. Perhaps we could discuss this again next week and see what Melvin wishes to do". Dorothy was so angry and wanted to say a lot more but she had no choice but to leave the shop because other customers were coming in and waiting to be served. She had said her piece and she wanted to say a lot more but she stopped the conversation as she felt that it was not for everyone else's ears. She went back down the street mumbling to her self. "I will give him Melvin if I get my hands on him. Discuss it with Melvin she said. She was glad to find Fred and she was still feeling very angry

"I have been to see that Mrs Fryer" she told Fred when she caught up with him in the car park. "Well what has she got to say?" Nothing she says that she will talk to the lad tonight. She had better that is all that I can say"

"See what comes of it. Perhaps they will be able to get married". "But when and where and who is going to pay for it? That's what I want to know. That Lad had better agree to marrying her and finding somewhere for them to live I'll not have the disgrace brought to my door. He will have to find another job that has a cottage to go with it and get married as quickly as possible. You know Fred this is something that I have always been dreading so far we have been lucky. Thank goodness none of the others have got them selves into this mess I just cannot believe that young Helen could be so stupid. The times that I have told them that I will not have disgrace brought to my door and to think that she has taken no notice"

"Now steady on a bit Dot as you say we have been lucky so far and between us I am sure that we can work some thing out"

"Work some thing out. Is that all you can say. It's too late now As far as I can see we have just got to make the most of it. Fred she is so young to have to go through this" For a moment Fred thought that Dot had some sympathy for her daughter. He continued

"Like you say I agree that it will be a good thing if they could get some where to live fairly quickly and get married we had better ask her to bring the lad to see us and see what he intends to do"

Helen persuaded Melvin to see her parents and face the consequences as she called it. He was neither keen to meet them or to change his job and as for getting married he had no intentions of doing any such thing. He began to change his mind after Dorothy had told him exactly what she thought about him for bringing her daughter's name in disgrace and ruining her reputation. As Dorothy had pointed out very sternly to him that he had now had his fun and that he must now face the consequences

After talking with his Mother and Father who were not very pleased either when he had confirmed that he had gone too far, as they had put it and got this girl into trouble. They had given him the biggest lecturing that he had not heard from them before and he was beginning to think how foolish he had been. He had to promise them that he would both change his job and get one, which could provide him with a cottage and also marry Helen. He dare not let them see that he was doing this very reluctantly. He was only seventeen coming eighteen and he was certainly not prepared for this big upheaval to his life. But both his parents and Helen's offered him little choice. Helen and Melvin married at little Wenlock church, three weeks later by special licence Dorothy would not allow Helen to wear a white dress that was only for virgins and seeing as Helen was no longer a virgin. Dorothy considered that if she allowed Helen to wear white it was against the religion of the Church of England and no way were they going to flaunt it in the face of God. That she was supposed to be a virgin when she was not

Helen wore a pale blue dress and coat and only a few friends were asked. Dorothy did not ask any of the uncles or aunts she felt that she could not face them laughing behind her back and saying that she had not brought her daughters up properly. Hannah stood as a witness and being as it was such cold weather she wore a very pale grey coat and hat to match. Dorothy insisted that there would be no publicity of any sort, not even photographs to be taken. They all returned to the farm for a meal of cold meats and salad. With cakes and a drink of sherry and that was that. Melvin had changed his employment and had taken a job working on a farm outside of Wellington All the family gave them items for their new home as wedding presents. Hannah and George gave chairs, another sister gave a table and so on between them all things were not going to be too bad for Helen. They had some where to live and a weekly wage coming in and both she and Melvin knew that they had to make the most of their situation. Helen never forgave her Mother for refusing to allow her to have any photos taken after all it had been her wedding day, Dorothy had been adamant she was not going to allow anyone to take pictures of her daughter who was now about five months pregnant,

Hannah had cycled to Wrockwardine in the after noon and seen to several of the chores when. George came in from work for his tea

"I think that we will go to see a film tonight," He said to Hannah as she washed up the plates and dishes from the meal. Judith had come in tired, eaten her tea and had gone to have a bath, she had said that she was going to have an early night and go to bed with a book.

"O.K then that would be nice we have not been to see a film for such a long time Yes George I would like that"Hannah smiled

There is something that I want to talk to you about. I heard something that just might be of interest to us. I only heard about it yesterday".

"That sounds intriguing does it not. Would it not be better to skip the film and have a talk here" Hannah was wondering what George could possibly want to talk about that was so important? They usually worked together in the caravan on Wednesday evenings because George found that as they had been working together Hannah had picked up the rudiments of carpentry and being a quick thinker she was able to pass him this screw or that nail as he had needed them. Hannah had been his right hand man so to speak. She was such a help and with out her ability to recognise his next move whether it was to use a hammer or a saw he knew that the building of the caravan could have taken almost twice as long to build. It was now almost completed. There was the upholstery to be chosen for the seats and the bath, cooker and other interior things. The villagers had been intrigued when they saw what George was building on the far end of his Dad's garden. He told any inquisitive ones that he was starting a business of letting caravans at the seaside. It was amazing how many asked if they could have a look at it and asked which seaside town that he was going to take it to, some said that they would like to book up in advance. George just told them that he would let them know when it would be finished and that he was taking no bookings until then, this was much to Hannah's amusement. "My goodness they are going to be very disappointed "Hannah had laughed.

Hannah was intrigued as to what George could want to talk to her about. She was thinking that if it was a piece of ground that he had found that was for sale it would of not taken him five minutes to have said so. He put his motor bike as usual at the back of the Clifton cinema and in they went to watch the film that was showing. It was one of George's favourites a cowboy and Indian. Hannah had difficulty trying to concentrate she just could not think of any thing so important that George had wanted to talk about and given her no clue as to what it was after the film George suggested that they go to a pub for a drink. Some thing that he had rarely asked her to do before as far as pubs were concerned Hannah had been brought up to believe that pubs were dens of iniquity.

"But George it is five past nine already and you know that I have to be in by ten o'clock. What on earth is it that is so important?" Hannah was beginning to wonder if he was going to suggest that they go away and get married. But that was not the case George took Hannah to the Queens Hotel that was just up the road from the Clifton cinema. He went to bar and bought a pint of beer for himself and an orange juice for Hannah He chose a fruit juice because as far as he knew Hannah had never been used to drinking any thing alcoholic. She had always refused to have a drink with any alcohol in it. She had once told him when he said that she ought to try something stronger than orange juice. "I can't go back to work smelling of beer I would be thrown out" He picked up the drinks that he had ordered and directed her to a table in the corner away from any other drinkers. When Hannah was seated she was amazed at how nice and comfortable the room was. She placed her drink on the mat provided on the round polished table in front of her. She was taking in her surroundings and found that where George had chosen for them to sit was very comfortable. The chairs were upholstered and not wooden ones, which could prove to be very uncomfortable if sat on for any length of time. The floor was carpeted in a nice pattern of reds and greens. Pictures hung on the walls and there were shelves on which stood rows of Toby jugs. This did not look like a den of iniquity as her Mother had insisted that all public houses were. George sat down beside Hannah and took a long drink from his pint of beer. What was it that George was about to say, Hannah could not have guessed. "George; For goodness sake what is it that you want to talk about, can you tell me what this is all about and be quick or it will be too late and I will have to go even if I have to walk up the street by my self?" Hannah would not be late in if she could help it taking a deep breath he started to talk

"Hannah. I have been talking to some one who is related to the people who took on the Wrekin Cottage when Eric Watson died. We had to fetch a body in yesterday and the fellow there who had just lost his wife told me that it was his daughter and Son in Law that had taken on the Cottage after Eric had died. Now that he had lost his wife he said that he would no longer be able to run his own business single-handed and that he was considering asking his Son in Law to help him out and then between them, they could form a new partnership. It would help him to know that his Daughter and Son in Law would be more secure and that he wanted his lifetime's work to be a benefit to them and his Grandchildren. He said that his one Granddaughter had not been very happy since her parents went to live up the Wrekin". George took another long drink from his pint glass." But what has this got to do with us?" Hannah wanted to know.

"Well I have been doing a lot of thinking over night. What do you think if I were to apply for the tenancy and see if we could get it"? George was getting quite excited at the idea. He had given it a lot of thought. If he could get the tenancy of the Cottage there was seventeen acres of ground that went with it. He would then become a farmer and be more acceptable to Hannah's parents. He would be able to once again enjoy his favourite sport of shooting of which he had done very little since he had stopped going up to the Cottage. Going out with his gun and shooting rabbits, Magpies and such. Oh yes he felt that he could be quite the little Lord of the Manor.

"Well what do you think about the idea?"

"The first thought I have, is that you are crazy. Have you stopped to think about how much work that there would be involved? We would have to find so much money to be able to take a place like that. Would we not?" Hannah exclaimed. She was absolutely amazed at George's idea. "It would be one heck of a challenge, have you any idea what we would have to do and are you certain that those people who are up there at the moment are prepared to give it up"?

"Yes I am pretty sure that they will give it up according to what the old boy said. If you must know, last night, when I finished work I called at his house and had a word with him to see if there was any truth in what I had over heard him telling the Gaffer. He said that his daughter had been thinking of giving the Cottage up for some time and now that her mother has died it would be much easier for them all if they came to live in Wellington and be a bit nearer to him. They would be a great help to him with the running of the business. He said that they had provisionally given their notice to the Estate at the end of September so that they could give it up at the end of March. They had been told that it would depend on the Estate being able to find a new tenant because the premises could not be left empty for any length of time, especially at a bank holiday".

"What have you got to do if you want it and another thing, I am not so sure that I could run those tearooms and think of all those cakes that have to be made every week and all the water that is needed. Who on earth would you get to carry it all?"

"Stop worrying there will be no need to carry water, there has been a pump fitted on the well and this old man told me that the kitchen had been modernised there is a four oven Aga cooker as well as Calor gas for lighting and heating boilers."

The thought of an Aga cooker like the one that the Corfield' had, did cause Hannah to sit up and take more notice.

"George it would be an enormous challenge. Of that there is no doubt, but firstly what do you have to do."

"Write to the Estate and ask if there is a possibility of us making an application. Then wait and see what sort of a reply that we get, you never know we might get an appointment to go and see the owner he is the Earl of Powys." Where does he live?" "Orleton Hall, that big hall just out of Wellington on the Shrewsbury road." I want you to write the letter for me. Your spelling is a bit better than mine is. Do you think that you could get an hour off tomorrow night so that we could do it and send it off? Make up some excuse and don't tell Charlotte why or she will just try to talk you out of it. You have been with her for so long and she will be reluctant to let you go. In fact don't tell a soul or there could be a lot of others putting in for it. The old Boy that I went to see said that if I were interested he would not say anything about it to anyone else. I have told him that I will let him know straight away if we decide to apply for it".

"I will see what I can do." Hannah looked at George's wrist watch and saw that it was ten to ten." George come on we are going to be late and if you want me to ask for time off. I don't think that it would be a good idea to put Charlotte in a bad mood I think that we should go quickly so that I can get in on time."

"Ok. I suppose that we had better any thing to keep the peace" Hannah could see that George was reluctant to make a move. He was rather annoyed there was so much more that he wanted to say to convince Hannah that it was a good idea for them to have a go at being able to take the Cottage up the Wrekin.

When Hannah went to bed that night she was filled with trepidation. No way could she go to sleep. All she could think about was the thought of going to live up the Wrekin. Then the idea came to her. If we were able to do that it just might shut her mother up for a bit and just think they would be neighbours our fields joining theirs. The more Hannah thought about it the more pleasing the idea seemed. We would be farmers just like Lizzy and Beccy but first we have to get the place and the fact that we are not even married I doubt very much that the Estate would give us any consideration at all. Still I will go along with what George says and do what he thinks is best. Charlotte let Hannah have the following night off proving that she was prepared to forfeit the following Sunday after noon and only have the evening off. Charlotte politely put it that it would mean that she would be unable to go out on any taxi runs, because there would be no one to sit in with Oliver. Hannah thought that this was a bit much because Charlotte very rarely went out on the evening runs, part time drivers came in to see to the evening calls. When Hannah saw George he was still quite excited about the idea and he and Hannah went into the Caravan and decide how best to word a letter to the Estate manager. It was a week later that George received a reply asking if the two of them would like to attend an interview at Orleton hall in the presence of the Earl of Powys. It stated that he was prepared to discuss the tenancy of the cottage with them. George was so excited and he asked Hannah to write back confirming that they were prepared to do this at a convenient time to suit the Earl.

"But what if I can't get the time off? Protested Hannah; when the appointment came through for them to be there at Ten O'clock the following Saturday morning. Charlotte has a wedding and there will be no one to answer the phone."

"Well she had better find some one who can" George sounded really angry to think that Hannah would put Charlotte before him.

"Well what am I to tell her that it is so important for me to want the time off on Saturday morning. Can I say why?" "No you bloody well can't we don't want any one to find out about what we are doing. I want to get this place if I possibly can, so don't 'you to go telling any one and spoil our chances.".

Hannah had not seen George so angry and was wondering what sort of excuse that she could possibly make to Charlotte to warrant taking Saturday morning off especially when there was wedding cars to be prepared. White ribbons to be tied on the cars and silk flowers to be arranged around the interior of them. Charlotte's wedding cars were always in demand they always looked so smart. Dressing the cars was the job of Hannah and herself. Washed and polished and immaculately clean, the drivers always wearing uniforms as well as white covered peeked caps. Charlotte always drove one of the cars herself and she too wore a navy blue uniform and a special cap. Hannah decided to ask Charlotte's sister if she would help out before she asked for the time off and confided in Rosie that she was scared stiff to ask Charlotte for a Saturday morning off.

"Don't you worry I will come and help out for the morning, it must be important for you to want a Saturday morning off. Something to do with George is it?"

"Well yes but I can't discuss it at this stage. As he says that if it gets out what we are trying to do I could jeopardise everything for him. I tell you what, if every thing goes Ok. I will tell you both all about it. Do you think that would be fair enough"?

"Yes I do and I will tell Charlotte that you are going to ask for the time off and that I will come and take your place I don't think that she will argue about that. You leave it to me"

"Oh thank you she will probably wonder why I can't ask for my self but I can't leave her to do every thing on her own and have no help with the cars. It takes us so long to prepare them and then she must have some thing to eat before she goes out. Oh thank you Rosie I will make up the time don't you worry".

"Don't you worry Hannah you work long hours you are always on call and have very little time off. I should not worry too much about making up for lost time"

Hannah told George that she had arranged to have the Saturday morning off thanks to Rosie. They were both excited and apprehensive about going to the Hall to meet the Earl of Powys. I will see if I can borrow the Boss's car, George informed Hannah "I think that may be it would look a bit better than turning up on a motor bike. Put that smart suit on, you know the one that Pricilla gave to you. I will wear my best suit; the dark one I had for my Mam's funeral. Its dark navy blue I think that I should look all right in that. We have got to give a good impression. The more I think about getting that tenancy of the Cottage the more I like the idea. I could still keep my job it would take me no longer to get to work than what it is doing now. Another thing it would certainly shut your Mother up. There would be little that she could complain about, I think that she would shut up about me not being good enough for you."

"I agree with you George. What time will you pick me up on Saturday Morning?"

"Oh about half past nine I don't want us to be late we have to be there for ten and we want time to get our story straight before we get there We have to know the answers to any questions that we may be asked"

"I am surprised that you can't confide in me as to what you two are up to" Charlotte said to Hannah on the Saturday Morning when she saw Hannah dressed as smart as she could be.

"If you and George are planning to run away and get married I do hope that you will tell me. I should hate to lose you, we have got on so well since Geoffrey died and I would have to find some one whom I could trust to replace you."

Hannah was very tempted to reveal where she and George were going but knew that if she did and George found out. He would be very angry indeed, if he felt that he could not trust her to keep what he considered was their business to her self.

"Don't worry we are certainly not planning to run away. This is only an interview which George wants a bit of support with. I will be back well before lunchtime".

"Oh that is a relief. I have Rosie to help with the cars so I guess we will be alright"

George is right Hannah said to her self as she waited for him to come to collect her. All Charlotte considers is what is for her benefit and not that I have earned a couple of hours off. Charlotte was also thinking to her self. I suppose that George is thinking of borrowing money probably to put that caravan on a piece of ground I bet it's the bank manager that they are going to see and he needs Hannah's support. The fact that they are engaged and that she is a farmer's daughter might help to swing things in his favour. But then on second thoughts why would they want to go by car if it was to see a bank Manager they could walk down the street or perhaps they are going to Shrewsbury. That would make more sense and I know by what I have seen of George. He would not deal with any one in Wellington. He likes to keep his business to him self. Oh well I think that I will have to wait and see. George collected Hannah in the firms little black Morris eight, it was a beautiful dry morning with a touch of spring in the air so neither of them had need for raincoats or umbrellas. The wind was cold but they were not worried about that, off they went. He stopped the car in Haygate road.

"You have not told Charlotte where we are going have you? Now that your Mother has the telephone I would not put it past her to ring her up and let them know what we are up to. Especially if she thought that they could stop us and if that happened she need have no fear of losing you".

"Of course I have not. You asked me not too but I think that she was really put out because I did not say where we were going. "

The two of them sat and discussed what answers to give if asked certain questions about them selves. They both agreed that the fact that they had both worked at the cottage up the Wrekin should go in their favour.

George drove up the tarmac drive lined with shrubs and trees to the front of the hall, he parked the car to the one side of the front door, but in such a way that it would not cause any obstruction to other cars that may come to the front entrance. He quickly ran a comb through his dark hair. He made sure that his tie was straight and in the correct position.

"Right lets go in and meet this Earl. And for goodness sake try not to look scared stiff, try and relax a bit he is not going to eat you, we are only here so that he can have a look at us. There may be many others who want the place"

"I hope not for your sake don't worry about me I will be alright its just that I don't want to let you down the Earl is rather an important fellow. I have not met an Earl before".

"And neither have I" said George as he pulled on a bell rope that was fitted to the one side of the large oak front door of the hall. They could hear the sound of it ringing inside and it sounded as if there was a very big hall the other side of the door. After a few minutes the door opened and a tall man stood in front of them. He was much taller than George was and as he looked down at him he said.

"Ah yes you must be Mr Fleming. I am his Lordships Agent I help to manage his Estate. Do come in, his Lordship is expecting you. Just follow me" Hannah was amazed at the size of the entrance hall it was bigger than the one where she had previously worked. The walls were of oak panelling and there were heads of animals hung as trophies on the walls; deer foxes and badgers. They were very impressive. George and Hannah followed the tall man until he stopped and turned to knock on one of the big oak doors. After hearing a faint voice call "come in" from with in the room the Estate manager entered and introduced George and Hannah to a small man who rose from a well worn leather armchair placed by a fireside which had an enormous fire grate. There were big logs of wood burning and giving out a tremendous amount of heat. There were logs stacked in a pile at the one side of the grate The Earl of Powys stood no more than five foot three and he had the most wonderful smile.

"Come in my Dears" He shook hands with both George and 'Hannah and then he pointed to a leather covered seat, and asked both George and Hannah to sit down. The seat had some very nice embroidered cushions on it

"Go and bring a pot of tea "He said to his manager. This was an unexpected pleasant surprise to both George and Hannah they most certainly were not expecting to be offered a cup of tea.

"I like a pot of tea at this time of the morning" he said. "Much prefer it to coffee I have to suffer that at dinner and so I please my self what I drink during the day if at all possible. This man that they both had dreaded meeting was so friendly towards them that George and Hannah immediately relaxed. Hannah noticed that there were several large paintings hung around the room. Although she was not all that intellectual regarding art she could see from what she had learnt at school that the paintings were probably done by famous artists especially the one of a lady seated and wearing a pale pink and mauve dress. It looked like one that she had seen a picture of and it had been painted by Gainsborough. The Earl had noticed Hannah looking at the paintings and he was quite impressed. He distracted her attention by starting to make conversation about the Cottage on the Wrekin. His Agent returning with a tray of tea, cups and saucers interrupted him. The Earl stopped talking until all four had their tea placed before them on an occasional table. His Agent sat and did not take part in the conversation. The Earl continued to ask relevant questions as to why these two young people as he referred to them should want to go and live in such an isolated place. Had they considered how much work that would be involved, that was if he were to consider them for the tenancy? Would they be going to live there as a married couple? He had noticed that Hannah wore an engagement ring. George quickly assured him that they could. He seemed interested in the fact that her parents farm came so close to the ground belonging to the Cottage and how much acreage that they were farming. He assumed that there would be help there if it were needed. After about half an hour The Earl brought the interview to a close. He stood up and said Goodbye to them both informing George that he would be making a decision with in the next few days. He said that he considered that it was imperative that the Cottage should not be left empty. He said that the present occupiers were hoping to leave at Easter; we're now only weeks away. George re-assured him that if he was considered that moving in for Easter would be no problem. The Agent who said good day as he shook hands with them both showed them to the door.

"Be in for Easter if we are lucky enough to be considered", Hannah said to George when they were seated in the car and out of ear shot. He said nothing. Instead he started the engine and drove out of the drive back towards Wellington.

Hannah continued "I sat listening to you and by what I heard I think that you gave the Earl the impression that we could be married. I am not twenty-one until June. If Mother has her way you know that she will not allow my Dad to agree to us getting married, I am sure that she will make things as difficult as possible. How on earth can we possibly do that? Be married before Easter." George are you listening to me?" Hannah raised her voice.

"I can hear you there is no need to shout. We have not got the tenancy as yet and if we do we will just have to get married" "What get married? Easter is only weeks away and we have no money for a wedding? I would have to leave my job. What ever would Charlotte do with out me I just could not let her down with such short notice? No George that just would not be fair at all" George pulled into a gateway and stopped the car." "Hannah" Now you just listen to me. This is one chance in a life time If we are lucky and get the Cottage we have to get a move on there will so much to be done and all you can think about is letting Charlotte down. I just don't believe it. As for getting married we can soon do that we have only got to see a vicar or go to a registry office. We can be married with in weeks." George went on to tell Hannah of all the plans that he had been making. They would have just about enough money saved to be able to pay for what he called the ingoing. That would be all the tables, chairs all the crockery and cutlery and what ever else had to be paid for. He would use the money that he had saved and was hoping to buy a piece of ground with but there would be none left over to pay for a wedding.

"Let us wait until we have the letter saying one thing or the other; if we don't get it we still have nothing to lose we have the caravan more or less finished and we can go back to our original plans. Come on let us get back into town, so that I can take this car to the yard, in case the boss is called out you never know he could be waiting for me to bring it back. I told him that I would not be that long away.". He started up the engine and drove into town where he dropped Hannah of at the top of New Street and reminded her to keep quiet for the time being.

"There will be plenty to talk about if we are lucky and then we can satisfy their curiosity" Hannah knew that he was referring to Charlotte so she said nothing she just walked away from the car and went back to work. She was so glad that Charlotte did not ask questions when she came in she looked at Hannah and seemed a bit peeved but Hannah got on with her work ignoring her

George called at the garage to see Hannah on the following Friday evening she was quite surprised when she answered the knocking at the back door and saw George standing there. Charlotte was also surprised. As a rule when Hannah had her off duty George would usually wait out side with his motor bike until Hannah went out to see him. He always knew that she would hear the engine of the bike as he went around the back to turn it around.

"George what are you doing here? I was not expecting to see you before Sunday afternoon." Hannah asked

"Can you come out for a minute? Come around the back". He sounded very agitated.

"OK what is that you want?"

“Just come out for a minute”.

“Won’t be a minute “Hannah called to Charlotte as she closed the kitchen door. What are those two up to Charlotte thought? There is definitely something in the wind that is for sure. Charlotte decided not to ask any questions for the time being she was sure that Hannah would not be able to resist telling her what was going on. Minute’s later Hanna walked around the back of the garage where George had taken his motorbike and promptly sat astride

“What is it George?”

“I had a letter from the Estate yesterday and I could not let it wait until Sunday” He took a brown oblong envelope from his inside pocket.

“What does it say”?

“You will never guess. It says that we can have the Cottage if we want it. We have to confirm in writing that we are willing to accept the tenancy. I want you to help me put a letter together to tell them that we will take it”.

“That is wonderful George. I can’t believe it. Oh my goodness George what does this mean? When can we tell any one about this? There will be so much for us to do.” Hannah was as excited as George was about the news.

“Well I have been thinking that because Easter is at the beginning of April we have to take the tenancy and have it signed up by the twenty fifth of March”.

“But that makes Easter only five weeks away. George we can’t possibly be ready in time.” Hannah was now sounding very alarmed.

“We will just have to. Let’s talk it over on Sunday. We could go and see your Mother and Dad and see what they have to say. Not that they can say much can they? After all it is our life is it not. I will tell my Dad tomorrow if I can get him on his own for a bit. If not it will have to wait until Sunday dinner time”.

“I suppose that you could tell Judith. Oh George how we are going to do it all.

"Well first things first. We have to answer this letter. We have to get married you know that I told the Earl that if he gave us a chance we would marry and take the Cottage as a married couple"

"Oh yes you did. I remember but I did not give it much thought at the time but now it is a reality".

"I can't wait to get up there, to be able to walk the fields with my gun and get away from the nosy neighbours of the village. It will be so good you see if it's not. I think that you had better tell Charlotte what we are proposing to do."

"Yes I think that I better had and she is not going to like it one little bit Ok I will think how it would be best to answer this letter and what we should tell the Earl. I will make a rough copy for you. We can write it out on Sunday afternoon and then you can post it on Monday morning. What do you think?"

"I wish that we could do it tonight so that the Earl would receive on Monday morning."

"I can't get time off tonight, Charlotte is going to a dinner party I believe that she has a new man in her life and there is no one to take my place at such short notice. Sorry George."

"Always Charlotte this and Charlotte that. In another few weeks you will not have to consider Charlotte any more". George put the envelope back into his pocket and his crash hat on his head.

"I will see you on Sunday at two. I hope that you will be ready we have a lot to sort out and I can't wait to get started".

"George you know that it is very rarely that I keep you waiting I will be ready" Hannah was beginning to resent George's attitude a little she had been so over whelmed by him since she had first met him. She had not noticed that he could be so sarcastic. She now put it down to the fact that she was expected to work such long hours and that she did not have as much time for him as he would have liked when he needed it.

“Ok I will go back in now. Charlotte will be wondering what we are up to if she has not already started to wonder what on earth is going on between us.

“OK “George said reluctantly “I will pick you up on Sunday at two as usual” He gave Hannah a very passionate kiss and started the engine any animosity Hannah had felt for him quickly faded.

“It is unusual for George to come on a Friday night. What ever are you two up to” Charlotte was eager to find out what was going on. Hannah sat on the chair at the kitchen table opposite Charlotte.

“It is like this. I am sorry that I could not confide in you a bit earlier but. George swore me to secrecy. We heard that the people up at the Wrekin Cottage were giving up the tenancy. We have applied to the Orleton Estate for the tenancy of it. We thought that if we tried for it we had nothing to lose and we certainly did not think that we would have been considered. George has had a letter back to say that we can have it. He came to see if I could go out for an hour tonight to help him write a letter in reply, saying that we will take it. I told him that it would have to wait until Sunday because you are going out tonight and there is no one that we can get hold to look after things here at such short notice”.

“Quite right I can’t get any one at such short notice Rosie will have made her arrangements for the evening. You sit there and tell me if you are thinking about going to live at that Cottage up the Wrekin. Just tell me when is this to take place? will have to find a replacement for you and that can sometimes prove very difficult not all young girls want a job where they have to live in they much prefer to work in offices if they can. And another thing I cannot just have any one living in. I hope that you will give me plenty of notice. I will most certainly need it”.

“We have decided that we will definitely take the Cottage, it is something that George has always wanted. To have his own fields; to walk with the gun and to have our own business.

We have to take over on March the 25th and have the place ready for opening at Easter. Not only that. George told the Earl of Powys that we would take it as a married couple".

"He has said what? The two of you have to be crazy, have you thought of all the work that is involved trying to run your own business?" Charlotte said very severely. Hannah was about to say that she had helped to run this business for long enough but thought that it was best to keep quiet.

"To be in for Easter you say, you can't possibly organise a wedding in that short time, Goodness me, it is only weeks away". Charlotte sounded really alarmed and angry" She looked so amazed this was not what she had expected. Hannah sat at the kitchen table and told her the whole story of what they had been doing. She also said that she was so sorry that she not been able to confide in her before this.

"We were so worried that if the word got out too many other folk might apply for it. George had set his heart on being able to go and live up there. He swore me to secrecy."

"I see, so it looks to me that I must look for a replacement immediately. I guessed that you two were up to something. I only hope that you know what you are doing? Going to live up there, it seems to me that it will be very lonely for you in the winter months. You say that you will have to get married. You had better go and see what your mother and Dad have to say about all of this"

"Yes I know that is why George came this evening, so that we can make a start but it will now have to wait until Sunday"

"Indeed it will. How do you think that I can find a replacement for you in such short time, most inconsiderate? That is what I call it; most inconsiderate it is. I wish that I could have been told what was going on Hannah it's a pity that you could not trust me? Farmland with this place is there; well that should please your parents. Have they been told of what you two have been up to?"

"No not yet, we thought that we could go and see them on Sunday. You are the only one to be told as yet" Hannah stammered.

"Really". Charlotte rose from her chair and walked swiftly towards the bottom of the stairs to go and have a bath and prepare herself for her evening out. Well. I never. Thought Hannah, George was quite right. All Charlotte thinks about is her self. She made her self a cup of coffee to regain her composure before Charlotte came back down stairs dressed up to go out. George came to collect Hannah after lunch on Sunday and he was on time. It had been raining all morning cold wet clingy rain the sort that seemed to penetrate through to ones bones. Hannah was not looking forward to riding on the back of George's bike.

"Where are we going? Not far in this rain, I hope?" Hannah asked, ""Home "Said George. Hannah said no more until they were at Wrockwardine and had put the motorbike on its stand. As they were about to go inside Hannah asked

"Have you had chance to talk to your Dad and Judith "? Hannah was a bit apprehensive as to what their re-action would have been.

"No not yet, I thought that it would be better if the two of us were there. Especially that we have to tell them that we are planning to get married"

"OK just as you say their re-action can't be any worse than Charlottes when I told her what we were planning to do. She was not very pleased".

"Well I told you that would be the case; all she has thought about is herself. You know that her business is quite a profitable concern and you have been muggings there for far too long. Thank goodness that it is all going to change in the near future". Hannah decided that she would leave it to George to do the talking and go along with what ever he said. They put their wet waterproof coats in the porch by the back door along with their crash hats. Hannah was relieved to see a good fire burning in the living room it looked so inviting. They settled them selves down at the back of the living room table. She would have liked to have sat in one of the more comfortable armchairs by the fire. With it being such a wet day; Hannah had got quite cold riding on the back of the bike. She would help George with his letter and then she decided that she would move to sit in one of the more comfortable chairs. She would be so glad to be able to warm herself properly nearer the fire her feet felt as cold as ice. Hannah had made a rough copy of a letter that she had thought would be good enough for their reply of acceptance and George was just finishing copying it, when his father returned from work.

"What are you two doing? It's not like you to be writing letters. Is it" When Judith heard her father's voice she came from upstairs and joined them in the living room and she too was wondering what or whom George could be writing letters to.

"You have your dinner and then we can tell you both what we are about. George addressed and sealed the envelope that he had in his hand.

"George Can I go and put that letter in the post box for you?" Judith asked as she put a large dinner plate of food in front of her father. She was hoping to see whom it was that George could be writing to.

"Not likely. I do not want half the village to know my business".

"But they would not know who has put what in the post box. Would they? What is so secret about that letter that you don't want any one to know about?"

"I will tell you in a minute and I will post this letter on my way to work in the morning at the main post office in Wellington". He said with authority and Judith decided to back off somewhat.

"My goodness it must be very important. What are you two planning? Simon will be here in a minute so you will have to be quick if you do not want him to hear what you are going to tell us".

"It will be alright for Simon to know because I have to ask a favour of him".

"Really? This does sound intriguing, I can't wait". She looked at Hannah thinking that she might be pregnant and a wedding on the cards.

"Well in that case go and put the kettle on and make a pot of tea because I think that you might need one. Judith said no more, she made her way to the kitchen but she gave Hannah the most peculiar look as if to say come and tell me what is going on. Hannah stayed where she was by the fire and just smiled when Judith looked at her hoping for an explanation. Hannah was determined that it was going to be George who did the talking. If his Dad blew a fuse and started an argument it was then left to George to calm him down and convince him that this was what he wanted to do. The sound of Simons's motorbike saved Judith from any further questions she went out to meet him.

"George is up to something He says that he wants to ask a favour of you, come inside and let's hear what he has to say. I have made a pot of tea." Simon noticed how excited that Judith was he put his crash helmet and over coat, which was quite wet in the back porch along with George and Hannah's coats. He followed Judith into the kitchen He said a casual hello and sat him self down in the other vacant armchair. Judith took the dirty dinner plate from in front of her father and brought the cups of tea from the kitchen.

"Now George are you going to tell us what this is all about?" Terry asked "So that I can go and rest for an hour. We have a lot of work on at the moment and I could do with getting my head down for a bit. We had to start at five this morning and it looks as if we will have to start early all next week" George told them how he had heard of the Cottage coming vacant and that he had applied for it and that he had been told that they could take on the tenancy if they wanted to.

"That's the letter to say that we will". George finished sealing the envelope with his tongue and pressing the flap firmly down.

"You have what?" His father asked? Looking absolutely astonished. "You two are thinking of taking the Cottage up the Wrekin Did I hear you right"?

"You heard right and what is more we have to get married and move in by the end of next month ready for the Easter trade. The Estate does not want it left empty over the Easter Bank holiday, and the folks up there want to get out before Easter. I have been thinking Simon," George looked at Simon sat by the fire. "I wonder if you would stand as best man for me The Army has sent our Thomas to some island near Australia so he will not be able to get back in time."

"Yes I will do that for you. My goodness you have got a lot of sorting out to do".

Judith looked gob smacked at Hannah and quickly asked, "Can I be a bridesmaid at your wedding?"

"Oh course you can if it is at all possible, but we have to tell my Mam and Dad as you know that I am not twenty one yet. I can't marry with out their permission. George says that we will go later tonight when we know that they have finished milking.". Terry had sat there listening and then he decided that he would have his say.

"Now just a minute you two hold your horses a bit. Molly and I were thinking of getting married at Easter and I can't see how we can afford two weddings in the same family and in the same month."

"You and Molly were thinking of getting married. You have kept that a secret "Judith looked at her father. She had been hoping that her Dad would remarry. She liked Molly and she was looking forward to handing over the responsibility of the household but she had not expected to hear this.

"So what do we do now?" Judith looked around the table for answers. As much as she would have liked to have a lovely white wedding Hannah knew that it could not be a possibility.

Neither she nor George had money to spare to pay for a big do." We were thinking of getting married at Easter." Terry continued." Well that could easily be resolved How about us doing a swap with you We were thinking of getting married at the end of June when Hannah had become twenty one with or with out permission from her parents. I intended having the caravan finished by then and we would not have to have any ones permission to get married?" George continued. "We could get married at the end of March and then we could have a really nice do for you and Molly in the summer." He started to laugh and saw the surprise on Hannah's face and he thanked his lucky stars that she did not say any thing untoward at that moment. "George. We have not posted the letter as yet, saying that we are prepared to take the Cottage. I think that we should wait until we have spoken to my Dad and Mam tonight and then we can make our plans about what has to be done. They will never let us live in sin and if they don't give their permission for us to get married what are we going to do then" She looked at Terry. Who had a frown on his face not fancying telling Molly that their wedding plans could have to be put back until the summer? "Would you be prepared to consider what George has just said if we are able to go ahead and take the Cottage. George has already got every thing more or less worked out. But there are one or two hurdles to be got over first. I can't see my Mam and Dad paying anything towards a wedding they have had to pay for Helen's do. Not that was very much. Poor girl I saw how disappointed that she was at not being able to have a nice white wedding. If we go ahead ours will have to be a quiet affair, just a service at the church or registry office and then a family meal some where. Neither George nor I can pay to have anything on a grand scale. You can certainly stand as my bridesmaid if you would like to Judith. I suggest that we all wait until I come on Wednesday and that will give us all a bit of time to get used to the idea and think things out".

"Oh really" George looked at Hannah "I am not the only one to have been thinking things out".

"Let's all have another cup of tea". Judith offered "As you say Hannah we have to think things out. My goodness you two taking on the Cottage Can we come and help you? Simon and I are going to need some extra money and we can come and earn a bit extra, we are both trying to save very hard. Hannah come and give me a hand and let's make a plate of sandwiches". Hannah rose from her chair and went to Judith's aid.

They spent the rest of the afternoon discussing the Cottage up the Wrekin. George told them how he had heard all about it. His Dad looked quite gob smacked when George said how he and Hannah had met the Earl of Powys. How the Cottage had been modernised and that it now had calor gas lighting and a four-oven AGA cooker. He shared his plans with them with great enthusiasm. He said that he would keep the motorbike that he had and use it for getting to work He had changed his 250 and he now had an AJS 500. He said that he would have to buy a tractor to get provisions up the Wrekin, as and when they needed them especially during the winter months. A van would have to wait until later when they saw how much money they could make. Thank goodness O.D. Murphy delivered all the minerals Crisps Etc. Terry, Simon and Judith were so excited about the prospect of George going to live up the Wrekin that Terry forgot about going for a lie down. When George thought that it was time to go to the Willowmoors. He told Hannah to get herself ready and that they would go and face the music as he put it. Thank goodness that it had stopped raining the roads which were mostly narrow lanes could be so mucky as well as wet. They had brought their overcoats to dry out a bit in front of the fire At least they would feel a little bit warmer to put on. It was seven o'clock when they got to the farm

"It's only us" Hannah called as they went into the kitchen, which was in darkness she found the electric switch by the back door and switched it on. Dorothy and Fred had a bigger generator, which now supplied the house with electricity. It did not give the same power, as they would have had if they were connected to the mains electricity supply. That did not seem to bother them because they no longer had to light the oil lamps. George and Hannah took off their out door clothes and put them over a kitchen chair, they put their crash hats on the kitchen table. Hannah found that her parents were seated in the front room listening to a new wireless set that they had bought. God she thought we could have been just any one coming in they would not have noticed until it was too late they could have been tied up and burgled.

"Oh it's you two". Dorothy said she looked up as Hannah knocked on the door and entered.

"Sit your selves down "She put another large log of wood on to the fire thinking that they would not be going to bed for a while now that they had visitors.

"Well what have you come to tell us? Got a bit of news have you?" Dorothy always used this phase when any of the family visited. She had got used to the girls only coming to visit if they had some thing to say or some gossip to pass on. Fred had made himself comfortable in an armchair in front of the burning fire. He stirred slightly and continued smoking his pipe. "Hello there" he looked really surprised when he saw who it was."Make a cup of tea mother and let's have a drink". Fred was always the first to offer a cup of tea.

There was no sign of Mary being there so Hannah did not ask where she was. William was away at school and Sandra had already been sent to bed.

"I will do it" Hannah made a move to go back to the kitchen. Her Mother did not object it meant that she did not have to move from her chair to make the tea.

The kettle which was sat on the Rayburn cooker did not take long to bring to the boil and by the time Hannah had gathered the cups, saucers, sugar and milk together and it was ready to be scalded. Nothing had changed places since she had left home over four years ago. The cups and saucers were still in the same compartment of the kitchen cupboard and she knew where to find a jug of milk in the larder

Hannah poured four cups of the tea and put them on a tray and took them into the front room she passed a cup to Dorothy, Fred and George. She sat down beside George at the back of the same polished table that had been in the front room for years.

It was George who started to speak first.

"We have come to see if we can get married. Hannah is not twenty one until June and we need to get married fairly quickly"

Dorothy put her cup and saucer on the table with such force the cup almost bounced off the saucer thank goodness that the cup was now empty and that it did not crash to the floor and break.

"What you mean get married in a hurry. I suppose that you are in the same mess as your sister". She glared at Hannah. Then she switched the wireless set off which had been playing some organ music.

"No Mother we are not in a mess as you put it. It's just that if we can get married fairly quickly. We are going to be your neighbours."

"Why what is going on? What do you mean that you are going to be our neighbours? You are not thinking of bringing that caravan anywhere near here are you? I will not have the two of you living like gypsies any where near me"

"No Mam we are going to live up the Wrekin at the Cottage, and the Estate would prefer it if we were a married couple."

It was at this point that Fred suddenly became aware of the conversation.

"Up the Wrekin. Aye surry that would be grand. When have you got to be in by?"

"We have to be in for Easter. The Estate will not leave it empty over the bank holiday and the people up there want to get out as soon as they can "

"You have been doing some planning have you not and have never said a word about it". Dorothy was determined to take control of the conversation again, and she sounded very annoyed to think that all this had been going on with out her knowledge and that she had not been in at the beginning of the arrangements.

"We could not say much until we knew that we had a chance and I only heard on Thursday that we have got it. If we had told any one there would have been too many after it." It was George who had now started to talk.

"The problem is that we cannot afford to spend on having a big wedding party so it will just have to be a very quiet one. Just a few at the church or registry office. What money that we have saved will be needed to pay for what they call the ingoing. We have to pay for six months rent in advance and pay for minerals, crisps, chocolate and things like that before we can start to sell", Dorothy stopped George before he said any more.

"I'll not have any daughter of mine getting married in a registry office. That I will not, it has to be in church." But" she spluttered" Easter is only about five weeks away. Do you reckon that we could organise something by then? What do you say Fred."

"Just as you say Dot; I reckon that we could arrange some thing if you say so." He answered philosophically knowing that Dorothy would have the last say if she could.

"Now what do you say if you had a nice little white wedding and then I could ask your Aunts and Uncles. The word has bound to have got out that we have had one of you getting married and this would act as a cover up for Helen' s mess. Yes I think that it would be a good idea". She was looking at the fire burning in the grate letting her mind run away with her as she was making a mental note of what could be done.

"Just hold on a minute Mam. George has said that we can't pay for a big wedding and as I have not stayed at home I don't expect you to pay for anything either. A quiet little do will be all we need. All we have come for is to let you know what we were planning to do"

"Quite a bit of ground with the place is there, what you think of doing with it" Fred asked.

"Well we have not given that any thought as yet. I will have to buy a tractor to get stuff up the hill and then I suppose a couple of cows will be a good idea".

"You will be farmers like the others" Dorothy smiled. "You had better go and see the vicar and have the banns read and fix a date and then we can go from there."

The conversation went on for another hour Fred saying what would be good for the ground and what would not as it was in such poor condition. George and Hannah had not given a thought as what to do with it. All that George had said was that he was looking forward to be able to take his gun out again to shoot rabbits and such. Before Hannah and George got up to go it was agreed that they would make an appointment to see the vicar because Dorothy insisted that they were to be married in church and of course it must be at Little Wenlock. The banns will have to be read and with Easter coming up he may have trouble fitting you in.

"Alright Mam"; Hannah agreed. "I will telephone him tomorrow and see if he can see us on Wednesday evening. If he can see us, we will call in and let you know what can be done".

"Mary will have to be a bridesmaid and Sandra. "Dorothy was thinking aloud again.

"I think that we had better be going". George announced and we will come and see what we can get fixed up again".

"You see that you do; my goodness another wedding to look forward to. And to think that you are going to live in the cottage up there. You will look down on us. Oh my goodness one surprise after another. But thank goodness this is good news".

George and Hannah said their goodbyes and quickly left the farm.

"Well I am amazed that they did not put up a fight" Said George as he started the engine of the bike.

"I can't believe it, I really can't It did not take much for my Mam to change her tune now did it "Nice little white wedding" Hannah mimicked her mother."

Wednesday evening George and Hannah went to see the vicar at Little Wenlock. The Reverend Barnfield had long gone. The new vicar the Rev; Fletcher seemed pleasant enough and when they had taken off their motor cycle gear in the hall and then he ushered them into a sitting room. Hannah was quite surprised at the difference in stature The Rev; Fletcher was a small man of no more than five foot four Very little hair almost bald infact where as the Rev; Barnfield had been at least six foot tall with such a mop of greying hair. It surprised Hannah that this little man could now be the village vicar. The three of them sat discussing as to what could be arranged so quickly for about half an hour. The Rev; Fletcher told them in such a quiet voice that the church was fully booked on the Saturday that George and Hannah said that they had in mind.

"I am sorry but the only other alternative as I see it, according to what you both have explained to me, is that you have your wedding on a day during the week if that could possibly be arranged to suit both families. I think that it could be the answer." The three of them discussed the matter further and a provisional date was arranged for Wednesday the twenty fourth of March. George and Hannah agreed to confirm this as quickly as they could do so because as the vicar explained to them that he must have three consecutive Sundays to read the banns. Starting this very next Sunday.

"I will expect both of you to attend the evening service and we can arrange a further meeting to discuss the wedding service". He sounded very serious. George and Hannah left the vicarage promising to do as he asked. If they agreed to marry on March the twenty fourth it would only give George and Hannah ten days before starting trade at the Easter weekend. They said their goodbyes and left intending to call at the

Willowmoors to tell her Mother and Father what the vicar had said.

"Well if we have to have the wedding on a Wednesday it will be alright for us" Dorothy stated. "What do you say Fred?" She looked at Fred for an agreement.

"Suits me" He refilled his pipe and tore a piece off the newspaper which he lit from the fire in the cooker. "One day is as good as any other". He said

"I have been doing some thinking" I'll bet you have Hannah thought. Dorothy continued.

"You say you can't afford a big wedding?

"Well your Dad and me reckon that if we pay for the reception at the Glen and I pay for the bridesmaids dresses and you two can pay for the rest. After all it is the groom who pays for the cars, flowers and the wine. Not that you should be charged for the cars, you should have them free. "

"Wine "George said not believing his ears.

"Of course"; Dorothy went on" I said we would pay for the dresses because Mary and Sandra will have to stand as bridesmaids. We have agreed on that. That's right isn't it Mary"? She looked across the table to Mary for support.

"Yes I think that Mam is right. Sandra would make a pretty little attendant".

"And" Dorothy went on. "You could borrow Liz's white dress that is if you can't afford your own, and you can borrow her veil. That would be something borrowed", She chuckled. Hannah could see that she was not going to have any say in this wedding at all. My goodness they had been busy arranging things and looked at George who she could see was thinking the same.

"See if you can go to morrow and see what Florence Dickinson's can get in the way of bridesmaids dresses for you. I will have enough to do tomorrow without having to walk to the top of New Street. I suppose that you will want Judith to be the other bridesmaid. Thank goodness that she has dark hair the same as Mary so it should not be too bad to get something to suit them both at such short notice"

"Yes Mam". Hannah said no more about the wedding arrangements. She changed the subject and talked with Mary about the Cottage and all the work that it would entail. Cakes to make for the tearooms; table cloths and tea cloths to be washed. Etc.

"We are thinking of going up there on Sunday afternoon and have a good look at what improvements and the work that has been done since we last worked up there". George gave Hannah a quick kick under the table as if to say keep your mouth shut. But it was too late.

"I'll meet you up there" Mary was quick to take up the opportunity to see for her self. "What time shall we say" Hannah turned to ask George who was not amused at the idea of having Mary with them but of what he had known about Mary in the past, he knew that she was not going to take no for an answer,

"I don't know as yet shall we say about three o'clock I will take a walk around the fields on Saturday afternoon and call on the folks who are living up there and ask if that is alright with them if we can go on Sunday afternoon. By then the Estate will have confirmed that it is ours to rent. If it is any different I will let you know".

"And don't forget to give your notice right away" Dorothy looked at Hannah "You will have to come home for the time that the banns are read. Other wise you will not be allowed to get married at Little Wenlock and I don't want to arrange anything with a different church. You know that you have to reside in the parish while the banns are read, and I can do with a bit of help in the house now that Helen has gone. Jack Munslow is coming to finish off threshing the corn the week after next"

"Oh dear; Oh Lordy". Hannah said to her self. She had not thought about what life back here would be like even if it would only be for two weeks. Oh Lordy the agony of it. But what choice did she have. None.

When George told his father of the arrangements; Terry was not amused at all; in fact he was quite angry.

"A Wednesday you say, you know that will mean all of us taking time off from work. It is all right for the Thomas's they can take any day off. Molly will lose most of a week's pay. You will invite her. I hope so. By the way I have written and told her what is going on and I have suggested that we put our wedding off until the summer and I don't think that she is going to be very pleased with that either. You say that you have been to see the vicar. So you are getting it all fixed up are you. What are you thinking of doing with the caravan? Have you thought about that? It's a pity that it is not quite finished so that you could have sold, it a tidy penny that would make to be sure".

George had given no thought about the caravan since he had heard about the Cottage and now that his father had mentioned it. It did give him cause for thought.

"I don't really know as yet, I will give it some thought. Wait until I can get every thing else sorted and then I will do some thing about it".

"I will see Molly this week end she is coming to stay with her sister I was thinking of asking her here for the day and was hoping that you would all be here to show her that she is welcome".

"Well what Judith has told me about her she sounds just what you need and could make you very happy? I have promised to go up the Wrekin but we will be back for tea time if that will be OK.

"That will have to-do and then we can tell you if she insists on having an Easter wedding".

"Weddings. Weddings Is that all every one has to think about". But George thought better than to voice his thoughts. He was more concerned about money and what had to be ordered to start the Easter trade and would Hannah be able to make enough cakes for the tearooms. Rationing was far less restricted but they would not have a clue as to what they would be allowed to use or sell in the shop.

Hannah went to order the dresses on the Thursday morning, Charlotte was at home working on some accounts, and she was there to take any telephone calls.

"Try not to be too long away" she had instructed Hannah "I want to get these accounts finished this morning. I don't want to be working on these all afternoon. I do not want to spend half of my time getting up to answer the telephone"" Oh still thinking about her self thought Hannah In that case I had better be as quick as I can. Hannah went out through the back door and down the street to Florence Dickinson's." Borrow Liz's dress not likely. I don't mind borrowing her veil but dammed if I am going to wear her dress "She said to her self as she went down the street.

Hannah was really pleased with what Miss Dickinson had to offer. She chose the colour lemon for the bridesmaid's dresses, because both Mary and Judith had dark hair. The style she chose would be that the dresses would have sweetheart necklines, short sleeves and full skirts. She spoke to Miss Dickinson the woman in charge of the shop about a dress for her self, dreading what she might be asked to pay for one.

"That depends on what you can afford". She smiled.

"Not a lot" Hannah looked down at the floor.

"Oh I see. You have to pay for that your self do you".

"Yes Mother is paying for the others.

"In that case I do have a very cheap dress in the back. It has been used for a modelling show in Wolverhampton so it has been reduced in price. Do take a look at it, not a mark on it to be sure and it looks to be just your size"

"Thank you I would like to see it."

Miss Dickinson fetched the dress and held it up for Hannah to see. Your mother is such a good customer of mine I was able to sell her the coat and dress for your sister's wedding the one that had to marry recently and the out fit for your mother and little sister.

"I guessed so My Mother has dealt with you for years, as long as I can remember. Mother says that she will come in on Thursday, as there are one or two other things that she wants. Please could I try the wedding dress on?

"Of course you can, come with me into the back from where I can still keep an eye on the shop" She led the way going between two hanging curtains, which reached, from ceiling to the floor.

The dress was a very plain one not what Hannah would have liked at all but it was at a price that she could afford?

"Yes I think that will do. I have not got time to go shopping around there is so much to be done."

"Yes Dear I understand. Such an expense for your Mother. Poor dear having so many girls" She looked Hannah up and down as Hannah was taking off the dress I know what she is thinking That I am having to get married because I am pregnant, but I am not going to make her any the wiser. She can think what she likes. Hannah left the shop and went back to work She made a pot of tea and took a cup through to Charlotte letting her know that she was back. Charlotte looked up from her work with quite a frown on her face.

"You know that I am not at all pleased with you Hannah. In fact I am furious, to think that you are leaving me two weeks earlier than I first thought; having to go home because of the banns being read. I have never heard of any thing so ridiculous. I can't see why you have to go home, that is an idea of your Mother's for sure I think that as long as you attended church on the Sundays that the banns are read you have nothing to worry about. You are leaving me in the lurch good and proper. Really Hannah it is too bad of you and you are doing all this to please that George. To go and live up that Wrekin you have got to be mad. I will not give it long before you are fed up with living up there and that you will be glad to get off that mountain and live somewhere decent. There is less than three weeks for me to find a replacement for you. Most inconsiderate I think. Most inconsiderate that it is." Charlotte sounded very angry. Hannah returned to the kitchen and felt quite upset at Charlotte's out burst. She felt that she had very little choice in the matter and George was right. All Charlotte thought about was her self and how inconvenient every thing was for her. Hannah had loved working for her they had got on so well and for Charlotte to turn on her now was quite upsetting.

Charlotte did not make conversation with Hannah after that outburst unless she had to. The day before Hannah had arranged to leave and go back home. Charlotte did how ever tell her that she would be glad to let her have the use of the two cars that Hannah had previously asked her if she could book them for the wedding. She said that there would be no charge but the one was return back to the garage as soon as it had delivered the bridesmaids to the Forest Glen. She her self would stay for the reception seeing that she had been invited but would leave immediately afterwards because she had the business to look after. Hannah thanked Charlotte

George had an invitation for his boss Mr and Mrs Cartwright he also wanted his work mates invited. His boss was not very pleased at the thought of his men having a whole day off during the week and he said that if they were prepared to work all day the following Saturday he would not reduce their pay.

The next time George and Hannah called to see her mother Hannah was so surprised at the guest list, she had sent invitations to all of them.

"I thought that this was only to be a small wedding?" Hannah said when she saw the list, "There were at least seventy names on it,

"Got to have a bit of a do and most of the replies that I have had back say that they are coming" Was all that Dorothy said.

Over seventy people watching me. This thought scared the wits out of Hannah; she had not prepared herself for this. When she told George he just laughed

“Think of the wedding presents that we will have”

Hannah had not thought about that, she had had far too much on her mind having to go back home for two weeks and the taking over of the Cottage. George surprised her with his comment

“Yes I suppose there will be presents I had not thought about that”

“Well let’s hope a few are cheques that will help us out a bit”.

"George that is not the way to look at presents, is it?”

“I suppose not but things are going to be a bit difficult for while. Let us hope that we have good weather at Easter so that we take a good bit of money. If we did it would give us a good start”.

“Wait until we get up there and then we can decide what to do and how best to do it. I have been thinking that if I have to make the cakes for the tearooms. I will have a go at it but I really can’t imagine me being able to make all that will be needed. There would be so many wanted. But on second thoughts I suppose that I could make dozens of small buns. Cherry topped cakes and butterfly ones as well as currant buns I also know a wonderful recipe for malt loaf. I can make scones. Yes George there is so much that I can do. Judith and Mary say that they want to come and help as well as Simon. Perhaps it will not turn out to be so scary. You would have to get some one to look after the swing boats for you. Once we get our first Bank holiday over with, we can then decide what the best way of running things is. Just think we will be our own bosses. I am looking forward to it all now that I have got over the initial shock. You know George I am certainly not looking forward to going home for two weeks. That is not going to very nice at all. Do you think that I could leave some of my things at your house and then they could go to the Cottage with your stuff”?

“Of course you can. Wait until we have had a look around the place on Sunday and then we can make up our minds on what we have to do. Thank God that a pump has been put on that well and the water does not have to be carried up to the house in buckets any more".

When George and Hannah arrived at the Cottage on Sunday afternoon, George parked the motor bike down the side of the house by the shop. Hannah noticed that although it was quite a cold day Mary was already there sat on the wooden seat under the oak tree. George was pleasant enough towards her but Hannah noticed that he was not too pleased to see that she was there before they had a chance to go inside and speak to the present occupiers. When the door was answered to his knock Mary followed Hannah and George into the kitchen and introduced her self. She sat down on the chair that she was offered so did Hannah, Mr Burrows the man who was the present occupier was quick to see that it was not a good idea to discuss business in front of Mary. He invited George to go through to their private sitting room at the back of the house. George was relieved at his suggestion and was glad that they were not going to discuss business in front of Mary. Mary and Hannah accepted the cup of tea that was offered and listened to Mrs Burrows telling Hannah what to expect and what not to expect. Hannah was so relieved to see the Aga cooker and a solid fuel stove that had been fitted in the corner of the kitchen to heat the water. The kitchen looked so much bigger and cleaner than what it had been when they were last working there. Painting the walls in a light colour had made it look so much lighter. Mrs Burrows went on to explain how the calor gas worked and that she had bought two boilers to boil water both heated with the calor gas. There was no more baking or washing to be done down in the old buildings as it used to be done. She gave Hannah the names and phone numbers of the different wholesalers and gave her some idea of what amounts of food to order such as bread, butter dried fruit for cake making and many other things. She explained that she had not made all the cakes required for the tearooms she had bought quite a lot in.

"With having no electricity it would have been a mammoth job to serve everything home made. I don't think that I would have managed that at all". Hannah had come prepared with a pencil and note pad and consequently noted as much as she could. Mrs Burrows gave Hannah and Mary some idea of the amount of trade that they could expect. The old wash place at the end of the passage had been converted into a proper bathroom with water on tap. What an improvement this was. George and Mr Burrows joined the women in the kitchen and further things were discussed. They arranged a moving day and when the property would be empty.

George explained that he and Hannah were to marry on the twenty -fourth and that they would like to officially move in the following Saturday. Mrs Burrows smiled and was quite in favour of this; Hannah thought that she looked as if she would not be sorry to get off the hill."

"My wife has not enjoyed living up hear as much as we anticipated" Mr Burrows smiled "I don't think that she will be sorry to leave".

"I certainly will not" His wife reassured him.

Oh dear, thought Hannah. I can see that there is a lot that can be done with the ground but I will leave that to George. I have been thinking as I have sat here looking up the hill. I could put a chicken pen up and have my own hens and eggs. There is so much that can be done I can't wait.

George and Mr Burrows had discussed the financial arrangements for the table's chairs and crockery Etc.

There was little else to be said as now all was agreed.

When they left George and Hannah walked as far as the buildings with Mary, Hannah saying that she would be coming to live at home next week end.

Back home at Wrockwardine George and Hannah shared their enthusiasm with his Dad and Judith and Molly who was spending the day with them.

Judith was thrilled that Hannah was having a white wedding; she had been to see Miss Dickinson to be fitted for a dress. She was so excited and could not stop chattering. It was Terry who stopped her by interrupting.

"I will tell you now that Molly and me have put off our plans to get married and have decided to have a summer wedding and then you can be a bridesmaid again."

"Are you sure" George asked.

"Quite sure. By what I can see of things you two are going to need a bit of help up at the Cottage and we are offering that is if we can be of any help at all. I can stand at a sink and wash dishes if I can't do anything else "He started to laugh. It was good to see him laugh again.

"I can look after the shop for you," Judith offered. "But only in the afternoon on Saturday but I will be able to come all day on Sundays, it is going to be so funny going back up there to work again. You will give me a job? You will" She looked at George for an answer.

"Of course we will" Hannah answered for him. "There will be plenty for me to do preparing the food for the tea rooms." Hannah went on to tell Judith of her plans that she had been thinking about for when they had moved in.

Hannah was very apprehensive when it came to leaving the garage; it had been her home for so long. Charlotte was quite cool, towards her but did wish her well and the best of luck as George came with the van from his works picked her and her belongings including her bicycle. They went to Wrockwardine to unload and then to take her to the Willowmoors where she was to be for the next two weeks.

She took only enough clothes to last for two weeks and they were the oldest and most worn that she had. The other things that she had she had put in cardboard boxes and was taken to Wrockwardine. George had put them in his bedroom. If she and George had to go anywhere that she needed to be really tidy she could always change at his house.

Back home Hannah gave a hand with most of the jobs around the farm she worked outside with Mary. When their Mother and Dad went into town the two girls gave the house a good scrub and clean. There would be relatives coming to the house before going to the church. "On the big day "as her mother had put it. William was away at school but they would pick him up the previous weekend and Dorothy had said that he need not go back after the wedding as he would be breaking up for the Easter holidays the following weekend. Hannah noticed that Sandra who was seven years old coming eight did very little. She would some times condescend to fetch coal and wood in for her mother to use on the cooker. Wash day had certainly not changed. The old copper boiler in the corner of the kitchen was still in use to boil the clothes. and it had to be filled before the fire was lit the same mangle was still standing behind the back door and it was Hannah's job to turn the handle once again as she and her older sisters had done year after year. George collected her when he could and took her out but Fred made as much use of him, as he was able to He had him doing general repairs around the farm buildings. George was put well and truly on the spot and was unable to refuse.

"You make as much use of him as you can" Dorothy had told Fred. "We are having to pay for some of this wedding He might as well earn a bit of it"

"I see what you mean Dot; there is plenty that I can find him to do"

George was so excited about going to live up the Wrekin that he was not the slightest bit bothered about being asked to do some repairs around the buildings he had guessed what her mother and Dad were up to. When George was alone with Hannah he could not stop talking of how wonderful that every thing was going to be when they had moved in and that they would be on their own and he carried Hannah along with his enthusiasm.

The Saturday before the wedding Mary and Hannah cycled into town to buy bits and pieces, which they required for the big day. They called to see Miss Dickinson to check that the dresses were ready. Hannah could not believe her eyes when Miss Dickinson brought the dresses out from the back saying how pleased she was with them.

"But those are not the ones that we have ordered" Sputtered Hannah when she saw them. These could not be the dresses that were to worn for her wedding. They were not the lemon ones that she had chosen. To Hannah these were horrible. The colour was a mauve colour and they had large collars on them and long ugly sleeves. The smaller one for Sandra was a pretty pink colour and Hannah did not think that it was too bad.

"Miss Dickinson I am sure that you have got it wrong, those are not the dresses that I ordered" Hannah said to the woman who just stood there smiling.

"I know that they are not quite like the pattern and colour that you would have liked, but your Mother was not happy with your choice so we had to alter our plans a little. Very smart don't you think?" She held one of the dresses up for Hannah to approve of it. What Hannah had not known was that as soon as she had chosen the dresses Miss Dickinson had telephoned her Mother and told her what Hannah had chosen and that she did not think that she would approve of Hannah's choice. She promised that she would wait until Dorothy could come into the shop before she ordered any thing for the wedding.

She continued "After all it is you who are paying is it not. I am so pleased that I rang you Mrs Thomas"

"I can assure you that they will look very nice and there is no time to get anything else for you at this late stage the wedding is on Wednesday is it not? Your Mother said that she would be collecting every thing with the car on Tuesday."

Hannah decided not to make a scene in the shop but she was so very angry.

"I don't believe it; the interfering old woman. How could she? Mary I am so angry that she has spoilt everything for me"

Whether Mary had known that her Mother had changed the dresses Mary did not let on. All she said was

"He who pays the fiddler calls the tune".

"I see what you mean. She had to get at me one way or the other. It's because I have stood up to her and that I am going to marry George. It is only that we are going to live up the Wrekin and that she can tell all the relatives that we are going farming and another thing I think that she wants to cover up for Helen's wedding. I think that is the reason that she has agreed to us getting married at all. She would have never paid for a wedding reception otherwise"

"Well she has never liked George and I don't think that she ever will. Like you say this wedding is just a cover up. You know that she has written a letter to the village school saying that all the children can come into the church to see the wedding and that they will each received a piece of wedding cake afterwards.

"She has done what? You are joking surely you are not serious? Hannah looked at Mary's face and she could see that she was not"

"Hannah. I think that Mam has done this just to please Sandra who wanted her friends to see how pretty she would look as a bride's maid at the wedding. And what is more the teachers have agreed to allow it".

"I don't believe it. She hasn't has she? Is there any length that she will not go to so that she can please that spoilt brat"?

"You are quite right; there is nothing that she won't give that child just to keep her quiet. It's a pity that she did not care a bit more for her when she was a baby. If it had not been for me the child would never have lived. Now Sandra can twist our Mam right around her little finger. You know if she skives off from school much more, that child is going to be as thick as two short planks. She only goes enough to keep the attendance officer away from the door."

"Really; what ever is to become of her?"

"Don't you worry about Sandra or William they know which side that their bread is buttered on They both know that they will never have to get a job and go out to work"

"You sound very cynical Mary but I suppose that you could be right. We will have to wait and see. Time will tell".

"Well Mam and Dad have made it quite clear that if the Willowmoors does not come up for sale they will look for another farm for William to Inherit. You know that Granddad is not very well these days. I think by what I have heard our Mam saying she hopes that if he dies, he will leave her the Manor or if not that he will leave her quite a bit of money and then they will be able to buy a farm of their own"

"For William".

"Yes you are quite right just for William You see if I am not right?" Mary continued "At a guess I would say that Uncle Gordon will inherit the manor as he is the eldest son. He has more or less run the farm for a long time now, since he gave up his own place and moved into Yew Tree house that belongs to Granddad. I wonder if he really did go bankrupt. No one has ever let on but by what was said at the time he certainly did. How Aunt Lucy looked down her nose at us. She was such a snob" Mary caused Hannah to laugh

"There are so many of you I don't know which one you are." Hannah mimicked her Aunt Lucy, causing Mary to chuckle

They say that old Mr Bromley is on his last legs so this place could come onto the market. That would give them a chance to stay here right where they are. What ever they do Mam will always want some one to stay and help around the house, and I reckon that is where Sandra will come in handy."

"But what about you Mary; have you not thought about your future? won't you want to marry one day?"

"Oh yes if the right man comes along but I can't leave them in the lurch at the moment they need me far too much". Mary sounded so forlorn.

"Fiddle sticks. If the right man comes along, you grab him, and let them pay for some help with the work"

"They moan about having to pay Bernie and the young lads that come from the village to help us now and again.

There is far too much work for just the three of us. I think that if Bernie could find some where else to live, he would be off like a hare; he wants to earn more money than what he is paid at our place.

Hannah found that it was good to share things again with Mary just as they had when they had been growing up. They walked the top fields as they had used to do to count the sheep and check for newborn lambs. Hannah paid a visit to see Joyce and Wilf at the Hatch. They were very pleased to see her and said that they were looking forward to attending her wedding. They could not see what Dorothy's objection to George had been They knew quite a few of the Fleming's who still lived in the area and seemed a straight forward family having never been in trouble with the law. As Wilf said if it had not been for George's grandfather dying the family would still be farming today. Hannah sat and had a cup of tea with them. She noticed that little had been changed in their living room since she had been a child, the round polished table and chairs were still positioned in the centre of the room. The same two leather armchairs with the hand embroidered chair back covers and cushions were in front of the black leaded firegrate. The polished writing desk was still under the window; the same ornaments and pictures on the walls. The rag rug that used to be just inside the door was replaced with a modern one. The only thing that had changed was Joyce and Wilf they had gone to look much older. Joyce still had the same hairstyle but now her hair was showing signs of grey. Wilf looked several years older than when Hannah had last seen him. She guessed that he must be at least sixty-five years old and then perhaps he could be in his seventies.

Grandma Wainwright had been telephoning that granddad was not at all well and she had sought medical advice and that they had said that it was because of his age. After all he was now at an age of eighty and that the prospects of him living a great deal longer were very slim. She had said what a relief that it had been for her to have Gordon to run the farm for her and also that Lucy was giving her a hand with the running of the house. A woman from the village was now engaged to do most of the household washing and cleaning.

"You don't think that they will leave it all to Gordon" Dorothy had said to Fred "I shall want to know where my share is if he does. I don't think that for one moment the old chap would do that after all he does owe us others quite a great deal"

"Don't bother your head about it". Fred had said "We are on our feet now and we have reared our family and we hardly want for anything. No Dot I reckon that if Gordon does inherit the Manor well good luck to him I never liked the bugger that I have not". Dorothy was not to be pacified the thought of Gordon inheriting the Manor niggled her and she went on and on about it.

"But the old fellow is not dead as yet "Dot "Wait and see what happens I hear that old Mr Bromley is also on his last legs it will be interesting to know what will happen to this place. They can't turn us out on the road we are what they call sitting tenants. You know we have to be given the first refusal of the buying of it, if they do decide to sell it and that will only depend on if their son whether he will want the bother and meither with the of keeping it".

Dorothy had not heard this bit of news and her mind promptly went into over drive." Well if the old chap does not leave me the manor which being the eldest I think that I am entitled to it, he might leave me some money to compensate for his leaving the manor to Gordon. After all he did set the other two lads up with their places. He might not have paid for them out right but I know that he gave them a better start than what he gave us. He only acted as a guarantor for us for the first years rent and then we did it all on our own and we did not have to ask for a penny from him we managed it on our own. He had those three heifer calves for moving us here Do you remember? Them brothers of mine would not be where they are today with out his help."

"Just a minute Dot they all had to work hard for him".

"May be so and so did I and if it had not been for that brother of yours Henry we would not have to have asked the old chap to have been a guarantor. We could have had no trouble and we would have had spare money in our pockets".

"Steady on Dot we have managed all these years and paid our way, let's not look back on the past it has gone now. No use grumbling about what could have been".

"It's gone all right Fred Thomas and so did your money, never paid a penny back he did not"

"Fred got up from his chair put on his cap and went out through the back door A practise which he had done over the years when Dorothy had started to grumble and bring up the past especially Henry and the hundred pound loan.

Monday morning Hannah saw Joyce Wilkins coming down the field to the gate under the walnut tree. Here comes trouble by the look of it. She is walking so quickly its looks as if she has some gossip. The family had recognised that when Joyce Wilkins was coming down the field at such a pace, she sure had some news that she could not wait to pass on. She looked just like the time when she had come to tell them about the murder at the Glen.

Hannah and her Mother quickly cleared the table of dirty dishes and while Dorothy went for a clean table cloth Hannah started to wash the dishes. Joyce Wilkins did not wait to be asked in. She came through the door and she pulled a newspaper from under her arm.

"Joyce, you look proper agitated what's the matter? Asked Dorothy.

"What's the matter Dorothy? I feel so sorry for you. I can't believe it but here in black and white it is I have seen it with my own eyes"

"What have you seen?"

Joyce put a newspaper on the kitchen table

"Just you read this". The newspaper was the News of the World.

"My Wilf will not have the paper in the house. He says full of filth it is, and that is what no decent person would contemplate buying it never mind buy it and read it. I have to wait until one is passed on to me and I make sure that he does not see me reading it. She opened the paper to second page and pushed it further across the table so that it was under Dorothy's nose.

The Headlines read. Shropshire Farmer, Ian Waterford was being sued for Divorce. Dorothy read on. He was being divorced from his wife because of a certain Grace Thomas. Dorothy finished reading the article and then sat down in Fred's chair.

I can't believe it. She told us that he was not married and that he was single. I don't believe it. He seemed such a nice fellow". She sighed. "Well you had better believe it. The papers do not dare print a pack of lies. This is too bad of her and to think what a good upbringing that you gave those girls. I my self am having a very hard job to convince myself that it could be true".

"I bet you are", thought Dorothy, and took the cup of tea from Hannah who had been keeping herself busy making a pot of tea and pouring a cup of tea for the both women sat at the tale. Hannah did not bother with one for her self she quickly disappeared out of the way around to the cowsheds to find Mary and tell her what was going on in the kitchen. And that it would be best to keep clear for a little while until Joyce Wilkins had gone back up the fields. They could expect Dorothy to be in a very bad mood for the rest of the day.

When Joyce Wilkins had gone Dorothy quickly put the newspaper in the front room cupboard and said nothing more about it she was not going to discuss the subject. She kept quiet about it the subject was not discussed again if she had told Fred about Joyce's visit no one knew. Hannah was sure of one thing Grace would not be at her wedding and she felt a bit disappointed. They had been together so much as kids and Grace would not be there for her on her big day. So that was the reason that she had not answered the wedding invitation. What none of them had known was that Grace and Ian had married secretly in a register office on the Tuesday before Hannah's big day.

Chapter Eight
Wedding Bliss

Hannah had tossed and turned until late into the night before finally falling asleep, she had been lying thinking about her wedding. Her big day tomorrow and she could only dream of sleeping in George's arms this time tomorrow night. The night she had only dreamt of in the past was to become a reality. They were at last going to be married and with the blessing of both their families. There no need to think about waiting until she was twenty-one and then going away and marrying in a registry office. She could now hold her head up high she was going to marry the man she had loved since she had been at school. Taking on the Cottage had seemed such an enormous task and she was still a bit apprehensive about it but she realised that George had been quite right about her Mother's attitude changing as soon as they had told her.

In the darkness of the night she had said a silent prayer and thanked God that she had not given in to George's demands and not taken the risk of getting pregnant she knew that he was not happy about it. And many were the time when she was almost persuaded to give in. At least her mother could not say that she had brought disgrace to her door. Hannah smiled to her self "I'll not have you bringing disgrace to my door", there was only Mary and Sandra now to go her mother had not mentioned Grace's name since Joyce Wilkins had been down with the paper, The News of the World. Was it the fact that Grace had lied or was she a little more than jealous and envious of Grace being mistress of such a big farm? Grace would be lady of the manor so to speak where as that was something that Dorothy had always dreamt of being. And now she was still scratching and scraping every penny to buy this farm or another one for William. No one would ever know how envious that she was of her brother Gordon who was running the manor and it looked inevitable that he had more or less taken over from her father. If that eventually happened to be the case her sister-in-law Lucy would be the next lady of the manor. Dorothy did not like the thought of that one little bit and she knew that only time would tell. Hannah wondered if Grace had found that knight in shining armour, which she had talked about now so long ago.

Hannah awoke and was trying to come to terms with her surroundings Daylight was just creeping through the net curtains. Although she had slept in this room all her child hood it seemed different now. There was only one double bed not two the other one had been moved into the far end room for William the one where they used to put the apples and pears to ripen on news paper on the floor. There was a carpet of sorts covering the bare floorboards and a wardrobe and other bits of furniture had been added since she had left...

She crept out of bed trying not to disturb Sandra. She moved the net curtain to one side and looked out of the window across the cattle yard. It was not raining, thank goodness for that, putting on her old jumper and skirt she tiptoed down stairs holding her socks in her hand; it must be at least six o' clock. There was no clock in the room. Sandra had not wanted one, she just did not get up unless she was called or she was hungry. As Hannah went into the kitchen she was surprised to see her dad sat by the cooker.

"Want a cup of tea lass"? He said smiling "I've just made a brew"

"Yes Please" Seeing as there is one already brewed I was not expecting anyone to be about as yet"

"We have a busy day to day; you all seem to be leaving us one after the other. Still I suppose that it is to be expected." Hannah took the cup of tea he had poured for her but not liking the cream that he had generously added to it. He saw her face as she looked at the tea.

"Drink it down lass, do you good "He added when he saw that Hannah was a bit reluctant to start and drink the tea.

"Ok just as you say; It is going to be a busy day for us all. I just want to thank you Dad for today although our Mam would have it no other way as much as she does not like George. Do you think that she ever will?"

"I can't answer that but it is he that you have chosen and it is he that you have to live with. "As you make your bed so you must lie on it", that is what my father told us. There will be no turning back saying that you have made a mistake. It's until death us do part. George has a good trade in his hands; a good job that will be there for him for life. It's a pity that he is not from a farming family that would have made your Mam happy".

"But his Granddad was a farmer at the Wrekin farm, and they could not help death changing their way of life, that can happen to any one". Hannah drank her cup of creamy tea not enjoying it for one minute; it tasted so sickly she wanted to heave. Since she had left home she had not had cream on or in any thing. She had felt that she had enough of it as she was growing up.

"Thanks for today Dad and being so understanding I did not want all this fuss being as I left when I did But it was so difficult then to get on with our Mam"

"You and Grace did what you had to do Your Mam is right vexed about this man that Grace has chosen I only hope that she does not live to regret it. Giving you a bit of a wedding reception is a little bit for the way you worked during the dark days of the war. Thank goodness that is all behind us now and it is time to move on. We are doing right well as yet but I fear for the future I only hope that this school that young William is going to does not put too many grand ideas into his head. I don't see him ever being a cattle and sheep man, he reminds me bit like your Uncle Gordon; tractors and machines to do the work." Fred sighed "He will be a tall lad when he is fully grown takes after your Mam's side of the family"

They sat talking for some time and Fred looked at the clock on the wall

"Aye surry the time flies its seven o'clock. He stood up to make a fresh pot of tea but Hannah was quick to take over "Leave it to me Dad I will pour this one. She emptied the teapot and scalded some fresh tealeaves and then she fetched the jug of milk from the larder giving it a good stir before he had a chance to put cream in her cup. He left the tea making to her, in stead he added more coal to the Rayburn. I had better take a cup to your Mam" He said putting a good helping of cream into a cup ready to take her. "She will be mad with us if we let her sleep too long She will want to be in charge of every thing today. It must go right for her. If things go wrong we will never hear the last of it. She does carry on a bit but I have got used to it over the years so it doesn't bother me that much. She had her hands full rearing you lot but we have got through it together".

"I know exactly what you mean". She poured them both another cup of tea and one for her Mother. She pulled on her socks ready to make a start out side she would see to the poultry and fetch logs and coal in ready to heat the boiler there would be so much hot water needed before the day was out. She would give Mary a hand with the feeding of the calves and checking the sheep and that all had to be done before breakfast.

It had been good to sit and talk to her Dad and after another cup of tea they put on old coats and went out to make a start. It was great for Hannah to listen to the birds singing their loudest she had missed this so much with living in the town the noise of the traffic moving had drowned the sound of the early morning bird song.

They stepped out together as one The wind was blowing from the North cold and bleak but at least it was not raining or snowing The clouds overhead were dark and dismal. Thank goodness for that Hannah said to her self at breakfast as her Mother Dorothy was taking control of every thing that was going on as usual, this has to be done has to be done. "You know what folks are like. They talk and I want you all at that church for two o'clock."

The family were not expecting many of the wedding guests to come to the house. It had been arranged that all the guests would go to the church for two o'clock. Hannah thought that her sisters might drop in for a cuppa, as they had to go past the gate on their way to Little Wenlock. Uncle Collin and Aunt Kathleen had written to say that they would attend and have a taxi from Wellinton station to take them from there to the church. Kathleen wrote that they were hoping that Fred and Dorothy would arrange transport for them from the church and back to the station in the evening.

"They've got some cheek," Dorothy said to her self when she read the letter.

"Don't worry your self about that "Fred had said I'm sure that Steve Evans will give them a lift in their car I will ask him next time I see him and I can pop them to the station later on.

Dorothy did not consider that it was her responsibility "Yes you do that Fred" and then she dismissed it from her mind.

Hannah's wedding dress and the bridesmaid's dresses were hanging on the out side of the wardrobe in Mary's room. She had shared a double bed with Sandra but to Hannah that did not matter. It had only been for two weeks and she was helping outside for most of the daytime or she was off on her bike to see George. So consequently she was extremely tired and was not too particular where she had to sleep as long as she could get a good night of rest.

She had been at George's home the night before her wedding to make sure that every thing that they both needed was packed and ready for their few days honey- moon. Hannah had been quite alarmed when George had said. "We will go to Blackpool on the bike it will be quicker and that will mean that we have not got to wait for trains busses or any thing else.

"On the bike? I can't leave the reception on a Motorbike". Hannah told him very firmly.

"Well you know what I think we should do. We will pack the bike and leave it at my Dad's when it is time to leave the Glen, the wedding car can take us to my house and then we can change and be off before anyone knows what is going on. "Hannah had agreed to this but a bit half heartily. She had not imagined this to be the romantic start to a honeymoon that she had looked forward to for so many years. Judith was so excited it was her first time to be a bridesmaid it had been agreed that Simon would take her to the Willowmoors on the day to dress and get ready to go to the church with Mary and Sandra. He would then go back to see that George was ready and to wait for Charlotte's car, which was to pick up Molly and Terry with them.

As soon as the necessary work was done Hannah and Mary went in to wash their hair and put curling pins in it hoping that it would be dry by one o'clock. Both Mary and Hannah wore their hair cut short. Mary's was still very dark almost black like that of her Mothers which although her mother was now fifty years old, her hair showed no signs of greying what so ever. Hannah's was still of a light auburn colour and had a natural wave. To day she and Mary wanted their hair to look its best.

"Oh to have my own bath room". Hannah said to her self as she and Mary were trying to wash them selves from top to bottom in Mary's bedroom and it was not easy. They only had the galvanised tin bath and they had to share the water.

Hannah thought how dreadful that it was not to have a modern bathroom Mary had bathed Sandra and washed her blonde hair earlier and told her in no circumstances was she to go outside. If she did and got her self dirty, she would not be dressed as a bridesmaid when Mary came down stairs again. The small room at the bottom of the stairs was now reasonably well furnished so Judith was told to change in there. Dorothy stated very firmly that she would not have strangers going up her stairs. Mary and Hannah had cleaned and scrubbed every thing that they could the day before

While her mother had been in town. Fred and Bernie had to clean the yards out side. The two of them had to see that all the animals were fed and watered so that they would be all right until they returned at milking time.

Because of Granddad's failing health. Grandma telephoned Dorothy and said that they would not be coming; she said that he was so miserable these days and was so cantankerous with every one. She considered that it would be for the best if they went ahead with the wedding and not to worry about them.

Dorothy had commiserated with her Mother and said that she quite understood. She had said that she was very disappointed that they were not coming. She did not say how ever that it was a relief not to have to watch their P's and Q's through out the day's events

The morning had gone by so quickly, every one was ready but only just as Charlotte's cars began to arrive. Both Beccy and Helens Husbands had bought second hand vans. They called in just for a quick cup of tea and seeing that every thing seemed to be chaotic they quickly left and went on to the church. Helen did not voice her thoughts but she really felt it when she saw what a fuss was being made for Hannah and she had not been allowed to wear white or have a proper reception for her wedding how could her mother have been so cruel. She was happy enough and she and Melvin had settled down in his new job but this did not compensate as to her feeling today. She felt that she could never forgive her mother for making all this fuss considering that Hannah had left home and she her self had done so much hard work on the farm

Hannah was so nervous she just prayed and hoped that George would be there before her. If she had known there had been no need for her to be worried at all. Simon had seen to it that they were ready in plenty of time. Charlotte was picking them up at Wrockwardine to deliver them to the church before going back to collect Hannah and Fred.

Much to Hannah's relief Charlotte turned up as arranged and drove Hannah and her father to the church the other driver had taken Dorothy and the bride's maids before them.

"You do look beautiful". Charlotte gave praise, much to Hannah's relief. "I was so sorry to see you leave us, but we are managing I have a new girl starting next week and I hope that she turns out to be as conscientious as you were" Hannah was quite surprised to hear a bit of praise from Charlotte. She had not forgotten what she had said about her leaving and now she had said this it certainly made Hannah feel a lot better.

Hannah felt that she did not look too bad considering the rush that there had been to get everything ready on time for her big day. Her dress looked good and she wore Liz's veil and headdress. She carried a bouquet of white heather and fern. The bridesmaids carried smaller bouquets of the same flowers. Hannah was still very disappointed with their dresses but decided that it was better to keep quiet than to have a row with her Mother because she knew that she could not win no mater how much she argued. Hannah now thought the sooner the better that the day was over. George had arranged to take her to Blackpool for a few days as a sort of honeymoon. They had to be back for Saturday as things were being delivered to the cottage and some one must be there to receive them.

Terry arranged with George that he would go up to the cottage first thing on the Saturday morning and be there to take a delivery of minerals crisps Etc; George had agreed to this as a good solution as any to solve many problems. The present occupiers had said that they did not want to be responsible for any deliveries, as they would have enough to do with moving out.

As the organ started to play the wedding march Hannah started the walk with her father down the isle followed by the bridesmaids. Fred was as smart as he could be. He wore a dark blue suit, his black shoes shone they had been cleaned by Hannah the day before.

He wore a small spray of white heather in his buttonhole His hair had gone quite grey but otherwise he had not altered at all. Hannah noticed the children from the school sat quietly in the pews towards the back of the church. There was George and Simon waiting for them at the front of the church. Hannah fixed her eyes on them and she walked slowly forward not noticing who else was in church. This had been the moment that she had waited for. Hannah felt radiant.

The Rev Fletcher started the service. First giving a welcome to all the guests. As the service proceeded both George and Hannah said their vows." I Do "Said Hannah" Yes she would take George for better or worse and promised to obey". She meant every word as she said it and she continued." In sickness and health and until death do us part" They were then pronounced man and wife. These vows were sacrosanct for Hannah and she knew that nothing would cause her to break them. After the signing of the register they walked down the aisle together. They were so happy.

Every thing seemed to go so quickly after that. A photographer was waiting when the stepped out of the church. He was from the Wellington Journal and Shrewsbury news. Dorothy must have booked him. Hannah had not expected this and was quite pleased and surprised. At the reception Percy Podmore gave the toast "To All Friends around the Wrekin". He was keeping up the tradition that his father Ossie Podmore had started years before. (His father was now dead and had passed on).

<u>THE TOAST</u>

To all Friends around the Wrekin and to her most Royal Majesty
The loyalty that she is seeking
To Shropshire Sons upon the sea
On land or in the air,
There never will be finer any where

For they that never bowed the knee
In Bondage to a foe
Nor never will while they have Breath
To fight the best they know
And may the good Lord rain down upon our foes bare shins
As many Holy pebble stones
As they have committed sins
In order that we'll know them
By the way they cringe and crimp
But more especially, so we'll know the Buggers by their limp.

After the applauding died down and the reception came to an end the guests started to mingle, all of George's work mates and others made their way to the bar for drinks of beer or what ever was their preference. Hannah and George made sure that they went all round the guests to thank them for coming as her Mother had said that they must.

It was half past five when George and Hannah said their good byes and left the Forest Glen in one of Charlotte's cars; to go on their honeymoon. She took them as far as Wrockwardine and left them there. George and Hannah quickly changed into their motorcycle clothes and were soon on their way to Blackpool where they had booked bed and breakfast...

George and Hannah enjoyed their few days together and spent most of their time going places on the motor bike during the daytime. They visited the tower and went up in the lift to the top. The view was fantastic.

How Hannah loved the sea they even went to see an evening of boxing something Hannah had never been to before. She was not sure whether she had enjoyed it or not. She felt much happier just going to see a film at the cinema.

Hannah enjoyed the few days alone with George they had so much to look forward to and spent time making plans for the future.

"George I do not want to start a family right away. I hope that we can leave it for a couple of years until we are on our feet and then consider a family. Lizzy is already pregnant and I do not want to be in that position until I have to. George was reluctant to give her any assurance on that point."

"I will have to try to be very careful in that case but does it matter when we start a family. We will not be committing a sin will we? You seem to forget that we are married now and I think that we should take things as they come along. "George was a wonderful and perfect lover; he was so gentle and kind. Hannah's response was sheer pleasure. Hannah could not believe that lovemaking could be so wonderful. They enjoyed every moment together she was blissfully happy. George pretended to Hannah that she was his first and only love she never suspected that he was telling her a pack of lies and that she certainly was not George's first love. All that she knew about making love was what George had taught her. Little did she know that George had been having plenty of practise?

When Hannah had asked him which bedroom that he would prefer to sleep in at the Cottage; she had said that she would like the one that looked out towards the East. She could see the bottom fields of her Dad's farm. It reminded her of her younger days when as a girl they had dragged the bags of sticks from the woods to light the kitchen fire George was very quick to reject the idea of them both sleeping in that particular bedroom.

"No I would not like to sleep in that one every night it has something about it that I do not like it feels creepy to me. Let us sleep in this one," He said moving into the room that looked towards the North. He dare not tell Hannah that it was the room where he and Gwen had shared so many secret nights of passion. Where he had been taught how to be a perfect lover and had learned positions in love making that he had never dreamed of.

Terry was up early on Saturday morning and set off on his bicycle to go up the Wrekin to the Cottage. O. D Murphy's would be delivering Minerals, crisps chocolate and such. George had arranged with Judith and Simon to load their personal things into a van he was borrowing for the day. He intended being back well before lunchtime so that he would be there to give his Dad and Simon a hand. Terry and Molly had bought them a bedroom suit for a wedding present and that too was being delivered on the Saturday. Anything else that George and Hannah wanted they decided could wait until they had settled in.

Thomas was rather sad when he eventually received Judith's letter telling him all about the wedding. But at the same time he felt glad that he had not been able to be there and that he had signed up for the nine years, His next posting was to take him to Africa so he knew that he would not be home for some time.

He did not know how he felt about his brother. George had taken the one girl that he could have loved He had won again. He just prayed and hoped that George would be fair and honest towards Hannah. He felt that it was a bit ironic that they had taken the Wrekin Cottage where they had all met up a few years back. Little did he know that when he and his comrades had been posted on Montebello island that they could have been exposed to radioactive material? The British were practising with nuclear weapons.

Hannah knew that they could not possibly afford to furnish all four bedrooms she did how ever manage to buy a single bed and start to furnish a second bedroom. This was the one that George had not fancied sleeping in but Hannah felt at ease in this particular room where as she did not feel the same about one of the other two rooms that faced the West. There was some thing creepy about them that she was not too sure about. She decided that if she started a family she would not use those rooms to put a baby in but all being well if she and George were very careful there would be no babies for quite some time. George had promised that he would do his utmost not to get her pregnant if he could help it.

As the weeks went by, Hannah was finding that she was so very busy in fact she never seemed to have enough hours in the day to get every thing done. Monday was taken up with all the washing that had to be done. Table clothes that had been used in the tea rooms all the tea clothes that had been used during the weekend as well as serving customers that called at the shop or came into the tea room. She had to be thoroughly organised so that they did not suspect that she was up to her elbows in soapsuds. Thank goodness for the two calor gas boilers, she was able to use one for boiling the washing and the other for heating water. Their personal washing was kept separate and done later in the week. . There were some times over twenty table clothes had to be washed and goodness only knew how many tea clothes. Hannah was so relieved that they had the Aga cooker and a wooden clothes rack hanging from the ceiling so that on wet days she was able to put a lot of it there to dry. The hot plate of the Aga was also useful to heat the irons that she used for the ironing. They heated up very quickly they were the same type of old fashioned irons that she had used before leaving home. The Aga did not soil the irons marking the clean clothes with spots of charcoal or soot

One thing that Hannah really loved was that she was now able to sleep with the bedroom window open at nights, a large beech tree stood tall outside their bedroom window. She was able to listen to the owls and the other night birds.

It was so lovely first thing in the mornings to hear all the other birds singing their little hearts out. It was wonderful to hear the dawn chorus again in the town it had been too noisy at night to be able to sleep with the windows open especially when there had been a dance held at the Majestic ball room next door to the garage. And the movement of the early morning traffic drowned out the sound of any birds that were singing. Yes it was good to be back in the country again. She would often wake to the sound of the woodpecker tapping away at the tree doing his best to attract a female or was it as some said, his tapping was to disturb insects so to have some thing to eat. Hannah was looking forward to be able to hear the cuckoo again later in the springtime. The trees were now in bud ready to open as soon as the warmer weather came. The row of beech trees still lined the path going along to the point and they too were waiting for the warmer winds to blow from the south saying that spring had arrived During the week it was not unusual for a busload of school children to come up the hill on a school trip and they would come to the shop window in order to spend their pocket money on minerals, crisps and sweets. Hannah would have to leave what she was doing and serve them. This had to be taken care of as well as coping with the dining room for afternoon teas. She had decided that it was best to keep the big tearoom closed during the week and only use it at weekends when she had more help. If the weather were a bit cloudy or dull, Hannah would light a fire in the smaller tearoom to give a welcome to those who stopped for an afternoon tea. George had put up a chicken run on the hill so that they would have fresh eggs; another job for Hannah to see to. She had to feed them, clean their pen and fasten them up at night in case a fox came and killed the lot. He bought a Jersey and a Guernsey cow to supply them with milk. Hannah would give a hand to milk them in the evening and if George was running a bit late she also gave him a hand in the mornings they both had to be up very early to get every thing done before George went to work. He still had to be there for eight o'clock. If by any chance they over slept it was left to Hannah to see to every thing. Every where in the cottage had to be scrubbed squeaky clean other wise a complaint from a customer to the authorities could cost them their licence to serve food. As the months went by they found that more and more people were coming to walk the hill. Terry and Molly were a great help they came to do what they could at the weekends. Terry cycled and George would fetch Molly on his motorbike. Molly loved this she thoroughly enjoyed the ride, when she had been younger she had owned her own motor bike and rode it to her work-place and where ever else that she could. She had given it up when she had married and moved to Birmingham. Terry was a great help with the washing up. He would stand at the kitchen sink in the back for hours and wash dirty dishes as they came back from the tea rooms Hannah continually had to tell him to change the water and not to smoke cigarettes while he was washing up. Otherwise he just let the ash from his cigarettes drop into the washing up water. This was certainly not acceptable and Hannah hated to have to tell him so.

The fact that they only had the motorbike for transport, this became very frustrating. George decided that they would have to buy a tractor, and as soon as they could afford it he would buy a van. What sort he had no idea it would have to be a second hand one of that there was any doubt. The weather had been very good during the first three of the summer months so consequently the tearooms were doing very well. So was the shop, Hannah had mastered the cake making and made dozens of different sorts of small cakes on a Saturday morning ready for weekend customers. George was still working full time and he felt that he could see no reason why they could not afford to buy a tractor. He saw an old second hand Alice Chamlers. Although it was fairly old it was in good condition.

George was very good mechanically and he could see that there was no reason why it should not be of good use for some considerable time.

When he drove it home he stopped it out on the front of the house and went to find Hannah. He was surprised that she had not come out to see it; he felt that she must have heard it coming up the hill. He turned off the engine and went in to find her He could see no sign of Hannah in the front kitchen. He went through and found her working away humming a tune to herself. Hannah could be often heard humming or singing softly to her self.

"What are you looking so excited about?" she asked, as she had sensed his presence and seeing that he was smiling as she looked up from the mixing bowl. "Come and see what I have bought" He sounded so excited about his purchase what ever it was.

Hannah followed him to the front of the house wiping her hands on her white apron and then she saw the tractor. Her face dropped with dismay. . Where it had not gone rusty the tractor was of an orange colour. She certainly had not seen one like this before. The steering wheel was not fitted in the centre like other tractors that she had seen. It was fitted to the one side.

"You will have to be able to drive this "George announced

"Me drive that," Hannah said looking at the peculiar looking tractor. "Why should I want to drive that"?

"Well you never know, if a delivery man refuses to come up to the house, it would be very handy for you to pop down the hill and meet him at the bottom. I will get busy and make a trailer to go behind it. I can't understand why you have never learnt to drive a car, and passed the driving test it would have come in very handy right now. Did you never think that it would come in very handy at some time or other, After all you were working where there were cars where you not?"

"Yes George I did work where there were cars but it was not my job to drive them. I have always wanted to but I was never offered the chance".

"Well you are certainly going to have to learn how to drive this I can't afford to give up my job as yet and we can't afford a car or van of our own either."

Oh I see, thought Hannah there was method in his madness some where. As if I have not got enough to do without having to pop to the bottom of the hill to meet delivery people. But on the other hand it would certainly come in handy. There was muck down at the cowshed that had to be moved and spread on the fields. The tractor would be very handy in the winter months there was no doubt about that.

Hannah looked at George and then at the tractor

"The fact is that I can't drive whether it is a car or a tractor. Besides George I would not fancy driving up and down the hill. You know how dangerous that it can be coming around that sharp bend that is about halfway up. There is only a foot of the track to spare and if I were to miss to steer properly over the side the tractor an me would go".

George was losing patience with Hannah "Well you will just have to be careful not to go over the side. You will have to learn how to drive it whether you like it or not".

"Very well I suppose that I had better have a try that is when you have the time to show me how to drive the thing". Hannah had not seen George so cross since they had gone to visit the Earl of Powys. But she felt that she had more than enough to do without having to learn to drive that thing as she referred to his new purchase of which he seemed so proud.

"Just think; Hannah we can plough the middle field and set potatoes on it Think of the subsidy that we could get" George was full of enthusiasm.

"George who is going to help us with all this extra work that you are getting so excited about."

"There's plenty of help if we want it. I am sure that your Dad will give us a hand with the ploughing; I have been thinking that it would be better to get him to plough it for the first time. They have a much bigger tractor than the one I have bought."

Hannah did not like the sound of George's plans; she did not want to get her family involved in anything if she could help it. Mary came and helped whenever she could. And as Hannah suspected her Mother moaned about that even if she did take home a few cakes if there were any left over at the end of the day and there usually was. Hannah found that it was not possible to use any that were left over the next day;

the little cakes seemed to come away from their paper casings. They did not look as fresh as they should She found that it was much better to make a few fresh ones every day during the week. George showed Hannah how to drive the tractor and she found that it was quite easy. In fact she was enjoying driving it. Mary had let her have a go at driving the Fordson, years before when their Dad had been in hospital but this one was very different but Hannah soon got the hang of it by driving it out to the point and back. George made a trailer to fit at the back so that they could carry quite a load at any one time. It was often needed to fetch provisions from the bottom of the hill and this Hannah often did. When members of the public were walking up the hill they would look at Hannah with amazement as she drove past them

The weather stayed good and the café and the shop was busy. On the Whitsun bank holiday there were a lot of people about. Suddenly a man came into the kitchen carrying a boy of about ten years old and he seemed very distressed. The child had a blood soaked handkerchief wrapped around his leg just below the knee. Hannah quickly moved things from the kitchen table. "Put him here "she said looking at the man who was holding the child. "What has happened?"

"He fell on some broken glass and I can't stop it bleeding. What am I to do?"

"Calm down to start with". Hannah called Judith through from the back kitchen

"Judith run up stairs and fetch a clean sheet, by what I can see we need some bandages for this leg and there is not enough for a job like this in the first aid box. Molly came through from the back kitchen and quickly weighed up the situation and she gave the man a cup of tea. As soon as Judith brought the sheet Hannah quickly cut and tore a strip and tied it tight above the child's knee. It stemmed the flow of blood which was now dripping onto the kitchen floor. She had learnt the basics of first aid at school never thinking that one day it would come in handy. Next she cut and tore wider strips and wrapped them around the gaping open wound

"Have you a car at the bottom of the hill that you could take your son to the local hospital "

"No we have walked all the way from the town" The man sounded so distressed.

"Is any one with you who can run down to the bottom and ring for an ambulance or a taxi."

"Yes my wife and daughter are now out side".

"Go and tell them to go to the Forest Glen and telephone for an ambulance or taxi to meet you at the bottom of the hill. (She quickly wrote down and gave him Charlotte's telephone number) I think that it would be best if you take this little lad straight to the Cottage Hospital where I am sure that they will know exactly what to do. My Husband will take you to the bottom with the tractor and trailer; you can sit on that and be quite safe. I don't think that it would be a good idea for this little lad to put any weight on this leg until it has been looked at by some one professionally and he is rather a big boy for you to carry to the bottom of the hill".

George came in and when he saw what was going on and when Hannah had explained he went to fetch the tractor and trailer from around the back.

It was very soon all over, as he went out carrying the child the man thanked Hannah and George for their help and he put his son on a blanket that Hannah gave him to put on the floor of the trailer. He then climbed up beside him and off they went down the hill.

"You know" Said Hannah to Judith and Molly when they had left and all was quiet again.

"I am going to see if there is the possibility of having the telephone installed up here; goodness knows that we could have done with having one just now".

"You could try "Answered Judith "But I can't see them bringing it up here don't you agree Molly?" She looked to Molly to support her.

"There is no harm in trying you never know, what can be done unless you ask." Said Molly. "It certainly would be a grand help; especially when you get some one like that little lad just now. I wish these idiots would not smash glass bottles. I can't see any sense in it; that I can't, young thugs that they are. I just wish that I were standing behind them. They would not smash another one when I had finished with them" Molly was certainly one who was brought up not spare the rod and spoil the child.

The following week when Hannah went into town to do some shopping she went to the Post office in Walker Street to make enquiries as to having a telephone fitted and she was given some forms to fill in. It was later in the summer that she found that she had been successful and that the GPO would install a telephone for her.

" It will be absolutely wonderful George Just think how it will change every thing for us. No longer will I need to feel cut off from every one." Hannah was so excited. When she had been working for Charlotte she was only allowed to use the phone for personal calls when and if it had been absolutely necessary.

"And don't forget another bill to pay" George reminded her; "Can't have you talking half a day on it. It will not take much to run a bill up, but you are quite right it will be a Godsend. I will be able to make good use of it. One day I want to give up working for my boss and work for my self. There are getting too many chiefs and not enough Indians at our place. I don't see why I should work my socks off for them to make all the profit".

"Let's see how they are going to get it up here first before we make too many plans" Hannah suggested now feeling a lot calmer. The realisation sinking in that George was thinking of giving up his job. There would no longer be a secure wage coming in. The thought was quite scary. They still depended on George's wage packet especially in the winter months. George was suggesting that he buy a van as soon as they could possibly afford one. He was now getting a little fed up with riding the motor bike in the wet and cold weather.

First telephone poles were put up the hill to the house it did not prove to be as difficult as every one had first thought. The telephone engineers were able to take a shot cut up the side of the hill opposite the Forest Glen and by September the job had been successfully completed.

When her mother Dorothy knew that they were having visitors she found it very useful she only had to ring if she wanted a cake making and she now had Sandra old enough to send for one instead of having to take Mary from her work. Although Sandra was only eight years old she loved to be sent for a cake. It did not take her long to get to the Cottage by crossing the fields and following the track. She knew that she would be given a bottle of pop and a packet of crisps or a bar of chocolate. Hannah was very generous towards her.

Because the weather had been unusually good since Easter, it had been a great help to George and Hannah financially. Trade with the shop and tearooms had been excellent giving them so much more enthusiasm to plan for the next year.

Hannah had been so relieved that she had not become pregnant because she felt that it was the last thing that she wanted. She felt that she had more than enough to cope with and in a way she was looking forward to the winter months when she could take things a little easier.

All through the month of October she had been feeling unwell and did not feel like pleasing George who had a very big appetite for lovemaking. He insisted on making love practically every other night if possible.

"What on earth is the matter with you" George had complained when Hannah had once again refused his advances.

"I don't know I just feel unwell and tired out" She had replied wearily. "Just leave me alone I will be OK in a day or two"

"I hope so. If not, go and see a doctor. I can't do with you being sick and bad now that we have got so much going for us.

We have shown that Mother of yours that we can do it and make a go of things and she now has nothing to shout about. I notice that she is very handy at sending Sandra for cakes every now and then I think that you are far too soft with her. Thought I was not good enough for her precious family did she. Well I am showing her different." Hannah did not like to see the sinister smirk on George's face. This was one side of George that she had not known.

"It is only a sponge cake or a few buns that she has and it does help to keep the peace" Hannah was trying to defend herself for being over generous. So her mother had been awkward about her marrying him but since they had taken the Cottage her mother had been much more amicable with them and she often rang to see if Hannah would make a sponge cake.

Her excuse was that Hannah had a much better cooker than the one that she had. The Rayburn can be so unpredictable it will either burn them or they flop, in the middle".

"Who is that sponge cake for?" George asked when he saw Hannah quickly beating margarine and sugar together and putting another sponge cake in the AGA.

"Oh just a quick one for Mother; Mary or Sandra will pop across for it later.

"Why can't she make her own?" George wanted to know

"She blames the Rayburn cooker but I don't think that is the reason. The fact is that she has never tried to make sponge cakes and it is not the cooker that is to blame". Hannah could only think it; she had not got the guts to say something like that to her mother.

Hannah promised George that she would call in at the surgery next time that they went into town to do some shopping. She had been put on the list of a Doctor Price a new doctor to the area. Hannah thought that he was in his late thirties very good looking and he seemed pleasant enough.

"You are pregnant "He told Hannah after giving her an examination.

"I can't be Doctor" Hannah stammered "I still have my monthly periods. If I am when am I to expect this baby?"

"You are and I estimate that you can expect to have it some time in next April. And as for having your monthly periods lots of women do exactly the same as you. There is nothing to get alarmed about they will stop and Baby will still be there quite safe. I want you to take this letter to the Wrekin Hospital so that they can keep an eye on you. You will need to have a check up every month or what ever advice the hospital give you. Don't look so miserable. What do you have to worry about you are a married woman and this happens to women in far worse situations. It will give you something to look forward to through the long days of the winter".

He smiled at Hannah as if this was no worse than having an every day cold. Hannah thanked him for seeing her and went quickly out on to the street.

When she met George as she had arranged, she was not in a very good mood.

"Cheer up you look so miserable, it is not bad news is it."

"Well I think it is The Doctor has told me that I am Pregnant and I don't like the idea of that one little bit You promised me that you could avoid it and said that you were being careful now look what a mess that I am in."

"Don't you go putting all the blame on me, so what if you are pregnant? Nothing to get upset about as far as I can see. When is this baby due? You can't be very far-gone you told me that you were not pregnant only the other day or were you telling lies just to avoid having to satisfy my needs because if you were lying how can I believe any thing else that you choose to tell me." George sounded really angry.

"George I have not been telling you any lies The Doctor says that it is quite usual to have my monthly and still be pregnant. He says that I am to expect the baby sometime in April He said that the hospital would be able to give me a more exact date nearer the time. I have a letter here to take to the Wrekin hospital." Hannah was quite upset at George's reaction, she decide to say no more,

She felt far too tired and worn out to put up with an argument and she was hoping that he would have been a little more sympathetic. There was so much that they had planned to do the next year and Hannah thought that she had enough to cope with as it was with out having a baby to look after.

"I will be another half hour. I have some shopping to do I'll meet you here again later "The two of them said no more. Hannah did what shopping she had planned to do and met George again at the Clifton Cinema car park as arranged. She put the shopping in the pannier bags of the bike and sat on the back when he had started the engine. Hannah had so much on her mind she did not bother to make any further conversation as they rode out of town and back towards home. George was now quite an expert rider and negotiated the bends up the track to the cottage with ease. Hannah went straight to the Aga and put the kettle on the hot plate to bring it to the boil and made a cup of coffee for both of them. They were able to buy large tins of powdered coffee made by a firm called Nescafe. The Americans had introduced the ground-powdered coffee. There was much more coffee being consumed in Britain. The coffee beans were dried and ground to a powder, a much easier way of making coffee than having to percolate the beans or use the liquid coffee such as the camp coffee that her mother used for so many years. George and Hannah still preferred their morning cup of tea but the new ground coffee made a very refreshing drink at mid morning and a lot of customers had gained the habit of drinking it. It was becoming very popular.

A baby on the way was all that Hannah could think about. This was something that she had not planned for. Well she thought that it was a bit late to get upset about it although the thought of it terrified her. She thought about Helen and how that she had given birth to a lovely healthy baby boy in June. Lizzy was pregnant and so was Beccy The saying was that every thing must come in threes and here was another instance. Hannah looked at the next year's calendar to see when the Easter Bank holiday would be.

"George unless this baby comes early I will be pregnant all through the Easter break and there will not be a lot that I will be able to do. Oh Lordy how will we manage"

"We will manage all right we will have plenty of help and besides you can always sit to decorate the cakes. I expect Judith will come and give you a hand to make them and there is always Molly. She says that the eldest Crosby girl who lives opposite her will always come and give you some help

Molly says that you can always rely on her to help with the washing and ironing since she has married she is sat at home doing practically nothing"

"But what if they want to make other plans instead of working up here"?

"Oh for goodness sake Hannah, stop going on, there are plenty who will be glad to earn a few shillings. You make it sound as if it will be the end of the world just because you are expecting. Just shut up and wait and see when the time comes I have enough to think about. I suggest that you get your knitting needles out and start knitting After all you will have all the winter months with very little else to do.

I have been thinking of fitting a door there "He pointed to the passage way leading to the stairs. There is quite a draft coming down the stairs I can't think why the last people did not fit one".

"George don't you think that it would be rather inconvenient for us to have a door fitted there It would be a bit of a bother trying to carry trays to the tearoom. I am sure that we don't want another door to have to open when our hands are full".

"In that case I could make a way through under the stairs and then there would be no need to come carrying trays through here at all". George swallowed the rest of his cup of coffee and went outside.

"Well I don't believe it" Hannah said to her self as he closed the door with a bang as he went.

Hannah was quite taken aback by George's re-action. Give me something to do during the winter months what about all the spring cleaning that has to be done ready for the Easter trade. And as for making a way through under the stairs, what a mess that is going to make still on the other hand if a door were to be fitted there it would keep the kitchen warmer during the winter months. Hannah had planned to give the small tearoom a coat of paint to brighten it up a bit and had planned to ask the Estate if they would allow them to change the old black leaded fire grate in there and replace it with a more modern one. The old one did not do a lot to cheer the room up. Hannah had decided to keep the smaller of the tearooms open during the winter months if there were any walkers about who wanted to take a break. She could quickly make some fresh scones to be served with butter and homemade jam. Hannah had made a little jam but not a lot because most of the jam that was needed during the summer months was bought from the catering wholesalers in seven-pound tins.

Her mind was in turmoil so many more things to think about now that she was pregnant. How big would she be? How much work would she be able to cope with? To her it seemed as if all her ready-made plans were now of no importance. I have enough to do with out sitting knitting she thought. But then on second thoughts she was going to be alone on the hill on the cold and wet days though out the winter months and the thought of knitting baby clothes might not be as bad as she had first thought. Yes next time she went into town she would go to the wool shop in Market Street, and see what baby patterns that they had and some baby wool. The more she thought about it the more exciting the idea became then she had to think about whom she should tell about the new baby that was coming and who should she not tell. Hannah knew that Terry and Molly would not be amused as they had all ready said that she was working far too hard as it was. Now that a baby was on the way, was it all going to be too much for her, and if so who was going to do all the work that there had to be done. They had noticed when they arrived on a Sunday morning to give a hand, the amount of cleaning and the washing she had done during the week. Hannah had already scrubbed the red quarried kitchen floors as well as scrubbing all the wooden worktables. She would have checked that the white table clothes in both tearooms to see that they were not soiled and if so had already changed them from the previous days use. Dusted Etc;

`Hannah thought that Molly would be the first to be told because she had been such a good friend to her and confidant. Molly and Terry had married at the end of June Theirs was a lovely wedding every one was so pleased for them, the reception was held at her sister Else's home and then after having a holiday together. Molly moved to live with Terry in the same council house in the village of Wrockwardine where George had been reared and brought up. She had been offered a part time job at the local shop in the village and she had accepted it. Much to the amazement of the locals. They did not take to the idea of some one new to the village having the job, which a lot of them felt should have been offered to a local person. This did not bother Molly one little bit, as far as she was concerned they could like it or lump it. She was good at her job and as long as she did the job required of her and was civil to all the customers who came in to shop and use the village post office. That was all that she had to worry about and she loved every minute of it and meeting the people of the village. She had some how persuaded Terry to set a lawn on the front garden and plant some flowers instead of growing the annual crop of potatoes like he had been growing all through the war years. The Government had told every one to dig for Victory and that every one had to try to be as self sufficient as much as possible. Stocks around the country were depleted, had it not been for the amount of produce that had been grown in one's own gardens to help the war effort? The country could have almost starved to death as it had happened in Holland. The Government had only revealed after the war was over, how short of food that they had become at one time during the war when the British Navy was taking such a hammering from the German U-boats. Molly had all so persuaded Terry to have a go at growing some tomatoes like her brother in law was doing. She spent her first earned money on a little greenhouse for him to try and see what he could do. She had brought Terry some plants from Elise's and he could now move the plants in to it and finish them off under glass Terry thought that she was wonderful, he idolized her and was a completely changed man from what he had been since the death of Ivy.

Hannah decided that she would wait another month or so before saying any thing about the forthcoming baby to Mary so that there was no need for her Mother to know as yet. That could wait a little longer. Perhaps at Christmas would be soon enough. The thought of Christmas made Hannah think about what she must do in preparation. George had completely ignored her twenty-first birthday not a card or a present. This had really upset Hannah but then she was always making excuses for George. Far too much on his mind to bother about birthdays she had quietly consoled her self. None of her family had started the habit of sending birthday cards. Hannah was so angry at first at the thought of George forgetting that it had been her birthday and when she saw an advert for a very nice cooking recipe book advertised. She had sent for it. It was called "The Good Housekeeping Cookery Compendium" Hannah was thrilled to bits with it. The book covered all types of cookery as well as preserving fruit and vegetables. She would use the recipe from it to make their first Christmas cake and Puddings. Yes she had so much to look forward to. Hannah made an appointment to attend the maternity Clinic at the Wrekin Hospital and was so surprised when she saw there were so many other women queuing up to be seen. Could all women be pregnant like she was, some showed little sign and others appeared to be very near to giving birth? Goodness I thought Hannah I will never be that big surely I can't imagine it. Blood samples were taken she was weighed. Hannah had put on no weight and was still the eight and a half stone that she had been since leaving school. There were so many questions that there was to be answered as the nursing sister filled in the necessary forms that were required Hannah was told to attend the clinic again in a month's time and an appointment card was made out for her. The next visit was not quite so traumatising but Hannah was given a green card which indicated as to what her blood type was and she was told that she was of the negative group and that she must always carry the card with her.

Hannah had practically no morning sickness and after feeling off colour the first few months she hardly knew that she was pregnant at all, and she was able to cope with all she had to do. Feed the chickens and keep the pen clean, and still cope with all the household chores.

Providing the weather was not too cold and wet. A few customers still came in for a pot of tea; Hannah still had to cook for them selves so it did not take much more to make a few extra cakes and scones for the tearoom just in case. The few extra shillings that Hannah made during the winter months gave her that little bit of independence. She felt that it was good not to ask George for every penny for personal things and preparations for the new baby like knitting wool, baby soap and powder Hannah started knitting baby clothes she had bought a pattern and wool for a lovely lacy pattered layette and shawl. She knit the layette first. Bonnet, bootees and a matinee coat. Then she decided that she would knit the shawl to match. Being that it was a very lacy pattern it certainly took a lot of time and concentration. Mary had called in unexpectedly and had seen Hannah knitting baby clothes wanted to know what was going on. Who was Hannah doing the knitting for and this gave the game away. Mary promised that she would say nothing at home before Christmas. Hannah was quite relieved at her agreeing to this, as Hannah did not want to start a family so soon especially in the first year of marriage.

Hannah was now beginning to see a different side of George's nature she had not envisaged nor was she prepared for this. Hannah could now see for herself that if George was denied satisfying his sexual desires his mood could change so easily and quickly. He was quiet and sulky. Surely if he loved me he would understand that it is not possible to make love whenever he feels like it. Now that she had a baby to think about Hannah was not the slightest interested in satisfying him? The baby that she was expecting was of much more importance to her and she expected George to understand this. Instead he would sulk and be moody like a spoilt child. Goodness me Hannah said to her self what is he going to be like when there is no satisfying him at all? I am not letting him near me if it means that there may be any risk to the baby. Dam it; he can't have it all his own way. He got me pregnant when I had asked him to be very careful. But then how naïve could I have been. After all I enjoyed his love making so I suppose that I must not complain. It takes two to make a baby.

In November George fitted the door to the kitchen so that it was much warmer to sit in during the winter months Hannah managed to buy two second hand fire side chairs to make it a bit more comfortable. The winter months did not seem to drag by too slowly as Hannah had at first thought that they would. She sat knitting whenever she could. Some days she would take a walk to the point and look down on the town of Wellington it was one way of getting some exercise and she felt that as she looked down at the town below she was not so isolated and she loved walking through the frozen leaves under the beech trees. It reminded her so much of when she had been a child fetching sticks from the woods in the winter months. On cold and frosty mornings she would have lovely sunshine up on the hill but if she looked down over the town, there would be thick fog below blocking out the entire landscape, blocking out the town and every thing else as it was engulfed in thick fog. .

"It's been a pea soup

George would complain when he came home from work at six o'clock.

"Not up here". Hannah answered. "I have had a lovely day cold but with plenty of sunshine.

It was Hannah's job to keep a record of the money that they were taking at the shop window and in the tearooms and also keep a record of out going expenses. She used to try and do this at least once a month sitting at the kitchen table. When Hannah realised that she was pregnant late in October she asked George to go ahead and fit a door to block the passage way off so that it would make the kitchen much warmer for the winter months. His idea of making a new way through to the small dining room coming under the staircase instead of the trays being carried through the kitchen now appealed to her. George made a new doorframe and a wood and panelled door to fit it. He was using some new manufactured wood called hardboard this could be bought quite cheaply. The kitchen certainly did feel much warmer after he had fixed it. It was one evening in January that George said that he was going to the motor cycle club but Hannah said that she would rather stay at home. The weather was bitterly cold she thought it best that she did not go out on a motor bike. After George had left, Hannah settled down to do her bookkeeping. She was quite engrossed when she felt a draught and turned to see the new door being opened and closed. It did not bother her at first. Until she realised that no one had come through the door and that there was no one else but her self to open it. It was quite scary for a minute or two. She got up from her chair and checked the door it was closed shut and there was no one about she checked the passage the stairs and their bathroom. That was funny she said to her self I will ask George why the door should open and close like that makes no sense to me, Must be the wind blowing out side and the door opening was caused by the draught. When she told George he laughed at her and said that it was just a draught. You will leave the windows open upstairs. Hannah made a point of closing the windows at about four o'clock in the winter months so she some how felt that a drought had not caused the door to open but she knew better than to make a fuss and annoy George. He would just say that it was her imagination. It was not until a week later when George was sat in his chair by the Aga and he had suggested that they go to bed when he saw the door open and close. Hannah laughed when she saw how pale that he had gone to look.

"What's the matter George you have gone to look quite pale. Did you see that door open and close? It is like you said that it is only a draught blowing through the passage".

"But" George stammered "There is no wind blowing to night". He quickly went out on to the front porch so that he could prove his point

"It could not be a ghost could it George "Just a draught" Hannah laughed.

"Well I don't rightly know but that door cannot open just like that, the catch fits too tightly" He went over to the new door and yes it was tightly closed. I will change the door handle and try another new one a different sort.

"I did tell you about it George. It has happened a few times since that new door was fitted. I have looked up stairs but I can't see anything spooky up there. "

"Never you mind about upstairs there is certainly something spooky down here. I am going to see what I can find out about this place. Old Eric Watson never mentioned that there was any thing strange going on and he should have known he had lived up here for a good many years."

"But George there had never been a door fitted there before for any one to open and close and perhaps you have disturbed some thing by knocking a way through under the stairs. Hannah had read about ghosts but had never feared one because she had never seen one, so she thought that it was all very funny especially for her to see George so scared about the possibility of the house being haunted. Hannah decided to be friendly towards who ever it was that was opening the door and then perhaps it would go away and leave them in peace. The next time that it happened Hannah was on her own so she spoke to what she thought was the ghost. She went into the passage leading to the stairs.

"Don't be afraid of us living hear we will not harm you we have only put the new door there to keep the kitchen warmer we will take it off for the summer months". Hannah felt such a fool talking to some one that she could not see but it worked and only a few times again did she see the door opening during the winter months and as she had promised George took the door away for the summer months

Their only means of transport was the motor bike or the tractor. One evening at the end of February Bill Harper came up to the cottage to see them both. He rode up on his bike to which he had now fitted a side car apparently Brenda preferred to sit in this to riding as pillion she did not like to spoil her clothes. The roads could be very wet and dirty in the winter months and it could be no joy riding on the back of a motorbike.

"Let's go and see a film and have a night out Bill had suggested and George was quick to take up his suggestion.

"Well you two go ahead, "Hannah said, not wanting to ride on the back of George's bike in her condition; her figure now showing that she was well and truly pregnant.

"You come with me" Bill was quick to make a proposal. "You can ride in the side car you will be perfectly safe I can assure you that no harm will come to you"

Hannah hesitated and then she could see by the look on George's face that it would be as well to accept and not cause any further argument.

It did not take George and Hannah many minutes to put on their coats and helmets. Hannah seated her self in the sidecar and tried to relax but that was not easy she felt most uncomfortable. Off they went Bumpity bump down the hill. Hannah at first thought that she was going to be sick or that she would start having the baby and was really glad when they reached the bottom of the hill; the ride down the hill had terrified her

"There that was not too bad "Said Bill smiling as they parked up in the Clifton Cinema car park.

Hannah did not answer she just went along with the two men feeling very conspicuous about her figure. Thank goodness that the public attitude towards women being pregnant was now changing a little.

One did not have to hide away for the last few months of a confinement and not be seen in public. If they did go out, the fashion now was to wear loose fitting clothes so as not to emphasise their growing figure. This had been the rule in the Victorian days. Large families were starting to go out of fashion as more women had started to speak up for them selves. Some of the younger girls did not seem to mind being seen in public when they were in the last weeks of their pregnancies. Hannah felt rather conspicuous.

The film was a Western about cowboys and Indians one both George and Bill thoroughly enjoyed and afterwards all three of them went into the Queens Hotel for a drink. Hannah quickly looked around as they entered the lounge and made for a seat in the furthest corner from where the drinks were being served at the bar. She thought of what her Mother would have said if she had known that a daughter of hers was sitting in a hotel drinking when she was seven months pregnant. She would never let Hannah live it down. Because Hannah had found the ride in the sidecar terrifying she was dreading the ride back up the hill. She waited until she thought that the time was right and then she suggested to Bill that he could drop her off at the bottom of the hill by the Glen.

"Don't be silly". He had answered "It is no trouble to take you back up to the house."

"Well if you don't mind I would rather walk."

"Now don't you go being awkward" George had interrupted. "What if you fall?"

"I know my way up the hill, practically every stone I will be perfectly alright" Hannah replied She thought that walking up the track would be much better than having to endure another ride in the sidecar. It was a clear moonlight night and except for any shadows from the trees the track would be well lit by the moon.

"OK" Bill agreed with her "I will drop you off at the bottom. "I have heard that you women can have some funny ideas when you are in that condition. "I dread to think what my Brenda would be like when it comes to her turn.

I can imagine her only being a Mother to One and that will be it. She certainly shows no sign of being the slightest interested in having babies.

When they came to the bottom of the hill Bill stopped the bike and asked Hannah if she had meant what she had said about preferring to walk up to the house; when she reassured him that she had meant it and that she would be perfectly all right. Hannah had great difficulty getting out of the sidecar and when she did manage to get out of it and stand on her feet, she vowed that she would never ride in a sidecar again no matter how long that she might live. She had certainly been frightened. Bill seemed quite miffed because he was not going back up to the Cottage, he just shouted Cheerio to George and turned the bike and sidecar around and sped off towards Wellington.

George had not believed that Hannah would prefer to walk and he was not amused. He was in a bit of a quandary not knowing what he was expected to do Whether he should leave his bike and walk up with Hannah or go ahead and leave her to get on with it He decided the latter.

I will see you later "He said and kick started his bike to restarted the engine",

"Yes that is all right by me. You go ahead and put the Kettle to boil I will not be far behind you".

"If you say so" George was soon gone up the track and out of sight. Hannah guessed that he would be quite angry but she did not care. No way was she going to sit in that sidecar to ride up the hill. The track was very bumpy in places where the rocks protruded, causing her to be tossed from one side of the sidecar to the other and sitting in such a confined space a second time certainly did not appeal to her. Hannah started to walk up hill thinking that as soon as George had taken the bike up to the Cottage he would walk back to meet her. She reached the worst bend in the track, which was about half the distance that she had to go; she stopped to rest a while. Hannah had not taken her pregnancy into consideration when she had said that she would follow George She had tried to walk much too quickly and was now needing to rest for a few minutes. She stood taking her time to breathe heavily until she felt better She found it quite pleasant standing there in the moonlight looking down on the trees and fields below her. It did feel somewhat a little awe inspiring being there on her own seven months pregnant. She had nothing to worry about there was nothing about that could be of any harm to her. She knew that there were Adders and snakes that lived in the blueberry bushes that spread up the hill on her right hand side but they would not be about in the late evening. Any foxes that were looking for a rabbit for their supper would be much lower down on the fields were and the rabbits would be feeding on grass. When she had got her breath back Hannah moved on only this time much more slowly. She reached the cottage and was quite surprised that there had been no sign of George coming to meet her she guessed that he was quite cross with her for not coming up in the sidecar.

She entered the kitchen George having taken off his overcoat and crash helmet was sat in his usual chair the far side of the table by the stove in the corner looking quite peeved,

"That was a bit bad of you not to let Bill bring you all the way. Don't you think"? He looked across at Hannah as she entered the kitchen. By the tone in his voice, Hannah guessed that he was quite angry and she decided to make light of it.

"I don't think so I did not like riding in that sidecar. I just did not feel very safe I felt so near the ground and it was so uncomfortable sitting on no more than half an inch of plywood. I felt every stone and rock that Bill went over. George; I never want to ride in one of those things ever again".

"It was safe enough. You would have been alright, there was so much that I wanted to talk to Bill about and the least that we could have done was to offer him a bit of supper".

"I am sure that you can arrange for him to come and see you another time. Have you made a cup of tea? Hannah asked hoping to change the subject,

"Not yet I was waiting for you to get here"

"In that case, don't bother I am going to bed" She picked up a box of matches from the back of the Aga so that she could light the calor gas lights on the stairs and in the bedroom as she went.

"Suit your self" George muttered.

Hannah did not bother to reply, she was tired and there was still a lot for her to do the next day. She had not seen much of this moody side of George and she wondered if it was because he was feeling left out now that there was a new baby coming. She was too tired to bother to reason why, the walk up the hill had been very exhausting and Hannah had to admit to her self that it had also been quite scary. She had been afraid of slipping on any loose stones causing her to fall. She had been very relieved to get to the front door and see the light shining from within. She had also been very disappointed that George had not bothered to come to meet her. She turned over until she felt that she was lying comfortable and was soon asleep. She was only vaguely aware of George coming to bed much later.

Hannah only went into town when she had to have a check up at the Wrekin Hospital, which were now every two weeks. She booked a taxi from Charlotte's garage to meet her at the bottom of the hill by the Forest Glen; after her check up she would walk into town do any shopping that she had to do.

This could not be a lot because she knew that she would have to carry it back up the hill later in the day. She would pay for a taxi to take her back to the bottom of the hill again. Charlotte always made her very welcome when Hannah called for a car. If she was not there Sally would offer her a cup of tea and they would have quite a little gossip. The girl who had taken Hannah's place had not stayed very long so Charlotte had not bothered employing another to live in. The new man in her life was there for her in the evenings so she was not on her own any longer.

Hannah was so pleased with her knitting; she carefully wrapped it in tissue paper ready for her new baby. She had placed it with all the other items White towels nappies, nightdresses and all the other things that were required by the hospital that she had purchased and put ready for the birth

Molly suggested that Hannah had a bit more help; she said that she should ask Hilda Crosby to come and give her a hand during the week days as well as helping out on Sundays. When George and Hannah had taken her on, she became a great help with serving at the shop counter when Judith was unable to come and she was also a great help serving in the tearooms. Hannah agreed with Molly that it would be a good idea and arranged with Hilda that she should come every day. Hilda Crosby was the eldest of thirteen children and had married a local boy from the village. She readily agreed to help out, she said that she would be only too glad to oblige and at the same time earn a bit of extra money

Easter approached in the middle of April and Hannah had not given birth she stayed in the background as much as she could. A young lad from Wrockwardine called Bobby Andrews had been given the job of looking after the swing boats and he said that he could come to work during the school holidays to do small jobs around the place so that George could go to work as usual. Hannah was glad of his company it saved her from feeding the chickens and carrying the coal hods full of anthracite to feed the Aga cooker and many other little jobs. She was certainly glad to have Hilda there to see to the tearoom and the shop.

It was the Monday after the Easter bank holiday; Bobby was due to go back to school the next day. Hannah, Hilda and Bobby got through the day quite successfully but by six o'clock Hannah knew that she was starting to go into labour. George arranged for a car to take her from the bottom of the hill to the hospital later that evening.

"I don't think that Baby will come tonight" Sister told George when they arrived at the Wrekin Hospital "You go home and telephone us first thing in the morning", After George had left, the nursing Sister brought a glass of warm milk and a tablet for Hannah to take, Hannah hated drinking milk she had so much of it as a child she wanted to refuse but Sister stood by the bed until Hannah had swallowed the lot. Hannah felt sick as she swallowed it but she soon fell asleep and remembered no more until six in the morning when she was well and truly into labour and she was delivered of a baby boy at about half past eight weighing eight and a half pounds. George came to see her that evening and seemed quite pleased with his new son. They called him Michael John. Hilda was a great help she coped with so much. She came during the week and while Hannah was confined in hospital for the two weeks which was the regular length of time that one was kept in hospital for the confinement. Hannah and baby Michael went home and did as she had been told during the first two weeks and found that she could cope OK. Every one was so supportive. Terry, Molly and Judith came to help with the work. It was the third Sunday that Hannah and her baby had been at home. Michael was crying much more than he should have been despite Hannah feeding him herself. In the afternoon Molly had heard enough of his crying and she was trying to console him

"This child is hungry" She stated very firmly Boil some milk and give him a good feed and see what happens" She handed Michael back to Hannah

"I can't do that, The Hospital said" She was about to continue that she had been told at the hospital that she was not too start him on powered milk until the district nurse advised her to do so.

"Never mind what the hospital says, give him some milk."

Hannah reluctantly did as Molly had said, she quickly found the baby bottle, which she had previously bought and then she boiled some cows milk cooled it and fed it to Michael and much to every ones relief he was asleep in no time at all.

"Now do the same tonight. The trouble with you Hannah you are working far too hard to be able to feed a baby I suggest that you get George to bring you a tin of Cow and Gate baby milk tomorrow and feed that child properly".

They did as Molly had told them and within a week Hannah had no more trouble with Michael He quickly put on weight and was a very contented baby. George began to idolise him. It had been while Hannah was in hospital that Granddad Wainwright had taken a turn for the worst and had past away. Hannah had been so disappointed that she was in hospital and unable to go to his funeral. There were a lot of assumptions between the family of his three sons and two daughters Dorothy and her sister Jane as to how he had made his will.

Her father's solicitor informed Dorothy that she and her sister Jane had inherited a small country cottage each and that was all. Gordon had inherited the manor and every thing that went with it including Yew tree House where he and his family had been living. His other two sons were left to paddle their own canoes. He had left it that they could pay off the remainder of what ever was owed on their farms.

Dorothy grumbled for days, she was so disappointed and furious that she had inherited no more than a workman's cottage. But there was nothing that she could do about it. Both she and Jane decided that it would be best that the cottages should be sold. They were practically uninhabited at the time. This was arranged and they each received a cheque for the sale of the properties. Dorothy promptly banked hers hoping that if the Bromleys did decide to sell the Willowmoors she and Fred would stand a chance of buying it. William's future was all that she could think about. The out come of Bill Wainwright's will left a very bitter pill for Dorothy to swallow and she made no bones of contention as to how she felt. The animosity between the family played on Grandma Wainwright's mind to such an extent that she became very poorly and only wanted to be with her beloved husband and she gave up the will to live, she died just six weeks later at the home of her daughter Jane.

Hannah and George had Michael registered and christened but not many of Hannah's sisters came to the Christening they were far too busy rearing babies of their own. Judith was his Godmother and Simon his Godfather. Every one who came to work up at the Cottage loved to take a turn feeding Michael. The following summer was dry and hot Hannah found that with all the washing to do for the tea rooms and the family she had very little time to her self and to enjoy her baby, it was a relief when some one offered to give him his bottle. That would save Hannah from leaving the work that she was doing and this was how she was able to get through most of the chores, which seemed to her be endless.

George was in his element. He was now very much the farmer. He loved to walk the fields with his gun and bring back a rabbit and sometimes a pheasant for Hannah to prepare and cook for their dinner.

This life suited him and although he had kept his job as a carpenter working for the Cartwrights he secretly looked forward to the day when he could give it up and be his own boss entirely.

It was later in the year that Fred and Dorothy were informed that their farm was going to be sold and as sitting tenants they would be given the first refusal. Dorothy could not believe their luck. With what they had saved and her savings from the sale of the cottage and may be a loan from the bank. It would mean that at last after all the years of renting they could at last own their own farm and she decided that nothing was going to stand in her way to stop them from becoming owner occupiers she had waited years to be able to achieve this.

Later in the year George purchased two baby calves to rear with the two baby calves that his Guernsey and Jersey cows had given birth to, He maintained that it was just as easy to feed four calves as feed two. Hannah thought that there must be some logic in that but where? Seeing as it was going to be her job to rear them. They were put in what was referred to as the bottom sheds. Galvanised lean-to sheds. George partitioned them off to make special pens for the calves. George planned that if they grew and he fattened the calves up he could take these to the auction in Shrewsbury the next year and all being well he would get a good price for them.

Terry and Molly heard from the Council that were to be offered one of the new bungalows that were being built by the council to re-house pensioners so that couples with families could be housed in the three bed roomed houses such as theirs. The bungalows were to be built on a piece of ground by the cemetery. Terry and Molly accepted the offer and Terry asked George what he was going to do about the Caravan that was still on his garden waiting to be finished.

George decided that he had no alternative than to bring it up the Wrekin He would then be able to put the finishing touches to it. He arranged for a friend who had a big Fordson Major tractor to tow it up the hill. They manoeuvred it into a position on a flat piece of land at the back of the house. There was very little to finish off just the seats that had to be ordered. There was some carpentry work to be done in the inside. Bernie often came to the Cottage for a cup of tea and a chat during the winter months. When he saw the caravan he wanted to know what was going to happen to it. He was looking for some where to live so that he could get a better paid job and hinted that if George changed his mind about sending it to the sea side he would be willing to pay him some rent so that he could live in it. Hannah was appalled at the idea. This had been their lovely caravan and to think that George would let it be used by some one like Bernie. Besides Hannah thought that if George agreed to this there would be more animosity with her Mother and Father they would say that George was encouraging their worker to leave and Hannah did not want to have any part of it. George thought that it was a good idea she was furious with him when he had said

"Save us bothering to take it to the sea side. And another thing we would be able to rent it all the year round and pay no ground rent".

"I don't like your idea one little bit. What will the Estate have to say about it if they find out? And besides George do you realise that caravan was to have been ours. Bernie will never keep it as nice and clean as it should be kept"

"Will you stop fussing How will the Estate find out unless you tell them and I don't think that you would dare do that and another thing if Bernie wants it I for one think that it will be a good idea. Your Mother would have to get others to do the work and probably pay them a bit more. It has been a pittance that they have been paying him, I know that they could argue that they give him the going rate for some one living in but they give him no extra pay for all the overtime that he works."

Hannah was getting really angry with George.

"It's just your way at getting back at my Mother "She said

"Please your self what you think, if Bernie can get a better paid job I will let him live in the van that is if he will wants to".

Hannah felt that there was no point in making a scene. She had got to know George a lot better since she had married him. She grew nervous of him if he became angry and she felt that if she were to push him too far, he could become very angry indeed, she felt pretty sure that he would not hit her but she knew when to back off in an argument. Now was the time to say no more even if she felt absolutely livid with him. Bernie found employment working for the County Council emptying the dustbins and took up George's offer to live in the caravan. He soon got used to using his pushbike to work and negotiated the short cut down the hill with great expertise. He was a much happier man now that he was earning a much better wage. Bernie had become a great Elvis Presley fan and had his hair cut and combed just like the pictures that he saw of Elvis. When he went out into town at weekends, he dressed as near as he could to what Elvis would have looked like.

Hannah was dreading her mother telephoning and start complaining that George had taken Bernie from them and she lived on tender hooks but as it happened, her Mother did no such thing Mary told Hannah that she seemed quite pleased that Bernie had left. She said at last she had one less to cook for and for the first time since the war her house was now her own, no strangers living in. She quickly re-decorated the room Bernie had occupied and bought some second hand furnisher and new curtains for it, she even had a carpet put down in it and when it was finished she was quite pleased with the result.

Hannah saw very little of Bernie except when he came in for water. If he were back up the hill before George he would sometimes give Hannah help with stacking the crates of minerals. OD Murphy 's men were often in a hurry when they delivered them, they would put them just inside the door or leave them on the front porch where George and Hannah had to leave the crates empty bottles so that the driver could make a quick get away. George decided that it would not be advisable to fit a water pipe to the caravan to give Bernie running water in case the estate Manager came snooping around, as George put it.

Good morning Molly said as she went into the passage to hang her coat and crash hat. "Are you OK?" Hannah asked. Molly did not sound her usual cheerful self "Come into the back kitchen a minute I've got something to tell you" Molly looked very worried

"This sounds ominous Molly. What is it that you want to tell me?

Hannah followed Molly in the back kitchen

"Don't say anything to Judith but for some reason or other she has finished going out with Simon "

"What? Judith finished with Simon. I can't believe it I thought that they were so happy infact a perfect couple. Well you do surprise me. That does take some swallowing. When did this happen?"

"I have no idea only that they have finished. Elsie is so upset. I said that if they were not getting on it is better that they split up now than leave it until after they have married. Her father is quite upset by the whole thing so I suggest that you tell George and then keep quiet about it. Judith will tell me all about it when she is ready to do so. At the moment she does not seem to want to talk about it but it seems such a shame Terry and me were planning to give her the best wedding that we could afford"

When Hannah told George he was astonished and would not believe it at first but when Judith came to help out a couple of weeks later there was no Simon with her. They decided that it was best not to ask too many questions as to what had gone wrong.

They did not see much of Simon again for some time. It was months later that Judith came to the Cottage with a new boy friend. This young man was totally the opposite in character to Simon His name was Carlton Bebbington Judith said that he preferred to be called Carl. Carl was very out spoken and continually cracked jokes one after the other and George did not take to him at all to begin with. Carl was a plumber by trade Hannah thought that they would have got on well being as they were both tradesmen but that was not the case. Six months later Judith announced her engagement to Carl. He had bought a Morris minor car and he was a very keen ball room dancer so Judith came less and less to help. She arranged to be married to Carl the following March and they took a little terraced house in the town. Judith was able to keep her full time job, which was a great help to both of them financially. They did marry in the March and Judith decided that they would do their own catering with Hannah's help. Judith was so good at organising anything and she had every thing worked out to the minute detail.

The next two years went by very so very quickly Michael was growing nicely and he was lovely little boy. He had dark hair and brown eyes just like that of his father'. But in other ways that was where the similarity ended, he featured Hannah and he seemed to be growing into a bright and intelligent little boy He was the apple of his father's eye and was spoilt some thing rotten especially by the part time staff.

The summer of 1957 Hannah found that to her dismay that she was pregnant again. The baby was due to be born early in February. Hannah was relieved in a way about the timing of the new baby. She could get it all over and done with before trade started at Easter. This was a totally different pregnancy to her first one. She was very miserable through out and she felt so ill. George did not have much patience with her, there was always so much to do and Hannah felt so rotten and tired. He had bought two young pigs to fatten up so that he could make a profit when he sold them.

Trade at the cottage had been good so far until this year 1957 which was cold and wet and Hannah did not make as much money with the shop and café as she had hoped. This took toll on their finances. Packets of crisps and biscuits did not keep for any length of time they went damp and limp so they had to be fed to the pigs. Hannah kept the tearoom open as long as she could, and especially if she saw people walking up the hill they just might come in for a pot of tea and some home made scones.

She would quickly light a fire in the dining room to make it look more cheerful there were always a few people about no matter how cold that it might be providing it was not raining and far too wet. As her pregnancy advanced Hannah was finding that she was putting on more weight and she seemed to be much bigger than when she had been carrying Michael.

"Is there any chance that I could be carrying twins," She asked Dr Price when she went for a regular check up is there any possibility that I could go and have a scan? Those new scans that are now available would tell us if there are two babies there".

"Don't be silly. He replied. "There is only one baby there I don't think that you could possibly carry twins never mind deliver them. You go home and just relax as much as you can. You have three months to go as yet and another thing we are a little reluctant to have pregnant mothers scanned I feel that we should wait a little while until we are sure that there is no danger to the baby. Don't get me wrong if for one minute that I thought that there was any danger to you or your unborn baby I would not hesitate to have you given a scan but as far as I can see I think that it is more rest that you require"

Hannah was worried, things did not seem right somehow At one time she had almost miscarried but after staying in bed for a week baby had settled down again. George had not been very pleased at all having to cope with all the extra work for a week. It was obvious that her Doctor was evidently quite right about her resting much more than what she had been doing. George did not seem able to cope and resented the fact that Hannah needed to rest when there was so much to be done. They had planted a field of potatoes and harvested them George had saved the small potatoes that were referred to as pig potatoes so he was glad that he had bought two pigs to eat them. Now there was another job to be done. The pig potatoes had to be boiled before being fed to the pigs. This certainly helped to eke out the feeding stuff for them. This had become another job for Hannah to do. George would empty sacks of potatoes into one of the old copper boilers that were still usable just down the hill in the old bake house and then he would leave the rest for Hannah to see to. Hannah had to cover them with buckets of water then light a fire underneath and keep an eye on it until the potatoes were cooked. George had said that he had more than enough to do and would be glad when he could give up his job and work at his own hours.

Hannah was too tired to put up any argument as to what George proposed to do. She felt that she could not cope with getting up and down the hill; every time that she needed to go to town. In November George decided that the time had come to buy a van. He told Hannah that they could not go on any longer as they had been over the last few months. He gave it a great deal of thought and decided that a Morris Minor would be about the best that he could buy he had been told what tough little vans that they were He went ahead and bought one He chose a dark green one. When he had taken possession of it; he welded some steel plates under the engine. Driving up the rough track up to the Cottage could damage the underneath of it and drain the oil out of the engine and then it would seize up and would cost another new engine. Oil could drain from an engine quite unnoticed and often it would be too late to do any thing about it.

This was now George's pride and joy. He had sold his motorbike to enable him to purchase the van. Hannah thought that he would be very reluctant to part with his beloved bike but to the contrary he seemed glad to get rid of it. No more biking in the wet and cold weather. After they had run the van for a while he and Hannah wondered how on earth they had managed so long with out it. The van turned out to be a proper little Godsend neither had realised what a difference it made. Hannah said that she would not mind having a go at driving it but George gave no indication that he was prepared to let her do any such thing. Hannah decided that she would wait a little while and then she was going to drive it whether he liked it or not. She was now beginning to stand up for herself a little more but she was finding it very difficult George could be very stubborn if he wanted to be

Chapter Nine
Help is At Hand

Hannah felt so pleased that George had been successful in getting the telephone wires brought up to the house. Having the telephone fitted had proved to be a Godsend.

Five weeks before baby was due Hannah went into labour "I believe that baby is on the way" Hannah said to George as she woke him up at six o'clock on the Friday morning. It had been hospital policy that second babies should be delivered at home but because of Hannah having such a rough and miserable time while she had been carrying. It was decided by the midwife at the Wrekin hospital to allow her to go to the Hospital to give birth.

"What? It can't be on the way yet you said that it was not due until next month are you sure? "He asked very sleepily getting slowly out of bed and putting on some clothes.

"Of course I'm sure"; she pulled her dressing gown around her and went downstairs. George followed Hannah to the kitchen where she had put the kettle on the hot plate of the Aga to boil and make some tea before she had to start thinking about going to the hospital.

"I will ring and notify the Hospital that I am coming so that you can take me in on your way to work. I am definitely in labour but I don't think that the baby will come before you go to work"... Who ever it was at the hospital answering Hannah's call said;

"I'm afraid that you can't come here. The maternity ward is temporally closed due to an infection amongst the babies. You must try to get in at one of the following hospitals she gave Hannah the choice of being admitted to four different hospitals.

Hannah rang them one by one two said that they were overbooked and that they could not admit her. The third one that she tried was the Broseley Cottage Hospital and they were prepared to admit her; when Hannah asked if they were taking patients from the Wrekin hospital. The person who had answered said.

"Yes we are taking Wellington patients,"

"Broseley did you say". Asked George "But that is miles away it's the other side of Ironbridge you are not going to have to go all that way are you?

"It looks like it they can't take me at the Wrekin and that seems to be the only alternative. It's the third hospital that is on the list that the Wrekin told me to ring. The only other one is the one at Much Wenlock and that is just as far away. I certainly don't want to have it here so let's get going" George reluctantly ate the breakfast Hannah put before him she could only manage a piece of toast and then she went to wake Michael and dress him giving him a cup of warm milky tea. They had no choice but to take him with them to Broseley. She sat him on a cushion between George and herself. Broseley was a way up the other side of Ironbridge about ten miles away. Hannah had arranged with Hilda to take care of Michael for the time that she was in hospital. George left her at the hospital and said that he would go home and feed the animals and get them selves a bit of dinner before taking Michael to Hilda's house at Wrockwardine. He would ring in to work and let them know that he would be in later probably at dinnertime.

After being in labour for three days until the following Monday evening Hannah was completely exhausted. No one at the hospital could say why baby was taking so long to come. The midwife insisted that if Hannah had not got any further forward with the delivery they would have to move her to the Women's Royal hospital at Wolverhampton. Thank goodness that during the next half-hour the Baby decided to come into the world Hannah gave birth to a baby boy at six fifteen that evening. He was a beautiful baby who had a mop of black hair just like his father. Although he was born premature he weighed five pounds twelve ounces. At last thought Hannah now it is all over but her labour pains continued and she asked the nursing sister if every thing was all right.

"What are you complaining about" The sister midwife snapped. "You have had your baby and it is no big deal He certainly took his time deciding to come. Not a large baby at all considering the time that you have been here but if you insist, I will take a look at you. If only to

Shut you up and stop you from moaning". Hannah did not think that she had been moaning she had only asked the sister if everything was all right because she was still having very severe pains in her stomach.

Hannah tried to ignore the Sisters comment and tried to relax. She looked around the delivery room she could hear her new baby crying from a cot at the far end of the room. He certainly sounded healthy enough. Another pain gripped her stomach and she held her breath for a few moments. The Sister noticed and came to see what was wrong.

"My goodness" She exclaimed as she prodded Hannah's stomach. "I do believe that we have another one. "We do have another one here. Oh my Goodness Nurse, Nurse". She called. A young nurse put her head around the door to see what she could be wanted for.

"Nurse I need some help here. Go at once and inform Matron that we have to deliver twins. Twins thought Hannah "Glory be Oh Lordy" Please let them be all right. Staff were hurrying to and fro another cot had to be prepared etc;

Half an hour later Hannah had a baby girl. The little mite had difficulty with breathing and after some time Sister was able to get her to cry. She weighed Four pounds six ounces? They asked what names that Hannah wished them to be called? Apparently it was the policy to give twins names as soon as they were born. Hannah could only think of David for the boy and she asked the two sisters who were now attending to her what were their names. One said Jennifer and the other said Rose so Hannah quickly decided that would be what the little girl was to be called Jennifer Rose By this time George had arrived for visiting and he was delighted that he was the father of twins; he had been completely fed up with ringing the hospital to be told that there was still no news. He stayed with Hannah for about ten minutes in the delivery room and then the nursing sister asked him to leave. Hannah was now quite exhausted and was told that she must rest.

Hannah and her babies were not allowed to go home for four weeks she had to wait until Jennifer gained enough weight and reach the weight of five pounds so that she could no longer be considered a premature baby. The weeks just dragged by so slowly for Hannah and although the Hospital considered that she needed the rest she could not wait to go back home.

George was managing all right at the Cottage. Michael had been taken to Hilda Crosby's, she had no children of her own and she was so glad to be able to look after him. Being as it was her second baby Hannah was expecting to be home with in a few days. Hilda did not have any other job than helping Hannah part time through the summer period. Bernie helped George with the outside work. The tearooms were kept closed

At last Hannah was allowed to take David and Jennifer home. Judith was all ready up at the Cottage on the Saturday afternoon when George came home with his new family she had wanted to give a Hannah a hand with the work and have a look at the twins who she had only seen once at the hospital. She told Hannah that she had bought a knitting machine. She said that she had been very busy using it once she had mastered it. She had knitted little baby cardigans and woolly suits. It was going to be a great help to Hannah with the extra baby clothes and she was really delighted to think that Judith had put her self out to such an extent She would certainly need more baby clothes. Hannah had only prepared her self for one baby and she was going to need quite a few more baby things like cot sheets and blankets which she had left and had kept from when Michael had been a baby.

What a mess George had made in the kitchens He had done no cleaning and he had used the café cups and saucers to save him washing up as he went along He had called at his Dad's and Judith's to get a meal when ever he could. Hilda had also cooked for him. It had not been only food that George had been having with Hilda

Hilda and her Husband Desmond had been allocated one of the new council houses that had been built on the edge of the village These were only being allocated to young couples with or with out children. Judith and Carl had put their names down on the list for one and were hoping to have theirs as soon as they were completed. They were much better designed than the old council houses that were down the village where Terry and Molly lived. The bathrooms were now situated up stairs and the kitchen was much bigger so that it had room for a table and chairs. The front room could be made much more comfortable.

George had been working near the village and had called to see Michael, after having some dinner he did not seem in a hurry to go back to work. "Haven't you got to get back to work" Hilda asked when she saw the clock saying that it was well passed half past one and George had used up his dinner hour.

"No hurry I am well forward with the job down the road. If the gaffer comes round he does not know what time I knocked off". He was sat relaxed in an armchair by the fireside Michael was content to play with his toys of which he had abundance.

Suddenly Hilda started to cry and poured her heart out to George; telling him that she and her husband Des. (Desmond was called Des for short by she and every one in the village) had been trying so hard for at least seven years to have a baby and that they were having no luck at all. They did not know whether it was one or the other who was at fault. It could be both of them and as the doctor had explained there was no way of finding out. He said that they should keep trying and if they had no luck they could always adopt a child.

"Well do you think that I might be of any help? I will have to see what I can do about it" George had teased her

"What do you mean by that remark?" She had asked with surprise. "You would not, would you? She stood up quickly and went into the kitchen dried her eyes on the kitchen towel and started washing the dishes they had used. George followed her

"Well that will depend entirely on you, "He said, standing very close to her as she stood at the kitchen sink with her back towards him. His hand came round to caress her voluptuous breast he pressed him self against her so that she could not move forward or backward. She pushed him gently back and quickly turned to face him. His body was pressed close to her and she could feel him aroused against her. He knew that she was responding just as he had thought that she would. Michael was playing in her front room with a new toy aeroplane that he had bought for him and the other toys he was quite content.

"I think that I could like this, she put her arms around him and pressed her self close to him and he did not back a way they both realised what it was that they wanted.

"Really" She said. He nodded. "Then follow me". As she passed the front room door she said." Michael I am just taking your daddy to look at some work I want doing in the bedroom. You be a good little boy and play with your new toy for a few minutes and Auntie Hilda will give you a sweetie when I come down. You stay there and no peeping or I will not give you a sweetie. She led George into the front bedroom.

The room was nicely furnished light and airy. George went over to the window quite a big one for the size of the room and it looked across the countryside towards the Wrekin. A white and pink candlewick bedspread covered the bed Hilda had really excelled her self with the décor. She had decorated it in white and pink and it looked very romantic. She had tried so hard to please her Des and Hilda had done this for his sake, so that he would not tire of trying to give her the child that she longed for. This is just what I needed George whispered to her as they lay under the bed cover on her double bed. He had already assured Hilda that because both he and her husband Desmond both had dark hair she had nothing to worry about if she did become pregnant so he was not going to bother taking any precautions.

"That is all that I ask for is a child of my own I don't know which one of us it that is at fault but this should help. Desmond hardly has any thing to do with me unless I have a go at him. He is thinking that it is his fault and says that he is tired of trying and of my moaning. I did ask him to have one last try last night because I knew that you were coming to have some dinner with me and Michael today and I was hoping that you would try something like this. I saw the look that you gave me the last time that you called and guessed that you would not need much persuading it must be some time since you were able to enjoy your self like this. You know George that I have never experienced any thing as good as this. Let us hope that you can do what Des can't. It can't be easy for you with Hannah being away as long as she is. Just you relax you do not have to worry about getting me pregnant. This should help to prove if it is Des's or me at fault. Just give me one baby and I will never ask again I can assure you that I would be content.

Des will never know unless you tell him and I can't see you doing that. George no one can know the longing that a woman has for a child of her own it gets worse as you get older. Des would be over the moon if I became pregnant. The Doctor has told us just to keep trying, he said that you never know and he felt sure that it would happen one day. I can't see any harm in wanting to help things along a little this might not work, it could be me that is at fault but there is no harm in us trying so that I can find out. I know that you are fertile and if this does not work there is nothing lost and it can be our little secret".

"Well let us wait and see if this has helped a little". With Hannah having such a bad pregnancy and being retained in hospital for so long George was getting desperate to be sexually full filled again and here was an opportunity and he was making the most of it. They had temporally forgotten about Michael down stairs. He was now coming three and he had got tired of his new toy and waiting for them to come back down stairs. He went to the bottom of the stairs and called." Dad Dad I want my sweet is Auntie Hilda coming".

The two of them got quickly off the bed and George put his trousers and shirt back on and went to the top of the stairs

"Coming Son Dad's coming now, be with you in a minute. Just you wait there I am coming so is Auntie Hilda".

After having a cup of tea with the two of them George lit a cigarette and went out to his van feeling very pleased with himself He decided to go back home he, had done what he considered was enough work for one day. As he drove down the narrow lanes towards the Wrekin a broad smile crossed his face. He thought about the different women that he had been with. Nell, Gwen and now Hilda He did not feel as if he had committed any crime. "What the eye did not see the heart could not grieve for". That was as the saying went. He was pretty sure that Hilda would not let on what she had been up to. She needed Desmond to support her financially Yes he felt pretty safe there. He was just filling in where he was needed and by Hilda's re-action today she had certainly needed him and by what she had said afterwards there was no comparison. Desmond was definitely no match to him. If Hannah did not come home soon there would be no harm in trying this again, just to make sure so to speak.

Bernie told Hannah that he had helped George with all the washing up the night before she was coming home and that it had taken them most of the evening. They had taken the centre burner out of the Aga cooker to clean it and what a mess that they had made. They had left a trail of the red powdered ash from the cooker out through the back door. Both the twins were being bottle fed; this had been decided at the hospital. They had thought that Hannah had no chance of regaining her strength if she were to try and feed twins herself. As soon Judith had left and Hannah had fed the twins they had settled down for a while, she set to and on her hands and knees she scrubbed the kitchen floors so that she could think about opening the shop and the tearoom again. She must make a start again so that they could serve food they were going to need the money. Later in the evening she cut blankets and sheets to cot size. She used her old hand sewing machine to sew all around the edges. Hannah had not prepared for two babies and now there was two to cope with and what a task that it was going to be. There was so much to do. Next day Sunday She asked George to collect Michael from Hilda's She had missed him dreadfully and she wanted him home to meet his new little brother and sister. Hannah was quite surprised when George came back home with out him.

"Where is Michael "Hannah asked as George came into the kitchen on his own.

"Hilda says that she will keep him for another day or two so that you can have a rest and get on your feet a bit."

"George I do not like the sound of this"

"Don't you worry about him he is ever so happy there. It will not hurt to let her have him for another day or two. Give you a chance to cope with that pair" He looked toward the new Silver Cross twin pram that they had bought. Hannah had felt that it was an awful extravagance when they had bought it but she had to have some thing to put the twins in during the daytime George had seen to the buying of it while she had been in hospital. They had Michael's old cot and another second hand one for upstairs.

George had called round to see Michael during the week when Desmond had been at work and see if Hilda would let him come home. Hilda had sobbed her heart out and George had felt so sorry for her he had left saying that he would leave him there until the weekend. He did not dare let on to Hannah that he had been to bed with Hilda and that after the first time they had gone to bed together they had been several more times They had been having quite a little affair going for the last four weeks and that he was terrified that she might tell all if he insisted on taking Michael away from her. Another week passed and George had called again asking Hilda to let him have Michael but she had refused. Hannah was getting very concerned. She did not know it, but so was George he was terrified that because of him they had lost Michael for good unless Hilda became pregnant herself, he could not see her handing Michael back and if he insisted she just might tell all. . Hannah arranged for Judith to come on the Saturday afternoon and keep an eye on the twins and she told George that she wanted taking to see Hilda.

"I want to know what is going on. I thought that you said that you would collect him for me during the week".

"I did not have the time "George lied. He was hoping that Hilda would not throw a sobbing tantrum like the last time that he had called. He had not told Hannah about it. He felt that Hannah would say that he was not strong enough to stand up to Hilda so he had kept quiet.

When Hannah walked the garden path to knock on Hilda's front door she saw Michael playing with Hilda's Husband Des inside their living room, he sounded very happy and excited. Hilda's face dropped when she saw Hannah standing on her doorstep.

"Hilda can I come in for a moment I have come to collect Michael; so that I can take him home". Hilda's face went quite pale. Hannah quickly stepped in to the hallway before Hilda had a chance to close the door.

"Why have you come for him it is just not fair, you have two new babies and I have none. We have tried and tried to have one since we have been married but we have had no luck. I don't think that you can cope with three little ones with all the work that you have to do. Please let him stay with me I promise that I will take great care of him. You will have no need to worry he will be quite safe with me and perhaps one day he could have a little sister or brother. Hilda still had no idea whether it was she or Desmond who was not fertile. Having a few sessions with George would give her the chance to find out. If she did become pregnant she would then know that it had not been her fault. I have looked after him for the month that you have been in hospital He will be quite safe with us. He will won't he Desmond?" She looked at her husband for support He had been listening and had come into the hall but he did not answer.

"I suggest that you make a cup of tea and let's discuss this properly dear. It is a very delicate business. Come into the front room Hannah while Hilda makes the tea".

George had been waiting in the van expecting Hannah to return with Michael very quickly. When she had not his stomach was beginning to churn what was going on in there? Had Hilda told them about his affair with her, He did not think so for Desmond's sake. He got out of the van and moved toward the open front door. He could hear what was being said so he came inside pretending to see what was keeping them. He had heard most of the conversation between the two women and was really worried that there might be an ugly scene. He took no notice of them arguing. He went into the front room he picked Michael up and sat down with him on his knee. .

He had heard Hannah telling Hilda "There is no question of you keeping Michael the law would not allow it unless you were to adopt him. And there is certainly no question of that happening He is our son and I am sure that George agrees with me that no way would we dream of parting with him".

"You were jolly glad for any one to feed him when he was little I did not think that you cared much for him at that time so why do you insist on taking him from me now, I have grown to love him over the last few weeks". Hilda started to cry and went into the kitchen. Her husband Desmond went to do his best to try and console her.

"I am sorry dear but Hannah is quite right they cannot just go giving a little one away just like that. I will promise you that if we still have had no luck having our own baby soon, we will apply through the proper channels to be able to adopt a little one. I just wish that there were some more tests possible to say why you have not come pregnant it has to be one of us that is at fault".

Desmond took the tray of tea from his wife and poured a cup for each one of them. Hannah and George quickly drank the tea and asked Hilda to pack Michael's clothes and toys and said that they would get going as they had left Judith with the twins. Hannah promised Hilda that she could come up the Wrekin as often as she wished to and give her help with all three little ones. What a relief that it was to Hannah to take Michael home. She had wondered why Hilda had held on to him as long as she had. Now she knew why and she could not help feeling quite sorry for the woman.

Hannah as usual was trying to make excuses for Hilda's behaviour.

"Perhaps she would stand a better chance of having one of her own if she were to lose some weight" Hannah said to George as he drove them home "She is certainly quite a buxom lady don't you think"

"Does not hurt to carry a bit of weight; quite cuddly infact" George chuckled."You know what the farmers say when they cannot get their cows in –calf; that it is time to change the bull" He burst out laughing. Hannah could not see what was so funny about that statement so she kept quiet.

Hannah found that she had a full time job just coping with feeding changing and washing. With having two babies, it was an endless task' as one baby settled the other cried. When Hannah took the babies to see her doctor for their monthly check up. Dr Price was very quick to apologise for not allowing her to have a scan when she had asked for one. Hannah did not know what to answer all that she said was

"Doctor it is nature's way of dealing with things, a mother knows when things are not going very well. "I think that is why I had such a miserable time carrying them".

It was a very cold wet spring Hannah did not realise that she was well and truly over working and consequently caught a bad cold which unfortunately she passed on to baby Jennifer who after a few days showed no sign of getting over it. Infact in Hannah's opinion she was getting worse.

On the Saturday morning at 7-30 she could not get her to feed at all and she seemed to be running a temperature. Hannah knew instinctively that some thing was really wrong and that she should see a Doctor. She asked George what she should do.

"George I think that we should pop Jennifer to the surgery I don't like the look of her".

"I have not got time to take you to Wellinton this morning. I have mixed a batch of cement I want to render that wall in the bedroom today. Ring the Doctor and ask he to come out and then he will tell you what to do and we can see what he has to say". He went out side and got on with mixing the concrete. He had borrowed some ones concrete mixer and wanted to make the most use of it as possible. Hannah did as George had suggested. She had to wait until a quarter to nine before she was able to get a reply to enable her to speak to the receptionist at the surgery to see if a Doctor could come out to see Jennifer. The receptionist told Hannah that she considered that it was unnecessary for a Doctor to come out as it sounded to her that the baby only had a cold.

"But I think that she is getting very poorly" Hannah protested.

"In that case why can't you bring the baby in to see the Doctor and if you do bring her in, you know that you would have to wait a considerable long time. Not exactly the right place to bring a tiny baby. I suggest that you let the District Nurse have a look at her and then she can decide if a Doctor should be needed or not" Damn thought Hannah I am getting no where. She put down the receiver No one will listen what is the matter with every one. Where the plaster had perished on bedroom walls over the years George started rendering and making good, so that they would be able to use the room later on. He filled one bucket after another with the mixed wet concrete and went through the kitchen to go up stairs. Hannah was really annoyed with him she thought that it was a pity that he could not stop what he was doing for the time being and take her and Jennifer to the surgery. He was making such a mess as he was going to and fro. If only he would close the doors as he was going through them. She was trying to keep the kitchen as warm as she could and it was practically impossible. She was trying to cope with a load of washing in the back and was a bit fed up with having to run and close the doors after he had gone through them,

Being Saturday it was two o'clock before Hannah was able to contact the District Nurse. She was very pleasant and said that she would come as soon as she could but it would be getting on for four O'clock before she was able to see Jennifer and by this time Jennifer's breathing was really deteriorating, she had become very poorly.

Nurse said that she was very concerned for her and said that she would telephone for a Doctor to come as quickly as possible, which she did there and then, and she explained to Hannah that she did not have the authority to send her to hospital. Although she felt that was where the baby needed to be. She left telling Hannah to keep the place as warm as possible.

Some flaming hope Hannah said to her self with George pathering backwards and forwards through out the day.

Hannah and George waited and waited Hannah put Michael and David to bed and still no sign of the Doctor she was getting very worried George started telephoning but was told that the doctor was on his way. He did eventually arrive at ten that night and took one look at Jennifer and said that she must be taken to Hospital immediately as she was very poorly indeed. Hannah could not believe her ears. This was a bit too much.

Dr Spencer said "I will take you to the bottom of the hill and you can meet the ambulance car there he will take you to Monkmoor Hospital. He had finished using the telephone. Thank goodness you have the telephone here it is such a help. It was quite late when I received the message to come out and I have been driving all around the Wrekin looking for you. No one told me that I had to come up here. This baby should have been sent into hospital hours ago".

"What are we going to do about Michael and David"? Hannah asked George.

"You go to the hospital I will stay and be here for them if they wake up".

Hannah left with Jennifer wrapped up in blankets. Dr Spencer drove her and baby Jennifer to the bottom of the hill. He was so kind He had quickly written a note for Hannah to take with her.

"As quickly as you can" he told the driver. Take them to the children's hospital at Monkmoor. When Hannah arrived at the hospital, a nurse was waiting to take Jennifer from her and Hannah followed quickly into the ward where she found the nursing sister to be so very nice.

"There you are "Sister remarked. "What have we here" She read the note that Hannah had passed to her. She quickly instructed for an oxygenated tent cot for Jennifer to be put in. She went on to explain to Hannah that Jennifer was very poorly and there was little hope for her.

"We will do all we can but it is very doubtful if we can save her. I want you go home and telephone in the morning. "If she gets through the next few hours there might be a slight chance that she might make it. Try and get some sleep you look worn out"

It was now two o'clock in the morning and Hannah was wondering how on earth she was going to get back home. She went out of the hospital and there was the car that had brought her. The driver said that he had to wait to see if he had to take her to another hospital and, as he did not have to. He offered to take her back home if she said nothing as he was still on call. Not far out of my way I have to return to Wellington in any case Hop in I can see things are not very good are they.

Hannah told him what sister had said and he was very sympathetic. What is your local church I will give them a ring in the morning when I finish my shift and ask them to pray for the little one"

"That is very kind of you. Thank you so much I think that I could do with some one saying a few prayers for us. Nothing has gone right since before the two of them were born".

As Hannah walked up the hill in the early hours of the morning she decided that she would learn to drive the van and pass her driving test Judith had passed her test so Hannah could see no reason why she could not do the same. She thought that it was time she became more independent. If only she could have driven she could have taken Jennifer to the surgery her self and that she would have been able to have some medication much sooner. It was a pity that George was not prepared to put him self-out for a couple of hours.

She went to bed but could not sleep she just lay wide awake praying that she would not lose Jennifer the Sister had given her such little hope.

She had not realised exactly how tired that she was when she eventually crept into bed along side George trying not to disturb him from his deep sleep. He had been exhausted from mixing concrete and carrying it up stairs to render the bedroom wall. Hannah's mind was in turmoil. She had not bothered with the Church since she had married and when she had Michael christened. She had always been too busy. She needed comfort now all that she could do was silently pray to her self that her baby would get better and no matter what she prayed that her little girl was going to be given a chance.

The news that one of the twins was so poorly quickly went around the village of Wrockwardine like clockwork. The parish Vicar rang Hannah offering help and hope and that they had said prayers for the baby in church that day.

By Monday morning Jennifer was still alive and had slightly responded to treatment but they could not say much more at this stage. By the Following Wednesday Hannah managed to get Hilda to come to take care of every thing while she went to see her for her self. When she got to the hospital she found that they had put her in a cot along side another little baby girl,

"Perhaps the one will give some willpower the other to hold on," Sister said

Hannah noticed that the staff had tied a small fluffy pink toy rabbit to the cot She thought how sweet that was of them. Jennifer was improving and responding to her treatment Hannah went home a much happier person.

Later that day when George came home from work, Hannah told George that she intended to learn to drive the van and try and pass her driving test."

"I don't think that I would bother if I were you. I have been thinking about buying a little scooter for you to get around on"

"A scooter George. That would be of little use to me, how I could put shopping on that and cope with twins and another thing what about the weather. I would be soaked through Can you imagine it. If I had not got wet through and caught such a bad cold Jennifer would not be as poorly as she is. And another thing when she comes out of hospital I can hardly take all three of them around on a scooter".

"Alright I will let you have a go at driving the van and see how you get on".

"Well there is a school of motoring started up Judith was telling me all about it she has had driving lessons and now that she has passed she can drive their Morris minor".

"Driving lessons do you think that we are made of money. It is costing enough you going to that hospital. No, I will teach you to drive as soon as I can get some spare time".

"Oh dear "thought Hannah she had not thought about the cost of going to Monkmoor to see Jennifer not that she had been there very often. But what was she supposed to do leave her there and not go to see her. George had not bothered to take a day off from work. He had not been to see his daughter at all and neither of them could go on a Saturday or Sunday. Hannah had the cakes to make for the tearooms and George had the farming side to see to. Sunday they needed to take as much money as they could with the shop and the tearooms.

Jennifer had been really poorly for about a week and then she suddenly started to show an improvement. Hannah visited her when ever she could during the week Hilda came and took care of things if she could It was four more weeks before she was allowed to come home.

George in the meantime was getting rather fed up with all the trouble the twins were causing. He felt that Hannah was pushing himself and Michael who was now three to one side. She was so busy running here, there and every where he was wondering if they were ever going to settle down as a family again.

On the Saturday afternoon Judith came to look after the other two Michael and David George took Hannah to the hospital to collect her. Hannah now had her hands full good and proper Both David and Jennifer were making good progress but they still needed a lot of care and attention. Hannah just did not know how she was going to cope with every thing that needed to be done. George did his best, but he found that it was too much of a struggle trying to help out with

The night feeds and get up and go to work next morning so consequently all the work was left for Hannah to do.

Hannah quickly arranged for the twins to be christened. She telephoned and asked the vicar of Wrockwardine church if that would be acceptable to have Jennifer and David Christened at Wrockwardine church although they officially belonging to the parish of Little Wenlock. Hannah asked Brenda who was now married to Bill if she would be Godmother to Jennifer along with Hannah's sister Mary. Bill and Mary's husband Graham and Judith's husband Carl were Godfathers.

Hannah closed the big tearoom for the Sunday afternoon and they had a little party in there afterwards. Dorothy and Fred also walked across to share in the meal.

After they had all gone home Hannah was completely exhausted and went to bed full of relief that the babies were now Christened and that they could once again get on with their lives. Hilda stopped coming to help out and Hannah put it down to her having to give Michael back. If Hannah had only known that Hilda had missed her very next period and hoping against hope that she was now pregnant. She did not want to take any risk by climbing up the Wrekin

Her sister Emily came at week ends in her place. Emily was no more then five foot tall and she was so thin. George gave her the job of looking after the swings and then Hannah had thought that she was far too petite to cope with that job so she found her some work looking after the shop and her brother Donald. Don as he preferred to be called took her place. Emily came inside and she was so quick and good with adding up money that Hannah let her look after the shop.

It was two months after Hannah had come home with the twins that Emily said that her sister Hilda was not feeling too well and she thought that it would be best if Hannah did not rely on her to come and give a hand during the following summer months

"Do you think that she could be pregnant? I hope so. They have been trying for years. I will be an Auntie Won't that be great, just think Auntie Emily. She smiled as she went to serve a customer at the shop.

"George "Said Hannah that evening Keep it to ourselves for the time being but Emily has told me that Hilda is not too well and will not be coming to help us again. She is hoping that she is pregnant so that she can be an Auntie. She says that she is pretty sure that is what is wrong with her. That will be wonderful for Hilda I am so pleased for her At last now that she is to have her wish I am sure that she will feel much better about having to give Michael back to us". George smiled and said, "That is good news I am sure Des will be so pleased if only to shut her up about wanting one".

As the weeks went by Hannah was getting to the stage when she found that she just could not cope with all that there was to do. Feeding changing washing it just went on and on there was simply not enough hours in the day and she was finding that it was impossible to cope. Hilda confirmed that at last she was pregnant so she no longer came to give Hannah a hand. She said that now that she was pregnant and as they had waited for so long for a baby she was not going to take any risks of losing the baby and she considered that climbing up the Wrekin would not do her or a baby any good at all.

"I'm thrilled to bits for her. At last she can know what it is like to have a baby of her own" Hannah said to George when Molly told her the news. And they pretended that this was the first time that they had heard that Hilda was definitely expecting.

"That's good news" Was all George could say. He did not let on what a relief that it would be for him that she no longer came to give Hannah a hand. He was dreading the possibility of Hilda letting anything slip out. But thank goodness she was as clever as George and convinced Desmond that he alone could only be the father and they were both so delighted. Neither Desmond nor Hannah had any reason to think otherwise.

Hannah was still finding that it was almost impossible to cope with everything

"What would you say if I were to advertise for a girl to live in and help with the feeding of the twins and perhaps she would be able to give me a hand with every thing else, like looking after the shop for me during the week days.

"Oh I don't know about that idea. I am not too keen to have strangers living in. The house will never be the same we will never be on our own. Just let's think about it for a while. I will give you a hand at nights again and see if that helps

"You sound just like my Mother did when she was told that she was to have the evacuees. OK I will give it another try and see if we can work something out between us. But as you know as one baby stops crying the other one starts and Jennifer is such a problem at taking her feeds. She will only take two ounces at a time so she needs a lot more attention."

One Saturday morning George had wanted some wood from the timber yard and he decided to fetch it with the tractor and trailer. He was driving the tractor down the hill and had not realised that he was so tired and he dozed off. It really scared him when he realised what he had done. He had fallen asleep and had almost driven over the side .If it had not been for the front wheel catching a prominent tree root and jerking the steering wheel causing him to wake up he would have driven completely off the track and crashed over the side. This had really frightened and worried him. He decided that he needed to have a proper night's sleep. He was now prepared to consider Hannah's suggestion about having more help and that it would be as well to advertise for some one. He felt that he would have given in to any thing just to get good nights sleep. He could not imagine how Hannah was coping with it all she seemed to be almost dead on her feet. Since bringing the twin's home every thing seemed to have become such a nightmare.

"Hannah" George said one morning when he was getting ready to go to work. Hannah was busy dressing the twins before Michael came down for some breakfast.

"I am fed up with working at our place; it seems to me that is getting too many chiefs and not enough Indians. I have had enough. Since the old man has retired and the Sons have taken over, one tells you to do one thing and another tells you to do something else. I am thinking of leaving and working for myself. I could make just as much money in a week as I am now. In fact I would probably make much more. There is plenty of work about that people need doing". George went on desperately trying to convince Hannah that he was doing the right thing. "Our bosses don't think that we know what they are charging for work to be done but we do and I reckon that I could charge the same and make a lot more money for our selves."

"I don't know" replied Hannah "Would it not be best to wait and see what sort of summer that we have before you do any thing that you might regret?"

"No I have made up my mind I am giving my notice in this week. I have been thinking that I could get that young lad, Hilda's brother Donald to help me. He could come and work for me during the week He could do a bit of fetching and carrying for me. He would not want paying such a lot and I am sure that at the same time I could train him to be a carpenter. He will be glad of the job when he leaves school in the summer not that he goes very often now. If I were to offer him a job now I think that the school would let him leave at Easter. He need not come up here every day he can cycle and meet me in town where ever that I happen to be working".

"I see that you have made up your mind. I am not going to try and persuade you not to work for your self. I am sure if things don't work out you will be able to get another job with some one else."

"Thanks for the vote of confidence. You are just like your Mother at times. You have not got much faith in me at all have you? Neville Tranter has left and he is doing well for him self they now have a television and other things that they could not afford before he left our firm"

"Now George don't take on so, it is just that I am so tired with not having a proper nights sleep. I was trying to give you re-assurance that I would not be too worried if you did not succeed with working for your self. I have got to admit having the twins it will be much nicer if you can work to your own time and not have to be at work for eight every morning"

"Well I can certainly say that since you have had the twins you have not been much help to me or any one else. It seems to have taken you all your time running to and fro here and there. I think that you should look after Michael a bit more and give him a bit more attention. Had his nose pushed out good and proper? As for needing me in bed you seem to have forgotten that I exist."

Hannah was quite taken aback by George's remarks.

"Really George Well I have noticed that you have not done much hospital visiting Jennifer is still having to go for check ups with her eyes they gave her so much oxygen she has squints in both her eyes or have you not noticed. And another thing what you expect of me in bed I really don't know. You know very well that when I went for my post natal check up the Gynaecologist at the hospital strongly advised that we have no more children because of my blood group and I have no desire to bring a malformed child or any blue babies into the world. I think that I have enough to do looking after these three, plus every thing else that there is to be done and what' s more I have decided that I need some help before I kill myself with work. I think that I already have one foot in my grave as it is; I am going ahead and advertising for some help whether you like it or not".

George did not answer; He had made his point of view clear so he quickly went out side and on his way to work. He intended giving up his job whether Hannah liked it or not. He would not have to get another lad to look after the swing boats Don as they called Donald could still come at weekends. Hannah did advertise for a girl to come and live in and she employed a girl from Shawbury called Constance James. She said to call her Connie for short. She was not exactly what Hannah had in mind but the only other two applicants seemed to be much worse. Connie was from a large family and she seemed as if she was desperate to get away from home. She certainly knew how to cope with babies so that was quite a relief for Hannah. Connie was of average height and she had her ginger coloured hair cut quite short. She was not a very attractive girl, in fact Hannah felt quite sorry for the girl she certainly did not to seem to have enjoyed much life so far at all. Hannah gave her all day Thursdays off and let her borrow her bike to get to Wellington so that she could catch the bus to Shawbury. It was such a relief to have another pair of hands to help with the feeding and changing of the twins. There did not seem to be enough hours in the day.

Hannah's worst days were when she had to take both babies to the out patients department at Shrewsbury. She had to set out early leaving Michael with Connie walk down the hill with the twin pram and walk to the station at Wellington. There was no point in taking two babies out of their pram so Hannah was allowed to travel in the goods van. Once in Shrewsbury she would push the pram across the town to the hospital and after waiting about for hours to see the paediatrician Hannah had prepared feeding bottles of baby milk before leaving home a junior nurse would help. She would see to the warming of the bottles and help by feeding one of them. Hannah would then make the return journey home. She would telephone home as she was leaving and if George was at home he would meet her at the bottom of the hill with the tractor and trailer. They would lift the pram on to it and ride up the hill. Little did Hannah know that she would be doing this for the next twelve months?

Hilda Crosby gave birth to a baby girl and every one was so thrilled for her especially Desmond they both idolised their new baby. When Hannah remarked that she was so pleased for Hilda George was reluctant to comment He just said, "It goes to show what they can do if they keep trying. Hilda did not come to give Hannah any help again.

George gave in his notice and soon he had plenty of work coming in and it seemed that it was the best thing that he could have done. He could now take some time off if and when Hannah needed help. He was popular with his customers who were very pleased with his work. Hilda's brother Don was a good working lad and George got on with him very well unless there were windows or such that had to be hand made, the lad would meet George wherever he happened to be working in town. Hannah only saw him at weekends when he came to look after the swing boats. Don was glad to work for George and earn some money for him self. . He enjoyed the good Sunday dinners that Hannah gave him and also some thing to eat at other times when he was at the Cottage. He especially enjoyed the home made cakes. Hannah assumed that he did not get many of these at home. His mother had given birth to thirteen children and as a result she now suffered very poor health. Bobby still came to help when he could but he now looked after the shop and Emily would help with serving teas and helping out generally.

Judith and Carl very rarely came to the cottage Judith had a little boy of her own to take care of. Some times when Hannah had to go to Shrewsbury on a Thursday she would leave the two boys with her until she came back and she would really appreciate the cup of tea that was offered before making the journey home.

Thomas came home from the army and decided that he would not sign on again. Mr Cartwright told him that he could have his old job back if he wanted so he took them up on their offer he would not have considered it if George had still been working for them. He often came to the cottage and he could see that Hannah was completely engrossed with George and the children. He was amazed at the amount of work that she had to cope with so he gave a hand at weekends with any general repairs and odd jobs. He helped Hannah with the painting of the small tearoom they painted it a pale blue colour and when finished it looked so clean and nice. He made him self quite useful and he enjoyed being back working up there. He was focusing his attention on Emily. He watched her as she worked and was quite impressed he liked what he saw. It did not worry him in the slightest that she was one of the thirteen children belonging to the family who lived opposite him in the village. He did not think that his Dad or Judith would approve if he started dating a fifteen-year-old. So he decided that he could wait until she had left school and then he would see how the land lay. He could see no harm in them cycling home together. Molly certainly took to him and he grew very fond of her. They got on like a house on fire and this was very re-assuring for Terry He would have hated any animosity between them but he need not have worried.

George did not see much of Simon he had a new girl friend they some times came to the cottage on a Sunday afternoon but it was not very often. He eventually marries but neither George nor Hannah was invited. That said it all as far as Hannah was concerned.

Their friend Bill more or less lost touch with them Bill started his own building firm, which went from strength to strength. He had married Brenda and she had one son and had no more babies. She considered herself quite a lady and chose her friends with great care and George and Hannah were not amongst them. George had dealings with Bill through his work but Brenda was not prepared to socialise with them Hannah called at their home to have a chat with Brenda just about the usual girlie things but Brenda did not answer her knock at the door. As Hannah walked to get back into the van. She saw Brenda standing at the bedroom window watching her. Consequently Hannah got the message and she did not call again and so they lost touch.

William had left boarding school and now worked on the farm with his father, with the knowledge that one day it would all be his. When Old Mr Bromley had died his son had given Fred and Dorothy first refusal of the farm and they had jumped at the chance William was really pleased that it had been offered to them.

Mary had married and was now rearing her own family she had married a well educated man who was a surveyor and worked for the Government He had been working in Shropshire which had enabled him to enjoy his hobby of Geology. He had put a tent in Fred's top field and had been working on the rock formation that formed the Wrekin. He had met Mary with going to the Farmhouse to buy milk and eggs. It was a very short courtship and they had married and taken a small holding with some ground at Lawley Bank. Her leaving the farm had been a dreadful loss to Fred he had become to rely on her so much and when she became twenty-eight he and Dorothy had not visualised that a young man would come and sweep her off her feet. For a while they were quite distraught but in the end they had reluctantly stopped grumbling about her leaving. She had a lovely white wedding and all the rest of the family were so pleased for her.

The twins began to grow and develop very nicely. Jennifer was becoming a little beauty she had dark auburn hair that was naturally curly and a ready smile for every one

Hannah had taken her to the Eye Ear and throat Hospital to see an eye specialist. Who assured Hannah that he would be able to operate when she was old enough and repair most of the damage that had been done to her eyes? Hannah was so relieved with this news. At last there seemed to be help coming from all sides. David's dark hair was almost black just like his father but he differed from Michael and Jennifer He had blue eyes. Both were growing into a sturdy little boys Hannah was so proud of them.

In 1960 as the spring came into summer the weather was very wet and what a miserable season that it turned out to be.

Trade for Hannah was very disappointing . Connie James was an absolute Godsend she proved quite capable at helping with the twins and looking after the shop. But after two years she proved to be untrustworthy with the handling of money. Hannah set a trap and Connie fell for it and it proved that she was helping herself and for how long that it had been going on Hannah had no idea. Hannah was so disappointed she had grown quite fond of the girl and had appreciated her help. Reluctantly she had to ask her to leave.

When Hannah was busy Sandra came across to give a hand with the children Hannah was not too worried if it gave the girl a chance to get away from the work at the farm As long as their Mother did not ring up complaining Hannah did not mind. Sandra was quite good with the twins and it was quite a help to Hannah. She always paid her for coming and it meant that Sandra had a bit of pocket money for herself. She would stay and have some tea and then run back down the fields in time for the feeding of the calves and seeing to the poultry for her mother. She always took with her some cakes if there were any left over and if not Hannah always gave her some crisps and chocolate, she was developing into a very attractive young girl. Perhaps not in her face her eyesight was still not good and she squinted badly. She was waiting to have surgery to improve her eyesight. The rest of her body was developing at an alarming rate. She had the figure of an eighteen-year-old not a thirteen year old. George often gave her a lift to school when he passed her on the road it was no trouble to him He would stop the van and put her bike in the back. She did not like going to school at all this and not having to cycle all the way to the secondary modern school suited her a great deal.

After a further very wet Summer Hannah could see that their finances were not good George was also getting a bit fed up with living on the hill He was doing exceedingly well with his work but maintained that if they were connected to the mains electricity there was so much more that he could do and things would be a lot easier for him. He did not bother with the ground much Hannah's father put some young stock on it to keep the grass down, He did not let on how ever that one of the first things that he would buy would be a television set. They often went over to see his friend Neville Tranter and his wife for a bit of supper; they would stay and watch a film it would mean that they arrived back late up the Wrekin. This did not seem to bother George one little bit he loved watching their telly as the television was now called. Hannah we are going to get off this hill and find somewhere where we can be on the mains for electricity. Then we can have our own television set you know the kids could learn so much more if we had one. Hannah had to agree she was getting a bit fed up with the amount of work that there was to do and as George had said it would be good to have a proper electricity supply. Time and time again when George, Hannah and their little family had been out to see Neville and his family, they would stay and watch the telly returning home late in the evening. Often when they reached the bit of the track by the old bakeries they saw all four swing boats swinging away as high as they could go and there was no one sat in them. All four would be swinging backwards and forward at exactly the same time. This was a bit awe inspiring because no matter how George and Hannah. Donald and Bobby and others tried to do this they had no success. They would start all four boats at the same time but to no avail one or the other swung more slowly and no matter how they tried they were not successful. They found that it was completely impossible. George had built two new boats, which weighed considerably heavier than the two old ones. The mystery was never explained so it was blamed on Jimmy the ghost they only wished that Jimmy could have told them how he had accomplished it.

Michael started school at the Wrockwardine village school. George would take him down the hill in the van to meet the school bus in the mornings but he had to walk back up the hill in the afternoon after school. He had grown into quite an intelligent little boy Hannah was so proud of him she was a bit concerned about his starting school it was arranged that he would go to Wrockwardine School as the previous children that had lived on the Wrekin had done. She was a bit worried about him having to walk back up the hill in the afternoons but George reassured her that he would be perfectly all right and that she could collect him with the tractor during the winter months when there were not many customers about._

It was arranged that Michael could start after the Easter holidays George would take him in the mornings to the bottom of the hill and wait with him for the school bus to come and collect him. Unknown to Hannah George had also arranged with Sandra to meet him there and then he would take her to school.

Sandra came across to the Cottage more and more often she was becoming a bit of a pain. She was now 14 years old. It was obvious that she was not going to be slim like the rest of her sisters. She was so pleased when George had suggested that if she could be at the Forest Glen when Michael caught the school bus that he would take her the rest of the way to school. He told her that it if she did it would be of no trouble to him. He told her that he was usually working some where in town. Sandra was thrilled with the idea and made sure that she was there on time.

George told Hannah about her being there because he knew if he did not Michael could say that he had seen his Auntie Sandra waiting for them He told Hannah what a little schemer that she was.

"The saucy madam;" Hannah had answered when George had told about her being there and waiting for him that one particular morning.

"You know that girl is growing into quite a stunner. I'll bet the lads will soon be looking her way I would not wonder; she does not seem to take after any of you others. You are all as thin as lathes".

"It's all the work that we do; we have no time to put on weight".

What Hannah was not aware that George had made the arrangements to pick Sandra up when ever he could? Sandra was relishing all the attention that he bestowed on her. He did not tell Hannah that it was most mornings that he gave her a lift. Hannah had enough to do coping with the café and the twins who got into as much mischief as they could and she had to keep a constant eye on them. When George did casually say that he had given her a lift |Hannah did not see any harm in it. It was no bother to her if George was able to give Sandra a lift to school if he happened to see her on his way to work. It was the winter months, which were often wet and cold first thing in the mornings. She smiled and said to her self. The crafty little madam I'll bet she makes sure that she is past the Glen by the time George goes down the hill to drop Michael off .She knows what time that he has to drop him off for the school bus. That little madam could wrap practically any one around her little finger just like she has done with her mother and dad and she has been doing it for years.

After Christmas George and Hannah decided to look for somewhere else to live, and to see what could be found. It was a great relief to Hannah when they found an old Cottage, which was for sale. It was down a country lane on the Little Wenlock side of the hill, George convinced Hannah that it had great potential the fact that it had no electricity or running water; he soon convinced Hannah that those problems could easily be resolved. We could build on the side of it and it would need the roof lifting about four-foot and I can see how we can solve the water problem. I have been looking at the well next door the water is not that far down; we could sink our own well. "

"Dig a well" Hannah exclaimed she thought what a daft suggestion that was. How far down would you have to dig?"

"25 to 30 feet I reckon"

"And who is going to do the digging".

"Oh we will be all right My Dad will give us a hand and there are plenty of lads that I can get to help me". George knew the owner of the cottage. Miss Hinge a spinster who lived in a big house in the village and she also owned several properties, which she had inherited from her late father. She had taken to George, with his good looks and flair for talking to woman, she always asked George to do any repairs that she needed to have done to her properties, and she had confided in him that she had been thinking of selling the cottage when he had asked about it. It had stood empty for some time and was no use to any one as it was. She could not re-let it unless she brought it up to standard specifications required by the council and as she was a spinster living on her own She only had her dog for company, she could not be bothered with it. George was full of enthusiasm and carried Hannah along with him. There was a very large garden and except for an identical cottage also owned by Miss Hinge next to them sharing their boundary, a farm on the other side, there were no other close neighbours. The woods that surrounded the bottom of the Wrekin were on the opposite side of the road.

George convinced Hannah that this would mean so much more to them and that they would be stupid not to go for it. He gave the Estate the required Notice to leave the Cottage and move off the Wrekin. They had one year to get the little Cottage ready for habitation. The asking price was three hundred and fifty pounds. First they must apply for the electricity to be installed and as soon as this was done the men; Terry Bobby and Don started to dig a water well Carl gave a hand when he could they had great fun. When Hannah had a proper look inside the cottage she just thought to her self. God what do we do with this. It only had one living room downstairs a larder of sorts and a tumbling down wash house. Upstairs were two bedrooms, one was quite a good size the other was part of the landing to the stairway. The access to these bedrooms was from winding stairs out of the living room. The windows were very small ones each one had been fitted in the gable end of the roof so that the rooms were dark and dismal. Looking towards the South and West was a wonderful view of the seven valley; the hills of Church Stretton and of Wales were in the background it was a beautiful view Hannah was beginning to see what the advantages that it could be and she could also visualise what it was that George could see. They would be living along side a tarmac road they would have electricity and that would certainly be very beneficial and make life be a lot easier. They could buy electrical gadgets as they could afford them the first priority as far as Hannah was concerned would be a washing machine but George was more interested in buying a television. The one thing that she did not like was the old fashioned out door lavatory. But George reassured her that they would only have to put up with it for short while.

"If we buy it and call it Woodside," Suggested Hannah.

Hannah decided that she must pass her driving test she did not pass at the first attempt. She had driven across an unmarked crossroads with out giving way and that had caused her to fail the test. Hannah had not been on those roads before and had no idea where she was being taken. Driving schools were just starting up There was one man in Wellington who had started a school of motoring.

Hannah suggested to George that she has a couple of lessons "Having lessons is a complete waste of time and money" George pointed out to Hannah. "You can drive better than most you are driving up and down the hill if you can do that I can't see any reason why you should not pass a simple driving test."

"That's all very well" Judith commented when Hannah told her about failing the test and what George's remarks had been.

"It was because that I had lessons that I passed first time. Any one can drive in the country but it is different driving in the town and you have not driven in the town before. Take my advice and say nothing to George and have a couple of lessons. And I am sure that the instructor will put you wise to such things as unmarked cross roads".

It took all Hannah's courage to oppose George He liked to think that he was boss and only his opinions should be considered, she took Judith's advice had a couple of lessons and passed the test. George passed no comment. This certainly made life a lot easier for her self and for the children, she only had one misgiving and that was why on earth she had not done this years before. She found that she had no fears what so ever of driving on the roads and she certainly enjoyed her new-found freedom. She would use the van and George could arrange his work to suit or use the scooter that he had intended for her to use.

George, Terry and any one else who would give a hand started digging the well. He would be there at the little cottage on Saturdays and Sundays

If George were busy working in Wellinton during the week Sandra knew that George would not only take her to school he would also give her a lift back home.

On some occasions she would let the air out of one of the tyres of her bike and would pretend that she had ridden over a thorn and punctured it. George would show such concern for her and offer to repair the tyre but she would refuse his offer, and say that she could put it right when she got home. He often guessed that it was just a ploy of Sandra's to save cycling home. George did not work so late in the winter evenings and if Sandra turned up where he was working he knew that she wanted a lift, He would just say. "Won't hurt for me to knock off a bit earlier, "Her face would light up with a big smile emphasising her blue eyes Her mother had noticed that George's van had often dropped Sandra off at the farm gate and when she had said something about it to Sandra asking how was it that George had gone out of his way to bring her home? Sandra had thrown a right paddy asking if there was any harm in her having a lift in the cold weather. She pointed out that it did enable her to be back a little earlier to help with the work and after all he was her brother in law so they knew that she was quite safe and who she was with. She dare not say that she had a secret crush on George infact she dared not tell any one especially George he might not like it and would stop picking her up when he saw her on the road. There were several lads at school who had offered her dates. Sandra had let one or two walk her home and they had stopped on the way up the Ercall and had kissed and sort of messed about a bit but they did nothing for her and she had dismissed them. They seemed such silly boys compared to George he was a man and there was something about him that gave her tingles all down her spine. But this was her secret and to be noticed by him was only something that she could dream about He was Hannah's husband and she knew that if he did notice that she had a crush on him there was nothing that he could do about it. She had to try her best to dismiss him from her mind but she was finding it so difficult.

Sandra was the only help and company that her mother had now that the rest of the girls had left home, her mother would not cross her if she could help it. She needed Sandra's help around the house. Dorothy was now getting older she also needed help with feeding the poultry and the calves.

They no longer had to pluck the chickens every week as they had done in the past the rearing of poultry was taking some dramatic changes now all the poultry was kept in deep litter sheds and the eggs were packed for distribution to the egg packing stations .Vans would come and collect the older birds when it was considered time for them to replaced by younger ones. They were taken a way to a factory to be slaughtered and processed and sold into the food chain.

It was Monday morning Hannah had been busy doing the weekly wash of tablecloths tea clothes Etc; she had washed and fed the twins who were now asleep in the pram. When Hannah had first brought the twin's home she would put the pram out under the front porch for them to sleep and have the advantage of the fresh air. The trouble was that women who patronised the café could not resist having a look in the pram and often was the time that when Hannah took them back in for their feeds their faces had traces of lipstick on them. It was evident that it could be dangerous if the pram net was not secured safely on the pram again. A wasp or bee could easily get into the pram and sting them. Consequently Hannah could not put them out on the front porch. She could not put the pram around the back because of the smell of the toilets. In the end she decided to put them in their little sitting room which she considered was the only safe place for them. She looked in to see if they were all right and she stopped for a cup of coffee and noticed that it was almost eleven o'clock and she suddenly became aware that Michael had not come down for his breakfast. She had been so absorbed in her work that she had not noticed the time. She quickly ran up stairs to wake him up. His staying so late in bed was so unusual. As a rule he was awake just after George had gone to work.

"The young monkey ", she said to her self as she went up the stairs I must put him to bed earlier if this is the case Poor lad he must have been tired out. Michael slept in the next room to Hannah and the door was always left open. She was surprised to find that it was closed Perhaps George had closed it so as not to wake him. Hannah pushed the door open and saw that Michael was still fast asleep. Then reality faced her the room was full of gas She looked up at the light fitting and the saw that gas had been turned on but the mantle had not been lit She quickly turned off the gas and grabbed Michael from his bed and carried him down stairs. She had thought that he was dead. Michael was very reluctant to wake. Hannah was really frightened why she had not realised that he had not come down for his breakfast. She cradled him in her arms gently massaging his little body and talking to him. Begging and pleading for him to wake up Relief flooded through her when he opened his eyes and spoke. She held him close for a few more minutes mostly from sheer relief. After having a warm drink Michael seemed none the worse for the ordeal. The whole episode had frightened Hannah so much that she did not let him out of her sight for the rest of the day in case the gas had adverse effects. If so the possibility was that he could be sick, in which case she must telephone for George to come home to take him to see a Doctor. It was so difficult now that they had the twins there had to be one or the other at home all the time. If George was not at home Hannah must be there for them.

When Hannah told George of what had happened he swore that the bedroom door had been left open and that he had not closed it before going to work. Hannah was convinced that she had not closed it and that it had been open the last time that she had been upstairs and as for the gas being turned on neither of them could explain how that had happened. There had been no need for the light to be lit Hannah could not dismiss it from her mind. She was continually checking each room in case it happened again.

It was some time later in the year that Hannah thought she heard Michael out of bed "That's Michael running about up stairs," Hannah said to George when they had settled down for an hour before going to bed. I'll go said George and see what he is up to. Hannah carried on with the knitting of a pullover for George.

"It must be your imagination "George came back down and was quite cross for having gone up stairs for nothing. "Michael is fast asleep and so are the twins". Hannah said no more she would take note if this happened again and sure enough she swore that Michael was out of bed but when she went up to see. He was in his bed fast asleep. It's that dammed ghost again she said to her self. I will call him Jimmy who ever he is. This happened several times and it was always the same when Hannah went up stairs. Michael was fast asleep. Jimmy was blamed for all sorts of things if any thing was mislaid and could not be found it was always blamed on Jimmy.

"You don't think that it could have been the ghost because he does not like us using the room. I am moving Michael out of there tonight he is not going to sleep in that room again.

"Don't be so daft "George was getting quite angry" How on earth could a ghost turn a light on. When he inspected the fitting there was nothing what so-ever wrong with it and the mystery was how on earth could a ghost have the strength to pull the light on? It was not that easy. You are letting your imagination run away with you". George repeatedly told Hannah

"Well you try explaining it will you, it practically frightened the life out of me I thought that Michael was dead. Just you check the fitting and see if there is a fault with it before the lot of us are gassed."

George did check the light fitting but could find nothing wrong with it. It remained a complete mystery. It was a couple of months later that one of the glass light fittings in the tearoom fell to the floor and smashed. George dismissed it saying that the fittings must have deteriorated and come loose. Hannah had a careful look at the fittings and there was nothing wrong with them. "Jimmy again" she said to herself."I'll give him Jimmy if I only knew what was going on". Hannah waited until she was on her own in the evening and then she went up stairs to the bedroom where she had previously put Michael to sleep. He was sleeping soundly in the other room. She lit the gaslight and looked around the room but nothing seemed untoward. Hannah pulled the chain and it put the light out. She moved toward the open door way and she turned and faced into the room .She said quite loudly and firmly

"Whoever you are and if you can not rest don't you ever touch that gas light again. I mean it. You almost killed Michael you cannot use a match to light it so don't you touch it again." It had made Hannah quite nervous and she was finding it difficult to go to sleep. She continually got up to make sure that Michael was all right. George got so cross with her disturbing him but she could not help it and thank goodness the incident with the gaslight did not happen again.

Chapter Ten
Fantacy And Reality

George had started picking Sandra up on a regular basis. He still did most of his work in the Wellington area and he did not mind giving her a lift when he dropped Michael off at the bottom of the hill to catch the school bus. November could be a cold bleak and a miserable wet month and he was glad to take her into town with him. On very wet mornings it saved her from being wet through by the time that she reached the Secondary Modern school. Some times he would be working at home making windows, doors and things which had to be made before being fitted. He still went out of his way to take her to school and then go back home to get on with his work. If Hannah happened to ask why it had taken him so long to take Michael to catch the bus, he always had an excuse at the ready and he would say that he had needed to go into town for more wood, screws and nails or something or other. The excuses always satisfied Hannah's curiosity some times he went in for her needs to save her leaving her work and as time went on she did not question what George was doing regarding his work. If Donald arrived before he was back Hannah set him on to do some tidying up or give her a hand filling the coal hods and other little jobs for her. If George were working at home he would go down the hill to pick Michael up in the afternoon and take Donald down the hill with him. He might as well knock off early as there is not much that he can help me with after dark. Dropping Donald and his bike off at the bottom of the Hill saved Donald seeing him talking to Sandra so there was nothing that he could tell Hannah. For some unknown reason to him he was getting that he was hoping to see Sandra, they would have a chat about different things but nothing of any importance. He looked forward to her being there, waiting for him to come to collect Michael. If she got away from school quickly and rode her bicycle as fast as she could she knew that she could be at the Forest Glen before the school bus had dropped Michael off. Michael was the first to be picked up in the mornings and the last school child to be dropped off in the afternoons. Some thing about Sandra intrigued George she always had a smile for him and she seemed so appreciative she reminded him of Hannah when she had first started work up the Wrekin. Sandra loved the time she spent with him going to and from school. He always had something witty to say and he always seems to have a smile for her. George could not believe how quickly she was developing into a young woman and he liked what he saw of her and he was making a habit of going out of his way to see her. He had not dared to try anything on with her she was his wife's little sister and that meant that she was completely out of bounds. But he could not get her out of his mind She bothered him. He would let his imagination run away with him. He would visualise making love to her but he knew that it was complete fantasy it was something that could never happen. He guessed that she had a crush on him she had given the game away by being so provocative and he enjoyed her toying with his affections. Hannah was still very good with him but she would only let him make love to her when she knew that it was safe to do so hoping not get pregnant again. This was difficult and how he resented it. He thought what a condescending attitude she had towards sex. To his way of thinking his needs should be her first priority not the fact that she could get pregnant again. What the child would be like he considered was of no concern of his even if things did not go quite right, that would be for her to cope with and had there not been enough bother with the twins and now they were doing alright.

George had been asked to do some work for the local veterinary surgeon He and his wife had bought an empty house next door to themselves Their only son who had also trained as a veterinary surgeon was helping to run the practice but he and his wife were not happy with the house that they were living in and needed to be nearer to his parents and the business Mrs Brown and her Husband decided that they would spend on it and have it brought up to scratch ready for their son and his new wife and baby son to move in and all being well in time for Christmas. It needed quite a lot of work doing to it; they had heard what a good carpenter that George was He had been recommended to them. George had jumped at the chance he could see that he would be there for several weeks and the weather could be bad in the months of November and December especially if he had to work outside. He saw very little of Mr Brown but Mrs Brown seemed to be in charge of things as far as George was concerned. She was a pleasant woman, she stood no more than five foot two her greying hair was cut short making it look very neat and tidy. She was a very down to earth woman she called a spade a spade and God help any one who was awkward towards her or tried to double cross her. She smoked like a trooper. She could swear as good as any man. Her husband was a popular veterinary surgeon in the town and consequently an extremely busy man.

It has now gone four o'clock George could do no more work the nights were drawing in and it was going dark much earlier; he had sent Donald home. He was driving up the Ercall when once again he saw Sandra heading for home pushing her bike He drew along side of her and offered her a lift. You are running a bit late are you not I thought that you finished at three thirty"

"Oh I had a bit of shopping to do I was hoping to see you save me biking any further it's a bit cold tonight. Dropping her off out side the farm gate he said "There you are; saved you from walking up the banks" as he lifted her bike from the van.

"You're my knight in shining armour!" Sandra teased She took the handlebars and moved toward the front gate of the farm. George got back in the van put it into first gear and he drove back towards the Forest Glen trying not to give any more thought to Sandra but the girl disturbed him and he tried to work out what it was about her. She was not yet fifteen but she certainly knew how to have an effect on a fellow. He wondered if she was having sex with lads at school. She could be for all he knew but he had not got the guts to ask her.

He lay in bed that night and he could not dismiss her from his mind he was glad when exhaustion caused him to fall asleep and that he would wake up next morning to the reality of his family and his work.

Sandra was beginning to take his giving her a lift for granted and started asking him where he was working in town. He did not take much notice of this and if she wanted a lift home she would know where to find him and it was no skin off his nose. Mrs Brown liked him and she was very satisfied with his standard of work. He was polite and always tidy in his appearance and cleaned up as he worked throughout the day. They had quite a lot of work for him to do. As soon as George and the decorators had finished the little family would be moving in.

It was almost four o'clock and they had done as much as they could for the day .He decided to send Donald home and that he would go home and start to make a couple of windows that were needed. He was just closing the back door of the van ready to leave for home when Sandra appeared as if from no where.

"Hello what are you doing here? I thought that you would have been well on your way by now. Could you do with a lift it's a good job that you came when you did or you would have missed me I was just off home. "

"Well my knight in shining armour, it is a good job that I came when I did don't you think. I had to go down the town again for Mother" she lied "Just a bit of shopping nothing much, I am a bit late starting for home. I would really appreciate a lift, it is so good of you and Mam and Dad know that I am quite safe with you"

"OK hop in I will put your bike in the back" She climbed in and sat on the passenger seat but when George got into the driver's seat she seemed to be rather close. He sensed that Sandra's closeness was a bit too much for comfort; she was sitting on the edge of the front passenger seat in the van leaning towards him. She had made sure that her school skirt was pulled up well back from her knees showing most of her legs. As they left town he could feel her leg brushing against his own. Sandra's hand came on to his knee; surely this was not what he was thinking it was? She wouldn't, would she? He felt her hand moving towards his thigh, gently but firmly stroking him. George placed his left hand on hers; she made no effort to move her hand away, she knew this was having the desired effect that she had been hoping for. He made no comment as they drove up through the narrow roads and climbed up the Ercall He pulled the van in as usual at the back gate and switched off the engine. First he lit a cigarette, he needed one.

"Care for one?" he asked Sandra" Yes of course"

"I didn't know you smoked"

"Oh I do when I can" she lied. He gave her one and held the lighted match for her. Their fingers touched, and then the moment was gone for George, he knew not to go any further. Quickly he said, "I had better get back," he drew heavily on his cigarette. He knew that if he did not get the van going and return home, he just might be tempted to try some thing with her. That he dare not do. Sandra reluctantly got out of the van, she waited until George had turned it around and gone back down the road. She threw the cigarette into the ditch and walked across the field fanning her face with her hand to remove the smell of the cigarette before she went inside. There would be one hell of a row if her mother found out that she liked the odd cigarette.

George returned home and to his chair by the Aga, Michael was sat at the other side of the table doing some drawing ready for school next day He wanted to impress his schoolteacher. George suddenly remembered that he had promised to pick Michael up when he came from school. Hannah took his tea from the oven and put it in front of him.

"Sorry I missed picking you up tonight son but we have a lot on at the moment Mrs Brown wants me to get on and finish so that the decorators can get in, "He said as much to Hannah as Michael.

"Oh that was alright he came home quite safely" Replied Hannah. "There is not many about on the hill at this time of the year and he was kept warm enough with walking up hill but give me a ring if you are not going to make it and then we can go a little of the way and meet him"

"Now that is not always possible I said that I would pick him up and I forgot so please don't make an issue of it. I've been thinking that it will be good to get off this hill and have somewhere that has mains electricity"

"Oh really I quite agree with you it worries me Michael having to walk up the hill on school days It will be so nice when he is picked up at the door" Hannah replied not knowing what else to say.

Not a lot of stock was kept during the winter months just a few crates of minerals and a few boxes of crisps and biscuits. The shop made a good playroom for the twins who having had their tea were playing in there. They soon stopped when they heard their Dad come in. There was no peace after that until all three were in bed. George lit another cigarette and then another, he could not relax. The wireless programme was of no interest to him.

"What's the matter with you?" asked Hannah as she sat with her knitting.

"Nothing I just feel a bit restless" he replied "I don't want any thing to go wrong with the Brown's job I am getting on well there, a couple of windows to make and I will see daylight at the end of the tunnel so to speak Be there for another two weeks They are so good to work for; she keeps a percolator of coffee on the Aga all day and it is good coffee the real stuff."

"I can see that Mrs Brown certainly spoils you perhaps you are overworking, you have had a lot on just lately. Perhaps it would not be a bad idea if we switch that thing off and have an early night" She pointed to the wireless set which stood on a shelf high up on the wall out of the reach of the children and out of the way of every thing else.

"They are a great couple to work for and they should pay up pretty quickly of what I have seen of them. Yes you could be right let's have an early night". Hannah put her knitting away and made their last drink of the day, it was Cocoa and they were soon upstairs and into bed. Hannah was dreading George wanting to have sex but to her amazement he turned his back to her and gave the impression that he was very tired and wanted to go to sleep; much to her relief. George was finding it difficult to go to sleep and he was only pretending, he mind was going around and round in turmoil he could not forget the closeness of Sandra when she had sat by him as he took her home.

Sandra was becoming crafty she found that if she sometimes left her bike in the yard at the back of the Glen and had started to walk on towards school nine times out of ten she would be offered a lift usually by George She hated school and she did not care if and when she arrived.

"Thank God I finish at Easter no way will I stay on until the summer break"

George was finding that he was now going out of his way to give Sandra a lift if he could. Percy Podmore had noticed her bike there and had thought the crafty little madam she knows that some one will give her a lift the rest of the way and he had noticed that it was George who was usually picking her up, that worried him a little but he decided to keep his thoughts to him self.

Sandra would be fifteen in the spring and had developed a real crush for her Brother in law. Not only was she trying to work it that George gave her lift to school or as she went back home. She made every excuse to go to the cottage on a Sunday afternoon to see Hannah and at the same time see George; she always had such a sorry story to tell. It was usually that her mother was in such a bad mood that she had to get out of the house for bit. Or it was that William would not do his turn with the milking leaving it all for her and her Dad to do. The lad who came from the village to give a hand did not work on Sundays. She complained that William only thought of getting him self dressed up and going out. Sandra was developing into a formative young woman; she had a very well developed figure although she was only 14 her bust size was already about size 38". She only had another full term to go before she could leave school. She could still wrap her mother around her little finger as she had done for most of her life. Now that her older sisters were all married with families of their own, she only had her brother William to confide in and she very rarely did that. He had been away at boarding school but now since leaving he worked along side of his father farming the farm and took it for granted that he would inherit the lot. He was extremely good-looking young man about six feet tall and took after his mother's side of the family. His Mother had thoroughly spoiled him and given in to him whenever he had asked for something that they did not think they could afford. Sandra was spoiled almost as much. Dorothy found that she was a great help to her around the house and with the feeding of the poultry. Sandra and William both knew that they could always persuade their parents into giving them what they wanted. William much preferred the tractor driving and working on any thing mechanical to doing any of the other farm work

On a bitter cold day early in December Sandra came to Mrs Browns hoping for a lift home and she was in luck. George was still there finishing off for the day, there was not much more that he could do. After Donald had left they both got into the van and started for home. He was aware of the nearness of Sandra as she leaned towards him. It bothered and excited him and he made no effort to move away from her. He dropped her off as usual and made back for home, her nearness had affected him and he could not dismiss it lightly later when he was lying in bed with Hannah he could not get Sandra out of his mind, and was fantasising about her voluptuous body. During the next week he was watching out for her hoping to see something of her, and of course he was not disappointed.

"Walking home again?" he said as he stopped to give her a lift no bike today, "How did you get to school this morning?"

"Oh William took me in after milking, I was late but there was nothing of importance to be learnt," She said so complacently. She had not bothered to take a great interest in schoolwork; the problems with her eyesight hadn't helped; the fact that her mother was quite happy to let her stay at home if she gave a hand with the chores. She had given no thought as to what she would do when she left, as far as she was concerned she could stay at home and do just enough to keep her mother happy.

As George drove out of town and into the darkness of the country roads; she leaned over towards him and put her head on his shoulder and her hand was on his leg as she had done the last time he had given her a lift. As they went up the Ercall he pulled off the road and he stopped the van. He put his arm around the back of the passenger seat and she did not pull away from him. He drew her close and gently kissed her on the lips. "Now see what happens", he thought, she would either slap his face or want him to do that again. He was not disappointed her arms came around his neck and she pulled him towards her. He kissed her again and again passionately she wanted him and he had guessed quite rightly. He eventually gently pushed her away and started the van. He knew that he dared not go any further. As he took her home they travelled in silence she moved close before she got out of the van as if waiting for another kiss but George refused her.

"No this is not on I am sorry it won't happen again".

She got out of the van and slammed the door shut. Boy oh boy was she angry, she had wanted more and George had dismissed her like a little schoolgirl.

"I don't believe it," he thought, as he drove home "I reckon she is no virgin, she wanted me tonight, but dare I?" It had been as much as he could do to control himself, "Let her try anything like that again and I will see how far she will go. She wouldn't dare tell anyone they would never believe her. In any case it would be her word against mine." She had reminded George of his youth when he had been with Gwen on Monday evenings and later when he had been with Hilda Crosby Sandra like them, she was a woman who was desperate to be sexually full filled.

Tonight she acted like a much older woman than the young schoolgirl that she was. It was another two weeks before he saw Sandra again. He had thought it best to keep out of her way if he possibly could. The weather had been pretty rotten sleet and snow so he guessed quite rightly that she would not bother going to the school He had been to collect some wood from the timber yard and was about to deliver it back to where he was working when he saw her. She was pushing her bike out side Bromley's. He pulled up along side her, and wound down the driver's window.

"Just going home, Care for a lift" He smiled.

"Just the job" her face lit up, she thought George had been avoiding her for the past two weeks. She had only gone to school when she thought that she could not get out of it. She had telephoned Hannah with an excuse and Hannah had said that he was working at home making windows for a job that he was working on and consequently had not been in town very much. Oh so that was why she had not seen anything of him.

Sandra got in the van her face all smiles; George got out and put her bike in the back on top of the new sawn timber. When he got back in and started the engine she kept her distance from him wondering what he was going to say to her but he kept quiet. Donald helped him unload the timber; he had done the little jobs that George had left him to do. He noticed Sandra sat in the front of the van he put her bike back in the now empty van, said goodnight and took his bike to head for home. "That's not the first time she has been sitting in the van, she got him running rings around her. Taking her home I suppose" he said to him self as he went and gave it no more thought

"I really admire the way you can make things George; you are so clever with your hands, Hannah is so lucky to have you as a husband"

"I've got my trade" he answered, "It's a living"

It was about half past five when they left the lights of the town and headed out into the country towards home. The moon was not high enough in the sky to give much light but the air was cold and it appeared to be already freezing. Sandra moved over towards his seat

"It's going to be cold tonight don't you think?" She pretended to shiver.

"Looks that way, you got much more to do when you get in?" he asked

"Not that I know of, Father will have already got the sticks and coal in. William can count the sheep when he feeds them. The lad from the village will have already gone home"

George drove the van off the road and into a clearing at the bottom of the Wrekin.

"Now what's all this leaning towards me feeling my leg and not slapping my face when I kissed you?" He lit a cigarette and the reflection from the lighted match in the driver's mirror showed that he was smiling, much to Sandra's relief. She did not answer him.

He leaned towards her to see if she would respond again to a kiss. She certainly did that all right, she clung tightly to him, and his hand unbuttoned the front of her blouse and felt the warmth and firmness of her breasts. Sandra made no effort to stop him. This was much better he thought. She loves it and he knew that she needed him, Sandra had dreamt of this moment. George was kissing her hard and passionately and they stayed this way for half an hour or so. George was really enjoying this he now knew that if he wanted to make love to Sandra she would let him, but he kept his head, she can wait, he would keep her waiting, he would make it worth her while,

"Come on, its time I took you home, there's always another time."

"Do we have to go?"

"Yes. Get your self respectable you will have to make an excuse for being late tonight"

"Oh don't you worry about me, the old lady will swallow any thing that I want to tell her." She was referring to Dorothy her mother.

He dropped her off at the back gate and went back home.

"You're a bit late" Her Mother commented as Sandra went in.

"I went to Sally's," She said. "We were talking and I did try to ring you but you did not answer"

"The phone has not rung" replied her mother.

"Well I rang; perhaps you had the wireless on too loud". Her mother could see that she was lying but did not want a row. She was getting older now and Sandra was all she had left to help her with the work.

"Well you are here now. Did you get a lift home?

"No" She lied I came home on my bike"

"Let us know the next time that you are coming late". Dorothy asking if she had a lift caught Sandra on the hop.

Had her mother or Dad seen the van pull up at the back gate? She did not think so. She guessed that they had sat listening to the wireless and appeared to be too engrossed listening to the programme to have seen any vehicles about.

"You don't know who is about. It was different with your sisters. It was safe to walk the roads and we did not have to worry so much." Sandra was fed up with the way her Mother went on and on. This was not the same. That was not the same when your sisters were at home. Times have changed since those days if only her mother could realise it. Sandra was getting her self something to eat; letting her mother's words go over her head, not listening. Later she went to bed she was so happy she felt so good She felt as if George was still close to her. Her breasts were firm and her nipples still tingled from his touch. She knew that he would not dare tell Hannah. She would kick him out over the doorstep had she known that he had kissed her little sister as he had tonight. Hannah would never suspect that her husband could do such a thing. Why should she? She trusted George implicitly Touch her little sister the idea was ludicrous, it would never cross her mind. Sandra looked in the mirror and studied her figure she knew that she could do with losing a few pounds but the boys at school seemed to like her as she was. The little liaisons, which she had with them, could not compare with the way that George had held her tonight.

Next morning before he took Michael to catch the school bus Hannah asked George if he would be working late. It took him quite by surprise.

"Why do you ask?"

"Your tea was not very good last night, If only I had known that you were coming in as late as you did I would not have cooked it so early. "

"No I won't be late tonight, I will be back about five". He had already decided that Sandra could wait for him. There was no hurry he would keep her in suspense for a while. It was now December and there were plenty of dark nights to come.

Sandra stayed away from the cottage the next weekend George decided that he would stay at home with the family. Mrs Brown could wait until Monday morning.

Hannah was so pleased; it was good to be at home as a family. George took the children for a ride to Wrockwardine village shop and treated them to sweets and a bottle of pop made a real fuss of them. He called on his Dad and Molly. Back home George said that he would be working late a couple of nights the following week.

"Mrs Brown wants her work finishing so that the decorators can finish and be out in time for Christmas.

"That's all right Dear, if I know what you are doing I will leave your tea and cook you something when you come in"

George saw Sandra the next Tuesday he knew which way that she would cycle home. She was pleased to see him when he drew the van along side of her.

"Jump in "He said "I will put your bike in the back". George drove a different way around the hill. He pulled up in a secluded stop where the van could not be seen from the road. George knew every track of the woods. He leaned over and kissed Sandra.

"What would Hannah say if she could see us now George?"

"Shh, don't spoil it"

Mentioning Hannah's name made a sense of guilt rip though George like a sharp knife. He resumed kissing and cuddling Sandra but he went no further. He knew by her responses that she was getting very eager and frustrated but he was not prepared to go any further tonight. Sandra mentioning Hannah's name had put him off. He knew that he would not be able to perform his best. They stayed for about two hours, and then George decided to take Sandra home. He lit a cigarette and smoothed his hair and started the engine. Sandra borrowed the comb that he had used and she combed her hair and smoothed her clothes and then she lit the cigarette that George had offered her.

"Are you still working at Mrs Brown's?"

"Yes I will be there for another week".

"Can I have a lift on Thursday, quickly thinking of a reason why she would need a lift? "If I come around to Mrs Browns It would save me from walking up the banks. I will try and persuade William to take me in the morning. A few of the girls want me to stay after school to watch a play that they are rehearsing."

"I will still be there I won't leave until you come", this gave Sandra something to look forward to. Thursday 4.30pm came; George had finished fixing a new door. He felt that he had done enough for one day and he wondered if Sandra would come for a lift home. Something told him that he would not be disappointed, He felt good, and he had shaved meticulously that morning and as he had been working that afternoon he had deliberately got his hands quite dirty; after Donald had left. He went to Mrs Brown's back door. He knocked and opened the door "Mrs Brown" he called. Is there any chance that I could wash my hands and clean them up a bit? I have to look at another job on my way home," He lied.

"Of course you can, George, Any time that you need to clean up you only have to say. Step inside there is the cloak room along the passage way." Mrs Brown smiled and quickly took a small clean towel from the kitchen drawer. "Here you are you can use this" she handed the towel to him.

While George was washing his hands with the sweet smelling soap he also washed his face drying himself on the towel Mrs Brown had provided for him. A quick comb of his wavy black hair and he was quite pleased with himself. He went out to the van and made it look as if he was putting tools away. In fact he was tidying the van to make room for Sandra's bicycle. There was no sign of her coming so he went out on to the street to see if she was waiting for him. He saw her standing waiting. He quickly said goodnight to Mrs Brown and handed her the keys of the next door property. He drove his van from around the back of the premises and pulled up along side of Sandra. Although she was still in her school uniform she looked stunning. Her blond hair shone in the streetlight and it was obvious to George that she had put make up on. She had made her self look as old as she possibly could.

"Want a lift" he asked smiling Pretending that he had only just seen her and that it was by chance that she happened to be near where he was working. She readily accepted. George quickly lifted the bike into the van as Sandra got into the passenger seat. He drove out of town as usual but he turned off at the Forest Glen and started to drive along the narrow back road, which led around the bottom of the hill. He parked in the same secluded spot as before and secured the handbrake firmly. Sandra could not believe her luck; she sat quietly beside George as he reached over to take her in his arms.

"This is very uncomfortable" George whispered, "The damn handbrake is in the way, just hold on a minute and I will make things a little easier"

He got out of the van and went around to the back door; he took out a thick sheet, which he kept for use when working in customer's homes. It was laid to protect their carpets from wood shavings and sawdust; he had given it a good shaking earlier in the day. He knew that he would have no further use for it until the next day, as the house that he was working on was empty and no carpets or furniture were being put in until after George had finished the required alterations. He moved to the bushes, a pheasant flew up from a bush where it had settled for the night causing him to jump slightly. Although the bracken had turned brown it was still thick and dense. After trampling on a patch with his feet he laid down the sheet, Sandra needed no persuasion to get out of the van. She had wondered what he was up to and had got out to have a look within seconds she was lying beside him. They lay down on the sheet, well secluded and hidden, there was practically no light. The moon had not risen and the only noises that could be heard were those of the wood. The flutter of the odd bird such as an owl or others looking for nesting for the night and a fox in the distance, barking. The call echoing through the woods, it was a bit early for foxes to be barking they would not start mating until after Christmas and then only if the weather seemed suitable. Wild animals seemed to know if there was to be a severe winter or not and that would depend on them mating. These were familiar noises to George and Sandra.

He held her tightly to him and gently unbuttoned her cardigan and blouse she had no undergarments on which pleasantly surprised him because the weather was rather cold. It had changed for the worst during the last week. He assumed that she must have taken her bra off before leaving school. He was delighted that there were no restrictive straps or hooks to be unfastened. He exposed her voluptuous breasts and kissed them, her hands were already inside his shirt feeling and stroking his body. Although the air was cold neither of them noticed they were too absorbed with exploring each other. George knew that he was going to have a treat tonight and he was going to make the most of it. He kept her waiting for as long as he could, she was young and eager but his need for fulfilment overwhelmed him, he had guessed rightly that Sandra was no virgin. She had learnt about lovemaking by trial and error with young lads from school and the village but she had never experienced the power of a man's body like she was doing now. She felt delirious with excitement as he entered her and with the perfect timing of their body movements they reached the point where they were utterly exhausted. George had had plenty of experience in lovemaking and knew just the right moment to withdraw so as not to get her pregnant. Afterwards they lay quietly together unable to believe that anything as wonderful as this could happen to them. George began to realise that it certainly wasn't like this with Hannah.

Sandra was overwhelmed; nothing had prepared her for this.

"We'll have to do this again", George whispered, waiting to see what Sandra's reaction would be when she realised she had been making love with her brother-in-law. He expected her either to welcome him gladly or have the screaming abdabs her reaction was exactly what he thought it would be.

"We must be together again George, I have enjoyed myself tonight. You know that I love you"

"Steady on a minute I don't know about the; I love you bit. You know that I am married. I am a bit tied down you know".

"I know that you are But we can pretend can't we and who is going to tell any one I am certainly not. Are you?"

"I dare not. I would be hung, drawn and quartered if this got out".

They got dressed quickly, the night air becoming suddenly chillier now that their passion had died down. They got back into the van and he lit a cigarette for them both to regain some sort of composure. When he was ready he took her home. As they pulled up George kissed her and she got out of the van.

"I will be in touch" was all he said. They had no need to exchange any other words to night had said it all.

In the meantime Hannah was getting worried as to where George was. It was getting late; if he decided to work late he was usually home by 8:30pm. It was now just turned nine; she had not eaten her meal with the children at tea time she liked to wait for George and keep him company, the children had long gone to bed Hannah waited until eight and then had some thing to eat. She was beginning to feel hungry. She decided that she would keep George's hot for him.

At nine thirty he finally drove up and parked out side the house. When he came in he was full of apologies for being late.

"I'm so sorry love; at last I'm on top of that job at the Browns. I didn't stop to ring you, it was quicker to get the work done and then come home. Mrs Brown gave me a cup of tea and a piece of cake to tide me over; she's a nice person to work for. I sent Don Home at four thirty there was no need to pay him overtime"

"I was getting worried" Hannah commented, Putting her knitting down on the table "I did not know whether I should give Mrs Brown a ring to see if you were alright You don't usually stay to work this late. I only hope your tea is alright"

"As long as it's hot," he said, going into the back to wash his hands in the sink so that she would think that he was still dirty from working., He came back and stood by the Aga cooker and looked at Hannah as she placed his over cooked dinner on the table.

"I'm starving; I can eat that although it looks a bit stale. Now you listen to me Hannah. "Don't you ever go ringing and meithering the customers to check up on me. Can't I stay over a bit to get on with the work? They have told me that they want their son to move into that house as quickly as possible. What sort of a fool would I look if the little wifey started ringing up to check on me to see if I was there? You know that you can trust me surely or are you letting your imagination run away with you. It's a good thing that we are getting off this damn hill before you go letting your imagination run away with you .I think that you are reading too many books, filling your head with rubbish they are, Mr and Mrs Brown are very busy people. Their phone is always ringing for one thing or another. I did not realise that a veterinary practice could be so busy Mrs Brown is running back and forth to answer the phone, as it is I am sure that she has better things to do than to reassure you that I am still working. That is the reason why their Son has come to help them with the business. No Hannah I would not like to think that you could not trust me to do a bit of overtime with out you getting your knickers in a twist. Don't you ever think of doing some thing so silly? It would make me look such a fool and quite rightly so, I would be so angry. Let's say no more about it but don't you ever check up on me. I will tell you where I am in case you need me, have no fear of that. Be quiet now and let me have my tea in peace".

Hannah was reeling from the lecture that George had just given her He had sounded so angry.

"Don't worry George I am not that stupid, and I would not embarrass you, I believe you if you say you have been working. What Hannah did not know George had prepared this little speech in case as he had rightly thought that Hannah might just check to see if he was telling the truth.

What excuse Sandra made to her Mother he did not care. That was her problem but he knew that after tonight she would be making many more excuses for being late home from school.

He had no idea what he was eating as his mind was still in the woods with Sandra, so he didn't comment when Hannah casually asked if his dinner was still all right. Not that she cared if it was not. She had considered that there had been no need to give her a lecture. Hannah took the dirty dishes through into the back kitchen and placed the in the bowl in the sink and covered them with water, she decided to leave them until morning She packed her knitting away and she went to bed. George stayed up a bit longer to calm him self down and get a grip of him self. Hannah going to bed before him was exactly what he had wanted. He decided that he would go to bed later when he thought that she had gone to sleep. Hannah was glad to go to bed and quickly fell asleep. She did sense George coming to bed some time later and she turned her body towards him and went back into a deep sleep.

The next time George saw Sandra she voiced her concern about him moving from the cottage on the hill. He drove up the Wrekin and parked along side the farm buildings. It was quite safe no one would be on the hill after dark at this time of the year and they were far enough away from the house for Hannah to see any vehicle lights. There had been a raw cold freezing fog hanging over the town all day. The frozen fog clung to the trees as they drove up the Ercall the overhanging branches looking very picturesque in the van headlights. As they started to climb the Wrekin their visibility became much clearer. It was to be quite a frosty night. George did not fancy lying under bushes on a night like this. The idea of bringing

Sandra here had suddenly dawned on him the other day when he had been looking for a saw that he had left in the building some time ago. He had no cattle they had been sold off and so had any heifers that Hannah had reared.

She took the last pair to Shrewsbury auction. It was a Tuesday in late November that they had been booked in to be sold. That particular morning it had started to sleet and snow. George had not fancied a ride to Shrewsbury cattle market on a tractor He would be cold and wet sitting on the Ferguson tractor exposed to the cold winter elements. He did not fancy it at all He decided to pretend that he felt really ill. "Must be the influenza or something" he complained when he came in from out side about eight o'clock He had made sure that the two heifers had been given a good feed and water before going to the auction. He pretended that he felt too ill to eat any food.

"Put it in the back if I feel that I can eat it later I can always warm it up a bit. He and Hannah had risen at six that morning. I really don't think that I would be safe with the tractor and trailer today. I think that you will have to go in my place"

"But George I have never been cattle auction before I just don't know what to do"

"Well it is time that you found out Take Don with you, he will help you see to things. I asked him to meet me at the bottom this morning. I will give you a hand to load them and then I am going back to bed".

"What about the twins? You can't go to bed and leave them to look after them selves".

"All right all right I will keep an eye on them you should be back before dinner time. You will have to stand in the box while they are being sold".

"What? Stand and be stared at by all those farmers"

"And what is wrong with that"?

"I will be scared stiff that is what".

"Don't be such a baby". He thought of Sandra she would never put up such a fuss.

He gave Hannah a hand to load the two Aberdeen Angus heifers into the trailer She wrapped her self up as warm as she could. Gloves a woollen Headscarf tied around her head and a topcoat. He had already fixed it up for Donald to meet her at the bottom of the hill. The night before when they had finished work George had said that he needed him to go to the auction with him and to be at the bottom of the hill next morning. Hannah drove very gently down the hill and was so relieved to see Donald waiting for her; the two of them set off for Shrewsbury. They had to be there for ten o'clock to have their cattle entered before the sale started. They went via Atcham and then turned right for Upton Magna; so that they came to the auction at Harlescott through Featherbed lane. Hannah was glad to get there she felt that she was absolutely frozen. She was wet through from the sleeting snow and so was Donald. Men came quickly forward and told her where she was to unload. The noise of the auction was deafening. Men were running here and there, cars with their trailers all trying to get a place to unload; the noise of the Lorries moving and reversing to unload their stock of sheep, pigs, cattle, and calves which were calling for their mothers. Once that was done, she and Don parked the tractor and trailer and went for a cup of tea to warm them selves up. Hannah took off her scarves and tided her self-up a bit; they went back to the selling ring to watch and to wait for their turn. When that came and the auctioneer announced the next lot to be sold and asked if any one was with them to take the stand Hannah went forward very gingerly.

"Come on my dear "he said He had not seen her there before. As Hannah stepped forward to the stand the men around the arena shouted and gave wolf whistles. Hannah could feel her face going bright red not from the cold this time but from embarrassment. Her two heifers sold very well and they topped the market in their class.

"Come on Don Lets get back" She said when she had collected her cheque from the cashiers office they went to the tractor but it refused to start. Men gathered around each trying to solve the problem. It had no petrol in it. Hannah had forgotten to check the petrol gauge before leaving. Petrol was needed to start the engine before switching over to the tractor paraffin oil TVO as it was called (Tractor vaporising oil) when the engine had warmed up sufficiently. George had never told her that was how one started the Ferguson and many other makes of tractors. He had not refilled it. She quickly borrowed a petrol can and sent Don for some petrol and then they had no further trouble and were able to go back home. She dropped Don off at Wrockwardine; there was no point in her taking him back with her if George had been as ill as he had made out that morning he would not want to do any further work after she arrived home.

George seemed to have miraculously recovered when Hannah got back up the Wrekin There was no sign of him having a cold never mind influenza, I don't believe it Hannah said to her self. She noticed that the plate of eggs and bacon had been eaten and the dirty plate was put in the sink for her to wash up. He has soon recovered she said to her self as she made her self-a cup of tea and a sandwich and she sat by the Aga to warm her self. She took the cheque from her handbag and gave it to him.

"George they did very well but you get one thing straight. I will never go to a cattle auction again as long as I live. I have been for you today but don't you ever ask me to go again. I will not go for you or any one else."

"Well what are you going on for, that is the last of the cattle for us to sell and you say that they did well so what are you moaning about, you had Donald to help you"

"You never said that I needed petrol to start that damned thing of a tractor and that there was none in it I have never felt so embarrassed in my life before today".

"You did not know that. Well I don't believe it everyone knows that and you should have known it "Hannah did not like the sneer that crossed his face so she decided to say no more. She vowed that today would be the last time that she would ever take cattle to the market again no matter what might happen to her in the future.

"George what am I going to do when you move to that horrible little cottage. I will not be able to see you as I have been doing. There will be no taking Michael to catch the school bus. George had prepared a little nest of sacks and straw in the back building behind the cowshed. Hannah was not likely to go there for any reason to night she would be with the children staying in the warmth of the kitchen. He had sold every thing that was not wanted and now there were only working tools housed there and she would have no need for those she had enough to do up at the house for the rest of the winter months.

"Stop worrying my little love we will certainly sort some thing out I won't let you down. Don't you worry your little head? I will have to keep my work and as it is now and most of it is in the town infact I will be passing the gate most days. I am sure that we can think of some thing.

George was getting nervous he was finding himself in a right mess and he was getting a little scared. He was pretty sure that no one could have possibly seen him making love with Sandra. She was getting more and more possessive and what was more frightening for him she certainly took a lot of satisfying. She was under age and he knew that if he upset her and she told of what was going on it could be prison for him that would be if her dad had not shot him first.

What he did not know was that Ted Locket's eyes had not missed a great deal of what went on in the woods He had noticed George giving Sandra lifts to school and by the looks that he had seen the two of them exchange. He had guessed that there was something going on but was reluctant to believe what he was seeing, he even wondered if he was letting his imagination run away with him because of all the other courting couples that he had a habit of watching in the woods.

He decided he could wait his time and one-day he would be in the right place at the right time with his little box camera.

George decided that there was a risk of Donald finding out too much of his feeling towards Sandra her provocative smiles and innuendo when she was waiting for a lift home just might give the game away so he decided to finish with him

He had the good excuse of his moving off the hill it would be too far for Donald to come on his bike. The lad was so disappointed he had a great respect for both George and Hannah they had been so good to him

March 1962 came Hannah and the family had to move into their little brick cottage behind the Wrekin. New tenants were taking over their business. Hannah decided that she had no choice but to make the most of things until the alterations of the cottage could be completed. It did have really good prospects. The view across the Severn valley to the Welsh hills was fantastic and a wonderful sight. They had the wood on the one side and the fields on the other, the smell from the farm at the far end of the garden did not worry Hannah she had been brought up to the smell of the farm.

Plans had been drawn up and presented to the Council to have a large extension built to the cottage. There were to be four bedrooms a big kitchen and dining room. Hannah designed an Inglenook fireplace in the main downstairs room, so that it would be with in keeping with the oak beamed ceiling which would eventually be their lounge or front room, what ever they decided to call it. It was such a relief to have the main electricity. The television had been the first big electrical expense they had bought they were also able to buy a washing machine. George was able to use his electrical tools and this saved him so much time and work. The telephone had also been installed.

George seemed happier now than what he had been for a long time; when they discussed the buying of a television set. Hannah had asked if they could afford it. George had argued that "The kids will be able to learn such a lot if we get them one." Hannah later found that it had not been bought so much for the children it had become George's prize possession. If George were at home he would sit smoking cigarettes and watch it until it closed down towards midnight. George was able to still enjoy his hobby of shooting but not very often since having the television he had lost interest although different farmers he knew were glad of him to go around with his gun and shoot a few rabbits for them. He did not have the time, there was so much to do and there was so much that could be done. He was still seeing Sandra whenever he was able to but he now had to be much more careful. She had left school at Easter and they made their rendezvous in the woods behind the lime kilns lane and when they were able to meet he certainly made it worth her while. Old Alec Hollis was dead and his wife lived alone in the cottage in the middle of the wood. Telling her mother that she was visiting her gave Sandra a perfect alibi. The old lady had no telephone so Sandra had no need to worry about her mother checking up on her.

Hannah and George were so happy, but un-aware to Hannah He was having the best of both worlds she had no reason what so ever to suspect that he was meeting her little sister. Hannah looked at the garden and worked out where best to make a lawn for the children to have a play area. There was about an acre of ground altogether but it was terribly over grown with weeds and brambles. It was going to take a lot of hard work. It would be no worse than when she had given a hand to clear a field of bushes when they had been up the Wrekin She decided that she would also like to have a vegetable patch. In the meantime George was busy fitting himself up with a workshop and coping with work for others as he was needed there was so much more that he could do now that they were connected to the electricity Although it looked a mammoth task to complete the house, they knew that they could do it. The children were so much happier Hannah had far more time for them Michael caught the school bus just out side the door there was no more walking up and down the hill for him. No more cakes to be made by the hundred and no more worry about the health and hygiene inspectors calling unexpectedly.

A well had been dug and as George had anticipated it had filled with clear clean water. He had it tested to make sure that it was fit for human consumption and thank goodness it passed the tests because they had no idea where the nearest main water supply was. At first George had not been able to set up a pump on the well so Hannah had to drop buckets down the well on the end of a piece of rope and pull the bucket up again. This however did not last for long Hannah gave George an ultimatum put a pump on the well and a cover on it in case one of the children fall to their death. If he did not he could get the water himself and enough for all the family and enough to do all the washing as well. Once he had fixed a pump Hannah lost no time in buying the washing machine. She had brought the calor gas cooker and one of the calor gas boilers from up the Wrekin so that she had a cooker but how she missed the Aga

George and Terry and with the help of Bobby they dug a hole deep enough to build a septic tank ready for when they were able to have a flush toilet. In the mean time George put in pipes to take the waste from the improvised kitchen sink. George had the caravan towed and put it in the yard under the wall of the next door cottage. Bernie was now sharing the caravan with a friend called Arnie who was in his twenties and he had fallen for a local girl He was not a fellow that Hannah had taken to at all He seemed a shifty fellow, sort of underhanded, she had not liked him one little bit. Where he had come from they had no idea but he certainly fancied him self. When they were still up the Wrekin George had not bothered to put some money in the safe. They left to go to work on the cottage and when they came back the money was gone. Hannah knew that he had taken it She could see his foot marks on her clean floor He had used Bernie's key, but he would not own up so consequently they were unable to prove it, and Arnie knew it. Bernie had decided that it was too far for him to cycle to work from the cottage. Much to Hannah's relief, he was offered lodgings with his girl friend's family so he took up the offer; He did ask George to build him a smaller caravan so that he could live on his own again. George agreed to do this for him. And he made a start straight away. He bought the chassis and started it according to Bernie's instructions but it was left as the plans for the alterations of the Cottage were passed and that had to take precedence. Hannah took one look in the caravan after the men had left it and she was so disappointed and horrified with the condition that it was in.

"What a mess they have made of our beautiful caravan what are we going to do with it now? George you just take a look at the inside"

"Leave it be for a bit until we can decide what's best to do with it".

"My goodness is that all that you can say" she said to George who appeared not to be the slightest bit put out by the state that it was in.

"Well what did you expect it to be like with two men living in it"?

"I don't know but it is going to have to have quite a bit of work done to it. It will have to have new seats made and I will have to give it a good scrub and make some new curtains for it. That is before you decide what you want to do with it.

"Well don't you start meithering me about it right now I have enough to think about at the moment this house has to be altered".

Hannah decided that it was best to drop the subject for the time being. She took the seats and curtains out and burnt them it was no use what so ever trying to clean them, they were so dirty. She gave the caravan a really good scrubbing inside and out and it looked much better for it. It was a lovely Sunday afternoon in July that George suggested that they take the children for a ride out to the Stiper stones near Church Stretton, he said that he had always wanted to see what they called the Devil's chair. And they just might be able to pick some blueberries at the same time. "I've heard that there are a lot of them up there. Bring something to put some in and we will pick a few." Hannah did not know that he was beginning to feel guilty about seeing Sandra and thought that he had better give Hannah the impression that he cared for his family. How they enjoyed that afternoon it was so good to be out as a family and not have to worry about the café and all the work as they had done on a Saturday and Sunday as in the previous years. The blueberries grew there in abundance Hannah gathered enough to make a pie. George and the children explored the hill and they found the rock that was known locally as the Devil's chair and each took it in turn to sit on it. On the way home George decided that he would call and see an aunt and Uncle of his. They lived at Pulverbatch. They were offered a cup of tea and while making conversation the topic of the caravan came up and they told George about a caravan site at Ynyslas beach at Borth North Wales where they had a van. They gave him the site manager's name and phone number.

"It sounds just what you could do with. If you put it there you could hire it out for the rest of the summer and you could still go to it when you wanted we don't let ours because we spend every week end that we can up there. We love it. It is only because Betty has a bit of the flu that we have not gone this weekend but she seems to be OK today. We will be off again come Friday evening"

Next day Hannah made the family a pie with the berries that she had picked and it was the best pie that she had ever tasted and the rest of the family agreed with her. George and Hannah decided that putting the caravan at the sea was the only answer to their problem. The council was very reluctant to allow caravans to be lived in just anywhere. They decided to go and have a look at the site one Sunday and to see the manager who agreed to take the van. They had a lovely time Hannah had packed a picnic lunch for all of them. The children loved it. She and George sat and watched them building castles in the sand and they played passing a ball with them and a game of football. They played hide and seek in the sand dunes

"George it was the best thing that we did giving up the cottage Just look at the three of them now. See how they are enjoying them selves it is so good that we have much more time for them. We are now able to do so much more as a family."

"I see what you mean. We could get used to this"

"Just think George that we could come here and bring them and all being well stay for a few days it would be lovely. George did a few necessary repairs to the van and ordered new seats. Hannah made pretty new curtains for it He arranged for a low loader lorry to take the caravan to the sea he went with it to make sure every thing was OK. They were able to let it for a few weeks before the site closed down for the winter and the money that they were able to take in rent paid for the site rent, which certainly was a great help.

The winter started very early before George and Hannah had a chance to make a really good start of the work needed for the cottage and it turned out to be one of the worst winters since 1947. Jennifer and David were due to start school on January 6th The night before it started to snow and the wind blew from the North East By morning the lane was completely blocked and there was no chance that any one could get up the lane to the village. George was missing Sandra dreadfully and could not wait for the snow to thaw so that he could get out and be with her again. The roads stayed blocked for six weeks George had to walk to the village shop to fetch supplies of food; the children were at home and under feet. They sat and watched the telly as it was now called. Or they would be out playing in the snow. Once the snow had been trodden down and a good path was made Hannah decided to send Michael back to school George would walk over the frozen snow with him to the to the village in the mornings so that they could to meet the school bus at Little Wenlock, the drifts were too deep to try and take a vehicle. Hannah would take the sledge to meet him in the afternoon and bring him back down the lane they loved this time that they spent together. George was restless and irritable because of not seeing Sandra; Hannah thought that he was fed up because of the bad weather. She had changed her mind about the buying of the television and she was now quite pleased that they had gone ahead and bought it. George would sit and watch it until it closed down at midnight. Hannah did not know it but it did help to take his mind off Sandra a little, he could not wait until they were together again. He was now beginning to realise that he could not do with out her.

The old washhouse that Hannah had for a kitchen had a couple of tiles missing, allowing the rain to come in. They had put the washing machine in it but the severe frosts at night froze it up and damaged it. Later it took the repairman an hour to walk with his bag of tools from the village. After that the machine was wheeled into their one and only living room at nights until the thaw started. Rats got through the hole in the roof looking for food most of them came from the farm next door Hannah blew her top about them so George reluctantly set traps and tried to temporally repair the roof. Hannah was well and truly fed up with the situation that they had put them selves in and she missed having the Aga cooker and she wished that they had never set eyes on this little cottage.

It was Easter before things got going again, This had hit George's finances very hard no one had wanted any repair work doing. It had been as much as any one could do to cope with the bad weather. . Hannah was not content to just sit and watch the telly she considered just sitting watching it was a complete waste of time she always kept her hands busy with her knitting, darning or embroidery. They both knew that it had been almost impossible to tolerate the condition of the Cottage let alone the bad weather conditions; she never wanted to have to manage like they had ever again. When the weather warmed up she decided that she must get busy and plant a vegetable garden so that they could grow as much as they could for them selves and make quite a saving financially. George was quick to get started with work again when the snow had all gone and as the days warmed up he was now able to see Sandra again and he was much more content with life she gave him complete fulfilment something that Hannah did not seem to do. He set to and started to build a new garage around the old wash house and that was left standing as long as it was possible, Once the garage was more or less completed it was knocked down and the last details of the garage were finished. It was about twenty feet long and George had put a large window that faced south and it had a good concrete floor. It was wired for electricity. Hannah painted the inside and turned this in to a temporary kitchen. This was a blessing; it was a great help. Their next big job was to lift the roof off the cottage and build up the walls to a reasonable height so that the new part could be built on the side of it.

Hannah suggested that they build the new Kitchen and dining room along side of the old house first before taking the roof off. George disagreed and said that it could not be done that way He argued that once he had the roof off it would not take long to do the job. The Council had offered George a loan of a thousand pounds so that he could get the work completed fairly quickly. He would then comply for the benefit of grants that were on offer. This seemed a really good idea to Hannah and when she voice her opinion to George he was really annoyed,

"I'm not going to have a debt hanging around my neck I'll pay for what I do as I do it. "But "argued Hannah. "We can't afford to do much work at any one time Why not accept the council's offer of a thousand pounds We could get on so much quicker".

"A thousand pounds. Not likely Woman I will get it done in my own time". Hannah had to give up on the argument but she was very angry.

October came the weather had been beautiful, Hannah was now making the most from her garden she had grown some potatoes, they were always good for cleaning the ground of weeds. She first had to dig the ground and then get the soil ready for planting, as the potatoes grew the soil was ridged up around the plants so that the weeds did not get much chance to get established. Finally the soil was dug again to harvest the crop. She had grown peas, beans, cabbage and cauliflowers. She had cleared a good area and sown a lawn and planted a few geraniums around it. She planted them in leaf mould she had collected from under the trees in the wood across the road from the cottage.

Hannah was very pleased with her efforts the flowering plants looked so pretty. Next year she was going to try and grow other things like a row of swedes and some celery. The children loved to play in the wood although they were not allowed to go too far unless Hannah was with them they soon made friends with other children from down the lane. They would arrange to meet at Hannah's cottage where they knew there would always be a drink of squash or lemonade with a cake that Hannah had made just like the ones that she had been making for the tearooms up the Wrekin.At the end of October George decided to take the roof off the cottage. He told Sandra that he would not be able to be with her again for a few weeks "I can still come on Sunday afternoon Can I?

"Yes of cause you can".

"Three weeks should do it", he boasted, "We will soon have the new roof on I have already made the new windows and every thing else is coming. The new roof tiles are ordered". He had some second hand bricks delivered. Because, as he argued that the outside of the house was to be rendered with cement. George considered that there was no sense in paying for new bricks. The bricks that were delivered were dreadful they still had old cement adhered to them. George asked Hannah to spend as much time as she could during the daytime cleaning them so that he could get on with working with them when he came home in the evenings.

"But it is going to take ages if you are expecting me to clean all of those bricks George I will just not be able to cope". Hannah pleaded

"Well you will just have to I have told you that we will do our best and that it will not take that long. Surely you can clean a few bricks and cope with things for a few weeks the kids will be at school during the daytime. Neville says that he will come and give me a hand."

"What? All the way from Turnhill?

"Of cause where else is he going to come from?"

"But George" He stopped her there "Where else do you think that I can get any help from. The old chap can't come now that he is not feeling so well".

"I don't really know".

"Well be quiet and don't keep going on" I have enough to do as it is".

Hannah said no more but she was seething there seemed to be several tons of bricks dumped in the yard.

Every thing upstairs had to be moved down stairs or covered up. The old larder downstairs was cleared and mattresses were laid on the floor for the children to sleep on. George and Hannah made the most of it by putting a mattress on the living room floor for the night. And having to move it again next morning George and Neville worked late at night; they had fixed up temporary lights so that they could carry on well after it had gone dark. George was so tired that he was reluctant to get going in the mornings and it was no joke for Hannah trying to get three children ready for school with him still asleep on the floor in the living room. The two men did not start work until after George had eaten his tea and Neville had arrived and then it was Hannah's job to carry the bricks and the mixed wet cement up the ladders to them. She was their labourer

They got on very well and Hannah was quite pleased with the progress that they were making but after the first week it started to rain and it rained and rained practically every day.

Every where was in such a mess George laid tarpaulin sheets across the upstairs floors but the water ran through where there was the slightest hole in the sheets? Judith offered to have the twins when they were at home at the weekend if that would help. Hannah tried it but David and Jennifer would not settle and it just did not work. George and Neville put in as many hours as they could until every one including Hannah was on the verge of exhaustion. How Hannah wished that the caravan had not gone to the seaside they could have slept in it until the roof was back on again. George argued that he was not going to the expense of having it towed back just for them to use it for a couple of weeks. It was while Hannah was carrying bricks up to George that they heard on the radio that John Kennedy the American president had been shot. That was beyond belief. They stopped work and went down and watched the news as it came on the television.

At last they managed to get the roof back on. Ceilings put up and the inside walls covered with plasterboard and rendered. They just managed to get back up stairs in time for Christmas. What a relief for Hannah the three children were able to share the bigger bedroom and George and Hannah had the little one but there was only enough room in it for a bed and the dressing table. The stairs were to be taken out and new ones made and fitted coming from what was the old larder and George was going to make that the front entrance hall.George could now go ahead with his plans to build the new kitchen and dining room on to the old part making the house a four bed roomed house with a bathroom and a down stairs cloakroom. It was now looking as if they were going to get their dream home.

"I can't wait until it is all finished," Hannah would say to George. "It will have been worth all the hard work". During the coming spring trenches were dug and the footings were put in ready for the new part to be built. Hannah was so pleased now because things were really starting to show progress.

Sandra would often take the short cut through the woods on a Sunday afternoon and stay for some tea. She and George had pre-arranged this as a cover up and it had worked Hannah would listen with patience as Sandra complained about her Father Fred and mother Dorothy. She considered that they were expecting too much of her. She complained that William was trying to get out of doing any more work than he had to.

"I don't mind you coming to have some tea as long as you keep the peace at home." Hannah told her. "No way do I want Mother shouting down the phone at me saying that I am encouraging you to get out of doing your share of the work don't forget I was reared there and I know what they can be like. So don't you think that you can kid me I know just as much about them as you do"?

Hannah did not have much to do with the family at all these days her mother had not approved Hannah allowing Jennifer to have an operation on her eyes she did not agree with having operations of any sort. And she had certainly not approved of them giving up the Wrekin cottage. But it was as Hannah said she did not have to live up there. Hannah went to any family gatherings that she was asked to. Fred and Dorothy were very independent, now that they had William to eventually take over the running of the farm Dorothy saw to it that what William asked for they gave him the farm machinery was William's toys. He was not interested in the milking of cows or the looking after the sheep unless he had to. William had much bigger ideas of agricultural contracting combining Etc.

George would some times make out that he was working late in the evenings. Hannah did not mind they needed the money to buy the materials to be able to get on with the house. She would prepare the children for bed and keep George a meal ready for when he came home. Hannah was always busy knitting Pullovers, for George and the children cardigans and jumpers for her self and Jennifer, she was never bored. Worn jeans and socks were patched and darned for use as play clothes. Hannah used her old hand sewing machine to make all Jennifer's and her own dresses. Hannah was a very thrifty housekeeper she had her vegetable patch in the garden and she was quite happy to make do and mend.

"I can make a meal where others would starve" She would say to George as she made cauliflower cheese with new potatoes and fried bacon the cauliflower cut and the potatoes freshly taken from the garden.

1963 Hannah had been so busy with working the garden she had not noticed how quickly the summer went by. There was so much to be done George had worked on the septic tank and had finished and connected it ready for the new kitchen and bath room, after that it all seemed to come to a stand still Hannah did the accounts for George and by the autumn she was becoming really worried about how much that he owed.

"You know George" Hannah remarked one evening when she was able to have him at home and time to talk to him. "It is time some of your customers paid up. I see that the timber yard want their money and you still have not paid for the cement that you used for the footings of the new part of the house. I see that you have not paid Bill and Brenda their last bill. I really think that you should. I would not like to lose their friendship. You know I am sure that Brenda thinks that I am just a country bumpkin I could be wrong but I feel that because Bill has done so well with his business she likes to be a bit of a snob and she looks down her nose at me. Hannah did not let on that she had been snubbed when she had last called to see Brenda". She had driven into the drive at their house in Wellington She got out and rang the doorbell but there was no answer as she went to get back in the van she saw Brenda standing at the bedroom window looking at her. Hannah got into the van, turned it around and drove away and vowed that she would not call again where she was not wanted George did not want to listen to Hannah going on about money He looked away from the telly and said sleepily.

"I will have to chase a few of them up, there are a couple of jobs that need finishing and then I will put my bill in. As for Bill we are mates and you have nothing to worry about my paying them for the bit that I owe them. Brenda means no harm it's just that she comes from a better family than us. "You will let your imagination run a way with you",

Better family! Thought Hannah, she is an absolute nobody her father only manages a shop. Better family than us indeed what would he choose to say next.

Things was now beginning to tell on George He was beginning to appear to be tired out and very reluctant to get up and get going first thing in the mornings.

Just before Christmas Hannah was beginning to despair. George was so reluctant to get up. The days were drawing in and it was darker much earlier in the evenings.

It's that damned television Hannah had said to her self when she had called George to get out of bed for the third time one morning. I did not hear him come to bed again last night.At about ten o'clock the previous evening," Hannah said, "Come on George. I am going to bed; I don't want to watch the telly any longer." She stood up and put the pullover that she was knitting for him to one side. "We have to get up in the morning or the children will miss the school bus. I think that you should come to bed. Oh by the way Mrs Mathews has rung to day. She wants to know if she can have those windows that you have made for her fitted tomorrow. I am surprised at you leaving her with out windows fitted in this cold weather. Hannah took the tea cups that they had used for their supper into the back and ran some cold water over them. She went out to the lavvy in the garden before turning in for bed as she went outside she felt that there was snow gently falling. She went back in and washed her hands in the sink.

"A bit of snow is falling out side". She remarked to George as she went through towards the stairs." Please George do try and put the glass in those windows that you have fitted for Mrs Mathews, they have small children"

"Oh stop going on. I am getting back there as quick as I can" George answered, still keeping his gaze on the television set. "They have only had to manage one night".

"She said that you promised to have the bathroom and her kitchen windows fitted today but when she rang at about five you had not been there. It was a dreadfully cold night last night. And it looks as if it is not going to be any better tonight" Hannah was concerned for his customers. There were times that she well and truly blessed the day that they had bought the television set. George was quite right that the children were able to learn quite a lot from it, but it was George who was beginning to be obsessed with it and as soon as he came in, he monopolised it. There were talk about the television companies producing coloured pictures instead of showing every thing in black and white and that in the future there would be many more channels to choose from. Hannah had thought that if they were able to do that George would be one of the first to have one and then she would never get him away from sitting and watching it.

George did not like Hannah reminding him about his work. He did not like it at all. "Some of you women will moan about anything" Who and where he was working he considered was his prerogative She was there to look after the kids and garden.

Yes she kept the accounts for him and took messages for him and he considered that was where it should stop. He certainly resented her making comments as to which job he should be working at.

Next morning Hannah had been up early, she saw that there had only been a skittering of snow but it was very cold outside there had been a quite severe frost. There was still no sign of George coming down the stairs. She had got the children wrapped up well and sent them off to school. She decided to give George a call and get him out of bed some thing that she had been very reluctant to do. He was getting to be more and more like a bear with a sore head when he got up in the mornings?

Hannah came through from the temporary kitchen wiping her hands on her pretty home made apron "Get moving", she said to him when he eventually came down stairs. "Go and see Mrs Mathews and calm her down a bit before she starts ringing here again asking for you. Its gone ten o'clock now and it will be dark by four you will not have a lot of daylight today".

"Alright. Alright I am going," He shouted and sounded so angry Hannah was not going to be put off

"You have no need to shout I don't think that having no glass in the window frames at this time of the year is anything to dismiss lightly. Why did you start the job if you knew that you would have difficulty in finishing it? And another thing I will be glad when we can get on with this damned house again That bloody old earth toilet in the garden is no joke You promised us that if we put up with it until you got a bit of spare cash. You would soon be able to get going again on the new part. Have you considered having that loan which the council offered you? I am been thinking of looking into it again? George it is not very often that I am angry with you but I have noticed that you have more interest in that damned television in the corner than what you are in any thing else. You can't be getting work done and bills settled sitting watching that thing every spare minute that you have."

"Well you don't seem to show much interest in me. Gone to bed and asleep always too tired "

"What more do you expect I have the entire garden to do, three children to look after and do all the knitting of pullovers and do what ever else that I can to save you money. If you were to shut that television off at night and come to bed at a reasonable time you just might find things were a little better for you. Besides I am quite happy as I am and you know that I have been warned not to have more children." She almost added that she did not trust him any more not to get her pregnant. It was then that she realised that she had said too much and that George would get the message that he was not trusted.He went quite pale and hissed "What a little martyr you are. Such a goody goody. It's a pity that we can't all be like you. You will believe any thing that you are told those doctors think that they know it all but there is nothing wrong with the kids that we have got. Just a dammed good excuse if you ask me" He went into the back before she could answer and quickly shaved his face in the sink Wiped it on a towel. Took a cigarette packet from his jacket pocket and his matches. Lit one from the packet and walked out though the back door causing it to close with a bang. He went out to the van with the cigarette in his mouth, quickly wiped the thin layer of frozen snow from the windscreen.

He got in and started the engine took a comb from his pocket and straightened his untidy hair and left the premises holding the accelerator flat down as he drove up the lane Hannah could hear the engine making a dreadful noise as he drove away.

"Oh Lordy "She sat down in a chair to gather her wits together. I think that I went a bit too far but I don't care I think that it is about time that I said something The man's tired out," She muttered to herself, "If only he got to bed at night. Sod it! What with watching that damned thing and working late he does not know if he is on his head or heels. She went and boiled the kettle made her self-a drink and sat down again until she felt better. I hope that he has calmed down by the time he comes home to night or we all could be in for a silent evening.

George had also been thinking as he drove into town. He had not liked Hannah criticising him for watching the television. It had been the best thing that could have been invented as far as he was concerned. He found that he was able to sit and watch the late evening films and completely relax with out having to go out through the door. So what if he did stay up late He could not see what Hannah had to shout about he was not out at nights swilling beer and drinking money away. So he said that he was working late when he was still meeting Sandra that was something that she did not know about. Nor was she going to find out about it if he could help it .She did a bit of gardening and knitting Oh how the clicking of those knitting needles got on his nerves when he was trying to watch the television. Did they have to be made of metal or could she not use wooden ones. She did not go out to work like a good many other women well so the house was not finished but it soon would be when he could get some more jobs finished and collect the money in. . . .

George arrived at Mrs Mathew's house at about eleven o'clock. He had to pick up the required amount of glass that he needed to finish the glazing that day. She heard the van pull up outside and when she saw that it was George's van. She went quickly to the back door to say hello and what a relief that it was to see him come to make a start. The pieces of plastic sheeting that George had temporally tacked over the window frames had done very little to keep out the cold.

The whole house had been very cold through out the night, and she had been worried about her two small children.

"Sorry I'm late," he said as he got out of the van and a lovely smile on his face. "Had to fix another window this morning and have the glass cut for this job" he lied.

Mrs Mathews replied "I'm hoping you can get the glass in all of our windows today that sheeting you put up for the night did nothing to keep our bedrooms or our bathroom warm."

"I will stay until it is all finished today I have seen to it that there is plenty of glass here. I will not have to leave you to fetch more" confirmed George.

"Good in that case I will make you a cup of coffee". George quickly got his tools from the van and was working some putty with his hands when Mrs Mathews brought him a large mug of coffee and some biscuits for which he was very grateful. He had left home without having any breakfast. He had not stayed to hear Hannah continually going on about getting the house finished and having a go at him for watching the telly.

He had missed his usual eggs and bacon and his toast and marmalade.

George worked steadily though out the day and he made good progress .He was finishing puttying the last window at about a quarter to four in the afternoon. When a voice said

"Soon be too dark to see what you are doing" It was Sandra who had come up behind him.

"Hello there, what are you doing here?" asked George all smiles.

"Saw your van and thought you might be good enough to give me a lift home?" George knew that Sandra could not have seen his van from the main road even if she had decided to go home the long way round through Cluddely and not up the Ercall. Ah so that was why she had asked him where he would be working this week the crafty little madam George said to him self. Can't do with out me.

"Can you wait about for half an hour I should be finished by then?"

"Of course I can" she smiled provocatively "I'll sit in the van It has to be a bit warmer than it is out here I've got a book that I can look at while I wait for you".

Mrs Mathews had heard voices, she came to the back door "Who are you?" she asked.

Sandra was quite surprised and quickly replied

"I'm just a neighbour of George's I was trying to scrounge a lift home if I could, its so cold cycling"

Mrs Mathews looked at the young girl and although she wore gloves on her hands her bare knees, which were showing below her dark brown skirt, looked very red and cold

"Come in and have a cuppa, you look so cold I am sure that George will not be too long before he is finished." She ushered Sandra into the Kitchen and motioned for her to sit on one of the kitchen stools. Sandra looked around the kitchen it was of a modern design Sandra had not seen one like this before. It seemed to be so small.

" I am so pleased that he has put the glass in those windows I do not wish to have another cold night like last night. I think that the frost will be equally as severe again tonight. We still have two more windows to be replaced as soon as he can fit it in, we were certainly not expecting to have to replace windows so soon, and these houses are barely ten years old. They make them with such cheap wood these days. I know that George is such a busy man, He seems to be so much in demand"

The two women sat on the kitchen stools and they discussed the weather and things in general while they waited for George to finish what he was doing.

George finished glazing the last window that he was working on then packed his tools in the van making room for Sandra's bike, He went to the back door to collect Sandra and say goodnight. When Mrs Mathews mentioned that she and her husband had decided to have the last two windows at the rear of the house renewed. George replied, "Give me a couple of days and I will be back. I can soon fit those other two windows they are already made and then you will have them all done and in time for Christmas".

"If the weather stays as bad as this, you leave them until after the Christmas holiday and don't you come and make a start of them unless you can finish them, we can then settle our account with you" she said Cheerio and closed the back door. George started the van and drove the long way round going up through Cluddely ""Sarcastic Bitch" Said George "When you fit them we can settle our account" George mimicked Mrs Mathews. I wanted her to offer to, pay for what I had done. I could have done with her settling up today". Sandra thought that George sounded very funny and started to laugh.

"It's alright for you to sit there and giggle I will probably get it in the neck when I get home I can just hear what Hannah's first words will be "Have you been paid George. All she seems to think about these days is money" Again Sandra chuckled at George sounding so funny. He headed out to their usual spot around the back of the Wrekin and spent the next hour together making love. When they arrived at the farm George pulled in along side the back gate. He got out and took Sandra's bike from the van.

"See you soon my little love" and kissed her goodnight.

"How did the job go?" asked Hannah as he came into the cottage, thinking that she had better be a bit more pleasant towards George than what she had been that morning

"Stopped her moaning for a bit I think" answered George. "She wants me to put those other two windows in before they settle up"

"Let's hope the weather picks up so that you can get it finished and put your bill in"

"Why do you have to bring money up as soon as I come through the door? I have always paid my way have I not" he said.

"Christmas is only two weeks away and we need some money" Hannah continued, "I will have to get the children something to say that Father Christmas has been. Can you possibly imagine how disappointed that they would be if they found that he had been to all their friends and not to them"

"There's plenty of time for that yet," he muttered.

"Jennifer wants Father Christmas to bring her a doll; she saw it in Woolworth's when I took them into town last week to have their hair cut, except for the bits and dabs I have more or less got everything else"

"Well what on earth are you moaning about if a doll is all that you have to get"

"George I am not moaning I am just a bit worried I do not want to let the child down she is looking forward to Christmas they all are and Jennifer is already so excited".

"So what? It is not my fault and there are kids far worse off than ours. At least ours can run and play and they have the woods to play in which more than what some kids has. He went over and sat in his usual chair Michael and the twins were already watching the telly George concentrated his gaze on the set.

"Hannah wondered if she was hearing straight Kids far worse off than ours in deed how could George say such hurtful things considering that he had promised to do so much at the house for them. She decided that perhaps that it would be better to keep her mouth shut and say no more. Thank goodness that she had already made her own Christmas cake, puddings and mincemeat.

"I've just got to finish a job at Bullocks, I am sure that they will pay their bill." The next few days were cold and wet with sleet and snow; George tinkered around in the shed but got nothing of any importance done. He spent most of his time sat in front of the fire watching the television as if he had not got a care in the world to worry about.

Hannah was losing patience, "Come on George, we will need some money before the end of next week. The Bank won't give you anymore credit."

"For goodness sake don't keep going on about money. It is beginning to look as if that is all you can think about"

"I do try not to mention money George but I get so worried". He did not answer but the next day he did go very reluctantly and finished the work at Bullocks taking his bill with him. Mr Bullock kept horses and the work that George was to finish was in the stables so he was in the warm and dry, Mr Bullock did not offer to pay the bill when George handed it to him He just wished George a happy Christmas and closed the door. So there was nothing more that George could do about it.

Mr Bullock said to his wife as he went inside their kitchen

"That fellow can wait a bit for his money seeing how he has kept us waiting for that bit of work to be finished. I suppose that he wanted paying so as to have a bit of Christmas money well he came unstuck. I saw his face drop when I walked away even if he thinks that I didn't"" He chuckled

Christmas Eve came and at dinnertime Hannah said.

"George I need to go into town and do the remainder of the Christmas shopping it is no use going on my own I can't lift the calor gas cylinder it is too heavy for me. And we need a refill if you are going to have any dinner tomorrow. When can you take me, I need some money and the shops will be closed at half past five."

"Get yourselves ready we can go now if you want to." He said to her surprise Hannah quickly put her self tidy, she did not bother to ask the children to change into better clothes they would not be getting out of the van so they could stay in their play clothes. As they were about to leave George put a five-pound note on the table? "This will have to do" he said "I will drop you off in Town and pick you up later." Hannah was unable to pay for anything by cheque or cash a cheque because George had every thing at the bank in his name he considered that it was his prerogative to handle all money transactions whether it be for his work or house hold expenses.

"But we need a gas cylinder refill for the cooker, I am pretty sure that the present one is about to run out" Hannah complained, "If we don't get one there will be no dinner tomorrow.

"Well that's all you're getting" he replied and walked towards the back door.

"What about the children it is so cold to keep them hanging about waiting for me I think that it will take me at least an hour you know that it is Christmas Eve and the shops are probably very busy".

"I will keep an eye on them they can stay with me"

When they were ready the three Michael, David and Jennifer clambered into the back of the van and sat on cushions that Hannah had put there for them.

It was about 3pm when George dropped Hannah off in Market Street. She reminded him to collect the calor gas before they closed at five thirty she would go and pay for it. She decided that the gas must have priority so that would be the first thing that she would do". She went to Bromley's and paid for a cylinder of Calor Gas and realised that there was not a lot of change from the five pound note". Hannah was looking forward to when the house would be finished. They were planning to have a solid fuel cooker in the new kitchen, probably an AGA. Next she went and bought other essentials, and, to her horror she realised that there was not enough money for the doll which Jennifer had seen in Woolworths the previous week and it was almost ten shillings. It was a lovely doll, blonde hair and blue eyes and it was nicely dressed in pink. Hannah entered the store. Yes there was still one there. She was in a quandary as to what were she going to do as she had now only got nine shillings and some pence left and she still had to buy a few things that were absolutely necessary? Jennifer would be so disappointed if Hannah did not get that particular one; Hannah wandered around the other shops but could not see anything that would make up for the doll. She went back to Woolworth's about three times and still the doll was on show. A customer knocked display toilet rolls, to the floor the woman made no attempt to retrieve them so Hannah bent down and put them back in their place. She was astounded when she turned to move away and saw that the store manager was close by her and had been watching her. Hannah's face went bright red and she quickly left the store thinking that the manager would wonder if she about to steal them. Actually the manager had seen what had happened and had been quite impressed. He had noticed Hannah looking at the one particular doll and he decided that he would reduce the price in case that doll was what she had wanted to buy and that she could not afford it. Hannah had seen a golliwog in another shop, which did not close until six o'clock, and she decided that it would have to do for Jennifer, it was less money. Thinking that there might be a chance that the doll in Woolworths could have been reduced at the last minute, which they often did on Christmas Eve, she decided that she would take one last look before she went to buy the golliwog. Hannah finally went back for the last time five minutes before closing time and she was delighted to find that the doll had been reduced to seven shillings and six pence; she quickly bought it and made her way quickly out of the store. She hurried back to George She had taken some brown paper from her basket and wrapped it around the doll so that she could leave it in the van Thank goodness George had left the children at home they had wanted to watch the telly.

"Where have you been?" George grumbled. Hannah tried to explain but all George said was "She could have had something else". Hannah didn't bother to answer, she was so relieved that she had managed to buy the doll and she knew that on Christmas morning Jennifer would be so pleased that Father Christmas had brought her what she had wanted.

Christmas and New Year went by and Hannah decided that she would have to do something to help out financially, but what could she do? When it came to Monday mornings and she asked for some money so that the children could pay for their school meals. George didn't seem to care very much. He would say "Give them a note to take until you get the family allowance on Tuesday".Jennifer and Michael didn't seem to mind this arrangement too much, but Hannah knew that David was quite upset by it. One day Hannah was polishing the old oak sideboard. George had made her some wooden photo frames when they had been courting she picked one up and looked at it The photo was of George with his new motorbike he smiled back at her George was a good-looking man, she loved him. He made this frame when they first started going out together, two upright pieces of oak wood grooved and fastened to a base of oak with two pieces of glass slotted between the grooves. He had made a good many of these for friends and relatives when training as a carpenter. An idea came to Hannah; if she could make these and sell them they would have a bit more money for the family. She was quite good at woodwork; she had learnt quite a lot from working along side George when they had built the caravan and often when she had put the children to bed. She would go and give George a hand if he needed help to complete some job or other. He had taken an order to make about twenty wooden bus shelters for the Wrekin Council. They had to be finished by a certain date and he had to honour the contract. Hannah spent many an evening knocking nails in for George as he cut and prepared the wood, if he failed to complete on time or they would deduct some money off when they came to settle the bill. She thought about it and the more she thought about it the more she thought that she could do it. She could easily make the time when the children were at school and she could work in the shed because George did not need it very often during the daytime

Hannah told George of her idea "What do you think?"

"You could have a go at it if you like" he replied noncommittally. He was not the slightest interested in what he considered was Hannah's hair brained idea.

The more Hannah thought about it the more she realised perhaps she could do it.

"George" she said enthusiastically when she showed him the first picture frame that she had made "Would you cut the glass for me if I were to make a lot more of these."

"Just a minute don't you go getting carried away with this scheme of yours? Have you thought of how you propose selling these? He said as he studied Hannah's handiwork "I have got to give it you; you have made a pretty decent job of this one". Hannah had not given much thought to how she was going to sell the frames so she did not answer at first but her brain was working overtime. She could not think of a solution. An idea came to her. She was busy in the shed trying to perfect a photo frame. I will try for a stall in the market she said to herself. Mother had one when we were kids so why should I not try to do the same. I will make some inquiries next time that I am in town. This she did and she became very excited about the idea. She may not make much money to start with but that would not matter she would have some money of her own and if they sold she would be sure of having the kids dinner money.

"Who is going to look after the kids while you try this crazy scheme? You know that I have to get this house finished. There is so much work to do that I can't stay and baby sit". George smirked, hoping that he had caught Hannah out, and that her plans were not such a good idea after all. If she was honest with her self she had not thought about the children as she had let her enthusiasm run away with her.

"I have to do something George; I am not prepared to let the kids go to school with out their dinner money on a Monday morning if I can help it."

It's a pity for them". He sneered" There are some kids much worse than what ours are. Some have no money at all and have to have free dinners off the state. And another thing I don't want you messing up my saws. I can't stop sharpening them every time I want to use them especially the band saw".

Hannah said no more for a couple of weeks. She could see that George was not going to be very co-operative and give her much help with what he had thought was a crazy idea. She would have to persuade him to bring the glass for the frames from town and cut it to size for her. She told Judith and Molly of her idea and they thought that it was very enterprising and should be all right. Once Hannah had their approval and they had told George they thought that it was a good idea. He reluctantly gave in.

Hannah was saying what she was proposing to do to a neighbour who suggested that Hannah could take the children with her and let them go to the Clifton Cinema as a matinee was held on a Saturday morning from nine o'clock to twelve noon. She said that she often took her boys so that she could do her shopping in peace. What a wonderful idea Hannah thought it would solve her problems. George could take them into town and call back for them and her at lunchtime. If he wanted the van. If not she would have the use of it on Saturday mornings. Although Hannah could drive George was very reluctant to let her use what he considered was his van. He always had an excuse that he needed it for this or that.

Judith told Hannah of a friend of hers called Joan who liked to sit and do hand embroidery and that she would love to share the stall with Hannah. Hannah went to see her at her home in Wrockwardine and was very impressed with Joan's standard of work and they agreed to share the stall. George backed down when he saw that he had no choice but to go along with Hannah's enthusiasm and cut the glass for her frames he smoothed the edges on the grindstone in the yard so that there was no danger of sharp edges cutting any one. Michael would turn the handle of the grind stone for him. Hannah washed the pieces of glass until they were clean and they shone. The stall started off well and soon Hannah was taking orders to frame all sorts of things. The hand embroidered items also sold well. Tray cloths cushion covers, tea cosies and all sorts of little hand embroidered things.At first Hannah hated standing in the market but she needed the money. She liked to be busy and the standing about waiting for some one to come along and buy some thing was not her forte. As it had happened, it worked out well, although it meant that they all had to get up early on a Saturday morning the children did not mind they were off to see the films at the Clifton cinema. George would then pick them all up at lunchtime and take them back home. The stall became busier. A lot of teenagers brought photos of their pop idols such as Cliff Richards Elvis Presley Adam Faith and so on. Hannah found out where she could purchase the photographs and added these to her stall and it worked very well. The youngsters would be they're waiting for her on a Saturday morning to see what new photos that she had obtained for them. And more often than not they would buy a photo and a frame to put it in. Hannah decided that if she paid a bit more she would be able to have her stall until four in the afternoon when the market closed. She hated standing there all day, she would have preferred to have been at home, but at least it brought some extra money into the house. David was much happier when he knew he could have his dinner money and pay it, on a Monday morning like all the rest of his pals at school.

More often than not George would collect the children at lunchtime and treat them to fish and chips. He was also benefiting from the extra money that Hannah was making. . The children were able to play around out side during the afternoons and were no bother to him. They had built them selves a fantastic tree house and they played for hours up there. It also gave Hannah a chance to buy the necessary weekend shopping from the other stallholders at a much-reduced price compared to the village shop. Sandra still walked through the woods as a short cut to Hannah's cottage on a Sunday afternoon. If the weather were good enough Hannah would be as usual working in the garden, David working along side her. Michael would be with his Dad working on whatever needed attention and Jennifer was very little trouble to any one. Sandra would help to amuse her and give a hand with Sunday tea, which Hannah was often grateful for. Hannah was a better cook than her Mother Dorothy was. Hannah always made a good Sunday tea. There would always be freshly made scones and sponge cake filled with home made jam and butter cream Sandra joined in as if she was one of them. The family usually sat watching television until Hannah decided that it was time to put the children to bed. This was the time that Sandra waited for, As soon as Hannah rose from her chair to see to the children, she would say that she had better go back home and not to be too late so that she could keep the peace with her Mother. If her Mother had been in a bad mood when Sandra had left the farm Sandra knew that she would have calmed down when she saw that Sandra was not there to help with the evening feeding of the poultry and the baby calves when she had it all to do her self.

Hannah had not taken too much notice that Sandra had casually asked where George would be working the following week. George would offer to take Sandra back home while Hannah prepared the children for bed and read them a story.

Hannah had not realised or noticed anything untoward with her little sister. The evenings were drawing in and it was getting dark earlier Hannah would say" George will take you back, it's getting dark and I don't like you walking back through the woods". George would stir from his chair and make it look as if he was reluctant to leave the fireside and watching the television. He would take her home he had more than a fascination for Sandra but he had to be very careful not to show it in front of Hannah. When he returned he and Hannah would settle down for the evening George watching the telly and Hannah getting on with some knitting, the clicking of her knitting needles would drive him mad but he knew that it was no use complaining. He had noticed that Hannah could not sit and relax like he could. She always had to be busy doing some thing with her hands. If she was not knitting then she would be darning or doing some embroidery. The children were growing so that Hannah did save a lot of money by knitting pullovers jumpers Etc for all the family. It did save quite a lot of money and George felt that he really did not have cause to complain. It would cost him a lot more to clothe them all if he said anything and she stopped knitting. Hannah had no idea that her knitting annoyed him. George really enjoyed watching a good film especially a cowboy and Indian one and there was usually a good one showing on the television on a Sunday evening. He still considered what a remarkable invention that the television was and now that most families could afford to buy one and sit and watch a film with out having to go to the cinema.

"Everything alright at the farm?" Hannah would ask when he returned from taking Sandra home. She assumed that he had stayed to pass the time of day with her parents and that was why it had taken him so long.

"Yes I think so; the van was out so I guess that William is off out enjoying himself somewhere"

"I feel sorry for Sandra", continued Hannah, "She has no one to confide in now that we've all left home"

"She can look after herself" commented George, "What a figure she is getting, she'll soon be bigger than any of you".

"It's all that sugar and cakes she eats; she certainly has a good appetite. I think that she likes coming here.

Her eyesight is not that good I wonder if she will be able to learn to drive a car. I have noticed that she's started to leave her glasses off, with her eyesight as bad as it is; I am inclined to think that she is being a little stupid, she squints so badly without them. But I would not dare say anything to her about it I consider that it is no business of mine. It is up to our Mother to reprimand her if she thinks fit to do so"

"Haven't really noticed", Muttered George as he lied. He was trying to sound uninterested and to keep his attention on the film he was watching.

Mrs Brown the vet's wife bred and showed her dogs. She bread the Elk hound and she offered one to Hannah if she would like to have a bitch which she did not want herself and she said that she had been so pleased with George's work. She said that she knew that it would have a good home in the country. There was just one snag and that was that she retained the dog's pedigree papers so no matter how much she trusted George and Hannah. She asked that they would not try to breed with her or try to show her. This was no problem to Hannah she loved that breed of dog. She had seen them so many times when she had needed the van and had dropped George off when he had been working for them. Mrs Brown had an Aga cooker in her kitchen and she always had a coffee pot full of coffee simmering away on it. She always offered coffee to who ever called. Hannah loved her coffee. Hannah was so pleased with the offer that she accepted the dog at once and the children loved her.

Hannah was able to take the children and the dog for walks in the woods she was able to teach them how to recognise things like the different trees and birds just like she had when she had been a child. They spent so many pleasant hours together how they loved those times.

Chapter Eleven
Day Of Bliss But For Whom

During the approaching days to Christmas, Hannah was busy with her market stall, and the making of the photo frames kept her busy. She had taken so many orders. The children were at home already broken up from school for the Christmas Holidays they played out side and in the wood for most of the time unless it was very wet. Michael and David had made friends with the neighbours children and they played for hours just inside the wood. Hannah had only allowed them to go a short distance into the wood unless she was with them. Jennifer tagged along whenever she could persuade the boys to take her with them They had built themselves a tree house, which was their secret hiden place. Today they were playing with two of the boys from down the road they had all been in for a break. They had something to drink and some of Hannah's cakes to eat. She went back into the shed and was busy working away looking forward to Christmas she had been being able to afford to buy what the children were asking Father Christmas to bring them. She had her suspicions that Michael knew who Father Christmas was but she had told him that if he did not believe in him then he was not to bother hanging a stocking up. She knew that he would not want to be left out and she said no more about it. Hannah had quite a lot to do so many frames had been ordered for Christmas presents and they were needed the following Saturday. Thank goodness that her orders were more or less complete. She could not afford to let her customers down. She could hear the boys playing just inside the wood the noise of the children playing gave her the confidence to get on with her work. They seemed happy enough.

Suddenly there was a screeching of car brakes. Hannah ran from the shed to see what was going on. A blue car had skidded to a standstill in the middle of the road. What had happened? Her worst fears were becoming a nightmare Jennifer was lying in the road in front of the car the other children came running from the wood and started to scream she hushed them up then they stood around looking on scared stiff. The driver got out of the car he appeared to be much shaken "I am so sorry. I am so sorry". He looked at Hannah her face now quite pale. "I had no chance she ran out in front of me. What are we going to do?" Hannah's inner strength took over.At first she began to feel quite faint seeing her little girl lying in the road. Then she quickly took over and gave orders to Michael to fetch a blanket from off her bed" She looked at the driver "Go and ring for an ambulance David go and show him where to find the phone". She tried to pick Jennifer up to carry her into the house but she cried out that she hurt when she was moved. It was her leg that seemed to be badly broken. As Michael ran back with the blanket Hannah wrapped it around her and with the help of the driver who was back out after ringing for the ambulance they used it to gently to carry her into the house. They put her on the front room floor in front of the fire. "We must keep her warm," said Hannah who was now trembling with shock "The ambulance is coming" The driver said. "I will have to report this to the police I'm afraid that I cannot move the car until they come" He picked up the phone and made the call. By this time neighbours had come to see what was going on and one woman called Alice was so relieved when she saw that it was not one of her boys who had been involved in the accident.

She quickly went into the back and made some tea. "Where is George working?" She asked. "Can we get hold of him?"

"I'm not sure. He said that he had one or two jobs that he wanted to finish before the Christmas break. He could be anywhere".

"Don't you worry I will look after the Boys Here drink this tea it will make you feel better "She passed Hannah a cup of sweet tea and she gave one to the car driver. Jennifer was lying still on the blanket softly crying. "It hurts it hurts." There is nothing that we can do for her; we must not give her anything to drink. The Ambulance will soon be here. You run upstairs and change so that you can go with her I will take the boys with me. She had noticed Hannah's worn jumper and threadbare skirt. Michael was trying to tell them what had happened. He and the other boys had crossed the road to play in the wood and he said that Jennifer was playing inside the house. She said that she was getting her dolls ready for Christmas and that she did not want to play with them. She must have changed her mind and ran across the road to be with the boys and she had not stopped to look for cars as Hannah had always taught them.

"Don't you go blaming your self" Hannah tried to comfort the driver, he was so upset Alice gave the boys a cup of tea they were so scared that they would be to blame that they were all chattering at once. When the ambulance came, the driver and his mate took a look at Jennifer and decided that her leg too badly injured to be taken to Wellington cottage hospital and after making some quick phone calls she was gently lifted and placed in the ambulance. Hannah was sat along side of her and they drove off quickly towards Shrewsbury leaving Alice and the driver to sort things out. George came home later and wondered where everyone was. He rang Alice to see if Hannah and the children were with her. Not that it seemed likely it was now quite dark and they would have been at home watching the telly. Alice told him the whole story and said that she would now send the boys up the road to be with him.

Hannah left Jennifer at the Shrewsbury hospital. She was told that she could not stay and they would see that she was made quite comfortable but they did not think that she would be staying there once the doctors had seen her and had taken X-rays and had made their assessments. She would probably be moved to Oswestry Orthopaedic hospital where they had much better facilities to deal with such a badly broken leg. They quickly administered some pain-killing drugs to help her in the meantime. Thank goodness that Hannah had picked up her handbag. She now had to get home and she had to have some bus fare. She caught a bus to Wellington and then rang home for George to pick her up. He left the boys watching the telly he did not have to warn them to behave themselves they were still coming to terms with what had happened to Jennifer. When he arrived at the bus station he was in a right bad mood.

"You and those damned frames. You should have been looking after her".

"I have not got eyes in the back of my head. I can't think why she ran across with out looking. George you give me a bit extra money to pay for everything and I will willingly give up my stall"

"That's right you have to bring money into every thing and put the blame on me". They argued for some time until Hannah decided that it was best to say no more. She was still shaken by Jennifer's accident. The next few days were a nightmare for Hannah After the doctors at Shrewsbury hospital had seen Jennifer and given her the necessary treatment for shock and X-rays to see what damage had been done to her leg and they also checked that her scull had not been fractured. They decided that it would be better for her to be sent to the Oswestry Orthopaedic hospital. The orthopaedic surgeon said the Jennifer would be there for at least four to six weeks and that they did not want her to put any weight on her broken leg at all because the break was rather high up on the leg above the knee. The visiting was going to be so difficult for Hannah

Visitors were not encouraged to visit the children's ward too often during the week. George said that he was too busy and in any case he did not like the smell of hospitals. Hannah visited Jennifer whenever she could, and promised that they would all come and see her on Christmas day. George and Sandra were still meeting whenever they could, trying not to raise the suspicions of Hannah and the rest of the family. Their lovemaking was beyond belief, neither of them had realised to what heights they could reach to satisfy each other. Hannah didn't question why George was working so late so often, she knew that she dared not. He had made that perfectly clear that one evening and Hannah had not forgotten. All the same she was very concerned that he was working so hard, He hardly seemed to be at home perhaps he was getting ahead with his work so that he could get on with the house after the Christmas break. She also knew that his customers wanted their work finished but he did not seem to be making any invoices out for them to pay for the work done.

"I must see you at Christmas" pleaded Sandra, as they got dressed after making love again in the place that they called their own secret hide away At the back of the lime kiln woods "It's going to be rather difficult" was George's reply.

"I'm sure you can think of something my Darling," Sandra said

"Well there is John from Leighton; he often called for bits of wood and things. He is doing his own house up; I could say I was going for a drink with him"

Christmas Eve he told Hannah he had seen John who had suggested that they go for a drink together;

"It's his way of thanking me for the bits and pieces wood that I have let him have"

"I don't mind," replied Hannah She loved Christmas time, it was the one time she could excel herself with the cooking and making things for the children. She never went to bed very early on Christmas Eve. There was the cake to be iced and the stockings to be filled the decorations to be put up and Hannah still believed that it was bad luck to bring the holly and the tree in before Christmas Eve

George had not come home by eleven o'clock, so Hannah went to bed, quite satisfied that everything that needed to be done was done. There was only the sprouts to be picked She liked to pick greens from the garden the day that she used them so that they ate them quite fresh. The brasses had been cleaned and shone on the fireplace. The tree stood on the oak table alongside the fireplace, sparkling with its decorations that Hannah had lovingly made and had been able to buy some fairy lights. The paper streamers had been pinned to the oak beams. Hannah had wrapped the new shirt she had bought George and placed it with the other presents under the tree. She had put a stocking for Jennifer alongside those of Michael's and David's. She was sad at the fact she was not with them, but they were all going to see her the next day. George returned home in the early hours, Hannah did not know what time it was when he had crept into bed She had been fast asleep from exhaustion. He was there in the morning as David and Michael leaped onto their bed with excitement as they found their Christmas stockings. Hannah liked the children to open their stockings when they awoke; they could play with their new toys. She found that this kept them quiet during the morning whilst she cooked the family dinner. After they had eaten and all the plates were cleared, the washing up was done, only after this could they all sit around a pleasant fire and open any presents that they had received from the family. This Christmas day was going to be difficult. Dinner had to be ready earlier as they were going to see Jennifer It was about eleven o'clock before George finally got up and got himself together. He sat in his chair by the fire drinking a cup of tea and some toast that Hannah had put before him watching the telly.

"Dinner will be at 12:30," said Hannah "It's early so that we can go and visit Jennifer"

"I don't feel up to it. You go you can take these two with you" was George's reply. He had thought that if Hannah took the boys he could settle down and catch up with some sleep.

"But you must come, it's Christmas Day, Jennifer will be so upset if you don't come with us"

"You go and take Michael and David and leave me here a bit I can then keep the fire stoked up for when you come back"

"But why can't you come with us?"

"I'm too tired"

"Too tired indeed! Really. Perhaps it would have helped if you had come in a bit earlier last night I have no idea of what time it was when you came in. I did not hear you but I expect the neighbours did", Hannah was getting annoyed, but she said no more as she did not want an argument on Christmas Day. She went out into the garden to pick the sprouts. The air was bitterly cold; she noticed that it had started to gently snow. Bother she thought I had better leave Michael and David here while I go to see Jennifer. A mans voice from over the hedge wished her a Happy Christmas. It was the neighbouring farmer, Mr Talbot. Ah there's an idea thought Hannah.

"I wonder if Ben would like to come with me to visit Jennifer this afternoon" Hannah asked him, "George is not up to it and now it is snowing I don't want to take the other two in case it gets worse as the day goes on. I think that I had better take some one with me in case I need a push".

Ben was a lad of fifteen and would be good company for Hannah especially if the snow continued and made it difficult to drive and then they might have to leave the van and walk down the lane before they got home. The lane could become snowbound very quickly.

"I'll see what the missus says", replied the farmer

"Thank you", replied Hannah and went back indoors with her sprouts.

"George I've seen Mr Talbot and asked if Ben could come with me this afternoon, it's started to snow. David and Michael had better stay with you in case it becomes heavy."

"That's a good idea "George replied from his chair keeping his eyes on the television programme. Hannah had no sooner started to clean her sprouts than some one knocked on the door. Hannah had no time to answer it. She saw Mrs Talbot walk in, ignoring Hannah she went through to George.

"Get off your idle backside", she shouted at George, "Take your wife to see that little lass, it's already snowing and my Ben is not going out today. You can leave the other two with me if you like. I heard you come in last night, you must have been the worse for drink I suppose seeing what hour it was when you crept in." She turned on her heals to go,

"Your too bloody soft with him you know, he needs a good kick and would get one where it hurts if I had to put up with what you do, your just too daft!" she said to Hannah as she closed the back door and went on her way. Hannah was quite shaken; she had not witnessed anything like this since she had left home. It did the trick though; George made the effort to take Hannah to Gobowen although he wasn't very happy at the idea.

Jennifer, as usual, was delighted to see her Mum and Dad. The ward had been beautifully decorated and there had been presents for every patient. Staff, patients and visitors all shared afternoon tea and the hospital had made a tremendous effort to give the patients especially the children a wonderful day. Jennifer opened the stocking that Hannah had taken with her. She was thrilled to bits with the contents. The snow had been gently falling throughout the afternoon and George and Hannah only just made it home. The van did its share of skidding and sliding as they encountered the narrow lanes. George didn't make much conversation as they made their way home; He was too tired to bother with talking. Hannah was quite happy to relax in the passenger seat watching the snow falling steadily. Jennifer had seemed so content in hospital, she had adapted to it very quickly but Hannah was looking forward to the New Year when there could be a chance of having her home again. George's thoughts had been elsewhere, he was remembering last night's lovemaking and how glorious it had been. He also wondered at what excuse Sandra had given her parents for being out so late, they had completely forgotten the time as they both satisfied their needs. She had told him how nice that it was to be with him when he was dressed in his tidy clothes."

"Makes a change from your working togs. You are so handsome "She had cooed" I am so jealous of Hannah"

"Don't talk of Hannah tonight my sweet "He was feeling so guilty but after being with Sandra for a while he dismissed all reservations. In fact he was already looking forward to the coming April when Sandra would be seventeen, but even then he had no desire to be caught if he could help it He was having the best of both worlds and he was enjoying himself. The weather had been mild at the beginning of January but the warmer weather did not stay for long the winter weather came back with vengeance it was a month later the snow that had fallen at the end of January melted away things had been quite difficult for a while. When George saw Sandra they had to stay in the van. This gave him the idea to take her to the caravan for a day later in the springtime.

"Sandra wants to know if you need any help at the weekend if you are going to see Jennifer. George asked when he got home after being with her.

"How come that you have been talking to Sandra?"

"I gave her a lift home today".

"Oh you did. Did you, crafty Madam she seems to know when you are driving home so that she can get a lift.

"I was thinking of taking Michael and David with me on Sunday to see Jennifer. What about you coming with us it would be nice for her to see all of us. What do you think? Are you coming?" "Michael gets so bored waiting around the hospital, I thought you could take him out in the grounds for a walk. If the weather is dry, we are allowed to take Jennifer in her bed for a walk. She likes that, those beds are not too hard to push, we could take her down to the café and shop"

"I don't know about that, it all depends on what I've got to do. I've plenty of work on just at the moment and you are waiting to have more glass cut there just does not seem enough time in the week to get every thing done." He said trying to get out of any hospital visiting if he could. When Hannah was visiting the hospital He knew where she was and about how long she would be away.

"I think that I will soon be able to buy some more bricks and cement to get on with the house."

"I hope you're right" Hannah went on, "Have you thought again about borrowing some money That thousand pounds the Council offered would certainly help you to push on with it We could pay it back as we went along." She saw the expression that crossed his face. As much to say don't you start about the house again"? "George we have got to think about having a bathroom, can't you see that the children are growing so quickly and oh to have a water toilet. I am absolutely fed up with that dammed stinking thing out side and the children hate it, all their friends have proper toilets it is just not fair and I am beginning to get fed up good and proper."

"I've told you before; I'm not borrowing money just to get the house finished. We can manage as it is for a bit longer can't we?"

"It's not easy George; I spend all my time heating the kettle and saucepans for hot water. Twenty times I boil that kettle on a Sunday night, just to bath the kids clean for Monday morning! And time and time again in the week"

"I know, I know. It is difficult but it won't be for much longer, things are looking up again" Hannah felt awful, perhaps George was right, and she told herself to have a bit more patience. George seemed to be working harder these days and she herself had got the garden producing well and she had the market stall. To be able to bring the children up in the country she thought was a lot to be thankful for. Hannah decided to give a little more time to George, perhaps she was expecting too much of him. She had been engrossed with Jennifer's problems and her days went by so quickly. George also had needs and one of these was the need for an active sex life. Hannah loved George deeply; she had even gone to the family planning clinic for contraceptive advice. The woman at the clinic had been very helpful and suggested that Hannah try a cap. George was not happy; he didn't think it was right to fiddle about so he dismissed it out of hand. Hannah had so much to cope with she was always tired out and was usually in bed long before George especially if he had stayed late watching the television she was not the slightest bit interested in making love with George every night and she had let him know it. Another thing she did not trust him not to get her pregnant. Sometimes he would complain but got no satisfaction. He did not realise that Hannah was trying to cope with far too much. He considered that he also was doing more than his share. Meanwhile Sunday came and Hannah took Michael and David with her to see Jennifer. Mr Rose had wanted to keep Jennifer as an inpatient for six weeks before he considered her being allowed home. While she was in hospital her diet was kept under strict control. It was important that Jennifer didn't put on too much weight or she would grow too big for her plaster cast and renewing it could disturb her broken leg. All sweets were under strict supervision of the ward sister, toys were shared and no one child was allowed to monopolise any one toy. All the children in Jennifer's ward had some education. A teacher came to the wards and did the best that they could although it was very limited and time passed very slowly for the children. If she could Hannah would visit in the week she did her best but she had to depend on George not needing the van for his work.

When the bell rang for the end of visiting time the three of them said goodbye to Jennifer. Hannah hated saying goodbye and she would be glad when Jennifer was able to come home again. Michael was already heading off towards the car park with David tagging along. Visiting was alright for a while but they soon got bored and wanted to go off to the hospital shop which sold every thing you could think of including all the various types of sweets. When Hannah got back home she drove the van into the yard and went inside ready to prepare a meal for the four of them, she was surprised to find that the table had already been laid, Sandra was there.

"I thought this was the least I could do, I rang to see if all of you had gone to the hospital. I was surprised when George answered the phone and said that he had finished work at four so I came across to give you a hand" she smiled

"You have been so good to me and William is at home for the milking today. I expect he will be off out before the day is finished and Mother and Father are not much company. They just sit and listen to the wireless they are now thinking about having a television set" She continued "There's been talk of bringing the electric across the fields, perhaps they could get themselves one, and they don't know what they are missing!" She did not let on that she and George had been on her bed making love and that she had no shame what so ever in what they had been doing. She was beginning to resent Hannah living with George although she was careful not to say too much to George in case he thought that she was getting too possessive and stopped seeing her.

"Ah it's the telly you come across for" teased Hannah

"Well it's the same as it was with you. Mother has never let me bring any friend's home from school and there is nothing much to do on a Sunday afternoon; at least you were working in the café. William is keen on that dark haired girl from Wrockwardine Road If he is not out with one then it is another you never know which one he is out with these days." Hannah's commented "I should leave him to decide that, he will settle down when he is ready". Sandra was not prepared to let the subject rest

"I can never see our Mother taking to that Sheila, you can scrape the paint off her face and her hair is just like a beehive, tins and tins of that lacquer stuff she uses and after all she is only a shop assistant."

"Yes you've got a point; I would not like to be in Sheila's shoes if she tries to marry Mother's beloved William, only the very best for him! She will want him to marry a farmer's daughter. Still Sheila doe's work in the hat department of McClure's which is considered to be quite a respectable shop"

Hannah had to admit she liked to listen to Sandra giving her a bit of family gossip. Her sisters were all too busy bringing up their own families to bother with each other. Elizabeth, Mary, Rebecca and Helen were married to men who had full time jobs and were also farming smallholdings. They did not hear much of Grace Hannah often thought about the times when they had been kids and Grace had said that she would only marry some one who could afford all she wanted. Now she certainly had her prince charming. The sisters sent each other cards at Christmas and met up for family gatherings, occasionally Hannah and George would go to visit but not very often as there was always so much to be done and the same applied to her sisters.

Hannah made a move to get the children to bed; "Do you want me to take Sandra back?" came from George's chair.

"Yes please dear, its dark now, I would not like to have to change a wheel if I were to have a flat tyre, the lanes are so narrow. Remember the time when I abandoned the van half way up the Wrekin? I turned it around on the ice and you had to go down to fetch it. I can remember you were not too pleased that day. I don't know what it is about women and vehicles but you men appear to cope far better! Still that's their prerogative, don't you agree Sandra?"

"I do," said Sandra, "I would hate to be stuck and not be able to get going again by myself, and still what are men for? To help damsels in distress are they not? I am thinking of learning to drive my self, not that our mother would let me borrow their car since they have bought the new Wolseley it is their pride and joy

They don't let William use it; he has to use the van. Can you imagine kissing and cuddling in that, it stinks of animals that have been taken to the auction?"

"I am tired out, having driven to Gobowen to see Jennifer I have had enough driving for one day there certainly seems to be more and more traffic going along that A5".Hannah got up to heat the water ready to wash the children for bed. George got up and went to start the van ready to take Sandra home George returned some time later. Hannah naturally assumed that he had been at the farm talking to her parents. Michael had heard his Dad drive into the yard, He waited a while and then he crept out of bed and down the stairs He did not like sharing the room with his twin sister and brother and he was looking forward to having his own room when the house was finished. He would then be able to hang all his model aircraft in his room he had made so many of them from kit form. He was very close to his father, they shared most things. His father always took him with him whenever he could. George was able to keep the lad occupied, which was what he needed. He was an intelligent child but he was also a bit highly strung and although Hannah loved him she sometimes found him a difficult child to handle, he got so easily bored, where he respected his father and they were able to communicate on the same level. George and Michael were chatting away together. Hannah was so proud of them, she was quite happy to sit back and listen to the two of them.

Sandra did not behave like a teenager; she behaved like a sexually mature woman and certainly took a great deal of satisfying. George was feeling absolutely drained of energy and would be glad when the day came to an end and they went to bed. In fact he was so tired that he suggested to Hannah that they had an early night and he was very grateful when she agreed with him. He was glad that she was not too demanding she always had so much to do that she fell asleep as soon as her head hit the pillow. Winter went into spring and Jennifer was allowed home. George was showing a bit more interest in getting on with the building of the rest of the house. The old staircase was taken out and the family had to manage with a ladder whilst a new set of stairs were made. The children thought it was great fun to climb a ladder to go to bed, the welfare lady who visited Jennifer, however, was most concerned and strongly advised George to get on with it for the safety of the children.Unknown to Hannah, George was still meeting Sandra. She was not very tall her height was about five feet two. One could not say that she had a fat figure and neither could it be said that she was slim. Her eyesight was poor but now that she was older there was a possibility of an operation to correct the fault on her eyes and give her a much better field of vision. Unlike her sisters her hair was still blonde and had changed very little since she was a baby. She had a very prominent bust that must be at least size 38D. Sandra had made no effort to get herself a job, There was plenty of work that she could find to do on the farm and Dorothy needed all the help that she could get in the house. Dorothy was getting older and so she was pleased that Sandra was not rushing off to work in the town, she could supply her with what pocket money that she needed, which as she had envisaged was not a great deal.

Sandra had not shown a great deal of interest in any of the local boys so she was not asking for any great amount of money for new hair do's and new clothes very often. She kept her blonde hair cut reasonably short. If Dorothy had known the truth about what her daughter was up to goodness knows what she would have done probably killed her without stopping to think of the consequences. Different young men came to the farm, who was mostly friends of William, One called Charles was taken on to help with the farm work, he came from the village and a well-respected family He was Miss Hinge's nephew. Secretly Dorothy hoped that Sandra would be attracted to him, but she showed no interest in him. He certainly was not cut out for farm work. It was not long before he left the farm to find work in Sankey's factory where he could earn much more money. Un-be-known to Dorothy Sandra had tried all her charms on Charles, but she found him very immature compared to George. The lad was far too reserved and shy, she knew she had to find an alibi from somewhere to cover her comings and goings, but Charles was of no use to her. She needed to be with George and she went out of her way to fix it. She was finding it quite easy to meet him Shopping days was Thursday and Saturday Dorothy rarely missed going into town on these days and if Fred and Dorothy were thinking of going to a farm sale. Which was being advertised in the Wellington Journal and Shrewsbury News, Sandra would find out in advance by casually asking if there would be anything of interest to them, they usually gave some indication if they were thinking of going to buy something in particular. Some times they would go just to socialise with others some thing which they both liked to do. Sandra kept George informed as to when there was a possibility of them being away from the farm. He would always telephone to see if the coast was clear. If for some reason or other they had decided not to go Sandra made sure that she was in the house when George called and would just say to her Mother that the telephone call had been a wrong number. She would have told George not to come to meet her. It was so easy for Sandra when her parents had gone out, she only had to wait till William was busy in the fields, then she could slip away for a couple of hours unnoticed. Both she and George knew every track in the woods surrounding the farm and they had their secret meeting places well hidden from prying eyes. Sandra was quite an expert; she knew exactly what George wanted but she loved to keep him waiting just to tease him, making him very excited. They used to lie together on a carpet of bluebells tearing each other's clothes off, anxious to reach fulfilment. The more that they were able to meet, the more possessive Sandra was getting. She began to resent George going home to Hannah and so she would prolong their lovemaking as long as possible, but she also knew that they had to maintain the secrecy. She knew that it would be devastating to so many if they were to get caught.

Sandra had made friends with, Mrs Hollis the gamekeeper's wife who was now a widow and getting on in years. Old William Hollis was now dead and buried. The old lady, Ethel was rather lonely living in the little cottage in the woods at the back of the Limekiln woods. She was glad of Sandra's company and knew she could ask Sandra to bring her shopping if she herself could not get into town which was not very often. She was very self sufficient, Sandra was able to make great use of this using Ethel Hollis as great alibi if her mother queried as to where she had been all evening.

The old lady's little cottage was still well off the beaten track. There had been no telephone connected. The woods surrounding the track were a really good place for Sandra to meet George. No one usually went into those woods except the odd courting couple and it was not a favourite place for them. They did not venture into these woods for fear of getting their cars stuck in mud and that would mean walking a great distance to a farm to get a tractor to pull them out. There were plenty of other places for them to go up the Ercall. William made many a pound or two pulling courting couples free with the tractor so that they could go back home. George did not know how to handle the situation he had got himself into. He was not prepared to stop seeing Sandra, he could not do without her, and she was able to satisfy his needs. Hannah made no such demands of him; she was such a contented person with her work and with the children she was satisfied with life. He knew he should get on and finish the house and he knew that it was not fair to the family expecting them to have to manage as they were for much longer. The main problem for him now was money. His keeping Sandra satisfied was taking up a lot of his time and his work was beginning to suffer. He was leaving his work during the day time when ever she wanted to be with him He was finding it very difficult to finish the work that he had started and so was unable to collect money for it. He would always have some good excuse or other as to why the jobs were not finished if Hannah asked him how such and such a job was going. She had wanted him to make out the bill for the work and collect the money. Consequently, he was getting behind with the paying for materials that he was using. He started to get worried in case Hannah would soon start noticing that his debts were increasing. He knew that the overdraft at the bank was getting worse, and he knew that he just would not be able to go on as he was for much longer.

Hannah had noticed that he was looking tired out and she thought that he must be working far too hard and she suggested that she thought that it would be a good idea for all of them to go to the caravan for a week. They were not able to let it to the public any more. The owners of the site had now stipulated that the vans were to be only used by the caravan owners or their immediate family The idea of taking Hannah and the children did not appeal to George one little bit .He did not fancy being with Hannah and the children on their own for a week at the sea side with out Sandra with them. He had got to the stage where he needed to be near her.

"You know that I can't leave the work for a whole week at the moment but we shall go as soon as I can fix it up. You are right I am feeling a bit tired but I can cope for a little while longer"

"As you wish George but think about it I don't want you over doing things we don't see much of you as it is"

"I know dear but I do have a lot on at the moment and we need the money I must get some jobs finished off so that I can have some bills made up and some money collected in"

"You are not too worried about money are you George I know that things do get a bit difficult at times but that is what happens when you work for your self. It was a pity that you did not keep Donald working for you. You have to do every little thing your self. I do understand and what ever happens I do not want you to be in trouble with the bank So far so good you have been able to get on with the house quite well with out having to borrow any money. I just wish that we could push on with it a bit more and have a decent bathroom".

"We will just be patient for a bit longer and then you shall have the house of your dreams"

"Get on with you George Fleming you are a proper charmer" Hannah went back to the sink to get on with her work.

Thank goodness for that thought George perhaps she will be quiet for a bit.

Meanwhile Sandra too had expressed a wish to see the caravan; George was working his way round to taking her there for a day at least. The more he thought about it the more he wanted her to be alone with him for the whole day, he would fix something up fairly soon, it could be arranged without arousing any suspicions. Sandra was so excited when he told her he was taking her to see the caravan for a whole day,

"Oh George that will be lovely"

"We can buy some food when we get there," he suggested.

"That's a good idea," she had agreed, "I don't think that we will need much that day. We'll have far better things to do than eat providing that you don't choose the wrong week for me," George was pleased to hear this "Leave it with me and I will arrange it." They fixed it up to go to the caravan on a Wednesday. Hannah did not need to use the van; she would be busy making frames for her market stall. Sandra told her mother that she was going shopping with a school friend to Shrewsbury.

"We will probably stay and go to the pictures. She lied. Dorothy accepted her excuse and gave her £20 for spending money; after all she thought that Sandra does work hard when they wanted her to give a hand with such as the sugar beet hoeing and the harvesting. William did so much of the work mechanically these days they now had their own combine harvester Dorothy had been so keen to say that they were now coming up in the world if you like. She was so proud of William.

George told Hannah that he would be working late and not to bother keeping his tea for him He said that he would get some fish and chips to keep himself going. Hannah did not mind she could have her meal when the children came from school. And that would mean that cooking was finished for the evening and she could clear things away and get on with the pullover that she was knitting for George.George could always have a sandwich later if need be.

George and Sandra met at the Forest Glen. She placed her bike around the back of the premises; the staff would not notice one bike from another. Bicycles were often put out of sight around the back while the owners walked to the top of the Wrekin and back. It being 8-30 in the morning no one was about as yet. She then waited out of sight until she heard George's van coming. Yes it was his She gave the usual signal that she was waiting. A handkerchief tied to a stick and put in a place where he would see it He stopped the van and she quickly got in and they were on their way without any one having noticed. Sandra had been looking forward to sharing this day with George for so long imagining a whole day with out the vision of Hannah hovering in the background.

By 11 o'clock they had arrived at the caravan site. George nodded to the site manager as they drove in to find his van. It was a bit early in the season for holidaymakers to be already on the site. He parked his van on the far side of the site, between the rows of caravans. Hannah would not have noticed that the spare keys were not in their usual place in the sideboard drawer, she would be far too busy making her frames ready for her market stall. They had called at a village shop on their way and bought some supplies that they thought that they would need, like tea sugar and milk. George quickly opened the van door to let the fresh air in. Sandra sat her self on the settee and made herself comfortable.

"Do you want a cuppa"? George asked her.

"Not yet darling". She had started calling him darling now and George had not objected.

"You come and sit closer for a little while. I will make one in a minute or two. I have waited so long for this moment. No don't draw the curtains back just yet, it is much cosier as it is". George looked at her he could hardly wait. "Let me show you how things work, He stood up and he moved seats and raised a dining table. Then he folded the table away to an oak panelled wall Just you watch this, he moved a couple of catches and the panel moved forward and downward producing a double bed which had been concealed in the panelling.

Sandra's face lit up as she moved from the seat where she was relaxing, she started to explore the wardrobe and store cupboards. She found the blankets which Hannah kept there. "Darling this is great. They lay on the bed together. "The tea can wait "She whispered" As George was removing her clothes. They took their time; they explored each other both now completely naked under the pale blue blankets.

Both knew why they had travelled this distance to be completely alone. They did not have to worry about peeping toms or jump every time a stick had cracked in the wood when a fox or rabbit had moved in the under growth.

"This is more like it". George whispered "Can't beat a good bed to lie on"

"Perfect" She murmured as their bodies were as one. They reached crescendo

Fulfilling each other's needs. They kept their lovemaking going until they were both completely exhausted, and then they lay close. Completely satisfied just relaxing.

They eventually stirred from their languor, Sandra made a pot of tea and they had something to eat... George was quite content with the way that things were going; Sandra how ever had other ideas. She wanted George for herself and she was not prepared to let anything stand in her way.

"Let's go for a walk along the beach before we go back George suggested.

"Not yet" was Sandra's reply; "We will go for a walk much later. Let's just enjoy being together. It was late afternoon before they strolled through the sand dunes hand in hand neither giving the slightest thought about returning home. George did not worry; he was content just to let the cool sea breeze stimulate him. They sat on the damp sand for a while watching the tide come in.

"Oh Darling I am so happy" Sandra leaned her head on his shoulder. "I never want to go back to reality. This is heaven. I wish that we could come here every day. Memories came flooding back to George, When he had first taken Hannah to the seaside how delighted he had been then to see Hannah so happy. He quickly came back to the present.

"Me too "He whispered "We will have to start back soon".

"Can we do this again" George I know that this is not the first time that we have actually been in bed together. Please can we do this again let's get something arranged".

George agreed with her Making love in a bed was much more preferable to being in the woods.

"Leave it with me I'll arrange something". They drove home, not a lot of conversation passed between them. Their perfect day was coming to an end. She had her head on

His shoulder and her hand resting on his leg.

Sandra's thoughts were in turmoil, she wanted George for herself. She had no interest in any other man all sorts of ideas were going through her head. Was there a possibility of George leaving Hannah, she couldn't see why? What would her father and mother say if they found out? How could it be solved? She had never heard of one man loving two sisters. What would happen if she got pregnant? She thought that Hannah might kill herself if she found out what was going on. But then on the other hand she had three kids to look after.

"Penny for your thoughts. Little one" George asked.

"They are worth far more than that my Darling. I love you so much"

"What is this word that you call love, bonking in bed all day, is that it?"

"No my love, it goes far deeper than that, there is bonking and bonking. You my dear have it worked out to a fine art; there is no man that could satisfy me as you have done today."

"You have certainly got something there I feel completely knackered, there won't be much work done tomorrow. I will have to do a bit of skiving; you are such a demanding wretch. I am completely drained. You are just like a bitch in season" He teased"

Sandra was quick to respond to his teasing. "George I only need one nice brave dog to satisfy me. Where are you working tomorrow? Its market day, the old folks will be off most of the day."

"Just a minute. Just a minute. Not again tomorrow"?

"Yes please my Darling. I can't get enough of you but it will never be the same again in the woods after going to bed as we have done today".

George waited a while before he answered; his mind was in turmoil. Hannah could never satisfy him as Sandra had done today. In fact she did not seem at all that interested in sex since she had the twins. Too scared of having any more that was what George had put it down to. He would have to get some thing worked out fairly soon.

"Leave it with me; we will get some thing worked out between us". He knew that he had no idea what. It was quite late when they got back to the Forest Glen. George drove into the car park and waited while Sandra slipped out and made her way quietly round the back and collected her bike, he quickly put it into the van and drove away dropping Sandra and her bike off at the back gate to the farm.

"See you tomorrow "he kissed her and went on his way.

When he went home the place was in darkness all the lights were out except for the one that lit up the yard. That was a relief he assumed that Hannah would be in bed. He was hungry. As he went inside and as he switched the light on

Hannah stirred her self from an armchair and gave him quite a fright. He had not expected her to be down stairs sitting in the darkness. He was quite startled for a moment and quickly had to get a grip of himself.

"Where have you been" She said as she became more aware of where she was and saw that the clock said five minutes to eleven" It is almost eleven o'clock"

"Coming. Coming" He repeated him self. He was trying not to show that he was nervous and caught by surprise. He was in no mood to have Hannah quibbling on to night. "Can't I stop for a drink with a friend if I want to?"

"I suppose so it's just that you are so late I stopped watching the telly and I must have dozed off. Do you want any thing to eat?"

"I could do with a sandwich or something" Hannah reluctantly rose up from the chair and made supper for him. She moved to go upstairs, she was quite put out that he had stayed out so late and she did not wish to share a cup of tea with him.

"I'm going up, will you lock up?" she called from half way up the stairs.

"Alright I won't be long"; George was beginning to feel over- whelmed with a mixture of guilt and relief.

The following morning Hannah greeted him with the news that Charles had been to see her. He was looking for you. His Aunt wants you to call in; she has got some more work for you to do. Will you look in as you go through the village?"

"Leave it with me". He replied. The children had left for school and he was getting himself moving to go and get some work done. Miss Maude Hinge considered herself to be the lady of the village. Her father had been Mayor of Wenlock and his daughter now in her late fifties had inherited his home and his other properties. She then sold the old Hall, which had been the family home and had another house built close by to her liking. She was a nervous woman who did not like to be a bother to other people she considered that she was far too well bred to have much to do with the other members of the village. She was actually a nobody, not very intelligent. It had been the gossip of the village that the daily cleaner did the school homework for her and her sister. She lived a very lonely life she only had her dog for company.

She was very fond of her nephew Charles and he pampered to all her needs running her errands and seeing that she was comfortable. She was so mean that little did Charles realise it she would send him with messages to George and other workmen to save using the telephone.

"He came here did he?"

"Yes dear he only stayed a few minutes, he had to go and baby sit for his mother. You know what that sister of his is like. Can't be left on her own for a minute. I reckon that she must be fifteen now. Don't you?"

"Could be I suppose, She is so thin she would drop down a drain if she did not walk around it". He started to laugh.

"There must be something wrong with her, but what? She is never allowed out unless her Mother is with her. It is said that she is an adopted daughter"

"Well can't say, must get going and get some work done or the day will be gone. I will have to cut some glass for your frames tonight".

"That's good dear. I could do with getting the frames finished to save rushing around tomorrow night".

George was in no mood to do any work; he was tired from the previous day. He went into town and called at Judith's for a cuppa. After and hour when he could see that he was outstaying his welcome .He decided to get him self moving. He drove up towards Dawley then working his way around the back lanes through Huntington to Hollins lane to wait in the usual place for Sandra. He thought that he would not be disappointed and he was right He did not have long to wait. They had conditionally made the arrangements the night before

"What excuse did you give today?" He asked as she climbed into the van putting her arms around his neck.

"There's only William about, they have gone to town. I've given the kitchen a quick whip around to make it look as if I have been busy. I told William that I had heard that Mrs Hollis was not well".

"We are OK for an hour," said George getting out of the van and carrying the sheet for them to lie on. They lay down thinking that there was no one about and proceeded to make love.

Ted Locket the ditch and drain cleaner for the Estate had seen the green Morris Minor van often parked in the woods and curiosity was getting the better of him. He was a bit of a peeping tom and always carried a loaded camera with him, hoping to get a few photos to drool over when he was on his own. He had no problem getting his films developed. A friend who was an amateur photographer and worked in town developed them for him and he liked to have a look at the results. It was surprising who was seen with whom. Today Ted Locket could not believe his luck. He had not expected the green van to come and park up. It had always been raining or something had happened when he had been around at other times. He lay in an empty ditch and watched well hidden, his body getting excited and his tongue moistening his lips as he watched the couple fulfilling each other's needs. My God what a body she has got, he would have loved to have those fulsome breasts close to him. Watching other couples and looking at the photos of them gave him the sexual satisfaction that he needed. His wife had been an invalid for most of their married life and this was the only way that Ted could fulfil him self. In his excitement Ted almost gave himself away, but thank goodness for him George and Sandra were too absorbed with each other. They had not heard him move to a better position. On one or two previous occasions, Ted had given his presence away and many an irate half-naked man who had been having fun with another man's wife had chased him. He watched the pair from a safe distance taking as many shots of them as he could. Eventually they had dressed and left.

He knew which way the van would go. He was only too glad to stand upright; he had been terrified of getting cramp in his legs and having to give his presence away. He knew that if George had known what he was up to he would probably kill him. He was well satisfied with the last hour's work. He left his hiding place and went on his way enjoying his afternoon chores. The memory of those two cavorting bodies kept a permanent smile on his face for the rest of the day. He would get this film developed as quickly as he could. He considered that there were quite a few people he knew who would enjoy looking at the results.

George let Sandra out of the van near a familiar opening in the hedge, she had only to walk across one field and she was back at the farmhouse. George went back to Wellington but he considered that it was too late to start any work at this time of the day, He decided that he would go and have a look around town for a while and then go back home. Work could wait until tomorrow.

Chapter Twelve
The Camera Does Not Lie

William was ploughing the field at the top of the Willowmoor bank there was 15 acres of it to be turned over ready for sowing. Most of this half of the field was practically out of sight of the farmhouse. The purr of the tractor made him feel good as he turned the brown earth over burying last year's stubble. Using a three-furrow plough behind the tractor got the work done at such a quicker pace than what his father had been able to do such work. It would have taken days to turn this amount of acreage over with only the use of horses. Where as William would have it turned over by dinnertime. He found it was hard to imagine ploughing so slowly and time consuming. He was a tractor man. He could relax as he went across the field to and fro. It was a wonderful spring morning the birds were following in his wake, feeding them selves on the grubs and worms, which were exposed as the shining shell boards of the plough, turned the soil over. There were pigeons, rooks and crows all hungry and looking for a tasty meal

William was fairly content with life for the time being, his father was getting older, he was now sixty-eight and so he left all the tractor work to him to do. This suited William extremely well. Having to get up in the middle of the night to help a cow give birth was not his idea of farming. The milk cheque at the end of the month was an essential provider with out it most farmers would go bankrupt including his father. His father Fred had learned that from experience over the years.

William saw himself as a contractor, doing tractor work for others and getting paid for it.

"You can't farm a farm in another farmer's fields" His father would tell him when William had told him about another job that he had promised to do for one of the neighbouring farmers. William took no notice, in his eyes he considered that he was right and that his father was far too old fashioned and he was not prepared to listen to his father's advice.

"There's plenty of tractor work that needs to be done and what's more I can get paid for it" William would argue when he had promised to go and do some work for some one else. He worried his father at times, the lad was so impulsive, and everything had to be done in a hurry. It was not like the old times any more. Fred had seen so many changes since the war. He some times wondered how they were going to keep up with it all the way every thing was getting mechanised What was it going to be like in another fifty years he dared not anticipate The future would not be for him.

He was proud of his son, William was now six feet tall and he towered above him. When Fred had first proposed to grow sugar beet. This particular field had been good for growing Sugar beet and had produced a good crop. It did not get water logged if it turned out to be a wet spring or summer. Last year it had been sown with wheat, this year the sugar beet was sown on the field half way up the bank William was now ploughing the wheat stubble to bury it; this field was to be reseeded for a good crop of hay later in the year. William was aware of the pigeons and crows grabbing for food, earth worms and slugs at the back of the plough as the plough turned the soil over. A peewit rose from the stubble, it was too early for her to have made a nest and laid any eggs so there fore there would be no nest for him to worry about. Farmers had respect for nesting birds and they would try not to disturb them if they could help it. If one had nested and laid her eggs

William would stop the tractor and climb down and remove the nest to the hedgerow where it would be safe the mother bird would soon find where he had placed it.

He took notice of how the rabbits had eaten the grass at least three to four yards into the field. I must ask the old chap. He thought to himself. He always referred to his father as the old chap, I will ask him to come and put some wire snares down before we sow the new seed there would be clover amongst the new grass seed. The rabbits would love that they would eat it away as fast as it started to grow

He was content with life, as things were at the present every thing was going well and it looked as if his father would eventually sign the farm over to him. He had met his present girl friend and he had fallen hook line and sinker for her. She was so different from any of the others that he had met. To him she was beautiful. She took great care in her appearance. Kept her dark long hair shaped up on her head in the latest bouffant style. She wore quite a considerable amount of make up. He felt that all his friends envied him having such a beauty of a girl friend. He had the feeling that his Mother and father did not seem so keen about his taking her out so he did not bring her to the farm very often. They will come round give them time. He had heard how they had carried on about Hannah marrying George. If it had not been for the fact that they took the Cottage up the Wrekin and his Mother could boast that another daughter was farming. He did not think that they would ever have taken to George and now what a good bloke that he had turned out to be. He had his own business and he was always giving Sandra a lift whenever he could. He was such a good kind bloke in their eyes He brought Sandra home on a Sunday to save Hannah the meither. Yes things were going fairly good in his eyes. He was hoping that Sandra would find herself a fellow and get married so that she did not become his responsibility if and when his parents passed on. He could not see Sandra and Jean getting on at all, they were as different as chalk was to cheese. It would be the same with his Mother. No way would Jean live in the same house as her. Some thing would be sorted before he got married and as he saw it there was plenty of time to sort all these things out. As yet there was no need for him to worry himself He could wait for a couple of years there was no hurry. He drove the tractor close to the edge of the wood to turn and go back across the field when he spotted Ted Locket. William slowed the tractor down to a stand still and switched off the engine. "Now for some fun "He thought. Ted waited until the engine of the tractor was turned off and William had climbed down from the seat before he spoke.

"Morning Will busy today" William sat down beside Ted on the grass verge.

"Aye got to get it turned over" William replied, he guessed why Ted had shown himself, he probably had some new snapshots of courting couples to show him Ted often did this. If Ted had some new ones he was quite willing to show them to Will as he had called William since he had known him from childhood. . Dirty bugger William thought to him self, but he is harmless enough. It gave them a chance to have a giggle at others expense and antics.

"What have you got today mate. Anything good and juicy?"

"Could say that". Ted reached inside his ragged edged jacket and took an envelope from the pocket.

"What do you think of these?" He handed some photos to William, who started to chuckle at what he was seeing they were various photos Ted had taken in the woods of courting couples.

Ted felt that no crime had been committed and as long as others enjoyed his snaps after all what was wrong with the odd couples snogging in the woods. William was enjoying what he was seeing of different couples enjoying them selves. Ted would never use any of the photos for black mailing any one although he knew that there was plenty of opportunity going for him if he were to try it.

Especially when married men were not with their wives. The working man being able to afford a motor car had a lot to answer for. William looked hard at one particular snap, the face of the woman looked familiar, the blonde hair,

"What a pair of knockers these ones got" he laughed to Ted.

"That's what I thought" Chuckled Ted. The photo showed the blonde sat astride her lover smiling down at him, her upper garments dropping off the back of her shoulders revealing her well developed breasts.

William looked again, recognition came quickly, and the woman was his sister Sandra. The bushes hid the man that she was with, the next snap showed a different position, and her lover was now on top of her. William's face froze he could not believe his eyes, was it really who he thought that it was. Yes it was his brother-in-law George. As reality hit him, his face paled draining of all colour with a mixture of shock and surprise. The next few shots were of the same couple. He turned to look at Ted as if not believing his eyes.

"Thought that might surprise you" Ted laughed as if he had found a pot of gold.

"Surprise me. What the bloody hell do they think that they are doing? What's going on? Ted has this been going on for long?

"Oh I could say so, a hell of a long time. As far as I know it's been since she was in school uniform. I just landed lucky a few weeks ago with the old box camera". William did not know how to answer Ted who was already slobbering at the corners of his mouth. William's mind was in turmoil. It was one thing to drool over a bit of pornography but it was a different matter when one recognised who the photos were of. His first instinct was to thump Ted Locket, dirty little man snooping in the woods and having the cheek to take photographs then he calmed down and the realisation of what he had been looking at dawned on him.

"George and Sandra Never" he said aloud.

"Guess so"

"Bloody Nora if this gets out the balloon will blow up and there will be the biggest bloody bang this side of the Wrekin. Ted what shall I do? Let them know that what I have seen or shall I keep quiet about it?"

"I reckon that's your problem Will" He quickly took the photos from William's hand and put them back in the pocket where he had taken them from. He did not want William to keep the photos they were his and he did not know what William might do with them and he was not prepared to take any chances. If he were to show them to his father, Fred Thomas just might wait for him with a gun many was the times when Fred had told Ted how he hated the peeping toms who walked the woods around his farm and the Ercall. Ted could see that William was really upset and he decided that it would be best to make himself scarce and leave him to think about what he had just seen. Ted had been trying for a long time to be able to catch this pair on camera and until he did he had decided to keep his mouth shut knowing that no one would believe him if he were to say what he had seen going on.

It was not very often that he went to the woods around the Hatch and beyond to take photos He usually stayed around the woods of the Ercall an ideal courting place. It had been said that at least a quarter of the children of Wellington had been conceived in the Ercall woods. It had taken time to find where George and Sandra were stopping He knew what was going on he had seen them many times. They had not seen him especially when George had picked Sandra up at the bottom of the Wrekin they thought that they had been so careful not knowing that Ted was watching them. He had watched far too many courting couples not to recognise the signs of an affair going on.

He had suspected that they must be having an affair some where in the woods but it had taken some time before he had the opportunity to find out where they had been. Then one-day luck had been on his side. The Estate had wanted some work doing in the woods behind the Hatch and it was there that he spotted the green Morris Minor van coming and parking up He had quickly hid himself fairly close to where they were stopping. Got it he had said to him self. It had not been until this day that he got the opportunity to be there in the right place at the right time. He was only just well hidden before George and Sandra had got out of the van. "Got em," He said At last now let them explain this if the film comes out all right.

"See you mate" He shouted to William as he went on his way swinging his ditching shovel over his shoulder. "That shook him he said to him self but it is about time some one let the cat out of the bag. That lass is just like a bitch on heat and there seems to no satisfying her.

William started the engine of the tractor and returned to get on with the ploughing he knew if his Dad happened to be watching from the buildings he would be wondering why the tractor had not come into sight to turn around and go back up the field. What the hell was he going to do? The more he thought about it the more it dawned on him that was why it was George who gave Sandra so many lifts home.

God help us all he said aloud as much to the birds still feeding behind the plough as to him self. If the old chap were to find out he will kill her or him and another thing did Hannah know what was going on. I'll bet that she doesn't It has been so easy for those two to meet. Thank goodness that he did not do his own courting in any of these woods he would have hated that little man to have been taking photos of him and any girl that he happened to be with. When he had finished the field he returned to the yard, he was still not sure if it was true what he had seen earlier in the day. He kept quiet for the next few days tossing and turning in bed at night trying to decide what was the best thing to do about it. Should he see George and have it out with him or say something to Sandra. Which of them had started the affair? He decided that one thing for sure he dare not tell his parents it could kill them. When he saw Sandra during the day and at meal times he just could not look her in the face He could still see those photos that Ted Locket had shown him they disgusted him and she abhorred him.

Looks as if he has fallen out with Sheila, Sandra said to her self when she had asked him something and he had just walked away from her with out giving her an answer. Miserable sod I suppose that he will come round give him time. William had not decided what to do when a few days later he saw both his parents going out through the front gate in the car. They must be going to that farm sale that they had talked about. He was going over to the tractor shed as it was called now and not the cart shed, when he saw Sandra going up the granary steps for some corn to feed the chickens. He followed her up the steps. She was so engrossed filling her bucket she did not hear him come up behind her.

"Boo" He shouted making her jump and turn around so quickly spilling some of the corn on the granary floor.

"What the hell". She said startled by the look on her Brother's face. What do you think that you are doing?"

"I want a word with you. What the hell are you doing I should ask. You and George carrying on together." Sandra looked as if he had slapped her.

"What do you mean Big brother?"

"What I said?

"You are talking through your hat "She pushed her blonde hair from off her face. A habit that she seemed to have inherited from her mother.

"Am I indeed. What were you doing with him in the woods?"

"I don't know what you are talking about?"

"Oh yes you do? How long has this been going on"?

"I still don't know what you are talking about. Can't I go across to Hannah's for half an hour now and then and give her a hand with the kids. It's the only way that I can get away from this place".

"You are not at Hannah's all of the time by what I have been seeing".

"What are you talking about?"

"Ask Ted Locket he carries a camera around with him". Sandra's face went as white as a sheet as it dawned on her that the game was up William knew.

"What do you know?" She screamed.

"Enough. Enough You and him take a good photograph especially when you are naked". Sandra knew that Ted Locket was a peeping Tom. George had told her about him walking the woods just to watch courting couples but she never dreamed that he took photos.

"What have you seen?"

"Wouldn't you like to know? Now what I want to know is what the bloody hell you think that you are doing. Of all the lads in the Country you have to go bonking around with in the woods. You little bitch have been bonking with your sister's husband. I don't know which of you is the bloody daffiest or the most evil.

"What are you going to do when the old chap and lady find out?

"You wouldn't you wouldn't". Cried Sandra. She had never seen any one so angry before she thought that William was going to strike her. She stepped back and sat down on the sack of cattle corn that was immediately behind her.

"You bet that I wouldn't as yet" He replied. "Do you want to kill them both? I would not like to have that on my conscience. Sandra looked at her brother, could she trust him? She was not sure

"Sandra for God's sake finish it Finish it I tell you. No good can come from it they've got three kids damn it" She had never seen him so angry "Get your self a young lad there are plenty of them about"

"Not like George "she spat back.

"I don't believe what I am hearing. "Not like George "he mimicked her. You stupid little bitch. You fool why have you not told any of us what is going on? And another thing he's old enough to be your father"

"Stop it, stop it" she shouted. "I love George and he loves me"

"You What? I don't believe what I am hearing. Well I can tell you one thing that it has got to stop and stop as from now. Stop"he shouted" Do you hear me You ring and tell that cheating bugger that he is to come no where near you or this place again or I for one will shoot the low down cheating rat"

"Alright calm down I will talk to George"

"Well if you don't, you know now that I will. I will tell all and then see what happens I know that for one thing the old chap will kill him if he finds out.

"You are not so bloody perfect. I know that you are first out with one and then another". She smirked.

"That's none of your bloody business I am not out with married women".

"We shall see "Sandra was now getting flippant. She picked up the bucket of corn and swept out of the granary. She went into the poultry house and closed the door behind her not knowing whether she was on her head or her heels. Her mind was in turmoil, if only George was here she could tell him what had just happened, and she knew that he would sort it all out for her. George was not here and the shock of some one finding out about her sins had well and truly shaken her. Sandra looked at the hungry birds squawking around her feet; take this she shouted at them, throwing the bucket of corn into the air not putting it in the feeding troughs or caring where it landed.

"I don't care I don't care. He's mine and I am going to have him no matter what. She stamped her feet just like she had done when she had been a little girl and had wanted to have her own way and was being denied it. She left the birds to get on with it. She went inside and tried to ring Hannah George just might be working at home and she could make an excuse to talk to him. She would say that she had seen Charles and had a message for him. She knew that Hannah would fall for it. She got no answer Hannah must be working in the shed and could not hear the telephone ringing "It is about time that they had an outside bell fitted "She said to her self.

Later when she saw William in the kitchen at dinnertime, she looked him straight in the eye, daring him not to say any thing. William had been giving this a lot of thought and had decided to keep quiet about it for the time being. Nothing could be gained about shouting it all out loud at this moment. He thought that it would be better if he could persuade Sandra to come to her senses and stop seeing George. What a mess. What the hell did George think that he was doing? What sort of man was he? Certainly not any good if he could cheat on his wife by messing around with her little sister. The whole affair was on the top most of his mind. His Mother Dorothy had noticed.

"Can't think why those two are at each others throats. They can't speak to each other without snapping and snarling". She remarked to Fred as they sat either side the Rayburn cooker.

"Leave them be Mother" He answered." Let them sort it out between them selves."

"I believe our William is pretty fond of that girl with the dark hair. Sheila, she is called. The one who works in Mc Clures". Dorothy went on.

"Never make a farmers wife" was his reply.

"I was hoping that he would just go out with that Doreen from the village, much more suitable, does not mind getting her hands dirty".

"I agree with you Fred that Sheila is just paint and powder, fancies her self too much she does. Looks down her nose good and proper at me when I go to buy a new hat I don't like to be served by her. Not the type William ought to go out with at all, he would never be able to afford to keep her dressed up like the china doll that she is. Now that we have bought the place William knows that it will his one-day. I hope that we have not worked and scraped all these years just to keep that bit of a girl in paint and powder".

"Hold on a bit Dot. I don't think that the lad is serious as yet. Give him a bit of time before marrying him off"

"Well I hope not. You were always the same Fred Thomas you can't see any further than the end of your nose. I keep my ears and eyes open you should do the same. I don't like our Sandra looking after that stall for Hannah on a Saturday either and I am going to tell them so"

"Leave them be. It gives her a break from here; she does not see many does she. Hannah has had it pretty rough with one thing and another. She is probably glad of a bit of help. I wish to God that George would get that house finished that he has started he does not seem to do much work he runs the roads in that van of his.

Fred always spoke up for his daughters if he could He was really proud of all of them especially the way that they had married and settled down.

"There are only two of them to go and then we will be on our own. We must give it some thought as to what's the best way to sort every thing out between them"

"Well William will have the farm that's what we have worked for" Dorothy was very quick to remind him. She was very quick to add. "The girls can look after themselves".

"Let's be fair Dot, they all worked hard as kids".

"Didn't we all "She snapped "I just hope our Sandra finds her self a good fellow".

"She doesn't seem bothered about them. I reckon that she will stay at home with us for a bit longer".

"That will not be a bad thing. I've got no help in this house" Dorothy always thought about her self and how hard done by that she was,

Sandra was desperate to contact George. They had their secret way of her being able to talk to him. She would ring Hannah and make some excuse for calling and ask if she could speak to George as she had a new joke that she wanted to tell him.

"I must tell him, "she would say. If he were there Hannah would hand the phone to him.

"Another of her funny jokes for you" When he put the phone down George would repeat it to Michael and Hannah saying that it had only been another of Sandra's silly jokes. They usually went Doctor Doctor or some thing else, which seemed to Hannah to be very childish.

"The pair of you need to grow up". Hannah would remark when George finished and told them the new joke. But what Hannah did not know was that George would get any message that Sandra intended for him. It was days before she was able to do this. Dorothy had now had the telephone moved into the kitchen. She said that her hearing was not as it used to be. There always seemed to be some one or other in the kitchen so Sandra could not get the opportunity to use the phone. Eventually she did and she was able to arrange to meet. George

"Just going to see how Ethel Hollis is" She told her mother one evening. "Be back just now the old lady gets so lonely these days"

"See that you are back in before it gets too dark" Her Mother reminded her.

Sandra closed the back door and quickly went along the path by the pig sties and up the field toward the hatch. Old Wilf Wilkins had died and his wife Joyce had moved to Jackfield to live with her friend from many years' back. Fred now rented all their ground. George was waiting for her in their usual meeting place in the Limekiln woods

“What are we going to do” She asked him after she had told him all about the row that she and William had had. “I can’t give you up I have decided that. I won’t you are the only man that I want”.

“There, there now my little love” George said consolingly.

“Let’s go away together George. Please don’t let any one part us”.

“Now we can’t do that, now can we. Let us think it out properly. Let us move from here in case big brother has been watching you leave the house and followed you. It would be so easy for him to do just that, just like that bloody Ted Locket has been doing You know my little love if I ever have the chance to get my hands on the little peeping Tom I will kill the bugger. I swear that I will He had no right to be taking his dirty photos in the woods.”

“Don’t kill him Darling. Just give him a damned good hiding one that he won’t forget. I would not like to think of you locked up in jail just for his sake. Darling just let us pack up and go away together and then we can really be on our own”.

What a mess thought George to him self, if they were to go away where could they go. They would need money and he was already well and truly overdrawn at the bank and the bills were now mounting up.

It would suit him very well just to up and run, but he had not got the guts to do that and he knew it. Neither had he the guts to approach Ted Locket and Ted also knew it He was in the wrong and his sins had been found out and he certainly did not like it. He did not like it at all.

Who else would he show the photos to? That was something that George would never know and he was a worried man”.

“I will find some way to see you my love you know I will. Hannah will be at the market stall on Saturdays. I have been thinking that I could bring the caravan back from the sea for the winter months”.

"Oh that would be brilliant Darling where would you put it?"

"Leave that to me I know of places. In the meantime why don't you go out with one or two of the local lads that should put William off the scent, He will think that you have finished with me. Give it some thought will you. If you do decide to go out with any of them, don't you dare let any of them do as we are doing" His hand was already down her blouse. Gently kneading her breast.

"Please George, not now. Move from here, I don't like to think that such as Ted Locket is watching us and now that he knows where we are meeting there is no telling what he might be doing. He could be already hiding here in the bushes".

Sandra became very nervous and edgy at the thought of being watched. George started the engine and moved from their favourite place, he drove to the other side of the Wrekin pulling off the road in a place that was well hidden by trees and a bit too far for Ted Lockets eyes.

"Alright now my love". His hand was back inside her blouse, while his other one was reaching under her skirt. He knew exactly how to get Sandra to relax and perform exactly as he wanted her to. Their problems forgotten for a while. He later took Sandra back but he dropped her off in a different place so that if William was about he would not see George's van anywhere near the farm.

Next day William asked her what she planned to do about the affair that she had been having.

"What do you mean?" She asked.

"You saw him last night, I know that you did"

"That's what you think" "

"I don't think, I know, Gone to see Mrs Hollis indeed. The old lady told me where you said that you were going but I don't believe that you went any where near Ethel Hollis" William always referred to his Mother as the old lady and his Dad the old chap. Sandra could not argue she did not know if William had been watching her.

"Snooping have you? You are no better than Ted locket".

"You were with him last night"

"Go to hell and mind your own business" She blurted out.

"Think of the family Sandra If this gets out. All their phones will be red hot they will burn the wires out and another thing it will take them all their time to believe that you could do such a thing". Sandra had not given any thought to what her sisters would do if they found out.

"I'll tell you when and if we finish and that will be when I am ready and not before".

"Well you see that you make it pretty soon".

"You keep your mouth shut," She said. "I am going to persuade George to go away with me".

"Now you are out of your mind. What about Hannah and the kids? Have you and your lover boy thought about that?"

"What about Hannah and the kids? She will manage"

"What about her, just think will you? Just give it a bit of thought as to what you are doing"

"I'm' eighteen at the end of this month and then I can please myself legally and then to hell with every one else"

"May be, but do you think that George is going to give up Hannah and the kids for you. I reckon that you have got another thing coming.

If you think that is what he is going to do. Hannah looks after him far too well for him to leave home".

"We will see she does not give him as much as I do".

"Oh really and what is that, pray do go on"

"Oh shut your mouth and leave me alone". William could not believe what he was hearing; she would not really break the family a part for the sake of a fling with her brother-in-law. William had no idea how long it had been going on. He thought of what Ted Locket had said about school uniform and if that was the case they had been seeing each other for years. He was hoping that Sandra would see some sense before that it was too late and the whole family devastated. William had not had a lot to do with his sisters; they had married and left home. His being sent to a boarding school he had only worked along side of Mary during his holidays. He remembered how Hannah and George had collected him from school the night before the wedding so that he did not miss going to it. Hannah had always been good to him. Bars of chocolate she had given him as a kid when she had the café up the Wrekin. There were always cakes made and sent across. His Mother only had to ask when she had visitors and Hannah had always produced the necessary. It was Hannah who ran down the hill and across the fields when mother had been ill and a doctor had been called. She would come and tidy up a bit as Sandra was not old enough and not very good at it. There were the white shirts that she had washed and ironed for him so that he would look good when he took Sheila out. His mother never made a very good job of the washing and ironing; she would mark the collars as she ironed them with the old fashion irons heated on the cooker. He only had to take them to Hannah and she would do them for him and keep quiet demanding nothing for her work. William remembered these things which made him more determined to sort Sandra out if he could. Hannah would be trusting George and have no idea what was going on behind her back. That Sandra is a pig headed little bitch and a fool, he said to himself.

If he came face to face with George he had no idea as to how he would react, he need not have feared. George kept out of his way having no desire to come face to face with William just yet. If they came face to face goodness only knows what could happen. William was a tall man compared to George and being much younger and doing agricultural work, he was much the stronger of the two. It would be god help George if William was to lose his temper and George knew this.

George now drove the long way home he did not go past the farm and if he saw William on the road he no longer stopped for a chat but he kept going. He's got a bloody nerve; rides the roads like Lord Muck he does.

It was well into June, some of the top fifteen acres that William had prepared earlier in the spring now needed hoeing. He had sown about an acre of it with some swedes and mangols as well as new grass and clover

Why it could not be done mechanically he could not understand or why his father insisted growing swedes and mangols at all. Every one who William could persuade to come and earn a bit extra and give a hand in the field with the hoeing and this including Sandra. William dodged as much of it as he could he hated the job. He saw a neighbouring farm hand was preparing the field next to his and by working his way around William was able to stop and have a chat. James Beddow saw William and stopped his tractor. He too like William enjoyed a bit of gossip. James, Jim as he was known locally was a tall six-foot fellow with dark hair and he was more than interested in Sandra and he asked William if he would introduce him to her. Couldn't be better William thought as he shouted to Sandra to come and join them. He made the introduction and then he moved away discretely leaving them to talk together.

Jim chatted to Sandra and they fixed up a date to meet. Sandra was still very upset at George's suggestion, now she could show him that he was not the only fish in the sea. She smiled to her self as she left Jim to go back to her work.

"OK" William shouted to her.

"Why not he's a bit shy and it looks as if I will have to teach him a thing or two". William did not care what she thought of him as long as she finished seeing George.

"I'll leave it with you"

"You never know he just might be my knight in shining armour, as long as you keep your mouth shut".

"Nothing to say if you go out with Jim and forget that other no good sod of George Any way you could do worse."

"We will see big brother we will see" William did not see the smile that crossed Sandra's face

Sandra was still very angry with George, very angry indeed. They had been lovers for so long; infact since before she had left school and if he thought that he could ditch her just like that in favour of Hannah She had made up her mind that he would have to think again., She decided that she would go out with this Jim so that it would look good to all the family. She could also imagine her sisters sharing tittle-tattle on their phones. Sandra has a boy friend. Well this is going to be news for them. Damn that bloody peeping tom Ted Locket. If it had not been for him William would not have found out about her and George and now she did not know how far that she could trust him. Damn, damn she said to her self. The more that she thought about what George had said, the more it made sense to her for the time being. Not that she wanted a date with this other fellow, she did not know much about Jim and she really did not want to know. He was polite and good looking. He came from a good farming family and Sandra knew that would please her mother, if no one else.

It did please Dorothy when Sandra told where she was going and who with.

"Seems to be very polite Mother and I think that he comes from a reputable family.

"Well the Hopley's would not have him working for them unless he had a bit about him and as you say he does come from a good farming family"

"This is good news," Dorothy said to Fred when Sandra had prepared her self and had gone out for the evening. "Our Sandra and Jim Beddow" Dorothy was letting her imagination run away with her as usual.

"Aye Mother Lets wait and see it would be nice to see her settled down". Fred replied as he was dozing in his chair his pipe laid on the side.

"Perhaps they could get their own little place" Dorothy continued, she always liked to have everything cut and dried.

"Wait and see "Fred reminded her sleepily.

"Well there is no harm in hoping" she smiled as she pushed another log onto the Rayburn. She returned her attention to the weekly paper that she had bought that day and looked to see if there was any local gossip to be read. She and Fred were so content these days every thing was going so well for them; they had bought a combine harvester a mechanical baler so that harvesting was nothing of a chore as it had years before. Fred still liked his herd of cows and his flock of sheep much to William's disappointment. If he had his way they would produce all grain, potatoes, peas and other crops that could be sown and harvested from the tractor seat.

Jim came to pick Sandra up as arranged he had a fairly old car a four door Vauxhall. Sandra was ready and waiting for him at the back farm gate.

"Where are you taking me" Sandra asked him as she seated her self beside him in his car.

"That depends on where you would like to go. To see a film or just a ride around and then some supper some where".

"Not fussy" She replied "Lets make it a film shall we I have not been to see a film for goodness how long".

"I don't expect that you have much time for going to the pictures with so much work that there is to do on a farm".

"You are quite right Jim There is not much time at all "

Jim Beddow was very reserved and behaved impeccably through out the evening, much to Sandra's dismay

"Can we do that again? "He asked as he dropped her off at the farm gate, making no attempt to give her a kiss.

"Yes please, I would like that. So they made a date for the following week

Jim was very pleased with himself, he had always fancied taking a girl out but being rather timid and shy he never knew the right way to ask in case he embarrassed him self. Now that he had actually done it, he was so chuffed with himself.

As Sandra walked across the field towards the farmhouse, Jim turned his car around and drove off towards Wellington and home. He lived with his widowed Mother in quite a smart house in the better part of the town.

"How did you get on with Jim" Dorothy asked Sandra the next day.

"Great we are going out again next week that's if I can find the time"

"What do you mean if you have the time You are hardly ever here you are usually running about after Hannah never have got much time to do much for me It's that damned television that you hanker after. What I hear the things that they show on those television sets does not bear thinking about. Folks are loosing all respect and decency since every body seems to be able to afford one. Hannah and that George would have done better spending their money getting that house finished instead of spending time sitting and watching that thing. The television set will be the downfall of a good many.

"George is doing his best and Hannah is trying to help out a bit. Sandra came to their defence. So you want to go out with this Jim again next week do you?"

"Well yes he says that he would like to".

"That's alright but just watch what you are doing. Did he tell you much about his family?

"No Mother only that he lives with his mother in a house in Leagomery; before you say anything it is the better end of the town".

"I believe that his brother runs a big farm out the other side of Shrewsbury, some where on the Welsh Border, quite big farmers they are" Here we go again. Matchmaking. Sandra thought if only you knew Mother, you think that you know every thing but I could amaze you a bit if I wanted to. Sandra saw George at the weekend when she happened to be in town She did not stay long to talk to him just enough to arrange a meeting with him. She asked him to pick her up in town and not in their usual place.

"How was your date?" Asked George after he had parked the van in the woods at the back of the Wrekin and they had been kissing and cuddling for a while.

"Quite the gentleman, dear lover, kept his hands to himself all evening". She said laughing as George's hands were already down the front of her dress.

"You would not let him go this far would you?"

"Let him what?

"Well go all the way".

"And why should I not dear lover I seem to let you have a good time?"

George felt a pang of jealously. "I don't want you to, that's why".

"YOU want your cake and eat it". She teased.

"I know that I do. I suggest that I fetch the caravan back for the winter it would make things a lot more comfortable for us what do you say?"

"That would be great, because at the moment I have no intentions of stopping seeing you. And in no circumstances am I prepared to give you up It might be a bitter triangle at the moment but I am sure that it will get a bit sweeter in time my love". He was arousing her emotions as they lay in their favourite place hidden away in the plantation of fir trees. The night was warm and Sandra was happy. She had not mentioned Hannah. She had convinced her self that every thing would turn out in her favour if she kept calm. The flies that bussed around them were getting a nuisance. George was relieved when he had exhausted him self and Sandra sat up. He lit a cigarette. Damn flies". He said aloud. He sat and watched the smoke drift upwards as he inhaled and breathed out. It was unusual for George to be irritated by any thing when he and Sandra were alone together. He felt hurt that she had been out with some one else even if it had been at his suggestion. He knew that he had been her only lover since they had first been together when she was still in her school uniform Now he wondered, could he trust her not to make love with any one else. There was nothing that he could do about if he was to try and save his own face. He took her back home and dropped her off near the farm but not out side one of the gates. He was still irritable when he arrived back home.

"Working late" Hannah casually asked as he went into the cottage. "Aren't I always bloody working" He snapped at Hannah.

"Sorry that I spoke. Do you want any supper? I have prepared some for you, it is obvious that you are not in a good mood so I will leave you to it and go to bed".

She picked up her bits and pieces of the socks that she had been darning and said to her self. I will have a word with him in the morning. Some thing must have upset him during the day.

"George dear, do you think that you could ease off the hours that you are working" Hannah asked him next morning." You have paid off Pearce's bill and we are a bit better off now are we not

"I can't ease off yet" He replied. Matterfactually, his mind was on other things and he did not want Hannah to start to discuss money that would be the last straw.

"George I'm worried, you really seem to me to be over doing things lately. Do you feel all right? I know that it is a worry for you Molly saying that your father is not at all well. What do you think about him? Molly was really worried about him last week".

"I don't know what is the matter with him. They seem to be complaining a lot about him these days its first one thing and then another. That cough that they say isn't very good, haven't they noticed that he's had that for years. Any way, stop pestering me I've got work to do".

Since Mr Bradley had been off-handed with him. George had made up his mind to make a better effort with his work and get some of the outstanding jobs finished up so that he could give them their bills for the work. His father was now a sick man; he had smoked cigarettes all his life and because of this his lungs were now in a dreadful state. It had also affected his heart and Shrewsbury hospital where he had been a patient reported that things were not too good. There was not a lot that could be done to save him the damage that he had self inflicted had gone too far to be medically healed

Hannah had always been fond of her father-in-law; she did not like to see him suffering so much with ill health.

Often when the children were at school she would catch the local bus which took the women from Little Wenlock and from all around the bottom of the Wrekin into Wellington for to do their shopping. She would get off at the Umbrella House on the A5 and walk up to the village and spend a little time with him and Molly. Having a little bit of lunch with them and then make the return journey. She was back at home before the school bus.

When Terry had retired. He looked forward to Thursdays hoping that Hannah would pop in to see them. He had always been fond of her. Hannah and Molly had always got on really well. Molly had little time for George these days she knew that he had another side to his character. She could see that he was not all the charm that he pretended to be and she could not see why Hannah was so completely blind to this. She only saw what she wanted to see and Molly was very concerned for her. Molly often voiced her concerns to Terry; he would only say that Hannah was good for George.

"Keeps him on the straight and narrow and that has always taken some doing with George. His Mother was the apple of his eye and he was inclined to listen to her more than he did to me. It was only when she thought that I ought to know something or other and that I got to know one half that he was up to. Thank goodness he has Hannah now".

"Well I don't want to see him do the dirty on Hannah." She thought about the times that George had called and dismissed her completely saying that I have come to see my Dad not you. It was at these times that Molly had known that George had come to borrow money and she guessed that Hannah had not known anything about it.

That's what you think thought Molly, he can twist her around his little finger, but she kept her thoughts to her self. Terry was pleased with his children; they had recovered well from the death of their Mother especially Judith. He had not seen much of Thomas over the last few years since he had been sent abroad with the army. The fact that he had not been so pleased with him when he had married that Emily. Thomas and Emily had bought a newly built house on the outskirts of the town. They had kept away from his father. Thomas had nothing to do with George since they had fallen out over some work that George had wanted him to do and George put the bill in for twice the amount that he had paid Thomas. The people who Thomas did the work for, told him how much that George had charged them and had thought that it had been a bit extreme.

Unknowing to Hannah George had borrowed money from his father to help with buying the cottage and he had promised faithfully that he would repay it but he had not got around to doing anything about it. Molly considered that it was of no business of hers, but as far as she could see he never would repay it. Molly considered what Terry did with his money that he had saved over the years before she had married him was not for her to comment on. Both Terry and Molly had worked very hard for George when he had been up the Wrekin and also in other ways and they had refused to take any thing from George for their efforts.

Hannah decided to seek Molly's advice; she was worried about George's recent behaviour. His continually snapping and snarling at her and the children and to Hannah this was not George's normal behaviour. She considered that he must be very worried about money or some thing perhaps he was not feeling well and did not want talk about it. Hannah had a different attitude towards money, she liked to talk about it, to have discussions to see what could be afforded or not. George considered that the bank account was his and only his own private affair it was a man's world and he considered that women should have nothing to do with it. Whether he considered that women' were not capable of handling and managing any thing to do with finance Hannah was not sure. She had been brought up with so many old fashioned sayings and one was.

That if No money comes in through the door. Love flies out through the window. She quite believed in the old sayings. Her Mother had been so Victorian in her out look on life and so she had become very superstitious. If a picture fell off the wall her mother reckoned that it meant trouble for the family. Not because the cord by which it was hanging was old and rotten. A woman must never be the first to enter the house on New Years day; under no circumstance would she walk under a ladder thinking that she would have bad luck for the rest of the day. Hannah used to laugh with Grace about their Mother's sayings, but as she got older the sayings began to make more sense to her.

"Helen rang today," Hannah said to George when he came in for his tea that evening.

"What has she got to say for herself?"

"Nothing much, except that she said that Sandra has a boy friend".

"And where did she get that bit of news from?"

"Oh you know what it is like with the family, a bit of fresh news is passed around very quickly. I'm really glad for the girl her eyesight has never been that good but I do believe that she can now have something done about it. I hope that she and this new boy friend get on well together It will be good for Sandra to have her own boy friend".

"Oh would it now".

"I think so, she needs some one special didn't we all. They say he works at Hopley's in the village, quite a good looking young man, so I believe".

"You women will gossip about anything".

"Not anything dear. Just that little sister has managed to get a date".

"So big deal"

"George Darling don't be so cynical, we were young once you know. I'm really pleased for her; it would be nice for them if it worked out alright".

"We will see".

"Perhaps we won't see so much of her now. You have been very kind dear always willing to take her home instead of me having to run her about. It had been so good of you putting your self out on a Sunday night. You know that I have a lot to thank you for it did give me a chance to get the kids ready for bed. I am not sorry that she has some one of her own at last. Now perhaps we won't see so much of her and I for one will be glad of that".

"At least I made sure that she got home safe and sound".

"I'm sure that this new boy friend will please mother who has no doubt got the pair of them married them off by now".

"I suppose that he is good enough probably from a farming family". Commented George and Hannah felt that the tone in his voice sounded as if he was sneering.

"I've no idea love, it will soon be known if the family have got any thing to do with it".

George did not want to discuss Sandra any more with any one especially Hannah it hurt him to listen to her chatting as she was. He ate his tea and went outside feeling very depressed with him self, he could not shake off his bad mood even when he went to bed,

"Are you all right? Darling," Hannah asked when he turned his back to her in bed.

"Just tired". He mumbled.

"I've told you that I'm worried about the extra hours that you have been doing". Oh don't start on that again"

"Sorry dear, Good night I love you".

George's mind was in turmoil, He did still have a certain amount of love for Hannah and he felt that he needed her but in a different way to how he needed Sandra.

He lay awake and thought about the eternal triangle but this was a bitter triangle, which left a nasty taste in his mouth. A very bitter pill to swallow. He knew that some one sooner or later was going to get hurt and he knew that he had gone too far to turn back and the horrible thought crossed his mind that sooner or later he would have to choose. He had not realised what a tough little woman that his Sandra could be. He could just imagine if he chose Sandra, how her parents would hate him. His own Father now a sick man would disown him. He tossed and turned for most of the night, like a condemned man about to go to the gallows.

When he did wake from sleep he stirred, and realised that Hannah was not by his side he must have dropped off to sleep eventually, when he became fully awake. It must be later than what he thought. He could hear noises down stairs it was obvious that the children were getting ready for school. He wondered if he had been dreaming, then reality struck, he had not and his problems were still facing him. He was hoping that if he went down stairs Hannah would not start asking if he was all right, he felt that he could do without her condescending attitude.

"Morning Dear" she called from the back. I have left you for another half-hour; you had such a tipsy turvy night. Who ever was chasing you in your dreams?"

"Did I "He tried to sound surprised. "I thought that I had slept all night". He lied.

Hannah let the subject drop and went about doing her daily chores.

Jim and Sandra had started to date on a regular basis and the family was delighted.

"You don't seem to have had much experience with women Jim" Sandra teased.

"What do you mean by that remark" Jim had pulled in at the back gate of the farm.

Sandra leaned over towards the driver's seat. "This is the third time that we have been out together. I'm waiting for my handsome prince to kiss me"

"Oh are you indeed" He replied taking hold of her very gently and kissing her quickly on the lips

"Ah that is better, but one could hardly call that a kiss. There was not the slightest bit of passion about it".

Jim let go of her and restarted the engine. He drove down the road and pulled in again in one of the secluded spots of the wood. Other courting couples often used these places. Before he had time to switch off the engine, Sandra was out of the car and into the back seat.

"Come my prince charming and join me".

"Very well my princess" He replied as he got into the back seat trying to make all six foot of him comfortable which was not easy. Thank goodness that he had a big car, it may be old but it got him to and from work and it was quite roomy inside.

He lay against the back seat. Sandra leant against him, her hands gently unbuttoning his shirt. Jim could not believe his luck, he had heard his mates talking but to experience a woman stroking him as Sandra was now doing was sending a thrill all the way down his spine.

She unbuttoned her blouse and guided his hand to her breasts.

Jim felt the warmth of her flesh but he felt a bit awkward and clumsy. This was some thing new to him.

"Are you a virgin?" She whispered. "Yes of course you are I can certainly tell that."

"May be not. I've read plenty of books so I think that I know what it is all about." Her hands had now unfastened his trouser front and were seeking his private parts. She felt him getting aroused and excited just as she had hoped. They managed to make love although it was not as Sandra would have liked. He was so awkward and clumsy and it was no joke trying to perform in the back of a car. "My God" she said to herself, "he knows very little about the art of lovemaking. I can see that I will have to teach him a thing or two as we go along". Jim was very happy, a girl had actually wanted him and he had risen to the occasion with out making too much of a mess of things through his being so nervous. He took Sandra home making another date to meet her, feeling very happy and contented with himself.

Sandra went into the farm kitchen and made herself some supper and sat down at the scrubbed table to think about the night's events. He is hopeless compared with George. Absolutely hopeless. Thinking about George made her stiffen as a chill went through her body. The kitchen was still warm from the heat of the Rayburn even though Fred and Dorothy had gone to bed some time ago. She was very pensive and she began to feel guilty as if she had betrayed him. George had asked her not to go that far She wondered what he would say if he knew. She felt angry and humiliated, and then she thought, "Blow him it was his idea so I am going to make the most of it. George is not going to know just yet. She knew that she had to see George she was getting that she could not live with out him. At least she could now pretend to the family especially William that she was with Jim. She realised that it was going to be tricky but she could not give George up as yet. She knew that she would see him on Saturday.

Jim was so pleased with the way his new romance was blossoming; to have a girl of his own made him feel ten feet tall. When he told his mother who he was taking out she was not too impressed.

"Take care dear" She warned him", "I have been hearing rumours about that young lady I would not like to see you hurt".

"Don't you worry Mother? I can take care of myself; I'm a big boy you know".

"So you may be, but remember that big boys hurt more than small ones if they fall" .Jim saw Sandra regularly until she started complaining that she was feeling tired and that she wanted to go home early.

"Sorry Jim dear we've been working so hard today darling, I will make it up to you. I'm so sorry. Don't look so crest fallen; it's not the end of the world. I just need an early night.

"All right, can I see you again on Wednesday? I don't really mind you going in early tonight, I'm a bit whacked myself the harvesting knocks the stuffing out of us. I will be glad when we have finished the corn harvest and then perhaps we can relax a bit".

"I know exactly how you feel she gave him a passionate kiss and got out of the car at the back gate of the farm.

It was late July and the nights were beginning to draw in a little. Sandra stood at the gate until Jim's car had disappeared down the road it was almost nine o'clock Dorothy and Fred would soon be in bed. She quickly walked across the road so that she was hidden from view of the farmhouse by the trees. There was no danger of William being about; he had gone earlier to take Sheila out. It looked as if they had become an item and would eventually get married she knew that it would be the early hours before he came back.

She walked quietly down the road to the edge of the woods, and then she heard the familiar whistle. George was there waiting in their prearranged spot. She quickened her pace and saw him leaning against the ash tree. His lighted cigarette was showing her where he was.

"You fixed it", He smiled "I saw the car go back".

"Of course darling. I will do any thing for you my love. I can't live with out you". They moved back into the wood to be hidden by the bracken and the bushes, lying down on the soft earth to make love together as if it was the most natural thing in the world to do.

"Feeling better" He whispered to her. "More relaxed now".

"Much better I need you. Poor Jim he was so glad to go early. He looked so knackered tonight."

"This could work well don't you think". George was quite pleased with himself this had been his idea.

"The family are already planning another wedding".

"Then let them that is just what we want them to think"

"Marry Jim I can't imagine it, he's not my type, he's all hands and feet. I'm sure that he takes size twelve shoes. Not like you my darling such a gentle lover, I could live with you for ever"

"I know my love; I know that it would be just heaven for the two of us. We will sort something out I assure you".

Sandra used this tactic of being tired several times with Jim It worked very well now she had a good alibi she was having the best of both worlds. Jim had taken her back early after she had pleaded she was not well he was irritated but he thought that it was best to do as she wished; he did not want to spoil the relationship. He had heard the lads talking about women's funny moods at certain times of the month. He went back home and it was only nine thirty

"You are early "Commented his Mother. Yes Sandra was not too well tonight so I have dropped her off early so that she can get to bed.

"Do you think that you should give her a ring and check that she is alright"?

"That's a good idea Mother I will be back in a minute." He went into the hall where his mother had the telephone on a small polished table.

"Who is that ringing at this time of night Dorothy complained to Fred when she heard the phone ring. She slowly rose from her chair. Dorothy was beginning to find that all the work that she now had to do was becoming very tiring. Although there was not the great amount of washing there was still a lot that had to be done. If Sandra was needed out side for such as sugar beet hoeing counting the sheep Etc. All the housework was left for her to do.

"No Sandra is not here" Dorothy said when she answered the phone. I thought that she was with you."

"No I brought her back" ages ago, "She said that she was not feeling well"

"I don't know what you are talking about; there is nothing wrong with Sandra"

"Oh I'm sorry to have bothered you I'll leave it for now".

"Where were you last night I did not hear you come in I thought you were out with Jim?" Dorothy asked of Sandra next morning.

"What made you think that I was not with him" Sandra looked surprised and her mother's question.

"Because Jim rang to see how you were feeling he said that you were ill and you seemed alright when you went out from here".

"Oh my God" thought Sandra; quickly making up an excuse "I just went for a walk"

"What do you mean. You just went for a walk," Asked the older woman.

"Well I felt better after Jim had left and it was rather early for bed".

"I don't know what you young ones think that you are doing, going for a walk at that time of night indeed. If you have any sense you would be in this house by nine o'clock and get your self to bed there is so much work that needs to be done I could do with a bit more help in this house"

"Yes mother if you say so".

Dorothy felt somewhat uneasy about the answers that Sandra had just given her but there was so much to do it was Thursday and she had to change and go into town to do the shopping so she let the matter rest for the time being. Now what is that madam up to? She wondered.

That was a close one. Sandra said to her self as she quickly left the Kitchen to go and make a start of the dairy. Sandra knew that no matter what, she could not and would not fall in love with Jim. George was her man. She continued to meet Jim but all though she allowed him to make love to her. Her heart was not for Jim. She was just using her body to satisfy his need to be with a girl of his own and not because she loved him. Each time she met him she would try to avoid having sex with him. Jim began to notice that something was wrong and they started to argue.

"Don't you want me to come and see you any more I can sense that there is something wrong?" He asked her one evening as they both cuddled up on the back seat of his car.

"I don't see why I should satisfy your needs every time that we meet".

"What do you mean by that remark? We rarely have a little bit these days. You are either too tired, if its not one thing it is another.

"Are you complaining?" She snapped.

"No but considering the way you could not get enough of me when we first went out together, you have certainly changed a lot just lately".

"Its you who have changed". She snapped again "You are not as gentle with me as you first were".

"Oh really is that what you are thinking I find that a very poor excuse".

"I'm not staying here to have a row with you, take me back. Take me back I said". She shouted as Jim turned to kiss her more passionately.

"All right, stay calm there is no need to shout, I get the message".

"Good "She said putting her clothes in order".

"Can I see you again?"

"I will give you a ring some time".

"Please Sandra don't be like that I think the world of you".

"I will ring you," She said firmly.

"All right but don't leave it too long will you".

"Goodnight Dear" She said as she closed the car door and went on her way.

"How am I going to tell George that I don't want to see Jim any more? Trying to make love with him is awful I know that I can't have the same feelings for him like the feelings that I have for George, I have no intentions of giving him up She said to her as she went inside? If any one else finds out that I am seeing him, I'll cross that bridge when I have to.

"George what do you think of getting Sandra to look after the market stall for a couple of weeks so that we can get on with this house a bit".

"That's a wonderful idea Love. Your Mother would know where she was. At least it would save her from telling lies about where she was and what she was doing. You know what your parents were like with us; no one was good enough for your high and mighty mother".

"I am going to look after the market stall for Hannah" Sandra told her Mother "I will be back at about four"

"And see that you are" Replied her Mother. "Hannah started the stall and it is her job to look after it" After spending one or two Saturdays at home, Hannah was enjoying her self. She preferred to be at home than having to spend time standing in the market. She knew that she would have to get back to it. She had now learnt that although Sandra did her best it was not the same as when she had been in charge her self. The takings were much less than Hannah's expectations and Sandra was spending too much on toys for the children Michael had taken up the hobby of model aircraft. He was aeroplane crazy he knew every model that was heard of and Sandra would bring him a new model to be assembled every week. He had hung the little plastic planes they were suspended from the ceiling in his bedroom. Hannah told Sandra that she was going back to look after the stall

"I will do it for the week or two; at least, it will help to keep the peace with mother". She said to Sandra.

"I suppose that you are right" Sandra agreed with her. She could not afford to ruffle Hannah's feathers.

"The boys have missed their Saturday matinee. They can't wait until I let them go again".

“Let me know if you want me to help you out again I can’t wait to oblige”.

“You know that I think that William is going to get engaged to that Sheila. Mother is not very happy about the idea at all she was hoping that he would forget about her and go for some one like Doreen Davies from the village”.

“I wonder what will happen if he marries her, and how they propose to sort every thing out they have never paid him a real wage so he will be entitled to the farm eventually,” Hannah was thinking.

“Buy him a cottage I should not wonder. Can’t see the old pair giving up the farm for her”. Sandra said flippantly

“They may be glad to hand over to William” Answered Hannah. “Have they spoken to you about retiring? Father is getting on a bit you know”.

“Retire “Sandra laughed. “I should not think so I can’t see the old chap ever retiring well not until he falls in a heap.”

“You’ve got some thing there, does he ever stop working.”

“Only when he is asleep”.

“What about you Sandra? I hear from the others that this young man of yours is quite charming. I’m sure that Mother has already got the pair of you married off”.

“She will be lucky. I will marry when I want and not before. Jim’s very nice but I don’t know if he is the right man for me. But I am quite happy to give it time”

“You have all the time in the world, lets see you are only eighteen now. I did not get married until I was almost twenty one and look at Mary she was twenty seven before she left home”.

“Have you any regrets? “Asked Sandra

“No not really it will be much better when George can get this wretched house finished. I can’t wait for my new kitchen. Jennifer is growing so quickly now she will soon need to have her own room”.

"But George works such long hours, you two should be well off by now" Sandra queried'.

"I know that he does, he is only at home when he is working in the shed and then it is because he has windows or something else that needs to be made for a job that he is working on. As for money it is so hard to get it in, No one is keen to pay their bills."

"I often see his van going past our place some times its after nine o'clock at night". Sandra was trying to convince Hannah that he was really at work.

"I know and he gets so tired doing the hours that he is. I don't like asking him to cut the glass for the frames any more. Even that seems to be too much trouble for him. I don't think that he could be seeing some one else. I have often let the thought cross my mind but I don't think that it is likely. If he was seeing some one she would have to put up with him in his dirty working clothes. The possibility could make more sense than he working late could, but I dismissed it. Judith said that I would be barking completely up the wrong tree. I don't dare ring the people where he says that he is working, to see if he is really there and that he is working late. I know if I were to do that it would make him very angry. But I am very tempted He would probably blow a fuse and I have not seen him angry very often and I certainly don't want to be the cause of an all mighty row. If he thought that I did not trust him any further than what I could throw him as the saying goes. No I think that he could be genuinely working to get more money to finish this wretched house. But on the other hand things don't make any sense at all. He is not in the pub drinking or I would smell it when he comes in. He could be staying talking before coming home. By the way I see it, there is something certainly going on. If it was not for being able to live in the country there are days when I wish that we had never come here and started of the damned house I know that I can't stick it for much longer. If he keeps working late as he is at the moment I am really going to do some checking up? We can't possibly go on like we are, we hardly speak civilly to each other and I know that it is not my fault. I can't 'do much more here, and the twins are too young for me to go out and get a full time job but don't 'you think that I have not thought about doing that. George says that his customers are reluctant to pay their bills but I have noticed that he does not make many out theses days. There is definitely something going on. I think I will have to see what I can find out. Sorry that I am having a good moan to you I know that George is not that bad really it is this blasted house that is getting on my nerves and he seems so moody these days". Hannah sighed as if it was good to have a good moan with some one but little did she know that she was playing right into Sandra's hands.

"Perhaps he's got a lot on his mind".

"Not that I know of. There's not much for him to worry about except getting the cash in and that seems to be a permanent problem to him".

The two of them chatted about the rest of the family none of the Sisters were expecting babies at the present time other wise that was the main topic of conversation.

Elizabeth had two daughters and two sons. Mary had not long given birth to a son the only boy with two older sisters. Rebecca had two sons but they were six years apart. Grace had given birth to a daughter and a son and then she had a hysterectomy. Helen now had two sons and a daughter so this did give the family plenty to gossip about when they saw each other. They had all acted as godparents for different babies. Grace had kept herself completely involved with her own family and she had cut herself off from the rest of her sisters. Her husband had considered that not one of them was good enough to have any thing to do with. Hannah had called in to see her as she was returning from visiting the hospital at Gobowen once or twice. Grace was always very busy with her hectic social life that she led. She was an avid member of the local Golf club Staff were employed to do most of the work including the house hold chores. When Hannah called she seemed to have so much that she had to see to. Cakes to be made for this charity do or telephone calls to be made to the people that they had to entertain. Hannah felt as if she was in the way and that it would have been better not to call. She felt as if there was no longer a close and friendly atmosphere between them. Sandra could not wait to see George and tell him of the conversation that she had with Hannah.

"Be careful George. She has smelt a rat and she is not going to give up until she catches it"

"Oh; she has as she. Well we will see about that".

"Well what I can see of things we are going to have to come clean and see what she says or you will have to leave and we can start together some where else with the caravan".

"Oh really you think that is what I should do". He sounded angry and Sandra did not like it.

"Don't you take it out on me Lover? You are in a mess and we both know why. I am not stepping out of your life just to please her. Got that straight. I will not give you up"

Hannah was beginning to notice that all was not well financially. The bank had returned a couple of cheques that George had written. The bank had refused to pay them. Hannah was most upset about it. One had been written to pay for her weekly grocery order. To her it was such a disgrace to have a cheque returned. George was doing so much overtime she could not understand it. She waited until the children had gone to school and he had washed and shaved at the kitchen sink. When he sat down to eat his breakfast she brought the subject up and she handed George yet another letter from the bank. He did not say anything to her as she gave it to him He put the letter in his pocket. He did not attempt to open it and neither was he prepared to discuss the matter any further with Hannah. He finished his breakfast in silence lit a cigarette and went out side saying.

"I will get some more money in. leave it with me. I'll see the bank, I just can't think what they are playing at, returning my cheques. I think that they have made a terrible mistake, and don't you worry about it."

"Should I make an appointment for you to see the manager?" Hannah had followed him to the door not wanting to dismiss or drop the subject.

"Leave it to me" George snapped. "I have told you that it is my problem and that I will deal with it. I can't work any harder than what I am doing. So leave it; will you?" He continued on his way to the shed. Hannah was quite shaken by his attitude this was not like George. She had been taken aback by his remarks and the tone in his voice. It was not like George to take it out on her if he had a bad day and what was more she had been quite prepared to talk things over with him but he was having none of it. She did not know it but he was still seething about what Sandra had told him. He did not know what Hannah was going to do about him saying that he was always working late; he was on edge and on the defensive. She was afraid to open her mouth for fear of having her head bitten off. Thank goodness that she now had her own little bit of cash coming in from the market stall.

George went to see the Bank manager Mr Henshaw and ask him not to stop any further cheques.

"You know your limit Mr Fleming and I can not let you go over it". He spoke very sternly "£500 is the limit of your overdraft and that is as far as I am prepared to go. I am not prepared to allow you to go any further than that amount. Mind you it would be a very different matter if you were to get a move on and finish that house. How your wife has put up with it so long I have no idea.

The manager then went on to discuss George's financial situation; this really irritated George. Who was wondering and thinking what bloody business was it of his. Was not the bank there to lend money? And as for finishing the house George considered that it was none of his business. He had always been a good customer in the past. George had to agree to make a better effort. He left and he was praying and hoping that Hannah would not find out how much he owed He knew that she was no fool and although he had kept all the bank statements out of her sight he dreaded her finding them. He would just have to get some of his jobs finished and collect some money in. George did this and things went smoothly for a few months. July went into August the evenings were starting to draw in and Christmas would soon on be here again. George did not fancy meeting Sandra and making love in the van which could be very uncomfortable and with great difficulty or in the woods during the cold weather. He had a brilliant idea but he did not know if he dared put it into practice.

"I've been thinking," He said To Sandra. "What if I fetch the caravan back from the sea? We could meet in it during the winter months"

"What a brilliant idea. Where could we put it with out raising suspicions"?

"Leave it to me I will think of somewhere"

"Listen, George darling. I will be nineteen next year. I am eighteen now and I can do, as I like legally. I want to know how I stand with you, are you prepared to leave Hannah for me? We could go away together and start a new life; we could take the caravan and manage for a while". George was so taken aback he was speechless listening to Sandra pouring out all these ideas of hers. The thought of leaving Hannah had never occurred to him.

"Leave Hannah", he tried not to sound too surprised.

"Well if you don't come away with me then you tell me what are you prepared to do? I am not prepared to give you up and neither am I prepared to be second hand fiddle much longer. I am not as daft as people are inclined to think. George; we have been lovers for so long now surely you are not going to tell me that you prefer Hannah to me. I would not believe it if you did. You have told me time and time again that I can satisfy you as no one else possibly could and I want to be more secure I have no intentions of being at home when William takes over He would make my life hell."

"My dear, as if I would compare you with any one else. You are quite right my little love no other has been able to please me as you have done. We will sort something out I assure you" George had never realised that he would be put in this situation where he would have to choose between the two women in his life He began to realise what a mess he had got himself into. Now laying on a sheet in the bushes the darkness closing in around them he wanted to give no thought to such problems. He was content with things as they were. He held Sandra close to him and murmured sweet nothings to her. She soon relaxed and they were making love as usual.

"Don't you forget to give some thought to what I have told you" Sandra reminded him when he dropped her off, hours later. It is soon going to be a case of her or me. If you won't leave her then you will have to get rid of her."

"Now my Darling don't spoil the evening we will talk about it another time"

"You are quite right we will. I am not going to stay working at home forever. As I see it there will be nothing for me William will have every thing and the old folks are getting no younger. If I know him He and Sheila will expect the old pair to get out, so that he is in sole charge of the place. As far as I can see it would be no use putting William in a cottage Dad is getting older, in fact too old to be up in the night calving cows"

"You leave it with me .I will think of something my love".

He reversed in to an opening in the wood to turn the van around and left her to walk the rest of the way home. When he got home the children were in bed and Hannah was ready for bed. She offered to make him some supper, which he readily accepted. Looking around the room, the furniture shining in the dim light. The fire still burning in the hearth which caused the light to flicker and dance on the brasses displayed there.

Leave this he thought, no way, how could he, to live in a caravan on a site some where. He had put all his spare time into the rebuilding of this house even if there was a lot more to be done. What about the children. Michael was the apple of his eye. The boy went every where with him when it was possible to take him. He knew that Hannah could cope with the twins but no way was he going to lose his eldest son. The very idea of it really frightened him.

The idea of being George's mistress for the rest of her life did not appeal to Sandra, As far as she was concerned she was going to see that he made a choice, he had to decide what he was going to do about Hannah. The fact that he was almost twenty years older than her did not worry her one little bit. George was every thing to her and she now knew that she could not live with out him. "I will not" she said to herself, he will be mine. She knew that he took Hannah to the market and left the children until he went back for them. Sandra got herself dressed ready for town. She started off towards Wellington. Her Mother was quite pleased to see that she was going off on her bicycle and that for once George was not picking her up. He seemed to always be giving her lift to one place or another. Still she thought that Sandra could come to no harm they knew who she was with and they knew that they could trust George implicitly. No harm could come to their youngest daughter. Sandra cycled into town she waited until George had unloaded the van then she made him aware of her presence. Hannah was busy unpacking the boxes and displaying her goods on the market stall. Sandra had already seen the children running to the cinema for the film matinee, but they had not seen her." What are you doing in town already?" George asked

"Just thought that I might see you around" She answered.

"It's my pleasure" He replied "where is your bike?

"Oh safe for a while". She smiled such and alluring smile.

"Jump in. I am hoping to get on with the house today".

"I'll come and give you a hand if you like?"

"I would like that very much".

They drove the back way around the Wrekin parked in the yard and went inside.

"I'll make a cuppa" Sandra suggested.

"Good idea". He smiled

They both sat drinking the tea but both knew what was going through the others mind. There was a bed upstairs and it was not long before they were both lying on it.

"How about this?" She whispered" Can't get any better can it.

"Just you watch me" George muttered. Appeasing both him and Sandra. He was full of energy after a good night's sleep. They did not move until well into the afternoon.

"Better go and collect them" He said as he made an effort to dress and go down stairs. "Goodness me, is that the time? George we must have fallen asleep. Drop me off in town. I am supposed to be looking after the stall. She dressed her self and smiled at the photo, which stood on the dressing table. It was of Hannah and George on their wedding day, "you are not as good as I am", and she had no recriminations about herself making love in her sister's bed. She knew that Hannah would not suspect a thing so they left the bed as they had found it. Hannah had not had time to make it properly before she went to the market she had only thrown the cover over it.

Hannah in the meantime was wondering why George had not collected the children at 12-30. The boys became very bored hanging around the market all afternoon. She was more than pleased to see him when he finally came as she packed up the stall.

"Been busy have you?" she queried.

"Not bad, not got on as I had hoped. Too many hindrances, I looked at a job in the village". He lied. Hannah was really dismayed when they arrived back home and saw that nothing had been done at the house. Even the sugar basin was on the table. George had apparently been making himself some tea and he had put the dirty cups in the sink.

What George and Sandra had not noticed was that the old boy that lived next door could sit in his bedroom and see practically everything that went on at Woodside. He had seen Sandra come back with George in the van and leave again but he kept his thoughts to himself. He could guess and let his imagination run away with him. Not having married himself he had never experienced the pleasures of the flesh, when his elderly mother had died he felt too old to bother. He was very fond of Hannah and chatted to her when ever she was working in the garden and could spare a few minutes, he felt quite pleased with himself when he saw that she had taken his advice about gardening. He took a great liking to David; the lad interested him as he watched him growing up. They would spend a lot of time in each other's company. He noticed that what ever the lad tried to do, he never gave up until he had mastered it no matter how long that it took him. He was very practical with his hands and he liked the lad the way he worked along side his mother in the garden, planting and weeding, nothing was too much trouble for him. While the older one Michael just did not have the patience. Old Tom did not like what he was seeing. Now why would that young Sandra be here on her own with George. He had taken a walk past the cottage but he had seen no sign of work going on. What are they up to? He wondered, like most old men he kept his thoughts to him self but he was going to keep his eyes open.

"Was that the postman"? George asked when he was about to go to work

"Yes" replied Hannah and there is a bill here from a firm in Craven Arms. I think that they must have got the wrong Fleming. Hannah was looking at the brown envelope "You don't deal with anyone as far away as that".

"Let me have a look at it. "George took the envelope from Hannah." Oh yes it is ours".

"What do you mean, its ours, you only deal with Pearce's and Corbet and Leeds"?

"OH. That bloke at Pearce's was a bit funny with me, he did not want me to get some wood out that I wanted for a job at Miss Hinges so I told him to stick it. George dared not tell Hannah the truth that the last cheque that he had paid Pearce's had bounced and there was to be no more credit until he had settled all the account that he had outstanding with them.

"How did you come across this firm dear?"

"Oh a rep came bothering me while I was working at Mrs Browns. I thought that there would be no harm in giving them a try. They certainly offer good rates. I thought that I would see how I got on with them .The trouble with Wellington there is so little competition so they keep their prices high".

"OK leave it; with you. I will be in Pearce's for some wood for my frames before next week.

If Hannah wanted to use the van, she had only to drop George off where he was working and collect him later. She would try to fetch wood for her self when he was working at home in his shed making windows or some thing that could not be bought ready made.

"Seen anything of Sandra in your travels?"

"No why should I" George sounded surprised at the question.

"She has not been across for a bit, all is very quiet"

If only she knew George thought as he went off to work. He did see Sandra as he went into town. She was already out with her bike. See you on Saturday she said. She told him that she would not come into town instead he could pick her up at the burnt cottage track. As usual she told her Mother that she was looking after Hannah's market stall. Old Tom next door saw Sandra come and leave later on the Saturday afternoon. That is funny he thought to him self, what can that pair being up to? No-good I'm sure of it from what I see of that little madam. He had been a walk again past Woodside taking his little dog with him. He had heard laughing coming from the open bedroom window. What are they doing upstairs there is no sign of hammering or knocking to indicate that George was busy working on the house. He was worried about the fact that Sandra visited when Hannah was not there. He again decided to keep his thoughts to himself, but his thoughts seemed to be turning into facts and this really disturbed him. Sandra came across again on the next day for Sunday tea. Hannah as usual made her welcome, they shared the family goings on and gossip and enjoyed each other's company. As usual George offered to take her home.

"Won't be long love" he said as they went out through the door to the van.

"That's alright. I'll get the jobs finished and then we can relax for an hour.

Hannah did as she had suggested and settled down but there was no sign of George. At ten o'clock the telephone rang. It was Dorothy her mother.

"Where is Sandra?" She shouted down the phone. "Time that she was in this house. You are encouraging her to stop out all hours and another thing its time that you looked after your own stall on a Saturday". This was always her mother's way of handling things when she was angry. She would shout it all out and not give the other person a chance to contradict her.

"Now just a minute Mother". Hannah said calmly. George brought Sandra back hours ago.

"Well she is not in as yet" Shouted Dorothy

"Some thing must have gone wrong and what is this about Sandra looking after my stall. She has done no such thing.

"You will say any thing to cover up for her"

"No I will not mother. I don't mind her coming across for a bit of tea but I look after my own stall"

"Well its time she was in this house and it has all got to stop" Before Hannah could say another word the phone went dead.

Hannah was amazed at the accusations, and was quite upset for some time she was glad to hear George drive into the yard and come inside.

“What’s the matter with you, you look all hot and bothered.

“Mother has been shouting at me down the phone she wanted to know where Sandra had got to”

“What’s she talking about. We’ve been sat talking around the kitchen table” He stood in front of the fire and looked Hannah straight in the face and lied. “The woman is going around the bend”.

“George nothing is making any sense she says that Sandra has been looking after my stall” That’s not true”.

“Now calm down lets think this out. You know that your mother does funny things and talks to her self”.

“Well don’t we all but that does not make us completely bonkers, I’ll bet Sandra has made the excuse of looking after my stall to get away from the farm and all the work. I would not be surprised if she has got another boy friend that she does not want them to know about. We don’t here so much about Jim these days.”

“Leave it with me I’ll have a word with your mother, Can’t have her going on at you like this. I will sort it out”. But how he had no idea.

Hannah listened to what George said. If he said that he had been in the kitchen then why had her mother rung?” George was adamant. If Sandra had been there all the time when her mother had telephoned was she really loosing her grip and going around the bend. George had swore blind that they had been in the kitchen and said that he had wondered why her mother had gone into the front room to use the phone they had heard her talking but he said that he could not distinguish what she was saying. If only Hannah had thought quickly she would have realised that the phone was now in the kitchen.

Hannah could accept the business about the market stall but not about Sandra not being in. She turned the whole business over and over in her mind. What was that madam up to?

The whole episode faded into the back ground as work gained precedence.

"Busy" shouted a voice over the garden hedge. Old Tom had seen Hannah working away in the garden.

"Always busy Tom you know me I can't rest for long there is so much to do.

"Well it's good of Sandra to come and give you a hand on a Saturday"

"Give me a hand".

"Yes she was here on Saturday while you were at the stall"

Hannah was puzzled, there had been nothing done in the house on Saturday. The conversation went from one subject to another.

"George". Hannah asked that night. "Old Tom next door said that Sandra had been here on Saturday. What is going on I'm hearing all sorts of queer things and nothing makes sense Can you throw any light on things or am I going around the bend What on earth was Sandra doing here when I was at the stall"

Oh hell thought George

"Oh that I gave her a lift and she came with me for a ride to pick up some tools. I dropped her off on the way back".

"Why did you not tell me"?

"There is no need for you to get upset there was nothing to tell. You know Sandra she comes here quite a bit. She would not touch anything in the house if you were not here. How long did he say that she was here?"

"He didn't, he just said that she had been here". Thank God for that George said to himself.

"Now don't let us have a row George If Sandra is playing them up a bit, I'm sure that it will pass over." Hannah was a born optimist as far as trouble was concerned; things usually were sorted out with patience.

George was getting worried things were beginning to catch up with him and he did not like it. He decided that he and Sandra must get together and sort some thing out between them. He had to decide if he could stop seeing her but that was something that he did not want to do. The girl had a hold on him as no one else had done. She was nothing to look at her eyesight was not good, neither could she cook nor clean properly. None of these problems had entered his head. She had a sexual desire and need of which there was no comparison. No matter what time of day or night that it was she was able to completely satisfy him.

Next day George drove towards Wellington, he had taken the long way round the bottom of the hill; he needed time to think. It was now well into May the new leaves on the trees were forty shades of green.

He pulled off the road lit a cigarette; he wound down the window of the van and drew heavily on his cigarette letting the smoke filter out through the open window. The birds fluttered from bush to bush they were far too busy to let the parked van disturb them. It was becoming obvious to George that he had to finish his relationship with Sandra he knew that he could not face the scandal if it became common knowledge. An idea came to him what if Sandra went out with some one else for a while

Then every one would be happy. He knew that he would hate the idea but it would throw the scent off him. Yes the idea could work. He sat and looked around him. If he brought the caravan back from the sea he could park it somewhere like this and then perhaps they could meet occasionally. All sorts of ideas raced through his mind. He would arrange to meet her and see what she has to say.

There were other problems; the work was not coming in as it had been. What he did not realise was that his customers were fed up with his starting jobs and not getting the work finished. The bills were piling up; he knew that the tax bill had not been paid. He was hoping that Hannah would not give up the market stall at least that kept her quiet so that she did not have to ask him for every penny that she wanted. There was no chance of there being any money to get on with the house. The new workshop that he was building needed a roof he had built it of second hand bricks so that he could save on the cost and have a more substantial place to work his present work shed was not the best place to be working with electricity. He stayed where he was for a couple of hours contemplating what to do He then decided to go and see Mr Bradley and see if he could finish the work there. No one was in at the house when he got there They knew that he had work there to finish As he drove into the yard a horse box was just leaving. The Son came from around another lorry.

"Oh its you "He said "And about time too. We need these jobs finished the gaffer is in a right mood. Does not want you on the bloody bank if you can't oblige us any better. We have got a business to run."

George reluctantly got out of the van and took his tool box from out of the back The stables had needed new doors and George had promised to have them finished for the winter months and had made no such effort. He started to get busy but was interrupted by Mr Bradley Senior.

Mr Bradley senior had seen George's van pull into the yard. I've got a word or two to say to him and he went into the yard to face George.

"Its you, Fleming, you promised to have these doors finished for the winter. Not good enough it is just not good enough you know."

George started making his usual excuses. "Sorry about this I have had so much on these last few months"

"Well get your priorities right" He old man growled "We have been good customers, not that I am saying that you don't do a good job, but this waiting not knowing when we are going to see you again is no good to us. Your little wife never seems to know where you are. We have found that it is a waste of time and money ringing for you," He turned on his heels and went inside.

"Piss off "George said to Mr Bradley's back. Meithering old goat he does not know what life is really about he has never been short of a bob or two. What George did not realise was that old Mr Bradley had worked from dawn to dusk seven days a week to build up their business. He had not been like George taking afternoons and sometimes-whole days just to go bonking up in the woods with a schoolgirl. Lost time cost money. George finished his work and made his way for home. He went back up the Ercall hoping to see Sandra he had avoided this way home for the last few weeks in case he ran into William There was no sign of Sandra being about so he went home knowing that she would be in touch.

Hannah seemed in a bad mood as he went in.

"Any thing wrong love" He asked with a smile.

"George what is going on? George gulped wondering what was coming next. Hannah was making the gravy for the evening meal, which smelt good. George was hungry.

"I rang Pearce's with the order for the wood to make my picture frames and they told me that I must pay for it before I could have any. They said that their account had to be settled before I could pick up any more wood up. I cannot put it on your account. George we don't owe them that much do we?"

"I expect that we do owe them a bit. And I don't want to discuss bills right now I want to have my tea in peace I'm hungry"

"Very well let's have our tea" Agreed Hannah "But we must sort this out afterwards. You agreed that it was best to book my bits and pieces through the trade so that we had the discount at trade price"

"Not now" He spoke firmly as the children came running in. The meal was eaten in silence. Michael sensed that there was an atmosphere and was wondering what was going on between his parents He had heard at school about parents splitting up and it was the one thing that he dreaded most.

Afterwards Hannah was determined to sort things out but Charles came with a message saying that his aunt wanted some more work doing on one of her cottages. This saved George for the time being, He thought if he was extremely nice to Hannah at bed time and make love with her she just might forget to question him about Pearce's. Not Hannah, she waited until the children had gone to school next morning and she brought the subject up again.

"What money have you got? George. If I am to pay for my timber I am going to need you to give me some. I only have the family allowance and Michael must have that spent on him he needs new shoes".

"I've got no money" George snapped "Where do you think that I get it from off trees".

"But this is ridiculous George I give you any money that I have surplus from my stall for your petrol and cigarettes after I have paid the dinner money, the milkman etc;"

"I give you a cheque for the groceries. Don't I "He Grumbled.

"Yes George but we have to be fed. The children cannot go hungry, providing that it does not bounce".

George was getting very angry. "You are always on about money".

"I am not I just want to know why the bank is refusing you any more credit to pay your timber bills. You did go and see the bank didn't you"

"Of course I did

"Well"

"We owe them too much if you must know"

"What do you mean you owe too much"

"What I say" George snarled

"George I want to know what sort of a state that we are in"?

"Pretty rough"

"I don't believe this I will not pay any more cheques for grocery, you will have to give me cash Can you imagine the disgrace that we are in. That cheque that was returned has given Mrs Timmins at the shop plenty of gossip and she will have it all over the village as quick as she can. Let us get the bank statements and sort some thing out I notice that the bank statements are not with the other accounts that I keep so carefully"

"Not now "George shouted I have to go to work"

Hannah waited until George had left and was out of earshot Money. Money why did he have such problems with money. He worked so hard so many hours Hannah was thinking as she looked to see where George had put the last month's bank statement. But she was unable to find it. The bank account was in George's name and she left it to George to deal with it Hannah only made accounts of bills that George made out for his customers and of bills that had to be paid by George. Hannah was always careful with George's paper work, but he was in charge of the banking, the account had always been in his name. What Hannah did not know was that the last statement had arrived on a Saturday morning after she had gone to her market stall and George had burnt it. Damn she thought when she could not find it. I will have to telephone for a copy of the last one it seems as if George must have lost it.

She went into the shed and got on with making her photo frames, which had been ordered for the weekend. As Hannah worked away smoothing the wood with sandpaper she went over the morning's discussion, some thing did not add up. George seemed to be working long hours or was he working. He could perhaps be sitting drinking tea and talking not bothering about the time. Or was he going to the pub and that was where he was spending money that he should be banking towards paying his bills. But he did not come home smelling of drink what was she going to do? She had never been in this situation before and she did not like it. She did have enough material to last a little while but what then. George was getting so reluctant to discuss money matters.

Hannah decided that she would stay at home for the next two Saturdays. She would ask Sandra to look after the stall for her. When she asked Sandra if she would look after the stall for a couple of weeks Sandra jumped at the chance. Now lets see what is going on Hannah said to her self there looks to me as if there are one or two things that need sorting out. What she had not realised she had played right in to Sandra's and George's hands. Sandra did not have to lie to her parents and at the same time she was able to see George. The next few days Hannah as usual prepared her work for her Market stall so that Sandra would not make any mistakes with the orders and the prices. She made lists and gave Sandra implicit instructions. George raised no objections to the idea and drove off picking Sandra up on the way and promptly returned home to work on the moulds for his idea of being able to produce kerbing stones. According to him this was going to save them financially. Michael and David worked along side of him. Later in the day he returned to collect Sandra and drop her off at home.

"When can we be together Darling"? She had asked him.

"Soon my love, I've got a proposition to put to you I will see you Tuesday night .

"I'll look forward to it. You bet that I will"

For the next few days George was pre-occupied, how was he going to tell Sandra what he had in mind? They met as usual

"George Darling" Sandra asked when they had exhausted themselves making love. "What are you going to do about Hannah?

""What do you mean,

"Well are you going to leave her and come away with me? Or what are you proposing to do?"

"My little love you know that I can't leave Hannah, there are the kids to think about and the house to finish. I can't. I just can't do that"

"Well you tell me what you propose to do?"

"You don't have to go to bed. Just make it look like it. William can think that you are not seeing me, we can still meet whenever we can get together".

"George what are you going to do about Hannah, If I did this as you say are you going to leave her eventually. I think that I could bear it if I knew that we were going to be together forever...

"I was only thinking that it would give us some time to decide what would be the best for us to do".

Sandra decided she would have to tell George that she could no longer go out with Jim and pretend that she loved him. She had not seen him for some time.

"I just can't. "She told him "It's a complete farce I can't go on pretending". She pleaded with George.

"But there is no harm done". He answered.

"I can't go on pretending. She pleaded.

"But there is no harm done" he repeated. "I can't see why? You only go out with him socially".

Sandra dare not tell him how far she and Jim had already gone.

"I will think about it" She promised.

"I have promised that I will give him a ring and agree to go out with him again".

"You do just that my love".

Sandra told George about her conversation with Hannah. For a moment or two he felt so angry to think that she might check up on him." The sneaky little bitch "He hissed" "Calm down a bit George" Sandra said "And put your self in her shoes.

"You can't blame Hannah; she is only worried for your health and as to when you can get enough extra money to finish the house. You must not get angry Darling if she were to find out the truth I think that she would be waiting with your shot gun and that she would make sure that it would be loaded. She has been confiding with Judith thinking that you are not well" She started to giggle. "I would say that you are pretty fit wouldn't you".

"I think that you had better start going out with Jim for a while. I will try and settle things down a bit at home".

"Not on your Nelly" she thought to herself. "I won't pretend any more. I'll not see him as yet. She decided that she and George would continue to meet when ever they could even if it was not so often.

William had noticed that there had been no sign of Jim coming to the farm and he asked Sandra about it.

""Didn't get on too well "She replied but we will probably make it up".

"Good" Said William. "If not look for some one else, we don't want a repeat performance of you and George thank goodness you're not seeing him any more"

"Don't you bother Big brother. You will have more to worry about than what I have if you insist on marrying that Sheila".

"There's nothing wrong with Sheila". He was quick to answer.

"Cost you a fortune to keep what I see of her".

"That's got nothing to do with you. There is no harm in making the most of ones self".

"Where would you live? This place is not good enough for her".

"It will always clean up, a bit".

"I think that is an under statement. The house will need a fortune spending on it. I can't see Sheila using an earth privy and having no central heating to keep her warm".

"We will wait and see".

"Now lets be sensible about this, Father's promised you the farm but I can't see him and mother getting out to make way for Sheila. If you have to wait for them to pass on you are in for a long wait brother. You had better start looking for a cottage I reckon"." "But they haven't' paid me any wages".",

"What's that got to do with it, they haven't paid any of us any wages of sorts. We have all worked on promises. The only money that I have had is pocket money".

"I've had no more" Grumbled William.

"They will see you all right I am sure". There is going to be some fun ahead, she thought as she left William to think about his future.

A month went by Sandra made no effort to contact Jim, she had met George a couple of times since she had last spoken to him. She had easily covered her tracks with out the family suspecting any thing.

Mary had seen her sitting in George's van when she had been calling in to see Fred and Dorothy.

"Where is Sandra? "She asked.

"Gone into town", Answered Dorothy.

"I've just seen her sitting in George's van. This side of the village.

"He's probably given her a lift to save her from walking. He often does that".

Mary said no more but she was disturbed by what she had seen. Perhaps there was no harm being done but she decided to keep her eyes open in the future. She had noticed George's van parked in the woods previously but she had given it no second thought. She had naturally assumed that he was cutting pea or bean sticks for Hannah to use in the garden. Lots of people did this; it was a common practise to cut a few hazel sticks for a row of peas in their gardens or to collect a bag of leaf mould, which was excellent for growing geraniums. Mary had called in to say that she was moving to south Wales with her husband and it was because of his job. They were going to rent an old rectory and that there would be plenty of spare rooms if the family wanted to visit. September came and Sandra to her horror found that her monthly period was late. Could she be pregnant? She thought back to the nights that she had lain in the bracken with George. If she were pregnant it would be his child she had not seen Jim since the end of July. She felt panic rise with in her, what was she going to do? Perhaps there was nothing wrong after all. She had heard her sisters talking about this sort of thing and then every thing had turned out all right. She thought back to one night in particular, she and George had been so happy together they had excelled them selves with their lovemaking and it appeared as if this was the result.

Should she wait another month or should she say any thing? What would George say? How would he react? She would have to see him and have a talk.

"Well can't you get rid of it" Was the first thing that he said when they had met and she had told him.

"And how do I do that?" she shouted at him She was completely over come by his suggestion.

"I don't know. You women know about these things, Can't you have an operation".

"What else are you going to suggest? An operation is out of the question. Who is going to pay for it? I would have to say who the father is. I can see that going well down with the family. George what am I going to do? Will you leave Hannah so that you can take care of me?"

"Leave Hannah".

"Yes we could go away together. We will have to".

"Let's give this some thought; I'm sure that we can solve things".

"I hope so Darling, it can only be your baby. Just think that I am carrying your baby. Oh George the whole idea scares the living day lights out of me. I know that it is yours. Isn't it wonderful that I have part of you inside of me despite being scared stiff it makes me feel so good"? Lying on the sheet hidden from view, Sandra felt safe in George's arms.

George was not feeling so safe. Bloody hell he thought to himself what a mess. This was not the news that he had wanted to hear when Sandra asked him to meet her. This had certainly thrown the cat amongst the pigeons.

"A child on the way. Are you sure or perhaps it's a false alarm, give it another week or two we will think of some thing.

"You must George".

"Are you still seeing Jim?"

"No I have not rung him as yet. I have not seen him since the end of July I'm pregnant and it has to be yours. What are we going to do?"

"But when did it happen I am always so careful".

"Remember the night I held you tight and you did not want to stop it must have been then."

"You have not planned this have you and held me so that I may have released before I was ready".

"What a wicked thing to say, as if I would do that George How could you even think it?" To hear them arguing, it was a pity that it had not dawned on them before, now considering the stupid risks that they had been taking that she had not got herself into this mess years ago. It appeared to never have dawned on them at all. The woodland creatures that were witnessing this carry on would never have under stood what all the fuss was about. When Sandra left George and went home. Sandra thought over what he had said. How dare he suggest that I deliberately held him tight? It's his child and he's going to be responsible. How, she had not got a clue, what she going to tell her parent's .At the moment she knew that she couldn't.

She saw George again. "Anything happened? "he asked" A week or so later"

"No not yet George and I don't think that it is going to".

"I bloody hope so "Give it another week and perhaps it will. I've been thinking that you should get in touch with Jim again and make a date to go out with him again and perhaps you could persuade him to go all the way. Your Mother and Father will accept him".

"Am I hearing right" She exploded. "You suggest that I go out with Jim and put the blame on him"

"You can always say that the baby came before its time"

"My God you have certainly thought this one out have you not?"

"And what am I supposed to do next? Marry him".

"And why not, he won't know any different"

"Marry him, I don't love him. I love you".

"It will give us some time Sandra".

"Give who time. Why can't you leave Hannah"?

"I can't I can't".

"I don't see why not. Just let us go away together. Sandra was not thinking rationally.

"And then what? Where should we live how do I get work what are we going to live on? What about Hannah and the kids"

"She can keep them. She can get a job. She said that if it were not for the twins she would get a full time job now to help you get on with the house".

"Oh it's so easy to hear you talk".

"If I marry Jim and put the blame on him then what?"

"We could still see each other"

"You do have a bloody nerve".

"Now calm down and let's think this out".

"It sounds to me that you have certainly done some thinking and it is all for your benefit".

"We have got to think what is best for you my love, you don't seem to realise that your Mam and Dad don't even know that you have been seeing me.

The shock would probably kill them just think of the scandal and if Hannah found out she would crack up".

"That would be alright you could then have her locked away and I could move in with you".

"Now talk sense, let's take one step at a time. I have given this a lot of thought these last few days. We have got to get a plan together just in case. We can't leave it too late. What I can see is that you have got to tell them that you are pregnant. In another month or so you will not be able to hide it. You will have no choice but to stay where you are and you can imagine what that will be like trying to bring a child up on the farm and who are you going to say that the father is. I think that if you were to go out with Jim again they would accept that. Blow their tops a bit at first but what I know of your Mother she would not be able to get you married quickly enough. You think about it Sandra. I will never be able to accept the fact that you are with another man carrying my child but what choice do we have"?

"Would it really upset you if I went to bed with some one else?"

"My god it would, I'll say so".

A feeling of pleasure ran through Sandra's body. George really did care, he really did care. I will give it some thought she promised as she let herself into the farmhouse in the early hours of the morning. She lay in her bed unable to sleep. Marry Jim that would be one way of solving her problems she thought of how that she was going to fix it. I've got to move pretty quickly if he's going to take the rap for this. Dare she. She thought of what George had said. Would he still see her if she married Jim? Where would they live?" Was George just trying to get rid of her? Who did he really love? Hannah or herself. What ever this baby was it would resemble George in some way or other. Now she would never be with out a part of him. This made her feel good. How was she going to face the future she did not know she could not visualise her future without George being part of it? She had been seeing him since when she was at school.

Next day she spoke to William. If you see Jim on your travels ask him to get in touch. I think that I will have to make it up to him.

"OK if I see him nothing wrong is there.

"Well you could say that. There might be but I must see Jim"

"You didn't you are not are you?"

"Well I could be, but don't say a word to any one as yet. There may be no need

"You know that Mary has been asking the old chap and lady to go for a holiday and have a break Perhaps we could persuade them to go for a week and have a party".

"What a good idea Big brother you sure can think of them pretty quickly",

Sandra waited until Fred and Dorothy had gone into town and then she telephoned Mary.

"Mother was talking the other day of coming to see you Is the offer still on for them to come for a break for a week? She said that she would quite like a change".

"You know that they can come and stay when ever. That is if you can talk them around to doing it. I can't see why you and William can't manage with out them for a week".

"Be glad to". Answered Sandra I will try and talk them into coming and taking up your offer soon.

"Yes you do that before the weather gets colder, the two sisters went on to discuss the rest of the family. Sandra waited until after tea when Dorothy was on her own in the kitchen.

"Have you and Dad thought any more about going to see Mary for a few days. Mary rang while you were out today". Sandra lied. "She wants to know if you could go for a break before the weather starts to get colder. She says that autumn will not be long".

"Well do you two reckon that you could manage for a week?"

"Of course we can. The sea air will do the pair of you good".

So it was arranged for Fred and Dorothy to go and stay with Mary and her family the last week of September.

William saw Jim and told him that Sandra wanted to see him. "Give her a ring" William asked of him.

"I'll get in touch" Jim answered. William left him and went back to his work in his own field.

"I'm so sorry Jim" Sandra said when Jim telephoned. "Can I see you again? To be quite honest I have missed you my darling".

"Really". Jim had a job to hide the enthusiasm he felt as he spoke to her. "What about Saturday night?" Ok pick you up about seven. I can't wait to be with you again".

"Same here. I have missed you too. I was hoping that you would get in touch again".

"Sorry Jim I can not think what was wrong with me, not to have got in touch before now".

"Never mind my love I will make it up to you on Saturday".

Sandra could not believe her luck as she hung up the receiver. She gave a sigh of relief. She would not have known what she would have done if Jim had turned her down. George was right Bless him, this just might solve my problems. She thought with great relief. She decided that she would have the best of both worlds, she would be able to carry on seeing George, and at the same time she could be seeing Jim. They could arrange something, she knew that George would. She felt no shame thinking of the two men in her life and she knew which one that she really wanted to be with, she now had to convince herself that she could make the most of her situation.

Jim arrived to take her out on the Saturday as arranged His Mother was not too pleased when he said where he was going.

"I wish that you had not made it up with that girl again," She had said. "I am not too happy about it. I am sure that girl will bring you nothing but trouble. You'll not be happy with her; there is something about her that I don't like.

"Oh mother she not bewitched you know". Jim answered in Sandra's defence

"Don't be flippant. I just don't want you to get hurt".

"I'll be careful Mother.

Jim decided to tread carefully with Sandra. They went to see a film, then after picking up some fish and chips for their supper and they sat in the car to eat them. When finished, he took her home.

Dorothy and Fred had not taken a holiday in all they're married years.

They went ahead with the arrangements and agreed to visit Mary and stay for the week.

"In the past when Dorothy had previously moaned to Fred about not having a holiday, His comments had always been. "Some thing all ways goes wrong when we are off the bank".

"Other people can manage it "She would grumble. Dorothy was really looking forward to a change of scenery and seeing Mary's family. Sandra and William organised a party to take place as soon as their parents went away Sandra quickly tidied up, they bought some extra food and drink, she polished the front room furniture. She had lit the fire to give it a cosy glow and she bought some flowers for the centre of the mahogany table.When finished she was quite pleased with the result. William collected Sheila, Jim arrived also a few more of Williams's friends from the village. Sandra made sure that she plied Jim with plenty of drink, she hoped to get him so drunk that next day he would not remember much of the evening's events. It worked a treat she mixed all sorts of stuff in the last few drinks that he had. Jim was well and truly drunk by the time the others had gone home in the early hours of the next morning. Jim stood up as if to leave at the same time as the others but found that he was incapable of standing up straight. Sandra was watching and quickly moved to his side. He had fallen into her trap.

"Come, my Darling you are in no fit state to drive home. You can keep me company for tonight; she led him upstairs to her bed where he fell into a drunken stupor. Jim could not remember any thing of the evening's events the next day.

"God what and how much did I drink last night" he asked when he saw that he only had his under pants on and Sandra was lying naked next to him in her bed.

"Oh don't you worry too much about last night we really did have a great time and you certainly did Jim you are so strong. Let us go and get a cup of tea or something shall we. They dressed and went down stairs where she made some strong coffee for him to drink and try to come to terms with his throbbing head.

"Was I so drunk that I could not go home"?

“Darling I thought that it would be safer for you to stay the night with me, you could have driven off the road and landed upside down in the woods some where”.

“That was good of you I had better get my self going”.

“No hurry I will light the fire and you can stay a while. I don’t think that your Mother would approve of the way you look at the moment. William is already up and is out milking”.

“Oh Lord Mother she will wonder where I am Can I use your phone? What excuse can I make for not going home?”

“Just tell her you fell asleep in the chair. After all you are no longer her little boy are you?”

Mrs Beddows was always accustomed to rising early in the mornings and as she passed Jim’s bedroom on her way downstairs she noticed that the door was open and that his bed had not been slept in. “He has had a good night some where and I will bet a pound to a penny that he is with that Sandra. She said to her self as she made a pot of tea which was usually shared with him before his going to work. Since her husband’s death and the handing over of the farm to her eldest son she had enjoyed the first cup of tea of the day with her youngest son Jim. She was as she had always been in the past an early riser. She was not a lonely woman she kept herself occupied with various charity work and with different organisations... She was quite pleased when he telephoned later to say that he was alright. She had guessed quite rightly that he was with Sandra and it disturbed her a little. On the other hand he was quite safe and had not come to any harm such as a road accident. For some unknown reason she took her diary from her hand bag and just marked the day with a small tick. She put it back thinking he will be home when he is ready and did not give it another thought

“Every thing alright” Dorothy asked When she and Fred had returned from their little holiday that they both had enjoyed

“Of course”. Replied Sandra.

"Thank goodness for that. You know I did not think that your father would agree to go. He always used to say that there was no place like your own when I have asked him in the past to go away I think that it to

See other farmers struggling to make ends meet especially those living up in those Welsh hills. You know we can be right proud of what we have achieved". She went on to tell Sandra all about her holiday How Mary had taken them out sight seeing they had been extremely well fed and had not had to wash a cup up Dorothy had smiled. They talked of Mary's growing family and the rectory where she was living; they had been out to the coast which she explained was not too far away. Sandra pretended to be interested but she could not have cared less. Wait until I tell you my news she thought and see how pleased that you will be then. Sandra arranged to meet Jim again. She had very little choice; she was at least eight weeks pregnant and could be more, she also arranged to meet George before she saw Jim again.

"Darling it worked" She recalled to George the night of the party. "Pissed out of his mind, he hasn't a clue what he did that night In fact he did nothing but he can't recall any thing. It paid off to put a little extra in his drink when he was not looking".

"It should work" George answered. "Leave it for a while and then you can tell him that he got you pregnant He won't be able to deny it. I am sure that you can pull this one off?"

"But what about our future" She protested. "If I marry him, I am not going to stay married to him. Once the baby is born at the end of April or at the beginning of May. I will have expected you to have sorted something out for your self and decided what you are going to do".

"I know my love lets take things one step at a time, when are you going to tell the family"?

"Not yet. I will have to tell Jim of course. Then I will keep it from the rest of them a bit longer. It could be a nice Christmas present for Mother."

"You know they will go clean up the wall" smiled George

"They will have to come down again if they do. I am of age now they can't do a thing about it can they? What ever is said they can't change what has been done? Now that I am getting used to the idea of being pregnant, I am quite enjoying myself. Just think there is going to be a wedding to arrange. Let's leave that bit until after Christmas. How are you going to like your mistress and baby living with another man"?

George swallowed hard, not having given any thought to that as yet He knew that the idea was not going to appeal to him, but it was the only way that he could see of getting himself out of such a mess.

"You will come to my wedding Darling Don't say that you won't I could never go through with it if you were not there to give me some support".

"Of course my love you just imagine that it is me who is standing by your side". Sandra told Jim some three weeks later.

"You are not are you?" he sounded so surprised.

"I'm afraid so". She tried to sound as scared as she could use a weak feminine voice.

"But when"

"Remember the night you stayed all night" It was then".

"But I was not capable was I?"

"Oh yes you were, there was no stopping you. Going to act like a man you insisted".

"I could not do much about it; you would not listen to me. I tried to get you to stop but you are such a big strong man. You insisted that I was to be naked. I prayed and hoped that this would not be the result and I can't do you for rape because I let you sleep with me. What am I going to do Jim?" Sandra pleaded crocodile tears falling down her face

"There, there now I am sorry. I am so sorry I would never have let this happen if I could have avoided it. What a bloody fool that I was. Just showing off to see how much that I could drink and a hell of a lot of good that it has done me. Sandra I am sorry. I will do what ever is honourable, believe me I will. No way are you going to face this alone".

"Jim Darling it is not all your fault. I persuaded you to stay the night remember".

"I don't remember much at all that is what is so sickening. If I intended getting a woman pregnant I would rather have known what I was doing. Sandra what can I say? I am so sorry".

"I suggest that we keep it quiet for a little while you never know how things may turn out it could be a false alarm".

After Sandra had said goodnight to Jim and gone to bed she was over the moon that it had worked and for the first time in weeks she went into a deep sleep she could now face the consequences of her predicament. Next morning she quickly told William that it had worked and that Jim would marry her. He was already out and doing the milking.

"Well, thank god for that and thank God that you have finished with that George so that it cannot be one of his just think what damage you could have caused to every body. Now to face the music when this is told to the old pair. The old chap will calm down after a while he usually does; never carry's a grudge for long forgiving old sort he is. I can see a wedding quickly arranged."

William thought thank goodness that will only leave me, I won't have to worry about keeping her when Sheila and me take over this place. That will be one worry less I can see that with my contracting and if I get some help with the stock we can certainly make a better go of this place than what the old chap has done over the years. Just they wait and see.

Chapter Thirteen
What An Evil Web We Weave In Order To Deceive

George had decided that now Sandra was expecting, he could not expect her to meet him and lie along side of him in the van and in the woods He made up his mind that he was going to tow the caravan back home for the winter months. He started to look for some where suitable to put it. The place where he proposed putting the van had to be some where off the beaten track and still not look suspicious for a caravan to be parked up. He came up with the idea of putting it in one of the tracts that led into the tree plantations at the backside of the Wrekin. If any one saw it they would naturally think that it was there for the estate workers and would not query it. A caravan as big as this was not likely to be put there with out the permission of the Estate The Estate workers could be planting a new plantation or it was there ready for the men to use when they cut the Christmas trees. Once in place he would make sure that practically no one would be able to see it from the road.

He looked and looked and then, yes he had found the perfect place, He arranged for a low loader lorry to fetch it home. He told the site manager that it was to come home to be painted and some work done on it during the winter months.

The van had not earned much money since the site owners had said that there was to be no re-letting of vans to the public, they could only let it to relatives that could be trusted to keep the site tidy and that George was not going to commit him self or vouch for that. The Manager informed him that the owners did not want their site getting a bad name like some of the other caravan sites that were springing up in other seaside resorts, especially in places like Rhyll. Having a holiday in a caravan was fast becoming big business. So too were Holiday camps such as Butlins. George had promised Hannah that they would consider moving their van from where it was in Borth so that it could earn some money again but he had done nothing about it.

Sandra had to play her cards right she could not afford to make the wrong move. And she could not make a mess of things now. Jim had played right into her hands; every thing was going much better than she had anticipated. Jim was so kind and had not been in the least bit angry when she has told him that she was expecting. She cuddled up to him on the back seat of the car and let him kiss her.

"You know I think a lot of you Sandra," he said.

"I really do love you too Jim" She lied. "It would really make my day to think you actually loved me. Knowing that, I think I can cope with anything".

"If it is true what you say, what do you think your parents will have to say about it? I for one will not look forward to meeting them once you have told them"

"I'm not going to tell them, let's wait a bit and then if nothing has happened and I am sure that I am pregnant there will not be much that they can do about it. Is there? We are both old enough to know what we are doing don't you think"

Jim had been doing some quick thinking.

"You know I would marry you if you wanted me to." He proposed. Giving Sandra an option

“Would you really. I don’t think I could expect that much of you.”

“I would you know” he said. More convincingly. “I could not let you face this alone and what is more I am not going to let you.

Your parents are not going to be very pleased with us. I don’t expect and my Mother will not be very pleased either but I think that I will be able to talk her around”. Sandra was hearing just what she wanted to hear.

“Let’s wait and see my darling” She whispered. “Then if the worst comes to the worst we can decide what is best for us to do. You will help me won’t you?”

“Of course I will, I can’t believe it, I am to become a father”.

“Just hold your horses for a week or two before you get too excited” But Sandra knew there was no need to wait she was definitely expecting a baby.

Christmas was approaching and Dorothy was beginning to notice something was wrong with Sandra. She was starting to look pale first thing in the mornings and no longer wanted egg and bacon for breakfast A piece of toast was all that she was eating. And this was not like Sandra at all.

When she mentioned it to Fred, he just said, “Well, you have a talk to her”

“I hope that she’s not pregnant but it looks very much like it to me.”

”I hope not” answered Fred. “She’s the last one left with us more or less and she is a grand help to you in the house. I quite liked that Jim but not so much if it is true what you’re saying. He must have taken advantage of her.?”

“I should know”. Dorothy said. “I have seen enough in my lifetime to recognise the symptoms I am pretty sure that I am right. The stupid little madam. If I am right she will get a piece of my mind I can tell you. And as for being much help to me in the house I notice that she only does as much she wants to.

There's a lot more that she could help with if she wanted to. Hardly earns her keep she does."

Dorothy waited for her chance to speak to Sandra It came one morning when the men folk had gone outside after breakfast and she guessed that Sandra had been sick. "What is wrong with you?" Dorothy asked

"Nothing, why?" Sandra lied she did not feel like an argument with her Mother. She had gone out to feed the poultry and had been sick again. Damn this! She had said to her self I wonder how long that I have got to put up with this. She decided that she could not face eating egg and bacon when she went in for some breakfast the very smell of the frying pan made her feel much worse. She went into the kitchen; her mother had the frying pan in her hand and offered to cook her egg with some bacon."I don't want any today I will just have a piece of toast." Sandra picked up the loaf of bread from the table and proceeded to cut a slice from it.

"Don't give me that, I reckon there's more wrong than you are letting on. It looks to me as if you are expecting the state that you are in these days."

"And what if I was?" Sandra replied flippantly. "What can you do about it?"

"Oh so you could be could you, well if you are you had better start doing some quick thinking because I have already guessed what is wrong with you and it looks to me as if I am not far wrong. I want to know what you are going to do about it. If you are in that mess you can't stay here. I will not have another fellow living under this roof and I will certainly have no more squawking kids to have to listen to. I suppose it's that Jim Beddows. Comes from a good family he does. I would have thought that he would have had more sense that to let his family down? Your father really took a shine to him, thought he was such an honourable lad"

"So he is mother. I'm afraid we shared a bottle of wine one night".

"And this is the result is it?

"As you know you have never encouraged any of us to have a drink of any kind and I suppose that I was not used it."

"Don't you go putting any of the blame at my door? You are quite right I have never brought any of you up to go to the pubs and drink yourselves silly.

Dens of iniquity that they are. You'll never do any good going to them places. When can we expect this event to occur?"

"End of May or there a bouts"

"Well we might as well keep it quiet until after Christmas and then you can start thinking about a wedding. In the meantime think of getting somewhere to live".

"Yes mother I am sure that Jim will take good care of me and he will find us somewhere to live". Sandra did not feel like being cross-examined.

"Now that she knows the worst is over" Thought Sandra. She now knew that her mother would organise everything and everybody. It was two weeks later when she met Jim again. He had suggested that he kept away from the farm for a couple of weeks so that it would give her time to tell her parents and for him to break the news to his Mother knowing that she would not be amused. Sandra was so relieved it gave her a chance to see George in the meantime. If only she had known what a relief that it was to George to know that her mother was planning to get them married off and he was hoping that would then be the end of it as far as he was concerned.

"I thought that they would come round when you told them that it was Jim who was to take the blame. I have to give you credit for sorting things out my little love"

"No thanks to you. Darling But it looks as if this hiccup can be sorted."

Sandra was able to tell Jim that her parents had been told and that her mother was already planning what they should do. "A wedding after Christmas I guess" She giggled

"I guessed "so he replied. Your Dad avoided me the other day I guess that he must be a bit miffed about it".

"Mother must have told him. He can be a funny old stick when he wants to be. He will come around, I'm sure. Give him a bit of time. I expect that they are a bit disappointed knowing that I will not be there for them in their old age. One hears that the youngest daughter is often left to look after the parents when the rest of the family has flown the nest. Well I am pleased to think that it is not going to happen to me".

"I have some good news for you. I've asked the boss if he knows of any cottages coming vacant and he told me that they own that row of three just as you go into the village on the left and one is already empty; he says we could have it if we've nowhere else to live. Wants quite a bit doing to it. I believe He says that they are not prepared to spend on it for the time being but it is there if we want it, to start with and if we have no where else to go. I will make enquiries in town there just might be some thing that we can find in a bit better condition".

"Don't worry my darling" Sandra reassured him. "I'm sure we can manage, It will be good enough to start with as long as we can be together I am sure that we will cope".

"It's so good of you to take it like this; I did not want us to have to start like this. I will do my best to make you comfortable, at least I've still got my job and if we live in the village it will be very close to my work. I will be within walking distance. That will help quite a lot. I will not have to spend any thing on travelling, it will be so handy. Don't worry; I'm sure everything will work out great".

Sandra was not thinking of him; she was thinking how handy that she would be to George if they lived in the village. She would see him everyday as he went to work.

"Yes see if you can get the cottage in the village we can make a start with that"

"But I really want my own place with a few acres. I've saved like hell to make a proper start in farming."

Sandra smiled to herself. "Have you really?" This was music to her ears, very good news to hear. If we try really hard

I am sure that you will have a smallholding one day and if this is a little boy, he will be a grand little helper for you".

Jim felt good to think that Sandra was prepared to plan the future with him.

Christmas went by; Dorothy started to make plans for Sandra to marry Jim. She planned for a February wedding. She was not going to let her have a white wedding she had disgraced the family and that in her opinion was bad enough no daughter of hers who was in that mess was having a white wedding, it would not be a very good idea. She considered that if the weather was very cold it would not be good for Sandra in her condition to wear thin clothes so she would see to it that she wore a warm coat. The news had quickly spread around the family that Sandra was to marry Jim and that she was pregnant. In a way Dorothy was disappointed that it was not to be a white wedding but decided to make the most of it. She would have liked to have made a splash and had quite a big do when the last of her daughters married. Now her dreams were shattered once again. "I just can't win, "She said to her self as she left the Forest Glen where she had just been to book the reception.

The church wedding was booked. Sandra was to wear a pink dress with pale blue coat and hat.

Jim's mother was very disappointed with her son when he told her, but she was relieved that he was going to marry the girl, at least he was doing the most honourable thing for Sandra. She had not liked Sandra at all but she had only met her once or twice when Jim had brought her to their home. Mrs Beddows sensed that Jim was letting himself in for a lot of trouble and that this was not going to be a very happy marriage but there was nothing that she could do about it. She could only stand by for when her son would need help. She had heard rumours about Sandra. Rumours that she did not like about this Sandra Thomas. She was thinking that it would not be very long before her son was going to need help.

"I just wish I could feel she was going to make you proud. Do your best for my sake Jim"

"I will mother. I think the world of her."

"I know you do dear, I only want the best for you." You are certainly not going to get it with her. She thought to her self. He must be blind not to see through her.

"Thanks Mother, I'll do my best" Mrs Beddows felt she could do no more. The arrangements were being planned. William's girlfriend Sheila was going to be bridesmaid and a sister Jim's would be the other attendant. Dorothy looked forward to a family gathering. It would please both her and Fred to have all the family all together at one time. She guessed and quite rightly that Grace and Ian would not turn up but she did not let that bother her. She and Grace had never seen eye to eye in the past and Dorothy would never accept her husband as part of the family He had caused a scandal and she was not going to forgive him at any price. When Fred had seen Ian in the cattle market and had gone out of his way to speak to him, Ian had turned his back on Fred and walked away. Fred had felt well and truly snubbed. When Fred told Dorothy, this had not helped one little bit. The fact that he had turned his nose up at Fred had infuriated Dorothy. "Jumped up little bugger If it had not been for his parents Ian would not be farming in such a big way as he is" She commented.

Both Mary and Helen were expecting babies in the spring so that meant there would be three more grandchildren. Neither Fred nor Dorothy bothered much with their grandchildren. They both considered that they were of no responsibility of theirs. Dorothy's logic was that they had them so they could look after them. Dorothy was resentful of the fact that their daughters were giving birth to sons and not all daughters like she had but that was now in the past and there was nothing that she could do about it.

The fact that her daughters were entitled to family allowance really did get to her. She argued that she and Fred had no financial help from anyone to rear their children.

“There was nothing like that for me when I had to rear you lot”. She would often grumble when any of them called in to see them. You all have it far too easy these days.” Consequently her daughters kept their families to themselves and did not visit too often. They knew that no matter how hard life was they dare not ask for any financial help from their parents. And if they had they would not have been given any Their Mother would have seen to that. Every last penny was spent to improve the farm or to buy machinery for William to do agricultural contracting

Her only concern was for William. She was very worried that he had been hinting about him and Sheila getting married and that there was a lot of sorting out to be done. Now that Fred was getting older Dorothy knew in her heart that she and Fred would have to look for some where else to live. It would not be fair for him to be left with helping cows calve if need be during the night but she also knew that he did not want to give up farming completely They would be very reluctant to move from where they had farmed for so many years.

It was such a relief for Sandra to have it all going her way; she was most certainly not looking forward to living with Jim. Not at all, not one little bit, she told George as much on one of the occasions when she was able to see him.

“To think I will be expected to treat the man as my husband. Wash his dirty socks cook his meals and knowing that I don’t intend to stay with him for any longer than I have to. You know George that I am only doing this to save your face. To think that you are getting away Scot-free. Don’t you worry dear you are not getting away from me, I can assure you of that and we are going to have to work something out between us, so that it will not be long before we are together for good”.

“What else could we do?” George looked into her blue eyes giving her the impression that he was full of concern.

“Not a lot can we”.

"It is much better to go along with what we have planned than have the truth come out and blow the family apart.

"Much better for you than me. I don't love the man. It is not his child and I don't want to live with him, never mind satisfy his needs in bed and what if he gets me pregnant after this one is born the idea does not bear thinking about".

"I know you don't want to go through with it my love" he tried to soothe her.

"Well what are you going to do about it?"

"There's nothing I can do until after the wedding".

Secretly George was hoping Sandra would settle down with Jim once she had her baby. How ever unknowing to him Sandra certainly had different ideas.

"I will wait until after the wedding, I will then be the most dreadful wife to him. I won't cook for him not that I am much good at it now. I'll give him hell so that he will be glad to go back to his mother"

"What about the baby?" George was wondering what she was going to say next.

"Well I thought it out. You could leave Hannah and move in with me we could look after your baby between us"

"What will you do if you're not allowed to keep the cottage if Jim went back home?"

"No one would dare turn a deserted mother and child on to the road now would they. Think of the publicity I could create".

George was beginning to think he had under estimated Sandra...

"Stay calm for the time being".

"Only for the time being "she informed him.

"You are a devious little madam I can see"

"You just wait and see my darling. I am a much stronger woman than what you think I am. Together we could make something of ourselves"

She sat up from the bed on which they lay her blue eyes penetrating George's brown ones. Her body was now beginning to show the signs of pregnancy although she had not put on too much weight as yet.

"Darling I love you" She teased. "This baby of ours can only bring us closer together."

The glow from the Calor Gas fire caught the shape of her breasts and George knew he could not resist her. The fact that she would soon be marrying Jim played on his mind. To his knowledge he had only been her one real lover. Granted she was no virgin but since she had been in school uniform she had been his and only his until now, it hurt to think he was losing her to someone else especially a great awkward farm worker. He leaned forward and took her in his arms and held her close to him. No one not even William knew of their secret meetings, which were not so often now. No one had discovered the caravan parked in the woods and if they had nothing had been said about it. When they were able to meet George parked his van just off the road, so that if any one saw it, the possibility would be very slight for some one to be driving around the country lanes after dark. Not many of the locals would be out and about they were country people who were in bed early and up early in the mornings. He and Sandra only had to walk a few yards to where the caravan had been put. Sandra was playing her part of the bride to be to her utmost. She had to pull this off. She was surprised how easy that it was. All she had to do was to go along with the arrangements that her Mother and Jim were busy making for her, she and Jim decided not to have a honeymoon, and Jim thought that it would be much better for them to enjoy a holiday later in the summer. He had suggested that perhaps George and Hannah would let them have the caravan for a week.

"I am sure that they will" she had smiled as she said it. If he only knew.

Jim had suggested that they go away and spend a night in a hotel after the wedding it would have to be a fairly local one. They could not afford to travel nor could they be away for a whole week there was so much to be done at work and with the cottage. Sandra had agreed with whatever Jim suggested she had no intention of upsetting him. She was certainly not going to rock the boat. Not now. She had left all the arrangements to him she did not care where they went for the night she would be just glad to get it over with. They could then go back to their cottage and prepare it for their own liking and for the new baby.

"Going to the wedding are you?" Hannah's neighbour Mrs Talbot sounded surprised when Hannah had been chatting over the garden hedge telling her about the arrangements that were being made for Sandra's wedding.

"Of course, we had better wish them all the best had we not? With a baby coming they are going to need it and Jim seems quite a nice sort of chap. My Mother is not very happy that they have to marry but times are changing. It does not seem to be as dreadful as it used to in the olden days. You sound surprised as if I should not be going?"

"Oh nothing" she replied. "What are you going to wear?" She decided to change the subject quickly.

Mrs Talbot's remarks disturbed Hannah but she went about her work and then gave it no more thought. Hannah was looking forward to the wedding and catching up with the family news and seeing all her sisters together again.

"No need for bitchy remarks like that" George said when Hannah told him about the conversation that she and Mrs Talbot earlier in the day.

"I've never taken to that woman" he went on. "I reckon that she has got too much to say for herself. Nosy beggar"

"She's all right", Hannah passed it off. "I don't think that she gets out enough. His mother living with them must be quite a strain for her. The old lady must be 85 now"

Hannah no longer had her market stall. George was getting difficult about cutting the glass and she found it impossible to keep up with demand for photos of the latest pop stars which changed every other day as new records were made daily. Hannah did not seem able to obtain the latest ones to keep up with it all.

Giving up the stall gave Hannah much more time to work in the garden and cope with the children's needs consequently they were all much happier

George seemed to be coping with paying his way and there seemed to be no money problems thank goodness although Hannah did miss that little bit of independence that the money from her stall had given her.

Sandra's wedding day arrived, she looked very smart and Jim was proud of her. After the reception at the Forest Glen the sisters returned to Willowmoor farm for a cup of tea etc which Dorothy had gone to great lengths to prepare. Sandra had come back with them. Being as Jim had said they were only going to a local hotel and there was no point in their going too early eight o'clock would be a good time to leave.

"Coming to have a look at the stock?" Fred asked of Jim when he and William came in from finishing the milking. William quickly changed and took Sheila out for the evening to finish the day off as he put it. He was so glad to get the day over with and Sandra married off and as far as he knew no one had been any the wiser about her seeing George. He had not said a word about their affair not even to Sheila. He could not take the risk of telling a living soul. If he and Sheila they were to have a row she might just go and let the cat out of the bag for spite. He was madly in love with her but she could be a bit temperamental at times especially if she could not get her own way. He did not speak to George at all and George knew why and it did not worry him the slightest that he was ignored. None of the other family members had noticed they had all been far too busy catching up with the local gossip.

"Of course" Replied Jim as the two men went out to take a look at the dairy herd Fred was and always had been so proud of his cows.

"Now" Said Sandra to George as she stood at the back of his chair"

"Hannah I've left something at home. You don't mind do you if George just takes me to collect it, won't be many minutes away. I can't see Jim coming back in for a while. Dad would be really upset if I drag him away just when he was more amicable with him. You know what men are like when they get talking about cows, milk production, this new stuff that they call silage and all that farm stuff".

"Why are you going away after all?"

"Only for a night. Can hardly pretend to be a virgin can I?"

"You've got a point there of course I don't mind if George takes you. See that you are not long away will you? We must get back and pick the kids up can't sponge on the neighbours for too long now can we? I can give a hand here with this washing up while you are away. It looks like Helen and Rebecca need some help now that the others have left."

"That is good of you to clear up a bit. Mother won't have me here tomorrow to clear up, will she?"

It was almost two hours later that the sisters noticed Sandra's absence

"Where is Sandra? Asked Rebecca. Jim and Dad have come in some time ago and Jim is getting fidgety" She had just taken a cup of tea through to the front room for her parents and the men folk.

"Sandra! "Said Hannah. I forgot about her; we have been chatting for so long the time goes so quickly surely she is back she is she? George took her to collect something that she wanted from their cottage"

"Which way have they gone? All the way around the Wrekin to get there." Laughed Beccy

"Oh there you are". Rebecca stated as George and Sandra reappeared into the kitchen from their rendezvous.

"Found what you were looking for? It certainly took long enough Jim's ready to go"

"Leave him to me" Sandra replied "I can handle Jim". She put her shoulders back as if in defiance and strutted towards the front room.

"So it seems. Remarked Helen. "A really nice chap you've got there in case you did not know." Helen called after her.

"I'm sure" said Sandra in a non-committal voice and she waltzed into the front room leaving her sisters to get on with their chin wagging around the kitchen table.

What they did not know was that Sandra and George had gone straight to the bedroom at the cottage, stripped off and stayed there for an hour or so.

"I can't believe you are going to sleep with him tonight" George had said.

"Don't worry my darling I will pretend the day's excitement has been too much for me. Being so tired the baby and I will just have to get some sleep."

"You do that my love. I know now that I can't live without you. I really do love you we will sort something out soon"

With that knowledge Sandra had been content to continue to go along with their plans

Hannah was telling George when they were home later that evening. The children were in bed and it was peaceful and quiet she said of how proud she was that they were so much in love and still together. She told him how it had taken her back to when she had stood by his side in the village church where they had made their vows so many years ago. She had witnessed Sandra and Jim making their promises to live together until death did them part. She loved the church music; she always had ever since she was a child attending Sunday school.

Even George was moved." It took me back a year or two," he admitted. "You women are a soppy lot

"Not really" Hannah replied as she put away the dishes after their night cap. I just hope Sandra and Jim will be happy like us. We have had our ups and downs but have survived

"I suppose so" muttered George.

"I know." Said Hannah. "Let's make this our year too and get on with the finishing of this house. You've got plenty of work on at the moment. Perhaps there will be a bit of cash to spare.

"Here we go again bringing money into everything you talk about "

"I was only speaking methodically dear we can't do anything without money"

"I suppose I don't earn enough for you"

"I didn't say that now did I?"

"It sounded like it to me"

"George I'm not going to argue with you tonight we've had a lovely day let's not spoil it. Sandra's wedding went off a treat. Incidentally why were you such a long time away with Sandra tonight we thought that you two were never going to return? Our Beccy wanted to know where you had got to. If Sandra was not so far advanced with her pregnancy I am sure that she would really have wondered what you were up to. She as good as suggested that something was going on between you. I tried to smooth it out?" I thought how funny she sounded. You and my pregnant sister I don't think so. Do you. Besides she seems to have met the love of her life or she would not be in the mess that she is in now."

"What do you mean, we were a long time. Tell me; were you lot watching the clock? She couldn't find what she was looking for and then she showed me a lot of work that needs doing to that cottage and she wants to know if I'll do it for them. Is that what you want to know?"

"Not really, are you coming to bed? Hanna would have loved to finish the day in George's arms, cuddled up close to him but he did not seem in that sort of mood in fact he seemed in a really bad mood. Oh well I suppose it had been a long day.

"I'll be there in a few minutes" replied George. He was in no mood to make love to Hannah. The fact that Sandra was with Jim was playing on his mind far more than he had realised. He knew only too well he was being stupid and should have been counting his lucky stars that Sandra had not revealed the truth.

If it all came out that he had been seeing her since she was fourteen. There could be a possibility that her parents would have him sent to prison. This was some thing that he could not contemplate It did not bear thinking about. He had to accept the fact she was now a married woman and try to leave her alone yet deep down he knew that it was going to be impossible

Hannah longed for George to behave with her as he had when they had first got married. It was her nature to love and to want to be loved in return.

Hannah felt desperately lonely and rejected; she managed to hide her feelings the best that she could. George was totally unaware of this. Always trying to show her capability made Hannah very moody at times one moment she was on top of the world and the next in the depths of despair. She could not go to sleep. She lay awake going through the day's events. It had been very kind of the neighbours to look after the children for her when they had come home from school When George eventually came to bed she pretended to be asleep [and in no time at all he was fast asleep. Now that Sandra was married Hannah hoped they would not see so much of her. Her getting pregnant had solved many problems for Hannah. Now that she had a husband to look after and a baby due in May. Hannah hoped that she and George could get on with their lives. She was sick of Sandra always being with them. Hannah had become afraid to reveal to Sandra about their plans of where they were proposing to go or what they were proposing to do Whenever Hannah and George were taking the children out for the day Sandra seemed know what they were doing and would ring Hannah with some lame excuse that she was having such a hard time at home. Would it be all right if she tagged along with them?

She would say "You don't mind if I come along with you do you Hannah. I can help keep an eye on the kids for you". Not that she ever did. Hannah as usual felt sorry for the girl. Of course she was completely ignorant of the fact that George had kept Sandra informed of their every move.

Hannah gave a sigh of relief and yawned she was dreadfully tired it had been a long day she just hoped George would feel better tomorrow, after all he had had a few drinks during the day and with that thought she went to sleep.

"Is George there?" It was Sandra ringing.

"Why? What do you want him for?" Hannah asked

"I've got a problem with a door. Jammed I think. I can't open it properly. Jim hasn't time and I don't think he knows what to do if he had the tools to do it with. By what I can make of him. It will have to be taken off and re hung

"I'll give him your message when he comes in" They went on to chat about different things. Hannah promising to give George the message.

"I would be grateful if you would I will end up doing myself an injury if something isn't done with it soon.

"OK leave it with me I'll see what he says".

Damn Damn Hannah said to her self there is still no peace from that madam. Hannah told George about Sandra's call when they sat having tea

"Still no peace" protested Hannah. Reckons the door is dangerous. Could do some harm.

"Yes, there is one door which badly sticks it's a bit of a struggle to open and to close it. I will try and have a look at it for them" He finished eating and picked up the phone.

"Be with you tomorrow" Hannah heard him arrange. "In the afternoon. Yes alright I'll be there"

"That little madam has us running to her aid already" Hannah said to George and she was not amused. She had seen more than her fair of Sandra If she did not see her for a very long time Hannah felt that it would be of no worry to her.

Why oh why did they have to get a cottage in the village. Hannah was hoping that they would have to move miles away and that it would be a long time before she saw her again. She knew that George would never understand if she complained to him so she said no more. Why did they have to live within shouting distance of her parents? Sandra had run to her whenever she could and Hannah was beginning to realise that it was when Sandra had tried to get out of doing her share of work at home. Hannah had never suspected for one single moment that Sandra and George were having an affair. Why should she? She trusted George implicitly Sandra was eighteen years younger and she and George had treated her as the little sister and no more than that. Hannah had always been there for her when she brought her tales of woe and had listened to her so many times but if Hannah had known how Sandra was repaying her she would not have hesitated to have shot the pair of them and they knew it. Hannah was quite capable of firing a twelve bore shot gun.

"Don't be like that. Jim would be no use trying to re-hang a door. Put it back in its frame upside down I wouldn't wonder. It won't take me long"

Hannah could say no more but she was not happy. George could not afford to work for nothing and she knew he would not charge Sandra and Jim because they would have no money to spare. Because of the baby coming they would need all that they could get. The house needed decorating all the way through from top to bottom and with the baby to prepare for what more could he do. Her Mother had given her quite a lot of bits and pieces to make it easier for her to make a start and with having quite a big wedding she had the advantage of the wedding presents.

"How are you coping? George asked Sandra next day as they lay on the double bed upstairs.

"Bloody awful. I don't like this house. I don't like being pregnant. Oh it was alright the first few months but look at me now I feel so big".

"Won't be for always love only a matter of weeks to wait and then it will all be over"

"Thank god for that, living with him is no joke"

"Try to make an effort for all our sakes will you"

"Well what the hell do you think I'm doing? It's your child and I want to be with you. I can't cope with this forever. You don't expect me to do you?

"Just wait until you've had the baby before we do anything"

"I've got no bloody choice have I? You men have all the fun and get away with it.

"Come now my little love it's not all roses for me having to pretend with Hannah when you know how much that I prefer to be with you" He lied as he held her close to him.

"You won't stop seeing me will you George? I couldn't bear it if you stopped coming I watch for you to go by every day."

"Come on let me have a look at that door that I'm supposed to be fixing or Jim will be back, it's almost five o'clock now, you said that he comes in at half past.

"You are right," She said getting her self-dressed. He will want some thing for his tea. I will pop to the shop and get some thing for him; you make a start of the door. Look busy if he comes in and say that you have just arrived".

"Hello there" Said Jim as he came from work His height and build filling the doorframe. "I'm so glad that you could stop by and fix this. He looked at the door that George had started working on. "Sandra is struggling with it and I don't want her to harm her self in any way. You know George that I am hopeless with wood working tools. I can fix my car if need be and do a few jobs around the farm but I'm no good when it comes to this. He passed the hammer off the floor to George just as he reached for it.

"I'll soon have it opening properly for her. The damp has not done it much good this winter, its because of the cottage being left empty all winter no fires burning but now that it is occupied again it will quickly dry out Get as much fresh air in the rooms that you can during the summer months."

"There seems to be quite a few jobs to be done around here. I would be grateful if you could give me a hand with them. As soon as something better comes along we will move Even if it does mean that I will have to change my job. I've got Sandra and the baby to think about now".

"I know what it is like" Agreed George. "Hannah wants me to finish that house of ours. I must get on with it if I am to keep the peace. You will soon learn these women can be temperamental that's for sure. I expect one can get used to it as the years go by"

"Jim, I have you some tea," Sandra shouted from the kitchen.

"Good, I'm hungry what have we got tonight"

"Its steak and kidney pie with chips"

Not again thought Jim, He said no more because of George being there." Any thing is better than nothing when you are hungry" he commented to George

"I guess so. Talking of which I had better get going and have mine"

"Thanks for coming, it was good of you "Jim said as he tried to swallow some of the now cold chips.

"My knight in shining armour is he not," Sandra added smiling at George.

"I will be in touch. "He looked at Jim "Don't be afraid to shout if you are stuck I can always drop by on my way home no trouble at all. I am sure that Hannah will not mind she is of a pretty good nature that she is".

"Yes thank you it is very kind of you what do I owe you"

"Nothing mate I have not used any new wood and a few new screws don't cost much some one else will pay for those on their next bill if you see what I mean "He started to chuckle.

"Thank you George. Sandra smiled as she saw him out through the front door and to his van.

"That's fixed that door for them" George said to Hannah as he went in for his tea, which smelt good.

"That's good of you perhaps we can now have some peace for a while"

"Oh I don't know about that Jim says that he has a lot more jobs that need fixing".

"The children said that they saw your van parked there when they came from school"

"Oh did they now. Must have just got there". George had not thought about the school bus passing through the village. He now realised that he was going to have to be very careful not to tell lies when he had been to see Sandra. His grey Morris Minor van was very recognisable. It was a fairly new van He had bought it during the last nine months George had really made an effort with his work and it had paid good rewards. He was quite proud of his van. Hannah often gave it a good wash and kept it looking good. George had always seen to the inside. Sweeping it out regularly he could afford to slip up and leave any tell tale signs that he and Sandra had been in the back. He always very careful to check that nothing had been left in the van that could give his little game a way. Once Sandra had forgotten to put her knickers on again. They were only some flimsy Black lace things but if Hannah had found then he would have some explaining to do. He had thrown them away over a hedge and had told Sandra to be more careful in future. The little things that he sometimes found in the van He some times wondered if she wanted Hannah to find out. That thought certainly scared him. He knew that she could not only be clever she could also be devious.

"I wonder what her baby will be "Continued Hannah. "I think she was saying that they wanted a son. Jim would be so pleased if it was. He seems such a gentle fellow, he will love the baby." Hannah was beginning to irritate George with her idle chatter and keeping on about babies.

"Do you have to keep going on about Babies?"

"No not really But new babies are like weddings some thing to look forward to and also a topic of conversation".

"Next you will be saying that you want to have another. In fact that might not be a bad idea".

"No thank you George I think that we have done our bit for queen and Country. Enough is enough I have no desire to start again"

"What about me? Don't I count" He asked sounding quite angry and alarmed.

"Of course you do dear, but you know the difficulties that we would have to face if we were to try for more. I don't think that I ever want to go through that again".

"Some hope of that you are as cold as ice, we would be so lucky if you ever got pregnant, "He sneered and Hannah did not like the tone in his voice.

Hannah stood up and looked him straight in the face she was beginning to feel furious.

"That's not true and you know it. You are the one who is always too tired because you are working so late. You're the one who stays up so late watching the telly until it closes down"

"Grudge me watching the telly what will it be next. Having some dinner I would not wonder". George said accusingly

"George that is preposterous, how you can say such a dreadful thing. You know that I don't grudge you anything but we agreed not to increase the family. Thank goodness the kids have gone to play in their tree house I would not have liked them to hear you says such things".

"You are my wife and if I want to increase the family I consider that it is your duty to agree to what I want"

"Fiddle sticks" Hannah shouted at him. "I might be your wife but I am not a reproduction machine for you or any one else" Hannah was amazed that she was standing up for herself.

"What do you mean by, the any one else". George sounded angry

"Nothing just a matter of speaking. George what is the matter with you. Just calm down will you. I don't want any more children and that is that. This house has to be finished surely that is your top priority and if it is not then it is certainly mine".

George turned the telly on and sat in his chair by the fire and said no more. Hannah knew that he was now going to sulk for a while so she cleared the dishes away and stayed in the back to wash them up. She was quite shaken by the argument. Increasing the family had not occurred to her. Finishing the house was her top, priority. She decided that she could not leave things as they were. She had a bit more to say on the matter She picked up the tea cloth and wiped her hands on it as she went back to the living room; she looked down at George relaxing in front of the fire,

"Now look here George lets get one or two things straight. I do not want any more children until this house is finished and then not at all. Certainly not if I can help it we need to have a decent kitchen bathroom before you think of increasing the family

"Oh is that so "George looked up at Hannah. He looked so angry.

"Yes it is. Like it or lump it Finish this damned house will you".

"Well I always had it in mind to have a family of six" He was now being sarcastic

"Oh you did, did you now". Hannah was starting to feel angrier "Well you can think again. I have a say in this and another thing you have not seemed interested in making love with me very often lately. If you are not sat watching that damned thing in the corner you are working late or having a drink in the pub with that pack of bikers that you tell me that you are meeting. If I did not believe you I would be thinking that you were seeing another woman. The next time you tell me that you are working late I think that it is about time that I did a bit of checking up don't you agree".

"You would not dare. If you go spying on me you will live to regret it. I am warning you. Do you hear me don't you dare make a fool of me. Spying on me indeed. So I can't go out now "He sneered.

"I did not say that. It's just that I feel that I am bringing these three up by my self".

"And who do you think is earning the money to keep you all"

"I am not disputing that, I am making it clear. No more family .Got it". Hannah turned on her heels and went back to her work. Neither of them spoke at bedtime, Hannah as usual had gone to bed first. George had stopped watching the telly.

Standing up for her self and answering George back had left Hannah feeling mentally exhausted and consequently she found it hard to get much sleep.

George sat there for some time after the telly had closed down. Thank goodness that Sandra was now married he was secretly hoping that she would settle down and that there would be no more risks to take. But he knew that from now on he would have to be more careful. He had a good excuse to call at the cottage in the village. A bit of knocking with his hammer let the next door neighbours think that he was there working so that it did not raise any suspicions.

March went into April Sandra did not go out very much now that she was so advanced with her pregnancy. George called regularly at the cottage to see her and to sit and have a talk with her. Sandra had convinced Jim that the baby was not due until the end of May beginning of June where as George was expecting her to have it at the end of April. The end of April came and George was getting worried for Sandra in case every thing was not all right. Jim knew nothing what so ever about pregnant women the only thing that he knew about was when he had witnessed some of the difficult births with cattle on the farm. Sandra went into labour on the 15th of May George was worried she was at least two weeks over due. She gave birth to a son on the 16th at 3-30pm. Jim visited her in the evening and he was so proud of them both.

"I can't tell you how proud that I am of you Sandra my love" He told her. "I was not expecting this to happen quite so soon. Well not just yet. Has the baby come too soon if he has. Will he need special care?". Sandra realised how she had conned Jim in to being the father of her son.

"Oh he is a bit early I suppose," She quickly turned her face away and said" But he looks none the worse for it. He's a good weight 8LB 9oz Thank goodness that I did not have to carry him any longer or he would have been a ten pounder.

"He certainly looks a bonny baby never the less "Smiled Jim.

"Looks like his father, don't you think. He has your dark hair and I am sure he has your nose". That's all that he needs to convince him, she thought to her self. George will be so pleased when he knows. She suddenly knew that she must let George know about his new son" Have you telephoned any of the family as yet?"

"No I came to see you and the baby first; there will be plenty of time to do that tomorrow. I might just ring my Mother when I get home and tell what a little beauty that her new grandson is".

"Please ring George and Hannah. Ring them as soon as you get back they have been so good to us".

"Ok I will do that if you want me too, you are quite right they have been good to us Remember that door we could not close or open it properly when we first moved in."

"George "said Hannah when she put the receiver back down "Jim has just phoned Sandra has had a little boy she apparently had it this afternoon at half past three He says that they are going to call him John.

"Oh she has. Has she. I'll bet Sandra's glad that it is all over"

"Well it's like us all once pregnant one had no choice but to get on with it"

George was so relieved that Sandra and the Baby were all right. Once that the birth was all over he did not think that it would bother him. But it had.

George sat at home that evening and was gazing at the television set; His mind could not concentrate on the programme. He was feeling worse than when Hannah had the twins. Now why he wondered, why had it bothered him. He could not get Sandra out of his mind. He tried to hide his feelings but at eight o'clock he decided to go out and have a drink. He had to get out of the house. He knew that the child that had been born earlier in the day was his son, but as things were he also knew that he never dared admit it to any one. He tried to hide his delight that he had a new son and he was finding it extremely difficult. Hannah put the twins to bed and was trying to persuade Michael to come in and prepare for bed. He was very reluctant to tell his pals to go home because his mother wanted him indoors. The nights were drawing out and to him this meant more time to stay out doors. It was almost eight, George decided that he had witnessed enough of family life and that he would have to go out.

"Won't be long away" He said to Hannah as he went out to the van. On his way out he told Michael to go inside in side and do as his mother had asked him.

"Anything wrong?" Hannah called after him.

"I don't think so; just want to check a water pipe that had to be disconnected on the job today". He drove up the lane and headed towards Wellington not knowing where he was going. Eventually he parked at the back of the railway hotel. He went into the bar which seemed quite busy, he looked around the smoke filled room, and there was only one or two that he recognised. He sat on a bar stool and soon relaxed with a pint of beer; one or two other men he had seen were having a game of cards in the far corner of the room. They were using three-penny and sixpenny coins as stakes. George smiled. The men sat around the table beckoned that he should join them. George walked over, pint in hand and sat on the empty chair at the table. Several more pints were downed and games were lost and won. All four men completely lose all track of time.

Hannah had long gone to bed before George arrived home. She was up before him next day the children already gone to school when he decided to show his face.

"Where did you get to last night? Wetting the babies head?"

"What are you talking about?" her words stabbing every nerve through his body.

"Well you were so late and you stank of fag smoke and drink, by the look of you it is a right hangover that you have got this morning"

"No need for you to go on. Just got carried away a bit"

"It looks as if you did; best place for you is back in bed!"

This was enough for George. He ate a bit of breakfast and went out and got into the van and drove off up the lane, not knowing where or what the day would bring. The only thing that he knew was that he could not cope with Hannah's patronising voice.

Jim went to collect Sandra and baby John from the hospital the following week. As they were about to leave and while Sandra was getting her things together Jim hurried to the car and came back with a bunch of flowers and he gave them to the nurse who was telling Sandra about attending the postnatal clinic. "Thank you" she said as Jim offered them to her. Now you take the two of them home. You have a lovely baby son to look after. Sandra was walking ahead carrying the baby.

"I will to be sure especially as he has come before his time".

"What do you mean come before his time I think that your wife had most certainly gone full time? If he had not arrived when he did we would have to have done something about it. Personally I think that he was a good two weeks over"

"Really" Jim said no more, they had reached the outside door and had caught up with Sandra. He told Sandra what the nurse had said about that the baby had not come early. She had to think very quickly.

"What? She thinks that I had gone full time did she? What sort of a nurse is she? I reckon that she could do with going back to do some more training if she can't tell a premature baby when it is born. You certainly came before your time, didn't you my little son" She cooed to the baby she held in her arms.

"Jim you have only to work it out for your self you know that it was the week my Mam and Dad went on holiday and any baby can come three weeks early or three weeks late". Doesn't know what she is talking about she does not". Jim could not recollect when it had been that her parents had gone on holiday and the baby was here now so he had to get on with it He decided to say no more about it. The baby was a healthy one and that was all that mattered as far as he was concerned. He had wondered why his mother had been so surprised when he had telephoned and told her the good news. "I was not expecting this to happen quite so soon" she had replied and at the same time thinking are you sure that it could be yours. Jim did not give it any more thought. Sandra had convinced him and that was all that mattered.

Chapter Fourteen
When The Cat Is Away The Mice can Play

Both Mary and Helen had new baby daughters round about the same as Sandra had given birth. Helen had a very difficult time giving birth. It had been touch and go for both herself and the child. It would be a while before she was out and about again. It apparently looked as if Melvin had given no regard what so ever to the advice that the doctors had given to Helen. It had been the same advice that had been given to Hannah about not having any more babies because of the difficulties that could occur.

On appearances Melvin had turned out to be a hard working family man, but behind closed doors he had turned out to be an unholy tyrant. Like George watching the television was paramount and the fulfilment of his sexual desires was also on the top of his list. The fact that Ellen had become pregnant again this being her fourth child. He considered was not his responsibility and there fore did not let it be of any worry to him. When he had almost lost both wife and child, a neighbour said that he had been a little upset.

When she was at home Sandra was surprised how much she felt for the baby. Previously all she had wanted to do was to get it over and done with, now every time she looked at her baby he reminded her of George, she could see that he had the same dark brown eyes, same black hair.

"You grow up to be just like your daddy" she would coo to him

"What do you think of your new son?" she asked of George when he called in to see the baby on pretext.

"He's great, but just keep your voice down! He's supposed to be Jim's. We don't want you slipping up and letting it out now that we have got the worst over with. Now do we?"

"What do you mean George? This child is yours and don't you forget it. I have no intention of staying with Jim. I can't George, please don't expect me to. You don't really want me to, do you? I will not, you cannot be that cruel not to me and your baby"

"Alright we will have to see what we can do."

"We certainly will do that, now he's here we can start making plans for the future for the three of us can't we?"

George did not stay too long; for one reason his van was parked outside Sandra's house, which was the middle one of three terraced houses and the neighbours did not miss much! The other he was not prepared for Sandra's wanting to leave Jim so soon.

For some unknown reason Hannah did not hurry to see Sandra's baby, she could not explain why, but she had no desire to. George had said what a bonny little lad he was and that was enough for Hannah.

Jim was so proud of the baby, He bent over backwards to help Sandra with him. His name was to be John Allan Beddows. Jim worked so hard at the farm; he was putting in all the extra hours overtime that he could.

"We have a future my love," he said to Sandra As they sat either side the fire place in the one and only living room"Someone to work for, we will do the very best we can for this little man"

"So we shall" Sandra agreed "So we shall"

"What are we having for tea tonight love?"

"Not a lot" was her reply; "I didn't feel up to cooking, we will have to manage with a pie or something" Not again thought Jim, this is the fourth time this week, it's either a pie with baked beans or just beans on toast

"Sorry darling, I will get something from the butcher tomorrow, he comes around with his van"

"Yes you do that; I could just fancy a nice pork chop now and again I suppose that you could buy some from the shop now that they have a refrigerator. Deep freezers they are called and they are able to keep quite a bit of stock in them"

"I will try dear, but mother did all the cooking at home, I didn't get much chance to practice"

"What are we going to do about getting John registered?" She wanted to change the subject.

"How much time do we have?"

"I believe that he has to be registered within six weeks of birth. That's if I have got it right"

"You must find out Jim and then we can get it dealt with, We must get our little man registered or no one will know if he is legal or not." She said going over to the pram to look at the baby who was now beginning to stir and wake for his feed.

"You know he's a beautiful little man, isn't he?" She cooed

"Yes he sure is we have been so lucky to have a boy first time.

"All babies are wonderful in their father's eyes, its mother who has to shut them up in the middle of the night!"

"But you don't really mind? He won't be so tiny for long. How many children would you like us to have Sandra?"

"This one will do nicely for a few years, I don't want to have one after the other, let's wait until we have a better home with proper sanitation before we think of having more"

"When can we make love again, I just can't wait. Its agony lying by the side of you at night and not being able to touch you. Still I'm content to do whatever you say love, we won't be in a hurry but I will be glad hold you and make love to you properly."

"Will not be much longer, doctor said about six to eight weeks after giving birth would be ok, then we can enjoy ourselves, just promise no more babies for a while There is talk in America of a pill being made, that when a woman has taken it, It is said that she can not get pregnant. That will be one of the seventh wonders of the world, don't you think?"

"You mean to tell me all a woman would have to do is take a pill and you would be safe?"

"Yes, that's what I have been reading; it was all the talk with the other women at the hospital. We women reckon the sooner they bring a pill out for the men the better. Then we women can have all the fun"

"I see what you mean. What were you saying about having to register this wee one?"

"Oh that, I must go to Shrewsbury and get his proper Birth Certificate, just to say the little man is actually born and alive"

"I suppose it will be in office hours. I am surprised that you can't get him registered at Wellington I thought that there was a registry office in Walker street"

"I think that is only to register deaths not births Oh don't worry love I'm sure Hannah won't mind taking me. I'll see what she says. They said at the hospital that I had to take him to Shrewsbury" She quickly lied.

"Well you do that and if not don't worry I can always take a bit of time off and take you both. I am due for a bit of holiday. But I said that because of the baby coming, I would work my holidays and have the extra money instead".

"Darling you are wonderful to baby and me. I will try to be a good wife to you; just give me a bit of time to get used to it all. I will try I promise you."

Sandra sounded so convincing that Jim believed every word she said

The next week George called in on her with the pretence of fixing a shelf, which Sandra had told Jim, had fallen down. It hadn't, she had knocked it with a hammer until the one end gave way to make it look as if it had fallen with age.

"How's my little man?" George asked looking into the pram.

"He's looking more like you every day my darling. George I have to get him registered, will you take me?"

"Of course I will, I'm sure we can sort something out."

"I want you registered as his father"

"I don't think you can do that can you?"

"I don't see why not, you are his father darling, and you have promised that we will be together as soon as you can fix it."

George had not given the idea of leaving Hannah any more thought. Sandra's words were shaking him more than a bit.

"What if Jim insists on seeing the Birth Certificate?"

"He won't even know I've got one, I can always say it's being posted later."

"Do you think he would believe you?"

"My darling I can convince Jim of anything if I put my mind to it. "We've got until the end of June to get it done. It's got to be within six weeks of birth. I don't want him registered at Wellington. I want to take him to Shrewsbury where we are not so likely to be recognised and I want you to come with me."

George assured her that he would arrange to take her no matter what; He quickly said that he must go and he kissed her passionately when he left

"I love you George" she whispered.

"I know you do" was the reply. But he did not dare say that he loved her. He was still hoping against hope that she would settle down with Jim even if he did not care for the idea very much. He wanted her for himself and he knew that there was so much at risk for him to be able to have what he wanted. As far as he was concerned having an affair with Sandra had like many other men only been to satisfy his sexual desires and that she could be dumped when he had chosen to. Now he was concerned to hear her talking as she was. He thought that he could relax a bit and try to forget her. Now it seemed there was no such luck.The next few days George thought about taking Sandra to Shrewsbury to get their baby John registered. It was something that at first he did not want to do, he felt the less he saw of her easier it would be to make a break but he was finding that when he was not with her she played on his mind. He now knew that he could not do with out her b but how was he going to fix it? He had no idea and then after giving it some thought he decided that it just might be possible. If he were to take Hannah and the kids to the caravan, he could make up some excuse to come back on his own and then he could take Sandra and John to Shrewsbury. Yes that's it, It could work Hannah must never know or suspect any thing. She would wonder why I was taking Sandra and that Jim was not. George knew that Hannah would question why they had to go to Shrewsbury and not to Wellington where they could now register babies instead of having to go to Ironbridge as they had to register their children.

He knew that as far as Hannah was concerned He was doing more than enough as already running to fix this and to fix that each time Sandra rang up, moaning how dreadful that their little cottage was. Hannah considered that they had been really lucky to find accommodation so quickly and had said as much to George they had also had a telephone fitted as quickly as possible within weeks of moving in. Sandra had used her charm and desperate situation saying that her husband had to work such long hours because of their financial situation and that she was so nervous left in the house by her self and it had worked; she had been given top priority.

George waited for his chance. Hannah had been busy in the garden and she had been giving a neighbour some help with some sugar beet hoeing. Hoeing the beet gave her a bit of backache but it also gave her bit of extra cash.

"How about having a few days at the caravan?" He asked Hannah one morning before he went out to go to work

"You're looking tired and you love the sea"

"Are you coming with us dear?"

"Of course I am"

"In that case, yes let's go"

"Well, what about next week? There's not much on"

"As soon as that?"

"Why not? There is a bit of work to finish off at Bullocks but that can wait a week" He lied.

"Do you not think that you should finish their work before you go they can be a bit funny if you leave them too long".

"No I will not be dictated to by the likes of them, if I want a day or two off I will take it" George said dismissing the subject.

"Ok I will get organised, I really could do with a break. What about going to see Mary while we are there?"

"That's a good idea, we could go down the coast and it would not take us that long to get there. We could go on the Friday Give Mary a ring and see if that is alright"

"Well why not make it the Wednesday and then we could have a day to rest before we have to come home. If we leave it until the Friday it will mean that we will be late getting back to the caravan and then we must come home on the Saturday. I will have to leave the van clean tidy and pack every thing up. George had not expected Hannah to disagree with him and he had to think very quickly.

"No make it Friday that will give us a bit more time to be together and me a break from the driving for a day or two.

"No matter George. I suppose that one day is as good as another as far as |I am concerned but you know that I can do some of the driving if you want me to",

"No need to bother your head about that you have enough to do coping with the kids" Hannah gave it no more thought.

She did as he had suggested and she was trying any thing to keep the peace. She thought to her self that there was no point in arguing with him she would go along with what ever he wanted to do. She decided that she just might as well enjoy the few days and make the most of the rest.

Not that she considered that she had that amount of rest. By the time she had fed them all including the dog and got the beds ready at night time and folded them away in the mornings so that they could raise the table and seats for their breakfast. There was the washing up still had to be done, carry the blankets and things that the children needed to the beach. George was never keen to go on the beach with them he said he preferred to lie in the van to have a rest. Not play around on the beach and sand dunes like silly fools He would leave all that to Hannah and the kids. Some times he would condescend to have a chat with people in neighbouring vans and his cousin if they happened to be at their van at the same time.

This was to be the first break that George and Hannah had taken since last summer. They had to go to the van at the beginning and the end of the season to turn the water off and on again. It was not making them any money and George had talked about moving it to another site but he still had not got around doing any thing about it.

Hannah rang Mary "Yes" she answered "I will have a meal ready for you at lunch time and then that will give us the whole of the afternoon to chat."

Hannah was really looking forward to going up to the caravan she let her friend and neighbour know that they were going to be away for a few days.

"Make sure you bring some money with you George, no point in carrying too much food when we can buy most of it on the site or in Borth"

"Leave it with me," George answered her "Let's go on Sunday afternoon"

George called in on Sandra; she was giving John his bottle when he called. "Your real daddy is here to see you my baby" she cooed, John was now three weeks old and he was looking more acceptable as a baby .He confirmed with Sandra that they would have the baby registered the following week. He told her of his plan to take Hannah and the children to the van and then he would come back home on some pretext or other so that he could be with her.

"Oh thank you darling, I knew you would help me out, Jim can go to work and we can spend the whole day together! That will be wonderful"

"Be careful," warned George "Or you will slip up."

"I won't George, I'm not that daft! Not as daft as a good many think I am. How are you going to get away from Hannah without her knowing where you have gone?"

"I'm going to take them to the caravan. Thank goodness that I had it taken back You know Hannah did not suspect a thing. I'll get them settled in and then come back I have some pretext or other already worked out, don't worry I can handle it," He said, "I've been thinking, you will have to put Jim down as the father, in case your asked to produce the Birth Certificate at the Christening"

"Damned if I will!" Sandra said, "And if I have to I won't have him christened, then no one will know."

"I'm sorry love, you can wangle your way out of most things but I can't see you getting out of this one, and if your mother found out she will go ballistic."

"We shall see," Sandra retorted, putting the baby against her shoulder to bring up his wind but all John did was howl.

"I'd better be going," George said, getting out of the armchair by the fire. The baby's crying was getting on his nerves and he did not like it.

"Alright Darling, make it Tuesday, we will be ready won't we little man?" she spoke to the still crying baby.

Hannah organised everything to take to the caravan so she was making sure there was no slip-ups. Hannah loved doing things as a family; it would give George and her time to talk and the rest would do him good. Sunday came and off they went, arranging the seats in the van so that the three children sat directly behind them to give them a clear view of the road in front of them. Hannah did not mind the usual banter between them as they pitted their wits against each other. Michael almost always won. He considered it his right and privilege to be superior to the twins.

Hannah sat back and relaxed it was good to be going away without taking Sandra with them. It was such a relief for her to be with just her own family.

The sight of the sea calmed Hannah and excited the children. Yes, the caravan was still in its usual place and they were all glad to tumble out of the van and run loose, "When are we going to the water?" they asked.

"As soon as the van is unloaded and we've had a cup of tea," was Hannah's response, "Your dad is tired from all that driving, just give us a little while.

"Why don't you drive, then he won't be tired" argued David

"Your dad prefers to drive so that he knows who is in control of everything." David was always the one who asked the why nots and the why fors

"Who had this caravan last!" exclaimed Hannah as they were carrying the sheets and putting every thing away in cupboards and places. "Look at the state of it, It looks to me as if a heard of elephants have been through it! Where has all this mud come from? I will have to think who had it last and I will not let them have it again if this is the state that they leave it in. Really it is just not good enough It really isn't?"

"Perhaps the caretaker has been to check all was well?" answered George; "It's a long time to be left, all winter"

"I will have to have a word with him and ask him to wipe his shoes in future. What a mess He must have been in here a few times the state that it is in."

"For goodness sake Hannah shut up and make a cup of tea, you don't want to go bothering the care taker He can be a funny bugger when he wants. I would not like to upset him before we can arrange for it to go to another site."

"Never mind, perhaps you are right; I will give it a good clean while I am here."

"Yes you do that; I can take the kids to the beach tomorrow."

"Of course dear, I will just sweep it out for tonight."

"If you don't mind I'll put my feet up for a bit, care to take them for a walk?"

"Are you so tired? I was hoping you would come with us"

"I am knackered!"

"Alright" said Hannah.

After having a cup of tea and giving the children glasses of lemonade with a piece of fruitcake that she had brought with her, she gathered a couple of towels and rugs and they left George to have a rest. The four of them went off to build sandcastles. It was now 3:30 so they did not have a lot of time before they would have to return to the caravan for a meal, so consequently they intended to make the most of it and set off happily chatting sixty to the dozen. The children ran on heading towards the water, fortunately the tide was out so there was plenty of beach for them to play on.

"Thank God for that" George had said to himself when they had left. If Hannah had gone to the office the Manager might have let slip that the van had been taken off the sight for the winter and he did not want that to happen. He lay down on the long seat forming the settee and thought of the times that he and Sandra had made love together in the van. He smiled as he fell into a deep sleep.

Much later when Hannah and the children returned George was still asleep, but he was soon awakened by the noise. The children were all wet and sandy and excited, they loved the seaside, and Hannah was planning what they were going to do the next day.

"Tomorrow would you take them out for an hour, so that I can give this van a good clean" Hannah said to George when he realised that Hannah had a meal ready for them all and he decided to move himself.

Next morning the children were up early and were eager to get breakfast over with and get going to the beach again.

"Would you pick some milk up at the store on the way back please dear"

"Alright "he answered.

She watched them walk away and was thankful for the peace and quiet Now lets get this spring-cleaned and all being well a bit of time left for me to have five minuets peace! Hannah said to her when they had disappeared from sight.

George returned with them at lunchtime,

"Here's the milk you wanted." "Oh thank you. We will need more tomorrow and some more general supplies" I can get them in the morning from the shop on the sight or you could take us down to Borth so that the kids could play on the rocks for a bit. You know how Michael loves looking for fossils and allsorts of little creatures in the rock pools"

Hannah, I've just found out that I have come without enough money to last us the week.

"You've what!" Hannah spun round,

"Look Hannah I'll tell you what I can do. I will go back this afternoon; I've certainly not got enough money with me to last us through the week. I thought that I had put those pound notes in my jacket pocket. They are not there I must have left them in the sideboard drawer. I've only got a ten shilling note and a bit of change with me, and that is not going to be enough for the week do you think"

"Got to go back"

"Back where?"

"Home of course, now don't get upset, I'll be back by dinnertime tomorrow, I will have to go; we simply have not got enough money, we can't stay the week with what I've got"

"Well how much did you think that you had with you?"

"Enough "

"George you promised"

"I know I did, I've only got ten shillings and a bit of change after paying for petrol. "He put the money on the table. You can manage with that until I come back can't you?

"Well we've got no choice but I think that we might as well all go back I can't see any sense in you going back by your self just to back here again tomorrow"

"Do we have to?" said Michael, then the twins joined in, both not wanting to go home. So it was agreed for Hannah to stay with them until George returned next day. Hannah saw him off but she was not only annoyed, she was angry. She tried not to show it too much in front of the children but she was so upset. She was beginning to realise that it was no good relying on George what so ever, he could not get things right! She would have to remind him in future.

By Tuesday evening there was no sign of George returning back to the site, Hannah and the children had spent most of the day at the waters edge and playing hide and seeks in the sand dunes. I'm glad that I did not take them back home Hannah said to her self when she saw what a great time they were having.

George had not returned by Wednesday lunchtime. Hannah was getting worried. She went to the public phone box and rang home but there was no answer to her calls Where the devil had he got to She told her self to calm down He was probably on his way back to them. She told the children that they must stay and play around the site in case Dad came back He would not be able to get into the van if they were not there. He would not think about bringing the spare keys He would have no need to bring them because he knew that they were there. Hannah was running short of, food she had spent the last money that she had the previous day. She went to his cousin's caravan to see if she could borrow two shillings to get some milk, she did not dare to ask for any more. His cousin Ruth was very sympathetic and gave it to her, but she said that they were leaving to go back home later that day. She hoped that George would soon be with them and that he had not had an accident or anything like that. Hannah had not given any thought that he could have had an accident. It suddenly dawned on her that the police would have been to the site if that had happened because the neighbours knew where she was.

By Wednesday evening there was still no sign of George. Hannah was desperate, she had no money to buy food and she had almost depleted all the stocks that were in the cupboard, which had not been very much at all. By Thursday she was really worried, she had tried to telephone George but there had been no answer. Hannah knew there had been no accident otherwise the police would have contacted her, Where the hell had he got to? Hannah was worried sick, why had he not returned? He had promised he was coming back for them. She was reluctant to leave the caravan in case something really bad had happened. The children were fed up because they preferred to play on the beach instead of on the caravan site. They had no milk or bread to eat so Hannah had to make some pastry without fat and to make it taste better for the children; she smeared it with the remainder of a jar of marmalade. They drank the remainder of the orange squash with water and she drank tea with out milk or sugar what was she going to do? At five o'clock she decided to go and see the site manager to see if he could help them get home, there was no way they could stay another night. As she was making her way to his office George pulled on to the site and stopped the van along side of her.

"Where the bloody hell have you been!" she screamed at him.

"Coming" was all he said

Hannah had been beside herself with worry and the relief of him coming was too much for her. Thank goodness he had the sense to pick up a box of groceries and bring them with him. He unloaded what he had brought

"Now go and fetch some bloody milk from the shop "she shouted at him "We have had practically nothing to eat for two days.

"But I thought that". She cut him short, "You are always bloody thinking but never about your wife and kids and get out before I throw some thing at you she picked up the empty orange juice bottle and threatened to throw it at him. Then she realised that Michael and the twins were waiting to be fed. He must have felt guilty or he would not have brought this lot as she said as she was looking in the box containing the groceries to see what was in it that she could make a meal of.

When she had pulled herself together she made a meal for them all.

"I'm sorry," said George, "I got held up with some work for Mr Bullock. He rang when I got up on Tuesday morning and I had to go and see to things there because they would have had problems with the horses. I was about to come I knew that you would cope for a bit.

"Cope for a bit" She shouted back at him. How the hell could I manage with out any money? It has been almost a week; I was just going to see the manager before the office closed. I was hoping that he might be able to help me. I thought that he might get us home or give me some money to buy some food. Thank God I saw you coming"

Thank god that you did, thought George the manager could have told her every thing. He would have told her about the van not being there the winter He could have remembered him bringing Sandra with him for the days that they had spent together. He had brought her a few times. George had not realised that Hannah had taken so little food with them. What made him collect a box of groceries he had no idea He thought that they might be getting a bit low and that it would save Hannah running to the site shop again before they got back home.

"I brought you a present" He smiled and fetched a brown paper bag from the front of the van and put it on the table.

"I don't want your blasted presents you can keep it she put the paper bag to one side out of the way of the table they were hungry and wanted to eat.

Hannah said nothing more she waited until they had eaten George decided to take the children and the dog after he had fed it for a walk to the beach hoping that Hannah would calm down when the got back. Hannah took a look at the present; it was two cheap imitation ornamental lamps that stood about 6" high.

She could have cheerfully rammed them down his throat. She put them on a shelf in the van, not caring whether she ever saw them again. If he thinks he can get around me with that sort of rubbish he's got another thing coming! She was livid

After she had calmed down a bit she decided that she would not make any more fuss in front of the children,

George had never seen Hannah so angry before and it had quite un-nerved him. Their holiday had been ruined and besides they were going to see Mary the next day. She was not going to forgive George for a very long time and only spoke to him if it was absolutely necessary, so consequently the journey from Borth to Pembrokeshire was not a happy one. If they had not promised the children and Mary had not prepared extra food Hannah would have refused to go. Thank goodness they were going home tomorrow Saturday.

"Look who's here?" Sandra said to Jim on Monday evening she made sure that she was sounding surprised, "George has just pulled up"

"Hello George"

She let him in through the front door, which opened into the living room.

"Take a seat, care for a cup of tea?"

"Aye I'll have one with you, just got back from the sea"

"Has Hannah come back with you?"

"No she wanted to stay a few days with the kids, how's life on the farm Jim, keeping busy?"

"Yeah, the Gaffer is having a go at making this so called silage instead of hay, stinking stuff it is, bound to affect the taste of the milk, that's what I reckon!" Jim felt he was now quite an authority regarding farm work. He was a married man and had the responsibility of a son.

"Can I make you a sandwich George?" Sandra asked

"Alright I will have one, a bit of cheese will do"

"No trouble, will just be a minute"

"What are you going to do about getting John registered tomorrow Sandra?" asked Jim.

"Well being as Hannah's not come back I suppose you will have to take the morning off," replied Sandra

"Oh that's why I called in," George piped up, "I'm going to Salop tomorrow to pick up some glass, can I be of any help?"

"Well it would save Jim losing time," said Sandra coming in from the kitchen with George's sandwich on a plate.

"I don't mind Jim I could see to it while George collects his glass. Better keep that boss of yours happy, it is such a busy time for you"

"Alright" agreed Jim, "I don't mind as long as we get little John registered"

"Oh thank you George" Sandra beamed at him, "What time in the morning? I can be ready for about half past nine; do you want me to come down the lane with the pram?"

"No need, I'll come around this way and drop some timber off at Miss Hinge's while I'm at it. She's been sending that Charles Leonard down wanting this doing and that doing, only fiddling little bits of jobs. Gets on your nerves after a while"

"It's a pity she never married and had a family" Sandra joined in the conversation,

"Who would she have chosen? No one would have been good enough for her! I guess that's what that woman needed, a good fellow to live with who could have kept her happy" said George laughing out loud and Sandra joining in.

George was still there talking and joking at nine o'clock He knew that there would be no cause for the neighbours to gossip if they had seen Jim come home and they did not miss much that went on in the village.

"I'm turning in" said Jim, "Got an early start these days, besides sonny Jim will want feeding at six in the morning and it's no good leaving it to Sandra, Getting her up at that time in the morning is like trying to waken the dead!"

"I've got to feed him tonight," she answered quickly "And it's me who has to get up in the night if he wakes is it not,"

"And so it should be" said Jim, getting out of his chair and made for the back door, to go to the toilet which was in the garden The same as the toilets in the rest of the row of terraced cottages. "You can get forty winks during the day"

"Oh can I indeed!" Sandra snapped.

Jim was already at the back door. Nothing else seems to get done, said Jim when he was out of earshot just stumbling over a pair of shoes left at the back door. He returned to the kitchen had a wash at the old sink and said goodnight to George emphasising how good it was of him to take Sandra the next day to save him losing time and money.

"It's no trouble" George assured him.

Sandra put another log on the fire, although it was now warmer in the daytime the cottage needed some warmth and the fire was the only means that they had of warming the room and airing the clothes. Consequently Sandra did not do anymore washing than she had to. She drew her chair closer to George's and put her hand in his.

"He will go to sleep soon," she said referring to Jim.

"Darling I need you" she whispered to George, "Any chance of us being together tomorrow?"

"I don't see why not, you have no need to come home straight away after we have been to Salop. (Local people sometimes referred to Shrewsbury as Salop)

"I only have to get Jim some tea. He will take some sandwiches and have them to eat as he goes through the day.

He says that the grass has to be cut and lugged the same day to make the silage properly so he will not be coming home until evening. May not until later if they can not get the field finished. It is no use waiting until it rains, they say that they can't cut it wet."

"I'm sure you will find something for him to eat"

"You bet I will and I might as well do some thing for you while I am at it"

George picked Sandra up the next morning at 9:30. He had swept the van clean, not that it needed much, and there were only a few sweet wrappings in it. Hannah had given it a good clean before they had left for the caravan. George gave Sandra a lift with the pram into the back of the van; she sat by the side of him with the baby John on her knee. "Now for a day with your real daddy" she cooed

Once the van moved away baby John slept all the way to Shrewsbury.

"I've been looking forward to this my darling" she addressed George, her hand already placed firmly on his leg, "I hope your feeling fit!"

"You are coming with me to register your baby"

"Of course I am my love"

"Are you sure we can't put you down as his father on the register?"

"Well I suppose by law there's no reason why we can't but if Jim found out he could kick you out and divorce you for goodness knows what, a scandal that would be! Just let's play it cool as I have already asked you. We will sort something out eventually; I know one day we can be together for good."

"You really believe that?" her face lighting up as the morning sun shone through the van window

"Yes I do"

The baby slept peacefully, his dark hair appearing quite black against the white of the shawl that he was wrapped in. Sandra leaned back against the seat letting the sun shining on the glass windscreen warm her body and she relaxed. She was with George and that's what she wanted, living with Jim was all-right to a point but she wanted to be with George and no one else. It she knew that she was living in dreamland and it was a complete fiasco but she was getting through it bit by bit, day by day. George drove in silence letting the fields rush by. The river at Atcham was still quite high from the spring rains. He had found a place to park and went with Sandra and the baby into the stone building of the registrar office. She gave the babies particulars as requested but hesitated when the woman behind the desk asked for the father's name. She glanced at George, his face told her enough and she said "James Beddows"

"Thank you Mrs Beddows" the woman said as she completed the certificate tearing out the appropriate page and handing it to Sandra. Sandra took the certificate and made no acknowledgement; she turned and walked out of the building with George behind her.

"That's that" he said

"One day I will change his name for yours" she reminded him

"Yes we will probably do just that" he replied. They then walked in silence to where he had parked the van.

"What about the glass you wanted?" She reminded George when she realised they were heading out of town.

"Oh that, that was just an excuse, let's go home shall we?"

Which home she wondered but said nothing. When they arrived back at George's Sandra's face lit up; they were going to spend some time together after all. In fact they had the rest of the day and it was not twelve o'clock as yet. She went inside with baby John as George unloaded the pram and followed her inside the back door.

"I will make some tea" she announced, "and give the little man his bottle, that will keep him quiet for a while, what do you think George? While the cat is away the mice can play" She giggled.

"Quite so, you are right I could do with a cuppa" he smiled," he replied as he looked to see what he could find for them to eat. He had picked a loaf of bread up on the way back and with what Hannah kept in the cupboards it was not a big deal. After feeding the baby and themselves Sandra put the baby back in the pram leaving him quite contented. She and George went upstairs to bed; this was the moment they had both waited for, to make love undisturbed as they had done when they had first started in the bushes and bracken such a long time ago. They simply could not get enough of each other, Sandra had not lost all the extra weight she had gained throughout her pregnancy and she was still very well endowed. Her breasts were now larger and it certainly suited her figure, George couldn't get enough of her and he now also knew that he could not do with out her. Completely exhausted they dozed together in each other's arms and were only disturbed by the hungry cries of the baby downstairs. Sandra jumped out of bed and paraded herself around the room for George's admiration.

"Do you think I should try and lose some weight darling?" she enquired.

"Of course not you are beautiful as you are"

"Well I don't get much exercise with only that little cottage to clean"

"We will have to get together more often for exercise I can see, "he laughed, "you've absolutely knackered me!"

"That's how it should me my love" she smiled at him now, covering her body with her clothes. They had not realised that old Tom was watching who was coming and going at the cottage next door.

"Where have you been?" Jim asked of her when George dropped her off at the cottage gate later in the evening.

"Don't come in" she whispered to George, "I will deal with this"

"Coming my love" she called to Jim as he took the baby from her and she and George lifted the pram from the van and she went inside,

"I'm so sorry that we are late and that you have been worried. I didn't get out of the registry office until dinner time. George wondered where I had got to because he was late going to finish a job for some one, so I had to go to Wellington with him. I took baby John to see Sally, you know she is so envious of us having a beautiful baby like John" she lied, "He's only just picked me up, it took him longer than he thought to finish the job Don't be cross darling I will soon make you some tea"

"Sorry love, I thought something had happened to you when you were not back at six. I don't mean to sound cross but I still have to pinch myself to believe you and baby John are both mine. So much has happened this last twelve months I have to take a breath now and again to believe that it is all true and that I am not living in dreamland"

"I have to agree with you so much has happened this last twelve months it sure takes your breath away if you stop to look back and neither of us are going to do that are we. My love "She said smiling sweetly as she closed the door behind her.

Chapter Fifteen
When Money Stops Coming Through The Door Love Flies out Of The Window

Back at home Hannah was still upset about the previous week; George went off to work saying very little.

"Did you enjoy your holiday?" the old boy from next door asked when Hannah was out gardening.

"Yes thank you," replied Hannah

"I see the boss didn't stay with you" he went on enquiring

"No he had to get back and do some work"

"Work my foot, I saw him charge in here on the Monday about six o'clock. Then he shot up the road as if all the devils in hell were after him"

"Oh he did now, did he?"

"Oh, he couldn't get to the village quick enough. They reckon the van was parked outside your sisters for goodness how long," The old Boy always went for a pint of beer on a Saturday night to the Spread Eagles He was picked up and brought back by one of the other forestry workers.

"Perhaps he was hungry and went to scrounge some food"? That was the only answer that Hannah could quickly think to give him and she did not want to say how George had left them at the sea. It was none of his business.

"Perhaps so, perhaps so"

Hannah did not continue with the conversation and left it at that, but it gave her food for thought.

"My word that old boy does not miss much does he?" she mumbled to herself as she got on with her work. She was still so angry with George for not returning to the caravan the previous week, that she did not care where he had been able to get his tea. Too idle to get something himself he had to run to my sisters to get someone to wait on him did he? She finished weeding the row of carrots; the potatoes were looking good now that they had the dark soil mounded up either side of the plants. A good row of peas, she said to herself as she walked past them. Hannah was very proud of her garden. While making a cup of tea before the children came in from school the phone rang, it was Judith,

"Dads not at all well," she said, "He has gone back into hospital, will you tell George, and we are all getting very worried about his condition"

"His breathing has been bad for quite some time, I'm sure he will be alright after a few days in hospital. The staff will take good care of him and I will tell George as soon as he comes in. Don't worry I'm sure he will be all right" said Hannah trying to comfort her sister in law.

"I hope you are right," said Judith as she rang off.

Hannah had enough common sense to know her father in law was a sick man, but she never knew with George if he was concerned or not, he seemed not to bother one way or the other. She would ask him to go and visit that very night.

When George came in for his evening meal Hannah told him what Judith had said. "And another thing I hear that you were too idle to get your own tea last Monday you went running up the road to be fed by my sister and as for working at Bullocks the old boy next door said that your van was here most of the following day."

George was worried what else had he told her.

"He needs to keep his nose out of our affairs Nosy bugger Can't come home to do a bit of work now with out him telling tales It's a pity that the pair of you have nothing better to do than talk about me".

"He only keeps an eye on the place for us". Hannah stammered .She had not seen George look so angry. What she did not know was that George now knew that there could be no more taking Sandra there when Hannah was out of the way.

"Well he can bloody well mind his own business or I for one will soon tell him what a nosy bugger that he is" He went out and slammed the door so hard it was a wonder that it did not fall from its hinges. As for going to see his father he had no intentions. In his view the women always exaggerated things and got every thing out of all proportion. He drove off out of the lane not knowing where he was going.

William has decided that he and Sheila were to marry, they had set the date for the 11th of August and it was to be quite a big do. Fred and Dorothy had decided to hand the farm over to them, so that they both could carry on with the farming of it. They themselves had bought a smallholding some 18 miles away. They had not wanted to move that far away but it was the only thing that they could find on the market at that time. They thought that perhaps it would be for the best and it was what they could afford. Although Dorothy had tolerated Sheila she was not very happy, in her heart she knew that the girl would never make a proper farmers wife, but she had agreed with Fred not to make a fuss for Williams's sake. They had agreed to leave the farm just before the wedding. They took what furniture they wanted, which was not a lot. The house they were moving to was a much smaller one. Fred took with him some cattle to keep up his farming with the promise from William that he would help with the harvesting and tractor work on the smallholding.

Mary, Helen and Sandra decided it would be a nice idea to have the three babies christened on the day after the wedding and have one party for all three. Sandra was very persuasive in asking Hannah if she would make her christening cake.

"I've got enough to do" Hannah remarked to George

"You can fit it in I'm sure"

"But Mary has asked me to make her one to save her bringing one with her; she will have enough to pack as it with out having to carry a cake"

"So make two, its not much more effort than making one, you were always quick to make one for your mother when we were up the Wrekin," said George

"Oh really and it seems as if you are quick to remind me I suppose in that case I had better make her one if only to keep the peace with you But after the holiday that you promised turning into a nightmare I can't see why I should." Hannah was not going to let George off the hook that quickly.

Hannah was used to making cakes so what was one more.

"I can't imagine what it would look like if it was left to Sandra"

"It would be alright I'm sure," said George, "She doesn't have much time now with the baby"

"And I suppose I have?"

"You know what I mean; you seem to take everything in your stride"

"It's a case of having to; it would be no use relying on you for every job. Which reminds me, what are you going to do about this damned house? Are we ever going to get it finished? George I'm not prepared to put up with this much longer. If I have to spend another winter here with this house as it is I will find us somewhere else to live. No don't look at me like that," she said fuming as she saw him smirking, half a grin on his face.

"I mean it George; I will take the children and leave you. A council house would be better for us than this; at least we would have a proper roof over our heads. I am thinking of putting my name down for one"

"Alright, alright, don't go on now so you are thinking of having a council house are you.

"Well at least we would have a proper bathroom".

"Well don't expect me to live in a damned council house"

"And what is wrong with a council house you were brought up in one

"You sound just like your mother, I came from a council house or have you forgotten what your mother's opinion was of council houses. I will see what I can do about getting on with it a bit and as for leaving, you can forget it, you are my wife and you will not be taking those children anywhere"

"Its all very well George, you are well looked after but it's not fair for me to manage as I am having to do"

After George had gone back into his shed Hannah gave some thought to what she had said. Would I really leave him? Hannah was amazed at herself for thinking the idea. No way would I ever leave George, the idea was ludicrous, she loved him and he was the father of her children, she made her marriage vows for better or worse and she was determined to keep them. Besides she thought, her family would never let her live it down, the disgrace of not making her marriage work, the idea would be unthinkable, and anyway where would she go? Hannah smiled to herself at her thoughts; still it did no harm to give George something to think about. He knew they had to get the house finished but when? August came and Hannah found to her horror that George had no spare money to buy clothes for them to go to William's wedding.

"I've got no money to throw away on glad rags. My suit will do and I'm sure you can manage" Hannah was very angry, no way was she going to make do. Not only that, she had nothing suitable that she could make do with. After several days of thought she found that the only way to solve the problem was to make something for her self. She had done this previously and decided to go for it. She bought some beige woollen material, which she knew, would match the colour of her hair, she could then have brown accessories. Hannah was very pleased with her outfit, a slim fitting dress with jacket George said nothing, he was more concerned about Sandra, praying and hoping she would not put him in any embarrassing situations during the day. by sheer coincidence George, Hannah, Jim and Sandra all arrived at the church at the same time, after the usual exchange of pleasantries Hannah started to lead the way into the church. She turned sharply on her heels to glare at George, as she heard him swap a dirty joke with Sandra and Jim who were following close behind her. Sandra's loud laugh proceeded over her head into the church; the guests that had already arrived and were seated inside turned to see who was making so much noise.

"Do you have to?" whispered Hannah to George, "Be quiet will you, don't start her off laughing again" The wedding was beautiful, a right show piece, Hannah was so proud of her brother standing up in front of them looking so smart. Being 6ft tall and his hair had been neatly cut for the occasion; this together with his grey suit made him look very handsome and prosperous. Sheila was a picture of perfection, wearing a gorgeous white dress, her dark hair piled up high on top of her head in a bouffant style, and she looked just like a dress model. Hannah studied the stained glass windows whilst the register was being signed. Her thoughts were miles away and she had to be jolted down to earth when the bride and groom walked down the aisle, they looked so happy together. The reception was held at the Forest Glen and this gave the family a chance to catch up on all their gossip. The next day was Sunday and the three babies were going to be christened at the same church Wrockwardine and then a party was being held at the Forest Glen. Hannah had her work cut out to get every thing on time, to cook the Sunday dinner, dress the three children, deliver the christening cakes and get to the church on time. The christening gave the family a second chance to discuss the wedding of their one and only brother and to catch up on with their usual family gossip and a chance for the cousins to meet and play together. Hannah loved these family occasions, the men would get together and that would leave the women free to chat for as long as they wanted, keeping an eye on the children at the same time. The weekend had been very successful and Hannah was feeling very content with her lot. The health of her father-in-law was deteriorating and it was obvious to Hannah that he would not live to see another winter, so she visited him whenever she could. Molly was a very capable woman and thought along the same lines as Hannah. She nursed Terry at home for as long as she could and when he got very bad he was admitted to hospital.

"I've got a copy of the parish magazine" she announced one day when Hannah visited

"Anything in it of importance?" asked Hannah

"A report of your brothers wedding. My what a show that it was, Sheila looked lovely as if she was one of royalty, the village are still talking about it"

"Yes it was a lovely wedding" Hannah replied as she sipped the warm tea that Molly had given her

"Look there's another picture of the christening with the three babies, just look"

"Well, so there is"

"Just take a look at that one of your Sandra's baby!"

"What about it Molly?"

"Well if that child is not a Fleming, I'm the Queen Mother!" she said holding the magazine under Hannah's nose

"What do you mean?"

"I'm telling you that child is a Fleming and there's no mistaking it!"

Hannah looked hard at the photograph, which was not very distinct now they had printed it in the magazine.

"Well there is bound to be a resemblance" Hannah assured Molly "Jim has very dark hair and Sandra is my sister, but you are quite right; baby John does resemble our Michael when he was that age, there's no doubt about that"

"No doubt whatsoever I reckon! You mark my words, there will be trouble yet"

"Molly what are you saying?"

"I'm saying nout, nor implying nout, but it's very uncanny to me"

"Molly you are tired and worn out from nursing Terry" Molly was looking older. Her hair was quite grey and she was beginning to walk with a limp she certainly was no longer the bubbly bouncing chirpy Molly that she had been when she had first come to the village

"Not that tired" she mumbled as she carried the cups back into the kitchen

"Can I borrow that magazine to show George? See if he can see the likeness"

"What a good idea" agreed Molly "You do that, but let me have it back will you. Let me know what his re-action is"

"Of course I will but what are you suggesting."

"I'm suggesting nothing .All that I am saying is that baby looks like a Fleming. There is an uncanny resemblance there"

Hannah stayed for a while longer then said her goodbyes to the old couple and went on her way; looks like a Fleming She laughed to herself Molly must be tired.

That night after tea she remarked to George,

"There's a photo of the christening in the parish magazine. I have brought you the copy to have a look at Molly suggested that I show it to you. Guess what she said to day. She remarked about the resemblance of Sandra's John to that of our Michael when he was a baby she said that he could be a Fleming the resemblance was so alike"

George looked at the photo and his stomach began to churn. This was something he hadn't given much thought to,

"I can't see much likeness, although there is bound to be something about them after all they are cousins, what's Molly doing? Flipping her lid? These Brummies are a funny lot; they will stir a hornet's nest if you let them. I can't see that much resemblance at all. Silly old woman"

"No dear I think that she is just tired, and it can't be easy with your father being as ill as he is"

"What? The old chaps good for a few years yet"

"I suppose your right, if he gets over this bad spell he's going through. He could go on again for a while but you know dear, I think he's a very sick man."

"We shall see" He made light of it and laughed telling Hannah that he considered that Molly must be loosing it to talk so daft about the babies after all families bore a slight resemblance to each other. George got up from his chair and went outside. He was a worried man. How much had Molly suspected? What did she know? He knew she was no fool and he also knew that she did not trust him. Molly was perfectly capable of putting two and two together and making five if not ten. He looked around his shed, he was running short of timber he must get some more bought but he was having financial problems again. He was running up bills at the timber yard and he knew that before long his credit would run out. He didn't know what he was going to do. Hannah would go mad with him when she realised what a mess he was in again. Things had run fairly smoothly over the last twelve months regarding the business, oh well he thought I'd better keep it quiet for as long as I can.

A month went by, Terry was not making much progress with his health, and he was now spending most of his time in hospital. He was only 65 years old and that was no age to die. The family were all worried about him, George was now aware of the fact that he was a very sick man and the realisation was beginning to dawn on him. He knew he would miss his father very much, they had worked alongside each other for many an hour, and the last thing he wanted was for Hannah to start moaning about money troubles. He saw Sandra whenever he could, she and Jim had moved into another cottage away from the village and she was a bit happier with modern sanitation and better facilities. She was also away from the prying eyes of the village. Hannah had taken care of baby John for the night whilst George helped them move their furniture with his van. If only she had known whose baby it was George dared not think of what her reaction would have been. She might have done it some harm. Hannah complained about the state of the babies' clothes and promptly dressed him in some old clothes of the twins. She gave the baby and his clothes a good wash and sent him back looking neat and clean

George knew that the cheques would soon start being returned again but he said nothing to Hannah, he decided there would be enough said when she found out and he didn't have to wait long!

"George" said Hannah when he went in for his tea one Tuesday "Mr Timmins said the cheque I gave him had been returned"

"What do you mean returned?" he said

"I paid for the grocery that we had last week with the cheque you signed for me. I hope you're not in trouble with the bank again"

"Well things are not too good"

"Whatever do you mean not too good? You certainly seem to be working very hard; you're never at home these days"

That's what you think; thought George He had just left Sandra where they had spent most of the afternoon in bed together.

"I will look into it," he promised

"George I am not going to get into a row about money, but you had better get your act together. It will be all over the village that your cheques are bouncing. How could you let this happen again? Think of the disgrace"

"Alright there's no need to go on"

Joe Timmins ran the village shop with his wife Sarah; they also owned the butcher's shop in the next town. It paid them well enough for Joe to take meat and groceries around the country areas with his van. His brother Frank was married to Hannah's sister Elizabeth.

"If it gets back to our Lizzy it will be all round the family" Hannah went on. George had heard enough and did as he usually did, made himself busy outside, out of the ear shot of Hannah at the same time promising to put the matter in order as soon as possible. In the next few weeks more cheques were returned, then came the court orders

"George what is going on?"

"Bloody bank has tightened up"

"George we have had this trouble before, I don't think I can cope with it all again. Can you not sort it out?"

"Of course I will" but he did not know how, "I will see the bank and sort it out, it's just a bad spell" He said trying to reassure Hannah.

"But the winter will be here again and you've done nothing about getting on with the house."

"Don't go on about the house, I've got enough to worry about"

Hannah knew it was no use continuing to argue with him so she let it drop for a few days. She was thinking things over when George had gone to work and she realised that there had been very few bills made out for recent work that he was supposed to have done. He's not getting jobs finished off she said to herself. Weeks went by. Hannah had washed the children and put them to bed, she was tired, and it was hard work trying to keep things going smoothly. She and George settled in to watch the television for an hour. "George can I have some money for the children's school dinners please? They need to take it with them in the morning and I've not got enough.

"You're always asking for money"

"George I only ask for what is absolutely necessary"

"You've had the family allowance, what have you done with that?"

"I had to pay cash for food from Joe Timmins, last week your cheque was refused again"

"That bloody bank manager, he's a miserable sod, he knows I'm trying"

"Well what have you told him exactly?"

"Does it matter what I've told him?"

Hannah was losing her patience, "George this really is too bad of you, I was worried sick the last time, and then the market stall helped to save us."

"Oh you are always the life saver" he quipped

"I'm not saying that George, but it is obvious that you are not able to provide for us on your own. I will have to get a job or something"

"You'll do no such bloody thing! You're place is here looking after the kids and the home"

"What home? Only half a one you mean, and from what I can see it's another winter in it as it is. What's the matter George? Why haven't you got on with it? I have had enough of living like this! God how I wish that I had not let you talk me into giving up the market stall"

"Don't go on, there's no money to do anything with and that's that"

"Well in that case I will have to get a job of some sort, a full time one if necessary" "You will do no such thing"

"But George could you have that money that the Council offered when we first came here"

"Don't but me, we've got to manage I am not borrowing large sums of money just to please you"

"And how the hell are we supposed to survive? What am I to tell the kids in the morning when they ask for their dinner money?"

"Oh you'll think of something I'm sure"

"I will think of something! That's what I'm asking you to do!"

"Do bloody wonders" replied George, now getting angry

Hannah got out of the chair and put her knitting to one side "My kids are not going to school embarrassed about money. I will get a job, and at least I will be able to save them the misery of not being able to pay for dinner on the day it is required. How would you like to be in their shoes?"

"I'm doing my best" George shouted

"Well your bloody best isn't good enough" Hannah shouted from the back kitchen, "Look around you, this isn't a kitchen it's a bloody garage, and what about the rest of the house? When is that going to get finished? Never by the look of it!"

Hannah was angry and George was getting angry too

"If you don't shut up about this bloody house I will shut you up"

"And what do you mean by that remark?"

"You will see you are getting on my nerves keeping on about money"

"Well what do you propose to do about it?"

"There's nothing I can do until someone pays up"

"And who is that someone, from what I have seen of you making out bills for customers it doesn't look like it to me that you have many jobs completed so that the customers can settle what they owe you. What the hell are you doing George when you leave here? The times that you have been working late My God how I wish that I had checked up on you, then perhaps I would know and understand why it is that you get into such a mess with your money. I am damned sure that it does not take all that you can earn on just keeping the house going. I am as careful as I can be It costs nothing for vegetables and little more for clothes. She saw his face and knew that she was treading on thin ice.

"That great scheme to make curbing stones fell flat on its face and came to nothing" Hannah knew she should stop, but she was wound up like a clock spring and she had lived through just about enough of George's money problems. She could see another Christmas short of money and another winter with nothing done to improve the house.

"I'm sick of that stinking privy in the garden it's not fair on the kids. When you bought this place it was going to be wonderful. If I'd have known what I know now, we would have stayed on the Wrekin; at least I had the café to make a bit of extra money"

"Oh you did wonderful" George mocked, "So very wonderful, I suppose it's my entire fault we are in this mess?"

"Well it's certainly not mine! You are supposed to be the breadwinner are you not? I've had enough, had enough do you hear" the tears were coming into her eyes, no way was she going to cry

"Are you listening? What the hell is wrong with you? Other men provide for their families without this misery. What is wrong with you George? What is wrong? We've been married for ten years and nothing has improved."

When she received no answer she shouted, "ARE YOU LISTENING TO ME?" she was putting a jar of marmalade back into the cupboard when she realised George was coming through. She had never seen him look so angry, his face twisted and he looked evil.

For the first time in her life Hannah was afraid, before she knew what she had done the jar of marmalade went splat on the floor at his feet. The broken pieces of the jar flew in all directions and a piece caught in George's foot, He had no shoes on his feet. He looked down and saw blood. Before Hannah could get out of the way he caught hold of her and slapped her hard across the face. Hannah reeled back with shock; she had never been hit like that before. George hit her again and again. Hannah felt numb; she thought she was about to pass out and the room started to swim around her. She saw the outline of the door leading to the hall and the stairs and made for it. Her legs were ready to give way beneath her as she scrambled to the bedroom and lay on the bed. The room was swirling around her as she closed her eyes; her face still stinging from the blows that George had given her. She remembered nothing more until she heard George's voice saying sorry next morning. He had not known what had come over him to hit Hannah like that; he had sat downstairs and thought very hard about it.

The pressure had been getting to him for several weeks now. Sandra was pressing him to leave Hannah so that they could be together for good. Only a few days previous he had almost been caught in bed with Sandra when Jim had come home earlier than they expected. If he told the truth he really did not want to leave Hannah and go away with Sandra. She was his wife and the kids were his family. It was too much to give up. Would Hannah ever forgive him? He would have to wait and see. Hannah got up and sent the children off to school. She looked in the mirror, what a mess. Her face was badly bruised, her one eye blackened and she felt dreadfully sick; consequently she returned to bed not bothering to speak to George who had made himself scarce in the shed. The shock of being hit had well and truly shaken her. Later George pleaded for her forgiveness, promising never to do anything like that again; he knew he had gone too far. He asked her time and time again to forgive him and stay with him and the children. Please don't leave us he had begged.

During the next few days Hannah did a lot of thinking. Could she ever forgive him? She did not think so. Not for a long time to come she knew that for sure. Over the years George had just gone from one money problem to the next, something had to be done.

"I will get a job Hannah, so that we can get a regular wage coming in, I will do anything you ask"

"Finish this bloody house" she had answered

"I will, I will, but let me get a job first"

"Well what if I got a job? Now the children are older I'm sure I could help"

"We will see" he said, "They are advertising for carpenters at the new power station they are building down at Ironbridge. I will go down there tomorrow and see about being taken on."

"You do that" agreed Hannah.

It was almost a week since the row and her face was looking much better so she agreed to call in and see Molly and Terry.

"Don't try to convince me you walked into a cupboard door" Molly stated when Hannah had given her the excuse for her black eye. "I've heard that one before"

"George is going to get a job again" Hannah quickly changed the subject

"I should think so and not before time, you need a weekly wage coming in"

"I've been thinking I might get a job myself to help out"

"You've got enough to do don't you think?"

"I've given it a lot of thought Molly; I can't see the house getting finished if I don't. George just will not borrow anything or take on a mortgage."

"That mans not right in the head, doesn't know what's good for him. Why you put up with it I just don't know"

"Things will get better" Hannah said full of optimism

Hannah gave the idea of getting a job more thought, but how?

There was the grey van in the yard, it was only 18 months old, if only George had kept a check on the engine for oil and not let it seize up as he had. It would cost a few pounds for a new engine to make it roadworthy. How could she do it? Hannah put the idea to George, "If I can raise the money for a new engine would you put it in the van?"

"Of course I would" He was prepared to agree with anything that she suggested if she would forgive him for knocking her almost senseless.

"I could use it then to get to and fro if I were to get a job"

George listened quietly but did not argue. Hannah made an appointment to see the bank manager Mr.Henshaw She proposed to pay off George's overdraft by getting a job if she could have the money to fix the van. Hannah sat nervously on the edge of her chair.

"That's a good idea" agreed Mr Henshaw from the other side of his desk. "I will do that on one condition, I want your husband to put the property into joint names to give you some security for your money"

"That sounds reasonable enough," agreed Hannah, "I will have to discuss it with George and then I will get back to you" later Hannah broached the subject with George she had been into town and when the children were in bed that night she told George about going to see the bank manager He was so angry, she had also told him that she was looking for a full time job. His first thoughts were that she was seeking her independence from him and he wondered what she was planning was it to leave

"George, Mr Henshaw will give me a loan, and then we can fix the van outside"

"There you are dear; I knew you would fix it"

"Ah, there is one condition attached. If I do that and help to pay your overdraft off he suggests I ask you to put the property in both our names."

"Oh he did, did he?"

"I thought that was reasonable enough, don't you?"

"You must be joking, crafty move I reckon" George sounded evil "Go behind my back, smarming to the bank manager, yes you can have a loan" he jeered "Just put the property into joint names, sounds good doesn't it? Get this straight, this house is mine and it's staying in my name, do you hear?"

"George you are being unreasonable, you are up to eyes in debt and I have offered to get a job to help pay off your debt, but Mr Henshaw is quite right, I need some security for my money"

"The way you have been behaving just lately I need some security for my work, damn it George I've worked hard for the last twelve years"

"And I suppose your saying I haven't?"

"No I am not, it's just that you seem to be working all hours and we don't seem to be any better off"

"I've told you I will get a job"

"Well how did you get on when you went for that interview at the power station?"

"That job is not for me, I want something better than just doing shuttering for ready made concrete" He lied. He did not let on that the firm would only employ men who had their City of Guilds certificate Otherwise their insurance would not cover them in the case of an accident. George had told them that he was one of the best of carpenters and he could have references to prove it but it was of no good the site manager had stood firm Get off the bank and only come back if you have the appropriate paper work.

"Well you look for something better" replied Hannah "I will get myself a job"

"You do that" he jeered, "Go ahead and see what you think you can get. Nothing if you ask me" George I have been thinking that if I were to find some way of raising the money to buy a new engine for that grey van that is standing out there in the yard. Could I have it so that I can get a job, I am sure that I can find some thing that would fit in with the school hours. If I did that would you prepared to fit it? If not I will get someone else who would do it for me but it would mean that I would have to raise more money to pay for a mechanic"

"Independent are we not?"

"I am not being independent, there are kids here that need feeding and clothing and one of us has got to do something about it, if you wont then I will!"

Hannah went into the garden slamming the back door behind her. Working in the garden usually had a calming effect on her, I will get a job, I will, she said to herself, how I can raise the money to put a new engine in that van. It's wicked the way that he has left it there to rot. That van cost us a lot of money? And when he had seized it up he just went out and bought another. She went back and had a chat with Mr Henshaw. He was very sympathetic towards her and he could see that she must be desperate to come asking again for help. To him here was a very determined young woman who he felt that a little bit of help from the bank would be of great help to her and he could see that she would honour the loan even if her husband would not. He thought that it would be a good idea to let her have the money. But it would be preferable to put it in her name only. But she was very reluctant to do that. She had told him that her husband had always managed the financial affairs and he might be extremely up set if she put any money even a small amount in her own name. Sat the other side of his desk he got the impression that she was more than a little bit afraid of her husband. The dealings that he had in the past with Mr George Fleming he had not taken kindly towards him to him her husband appeared to have a very arrogant self assured manner, Mr Henshaw sanctioned her the loan but made a note in her husband's file that the loan should be a separate one, which Mrs Fleming had agreed to repay. He had given the money to buy an engine in order that she might work, to provide for herself and her children.

"Will you pick a new engine for the van?" she asked George a week later.

Both had forgotten about their quarrel of the previous week.

"I suppose so," answered George, thinking the van outside would be a much better one for him to use. The one that he used every day. He had bought it for what he could afford at the time which was not a lot and which was some time ago and the price had seemed not a lot at the time. Yes, he would fix the engine, how Hannah was going to repay the bank for the loan did not interest him. Hannah scoured the local paper for jobs available, but nothing seemed suitable for her with the three children to cope with, she was determined to do something though. She would never forgive George for hitting her as he had for some time to come; she put it to the back of her mind for the time being. But she would be very careful not to antagonise him any more than she could help; she knew that she had to play her cards very close to her chest. It was more important to get some money to keep the children. But she was careful not to give him a chance to repeat it.

"I can't think how you got around that Henshaw at the bank" he commented, "How have you promised to pay the money back?"

"I will get a job" Hannah announced

"And who's going to look after the kids?"

"They will be alright, I will see to that" answered Hannah, "If only I could find some part time work"

"But what good will that be?"

"Better than nothing," she replied, "It will buy the children some new clothes and goodness knows they are at a stage where they need it, I can't make everything for them now they are older"

George decided not to argue with her, he knew he had gone too far by hitting Hannah so he just kept his cool and made sarcastic comments whenever he could.

Terry died whilst in hospital; Judith took the responsibility of arranging the funeral. Hannah was quite amazed to see her mother and dad attending. She felt quite pleased about it. Judith and Carl helped Molly all they could; she was a very independent woman and coped well. Judith now lived just around the corner in the same village so she was close at hand. Judith had a go at George to repay money he had borrowed off his father and give it to Molly Hannah over heard them arguing she had no idea what they were talking about. She bided her time she waited for a couple of weeks until she was able to ask Judith what they had been talking about.

"What you don't mean to tell me that you did not know what money George had been borrowing over the years. It began when you first moved off the Wrekin"

"Honestly Judith I have no idea what you are talking about but I will make it my business to find out. If it is as you say then I agree with you that George should repay any money that he has borrowed to Molly. Honestly Judith I know nothing about it. It sounds ludicrous to me for him to have been borrowing money from his father How as he managed to keep it so secret for so long I don't believe it."

"Hannah I am not joking and I think that it is about time that you woke up and did not bury your head in the sand like you do you evidently have not got a clue what he gets up to". apparently George had borrowed some money from his father promising to pay it back but of course had never bothered to do so. Judith was very annoyed with George. His father died before he was sixty-five so therefore Molly was going to have to live on a widow's pension which was a very poor pension. If Terry had lived until he was sixty-five. Elsie would have had a better pension. In the meantime she would have to manage and make up the difference by keeping her job working in the village store. Why should George not repay is what Judith wanted to know?

"Well there's not a cat in hells chance of him paying anyone at the present time. He's in such a mess financially; I'm getting a job of some sort if I can. I'm so desperate and I have got to do something."

"How the hell has he got into such a mess? Is that what you two have been arguing about?"

"What do you mean?" Hannah asked

"Well don't tell me it's a bed of roses at your house because I would not believe you"

"I don't understand, George works such long hours" replied Hannah trying to protect him

"But is he working?"

"I suppose so; I have no reason to think otherwise"

"Do you ever check where he is?"

"Why should I? George would not lie to me as to where he has been"

"Well if he is working the hours that he makes out he is, you two should be wealthy"

"That's what I can't understand Judith, he puts in such long hours and yet he can't afford to pay any bills. He's trying to get some employment and finish working for himself"

"That would be a damned good idea, and about time too I say. You would be a lot better off. Thinking of getting a job are you? Well if you do, see that you spend your money on yourself and the children"

"I have no choice, we need the money"

"Well best of luck, let me know if I can be of any help"

"I think you did enough for me when the twins were small"

"Well you never know, I just hope that big brother of mine will come to his senses and sort himself out a bit and if I get the chance I will certainly tell him what I think of him and at the moment that is not very much. It will be a long time before I speak to him again at least until he pays Molly what he rightly owes her"

"Yes; so do I hope things will get better? You know, despite his faults I love him so very much"

"Love is blind sometimes" muttered Judith under her breath

"Judith I have threatened to leave him if he does not get that house finished. He says I wouldn't dare but when he has one of his off days I could just walk out but I just can't do it and he knows it"

"Well you don't just give up, but remember there are limits"

"Well just tell me where on earth I could go and what would I do for money?"

"There's always a way of surviving if you are strong enough to do it"

"Well let's hope it never comes to that. I couldn't imagine leaving George or trying to cope on my own. I'm sure if I get a job and help out a bit things will sort themselves out. You know I feel better already, just being able to talk to someone helps"

Judith then told Hannah that she was very worried about Molly, what would she do now that she was on her own?

"She has been a wonderful mother to us all. She has talked about returning to Birmingham to be nearer her own daughters, I don't know whether she will or not, they've not been that close over the last few years"

"Give things time" replied Hannah "If she decides to go you must not interfere, she loved the city life and it must be very quiet for her here now that Terry has gone"

"The thing that she hates most here is having no street lights, she can't get used to going out at night in the dark, especially with the winter coming on again. The evenings are very lonely for her"

"I wonder what she will do if she does go back to Birmingham? Perhaps she will stay with one of her daughters at first"

"I know that she worked for Cadbury's for many years, she has applied for one of their bungalows. If she gets one she will be near both her daughters. I will just have to wait and see how things go," replied Judith, she went on, "I know that if Molly decides to do something nothing will change her mind. We will all miss her dreadfully if she were to go back to the city."

"Perhaps she thinks we don't want her, especially now Dad has died, I think that we all should tell her how much we love her and how much we are going to miss her if she were to go"

Hannah told George that she had been talking to Judith and asked him if it was true that he had borrowed money from his father. When she saw the look on his face she wished that she had not said anything. He looked just like he did the night that he had hit her and she was terrified.

"What the bloody hell have you been gossiping about with Judith" He was sitting watching the telly but looked at Hannah and she could see that he was angry. Very angry indeed".

"We were casually talking about Molly going back to Birmingham that was all and Judith just happened to mention that she only had her widow's pension to live on and it would be so nice for you to pay what you had owed your father. I did not know what she was talking about. Is it true George that you borrowed money with out telling me? How could you? I don't believe it". She saw the look on his face and that told her that Judith had been right he looked as guilty as sin.

"Mind your own business and tell that sister of mine to do the bloody same" He hissed and rose from the chair; Hannah took one look at him and was scared stiff. He looked murderous, she made for the back door and before he had time to grab hold of her she was out of his reach. She went to the garden shed and took a hoe and did some gardening to pass the time away until she had calmed down a little. The evening chill was good for her she worked steadily for about an hour until she found the light fading too much. When it was getting too dark to see she went back inside taking the hoe with her She would use it if he came anywhere near her. As it was, she need not have worried he had calmed down and was full of apologies for losing his temper. She did not answer him she was still angry with him. She quickly washed and made a drink; she put one before him but took hers to bed with her. She lay awake until he came upstairs and then pretended to be asleep until he had gone to sleep and only then was she able to relax.

Neither spoke next morning they made no conversation George ate his breakfast and went to work where to Hannah had no idea nor she did not care. Her first priority was to get a job and be independent if she could, after last evening she knew that she could not trust him not to hit her again. He would just keep saying sorry expecting her to forgive him but no way could or would she; she had lost all her love for him.

Chapter Sixteen

An Ultimatum but Which One to Choose

"Did you really hit Hannah that hard?" Sandra asked George as they lay in bed together, "You would never do that to me would you darling?"

"Of course not my little love, it's just that I cannot cope with Hannah going on about me not finishing the house, I must have lost my temper. He did not add that he had not been doing much work because of the time that he was chasing after her. No jobs were getting finished co consequently the lack of money coming in to pay his bills was also added to their problems.

"Well I heard that she certainly had a black eye for a week, do you think she will ever forgive you?"

"I don't know? You never know with Hannah, she does not talk when she has had her feelings hurt. I never know what she is really thinking. She has come up with the idea of getting a job"

"Well let her, we will know where she is won't we. Do you really need the money?"

"Of course not, it's just she wants to do everything better than what we can afford" he sounded so convincing

"Well I'm not satisfied with this pokey little place, just look at this room, not enough room to swing a cat around in. You know darling, if only Hannah would leave I could come and help you finish that house"

"That would be perfect my love, but what's wrong with this room? It's so cosy for satisfying you, quite big enough"

"I know, but Jim is talking about looking for a job that has a better house and that there might be a bit of ground that he could rent and make a start for him. I don't want to move again, especially away from you my darling. If he did see a better job advertised he would be keen to take it and it will be a step in the direction that he wants to go. Jim had told Sandra when he had married her that he would be looking for a job and a place that had a bit of ground

"But no way am I intending to stay with him forever when I can share moments with you like we have done tonight.

"If you moved to the end of the earth I would find some way of visiting you and getting into bed with you. You know I need you, and it looks as if I am the only one who can satisfy your voracious appetite," He said as he made love to her again, "We'll be alright for another hour won't we?"

"Yes darling, Jim is working overtime; he won't be in for some time yet. As long as the baby keeps quiet we will be fine.

Later when they had dressed and were enjoying a cup of tea Sandra remarked

"What are you going to do about Hannah?"

"Let's see what she does with idea of getting a job" he replied

"Well fix that van for her so that she's got transport"

"But I don't want to do it. Why should I put my self out for her benefit If she gets a job it will make her that little more independent of me. At the moment I have got her where I know where she is and another thing if she thinks that she only has to say do this or will you do that and I will jump straight away just to please her. Not bloody likely"

"Take my advice darling, we will sort it out, anyway I've got an idea"

"What idea?"

"Let's take it one step at a time, agree to Hannah getting a job if that's what she wants to do."

"You could be right," he said, knowing how desperate they were for money

"Play along with her. By the way are you going to get the caravan towed back this winter?"

"What do you think?"

"Well we can't really relax here after the other week, I only just got away with it, and we nearly got caught"

"What do you think he would have done if Jim had caught us at it?"

"I don't really know or want to find out. I've heard he has got a right paddy but he has never shown it with me. He believed that story that you had a violent attack of diahorrea and that's why you were coming out of the bathroom. You will bring the van back won't you darling?"

"Alright my love, I'll see what I can do, but how will you be able to get away?" "I will think of something, don't you fret about me"

"You're a crafty one to be sure," he said kissing her passionately as he left.

"Not half as crafty as you, be careful darling go home the back way"

"And why should I?"

"To keep me in mind as you pass our little hidy place"

"I will always be thinking of you" he replied

Would he ever leave Hannah? Sandra wondered as he drove away towards home. It was obvious that all was not well between them, this gave her hope that perhaps one day soon she and George would be together, and in the meantime she would have to be patient. He did not dare tell her that he owed money right, left and centre and that he was going to have to start paying some thing off the bills or he would end up in court. Bill Harper had sent a stinking letter saying that they would have to go to court if he did not settle the account with them. Hannah was furious with him

"How could you George? She had shouted at him when he had come in for his tea. Owe Bill for this amount for so long They certainly don't want you as their friend if this is how they write to you" George it looks to me as if I have no choice but to get that full time job that I have talked about".

"Oh trust you to come to the rescue with your big ideas."

"Well it does not look to me as if you have cat in hells chance of paying off your debt if that is how our supposed best friends are writing to you. I had no idea that you owed them that amount".

"It's not much for them to stand out considering the amount of work that Bill's firm is turning over"

"George I don't believe that I am hearing you correctly how can you stand there and say things like that. By the way what are all these court orders that are coming for stuff that is now owed to different firms? I can't see how the hell I can ask for money to clothe and feed the kids. That is why I suggest that I look for a job. At least I can feed and clothe us while you get and pay off your debts. I just cannot understand it at all you say you are working late to earn extra but where is the extra money. There is none that I can see. I think that you are telling lies and that you are not working. I am beginning to think that you are else where and you certainly are not working late. Well get one thing clear George Fleming if I am able to get a job it is for the benefit of the kids and me as far as you are concerned you can go and whistle. And another thing if I find out that you have been telling lies about your work, I am leaving you. Because I am beginning to think about doing some checking up on you, nothing makes any sense to me any more."

"On your high and mighty horse are you again well you go on and check up on me and see how far that will get you. You will just make a complete fool of your self. Think that I am telling lies do you". George sounded angry very angry indeed. Hannah was getting very nervous of him. And another thing you are not the only one looking for a job. Two can play at that game". He went out and banged the door as hard as he could as he went. The next evening George was sat as usual watching the telly after the children were in bed. Hannah sat with some embroidery that she was doing. George started to make conversation.

"I've been thinking," He said to Hannah that night in such a pleasant tones that it took her completely off guard. "I will fix the engine into the grey van. You are quite right, perhaps if you did get a job you could cope with, it would help us out, but only until we get over this bad patch. I've been looking round as well." He sounded as convincing as he had hoped he would. This is what Sandra had suggested that he said, let's see what happens now. He said to him self.

"Oh that would be great. If only I could get some part time work it would sure help us out a little we can't go on as we are that is for certain."

"I did that bit of beet hoeing down the lane for the Parker's, but I need something coming in every week if I am to be of any help to you."

"Well I will leave it with you; see what you can come up with. I can always give a hand with the kids, not that they need much now they are growing up"

"They need a lot more than you seem to realise"

"Alright let's leave it at that shall we?"

Hannah was relieved that he did not need to fulfil his desire for sex and was content to go to sleep. George had shown a different side to his character when he had hit her and she had not felt a great deal of love for him since. Okay she made excuses for him not doing this and that over the years but she did not feel the same for him as yet, at least he was now offering to help her. Perhaps it was his way of an apology It did not take Hannah long to find a job, it was not what she wanted but the money was good. After all the only qualification she had was her driving licence. How Hannah wished she could turn the clock back a few years and persuade her parents to let her stay on at school and get more academic qualifications. It was too late now for wishful thinking, money was needed and in Hannah's opinion the only way to get it was to go and work for it. The job that she under took, was to deliver bread for a man called Brian Martin, he had the local franchise for one of the bigger bakeries from Stoke on Trent. Her route was to deliver bread and their fancy goods Cakes, pies Etc; around the town and outside areas. It meant starting at Eight O'clock in the morning which wasn't too bad as the children were collected from the door by the school bus at a quarter past eight. This meant she only had to leave the children with George for half an hour. Hannah usually finished the round by Two o'clock in the afternoon and was back home before the school bus, except on Saturdays. She was a bit later that day because of collecting the money from customers. When George saw the extra money coming in he did not mind working around home on a Saturday so that he could keep an eye on things until Hannah came home

First things first, Hannah had said, as she bought the children new underwear and warm coats to wear for school. Despite the extra work Hannah was happy, she loved her job and the extra money gave her peace of mind. She honoured her contract with the bank and started to pay off the loan for the van engine, which had only been thirty-five pounds. There was a lot more to the delivery round than one was aware of and Hannah soon learnt the ins and outs of the job, she had a young girl with her to help They soon learnt which customers were good payers and which weren't. The poorer payers were the easiest to sell to, not that her employer was amused when he had the payment books handed in on a Saturday evening. Hannah felt that it was not her problem; it was the job of her boss, Brian to chase up bad payers. After all he wanted the goods sold and that was all he was concerned about. He had to get a certain amount of financial turnover otherwise he would lose the franchise, which meant a great deal to his income. Hannah could not take to his wife Beryl, she was a small woman, very pale faced, she helped her husband with the running of a grocery store. Brian was easy to get along with as he was a mild man hen-pecked and ruled over by his wife. He was tall and slim quite good looking Blue eyes and brown hair. Yes he was not bad at all that is if you fancied that type of man. He was definitely not Hannah's choice. Hannah could never work out whether to admire Beryl or to feel sorry for Brian. The job suited Hannah at long last she had some regular money coming in to the house and that was all she was concerned about for the time being.

Christmas came and went Hannah was still doing her delivery round as spring went into summer. She often took David or Jennifer with her on a Saturday; they liked to go with her, as it was something different for them. What was she going to do with them during the summer holidays? She had not sorted it out yet and six weeks was a long time to keep them occupied. George had not got a job but was still talking about it. Michael went with him when he was not at school Hannah managed to cope; William and Sheila had the twins whenever they could. Helen offered to have David for a week and he stayed with her for the rest of the holidays, enjoying life on the farm, anywhere away from the troubled atmosphere of home. Jennifer often played with her friend from down the road until Hannah returned in the afternoons. On the whole everything worked out very well and before they knew it, it was time to go back to school for the autumn term. George managed to get a job with a damp coursing company, but it meant travelling from one area to another. Often this meant he would be away from home and this in turn put pressure on Hannah. She had to go to work later and George began to lose interest in anything to do with the house or the family. Hannah wasn't too worried, Michael was twelve and the twins were going on for ten. They were capable of amusing themselves for half and hour or so.

George's moods worsened so that Hannah dreaded weekends. He would accuse her of having men in the house while he was away.

"Of course I haven't" She would reply "How the hell am I going to bring other men in the house with three children?"

"You would think of something" he sneered "You would sneak off and meet them some how"

"George you have got everything wrong, can't you trust me whilst you're away?"

"Why should I? You women are all the same, can't get enough of men."

"Your talking a load of rubbish George, we women as you say, have got too much to do .So that if we had any spare time. I can assure you that I can find some thing better to do with myself than to spend time chatting up to other men" who on earth would I bring here? I have no interest in anyone else. I married you and you're the only man I love. Are you sure you're feeling all right? Is the travelling with this new job too much for you? I'm really worried about you"

"There's nothing wrong with me" he muttered "You wanted me to get a job now you're saying you are not satisfied."

"No such thing. You decided to get the job, you had to do something. I don't want to have the Inland Revenue threatening to send the bailiffs again. It was a good thing that you were away at the time otherwise there would be no furniture in the house"

"Go on blame me. It seems to me as if you are making out that it is always my fault"

"George I am doing the best that I can to help you get out of the mess that you are in I am not blaming you. I just want to help so that we can finish this house. For the kids sake if not for yours"

"That's right you go on about the house. How the hell can I get on here if I am working away all week?"

"George you took the job. Not me. Why don't you look for something more local in the meantime? I am sure that good carpenters are always needed".

George was getting so bad tempered with Hannah. Working away did not suit him He was unable to get to see Sandra He had not realised that this would become such a problem. He did not get home very early on Fridays and because Hannah was working Saturdays he had to stay and work around the house so that he could keep an eye on the children. This only left him free on a Sunday and he could not go to see Sandra with the hope of going to bed with her because Jim had Sundays off and would be at home working around their place. He was missing Sandra so much that he decided that he would have to do some thing about it, but what could he do. He decided that he would bring the caravan back for the winter so they could meet on a Saturday evening. He thought that at least they would be able to meet in comfort, she would find any excuse to get out and he knew that she would find some way so that she could be with him. He went ahead and arranged to meet her making an excuse to Hannah that he had to go and see his friend Len and have a drink with him and see if he knows of any local jobs going. "If I am a bit late don't wait up for me"

"That's alright" Replied Hannah she was quite relieved that he was going out. "I 'm absolutely shattered I thought that we were never going to get the round finished today"

"Yes that is a good idea you get an early night, don't wait up for me you take it easy a bit when you can"

"So you don't mind if I turn in. I will wait up, for you if you want me to".

"I have said, haven't I. don't wait for me although I will try not to be too late". He said He had made an effort to dress him self up wore a nice clean shirt and a tie He smiled to him self as he drove up the lane. I'm glad that she is so tired she won't bother arguing with me. He doubled back along the winding lane to pick Sandra up at the pre-arranged place.

"What excuse did you give?" He asked Sandra when she got into the van and sat along side of him.

"I told him that I was going to see Sally and that I would make my own way back. Get a taxi or something. I said that I would be an hour or so He can't go far he has to keep an eye on John. He said that he would call and see his mother and go back and put John to bed. I've pulled the plug out of the phone so that it will appear to be out of order if he decides to check up on me. George made his way to where he had parked the caravan Hidden in the plantation of trees.

George turned the gas on and lit the fire. "A bit chilly in here "he teased.

"Not for long" She replied lowering the double bed and starting to remove her clothes.

"Come my Darling I am waiting for you"

"Do you think that I should keep you waiting?"

"That's up to you but I am not moving from here".

"It took George no time at all to strip off and join Sandra in the bed.

Their naked bodies became as one as he made love. Her appetite for him was insatiable. When at last he had exhausted himself. She relaxed and teased him as she so often did. She got off the bed and danced a little dance in all her nakedness, flaunting her body before him. This was a little ritual that she often performed as she turned and twisted in front of the fire. The glow from the fire emphasised the shape of her very full breasts. George knew that he loved her, He wanted and needed her and she in turn knew what he was thinking. Neither of them had any sense of guilt or shame as to what they were doing. She lay back on the bed beside him. "What was that idea that you said that you had in mind? You promised that you would tell me" He smiled at her.

"God you do look sexy in the fire light" he teased. "

Jim had seen and advertisement for a farm worker with Farmhouse and eight acres of ground to go with it. It said that there would be no ground rent to pay for a reliable and enthusiastic worker. Some Farm buildings would also be available

" This would be grand for us to be able to make a start of our own" He was reading the advertisement and he was becoming so excited about the prospect of being able to make a start. Sandra this would be great for us just think at last I could get baby calves and rear them. It says that there are some out buildings if we want them What about you rearing some chickens Ducks and goodness knows what?"

"Just a minute Jim where did you say that this place is?

"Oh it is some twenty miles from here the other side of Whitchurch the address sounds to me to be the Newcastle area"

Jim if you think that I am moving that far away you have to think again". Sandra was quickly thinking how would she be able to see George if they were to move such a long distance away. "No Jim you can think again".

"Well Sandra I am going to look at the place. It seems to me to be just what I have been looking forward to. Besides there is no reason why you should not learn to drive the car. Yes I will go over there on Saturday you can come with me if you feel that you want to or I will go on my own and then we can talk about it again. But I am not prepared to let this chance go by if I can help it". He thought with or with out your help. But he knew that it was best not to voice his thoughts out loud.

"Jim don't you be quite so enthusiastic you may not get the job never mind the house and the rest of it" I hope that you don't She thought I could not bare to be that far away from George. She continued "Yes I agree with you that there is no harm in going to have a look at it." I just have to hope that you don't get the job. She said to her self.

Jim went to see the farmer and had an interview for the vacancy. The farmer was quite impressed and after a cup of tea and a piece of his wife's home made cake. Jim left as happy as a little sand boy. His mind was forming all sorts of ideas and pictures for the future. Sandra was well and truly disappointed when he returned home and told her that he had been offered the Job and he could not stop talking of what an opportunity that it was going to be for all three of them." I gave him the impression that we would take the job but said that I must consult you first".

"I should think so indeed I have some say in this you know" Sandra had thought of nothing else She remembered George saying that if she moved to the end of the earth he would find some way so that they could see each other. Perhaps it would be better for them after all if Jim decided to take this job She was sure that she would be able to find little jobs for George to do about the place. If they were to move further away it would also put the locals off and then there would be no more concern for gossip. Yes she would go along with Jim's enthusiasm. The thought of a nice big farmhouse was quite pleasing to her. If Jim was offered overtime she knew that he would not be able to refuse it. If his new boss wanted him to do overtime Jim would jump at the chance of making a few extra pennies. He never kept her short of money and she did not have to scrimp and save Jim saw to that. By what George had told her she would not be out there very long he would find a way to get rid of Hannah she was sure that he had meant every word. Any way she was going to have another go at him about their situation the next time that she saw him.

The move was quick and successful one big van that Jim was able to borrow moved most of their furniture. Their other bits and pieces. George took for them. He had offered to move Sandra, John, Food and small items in his van. When he came home that evening. George was telling Hannah all about the place that Jim and Sandra had taken on. "A Nice place they have got there. They should do well" Hannah was non-committal secretly she was so glad to see the back of Sandra and was hoping that she would not be continually ringing for George to fix this or fix that. Peace at last she thought to her self. Peace at last.

"George what are you going to do about Hannah. You know that I can't go on any longer like this. Living with one man and loving another and besides you are missing out so much of baby John's ways. You have to do something to get rid of her so that I can come and bring John and live with you. I am perfectly capable of looking after you and your kids. You know that I am and you also know that you can't live with out me. Sleeping in bed with another man when you want me all to your self. I know that it is eating away at you. And what do you think that it is like for me. It is almost unbearable it is. Absolutely unbearable. George I simply can't take any more. You know Darling that I hate it. You will have to do something soon or I am sure that I will crack up completely and then I might give your little game away". What do you think that Hannah would do if she found out about us; it is a miracle to me that she has not suspected any thing before now. Even if you don't leave her, you will have to get her to leave you".

"Get her to leave me how do I do that?"

"We will have to think of some thing. If you were to get rid of her I could move in and look after the children"

"I could never see Hannah giving her children up, she is devoted to them. Their needs come before mine. They are her whole life our responsibility she is always reminding me, as if I did not know that it was".

"Well you had better start doing some quick thinking sooner than later".

"Now steady on a bit how do you propose that I get rid of her. You are quite right I hate the thought of you going to bed with Jim but what can I do about it. I can't just get rid of her like that can I? And why on earth should she suspect that her little sister is carrying on with me. She has no reason what so ever to suspect anything. You are legally married to the supposed father of your child. Why on earth should she suspect any thing untoward? If she said that she had any inclination that I was meeting you. It would be so easy to make out that she was going around the bend to even think of such things. No woman on this earth is going to suspect that her little sister has been doing what you have done, As far as I know there is only your William and Ted Locket who could shop us.

If William had wanted to do that he would have done it a long time ago. But he wants that farm and he knows it The fact that you and I are seeing each other and that John is not Jim's It could make them ill and it could kill the old pair, they are getting on a bit you know. What is the old fellow now he must be getting on for seventy if not older is he not. William has so much to lose; I don't expect that that for one minute that they have actually signed the farm over to him as yet and I reckon that they have not made a will leaving every thing to him. If any thing were to happen to them before they put it in writing the lot would have to be shared between all of you. Then where would he be I don't expect that they have paid him a decent wage and you know that he has been working so far on promises just like you were. What did they give you, they paid for your wedding and that was about it. Except for a few bits and pieces of furniture. Do you reckon that I am right? Who would believe a bloke like Ted Locket he dare not show those photos to any one, can you imagine what his wife would do to him if she were to find out about what he has been doing in the woods when he should have been working. She would kick him out and then what would he do There is no one who would want a peeping tom to live with them No I don't think that are many who would be glad to take him in. Would you? He could be locked up for taking that sort of stuff; Your Dad for one would most certainly threaten to shoot him."

George drew hard on his cigarette. It was mid afternoon George had telephoned to make sure that the coast was clear that Jim would not be there for some time to come. Hay making was being dropped in favour of silage making, farmers no longer wanted to rely on the weather. Now they cut the grass while it was still green in the month of May and then it was taken to what was called a silage pit where it was treated. It was then covered over with tarpaulin sheets until it was needed for feed in the winter months. The cattle seemed to like it and they certainly did very well on it. George and Sandra had been in bed and were now down stairs and sat at the kitchen table. Sandra kept the house reasonably clean but there was a lot more that could be done if she put her mind to it the kitchen certainly had a lot to be desired. She was not as fussy as Hannah was. Not that a bit of dirt in the corners and the rooms being untidy bothered George he was more interested in other things. Satisfying his sexual needs

"Have you been listening to me"? Sandra said quite loudly "My God you have got things worked out. Have you not? Aren't you forgetting one thing that it was not only me that started this affair as far as I can remember I think that you had something to do with it? She continued "I have been thinking that I could soon get grounds for a divorce from Jim. It would be no trouble to fix him up he is pretty gullible He fell hook line and sinker about getting me pregnant. All it took was a bit of black lace. It is up to you to get rid of Hannah before I do anything here. If she is not there then I can move in and he will have grounds for a divorce. Can you see what I am getting at?"

"I've thought and thought about it. I am fed up to the teeth with Hannah going on about money and me not getting the house finished but I can't work any harder now can I?" He started to laugh.

"But you would finish the house for me wouldn't you Darling" She brushed her face against his. "I have thought of a way that you could get rid of her, how about giving her a bit of poison. Just a bit to start so that no one would suspect any thing, You could always say that she had killed herself by taking an over dose when she died at a later date. I have been reading about some one who did this. She just gave her husband a little bit and a little bit and because he was always feeling ill he became depressed and finally took his own life and no one suspected any thing. We have some tins of warfarin in the buildings. Jim keeps it for the rats they are a bit of a pest and the cats that are about the place seem to be pretty useless at catching many of them".

"You are not suggesting what I think that you are. I can't do that I would get sent down for it and for a long time at that".

"Who would know? There are ways and ways of doing things. Just a little bit to start with and see what happens. Well now you listen to me George I am giving you an ultimatum you get rid of her one way or another or you finish with sneaking over here to enjoy your self when ever you feel like it. By the way I have been thinking that you ought to come one evening and bring all of them with you so that it looks as if you called socially it would not look so suspicious. The neighbours will see your van coming so often and they will start talking. I would not like Jim to suspect anything at this stage and I can't keep finding little jobs for you to do about the house now can I" She chuckled loudly He drank the tea that she had put in front of him and then he gave her a passionate kiss and went out into the yard to start the van his mind in turmoil.

"Don't you forget what we have talked about "Sandra reminded him as he started the engine to drive away? Things were going around and around in his head as he drove the miles back towards Wellington. What a situation to be in. He hated leaving Sandra, the thought of her living with Jim and he had to admit that it was becoming unbearable. It was slowly eating away at him and he knew that he hated to visualise her in bed with him. He thought of what she had said about getting rid of Hannah. It had really shaken him. Did she really expect him to go to such lengths so that they could be together? What if every thing went wrong he would be left to carry the can. He was completely amazed to think that Sandra expected him to go to such lengths but it also dawned on him that she must be getting desperate to be with him if she was capable of thinking up such a plan. Dared he try it? To poison Hannah the thought had never occurred to him before? It did not bare thinking about. If things went wrong he could just see Sandra saying that she was happily married to Jim and that she had their baby John to look after. He could see her playing the little innocent and every one would believe her. Why should they not? It would never cross their minds that she had been having an affair with him for so long and behind Jim's back.

He knew that he had to do something. They could not go on as they were. To his way of thinking Hannah was getting unbearable to live with and he now knew that she no longer loved him and she refused his advances he had guessed that she was terrified of getting pregnant. He now realised that he should never have hit her as hard he did that night. He could have killed her and thank God that he had not. She had pushed him to his limit keeping on and on about money. He had killed all the love that she had for him in one solitary night. She said so little and only spoke to him when she needed to speak Things could not go on much longer as they were that he knew for sure. He was going to have to do something there was no dought about that, but what? He had the sneaky feeling that Hannah had it in mind to take the children and leave him but he knew that she would have no where to go, so he had dismissed that idea from his mind. Besides if she did try to leave him she was not going to take Michael from him by hook or crook he would see to that. He knew that her parents would never take her back they had not approved of the marriage in the first place and even to mention the word divorce they would go berserk. Marriage was for life for better or for worse one had to see it through no matter what If you had stood up in the Church and made your vows there should be no way that you break them. Fred and Dorothy would never consider hearing anything about one of their daughters having a divorce, to them it would bring terrible disgrace to the family No she would not go to them. Now Sandra was actually suggesting that he try to poison her. "I don't think so"; he said to him self. I have no desire to spend the rest of my days behind bars in a prison. Why had things gone so wrong for the both of them and when had it started to go wrong. George tried to analyse things in his mind and it had all seemed to go down hill for him after the twins had been born and that she had been advised not to have any more children. He had never heard of such things Women had dozens of kids in the past. You only had to look at Hilda Crosby's mother Mrs Morgan, she had thirteen kids. What George did not realise that because Mrs Morgan had thirteen children, she had not only given birth to two boys who had admormalities and it had also cost her life at quite an early age. She had not lived to see half of them grow up. It was discussed amongst the women of how many still born babies had been born in the years gone by but now that the hospital laboratories were able to analyse blood samples and advise mothers of the dangers the death rate amongst babies had fallen dramatically. There was a choice now and the women were beginning to stand up for them selves and make choices

Hannah had spelled it out quite clearly to George that she wanted no more babies. She said that she certainly was not prepared to carry a baby nine months just to see it die because it was born with what was known as a blue baby. Not only that with the twins being such a hand full she had always been so tired out and she had not much time for him. She took it for granted that he felt the same and was quite happy to restrict having sex unless they were quite sure that it was safe. Little did Hannah know that he could not cope with the restrictions and that was how he had come to get involved with Sandra? He said to him self why oh why? Had he got himself involved with Sandra? George knew the answer she was a sex bomb waiting for the right man to set it off. It just happened to be him. At the beginning he had known that he was in the wrong, but he thought that a bit of flirting did no harm and even when it had turned out to be a regular affair again he was not too worried. He had it in mind to just drop her like a hot potato when he had had enough of her. He had well and truly under estimated her. She could satisfy his needs and she knew it

The situation had now grown completely out of hand and he knew that it was up to him to sort it out but how. He could not stop seeing Sandra he was sure about that. He was growing so angry inside with the thought of her sleeping with another man. But what was the answer if there was one. If they could get rid of Hannah it would be so easy for the both of them. Sandra could walk out on Jim and he knew that she would not hesitate to do so and to hell with what the family thought or said. But Hannah was still there.

Things were getting out of control and were going too far. He had to do something. The idea of giving Hannah some poison crossed his mind. Dare he? Could it be proved? He spent days thinking about it and then confided with Sandra.

"Oh George that would be wonderful, just think if she was not there we will have the rest of our lives together." They discussed what he would have to do. She fetched a tin of warfarin from the buildings and gave it to him.

"Here you are this should solve all our problems" She smiled sweetly.

"You know I would not have thought that you were capable of thinking of something like this but it is worth a try.

"Don't you give her too much you do not want the police knocking on the door and you are of no use to me if I could only see you from behind closed doors."

"I will be careful I can guarantee you that. I still have a bit of life to live as yet" He started to chuckle.

His mind went over and over what Sandra had suggested that he could give Hannah some poison but he did not think that he had the courage to do that as yet The tin of warfarin seemed to be burning a hole in his pocket. He would be glad to get home; he could then hide it in the shed. That night as he lay along side Hannah all he could think of was how best he could administer the rat poison with out raising any suspicion. He had to be sure of what he was doing. He could not afford for anything to go wrong. Whitsun bank holiday Monday had been a very hot day. A blazing row about his not getting on with the house followed in the evening. Hannah had slammed the door and went to bed. It had started because they still had to use that stinking lavatory in the garden she had cooked a large capon on the Sunday for dinner. They were chickens that were treated and fed to gain a lot of weight. They were quite like small turkeys; the family had eaten it cold that day so as to finish off the bird. George was fed up he could not pay for any more materials Sand. Cement and bricks, which needed before much else, could be done to get on with the house. He had creditors to pay off. He had ignored demands from the income tax people and they had sent the bailiffs to possess the furniture. Because he had not been at home at the time they could not touch anything unless he had been present. Hannah had been so angry with him and one thing had led to another. George decided to put his plan into action. He felt that he had had enough and that it was time to do some thing. He came to a decision about what he would do. He slept very little that night; he tossed and turned for most of it. He was awake at five next morning. He got up and made himself some tea. He was not going to go back to bed but neither did he fancy doing any thing at that time in the morning. It was later that he then went into the shed and took the tin of warfarin from the place where he had hidden it. His hand was shaking as he took it to the make shift kitchen. He sat and waited. He watched the eight o'clock news on the television keeping the sound down so not to wake the family He made a fresh pot of tea before Hannah had time to wake up

He crept quietly upstairs to check the bedroom; yes she was still asleep. He crept back down again. The children rarely woke early when they were at home from school; they played in the woods and were allowed to stay up a little later to watch the television. They were always completely exhausted when they went to bed.George poured the tea and took a cup of tea to the bedroom.

"I'm sorry for shouting at you last night "He pretended to apologise a thing that he very rarely did. George was never in the habit of apologising to any one and certainly not to Hannah. Oh yes he had said sorry that time when he really hit her He knew that he had gone too far and that she could have gone to the see the doctor and that he would have advised her to report him. His begging for forgiveness had paid off at the time.

"I have brought you a cup of tea. Stay where you are for a bit, have an extra hour and get up just now. I will keep an eye on the kids for a bit there is no school for the rest of this week"

"Oh George that is so kind of you, but you know how I hate drinking tea in bed, But thank you." She could not help but feel sorry for him He looked like a little whipped puppy dog. Hannah took a sip of the hot tea. "George; You have forgotten that I hate having sugar in my tea. My goodness this does taste sweet."

"Oh yes I forgot for a moment Sorry I will fetch you another one". He knew what the response would be and he was right.

"Never mind dear I will drink it to save you getting another one". She was so pleased to see that he was sorry for shouting at her the previous night.

Hannah was not a person who found it easy to stay in bed in the mornings she liked to be up and get on with the jobs that had to be done especially if the day was going to be hot. She quickly swallowed the sweet tea after George had gone down stairs. She stayed where she was for another half an hour or so and then decided to move. She made a start did some washing and pegged it on the line. Towards eleven o'clock she began to feel a bit light-headed. Hannah took no notice the sun was well up and it was already getting hot, I must slow down a bit. If I can, I will put my feet up for an hour this afternoon and do a bit of knitting. The garden can wait until it is not quite so hot. She said to her self and carried on doing the usual chores tidying up and preparing the dinner. Being as it was going to be another hot day, bacon and eggs with new potatoes would do for dinnertime so there was not too much to be done. She had not been feeling too good and by the time she had the dinner ready she felt really light headed and giddy.

Hannah knew that she did not feel well enough to be able to eat anything at all. She started to be sick and have to run to the lavatory. The pains in her stomach got worse as the day went on. She took her self to bed telling George to cope with what ever had to be done. How she got through the night she did not know she had never felt so ill in her life. Hannah told George that she would try and cope but if she felt no better she thought that it would be for the best that he must ring for the Doctor in the morning as soon as the surgery would be open. Sleep was impossible she was so sick. Early next morning she was so exhausted that she fell into a deep sleep. George got up and left her in bed. He began to panic, he rang Sandra and told her what he had done and she told him to keep an eye on Hannah and as long as she was breathing he was not to panic and frighten the children. Just to tell them that mummy was not well and was staying in bed for the day. It was late in the afternoon that Hannah awoke and although she felt better for the sleep her stomach felt as if she had been severely kicked.

The relief that George felt when he saw that she was getting better was indescribable he really thought that he had gone too far and given her too much poison. He really thought at one time during the night that she was going to die. It had been the longest night that he had ever lived and was relieved when dawn had risen and Hannah had gone into a normal sleep. He vowed there and then that he could not go through that again and no way was he going to do that again. He decided that Sandra could think again. He really thought that Hannah was going to die and that he would have to answer for it. Some other way would have to be found to get rid of her and right now he was too relieved to consider doing anything further.

For the rest of the week Hannah blamed her illness on the chicken that she had eaten. She said that it must have gone off and given her food poisoning. What else could she have possibly eaten that could have made her so ill? Nothing that she could think of. It took her the rest of the week to get over it. It never dawned on her that none of the other members of the family had been sick and that if it had been the chicken that had caused the food poisoning the rest of the family would have been ill and would also have suffered the effects of it.

George saw Sandra later that week. He told her that giving Hannah rat poison was not on. I only put a little bit as I thought in the cup of tea and I put plenty sugar in it. I can't see her suffer like that ever again. I have to think what would have happened if she had died I would have been for the high jump that is for sure." Sandra listened to him and thought. Thinking of your self again "For goodness sake George don't be such a wimp she is not dead and was not going to be. If you can't go through with this, we are going to have to think again. I had to marry this great Oaf of a fellow to get you out of one mess surely you can now do some thing for me. I'm getting that I hate bedtime coming and I can't bear to have him try to make love to me. George I don't want to have any thing to do with him if I can help it and I certainly don't want to have a kid by him. I keep running out of excuses to put him off. I am not going to put up with it any longer than I have to. It's all right for you. You still have the best of both worlds. You don't seem to realise what a lucky bugger that you are."

"Now don't you get all worked up my little love I will think of some thing I hate the thought of you sleeping with him as much as you hate it".

"Really George In that case you know how I feel. I hate having to do his washing in fact I hate having to do any thing for him".

"Well you marrying him certainly gave us a bit of time and I agree with you that things must be pretty unbearable Just give me some time". He said tried to sound as if he was worried.

"How much more time do you want George" Sandra was quick to ask.

I don't rightly know but I promise that I will think of some thing and soon".

"You had better or I will tell all. I feel like leaving him here with the kid even if it is yours. You should have done what I first suggested. You should have left Hannah and we could have lived in the caravan until we had sorted every thing out. But no! You would not agree and I can't see any reason why we can't still do that "

"Now don't go down that road again It would not have worked we would have to have money and work and no way could we have stayed around here Leave it with me. I will be over to see you again as soon as I can".

"See that you do and I hope to see you sooner than later I am waiting every day for you my love".

Chapter Seventeen
Only So Much One Can Take

George "Said Sandra "Have you decided what you are going to do about Hannah because if you haven't I have got a plan. I heard of a couple that wanted to be together just like we do. The husband gave the wife the impression that she was having a mental breakdown. She did have a break down and was locked away for several years. I have been thinking you know that couple Phillip and his wife who lived up the lane from you. That was practically the same as the one that I have heard of. His wife had a nervous breakdown and they took her away. The gossip at the time was that the woman who moved in to care for the little girl Karen had known the fellow for some time and that they had been lovers. She was quick to move in so that she could be with him and care for little Karen. What if you could drive Hannah crazy? I could say that I had come to look after you and the kids". Sandra smiled so sweetly, she sounded so convincing.

"How on earth do I do something like that"? George wanted know and seemed a bit alarmed at the idea.

"Oh it's quite easy actually. You just move things around the house and then blame her for moving them. You say that she has said things when you know that she hasn't Accuse her of having men in the house when you are away. All sorts of things"

"But I can't do that, Hannah is not stupid" George was quite alarmed at the suggestion.

"I know that, Of course you can do it. That is if you don't weaken. Well lover. Which one of us is it going to be? I can think of no better way at the moment, can you?"

"But I suppose that this new idea of yours is worth a try. I can give it some thought and see what she does. You may be right. It could work".

"Just have her put away for a while and I will come and help you with the children. I would only be doing what any good sister would be expected to do"

"Tell me, where does Jim fit into your little plans, my little love"

"Oh he doesn't" She replied. "I would just leave him. The way that I treat him it's a wonder that he has not left already. You try this idea that I have suggested, please darling give a try for my sake. Please Darling it won't be Hannah cracking up it will be me. I need you. I need you my darling "She cooed as she kissed him. .

George gave quite a lot of thought to what Sandra had suggested. He wondered if there was a possibility that it might work. He could always give it a try. He decided to play it quietly by deliberately placing an ornament from off the sideboard and put it on the windowsill. He would wait and see if Hannah noticed. A few days went by and it was obvious that she had not. The ornament was still there where he had placed it.

"You know" He said to her "I can't think why you put this ornament here in the window. It could get broken and I know that you think quite a lot of this one. It is the one that Brenda gave to you. You normally keep it on the sideboard"

"Why yes, so I have. Perhaps I was not thinking straight. You know what it is like when there is so much to do and I only get to do a bit of dusting at the week ends instead of every day like I used to". Hannah was finding it very hard going, keeping a full time job and at the same time trying to do the best that she could for the family so that her going to work did not disrupt them too much.

She picked the ornament up "There "she said. "Let's put it back where it should belong." She looked at it. It was a china figure of a young girl.

Hannah had always treasured it. I must be more careful and think what I am doing She muttered to herself. Now fancy me putting that in the window. It is quite true what George had said, it could have been broken and that would have been so disappointing. I had that given to me when I was in my teens. Hannah put it to the back of her mind and got on with every thing else that she had to do.

The next week it was the alarm clock. It was a blue enamel one and it was always on a little table on George's side of the bed. There was no room to put any furniture on Hannah's side of the bed it was too close to the wall.

"Where is the clock George? Hannah asked as she noticed that he was not winding it up, as was his usual habit when he got into bed.

"Have you put it your side when you made the bed"

"I would have a job. My side is against the wall. George I have not moved it, as you know you have always set the clock since the day we married. Remember you saying that it was your prerogative to wind the clock to make sure that we woke in good time in the mornings"

"I don't remember saying anything of the sort. You are letting your imagination run away with you. Why on earth would I say anything as daft as that? Any way we need it now where in heavens name have you put it"

"I have not put it anywhere but you stay there I will go and look for it." She got back out of bed and took a woollen cardigan off the bottom of the bed and put it around her shoulders. Hannah remembered quite clearly what he had said when they first married it was those little things that stayed at the back of ones mind. He must have forgotten. She could not find the missing clock she looked in the children's room she could not see it and she did not want to disturb them if she could help it. She then went downstairs in case one of them had been playing with it but she could not find it. She went back to tell George that it was no where to be seen and that they would have to do with out it.

"Where have you been?" He said as she reappeared in the room.

"Looking for that damned clock and I can't find it".

"Well I don't know why? It was there on the dressing table. You did not look very hard did you?" He did not say that it was under his pillow so that she would not hear it ticking.

Sure enough George was holding the missing clock.

"I looked there before I went downstairs" Hannah sounded so surprised. "That clock was not there that is one thing that I am sure about"

"Come on and get into bed and forget about it. We have it now and I have wound it up ready for morning. You must be getting a bit tired and forgetting things. You will be alright in the morning"

Hannah could not forget about it, she tossed and turned and it played on her mind for quite a long time that night, until she eventually she fell asleep. She was really worried. During the next weeks things settled down slightly and she put the business of the clock behind her. But at times it still nagged at her she knew that the clock was not on the dressing table and nothing that George had said would convince her otherwise. During the next few weeks other little things started to move and were not to be found in their usual places. George accused her of saying the most peculiar things. Hannah knew that she had not moved the objects and neither had she said one half that he accused her about. Leaving the fridge door open leaving the washing machine still switched on after using it. She was getting worried. What was the matter with her? She started to make a mental note of the sort of the sort of things that George was accusing her of. I will have a word with Molly when I next see her.

On a Wednesday it was the one-day in the week that Hannah managed to finish the daily bread round a little earlier than other days. She drove around by Wrockwardine on her way home from work.

"It's good to see you" Molly said as she and Hannah sat down for a cup of tea. "I guess that you have called to ask me something for you to be here at this time of day.

"You are quite right there is no fooling you is there Molly?"

"No. Not many have pulled the wool over my eyes and them that have I have let them have the sharp end of my tongue. Well what is on your mind? I can see that you are all flustered".

"I'm a bit worried that I might be losing my grip a bit"

"I'm not surprised the hours that you work. You want to take my warning before it is too late and that you crack up. Don't forget that I have seen it all happen before. Just tell me why you should think that you are losing your grip" Hannah sat and told Molly about things not being put un their proper places and things that George had said she had said when she knew that she had not said such things".

"You say that you know that you have not put or said these things. If that is the case then you also know that you are not going around the bend. The first thing that I advise you to do is take no notice. It is the oldest trick in the book"

"What do you mean? The oldest trick in the book".

"Woman stop and think for a moment if you were to have a mental break down what would happen to the children when you were taken away and locked up for may be months. My guess is that there is another woman waiting on the side for this to happen and then she will move in and take you place in your house and bed".

"You think that this is a plot to get rid of me. But who would be so cruel Not George surely".

“Well who else? It looks to me as if you had better be warned to be on your guard. Some one is cooking some thing up and it is not going to be pleasant to swallow. I don’t think that you have very far to look to see who is behind this”.

“But Molly. George has no reason to do this, He has not got another woman or surely I would spot some thing or other”.

“There is none as blind as them that don’t want to see. I will say no more but you think on and take my advice, Start looking for some where for you and the kids to take refuge it will come to it Mark my words”. They sat and chatted about the family until Hannah stood up to leave and get back home before the school bus. Molly gave her a hug and kiss as they said goodbye. “You be careful. I’m telling you. She said as Hannah climbed into the van to drive away. What Molly had said really disturbed Hannah as she drove back home. She was not going to let it get to her but at the same time it did worry her. She would make a better mental note of things that were moved and things that were said. But it would take a lot to convince her that George was seeing another woman He did not get washed and dressed up to go out at nights and it would have to be some one not very good to be meeting him in his working clothes

Christmas went by very quickly and the weather had been fairly good a little snow at the end of December and the odd day of frost and fog but there had been no deep snow. One Wednesday towards the end of January, Hannah was busy with the bread round; the weather forecast that morning said that there was a possibility of snow for the area later in the day. Hannah decided to push on as fast as she could to get the bread round finished with her helper Maggy so that they both could be home before any snow started to fall. Customers were gently persuaded to take the extra loaf or meat pie just in case. By twelve o’clock it started to snow. At first it came as a very fine snow. Just gently falling but not sticking to the ground it was just moving like a white dust in the wind.

Hannah was not too worried she finished the round and took the now empty van back to the shop and put it in its usual place.

"Am I glad to see you two have finished the round? You must have worked very hard to have it completed it and finished already". Commented Beryl. "Folks say that it is drifting quite a lot in the country. How are you getting home Hannah I noticed that George brought you to work this morning?"

"Yes" agreed Hannah; "He seemed to be having trouble with his other van so apparently needed the grey one today. I can go as far as the village by bus"

"Well that's alright, but let's hope that he is there to meet you at the other end the wind it is bitter cold"

"So we have noticed it was sure bleak up at Ketley this morning". Hannah said Cheerio See you on Friday unless we are snowed up. When Hannah saw the look on Beryl's face she quickly added, "I am only joking"

"Now don't you go saying anything like that my husband and I have got used to you coping with your round. It does not give us the amount of problems that the other round does"" They said Cheerio and Hannah made her way to the bus stop but there was no sign of the two thirty bus to Little Wenlock. She made inquiries at the office.

When Hannah asked about the buss". The woman sitting behind the desk informed her.

"It will be late love, the snow is drifting badly in the lanes, we will get a bus for you and you will be on your way as soon as we can. You could have to wait at least an hour. We have decided not to run any more busses than necessary

"What do you mean" Asked Hannah. "I must get home before the school bus at a quarter past four".

"Can't help you love. You will be lucky if we send one out before six tonight". Hannah was utterly dismayed. "Can I use the telephone please?"

"Of course you can. It's a bit of a devil that it is and by what they say it is getting worse" Hannah tried and tried ringing home. There was no answer. Where the devil was George? Obviously had not got home from work or he would have answered the phone He always seemed to Hannah to be quick to answer it if he was at home when it rang. He had a bell fitted in the yard outside He had said it was so that they did not miss calls in case it was some one wanting work to be done. He did not let on that it was in case Sandra rang. Hannah bought a cup of tea and a cake in the bus canteen, which helped to warm her up, a bit. She could not leave the bus station in case the management decided to take a bus out and she would miss a chance of being taken home.Half past four came and it was getting darker by the minute. The snow had been falling quite fast during the last two hours and was now sticking to the roads and making driving conditions treacherous. Oh Lordy I must get home she thought. Minutes later they decided to let a bus go out as far as Dawley and take the passengers that had now gathered in the café trying to keep them selves warm By the time the bus was leaving Wellington it had filled up. All the empty seats were now occupied. Slowly it made its way up the Dawley road towards Lawley. Hannah was so thankful to be on the way home.

"We are not going to make it". The driver's voice came from the front. "You will all have to get off and give me a push". He started to laugh.

"Keep it going "The passengers shouted "Keep it going".

"It will be no further than Dawley" he replied".

OH no, thought Hannah I just hope that George is at home in time to be with the children. There was one consolation that he was not working away from home this week so because of the snow he would have naturally finished work early. The bus crawled along at a very slow pace; it did get as far as Dawley where the driver made his decision that it would be too dangerous to drive across Coalmoor to little Wenlock the wind would be drifting the snow very badly across the moor.

"I'm sorry but you all have to get off here," He said.

"Get off here" the remainder of the passengers echoed".

"Sorry folks but there are no way that I am going to get through to Little Wenlock It is going to take me all my time to get this bus back to the depot.

"Oh well we will just have to walk it. Mr Armstrong who lived in the village commented to Hannah. What thought Hannah it is at least five miles. She gathered her shopping together and stood up to leave the bus forgetting that her boots had warmed up during the ride. Hannah stepped off the bus on to the icy pavement, it was covered with trodden snow, and now it was very slippery. She fell flat on her back and her shopping scattered among the feet of the other passengers. Her loaves of bread. Biscuits and tinned beans and soup Etc were all over the pavement. She got to her feet feeling very embarrassed. Once she had gathered together her shopping. She and the other passengers about twenty in number started off to walk towards Little Wenlock they diminished in numbers as they reached various places along the way. There were only five of them left to complete the journey across the moor.

It was very cold and the wind was blowing about as hard as it could It was coming from the North- East. Its icy blast stung their faces the freezing snow was now drifting deeply, trying to keep on the road and finding their way was becoming difficult. Their chatter had completely diminished Mr Armstrong's torch did its best to guide them to stay on the road but it was not easy. Hannah' feet were wet through and very cold. Her ankle boots filled with the snow very easily and were not much use at all. One needed to be wearing Wellington boots in order to have been able to keep ones feet dry and they would have been lucky even then. In places the snow was now knee high. Her breath came in gasps against the biting wind, she tried to keep going, and her white overall that she wore under her coat was a bit of benefit to stop the wind blowing completely through her. The numbness of her fingers carrying the shopping really hurt and was beginning to make her feel sick. The shopping seemed to Hannah to be weighing heavier with every step that she took. She wanted to drop the lot and leave it on the road but she knew that it was needed so she must keep hold of it.

As they neared the village the howling wind had ceased a little and the snow was not falling so heavily. There would be no way of going shopping tomorrow unless a snow plough could get though so Hannah was glad that she had hung on to what she had got They would need the loaves of bread. At the village she said goodnight to Mr Armstrong and the others as they went in to the warmth of their homes glad to be out of the cold biting wind. Hannah was glad that she had got this far as she made her way towards the lane to take her home. Only a mile to go now she thought I can do it. The whiteness of the snow emphasised the hedge banks, which grew high on either side of the lane. The wind whistled through the leafless hedges but it was now passing over Hannah's head she slithered and skidded as she made her way down the lane. Hannah was very cold, very cold in deed. At last the light of the neighbour's cottage came into view through the trees, what a relief. Not much further to go now. Down the bank over the bridge and up the other side. The thought of a hot drink in front of a warm fire kept her going for the last quarter of a mile. She was feeling completely tired and exhausted,

Relief flooded through her as the lights of their own house came into view. She thought that it must be at least seven thirty. The snow had more or less stopped falling "Thank goodness" she said as she turned into the yard. But where was the van? George, she thought where was George? He should have been home hours ago.

In her anxiety Hannah half tripped up the back step of the kitchen door and put the shopping down on the floor. She looked around the living room in dismay. There was no fire burning in the hearth the room felt icy cold. The children sitting there on log stools. They hadn't seemed to have noticed how cold that it was their attention was focused on a television programme. Hannah could see that they had made an effort to make a decent fire but their efforts had been futile they had covered it with coal slack. They had not known that it would never burn unless that was only used to back up dry logs of wood or of a good quality coal.

Some thing had to be done? Hannah took off her wet clothes and threw them over a chair in the back. She was hungry; she had not eaten since she had been sitting at the bus station waiting for a bus earlier in the day. Tins of soup were opened and the contents heated in a saucepan on the calor gas cooker at the same time Hannah toasted rounds of bread under the grill. First things first she thought lets eat. There is no point going out to the shed to chop sticks to make a better fire. Next job, hot water bottles and then they would go to bed. She told the children to keep their socks on and to put a pullover on over their night- clothes. They were soon settled down. But where was George what Hannah knew of him he would have left any work that he was doing and scurried home at the first sign of a snow flake falling. She decided that there was no point waiting for him to come home, she had no idea where he could be. The possibility of him driving home now was very remote, the wind had drifted the snow in the lanes and he would have great difficulty getting the van home. She switched off the down stair lights and went to bed. Thank goodness that she did not have to go to work next day. It was Thursday her day off. There would be no school tomorrow the school bus would not be able to come down the lane. She looked through the bedroom window to the woods across the road. The snow had stopped falling and as the moon shone through the trees they looked quite ghostly yet very beautiful and at the same time it looked quite eerie.

It looked as if there was to be quite a severe frost by morning. She got into bed. The hot water bottle felt good as Hannah held it close to her. Her feet felt better but her whole body shook with exhaustion as she tried to settle and sleep at first she dozed fitfully and the finally went into a deep sleep.

Morning dawned a bright crisp day. It had frozen hard during the latter part on the night. The sun was weak and low in the sky as it tried to rise and shine through the trees. What a contrast to yesterday thought Hannah as she put her woolly sock covered feet into a pair of George's Wellington boots and made her way to his workshop for dry wood to enable her to light a fire. There was always cut offs under the workbench plus plenty of wood shavings. She was busy chopping the dry wood into sticks when it dawned on her that he had not come home. I wonder where he spent the night she said to her self as she filled the bucket with sticks and took a fresh bucket of coal in with her at the same time. Back inside the fire was soon burning brightly she must have the living room warmed up before the children came down. She had knitted mittens and gloves for them. These would be wet in no time at all once they started to play out side in the freshly fallen snow. These would need to be dried and she knew that they would not be able to get out there quick enough. Drying wet clothes was a nightmare during the winter months. It all had to be put on clothes-maids and placed around the fire when they went to bed. If Hannah went up before George he would often forget about this when he had condescended to switch the telly off and turn in.

Drinking the freshly made hot tea, Hannah thought about the night before when she had walked across Coalmoor carrying three large bags of shopping in the blizzard. The realisation began to dawn on her "I did it. I coped," she said to her self "I coped I did it" Where? Was George? As far as she was concerned she did not care she was beginning to realise how much that she had taken on during the last twelve months and survived. Realisation dawned on her that she was coping with every thing more or less on her own. I'll not stay in this place another winter she said aloud as she looked around the room. Thinking how cold the bedrooms were up stairs. It's a wonder that we are alive and healthy and not dead from pneumonia .I will look for something which has got its entire roof on and not a house where you can see the stars from the landing.

And some where it will be bit easier to dry the washing in the winter months".

The idea appealed to her but how on earth would she go about it. At times Molly's words kept echoing around her head. She really surprised herself with her thoughts. It is time that we had a decent bathroom and Jennifer has her own bedroom. Her thoughts did not include George. He shall please him self she said to the now brightly burning fire warming the room. I could have died on that moor last night I was really frightened I did not think that I was going to make it at times I felt so exhausted. I wonder if he would have cared.

"Stop it Stop it", She told her self this is crazy thinking. Of course George cared for her. He had promised faithfully to finish the house this summer. And what had he done, bugger all, only get him self into more debt. Noise from the floor above let her know that the children had woken. Come down to earth and stop dreaming she told herself. She got up to prepare breakfast for them. All thoughts about finding some where to live went from her mind as she later watched the three of them playing and romping in the snow. It was afternoon before the snowplough came down the lane. George was still not at home. It was when they were having their evening meal that he did return and he was full of excuses as to why he had not been at home all night. "What a blizzard" he remarked.

No use of me trying to make it home"

"You could have rung"

"But I knew that you were here".

"Mum was late "chipped in Michael

"How late?"

"It was dark"

"Where had she been and why was she late? George was soon asking questions. He wanted to know? "Trouble with the busses you had the van remember. Where were you?"

"I called in to see Jim and Sandra and they persuaded me to sleep on their couch and not be silly enough to try and get home. I will be only too glad to get a decent sleep, tonight".

"Why had he been to see Jim and Sandra. Hannah did not ask and for some unknown reason she did not want to know

Now that Jim and Sandra were further away Hannah did not see so much of her. They came for tea on a Sunday now and again which Hannah gladly provided. Now that she was going out to work there was no time to communicate with the rest of the family. Where as Sandra seemed to know how each one was getting on and what they were doing? She kept close contact with Elizabeth whose two girls often stayed with her.

"Thank goodness that the snow plough has been" Hannah remarked to George "Will you need the grey van tomorrow. If not I will take it to work".

"That will be alright. There is not much that I can do in this weather".

"Well it is different for me the customers will expect me to deliver their bread what ever the weather conditions are. Let's hope that it is not as bad in town as it is here". As the evening wore on Hannah started to think what had George been doing over at Sandra's. Perhaps he had to help Len with some work they often did each other a favour; he must have called on his way back. She made up her mind to ask Sandra's next time that she spoke to her. George seemed to be so temperamental these days Hannah decided that it would be better not to ask too many questions as to where he went. Now that they were both working he was able to start paying off some of the debts that he had incurred while he had been working for himself.

George's moods swayed to good, bad or indifferent. Money was still a problem and Hannah could not see him getting on with any more building done to the house. There was getting a time when she could no longer understand him and she was beginning to feel afraid of him. Why was he so moody? Nothing seemed to be right for him. What more could she do? He criticised the food that she cooked for him this was not good enough or that was not properly cooked. Hannah was getting very puzzled she thought that she was a fairly good cook. May be a bit plain but it was always very wholesome.

There was no spare money to buy un-necessary luxuries but the family was not going short of any thing.

Spring went into summer. George was doing nothing further to the house. If she mentioned it he would snap her head off and start swearing about how ungrateful that she was. Hannah wondered if he could be suffering from depression. He seemed to portray all the symptoms. She decided that she would have a word with their Doctor. She found that she had wasted her time Doctor Price just dismissed her and saying that he could not prescribe any thing He explained that he would have to see George and if George was not prepared to go and see him that there was nothing that he could do. This later dawned on Hannah that it was plain common sense. Any Doctor could not prescribe for a patient with out a consultation.

"You should worry about your self not him by the look of you. You look very tired," Dr Price commented "Well I am doing some very silly things these days"

"What exactly are you doing that you could be worried about?"

"I keep putting things in their wrong places I forget what I am doing There are times when I think that I must be cracking up mentally"

"I don't think so" He reassured her "You come back and have a chat with me if you think that you are getting any worse I will then be able to advise you what to do or give you some medication to help you." He sounded genuinely concerned so Hannah promised the she would come back if things got any worse.

George's moods did not improve, infact Hannah thought that he was getting much worse and she was becoming afraid of him and she decided that she was not going to put up with it. She tried to talk to him.

"Why are you so moody George I am beginning to worry about you .You seem to be absolutely impossible to live with these days Why not go and have a check up at the doctors. Dr Price might be able to prescribe you some thing to calm you down. I don't think that there would be any harm done if you were to go and see him".

Hannah quickly realised that she had said too much and touched a raw nerve.

"What are you trying to say" He shouted, "You think that I am going around the bend. It is not me it is you. I don't go around putting things in the wrong places. I think that it is you who needs to see the quack not me".

"Well it just might surprise you that I have already had a check up. I have seen the Doctor and he says that there is nothing wrong with me"

"Huh that's what he thinks. You've been going around the bend for the last twelve months. You don't see your self and the daft things that you are doing" The smirk that crossed his face contained no love what so ever and Hannah had noticed it. He had looked evil. His words had stung Hannah and she was worried. Why should George be thinking these dreadful things about her? She could not win. I have one of two choices she told her self I live with it or I do some thing about it. But what could she do? The fact that she was earning some money gave her some independence. If she decided to leave him then the responsibility would be enormous and a totally different kettle of fish.

Where could she go? What about the children? Could she leave with out them? No she knew that she could never do that. Where ever she went the children would have to go with her. No way could she live with out her children. Every day Hannah found herself turning these things over in her mind. George's moods were not improving since she had said that she had seen the doctor he seemed to be getting worse and she was becoming more afraid of him she did not know what to talk about when he was at home. The slightest thing would set him off shouting what he would do for her. Hannah was afraid that he just might hit her again and how far he would go she could not anticipate nor could she afford to not to go to work if he were to hit her and she suffered injuries that she would not be able to go to work. She might lose her job. Brian had made it quite clear that she was to be reliable. Other wise he would not give her the job. Customers depended on having their bread delivered daily.

I will see the council and put my name down for a house or a flat she decided one morning when she had left the house. George had just given her a mouth full of abuse as she went out to work. What if he found out? He could be very nasty these days He would probably kill me. What should she do? If in doubt don't. That had always been her motto. In doubt to stay or in doubt to leave. She did nothing for a little while longer. George seemed to resent her independence by earning her own money not that Hannah spent it on her self. George gave very little of what he was earning. It was going to take him a long time to get back on top financially. Every penny that he earned was needed to pay of the debts that he had incurred.

Hannah plucked up courage to call in at the council offices on her way home from work one afternoon. She asked if it would be possible to rent a council house.

"We don't offer help to people like you". She was informed. "With a waiting list like the one our council has You have no chance what so ever. You have to be destitute and on the street before we are allowed to offer any help. We will how ever put your name down" Hannah sat and watched as the woman filled in various forms when finished she stood up and thanked her for listening to her and then left the office feeling completely disappointed. She made her way home.

Hannah was turning over in her mind what she had been told. She suddenly said to her self. I can't believe it, I really can't I only went into the council offices and put my name down for a house. I must be going out of my mind".

George had been working away that week and when he came home at the weekend he was in a foul mood.

"George "Hannah said to him "What is the matter with you. You have not spoken a civil word to any of us all weekend. Have I done any thing wrong"?

"You don't seem to do any thing right" He snarled

"What on earth do you mean by that remark? What more can I do for you"?

"You don't do any thing for me. You are too busy keeping that boss of yours happy"

"What do you mean by that remark?"

"It's Brian this and Brian that".

"That is ludicrous I don't see much of him I only see him when I get there in the mornings and have to load the van. The weeks that you are working away makes so much more for me to do here. You know that I have to get home as quickly as I can. There is so much to done, what with the washing cooking and then there is the garden. Don't forget that I even have to chop the wood for the fire."

"Oh call yourself a cook do you. In the digs where I have been staying. I had chicken cooked a damned site better than what you can cook one She could run rings around you"

"In that case why do you bother to come home? .If you are looked after so well. Perhaps it would be better if you were to stay away all together".

"You are my wife and I have come back for you"

"Well if you expect me to sleep with you when you are so nasty to me. You can think again"

"You're my wife and you will do as I say"

"Oh indeed lord and master"

"That's what you think is it. George caught hold of Hannah and roughly dragged her up stairs. No passion existed between them now Hannah felt as if she was being raped. George had no mercy, he had to satisfy him self. Hannah felt bruised and battered and dreaded the consequences. She hated him and dreaded being near him the thought of him making her pregnant terrified her. If that were to happen it would mean that she would have to give up her job, and then she would have no money to live on. If that happened she now knew that George would only gloat. When he came home at the weekends he was getting impossible to live with. Hannah was finding that she and the children were much happier when he was away. What she did not know was that he was missing going to bed with Sandra and he only had Hannah who he could take it out on. He knew that he could not go on living with out Sandra but did not know what to do about it.

As the weeks went by Hannah decided that she must do something, no way could she go on like this? Her health was beginning to suffer; she was thinking that she was cracking up mentally. The thought of having a mental breakdown haunted her. To be locked up in a mental hospital she could not contemplate. She knew that she had to keep sane for the sake of the children. The more agitated that she became the more George would try to convince her that she was going mad, so that she would start to believe it. The winter would soon be here again I must try and get out of this house and the lane. She started to make inquiries here and there for a house to rent but she had to be very discreet. If George found out what she was planning to do he would probably kill her. He wanted to keep his cake and eat it. He had made it quite clear to her that he would kill her if ever she dared to leave him especially if there was another man involved. Hannah knew that he meant it.

"Don't think of it that is if you want to stay alive"

"But George I can't live with you any more I can't cope with your moods you frighten me you argue that there is nothing wrong with you. You say that it is my imagination when I have asked you to see Doctor Price. Have you found some one else another woman perhaps"?

"No" bellowed George "There is nothing wrong with me. Get that idea out of your sick head. And you could not blame me if I did go with another woman you are just an iceberg"

Hannah was very careful who she confided in She told both Molly and Judith that she could take no more. They symphasized with her and told her that they had expected this for a long time and they convinced her to look for some where else to live as soon as possible before it was too late. They were very reluctant to say what they thought George was up to and whom he was seeing. They had talked this over at great length and had thought that it would be best not to suggest to Hannah that Sandra might be involved.

Molly had had her intuitions for some years now. She and Judith felt that if they named Sandra, Hannah would not believe them. If it dawned on her that what they said could be right. She would probably crack up altogether and neither of them wanted to be responsible for that happening. It did not bear thinking about. Hannah asked her sisters hoping that they just might know of a cottage that was empty and up for rent. They each said that they knew of nothing but promised that if they did hear of any thing going and that they would let her know if they heard any thing on the grapevine.

Sandra persuaded Jim to go for a ride and see Hannah and George and then we can call on the old folk on our way back. Perhaps Hannah will give us a bit of tea so I won't take any thing with us. Save a few pennies. She knew that if she was showing that she was interested in saving a few pennies she would keep on the right side of Jim She knew that he liked to take care of the pennies as he called it. It was not that he ever kept her short of house keeping money. Some weeks he often wondered what on earth that she spent it on. If she were to do a bit more cooking and not buy every thing ready made that they ate. He was certain that they could save a little more .He dared not say any thing he knew that she would fly off the handle and call him the most dreadful names. So consequently he kept quiet for most of the time but he was absolutely sick of fish and chips and meat pies.

Hannah had finished the washing up and then made an excuse to take Sandra to look at the garden. The two men and the children were watching a film they had eaten a really good tea. Jim could not help notice how Hannah had made a salad of things that she had grown in the garden Lettuce, celery, and beetroot. It looked as if she had only bought the tomatoes and salad cream she had boiled a piece of ham to have with it. There was buttered scones with home made jam and the sponge cake that Hannah had apologised for because it was still warm had tasted so good with the butter cream and Jam that she had put in it Being a hard working man he had a big appetite. He gladly accepted and he made the most of second helpings that Hannah offered him.

Hannah asked Sandra that if she were to hear of a cottage to let would she let her know.

"Why what is going on" Sandra inquired

"I can't go on through another winter in this house. Hannah told her. "If I were you I wouldn't visit any more. I don't intend to stay here if George does not improve".

"You would not leave him would you"?

"Oh yes I would".

"Then what?" Sandra tried to hide her smile of good fortune. George was winning. It was working.

"Divorce him"

"Really but what about the family

"Sod the family. I have had enough

"But Hannah what about the scandal"?

"So what I've had enough and I don't care any more"

Sandra had heard all that she wanted to hear. OK I will be in touch if I hear of any thing going. You never know "They talked about the family and other subjects and soon had to go inside as Jim was getting agitated he wanted to be off

"Best of luck, "Sandra said to Hannah as Jim drove away and their car was soon gone out of sight up the lane.

Don't bother calling on the old folks "Sandra said to Jim "Let's get back we can come another Sunday".

"They will not like it if they hear that we have passed so close to them with out calling in"

"That's a chance that we will take John is tired and I would rather get him home and now that we have moved there is so much more to do".

"I agree with you there. Perhaps you are right I will keep going and head for home".

Sandra could not believe her ears; When Hannah had told her that she was thinking about leaving George. Their plans were working". She sat in the passenger seat with John on her knee and she had the biggest smile on her face as Jim drove home. "What are you looking so pleased about" He asked

"Oh nothing in particular just some thing that Hannah had said.

"Must have been good news. Since we started back from their place, you have looked like the cat that had swallowed the cream."

"Oh it's nothing just a joke that she told me. Remind me to tell you sometime"

"Well why not now?"

"No it is not that important it does not matter". Jim concentrated on the road ahead and gave no more thought to Sandra's joke, it was nice to see Sandra in such a good mood and happy for once. Which he did not see very often?

It is working thought Sandra to her self. It is working. Once she leaves I will be free of this lot. George you are wonderful. I knew that you could do it. I know now that you need me far more than you need her. I knew you could do it

"By the way I saw that you ate plenty. Sandra suddenly broke the silence. "Hannah will think that I don't feed you properly"

"Oh do you think that I made a bit of a pig of myself. I do hope that Hannah and George did not think that. But I did enjoy that home made cooking. Reminded me of my mother".

Jim instantly realised that he had said the wrong thing referring to his mother Sandra had not taken to her and she had not taken to Sandra at all. There was very little love lost between the two women".

"So if that is how you feel you can go and live with your mother if you are not satisfied. Jim Lad"

"Jim did not bother to answer He had to be up early the next morning and they had stayed longer than they had intended watching the film and having tea. He was glad that they had not called on her Mother and Dad tonight, it would be too late and he did not feel like having an argument with Sandra tonight". To his amazement Sandra quickly snapped out of her bad mood and she seemed to be enjoying the journey back .At times when he glanced across at her she was actually smiling.

George was finding that he could not do with out Sandra He now knew that he needed her. He told Hannah that he would be working down south in Oxford the next week. Actually he lied he was not going down south at all He was working near Wolverhampton. This gave him a chance to visit Sandra while Jim was at work. During the week to save money he called at a friend's house in Trench for a cup of tea and a sandwich not thinking that he would bump into his sister Judith. They had a chat and Judith quickly went on her way not giving it any thought about meeting her brother except that Hannah had told that he was working away all week".

Judith told Hannah about seeing him when they had a chat the next week.

"I thought that you said that George was working away last week".

"I did he was working somewhere near Oxford"

"Not when I saw him in Trench".

"Surely you were mistaken"

"Hannah I know my own brother when I speak to him. You ask him when he comes home at the weekend".

Hannah did just as Judith had said. George was already at home when she arrived home from work on the Friday. This was unusual if he was working down South he would normally not be back until later in the evening.

When they had eaten the evening meal and the children were in bed. George had been quite pleasant and was sat watching the telly. He had been to bed with Sandra that very afternoon. He had made sure that the work that he had been asked to do in Wolverhampton was finished by lunchtime. This had left him with the entire

afternoon to himself.

Hannah looked up from her knitting and just casually said" I have been talking to Judith and she said that she was pleased to have a chat with you during the week when she saw you in Trench. I thought that you were working down South." Hannah was watching him quite closely to see what his re-action was going to be She was quite startled by the look on his face She could not make out whether it was anger or surprise.

George emphatically denied being anywhere near Shropshire.

"Tell Judith to get her specs changed. Spoke to me? How could she I was a hundred miles away do you want the proof?"

"No George I was a bit puzzled that's all I could not think why you would be in Trench when you said that you were working in Oxford"

"You bloody women are all the same Seeing things Imagining things She must be going the same way as you are completely daft. It is enough to get a body hung it is and you would between the two of you. Got nothing better to do than gossip on the phone".

Hannah did not bother to answer. She had seen Judith in town. They had not spoken on the phone. She concentrated on the pattern of the cardigan that she was working on. They went to bed that night but neither of them made any conversation.

Sunday morning there was a dinner to cook Washing, Ironing and getting every thing ready for Monday morning.

George had stood watching her she had not realised that he was standing there.

"What's this that I hear about you looking for somewhere else to live" Hannah was taken by surprise. How on earth could George have found out?

Stumbling over her words she replied "Nothing really George I haven't done anything about finding any where else to live its just that"

"Just that what," He caught hold of her so roughly, his voice was like the hiss of a snake." Get one thing straight woman. You can bugger off if you like tomorrow but you will never take the kids. Get that clear Never, he shouted and shook her violently.

Was she hearing properly, she apparently did not mean anything to George and this was just beginning to dawn on her? He did not love her, how could he if he was prepared to let her go just like that. He is cracking up He is ill Hannah was trying to convince her self.

She made an appointment to see Doctor Price and she told him of George's behaviour.

"My advice to you is to look for somewhere else to live and you must get out from there if you can and I strongly advise you to make it sooner than later. It is not you who needs help it is your husband"

Hannah thanked him and left the surgery. George's words played on her mind she went over and over what he had screamed at her, time and time again and then she convinced her self that the Doctor did have a point. She began to realise that she was scared stiff of George and that she now knew that she was afraid of him. I must do something but what?

Weeks went by Hannah thought of a plan it just might work if she had the caravan towed from the sea. You never know Mother and Dad just might have forgiven me for marrying him. Perhaps her mother and dad would let her put the caravan at their farm. She could get another job and they would be there to keep an eye on the children during the holidays what a good idea". She said to her self. The next time that she went to visit them she broached her idea to them. She quickly had quite a shock, their reaction soon brought her down to earth No way would they consider such a thing.

"You made your bed lady now you can lie on it" Dorothy shouted. "We never liked that George but you would not listen to us, now you can get on with it and don't you go bringing any scandal such as divorcing him to this family or you will not hear the end of it from us"

Hannah looked around the room at all the familiar objects of her childhood. The grandmother clock chimed. She got up and said that she must be getting back. I'll just call the children. They loved visiting the farm they liked to play in the farm buildings and in the hay. Hide and seek and kicking a football around the stack yard. They had much more fun playing outside than sat in the house listening to the family gossip and events.

Hannah and the children said their goodbyes and went off home. As she drove back Hannah realised exactly where she stood as far as her parents were concerned there would be no help from that quarter. She knew that she must find a way.

"What still here" George sneered. When he came home at the next weekend.

"Of course" Replied Hannah

"You haven't buggered off then. No where to go is that it. This place is not good enough for you? Well I want to see if you can get any thing better. Even your parents don't want you"

Hannah remained silent; it was better not to say anything He had come home in one of his foul moods. She must get through the weekend and pray and hope that he would be working away the next week. How did he know that she had been to see her Mother and Dad she had no idea? Sandra and Jim had been to see them and Sandra had told them that Hannah was not satisfied with George any more she wanted some thing better So consequently Dorothy had told Sandra that Hannah had been to see them about bringing the caravan home.

"I told her straight" Dorothy had told Sandra I'll not have them here She married him now she can get on with it" Sandra had been able to tell George all about it when they had been having their little tete- a- tetes on the phone. He had the audacity to reverse the charges so that Jim would end up paying the phone bill. He can pay the bill my Darling it allows us to talk a little longer.

The weekends were becoming a nightmare. Hannah and the children dreaded George coming home and it was beginning to show.

Hannah spoke to Molly about it. "You know Hannah I've told you time and time again that you would be better off with out that man. If the worst comes to the worst you can always come here. You know that we will manage some how. The council has offered me a flat that is if I am prepared to give up this bungalow so that they could let another elderly couple have it. I've made up my mind that now that Terry has passed on, I would like to go back to live in Birmingham and apparently I am eligible for one of Cadbury's bungalows. The years that I worked there have given me entitlement to one. What do you think?"

"I think that it would be a wonderful idea for you if you were to accept but we would miss you so very much."

"I have given it a lot of thought I would be much nearer Elaine and Joan and I do miss the city life. Perhaps the council would be able to help you its worth a try"

"Well Molly I did put my name down some time ago infact it was last year"

"Well I am going to tell you straight and that is I reckon that if you don't get out from where you are there will be murder done and it won't be you who stays alive. . .You mark my words that is if you live long enough to tell the story. That George has the look of the devil himself at times. I have seen it for a long time now and I reckon that he is mucking about with another woman".

"Molly what will you say next, another woman. George would not do that I am sure"

"I'm sure my foot why do you think that he is behaving like he is? You seem to forget that I am older than you. I have seen it all before. What ever he is up to, I am sure that he is up to no good".

"But he behaves as if he is ill I'm convinced all the worry about money is causing him to crack up. No man would behave as he is doing if he was in his right mind would They?"

"Hannah it is the oldest trick in the book. It has gone on since time began. Give the wife hell on earth then when you have got out or cracked up and been taken away then that opens the door for the other floozy to move in".

"Molly I don't think that he is seeing another woman".

"The trouble with you is that you don't look any further than the end of your nose. You only see what you want to see. Women have always been the same. The best thing that you can do is to get out. And the sooner the better. You and Jennifer can have the double bed in the spare room; we can manage the boys between us. Judith will give us a hand I am sure. Give me a bit of notice that is if you decide to do anything you know that we will help you all we can

"Molly I will certainly give it some thought. It is a great comfort to know that we will have a refuge to come to that is if the worst comes to the worst"

"It will. It will. You know. Just you don't stay in that house until it is too late if you crack up what are those kids going to do with out their Mum?"

Hannah pondered and thought about Molly's words for the next few days. Did George have another woman, but whom? He had said that the woman in Oxford cooked a chicken much better than she ever could. Perhaps that is who it is. There was no evidence of his wanting to hurry to work in that area, He moaned and moaned about the travelling that he had to do. No Molly was wrong Hannah decided. There was not another woman in George's life to her he was behaving like he was a sick man. The things that he had accused her of convinced her that he had to be sick and that he needed help. Perhaps if I were to leave and go and stay with Molly just for a week He might come to his senses and agree to get some help

Yes that was worth thinking about. Hannah suggested this idea to Molly next time that she saw her

"That might do him some good "Molly had replied "You could try it. Let us say the next time that the children are off school and are on holiday. If he comes home and finds no one waiting for him to wait on him hand and foot. It might work but I doubt it George is a clever one and there is no mistaking the fact". "OK now that's all fixed up and we will give it a try" Hannah, Molly and Judith agreed to carry out their plan. They fixed it up to try it in a couple of week's time. Hannah decided that she would take a change of clothes Etc; to Judith's next week. Jumpers, jeans and things that they would need.

George came home at the weekend and they all had a very pleasant weekend, no rows. Sunday evening Hannah had put the twins to bed and had settled down with her knitting. At the same time keeping an eye on the television. Watching a programme with George and Michael. But Hannah was not too happy about it.

"George do you think that we should be watching this. "Why what is wrong with it? He laughed. The film was about a newly discovered Amazon tribe in the tropics. Half-naked women were performing their tribal dance, they were bare breasted and were dancing in a much suggestive manner. Hannah felt that it was not suitable for a young boy to be watching.

"That's not what you said last week when you were watching one like it; you could not get me into bed quick enough"

"I have not seen a programme like this one before with you and I certainly did not jump into bed with you as quick as I could".

George suddenly realised what he had said. "You did Last Saturday night last weekend" He was trying to cover up his mistake

Hannah remained silent. So he had been to bed with some one else. But whom had he been to bed with? The very thought of him being in bed with someone else and then coming home to make love to her when he felt like it but thank goodness that it was not very often. The thought made Hannah feel sick. She felt dirty and used she felt really sick. Her thoughts were racing away with her as she tried to concentrate on the film. Molly was right. Hannah put away her knitting and picked up the supper things at the same time calling to Michael that it was time for him to go to bed.

"Leave him a bit longer" George said "Watching this won't do him any harm. He has to know about these things sooner than later".

"As you say I am going to bed" Once Hannah was in bed her thoughts were in turmoil racing around her head. Molly was right he does have some one else. That has settled it I am not staying here any longer than I have to I am getting some where else to live for the kids and myself. I will find some where. She knew better that to confront George and make a scene He could turn nasty and if he were to lose his temper she could end up getting seriously hurt. She had witnessed George when he had lost his temper many times before. That is not the answer she decided. I will take things one step at a time and get out when I am good and ready. On her next day off she took the box of cartridges from the cupboard where George kept them. These were for his twelve-bore shotgun. She took them down the road to her friend and neighbour Mabel Parker and asked her to keep them. I don't trust my self. She told her friend if he loses his temper with me again I swear that I will pick up his gun and shoot him. If you have the cartridges at least I can't be done for murder. "

"I would have killed him long a go if my Paul had been carrying on like George has"

"What do you mean? I have only just found out that he has some one else."

"Oh nothing it is about time that you came to your senses. You know that you can depend on me if ever you need help. You were a god send to me when I was learning to drive You took me all over the town and showed me how to pass the test

I could not have done it with out you. My Paul was far too scared to sit by the side of me". When Hannah arrived home from work on one Monday in October she prepared the tea for her self and the children Michael was now thirteen and the twins had turned ten. They were growing up so quickly. There was no sign of George He must be working away she thought. He must have left after she had gone to work. She was mistaken George came home in a foul temper. Finding fault with every thing and everyone.

"George if you don't stop it and leave us alone I will walk out of here and not come back". Hannah said very firmly.

"Walk out would you?" He sneered you wouldn't dare. You are crazy in the head. Do you know that you are crazy? Been talking behind my back you have making out that it is me who needs help. I'm not going daft you know. Not me. It's you and he raised his hand as if to strike her" She stepped back very smartly. And he sat down again.

"Well you tell me why are you behaving as you are if there is nothing wrong with you? Neither the kids nor I are putting up with it any longer. I have asked and asked you to stop coming home in such bad moods but nothing that I say makes any difference".

George stood up and started shouting the most horrible things at Hannah she really thought that he was going to hit her this time. With out stopping to think she ordered the twins to put on their coats and she picked up her own and her hand bag Michael put your coat on you are coming with me"

"Michael is not going anywhere "George screamed and raised his fist.

Michael looked at Hannah not knowing what was going on she had never hinted to them that she was thinking of leaving now he could not understand what he was expected to do. I'll stay with my dad He answered.

"Alright I will come back for you"

"You'll do no such thing" George hissed like a rattlesnake about to strike.

Hannah took hold of the twins by the hand and walked out through the door.

"And don't think that you are coming back" George shouted after her.

It was quite dark out side "Where are we going "whispered Jennifer"

"To stay with Auntie Judith Just walk along with me.

They walked down the lane to her neighbour's house. "Could you do a favour for me Mabel? "Hannah asked.

"Of course I will" she replied

"Take us to Wrockwardine "

"Of course. Just climb in the landrover, I have been waiting for this to happen for a long time now". She said as they drove down the lane the opposite way to where George was.

"What do you mean waiting for this to happen I have not long found out about him having another woman I think that it is some one down south where he has been working"

"Oh really Well I think that you are in for a shock or two. "

"What do you mean Mabel"

"I'm saying no more I think that it is best that I don't" They travelled the rest of the way in silence.

They all climbed out of the Landrover at Judith's and Hannah thanked her.

"No need for thanks Best of luck you are going to need it". She turned the vehicle around and was soon out of sight. No more questions were asked. Her friend Mabel knew what had been going on at that house just up the road. Old Tom had kept them informed a hell of a lot of what Hannah apparently did not know about. Boy oh boy was Hannah in for a shock when she found out what her precious little sister had been up to and sure enough she would find out. It had been the village gossip for years George's van being parked up out side Sandra's so often and old Tom had kept them informed when he went for his Saturday pint He told of the rows That George had not known that he had been overheard when he had come home and had started to row with Hannah. He knew when Sandra had been to the house with George behind Hannah's back. Little had passed his eyes even the night when George had come home in a vile temper and seen a stray dog in the yard sniffing after his dog. How he had taken a piece of wire and strangled it then he had dragged it up the wood. When the owner came around looking for it. George denied ever seeing the dog. What he did not know that he had been watched from the little bedroom window that looked down on his yard that moonlight night.

Judith opened the door to their knock and took one look at Hannah and guessed what had happened,

"We've been expecting this. Come in and let's get the twins to bed. Then we can and try and sort things out a bit"

"Oh don't worry I am sure George will come to his senses by morning and he will come to fetch us back." Hannah was trying really hard to hold back the tears.

"Well you just kip down on the settee for tonight. It won't hurt the twins to have a day off school tomorrow

Days went by; there was no sign of George coming to collect them. At least Hannah was able to relax but it was not very comfortable sleeping on Judith's settee. Judith persuaded Hannah to go with her and see George and fetch some clothes for the children. They decided to go one evening when Carl had finished work and that he could keep an eye on them.

Judith drove the Morris minor and parked it on the road out side of the house. They went in through the back door Hannah walked into the living room where she saw George and Michael watching the television.

Surprise showed on George's face when he saw her. "What the bloody hell do you want? He shouted," Not knowing that Judith was just behind her." Think that you can come bloody crawling back when you want to. Well get one thing straight you walked out on us so you can walk out again because you are not stopping here. I don't want you. Several swear words followed. When he saw Judith his face froze but he quickly composed him self

"You're here as well hasn't the guts to come on her bloody own"

"I'm not surprised," Judith said "If this is how you behave." She turned to Hannah "Go and get some clothes for the kids that is all that we have come for".

Hannah made her way quickly upstairs and left George and Judith rowing below.

She quickly grabbed what clothes she could and as she closed the dressing table drawer she noticed the wooden jewellery box that George had made her when they had been courting. Hannah had always treasured that box it was made of mahogany. The lid had been inlaid with other woods and it shone from years of polishing. She re-appeared in the living room George noticed that she had the box in her hand. He had promised Sandra that one day she should have that box .He had told her that he had made it with love and that she was the only one he had any love for now.

"You are not taking that with you "He shouted and jumped up from his chair. He grabbed the box from Hannah's hand"

"Its mine "Hannah said defiantly

"Well you shall have it" He threw it at Hannah. She ducked and it hit the wall with such force that it smashed into pieces.

"Get out of here "Urged Judith.

"Michael" Hannah pleaded, "Please come with me"

"George Stood in front of her Michael is not going any where so get out the pair of you"

"I will take you to court" Protested Hannah.

"You do that, but Michael is staying with me"

"Come on. Come on "Judith insisted. Before some one gets hurt". Hannah went out and got into the car and put the bundle of clothes that she was carrying onto the back seat. "Why would Michael not come with me" She started to cry the tears running down her face.

"He will" Judith tried to console her as she drove away and out of the lane.

"Not if George has his way. Judith I can't leave him here"

"He will be alright Now that he has got you out of the house if that is what you can call it. Half a one is more like it. He will not harm Michael but I can see that it is not safe for you to stop and argue any more.

"They drove back to Judith's in silence both preoccupied with their thoughts. At least we have a few clothes for the twins commented Judith as they pulled up out side her house.

"We will manage" Was all that Hannah could say. She was still in shock at George's re-action She had thought that he might have persuaded her to come back She had not prepared herself for the reception that she had received.

"Manage how? What about you?" Judith was still reeling from George's onslaught.

"Wash and wear" Hannah started to laugh more from relief than fright. I'll wear clothes one day and wash them at night.

"I still can't believe that it was George behaving like that Judith was telling Carl of what had taken place. He's flipped his lid"

"I did not want you two to go alone. The man's mad. Promise me that you won't go near that house again either of you with out some one with you.

"But what about Michael". Pleaded Hannah.

"George will take care of him," Judith said trying to comfort Hannah "He idolises the boy. Michael is an intelligent boy and can look after himself you know. It is amazing what they are capable of at that age. What you have got to do is to decide about George. No way can you go back to live there"

"Yes I understand that. When he is so angry he is dangerous but then I have seen it all before. Thank goodness that I have my job at least I can pay my way but firstly I have to find somewhere for us to live. We have to get our own place and get one quickly. I cannot impose on you a day longer than I have to"

"Molly and I have had a talk and she says that you and Jennifer are to sleep there and David will share Robin's room here, it's a pity that you had not got out long ago".

Hannah started looking for some where to live but she did not have much idea of where to start. She was finding that it was so difficult not having the van to get around in. She missed it so much Walking from Wrockwardine to work each morning certainly took more time and energy. She went around for a few weeks in the state of shock, what was she going to do. Molly and Judith were wonderful to allow them to stay but Hannah knew that it could only be a temporary arrangement. She really had to find some where for herself and the twins and then she could see what she could do about getting Michael to come and live with them No way was she going to leave him living with his father. That would be no home life for her son. She tried to imagine what it must be like for him to come in from school and finding the house empty. Who would do his washing? George had not done any washing in his life as far as she knew neither had he done any cooking. Was George still going away to work? A thousand and one things raced through her mind.

She was out now and she had to keep going. Her wages were the only money she had. The twins must go to school it would mean them having to catch busses to get there. Hannah was beginning to feel quite ill. Was it the relief of getting away or was it the fact that she was working too hard and had been for so long under such stress and pressure. Judith persuaded her to see her Doctor and have a chat she said that it could do no harm if it did not do much good He might be able to give her something to help her get some sleep at nights.

Doctor Price was pleased to hear that she had got out for her own safety and said that she was not to worry about Michael he would be taken care of but he failed to tell Hannah exactly what he thought. He said that he thought that it would not be long before another woman took her place. He prescribed her some capsules to be taken daily and with a genuine smile he wished her all the best and that she was to look to the future and not dwell on the past. It was alright for him to talk thought Hannah but the past is all that I have got right now and not all of that until I can persuade Michael to come and live with me.

Chapter Eighteen

Joy or be it No Joy

Later that night George did not know how he really felt after Hannah and the twins had walked out. He did not know whether he should feel disappointed or angry because she had gone. The one thing he quickly realised was that he had to keep on the right side of Michael in case he lost him as well.

"Don't you worry lad" He said to his son. "We will be alright I will be here tomorrow, I'm packing my job in and looking for something a bit closer to home You have no need to worry I will take good care of you."

"'I'm alright" Michael "replied. He did not have much idea of the enormity of his mother walking out.

"Next morning George was up early He began to realise what a relief it was to him that Hannah had gone Where to he did not care, One of her sisters, he had thought. He saw Michael off to school. He reassured him again not to worry, as every thing would be all right. He could not settle to do any thing, he had to ring Sandra. By nine o'clock He knew that Jim would already be at work. He rang her and told her that Hannah had walked out wondering how she would react.

"That is wonderful news. Darling you did it. You've got rid of her. You say that she has gone, you are wonderful. Have you any idea where she has gone? Has she taken the kids?"

"She has taken the twins Michael is still here and here he is going to stay I've sent him to school and I am going to look for some work closer to home and be rid of all the travelling".

Dam thought Sandra why had she not taken Michael with her. I must tread carefully. "Darling, I can't wait to get away from Jim so that I can be with you. John will get on so well with Michael after all they are brothers. Just think they are your very own sons"

"Just hold on there a minute Do nothing for the time being" George was getting slightly worried. Trying to answer all of her questions. He suddenly began to wonder what moves that Sandra was going to make next and to what lengths that she was prepared to go.

I will come over and spend the day with you, just tell me when My Darling what about next Thursday I can tell Jim that I am shopping with Sally."

"Are you sure that you can trust Sally?"

"You leave me to worry about that my Darling I will fix any thing just to be with you for a whole day"

George agreed that he would pick her up near Sally's the following Thursday morning.

"I can't wait to be with you. Thursday it is then".

After cooing and reassuring each other of their love they said Cheerio George promising to ring her every day until they could be together.

Sandra was ecstatic all morning she was so excited at last George had rid himself of Hannah. The way he had spoken to her this morning did not give any indication of him asking her to go back. Soon he would be hers. She now knew that all she had to do was get away from Jim She would make a start this very day She quickly found last weeks local paper so to look for a flat to let. She was in no hurry really but on the other hand there was no harm in looking Now that she knew Hannah was gone she just needed a stepping stone for the time being. She saw some flats to let some where near Wem. "Ah that could be a stepping stone half way between here and Wellington. She set about doing some telephoning Yes they had one bedroom and two bedroom flats that would be for rent as soon as the property development was completed. Would she like to put her name down as a prospective tenant? "Yes "She answered that she most certainly would. The person that she was speaking to promised to send her the necessary application forms to fill in and return them to her. Sandra did not have to worry about Jim seeing any post arriving, the postman usually came around eleven o'clock and Jim did not have a break until lunchtime. He also worked most Saturday mornings. He always filled a flask and made a sandwich to take with him to tide him over the morning's work. It was a large farm that he worked for and they had a large dairy herd .Jim was not the only one to be employed; there were others and some part time labour.

Now all she had to do was to get Jim to give her grounds for a divorce. She could now give that some thought.

She quickly worked it out how to get Jim to take her to Wellington the next Thursday. She cooked him a good dinner and waited until he had almost finished eating satisfying his hungry belly from a morning of hard work

"Jim, Sally has rung and has asked me if I could spend the day with her would you take a breakfast break and pop me over to Wellington say next Thursday. We could have a good look around the market and do a bit of shopping" Sandra was all smiles and spoke to him so sweetly that she almost choked on her own food.

"Say you will Darling Just take an hour off for me and our little man"

"OK if you like, I can do that and come for you later in the evening" Jim was so surprised to see Sandra looking so pleased he would have agreed to do any for her. She could be so moody some days he just did not know what to expect when he went in from work.

"Thank you darling, I know that you have a lot on at the farm at the moment but a couple of hours will not hurt the boss, surely seeing all the overtime that you put in for him.

"It will be alright I am sure. But you have to remember that I am paid extra for the overtime and we need all I can get if we are to make a go of this place"

"I know dear you are so good"

Sandra could not wait for the next Thursday she arranged with George where to pick her up near to Sally's house.

Jim did as he had agreed and he arranged with Mr Howells to take a couple of hours off on the following Thursday.

"That will be quite all right lad, the way you work you deserve an hour off Take your time I am sure that we can manage with out you for a little while" He said smiling.

"Oh thank you dear". Sandra said when Jim told her that it was Ok to go to see Sally. "So that is settled I will let Sally know that it is OK then"

Thursday morning although quite cold it was dry and quite pleasant. Sandra had arranged with George where to be in town to pick her up.

"Drop me off here "Sandra said as Jim drove towards the traffic lights it is such a good morning I will walk from here. You get back we don't want the Boss wondering where you have got to"

Jim agreed and slowed the car to a stand still." Have a good day, the pair of you "He said as took the push chair from the boot and unfolded it for her. He waved to them both as he drove away. What he did not know or see was that George was waiting around the next corner to pick her up.

"George this is wonderful," She said as she quickly got into the back of his van and sat down on the cushions he had placed there for her.

"Its better you sit in the back just in case any nosy beggars are about"

"I don't mind as long as I can be with you for the whole of a day"...

George drove the long way around to the cottage Sandra did not mind one little bit sitting in the back with John sat on her knee. She thought that George was quite right it was better so that if any one saw the van it would look as if George was on his own.

George carefully reversed the van into the yard so that it would make it difficult for the neighbours to see what was going on. But he did not see the face behind the net curtain at the little bed room window above the yard. News had quickly spread down the lane that Hannah had walked out so consequently old Tom was not going to miss any little thing if he could help it. He was going to see as much as he could that went on at Woodside His little terrier dog had heard the van and raised its ears as much to say to Old Tom that there was some one about. Old Tom despite his age was quick to climb the winding stairs and see what was going on in the yard below.

"I thought as much the evil buggers that is what all this has been about get one woman out so that the other can move in. But her sister how the hell could they. I thought as much. He looked down at the dog by his side and felt as if he was about to cry. Some thing that he had not done since his old Mother had passed a way and then it had only been in private. When it had all been over and he had gone to his bed and wept. The house was so empty with out her. If I was a younger man I would go around there now and I would knock him to the ground with my very own fists the wicked bugger. I would like to give him the hiding of his life and her as well the dirty little bitch.

Having eaten and settled John with some toys they had gone up stairs Sandra had been so excited now that she did not have to worry about Hannah.

"We will soon get this house finished Darling" She spoke with assurance. "I will help you my Darling. You have no need to go away from home to work. Let us think logically Let us get organised, I will leave Jim, but first I must get some grounds for divorce",

"Don't you go doing any thing irrational; we will take one step at a time? Do you realise what will happen when the family find out".

"We can talk our way around things, I am sure, tell me what reason are you going to give for Hannah going?"

"Don't know as yet"

"You don't think that she will want to come back?"

"Well I am not going to ask her? Any way I don't think that she will. Just let us take things quietly and see what happens" "Lets go down stairs, Michael will be home from school soon. What time did you say that Jim was picking you up?

"Won't be until after seven tonight. Jim had no reason to disbelieve her so he had accepted what ever she had told him

"I have already been looking in the paper for a flat so that I have a stepping stone to be nearer to you. I have found that there is a building being converted near Wem. If I can get Jim for a divorce I will have a good reason to get out"

"You have been busy thinking things out my little love".

"I will do any thing for you my love" They dressed and went downstairs. They did not realise that their laughing and giggling had been heard out on the road through the open window and old Tom had the ears of a fox. He had deliberately taken the terrier for a walk. He had guessed and guessed rightly that, the pair of them would be too busy bonking in bed to notice who went past the house. He had passed the cottage during the afternoon and had heard giggling and laughter coming from the bedroom. The pair of them thought that they had been clever but not to close the bedroom window before bonking on the bed.

Sandra prepared tea, she was already feeling quite at home she had not been slow to make mental note as to where Hannah kept every thing when she had been calling previously on the Sunday afternoons. She decided that the first thing that she must do was to get rid of any thing that she considered would remind him of Hannah. Clothes photographs etc; She did not want George to change his mind and go running to Hannah to ask her to come back. Sandra had to use her wits as she had never done before and she was determined to succeed. Her love for George would not waver. She idolised the man now more than ever before. She wanted him and now she could see that she was very close to getting what she wanted.

"Will you sit down and relax my Darling, "She cooed as George stood first on one foot and then on the other in front of the fire which was now burning brightly and giving out some considerable heat

"I will wash up and put the Hoover around"

"In that case I will go and do a bit of work in the shed. He did not fancy sitting by the fire with the noise of the cleaner and first having to move out of the way from one chair to another. Sandra was going to do her best to impress George and show him that she was quite capable of doing housework. She asked Michael to keep an eye on John for her she wanted the two boys to get on well together and there was no time like the present to make a start. She waited until George went out side with a huge smile on his face. Thinking that if Sandra was going to be willing to help with the housework Perhaps things were not going to be so bad after all. She dusted the chairs and sideboard the mantle shelf etc. She took notice of the armchairs and decided that they were getting to show more than a bit of wear. I will buy a new suite and bring it with me she said to her self. I am going to make a few changes around here.

She noticed that Michael was watching her.

"I'm so sorry that your Mums not here" She said to him; trying to smooth his hair,

The boy moved quickly away from her She continued "That was very naughty of her to run off like that I have just come to give a hand Your poor father can't be expected to do everything for him self Auntie Sandra will come and give you a hand. I can do the ironing. We can't have you men trying to cope on your own, now can we. You must go to school clean and tidy"

"My Dad will look after me" Michael responded sulkily

"I know that dear but even the best dads need a little help. I am so glad that he has given up the awful job that your mother insisted on him taking. He will be at home with you a lot more. Your dad is a very good man and he loves you so much, He will take great care of you so that there will be no need for you to move. If any one asks, you must tell them that you are very happy living here in the country with him. Goodness only knows where your mother is going to take the twins. Probably to live in a flat or somewhere just as dreadful. You would not like to leave your friends and have to change schools now would you?"

"Michael was giving this a lot of thought. The idea of living in a flat did not appeal to him one little bit despite the fact that he was already missing his mum being there for him. Perhaps things were not going to be so bad if Auntie Sandra would come and do the house work Michael stayed quiet and did not answer.

You can depend on me Uncle Jim will not mind my coming to give a hand. Are you going down the road to see your friends so that your dad can take me back he won't be long away? I think that I might be able to find you some pocket money to spend on some thing that you would like. She took her purse from her bag. Yes here is ten shillings you can have this to spend on what you like Your Dad won't mind I am sure"

Michael looked at the ten shilling note that was a lot of money, the most he had from his mum was half a crown piece He quickly worked out as to what he could spend it on. There was a model aircraft that he could buy and put together it was one that he had wanted for a long time. Sandra felt that it was essential that she made a great effort to be friends with Michael. She knew how much that his father idolised him and she must try not to cause any animosity between them. Off you go then and be good. Dad won't be away very long he's just going to take me to Wellington. She did not want Michael with them on the drive back; he just might overhear something that they didn't want him to hear. She looked around the room, that looks better she said to her self. It will be good when the other half of the house is built, should be very smart place when finished. Yes she decided that it would suit her just right. In fact just nicely. The furniture already looked better with out the layer of dust, which had accumulated over the last two weeks since Hannah had gone. A sense of pleasure rippled through her body all the stress and tension gone since she had been able to completely relax with George earlier that afternoon. Her doing some cleaning was bound to impress him.

"We had better get going" George called through the back door

"Ready when you are, Michael says that he would like to play with his mates down the road until you get back I told him that it would be OK Is that alright with you Dear"

"Aye if that is what he wants to do. It was dark now and Sandra did not bother to climb into the back of the van, she sat in the front her hand resting on George's leg. John sat quietly on her knee.

Round at old Tom's cottage his terrier dog lifted its ears and whined it had heard the van being started next door. Tom quickly scrambled from his wooden armchair and up his winding stairs he hoped to see what was going on. He had seen the van return earlier in the day now he wanted to be sure who was sitting in it as it left and he was not disappointed. George had put the outside light on in the yard so that Sandra would not trip as she walked to van carrying John. Yes he was taking the evil little bitch back to where she had come from. Old Tom felt angry and sick in his stomach. This is why he had heard George shouting at Hannah so many times as he had passed the cottage giving the impression that he was walking his beloved little dog. This is what George had wanted and he had got it. Hannah out and that little bitch in how could they.

He swore there and then no matter what, he would never pass the time of day with either of them. They had to be possessed with evil to turn his wife and children out and then go to bed with her sister. I will have a bit of gossip to pass on to the village on Saturday night he said as he watched the van drive away up the lane.

I wonder where that poor sod Jim Beddows fits in this plan of theirs. That will be the next thing He will be left high and dry she has the cheek of the devil to be sure who would believe such carrying on would take place down this lane.

"This has been a wonderful day Darling I have enjoyed it. You have enjoyed being with your real Daddy haven't you my little one" She cooed to baby John. The child was already sleepy when they had left the cottage and the movement of the van soon had him fast asleep. George drove into town and dropped the two of them off just around the corner from Sally's who appeared quite surprised to see Sandra and John on her doorstep".

"I am sure that you don't mind if I wait here with you Sally for a few minutes until Jim comes to pick us up"

"Of course not let me hold little John. Its ages since I saw him Come on in and tell me all your news.

"Jim thinks that I have been shopping with you today Sally. But I was about to arrange it with you when George rang me practically out of his mind. That sister of mine has up and left him. The cruel cow. He's broken hearted I've been there to give him a hand and see how he and the boy are coping. You won't tell Jim will you? Please cover for me Jim might not see it as there is no harm in it He has such a quick temper you know what these men can be like".

"Well not really Sandra My Arthur is a lovely chap I don't think I could find a better one. When we have saved just a little more money we are hoping to start a family just like you. My goodness hasn't baby John grown. What is he now turned two. Of course I will cover for you I should hate this little man to suffer in any way. They say rows in the house are not good for children even little ones".

"I have heard that too George and Michael were so glad to have me do a bit around the house. How could she have gone off and left them like she has. I do not know. Must be off her head and gone funny I should not wonder"

"Well where have they gone to?"

"George says that she has run away and could be staying with his relatives in the village what they must think, goodness only knows. I feel so sorry for George and Michael; you had to see them to understand,

"It was very good of you to give a hand Sandra, I am sure that it was very much appreciated. Poor devils. Why did Hannah do it to them is she mentally unwell How is she going to cope with the twins that you say she has."

"I honestly don't know the woman has flipped her lid. I say it although she is my sister.

"Well Sandra you give George a hand when ever you can. I will cover for you if you don't think that Jim will be happy"

"You are a real friend Sally I am very fond of you if there ever comes a day when you want a favour doing you will only have to ask". They sat in front of the electric fire waiting for Jim to come

"I am worried about Jim but that is another story, he can be so funny at times "

"Can't we all" Remarked Sally. Jim's knock on the door interrupted their chin wagging" Out in the cold night air they went and waved goodbye to Sally and Arthur.

"I hope that you have had your tea Jim" Sandra asked when he had started to drive them home.

"Not really, I thought that we could pick some fish and chips in town".

"I thought as much" Snapped Sandra I can't have a few hours off and you can't feed your self. Well get fish and chips if you want, because I am not going to start cooking you a meal when I get in I've got enough to do I have to put John to bed.

"Very well dear, but don't be so cross. I was late finishing tonight. I've been in and lit the fire for you so that it would be nice and warm for when we get back".

"I should think so" We don't want to go into a stone cold house Do we my little man" She spoke to little John who was now asleep again, None the worse for being woken up at Sally's.

"That house is as cold as a barn at the best of times"

"It's not that bad" Retorted Jim it is better that the ones that we have had before".

"Better really, what next will you say Jim Beddows."

Sandra was going to play her cards right. Nothing from now on was going to be good enough for her. She picked a quarrel with every word that Jim said. He said no more and drove the rest of the way in silence not bothering to stop for fish and chips. He decided that he would make do with a sandwich while Sandra put John to bed. What had upset Sandra today he did not bother to ask, it had only been a fortnight ago when she seemed to be on the top of the moon, he could not say a wrong word.

Jim had been content with life since they had moved again and that he now had a few acres of his own. Sandra's Dad had given them some help and Jim had worked long hours at his job and then he had come home and started work again. To him Sandra had appeared to be content with what they were doing but she showed little interest in any thing to do with the outside work she would feed the baby calves for him now and again. Jim was hoping that she would attempt to have a go at rearing some poultry and growing some vegetables in the big garden that they now had. But Sandra had made no effort to use any of the fruit in the garden such as gooseberries, Rhubarb and the blackcurrants to help out financially. She showed no interest, which did seem unusual considering that she was a farmer's daughter. Jim would have loved to have another baby but had not had much luck. Still he had John it was better to have one little lad than none at all.

Sandra had believed him when he had said he was very careful when they made love, which was not very often if she could help it. She took a lot of persuading to have much to do with him, so un- knowing to her he was not the slightest bit concerned if he did get her pregnant. Nothing had happened which did puzzle him. Had he become sterile or was there some thing wrong with Sandra. There can't be any thing wrong with me I have already fathered John he thought to himself. It would be no use of his trying tonight considering the bad mood that she was in.

The fire was burning brightly when they entered the living room Jim put John down on the couch to give Sandra time to take off her coat. He then went into the kitchen to make himself a sandwich "Not much here to put between some bread He said to him self."" "Have you done much shopping?" He called from the kitchen

"No why?"

"What no food/ there is nothing to put in a sandwich. Oh it's alright I've found a bit of cheese It will have to do"

"It will certainly have to" Said Sandra from the doorway holding John in her arms. "I have not done any food shopping it was my day off; we only looked at clothes and things. I will worry about feeding you tomorrow" She turned on her heel and made for the staircase. "I'm tired" She called back."I will probably go to bed when I have put John down don't wake me if I have already gone to sleep". No way did she want to please Jim tonight after being well and truly satisfied by George. To her George was wonderful; Sandra could think of nothing else as she went to bed and she just lay there making plans for her self. At last there was a possibility of her being able to live with George.

Tomorrow she would give Elizabeth a ring and see if any of the family knew that Hannah had left George. Keeping well ahead with any family gossip was essential to her. She thought that she would start to move things as quickly as she could. Little items of china could be moved to George's. She could put little bits and pieces in his van when he called .Now that he would be giving up working away he would be calling much more often. Jim would not notice what disappeared from the cupboards. He was far too busy working all hours and he just washed and crashed out when he had finished at night. She was certainly not going to leave the china teaset that Ethel Hollis had given her for a wedding present she had known that it was made by a firm called Aynsley and that it was a very old one and could be worth a few pounds in years to come. I will see about changing the three-piece suite so that if I can I will be able to take a new one it with me. That one at George's is getting a bit shabby. If only I could drive a car. I must do some thing about it. In the mean time I must get some sleep.

Sandra made a point of ringing Elizabeth next day and talking casually to her. She said have you heard? Hannah has left George"

"No, when did this happen? Oh my goodness what will mother and Dad have to say about this Fancy Hannah causing this sort of scandal?

"I can't think why she has left him they reckon that she is staying at Molly's in the village".

"Well Sandra I did hear that George has been behaving badly and that they were short of money why else would she be going out to work on that bread round in all weather like she is?"

"Fiddle sticks what I have seen there. Hannah was not kept short of money I think that she just wanted to live like a lady trying to keep up with Grace".

"Oh I don't know about that Grace would take some keeping up with" Lizzy laughed "Let me know if you hear anything more"

"Oh I will. You know that she should have a husband like this one that I've got to live with and then she would have something to grumble about."

"But I thought that Jim was a very nice fellow. He comes from a very well respectable family we all liked him very much. You have done very well for your self. It has not been long since you married and you have a lovely little boy John. I can't think what you have to worry about. Mother and Dad did their best for you; At least you had a proper wedding that is a lot more than what was given to Helen".

Sandra said no more about Jim she had said all that she wanted to, just enough to give Lizzy some thing to think about and what she knew of Lizzy she would soon spread the gossip when and if any of the other sisters contacted her. Just as Sandra had intended. She returned to the chores of the day. Happy days ahead she thought. To hell with Jim lad, you have had your chips I will get you one way or another and get away I will. I'm off at the first opportunity. Sandra sang to the music on the radio as she worked for the rest of the morning. She thought of what she had said to Lizzy Yes my little innuendoes would have worked a treat. When I go into town I will look what three-piece suites are in the sales. George's is a bit shabby

The days passed by; Hannah was hardly noticing what went on around her she was living in a dream world. Judith and Molly helped her with the twins.

Hannah and Jennifer slept at Molly's in the spare bedroom and shared the double bed. David stayed at Judith's in her spare bed in Robin's room. It was working well. I can't go back to the lane Hannah confided to Molly

"Don't you think of it" She retorted. "If you do you will live to regret it. That is if he lets you live at all. A leopard can not change his spots no matter how hard he licks. Oh he would probably be good for a couple of months and then he would be back to his own selfish self."

"You know that I said about George having another woman."

"Yes I suppose that you are beginning to think about it, are you?"

"Well he did slip up once I guess it was some woman where he had been staying in digs down south"

"Never mind about where he had digs you need to look nearer home a lot nearer home"

"What do you mean?"

"I'm saying no more but it is about time that you woke up a bit"

"Molly I must get some where for us to live, we can't impose on you any longer than necessary. I feel that we have already out stayed our welcome"

"You have only been here four weeks you will get some where that I am sure. I've had a word with the council and they have put you down as my lodgers. They are offering me one of those new flats that they are building. If I accept would you be prepared to go into one if they offer you one?"

"If they were to offer me a flat that would be wonderful it really would".

"Well you know that I want to get back to Birmingham and if we accept the council's offer they could put another retired couple in this bungalow and it would save a lot of problems all round."

"Molly just think, a brand new flat, oh no disrespect to you. You have been wonderful but to have our own bath and our own flush loo etc; if you hear from them again will you let them know that I will only too delighted to accept"

"Leave it to me I suggest that we both go to bed and get some sleep" A knock on the door broke into their conversation. Molly went through to the hall to see who could be visiting at this time of night it could be Judith coming around. Although it was only nine thirty. Hannah heard Molly say Hello Charles what brings you hear?" Go on in I will put the kettle on. She ushered him into the living room.

"Hello Charles "Said Hannah "What brings you here?"

"I called to see if you were alright and what we are hearing is true".

"That depends on what you are hearing?"

"Only that you have left George"

"Quite true".

"We can't believe it we always assumed that you were such a happy couple despite the rumours that have been going around the village".

"What rumours have you been hearing Charles?"

"Oh nothing really but will you consider going back?"

"Look sit your self down" Ordered Molly as she was coming through the door. "You are too big for me standing up"

Charles sat all six feet of himself into Terry's old wooden chair.

"Now fancy a cuppa you might as well we were just going to have one before turning in".

All right Charles replied, thanking Molly. "So good of you "

"So good be -damned we need a bit of cheering up, what do you reckon Hannah?"

"Could do I suppose what are these rumours that you were referring to Charles?

"Oh nothing except that for the fact that George was always at your sister Sandra's."

"Oh yes she was always a pain in the bum, wanting this done and that done".

"That's not all he was doing according to the village gossip"

"Don't be so absurd Charles you are not suggesting that there was any thing going on between George and Sandra"

"I've tried to tell her for years "Piped up Molly. As she brought in the tea tray from the kitchen where she had been listening to every word that had been spoken.

"The very thought of such a thing is incomprehensible" Said Hannah Looking from one to the other as they nodded in agreement. She was shocked at the possibility of George and Sandra having an affair. She looked at them with daggers drawn.

"Look I only came to see if I could be of any help. I always had great respect for you when I came to see George for My auntie Maude. You always offered me a cup of tea and by Jove those cakes that you used to make were so good. We only had bought ones at home.

"I reckon that there is some thing that you could do for us. The council have offered us a flat What about taking us to have a look at them?" Molly asked smiling at Charles as she handed him a cup of tea.

"No trouble I will do that for you"

"Right Sunday afternoon would suit us very nicely. We will be ready at two o'clock"

Molly had a gift of organising things to her own advantage. Their conversation moved from one subject to another Charles stood up saying that he must be on his way. He did not let on that if he were late going in at home his mother would want to know where he had been and who with. She kept him under her thumb as much as she possibly could.

"Thank you for coming "Said Hannah as she saw him to the door. "Those rumours that you mentioned, are you sure about them."

"Well it's like this Old Tom next door to you did not miss much that went on and he reckons that she has been there cleaning up ready to move in". Hannah closed the door and went to give Molly a hand with the cups. Molly you sure can get things organised when you want to Said Hannah gathering up the cups and saucers and took them through to the kitchen,

"Molly what do you think about what Charles says about the rumours going around the village is he talking through his hat?"

"I have told you before but you have taken no notice of me. I said about those baby photos in the village magazine but did you believe me of course not why should you? It is the oldest trick in the book gets rid of the wife so that the mistress can move in and by what Charles has just said she has not lost much time doing that".

"Molly do you really think that George has been having an affair with Sandra?"

"I'm not committing my self to say any thing and what I say is only what I think by what I have seen going on. What I think of you is that you must have been blind not to see what has been going on but to be fair you would not have suspected a thing. Well not with your sister and George. But you start thinking and then perhaps things will make a little more sense to you. That is all that I have to say and thank goodness that you have had the guts to get out before he did murder or throw you out on the street to get her in. You mark my words that little madam is evil through and through I saw it in her eyes the day you married and she was your little bridesmaid."

"Molly what will you say next?"

"I am saying no more but there are some that are so blind that they can't see".

That night Hannah lay unable to go off to sleep, it evaded her, what were these rumours Charles had spoken of. It was unthinkable. George would not touch Sandra her little sister. The more that she thought about it the less that she could go of to sleep. If there were any truth in it. If there was, it would make George a complete bastard but of course this was not true Get some sleep she told her self and think about it tomorrow. Jennifer was fast asleep by her side and she had a hard day's work to do. Hannah could not get to sleep and she was very tired and listless next day. Being able to have a flat would solve Hannah's greatest problems. She could not impose on Molly any longer than absolutely necessary It was not to be tolerated. As for furniture she would worry about that when she had to. The money that she was earning was only enough to pay her way. Living with Molly had enabled her to buy a few bits and pieces for her self such as knickers and stockings in the local market.

Tights were coming into fashion. Hannah had noticed them hanging out on clotheslines as she went on her bread round. They looked so funny; were they stockings with tops or knickers with legs. Did one wear both knickers and tights? Hannah decided to try them "The best thing since this sliced bread "she laughed with the girl Maggie who helped her on the bread round we don't have to worry about bending over this is fantastic. It does not matter any more about Brian seeing our stocking tops.

Hannah's up bringing was that one did not allow the tops of ones stockings to be seen even when bending.

"You will be alright for money" Judith assured her "George will have to pay some maintenance, but you must go and see a solicitor so that George is ordered to pay something to help you keep the twins and decide what you are going to do about getting a divorce"

"What?" Hannah said in amazement "Divorce".

"Well you are not thinking about going back to live with him are you?" She asked.

"Well it is obvious that he does not want me back or he would have come running by now it looks to me as if he was glad to get rid of me"

"So you had better get moving to sort some thing out legally".

The thought of having to see a solicitor filled Hannah with dread. I can't I can't she tried to convince herself. But I know that I must I am going to need some more money if I get a flat. I have no furniture no bedding nothing at all I am going to need so much What ever am I going to do?"

Where had she gone wrong why had George not come and begged for her to return to him? They had loved each other so very much, could all his feelings for her gone and died forever. Hannah could not accept that George no longer needed her. Who was this other woman? If he was seeing some one else or what were the real reasons for his bouts of depression. George had an affair with Sandra that was just idle gossip No matter what Hannah tried to convince her self surely there was no truth in such silly rumours. Sandra would surely have told some one? A member of the family perhaps Sandra would not sink that low to make love with her sister's husband. Surely no sister on earth would do such a diabolical thing. Any way Sandra was happily married to Jim with a lovely little boy. They were doing well Jim was such a hard worker and he was so proud of his family he idolised his baby son. No Hannah kept saying to her self, don't believe the gossip. Some people will say any thing to start rumours especially in villages. Sandra and George what a load of rubbish Who ever this other woman was Hannah did not want to know or care Her top priority was to get some where for her self and the twins to live and do some thing about getting Michael to come and live with her. The thought of the children being brought up living apart was some thing that she did not want to contemplate. Perhaps Judith was right she must go and see a solicitor but how does one go about such things. Hannah decided not to do any thing until she had looked at the flats, which the council had built about three miles from Wellington.

Charles came as promised on time and off they went. The block of flats was seven stories high and seemed to them to reach the sky. Charles parked the car and there seemed to be plenty of parking spaces made available at the back of the building.

I wonder where in the building we will be" Said Hannah when they had got out of the car and had a walk around.

"Well I asked to be on the ground floor" Answered Molly.

They walked around the building looking through the windows it looked so new and clean. The paintwork was all white and the floors were covered in soft grey Marley tiles. Hannah's spirits rose, wouldn't it be wonderful if the council were to allocate us one?"

"They will, don't you worry" Said Molly. Shall we go home now "She said to Charles. "? No "he replied let us go out into the country for a ride"

"That would be wonderful"

They all got back into the car. Molly sat by Charles in the front and Hannah and the twins sat in the back. "Where shall we go?" Charles wanted to know

"Oh any where" Was the reply from the twins. Charles decided that they would go for a ride to Wenlock Edge where they stopped for a while. The twins were soon out of the car and ran around to play and let off steam.

Hannah and Molly talked quietly Making plans for their flats.

"My flat will only be a one bedroom flat so you can have the double bed and a few bits and pieces if you would like. If I try to sell them I would have to get them to a salesroom and by the time the auctioneer has taken his fees there will not be much left worth talking about"

"Yes I could certainly do with the bed and any thing else that might be going, It would be great if I can have the double bed. I could buy a single for David. Jennifer and I can share for a bit longer until we can get some thing better. They returned back home feeling quite happy and relaxed "Stay and have a cup of tea "Molly asked Charles. He readily accepted. "You know I really did enjoy that ride. Thank you Charles.

"I will come again if you would like I have no commitments" Said Charles.

"What no girl friend?" Asked Molly

"Well there was one girl that my Mother liked" he replied. "But I can't see that working out. No matter what My Mother interferes. I had better be going or she will be on the warpath if I don't get back soon I didn't tell her where I was going."

"At your age I did not think that you would have to?"

"Oh yes I have to tell her or she moans for days"

He went on his way offering to take them out again. Hannah was not to sure about this what if he went straight back to George and told him that he had taken them out. She voiced her concerns to Molly.

"Well let him it will give George some thing to think about. By the way have you done any thing about seeing a solicitor; you are going to need some money".

"Yes Molly I have made an appointment.

"Good we should have it confirmed that we have a flat this week. They do look lovely".

"Molly, tell me how come that you are so sure that we can have one?"

"That's for me to know and others to find out" She laughed. "The rent man said that the council have already allocated this bungalow so I know that they are going to put us somewhere and that is not on the street. They said as you are my lodgers that entitles you to have one as well"

"I did put my name down almost two years ago when I first thought of leaving George".

"That's it then. That is why they are letting you have one that is good to know you should have told me".

"I would have done but I was told at the office that I had not a cat in hells chance of having a council house unless I and the kids were out on the street".

"Oh I see. But I have only done what I could you certainly need some help from some where". And some more to come I wouldn't wonder before you have finished, She thought but did not say out loud. Molly had always been suspicious about George having an affair with Sandra and if she was right it would all have to come out in time.

She was looking forward to be going back to Birmingham; Cadbury's had said that they would inform her as soon as they had a vacant bungalow. She had missed her own two daughters quite a lot, although she had visited them quite often. She had her job at the village shop and although she had enjoyed every minute that she had worked there it did not give her much time off. She missed her grandchildren greatly and now her life was very lonely with out Terry. She had always considered and treated Judith as a daughter, but she missed the hustle and bustle of the City life. She was now longing to get back there to live.

Hannah's appointment with the solicitor was made for the afternoon when she had finished her bread round. She was not looking forward to this. Not one little bit. She walked up the stairs and entered the receptionist's office. . When asked she gave her name and said that she had an appointment with a Mr Barnett. Nerves suddenly got the better of her and the room started to go round and she could feel herself starting to sway. The receptionist noticed and told Hannah to sit down and that she would fetch her glass of water. She quickly left and minutes later returned with it.

"Drink this. Mr Barnett won't keep you waiting very long"

"Thank you" Whispered Hannah "I feel better now I must have come up the stairs too quickly.

"You will be alright in a minute" I've heard that one before the receptionist said to her self.

Hannah suddenly felt frantic and scared stiff. George had threatened her with all sorts of things if ever she dared to see a solicitor about him when she had threatened to leave him. Now here she was doing exactly what he had threatened her about. Mr Barnett called her into his office and invited her to take a seat

When she did so he asked "Now what can I do for you?"

"I don't really know I have left my husband"

"Now tell me why you have done that. I am sure that there has to be a very good reason"

"I could not take any more of him" She replied tears coming into her eyes"

"All right my dear that will do for now" He said as he picked up a green form and started to complete it Just relax a little and give me your name and details Then you can tell me why you are here?

"I need some money to keep the children and I am going to have a flat that is if I am lucky.

Mr Barnett was very sympathetic and had such a kind voice Hannah did not feel quite as bad as she tried to explain what had happened. Mr Barnett said that he would write to George immediately to ask him what he was going to do about maintaining his wife and children. I will notify you as soon as I hear from him. In the meantime you go ahead and accept the flat if you are offered one".

A month went by before Hannah heard from Mr Barnett again, He said that he had written to George twice but he had not replied. He advised Hannah to make an appointment to discuss her future needs".

"Just what I expected" Replied Molly when Hannah showed her the letter. "He can't get away with out maintaining you and the twins. If I know him he will if he can"

Hannah was not very optimistic, she agreed to take the flat the council offered her and they were due to move in the next few weeks.

"What shall I do "She was in despair as she talked to Judith there is so much that we need.

"See Mr Barnett first before you do any thing "She advised. "I am sure that he will force George to see sense and then you will have a bit more money to live on"

Mr Barnett did not seem so terrifying the next time Hannah saw him.

"What happens now?" She asked

"You have to decide if you want to divorce him. If so we can then apply to the courts".

Divorce courts. The words echoed around in Hannah's head. The law Oh my goodness what am I doing here, she began to wonder.

"Can I let you know? "She whispered.

"Of course, make an appointment when you know what you want me to do. This husband of yours looks as if he is going to prove difficult and I think that it can only be the law that is going to help you. You know that we have to make him aware of his responsibilities"

Thanking Mr Barnett Hannah left his office with the word divorce court ringing in her ears,

"Judith I can't" she said "I have heard such stories about going to court they ask all sorts of questions. What will the family have to say about it? I simply can't go through with it".

"Well it's for you to decide. I suggest that you let Mr Barnett advice you He deals with these things every day Can you manage for money"

"Oh yes I pay my way with what I earn. I can pay for such as the rent of the flat Heating etc; .It will be a bit of an effort. Because you see neither you nor Molly have charged me any rent as yet and I have been here for a few weeks. I have managed to save a few pounds

"George will have to pay eventually you know. I have an idea why don't we go to the caravan and bring back the china etc; it would all help and it would save you quite a lot and it would be a bit less for you to buy."

"We could but George would kill me if he finds out"

"He threatened to kill you if you were to leave him. He threatened to kill you if you saw a solicitor but you are still alive He has been such of a bully threatening you if you do this or if you do that. It was all to keep you terrified of him."

"So I am. You could be right".

"I will see what Carl can arrange perhaps you and me could go on Sunday afternoon, after all don't you forget that you are moving into the flat next week, and you have to have something to use"

Judith I have worked it out if that I can pay the rent and heating and food but there will not be much left. I have put a deposit on a gas cooker. If you and Carl would spare next Sunday after noon yes let's go. They were unable to go for the next two weeks Carl was busy helping Molly sort Terry's belongings out such as the garden tools Etc Molly and Carl were hiring a van to move Molly and Hannah into their new flats. It was a very busy two weeks and Hannah could not afford to lose any time off from work she needed every penny that she earned. Hannah borrowed three cups and saucers and a few other things from Judith and Molly to tide her over the Saturday evening and Sunday morning until they could go to the caravan. Hannah was thrilled with the flat. My very own, she whispered to the white painted walls A real toilet my own bathroom It all looked so clean It was wonderful David was so pleased that at last he had his own room. They had no furniture as such Hannah had bought a bed for David in the sales so she got it quite cheaply It had a pink mattress, not the colour for a boy. She promised that she would get another one as soon as she could afford it and then Jennifer could have it. They put a tea chest with a board on top for a table and covered it with a tablecloth that Molly had given her. They made do with three old chairs that Molly was throwing out. Hannah was hoping to be able to buy some curtain material as soon as possible so that the living room would not look so bare but that could wait a little while They were situated on the second floor no one could see in through the windows.

Sunday morning Judith picked up Hannah and the twins at about ten o'clock they dropped the twins off at Wrockwardine for Carl to look after them until they came home. Judith drove the little Morris minor to the caravan site. They were amazed to find that George's van was not in its usual place. They went along to the site office to enquire as to where it had been moved. Then they saw it standing on a rough looking field along side of the site.

"Oh" Said the caretaker when Hannah asked why it had been moved

"No site rent paid you know the rules No money No site "

"Yes Hannah knew the rules. If the rent was not paid the vans were towed onto that field at the side of the site where they were held there until it was paid and if the caravan was not claimed with in a certain time they were burnt.

"Can we have the keys please? "Asked Hannah

"What do you want them for?" he asked as surly as he could

Hannah knew that she must tread carefully. The caravan and its contents now legally belonged to the site.

"I have come to collect just a few things "

"Does your husband know" The caretaker was not pleased at being interrupted from his afternoon nap. If he does not you had better sign for what you take"

"Oh that's quite alright" Judith said very quickly "We will come back to your office in a minute or two. We have no intentions of leaving with out giving you the key.

"OK Missus "It was obvious that he had no intention of getting involved in an argument with Judith. "What a shame" Remarked Hannah "Our lovely caravan coming to this".

"George obviously does not care or he would have paid the rent" Answered Judith" Don't stop to think about it Lets just take what we need and get away from here, it is so depressing"

They gathered together the china Cutlery and packed it into the empty cardboard boxes that they had brought with them.

"What about these two seats" Said Judith "If a frame could be made for them they would make a very useful seat."

"How can we take those back with us?"

"On the roof of the car. There is always some string in the boot Carl always carries things like that just in case we could tie them down well, Lets try, "They did. The two seats were as long as the car what a sight they looked' the two women went back to the office. The caretaker asked for a list of what they were taking from the van. "What are you taking those seats for? You know that you are not supposed to. ?"

"Well we thought that when we get back I will persuade my brother to settle the money that he owes to you and we thought that we would take the seats and have them recovered they look a bit dirty".

"Well are you going to be alright taking a load like that, it is no skin off my nose if he does not pay off his rent arrears. Can't think why he did not give that van a good coat of paint when he took it home. Damned good strong van it will get burnt I reckon, bit of a shame if you ask me."

"What do you mean, when he took it home? The van has not been taken home" Asked Hannah quite shaken at the suggestion that it had been home.

"Oh aye missus it has taken off a couple of winters; I will show you the book where he signed it off the site It has not been back all that long See hear he took it off once or twice by the look of the book. Only no rent no site

Hannah looked at the records in the logbook, which was kept for all movements of caravans on and off the site. Yes there was George's signature. They said no more to the caretaker". Thanking him, they drove away in silence along the coast road . Judith asked "Do you want to stop and take a look at the sea for old time's sake?"

"Not really I would rather get back and see how Carl is coping with the twins. Judith what do you think has been going on? Why would George tow the van back home which I know that he has not and if he did where did he put it or is that care taker lying"

"The caretaker has no reason to lie and that was George's signature alright. It is a complete mystery to me, forget it for now" But Hannah knew that she could not forget it. She said no more but kept her thoughts to herself. They headed away from the sea towards home, having taken what they had come for. These bit and pieces would make a great saving for Hannah not having to purchase so many things. She was filled with sadness this place would now be part of her past No more would she long to come to this place near the sea. She knew that Oliver Pearson had qualified as carpenter so she thought that she would ask him if he could make a frame to put the seats on and then she would have some thing more comfortable for them to sit on. She told Judith what she was thinking and Judith agreed that it would be a good idea. If George does decide to pay the rent, He can soon get some new seats, which I don't think that he will, by what you have told me, he does not have any money to pay off the site rent as it is. It is a wicked shame if you ask me. You spent so much time building it. What can he be thinking about to let it stand there and rot.

The twins coped with the travelling to and from school. They were able to stay at the school were they were settled. Hannah had to leave for work just before them in the mornings. She saw to it that they were up and dressed and that they had eaten some breakfast. Molly agreed to look out for them. She would listen for them going out of the flat she was situated on the ground floor directly below Hannah. She could see them going to the bus stop from her window. Molly always waved to them as they left the building to let them know that she was watching out for them.

Every day Hannah asked if they had seen Michael. Some times the answer would be yes and some times no. Hannah was always full of questions did he look tidy, Is he happy what did he have to say to you?"

Jennifer was missing her father very badly so she played up for a while. Money was the biggest problem. Go to the DHSS Hannah was told but this proved useless.

"You are working and your children are over five years of age. She was told. You have left your husband so consequently you must get on with it. You should see a solicitor and get your husband to pay maintenance for all three of you. Hannah could not believe what she was hearing. She had been told that it was so easy to get help But not so easy in her case. She felt very angry.

"Don't worry" Said Judith when Hannah told her about her visit to the DHSS office. "You go back and see Mr Barnett. Ask him to get things moving".

"But he will want to know if I am prepared to go for a divorce"

"You have to make up your own mind about that George certainly does not seem the slightest bit interested as to how you are managing"

"I've heard such dreadful things about divorce courts"

"I am sure that Mr Barnett will assure you of your rights".

Hannah made an appointment to see Mr Barnet again. He advised her about obtaining legal aid. Yes if she was prepared to divorce George he could then go ahead making it much easier to require George to pay maintenance.

Hannah agreed with Mr Barnett and instructed him to go ahead "We can't go on living on bread and margarine any longer than necessary" She laughed.

"I appreciate your difficulties. It cannot be easy for you. One is torn between the devil and the deep blue sea".

"I have heard such alarming things about divorce courts" Stammered Hannah

"Don't be alarmed they are not as bad as you think. Besides there is the custody of the children to think about. That is one thing that has to be dealt with legally."

"They could not order me to hand over the twins to George. Could they?" She said sounding quite alarmed.

"I don't know. That is for the court to decide.

"But I am hoping to get Michael to come and live with us".

"Now that will be difficult. Michael is an older child. He will be asked which of you that he would prefer to live with. You will have to wait and see.

"Michael will be allowed to choose, but he needs his mother I know that he will choose to come and live with me"

"Wait and see my Dear these things can some times not work out as you would like In the meantime cope the best that you can. It will be very important to the courts to show that you are managing and that the children are not being neglected in any way"

Oh Lordy thought Hannah what have I done.

Sandra had rung George most days and she had been seeing him whenever she could. If she did not give him a ring he would telephone her knowing when Jim would be at work more often or not reversing the charges. It was so easy using a public telephone and telling Sandra how much he missed her and needed her.

"My Darling ring me back if you have no change reverse the charges we can talk for much longer It will be a small price to pay to be able to hear you voice besides Jim can pay the bill when it comes in. I can't wait to leave him and be with you my darling she would coo to him"

She found it so easy to explain to Jim how lonely George was now that Hannah had left him. "How could she have done that to poor George?" .She would complain to Jim?

"George is a good man and did not deserve to be left with a son still at school. You don't mind dear if we give him a meal now and again do you?" I know that she is my sister but I for one don't want to own her, how could she have been so cruel."

"Well I never imagined that it could happen. I can't believe that Hannah was capable of such a thing she always seemed to be such a caring person and a hard worker; she was always doing one thing or another.

"Don't I work hard enough for you is that what you are saying?

"Of course not, you do try and you have little John to cope with He's getting such a handful now isn't he?"

"What are you implying?"

"I'm not implying anything I just said that it did not seem Hannah's nature to leave George with out good reason"

"Sticking up for her are you?

"No I am not I just came in for a bit of dinner I don't want another row"

"What do you mean another row?"

"Well not much but nothing seems to be right for you these days".

"Nothing is", she muttered. "

"What was that? Jim was getting angry He got up from the kitchen table and going towards the back door He said" Ask who you want if it will keep you happy "He strolled off down the yard. Jim had left the tractor ready to start an afternoons ploughing As soon as Sandra heard it start and move out of the yard she hurried to phone George She knew that he would be at home.

"My darling come over for some tea at the week end No don't make dinner so that if Jim is working overtime we will have the whole afternoon together she purred blowing kisses down the phone. I need you I can't wait"

That's great. She said to her self after George had confirmed that he would be over to see her. George had told her that Michael would be off with his mate so he could look after himself. You be careful darling you don't want those social lot breathing down your neck, If Hannah finds out that you have left him on his own She won't be able to get to a phone quick enough and you don't want to lose him now do you my love. You must make it look as if you care, get what I mean?"

George re-assured her he would take care and would be with her at the weekend. "Ring me again tomorrow please Darling the days are so long while I am waiting to be with you. Get my meaning I can't wait until we can be together for always. Saying a right sloppy goodbye she replaced the receiver on the telephone hook

"Now" she whispered to little John "Your real Daddy is going to be here on Saturday. Let us show him that we care for him. You are going to be a good boy for your mummy aren't you while I get busy and make this place presentable you know little man I hate housework but we will have to get on with it. It won't be long before we can live with your real Daddy for always. God I will be so happy.

"Goodness me" Commented Jim on the Friday evening. "Spruced the place up a bit haven't you He couldn't help noticing how tidy the kitchen was as he came home from work.

"Oh have I indeed, Well don't you go mucking it up".

"Who's coming, the duke him self I don't think that I have seen the place this clean since we moved in"

"There's no need for your sarcasm"

"Oh I for got you said that George might come for tea. Now I see why"

"What do you mean you see what are you implying?"

"Nothing "Jim said

"Jim you meant something by that remark or am I reading too much into it"

"Take it as you like but it is not very often that we get a spring clean now is it"

Sandra was now getting angry her conscience was beginning to niggle a little. Jim was right but she was not going to let him think that he was.

"I can't make a very good job of spring cleaning as often as I would like with this old furniture that we have got"

"It was the best that we could afford or have you forgotten what we started with"

"How could I forget" She wanted to taunt him as much as she could; we started in that stinking little cottage in the village, how I could forget".

"You were happy enough in those days what is the matter with you now?"

"We need new furniture I have seen some very nice three piece suites in the sales. Look very nice in our front room one would".

"We can't afford new furniture for a little while yet. It's not too bad. We will have to make do with what we have got for little while longer."

“I’ll not make do Jim Beddows I want some thing better. You had money to buy that young stock but none to spend on me”

“Well we can’t afford it and if you want a row about it you can have one

“I thought that it was too good to be true to expect something decent from you”

“As far as I am concerned I’ve been decent. We don’t owe for any thing and I am not going into debt just to please you. So get that into your thick stupid head Sandra I just don’t know what is the matter with you these days, nothing that I do seems to please you at all”

“Well if you don’t do some thing about it I will” Sandra spoke defiantly the fact that Jim was standing up to her had made her really angry

“You do that, if you want to but don’t you expect me to pay for it”

Sandra was now really angry she wanted the place to look good for George’s benefit All their furniture had been bought second hand .The armchairs in the front room were now looking a bit tatty. She left the kitchen and went into the front to have a look around it. Yes a nice three piece suit would look good in here the wallpaper is not too bad

I have my family allowance that would pay it off but first I have to get a cheque out of Jim for the deposit. Let’s hope that Hannah goes for a divorce and then George will be free. I could always take it with me when I move out, that one at George’s is getting to show a bit of wear but then he has had it for fourteen years. The idea of pleasing George one way or another did cheer her up a bit. Although the oak beams of the ceiling darkened the room, it was a large room and if some one really wanted to make an effort, it did have good possibilities.

Yes she decided she would do something about it. She would find a way to get the three piece suit it would be just too bad if it was not paid for when she had left him He could just sort it out. I must get him angry enough to hit me so that I have got grounds for a divorce.

George arrived as arranged for lunch on Saturday. Sandra went for fish and chips once he had settled him self in the kitchen. Won't be long my Darling she said as they kissed passionately. Stay with John isn't he looking more and more like you every day". Jim will be back in a minute. Where is Michael?" She enquired realising that the lad had not come with his dad.

"Decided to stay with his mates down the lane. He will be OK "He said smiling up at her"

As their eyes met they were full of love for each other

Jim came in for lunch; he politely passed the time of day with George. And was surprised that Sandra was not there putting some dinner on the table.

Where is Sandra?

"Said she was fetching fish and chips. She says that you need a few jobs doing around the place"

Jim thought not bloody fish and chips again that and meat pies were all they seemed to live on.

"Oh I expect she will show you what needs doing, not that I can think of much. This house is in much better state of repair than the one in the village. I can't stay to talk with you all afternoon I must get back to work I need all the overtime that I can get. Money comes in handy you know I could do with another couple of calves. The boss is so good to us, bends over backwards to help us, he does.

Sandra returned with the fish and chips. They ate the meal in silence; she had put them on plates instead of eating them out of the paper that they were wrapped in. Jim soon swallowed his down with a mug of tea pushed his chair back on the quarry floor making a bit of a noise and went out and on his way back to work.

"Now that he has gone my darling, tell me how you are coping is there any thing that I can do for you? Give him a minute or two to get on his way then I will show you what I intend to do with you first of all. They stood up from the table. She was pushing her body close to George. Her hand already feeling for his stiffness as she pushed her hand down the front of his trousers, causing him to draw a deep breath as she struggled with her other hand to release his belt and zip. Zips were now being used instead of buttons on the flies of men's trousers and there were a few that had a very uncomfortable experiences with the zips and George did not want to be one of them it could turn out to be very painful indeed'

"Go Steady" He muttered terrified in case she caught him in the zip. Trousers with zipped flies were the new thing; George had been used to button flies not zips.

"It's alright," She said. "I'll be very careful; she led the way carefully up stairs, not that George did not know his way to the bedroom, he had been there several times before. Sandra had spent a little time earlier tidying up. Fortunately John was quiet down stairs. John now coming four was used to being left on his own for an hour or so. Sandra often left him while she went for chips to save putting him into some clean clothes or when she went out to feed the calves. She knew that he would not touch the Rayburn cooker. It was far too hot to his touch. He could not open the firebox with out using the metal leaver that was supplied with the cooker. Sandra always put that on the mantle shelf where he could not reach it.

Sandra was desperate to be satisfied sexually. Jim had not bothered much with her since they had moved He was either too tired from working long hours or she was too miserable for him to make the time or effort. He did try now and again but Sandra was so glad that he had not got her pregnant again. When she and George were completely satisfied they dressed and went down stairs and sat drinking tea.

"What is happening about you and Hannah Are you going for a divorce, surely you could on the grounds of desertion. After all it was she who left you Did she not?"

"You have a point there I hadn't thought about that. You could be right. I keep getting letters from her solicitors but I just take no notice. If they want me I'll go when I have to and not before" Jennifer says that Charles Leonard has been taking them out in that fancy new car that he has bought"

"Oh he has. Has he When have you seen Jennifer"

"She and David came on their bikes on Sunday"

"On their bikes, what bikes?

"Had new ones for Christmas, Jennifer told me"

"How did Hannah pay for those? You don't think, do you, she and Leonard? "Sandra sounded excited"

"No from what I can make out Molly goes with them. Been to the caravan they have and taken a lot of stuff"

"Could you get them for theft?

"I suppose so I will look into it" He didn't tell her that he hadn't paid the rent for the site or that he hadn't paid Hannah any maintenance "

"Are you going to get a solicitor?" She asked

"I suppose that I will have to if she goes ahead with this divorce. She is threatening me with it"

"Well you oppose it, dig your heels in. Don't you let her wipe the floor with you What about Michael Do you think that you could lose him?

"Not if I can help it, he is staying with me" She dared not let on that she was hoping that Michael would be sent to live with his mother and would not be there for her to look after.

"By the way I am making some inquiries about some flats that I have found out about some near Wem. If I can get one, I can get out of here and use it as a stepping stone to be nearer to you

"It will be bloody good to have some one to sleep with again"

"Won't be long my Darling. If I can get Jim angry enough He might give me grounds to divorce him."

"See how it goes but be careful I don't want you to get your self hurt. Although he seems placid enough to me. He does not seem to have a lot of go in him; he looks a bit of an awkward bugger"

"Now don't talk like that Dear He has served our purpose "Sandra was jumping to Jim's defence knowing that she really could not have had a better husband, It was that she did not have any love for the man. "Every thing will sort it self-out".

"I had better make it look as if I have come to do some work. What needs fixing?"

George resented her speaking in Jim's defence.

"Oh just plane a few bits off the pantry door and leave plenty of wood shavings about but tell me when am I going to see you again? Darling"

"Come over and stay for the day that would be good if you could?"

"Of course I'll come and give you a day I'll arrange it"

It was late when George finally left Sandra to return home Jim and little John was already in bed and fast asleep. George and Sandra kissed passionately in his van before he left.

She got in bed beside of Jim trying not to disturb him and she relaxed.

"You stayed up late last night didn't you "Jim said the following morning.

"Not really, are you grudging me watching a bit of telly now and again?"

"Of course not dear." Jim wanted to avoid an argument.

"Not much use coming to bed any earlier is it? Your no use to me always too bloody tired".

"I work hard"

"Don't I.?"

"Oh I am going out to work"

"Work, work that's all you think about". I'll torment him she decided.

Jim was out in the field spreading muck by hand and he was hungry as it neared dinnertime He went in for a bite to eat. Sandra had got herself ready for when Jim came in. She put John in the front room with plenty of toys and closed the door on him .She had gone upstairs to the bathroom and filled the bath. When she heard Jim come in She quickly got her self undressed and called Jim to come up to her.

"I'm not coming upstairs I am all mucky" He Shouted back up the stairs' She went out on to the landing and stood completely naked looking down the stairs,

'"Oh Darling. Do come and make love with me"

'"What the hell is the matter with you Are you sex crazy?

"Oh I suppose that you can't rise to the occasion? Too tired. Too busy. That's all I hear about these days. Come my Darling and make love to Sandra She needs you"

"Sandra don't be so daft, I'm hungry and I've a lot to do" Said Jim going up the stairs

"Follow me my Darling or are you feeling hopeless as usual I Just fancy you. Join me in the bath or is that too much to ask? She cooed lowering herself into the water.

Jim had never felt so angry "Now look you stupid woman get some clothes on and come down stairs I have had enough of this bloody nonsense".

"Come with you, not until you have satisfied me or are that asking too much".

She stepped from the bath the water dripping from the nipples of her breasts. Pouting her lips, she continued by saying, "I could name many a man who would not be able to resist me"

"That's enough" Shouted Jim

Sandra knew that she now had him angry and she would not shut up. As Jim turned to go back down stairs he slapped her face.

"Hit me would you. How dare you" She screamed "I'll have the law onto you"

"Do that if you dare."

Jim took a piece of bread and cut a piece of cheese throwing the knife into the sink. He stepped into his wellies and went back to the field.

Sandra in the meantime had just what she had wanted she quickly dried herself and put on some clothes, she went downstairs and telephoned the police crying into the telephone that her husband had beaten her up and had threatened her with a kitchen knife. She did this hoping that they would put an order on him not to touch her again. She knew that now she had some grounds for a divorce.

Jim was working away spreading the muck throwing it across the green grass with a spreading fork He was trying to work off his temper He knew that he should not have hit her! She's driving me too far he said to himself.

"Mr Beddows" A voice spoke from behind him. Jim spun around with surprise and saw a police officer standing there, watching him "Working hard I see"

"And why not" replied Jim "What do you want?"

"Your wife has made a complaint against you"

"Has she indeed"

"I believe that this is not the first occasion".

"Believe what you like. Now get off this field or the grass won't only be covered with muck"

"Now, Now Mr Beddows. Just let us talk about it"

"You can talk all you like, I am listening"

"You promise me that this behaviour will not happen again. Not that I can do much because it is a domestic matter. Its up to your wife to press charges Thank goodness it was only a slap and no damage done, The law takes a very dim view of men who hit their wives. She says that you threatened her with a knife is that true? That could be a very serious offence"

"She did .Did she, the only knife that I picked up was to cut a piece of cheese for something to eat and she was up stairs at the time God she can tell some lies".

The police officer guessed that there had been a row and thought that by the look of Sandra face he had not hit her as hard as she was making out. He was inclined to believe the husband's version of events. And as for the knife incident he could see that she had stretched it to the limit.

"Now let me get on with some work." Jim was so annoyed that Sandra had called the police. Why had she done it? Finishing what he had wanted to do, He went back inside.

Sandra was sat quiet watching the television in the front room. Jim did not bother with her instead he got himself something to eat. He fried some eggs and bacon and sat at the kitchen table with his mug of tea by the side of his plate He had no intentions of discussing the previous events of the day. He went out and fed the animals, which needed to be fed then returned stripped off his shirt, and washed at the kitchen sink. He went to bed completely exhausted with the day's work. He remained silent as far as Sandra was concerned. He had been prepared to apologise, never having struck a woman in his life before He was not an aggressive man Getting the police involved had shaken him What the devil was she up to? Only the day before Sandra had seemed so happy. George coming had certainly not upset her. Now today his whole world was topsy -turvy. He knew that he should not have slapped her but she had provoked him. He was a hard worker and had only wanted to provide for his family. He wondered where she was. Then he turned over, relaxed, and fell asleep.

Sandra now had what she had wanted Jim had slapped her. Having the police gave her proof although her face had looked red it didn't hurt. The policewoman that stayed with her while the other police officer went to speak to Jim had looked concerned.

"Does your husband make a habit of this behaviour?" She asked Sandra

"I don't know" Answered Sandra "It depends on which way the wind is blowing".

"Do be careful Mrs Beddows there is always some one who can be of help to you. Don't be afraid to ring us if any thing like this happens again".

"Oh yes I will I get a it nervous of him at times Thank you for coming I must have panicked I will be alright now that he's calmed down"

"Well take care of your self and that little boy we don't want either of you to come to any harm"

"I have been thinking of leaving him all being well I hope to have a flat soon"

Sandra did not join Jim in the double bed instead she slept on an old single bed in one of the spare rooms.

"What the hell is the matter with you?" Jim asked next day when he came in at dinnertime. His working day started far too early for him to have seen any thing of Sandra earlier in the day.

"Nothing wrong with me you big bully".

"I have never touched you before. Tell me why did you drive me to it?"

"I didn't you are helpless and hopeless I'm not stopping here any longer than I have to"

"What are you talking about Not stopping here Of course you are staying What about little John?"

"I will take him with me".

"Take him where?"

"Never you mind where. I will find some where" Jim decided not to argue any further The very thought of Sandra actually leaving had never entered his head He did not take her threats seriously, instead he ate his dinner and went back to work.

Months later George had still ignored orders for him to attend court hearings. After having had three court orders served on him there was only one alternative left to the courts and that was to order an arrest for the next hearing. Hannah was finding it a struggle to make ends meet when she had been at the lane there had been no rent to pay and no Gas central heating this was added in the rent so that the council knew that it was paid. Hannah was managing but only just. Christmas would soon be here again, what was she going to do then? Worry about it when the time comes she said to her self meanwhile she just had to carry on. She still had Thursdays off so she would go into the market in Wellington. She could get more for her money than what she would get from the store by the flats.

"Hello there Hannah". She looked across the street and there was Mrs Brown who was crossing over to have a chat.

"I still can't believe about you and George splitting up. How are you coping if there is any thing that you want? Don't you be afraid to ask me? You know me well enough to know that you only have to ask. By the way my son and Daughter in –law are changing some of their furniture there is a kitchen table and chairs that you can certainly have, that is if they would be of any use to you?"

"Mrs Brown they certainly would. I am a bit short of furniture, I would be really grateful" She smiled imagining a table and chairs in her kitchen that would make life much easier.

"I am going to look at a wardrobe and a couple of arm chairs tonight they are no longer needed and I can have them if I can fetch them. I could collect the table at the same time.

"You know Hannah I can not under stand George" Mrs Brown went on. "Damned good carpenter but he just would not finish a job. He was always keen enough to start, that young sister of yours only had to show her face and he was off like a rocket with her" Hannah felt a shiver go down her spine.

"My young sister" She asked. Hannah was trying to sound calm.

"Yes the little madam needed a damned good hiding the way she was running after him and he was no better or he would not have encouraged her. It must break your parent's hearts just to think about it. Are you all right Hannah?" Hannah was now feeling very sick and she looked as if she was going to faint. Her sister's name was being mentioned all too often.

"You do know what has been going on," Mrs Brown asked.

"Not really "Stammered Hannah

"Well is that not the reason that you left him"

"No"

"Oh my goodness you come with me, let us go to my place. That is if you have got the time. I am so sorry; I would open my big mouth. You get in this car. She ushered Hannah and her shopping into her car. Hannah felt so numb that she did as she was told. The caravan being towed home George and Sandra; her mind was in a whirl.

"Now you sit down Mrs Brown ordered as they went into the kitchen Hannah sat where she had sat so many times before when she had been waiting for George when she had been shopping in town. The old coffee-pot was still sat on the Aga keeping hot. Mr Brown had passed away and her son now ran the veterinary business. She was glad of Hannah's company.

"Tell me what is it that you were saying about Sandra coming here. It seems that every where that I go there is a hint or a remark linking George with Sandra as if they were having an affair"

"Well put it like this. If she called on her way home from school there was no more work done here for the rest of the day"

"But But" stuttered Hannah "George worked such long hours here until ten o'clock on some nights".

"Ten o'clock my foot, he has never been here after five no matter what job that he was working on."

"Well tell me did you not give him tea and cakes so that he could work extra hours".

"Are you sitting there and telling me that you did not know that they were carrying on together". Hannah started to cry. "Of course I did not know. I had an inkling that he had been in bed with another woman, just before I left. But never in my wildest dreams did I suspect that it was Sandra My own sister. How could he? Do you really think that it was Sandra?"

"Of course it was Sandra. She has worked it so that she has got you out of the way has she".

"But she is married to Jim and has the baby"

"So what, that lad fell hook line and sinker"

"What do you mean?"

"Well you don't think that that the kid was Jim Beddows do you?

"Of course or why did he marry her and he has taken the blame. He's a wonderful father to the little boy"

"You only have to ask his mother, according to her He was never the father, That young bitch got him drunk His mother marked the calendar and no way was that baby born two months premature not at the weight that he was"

"That's nearly three years ago"

"Makes no difference if it was ten, that girl was not straight, you'll see it will all come out now that you have got out. Why did you get out if it was not because of her?"

"I got out because he was making out that I was going mad and he was accusing me of all sorts of things and he could be violent at times We got out for our own safety The bastard, he wouldn't would he not my own sister".

"Well he used to look bloody pleased with him self when she arrived here He was damned quick to put her bike in the back of that van of his I can't believe that you did not suspect any thing."

"Mrs brown why should I. I still can't believe there's any truth in what you are saying. Although Molly used to say different things but naturally I thought that she was tired or whatever. When I spoke to George about the things that she said He would try to convince me that she was losing her marbles. No not my own sister she would never do that to me I always treated her as one of the family"

"So you have". Replied Mrs Brown".

"Oh my God it does not bear thinking about" Exclaimed Hannah as realisation was beginning to dawn on her about what Mrs Brown had been saying.

"George and Sandra. OH no she is young enough to be his daughter No wonder he threatened me if I were to ring you and see if he was still working late. He said that he would never forgive me if I made a fool of him and that I could not trust him to do a bit of overtime".

"The oldest trick in the book. Drink your coffee and have another one. You are going to need it".

"What you have told me is now beginning to make sense. Others have been hinting but I have not listened. Molly has been trying to tell me but I did not pursue the matter Hannah went on to tell her about the caravan being towed back home".

"The evil buggers, "She said .You were such a damned good wife to him if I had a gun I would be the first to shoot the devil. Believe me I would. "

Hannah drank a second cup of coffee and then they said goodbye to each other Mrs Brown giving Hannah a hug and telling her to get in touch any time that she might need help.

Hannah made for the bus stop; she must get home before the twins came in from school. Entering the flat she put her shopping down on the kitchen floor and made for the bathroom where she was violently sick. She sat on the floor. George and Sandra George and Sandra kept going round and round in her head, she got up and made for the bedroom and flung herself onto the bed. God! I feel so ill, why did Mrs Brown say such dreadful things. Calm down she told her self, there is no truth in it. Whatever George had been like for the last three years even he would not have sunk so low as that. Would he? If he had not been working late and doing overtime where had he been and why should he make up such dreadful stories about working late. This was some thing that happened to other people, not her.

After giving the twins their tea she went back to the bedroom to think, completely forgetting about the wardrobe and the armchairs.

"Are you not feeling well Mumsie?" Jennifer asked peeping around the bedroom door.

"I'm alright Dear I just have a head ache I will be with you in a few minutes".

Pull your self together her mind was telling her body. This is just a nightmare. The best thing to do is to find out if there is any truth in the rumours. Any thought of eating was out of the question. Hannah sat on the seat and watched the television. There was no point in her running to Molly in the flat below her. If she confirmed what Mrs Brown had told it would be the end for her. The more that Hannah thought about it she began to realise that it could be true but the big question was why she had not seen it going on. She convinced herself that she would have noticed if George and Sandra were having an affair she was not daft and neither was she stupid. As soon as the twins went to bed Hannah also turned in but sleep evaded her.

The following morning she looked awful.

"What's the matter with you" Asked her work mate Maggie "You look dreadful, do you think that you should have come to work today".

"I'm alright. And who else is there to drive the van today" Hannah muttered. Having decided that she would not talk about her misgivings to any one. No one would understand how it was that she had not noticed that her own sister was having an affair with her husband. If what Mrs Brown had said was true and the woman had no reason what so ever to tell Hannah a pack of lies. Hannah had worried about it all night and the more that she tried to make sense of it all the more she could see there was a possibility that it was all true. That was the reason George had threatened her about checking up on him. She would have found that he was not where he said he was.

Not concentrating on what she was doing Hannah put the van into reverse so that she could turn it around in a cul-de-sac and bang, she had hit a car that she had not noticed when she should have checked her side mirrors.

"Not your day" had Maggie said laughing

"Oh Lordy what a mess", she looked at the damage that was done to both vehicles. "The boss will go up the wall

“The owner of the car seemed to come from no where, He looked at the damage to his car and was quite a nice sort of chap.

“Not too bad” Confirmed the owner providing your boss will pay for the damage”.

“Pay for the damage, Hannah thought to her self what will he say about the van?

“Some one is not going to have any wages this week” Maggie broke into her thoughts. Not for a few weeks any way”.

“But I need my wages I can’t afford to pay for the damage. It looks as if it will be the sack for me”

“Didn’t you see the car?”

“I was not concentrating I guess”

“You should have stayed home. You looked awful this morning”

“I’m alright, let’s get on with the round and then we can both go home”.

“What in the damnation were you thinking about” Stormed Brian her boss when he saw the damage to his fairly new van. “Still I suppose that it could be worse at least we can still use it but it will be difficult to take it off the road long enough to have it repaired.

“Get off home, you look to me as if you need a good nights sleep. Stop watching that telly at nights and get to bed”.

Hannah was so glad to be let off so lightly. She made her way to the bus stop. Sitting on the bus as it made its way through town she looked vacantly through the window. She decided to really think before she said any thing to any one about what she was being told of George and Sandra Just in case they thought that she was mentally ill to even suggest that her sister had been seeing her husband. No one was going to believe her especially the family. Proof had to be obtained and if that was the case she must do some thing about it. But who could she trust if she were to even suggest such a thing.

Her solicitor had informed her that she had sufficient grounds for a divorce from George IT would be quite possible to take it on the grounds of mental cruelty, brutal cruelty and desertion. Hannah thought that he would be the best person to talk to She made an appointment to see him. Sitting again in his office which was now getting more familiar to her. Hannah told him of what she had heard and that it could all be true. He listened to Hannah's story and then he told her that there was nothing that she would be able to do about that because now that her sister was married the court would not bring this matter up because she was now a married woman. To reveal all was not the thing to do. The reason being that it could wreck her prospects of a happy marriage, with the man that she was now with. What Hannah was hearing was beyond belief was it possible that George could do such things and get away with it and as for Sandra the scheming conniving little bitch. As she went down the stairs and on to the street she was feeling so angry. I'll never let her get away with this she vowed.

A few weeks later Charles called to see how they were getting on and how they were coping. He had joined the RAF. How smart he looked in his uniform.

"What about coming out for a ride next week end?" He suggested "We could go for a ride to the sea I am sure that it would do Molly good, what do you think?"

"I must not be seen out with another man because it could jeopardise my divorce hearing.

"Hannah what are you thinking about, We have been friends for a good many years I went to school with William I am only offering to take you out for a day".

"I'm sorry Charles" Replied Hannah "I did not mean to imply any thing, it would be wonderful to get away from here for a day. Let's go and ask Molly what she thinks".

"That would be lovely" Was Molly's reply.

"I'll make some sandwiches and bring some pop for the twins." Hannah offered she was already getting enthusiastic.

“That’s settled then I’ll be here for ten o’clock on Sunday morning so be ready”

Charles stayed for a cup of tea and then went on his way. Sunday they all had a really good day out visiting Black rock sands. Hannah sat on the rocks keeping an eye on the twins as they played Molly and Charles were far too busy enjoying them selves just strolling and talking. Hannah looked out over the sea why had George towed the caravan home? Was it to meet Sandra? Where had they put it? She felt that she could never visit that caravan site as long as she lived She knew that she couldn’t. All sorts of things raced through her mind. It was so good to be able to get away from the flat although it was wonderful to have some where to live. Living in the country had always been so quiet the noise from the Sankey’s nearby factory was a pain when the windows were opened. Hannah had always slept with the window open at night. Now the noises of the night were totally different Cars were continually coming and going Music was always being played in the flats above them. The noise of the lifts going up and down never seemed to cease. This was different to the country side She no longer heard the birds first thing in the mornings That was the one thing that she missed the most of all. As soon as I can find a little cottage in the country to rent I will take it.

Hannah promised her self. This was only a temporary step.

“Charles “Hannah said one evening when Charles had called to arrange to take them all out again. “Would you think that I was crazy if I said that I thought George and Sandra were having an affair?”

“Well didn’t you know? I thought that was why you got out”.

“Well I did not know”

“You must have known it was common knowledge all over the village Ask your William he saw some photos of them”

Saw photos of them. “What photos? You mean to say that he knew and never said any thing to me about them”

"Would you have believed him?"

"It would have given me food for thought I could have done a bit of checking up on George. I just might have been able to put a stop to it or killed the both of them"

"You must be joking, from what I hear he's been seeing her since she was at school"

"At school what do you mean?

"She used to wait for him to finish work just to be with him Mother had often seen them together".

"It's funny that you should say that Mrs Brown reckons the very same thing that she was always chasing him".

"Didn't you suspect that there was some thing going on?"

"Why should I? It would have been beyond all comprehension to even contemplate that your own husband and your sister especially that she was so much younger than he was. Charles every one is suggesting that they were having and affair and that John is not Jim's child, what do you think?"

"There is a possibility they could be right, she certainly did not want any thing to do with us lads. Then all of a sudden she and Jim are getting married. You don't think that they would have pinned that on him"

"I don't know I have found out that our caravan was towed home Charles keep your ears open and would you let me know if you can find out about a big caravan being put some where it should not have been"

"It would be very interesting to see what George and Sandra do if you divorce him" "What do you mean?"

"Well he would be a free man, so then they could marry. Old Tom has been saying in the pub that she is down the lane quite a lot since you have left. The old boy does not miss much that goes on down there. You can be sure of that".

"She has been in my house cleaning and what else I wonder, have they been doing Charles it does not bear thinking about. How the hell has she got the nerve? I could be sick. Oh no they could not marry. I don't think that they can by law. One can not marry ones sisters husband as long as the sister is still alive"

"Well according to what old Tom has been saying she was bonking in your bed when you were at the market. You remember that stall you had. Well according to what he was saying in the pub as soon as he took you into town, he brought her back for the day. I think that you had better watch out for yourself"

"Really as long a go as that, he didn't did he? Surely not? In my own Bed I will swing for her. That I will. Surely the conniving pair would not harm me just so that they could get married."

"Why not? They are making out to all and sundry that you were going off your head. Cracking up"

"Oh they are. Are they? I have got to admit that if I had not got out I'm sure that I might have cracked up and had a complete breakdown When I think about it and what I have heard since, I am beginning to think that was what he was trying to do. Well he came unstuck. I'm made a lot tougher than that. It will be interesting to see what happens next. Of all the nerve, she has got the most that any one can comprehend. To go anywhere near the lane I wonder if Jim knows what is going on. I'll bet he does not she is such a convincing liar."

"How are the family taking it?"

"I've no idea I haven't seen any of them I'm a bit cut off with out having the telephone I don't think that the parents will approve of my leaving George

"I wonder what they will say when they find out that it is Sandra behind all this"

"It does not bear thinking about. Disown her I should imagine, the little bitch Do you know that I can't think what is the worst thing that I could call her I just feel like killing her"

"Now don't you go doing that, nothing would be gained" Exclaimed Charles sounding worried. I would not blame you if you did. One could hardly call her a very loyal sister she has ruined your life and that of the kids. Tell me. Will you ever forgive her? If she stays with poor Jim She will have got away with it"

"I don't think that she will stay with him. If it is right that she has been with George since her school uniform days, she is not going to stay with Jim, not likely. I reckon that they have used Jim to cover up their sins. Poor sod. She will not get away with it and neither will he The lord moves in mysterious ways We will all pay for our sins before we die Well that's what we were bought up to believe."

"Tell me how you really feel about her?"

"I can't explain exactly how I feel about her or George, repulsive, bitter I feel that I've got to get revenge. It all keeps going around in my head. At the moment I only have hatred for them both. No wonder that he was so horrible to me. You know Charles I can't think why I am telling you all this. Don't take any notice of me I will get over it in time. Talk about eternal triangles .I thinks that this is going to be bitter triangles. If you hear of a cottage to rent perhaps you would let me know the noise here gets to me. The wheels that they throw around at the factory across the road create such a din at nights".

"Have patience Hannah sort your divorce out first I say. You do one thing at a time. I will keep my ears open for you if that would be any help. I'll get off now so that you can get to bed. That young Jennifer will not settle until you turn in."

"Its very difficult for her .She is missing her Dad dreadfully and she misses Michael's company".

"It can't be easy; just you let me know if there is any thing that I can do"

"You don't know any one with a van who would not charge too much do you? Mrs Brown has given me a kitchen table and chairs I have to collect them as soon as possible"

"Leave it with me I can borrow a van and give you a hand

"Charles I really appreciate it, you spend far too much of your time helping us".

"I don't mind it gets me from under mother's nose. There is never much peace at home she is always wanting me to stay in and keep that sister of mine Company".

"Can't be easy for you Charles If only your Mother would let the girl grow up instead of treating her like a baby".

"It's all Annabel, she has no time for any thing or any one else. Dad and I take care of our selves most of the time. I had better get back or it will be like the Spanish inquisition. Where have you been? What have you seen? What gossip is there to tell? It is only so that she can go to the village shop tomorrow with some thing fresh to talk about. When she is not out shopping with Annabel she is gossiping in the village shop. Aunt Beattie is always moaning about the way that she spends her time. No one would believe that they were sisters they are as different as chalk and cheese.

Hannah saw Charles out of the door of the flat.Back inside she sat down on the seat. Why have I talked so much?" She said to her self. I am a fool, but what does William know that I don't. I will ask him if he comes for David at the weekend. David got on extremely well with William He often went with him on the farm on a Saturday While Hannah was working so that she could keep her job Hannah needed her money it was all she had to live and keep the children with.

"Hannah was told by her solicitor, that the fact that she left George did not entitle her to any thing. Furniture a part of the property nothing. She would have to prove her case in the court to get a divorce.

"Oh Lordy what a mess Why did I get out? Why had I not seen how difficult it was going to be? When would the courts catch up with George so that she could have more money to live on? What if she did not win the case? It seemed all right for Mr Barnett to sit there in his snug little office and say that all being well she would get something. I am condemned to this flat with no garden to grow any vegetables to eke out the pennies. What had she done? Taking the twins from the country to live in a flat. She asked her self so many times why she had done it. Doubts often filled her mind what had she done? Sitting talking to Charles had brought so much of the times when he had called when they were living in the lane back again. Hannah missed the country and she knew that the twins did. Jennifer had not settled at all Hannah was really worried for her should she beg George to have them back Would he? There were so many questions to be answered. But when she thought about the fact that he had been having an affair with her sister she knew that she could never forgive him enough to be able to live with him again. No she could not. That was the one thing that she could never forgive him for how ever many times he asked to be forgiven. He had been repulsive in what he had done she thought that it was just about the worst thing that a man could do. I must have proof, at the present it is only just hearsay. I must see William and find out if it is true about him seeing photos.

"William "she asked when he brought David back on the Saturday evening "Charles called to see how we were coping and he mentioned that you might be able to throw some light on the rumours that are going around. Do you know any thing about George and Sandra having an affair?"

"Well all that I know is that they did but it is all over she went out with Jim She married him"

"How did you find out?"

"Ted Locket showed me some photos that he had taken of them in the woods"

"Ted but that Ted lives in the flats across the way in that other block just over there I have seen him coming in and out. That bastard George really did have an affair with her People keep telling me about it. They reckon that she is still seeing him".

"I dunna think so She promised me that she had finished it when she got married Any way I'm surprised that you did not suspect any thing"

"No of course not, He always had a plausible explanation to why he was working overtime".

"I'll bet the bugger did He does not look me in the face, Any way she was just as bad but then he had no right she was under age"

"You stand there and tell me that this could have been going on before she was sixteen. Never, He wouldn't He didn't. It was against the law".

"Bloody sex mad the little bitch she could not get enough of him until I put a stop to it"

"You did what?

"I threatened to tell the old folks if she saw him again"

"Why didn't you tell me?"

"Thought it best to sort it out if we could, it's past now she's married to Jim".

"Not what I hear, that child is George's not Jim's. Could there be any truth in that?"

"I suppose that there could be. But I shouldn't think so" Hannah notice his face drain of all colour and guessed that he knew more than what he was letting on. What Hannah did not know was that he had just realised that he had taken it for granted that Jim had been the father of that child and now he wondered if Sandra had been lying to him as well. He suddenly thought about the night of the party when his parents had been away. She had been all over Jim that night. He could hear her saying that Jim was her knight in shining white armour. It was now dawning on him that she had pulled the wool over his eyes good and proper.

"She married now I should let sleeping dogs lie"

"I can't do anything about it according to Mr Barnett the solicitor"

"Time will tell. I think that the best thing that you did was to get out. Leave him to it. "What happens about Michael?"

"There has to be a court hearing, George does not want him to come and live with me. But I don't think that he will have much choice. I'm not giving in I must get the three of them back together again. Jennifer misses him dreadfully but I can't do any thing until the court decides what is best for all three. I will be glad when they get the bastard to pay me some money. I need it".

"I hear that he has given up his job that he had and is at home most of the time. Some talk of him getting work building that new hospital at Shrewsbury".

"Oh he's working local again is he? That's a relief in a way for Michael's sake. Keep your eyes and ears open for me, she told him about the caravan being taken off the site"

"Bloody Nora the cheeky devils. They haven't have they? Surry what lengths did they go to so that they could be together"

"I really don't know but that's enough of talking about that pair, how are you and Sheila getting on?" Asked Hannah trying to change the subject.

"Alright I guess" But he did not sound too re-assuring.

"No problems?

"Not really" Hannah did not pursue the subject any further Sheila was a bit of a girl for the men. She loved to show off in front of them. Once when they had called on Hannah and George, Hannah came in from the garden to find her sat on George's knee sharing the same pullover as George. They were taking it as all good fun. Then they explained that they were only acting the fool and that if it looked bad don't give it any thought,

After William had left Hannah sat staring into space? Why did she feel so sick theses days? She was having trouble eating and she knew that she was loosing weight. I will see Ted locket and ask him if I can see those photos for myself next time that he stops for a chat. Photos indeed the thought made her feel worse than she did already. Every thing that had been said by first one and then another all pointed to the fact that it was all true and she had been the only one not to know. Hannah's mind refused to accept the facts, why didn't I see what was going on. Why did George need her? What was wrong with me? We had a fairly happy sex life up until the last couple of years. She had cooked and cleaned and done the garden where had she gone wrong? There were a thousand questions to be answered and where was she going to find those answers. If I ever get my hands on her I will wring her bloody neck and if I could get hold of a gun I would shoot him. I'll get even with them if it is the last thing that I ever do She promised herself. How could they have done this to me? If George had wanted another woman why pick her little sister and why had the pair of them not packed their bags and moved to the other side of the country.

Molly had been right she could see it now; George had set out to get her out of the house. Why had she been such a fool? She could not imagine Sandra leaving Jim to go and live with George. No that would be unthinkable she would not. Even Sandra would not have the nerve to do that. What if it was George's child, what had those two been planning? Poor Jim even Sandra could not be that cruel meeting her sister's husband was despicable enough but to use another human being to that extent would be deplorable. Hannah decided that it would be best to wait and see. I know now that I must get this divorce business sorted out. How am I going to go through with it? I've only been in a courtroom once for the inquest of Timmy.

Hannah made a point of having a long chat with Molly and told her all that she now knew.

"The low down stinking bastard. You take them to court. You take them all the way. You can do it "Molly re-assured her

"But I will have to stand in the dock and prove my case" Protested Hannah.

"But if you have a good case, your solicitor man has already told you that you have"

"Molly what happens if I can't win. I've been told that they could take the twins away from me"

"Don't you go listening to gossip and tittle-tattle" Molly said very firmly. If you do you will not be able to go through with it. The judge will be on your side, you can be sure of that. Once the facts are presented to him and besides I'm coming with you".

"You would"

"Of course I will I am not going to let you go there on your own. It is time that George faced up to his responsibilities like a man if you can call him one I certainly would not, I sure have my doubts about that".

The next time that Hannah saw Ted Locket she asked him. "Is it true that you saw George and Sandra in the woods?"

"Who said that I did? What have you been told?"

"Not much William dropped it out that you had seen them, some thing about photos".

"What did he tell you?" Ted started to stammer.

"Not a lot only that I would not believe that George had been meeting Sandra in the woods"

"Oh that is true alright. They had been at it for years when she was a kid at school. He was always giving her lifts and she did not see me when she was waiting for him".

"I still can't believe it Ted what would my Dad say if he had found out?"

"Well is that not the reason that you got out? If your Dad had caught the buggers he would have shot the pair of them"

"No I got out because of his moods and cruelty and the lack of money I couldn't take any more".

"Has he done any more to that house, expecting you to bring up three kids in that bloody hell of a house What was the man thinking about, Still I suppose that he had no time to do much. Bonking in the woods every other day like he did. Too busy satisfying her I reckon"

"No I don't believe it"

"Won't be long before the little bitch moves in with him. Like a dog on heat she is"

"You are joking, she wouldn't

"How much do you bet missus I've watched you lot grow up, but in all my time working in the woods I've never come across one like her. Man mad My God it looked to me as if she took some satisfying".

"Let me have those photos of them Ted"

"Can't do that Missus".

"Why not Ted?

"I'll have the bloody law onto me, don't want that now do I "

"But who would know Ted?"

"What are you going to say if you were asked where you got them from?"

"Oh I could make up some story".

"What when you are in court on oath. I know you women you get nervous and then every thing comes out"

"I wouldn't"

"Can't take a chance. Sorry missus its not that I don't want to help you mind, you need all the help that you can get but I reckon that you will sort things out alright I hope that you get the better of that pair of buggers. You deserve to see them rot in hell that you do. See you around. Best of luck, take care of yourself" He turned and quickly walked away.

"Bye Ted".

Blast and damn, thought Hannah when Ted had gone. The very proof that I wanted and I can't get my hands on it. Damn damn she swore. I'll do it with out his help. So he thinks that it is still going on, does he. I wonder. She returned back into the building and up the lift to her own flat. Sitting down she thought about what they had discussed. It is all true what every one has been trying to tell me and to think that I could have been so stupid as to doubt them. I'll get even with that little bitch, but how. How the hell could she go bonking up the woods as she has? It was revenge that Hannah now wanted most of all. She tried to recall some of the difficult times that she had had with George. No bloody wonder he had been so difficult to live with No wonder he never seemed interested in having sex with me, he was knackered from bonking in the woods with her. My god what a lovely time that they have been having I suppose that it was for her that the caravan was towed back from the sea. But where had they hidden it I will kill her I will I will I have to get her for this I'll never forgive them. Never.

Sandra telephoned the DHHS office and made an appointment for the next time that she went into town shopping. She wanted to find out what she was entitled to and what she was not. When asked why she wanted help she told them that she had to get away from her husband because he could be violent at times and that she feared for her safety and that of her little boy.

"Have the police been involved with this matter if so you do stand quite a good chance of getting help until matters can be sorted out for you."

"Oh yes .I had to call the police one afternoon when He hit me?"

"Really". "In that case we will check with them and see if what you are saying is true and then we will assess your needs." The woman in the office went on to explain to Sandra that she would be entitled to have her rent paid. Television licence and so many other things such an allowance for food and clothes until she had divorced her husband and the courts had decided who had to pay for what and to whom.

Sandra went home completely ecstatic she could hardly contain her self. Every thing was going her way. Once she had a flat it would be so easy to move in it.

Jim was some times asked to accompany his boss Mr Howells to cattle sales and he always knew in advance which day that he would be going. He would be away all day. He never knew in advance if his boss was going to do any buying of young stock and if he did the responsibility would be Jim's to see to any loading or unloading of the cattle. Jim quite liked going to the sales it was like a social gathering for the farmers and his boss always treated him with respect introducing Jim first to one and then another. At the end of the week Jim found that there was always a bit extra in his wage packet for the inconvenience of being away all day.

Jim was quite surprised when he saw the new three- piece suite that Sandra had bought it seemed rather small for the size of their front room. He thought that a much bigger one would have looked a bit better. He did not fancy a row with her; she could be so temperamental during these last few weeks he had decided to keep his mouth shut. What he did not know was that it had not been bought for his front room but for George's living room. Mr Howells stopped at a public house that served good food it had been well tested on many other occasions.

"I don't like to bother the wife to make me a meal when I get in. So you come with me Jim and have some thing to eat, there is a lorry load of young stock to unload when we get back and no man can be expected to work on an empty stomach. Tuck in Jim lad and order what you fancy." He said .It was not until that awful evening when Jim, after having a very successful day out with Mr Howells. He came home to an empty house. There no sign of Sandra or little John and when he looked around he was amazed at what else had gone. He was absolutely gutted. Where were they and why had she done this He went from room to room, There were signs of furniture and other things missing? God he said to him self this has been well planned.

Jim went back to the kitchen he was having difficulty in digesting what he thought that Sandra had done. She had gone and she had taken John with her He felt so angry and so sick. He went out side to check if his stock had been fed as she had promised that she would feed them in case he was late getting back from the sale but the way the calves were making such a noise he knew straight away that they were hungry. The feeding of them must take first priority. Back in the kitchen he looked to see if and what food she had bought but there was none. There had been no food shopping done earlier in the week He had not been too bothered he thought that she would be going into town on Saturday while he was away all day. But when he tried to think. He realised that she had been in town during the week. Yet there had been no food bought. What he did not know was that she had used the housekeeping money that he had given her to buy food and to buy as many other little things that she thought that she might need. She had packed it all into boxes and put it under the bed in the spare room. It would only be there for a couple of days. George was coming on Saturday with his van and while Jim was away and take the boxes, herself and John to the flat. She had hired a different van from a local firm to move furniture so that she could be reimbursed for the cost .She had been told at the DHHS office to keep all the receipts and they would see what they could do to get the money back for her. Jim went to bed that night completely exhausted and for the first time in his life he felt completely alone.

Chapter Nineteen
Finality and Inevitable

The doorbell rang. Hannah went to se who was calling. . She was so surprised to see her eldest sister Lizzy standing at the door.

". Come in "Said Hannah, Lizzy stepped inside looking about her as the she followed Hannah to what supposedly could be called the living room or lounge. "Have a cup of tea". Hannah offered as she looked at Lizzy. Lizzy had not changed much since she had married, still very slim she sat down on the seat that Oliver had made for her, as she removed her hat and gloves. Hannah noticed her hands were now showing signs of really hard work. Hannah referred to the seat as her settee. Well it was the nearest thing to look like a settee that she was going to get

"This is a pleasant surprise" Hannah smiled

"I can not stay long. I must get back," Lizzy quickly said "And I don't see much for you to smile about. Hannah did not answer that comment instead she said "Sit there a minute while I put the kettle on, It will not take many minutes boil on the gas cooker, this gas is wonderful it cooks every thing so quickly.

"Well why have you come to see me, if you have to get back so quickly?"

"It's because of all this talk about you are going to have a divorce. You know Mam and Dad can't believe that you would do such a thing. They and we all think that it is dreadful. What on earth is going on? Bringing disgrace to the family you are. I don't think that you should go through with it"

"They do. Do they? You have been busy talking to each other. Well you can ask your little sister Sandra what she has been up to. That is if she could say any thing that was the truth and not a pack of lies. Hannah told Lizzy her version of what had been going on" An hour later Lizzy left the flat. As she went down the stairs to the front entrance no way would she go in the lift? She was far too nervous to get into one of those things it might break down and she could die in it... If Hannah thinks for one moment that I am going to swallow that load of nonsense then she has to think again Just wait until I tell My Frank about it when he comes in tonight. She said to her self When Frank came in from work she told him of her visit to Hannah's flat. She told him what Hannah had told her were the reasons why she had left George". "You know Frank If Hannah thinks that I am going to swallow that load of rubbish she has to think again. I have known George since he first went to work up the Wrekin and no way would he do any thing so dreadful. He would not hurt a fly and as for Sandra she is happily married to Jim. They have little John to think about. I think that it is as Sandra says that Hannah is jealous of Grace and that she has left George hoping to find some one better. Well the best of luck to her, that is all that I can say. Living in a flat with hardly any furniture is not doing any better than what she had with George down the lane. No I don't believe a word of it"

"Well I don't think that Hannah would have left him for nothing I have never liked Sandra, A thoroughly spoilt brat that is how I have all ways seen her. I think that it would be best to wait and see what is going to come out of this business. I have heard rumours from the village that George and Sandra have been carrying on for years. But if I had told you what I was hearing I don't think that for one minute that would have believed me No I think that it would be wise to stay quiet for a while and see what comes out of this lot".

Lizzy was quite put out she did not like to hear Frank taking Hannah's side. Lizzy could not and would not believe what Frank had just said. There was always a rumour spread by drinkers when in the pubs and most of the time there was no truth in them what so ever.

"Frank she tells me that Ted Locket, you know the ditch cleaner has taken photos of George and Sandra being undressed in the woods. Well I have never heard of such things Ted Locket taking photos of courting couples in the woods. I cannot think what our Hannah is thinking about. She is getting confused that she is How can she make up such stories?"

"Well Lizzy. It was always known that Ted locket as a peeping Tom. Not much that went on in those woods missed his beady eyes when I was working at home he told us some tales He often had a cup of tea with us. I knew what he got up to and it does not surprise me if he hadn't taken a few photos. I say if it is right what Hannah has told you those photos would be worth looking at George and Sandra, Well I never. So the rumours could be true after all"

"Of course they are not true and I can't think why Hannah has made this all up and another thing Frank Timmins. I don't want you looking at dirty photos and certainly not in my house. Taking photos of courting couples indeed, I have never heard of such things". You have not heard of very much Frank said to himself but he thought better than to prolong the subject. He could see that Lizzy was getting proper agitated. But by-Jove was he going to keep his ears and eyes open from now on.

Lizzy was glad that Frank dropped the subject .She decided not to say any more but she was going to keep her ears open and nothing was going to convince her that Sandra and George had been having an affair. My goodness what ever will be said next, I wonder. I will not believe one word that Hannah has said. No I can't see George having an affair with her sister. That is complete nonsense, people don't do that sort of thing, and Of course they don't. George and Sandra how ridiculous. She repeated to her self. She started to chuckle to her self as she washed the dishes that they had used for their evening meal.

Hannah had to face the fact that divorce was inevitable. The very thought of it made her feel ill, her nerves were on edge. I must not crack up now, she told her self. No matter what proceedings took place today I have to go through with it but she did not look forward to it. To have to prove her case the words echoed though her brain. What if I don't? Her life to be discussed in front of strangers the very prospect of it all filled her with dread. She had spoken to her Doctor and he had given her some sleeping tablets, she told him why she thought that sleep avoided her and she was finding it difficult to cope with her work and the children.

When explaining this to Molly. Molly had no sympathy for Hannah what so ever. "You have two choices, she said firmly. "Either you get rid of him and have no recriminations; That George has been no help what so ever to you has he? Terry and I saw how you worked up that Wrekin, you did twice as much as he did and he has certainly done very little since you left there. Well certainly not in the last twelve months" And well before that, she muttered as she poured another cup of tea into the china cups, which she was very fond of. "Any way what about the twins? If he had cared any thing for them he would be sending some money towards their keep. I will be coming with you so don't worry about going into court on your own I know what an ordeal that it can be for you and I will see that you survive."

"You are still offering to come with me" Hannah's face showed surprise.

"Of course. You don't think that we are going to let you go on your own No way I think that you have been through enough already"

"Molly that would be great if you would, I was dreading going on my own". Hannah was so relieved. She sat back and enjoyed the cup of tea. A glance at Molly's mantle clock reminded her that the twins would soon be home from school.

"Don't forget what I have offered". Molly said as Hannah went out through the door.

Hannah received the official letter telling her to attend court The county Buildings Shrewsbury on the following Tuesday morning. There was no sleep for Hannah the night before. A thousand things were flashing through her mind. Firstly would George be there? If not there would be no case to answer and she would have to wait again to get the whole business settled. What would the Judge be like? Would he be more sympathetic towards a woman or towards George being a man like him self.

Tuesday morning finally came. Leaving Jennifer fast asleep Hannah crept out of bed. She went into the kitchen to make some tea she was tired and weary from the lack of sleep. She had decided not to take a tablet the night before in case she felt a bit woozy during the day. She sat at the red Formica table that Mrs Brown had given her and drank the tea sitting by the window watching the morning rush to work. It was so busy in the street below; although her flat was only on the second floor she still seemed high up. Later she tried to force her self to eat some toast. She must pull her self-together, her mouth felt like sandpaper. I will be glad when I can afford some butter instead of this margarine. Any sort of butter would be better than this. She studied the packet while she was trying to eat. I must eat she kept telling her self I must not faint.

She saw the children off to school and although she was constantly telling her self to calm down it was a relief when she was on the bus going to Shrewsbury sitting along side Molly. Hannah was sitting there in a world of her own. Molly was trying to make conversation Hannah was trying to answer her but a lot of it was just going over her head.

Was she doing the right thing she continually asked her self? Divorce was so final. The end of fourteen years marriage. Why had George made no effort to finish the house that had been their dream home Why this and why that.

She was wondering if Sandra would move in with him. Surely not. What would the family think? It would provide so much gossip for the village and for a very long time?

"We're here" Molly's voice broke into her thoughts "Come on, let's get this over with".

"I'm coming" Replied Hannah in a shaky voice as she came back to reality. They walked to the courthouse and entered the building; it appeared to be a very busy place People moving from one room to another Hannah caught sight of a man wearing a long black gown and a grey wig on his head.

Oh my goodness, he looks terrifying surely I won't have to face some one like that.

Her stomach started to churn; no you can't be sick now. She told her self. Take some deep breaths. Molly was making some inquiries as to where they had to present them selves. She found that they were too early but as she said it was better than being late. They were ushered into the courtroom and they sat where they had been told. They were in the public gallery. Hannah looked around her she was in a row of seats that were shaped in a semicircle and they were looking down on the proceedings of the court.

"Who are those that are wearing the wigs?" Hannah whispered to Molly

"Barristers" Molly whispered back. The barristers were sat and also the solicitors who were representing their clients; every one was talking in hushed whispers.

Ten o'clock came and the judge took his seat. To Hannah he looked very awe-inspiring. As she watched what was going on below her, she just wanted get up and run out of the building.

"Will you sit still and stop fidgeting" Came from Molly; the proceedings began Jones versus Jones. Hannah could not believe what she was witnessing. The barristers were asking questions one after the other. They were such intimate questions. First the husband and then the wife Surely she was not going to have to go through that? Where was Mr Barnett wondered Hannah There was no sign of him Hannah was beginning to panic? He said that he would be here. She felt a tap on her shoulder; Mr Barnett beckoned her to leave her seat.

Mr Barnett led her down some stairs and they sat in an office to await to be called "Now I want you to stay calm" That's alright for you to say thought Hannah I am terrified"" She did not know whether to be sick need the toilet or just faint. "Answer the questions as they are put to you"

Fleming versus Fleming. Please step forward the Clerk of the court announced from the door. Hannah stood up, her legs gave no response they would not move, Come along urged Mr Barnett.

"I can't. I can't go through with this" She pleaded

"Stay calm and follow me" Mr Barnett took her arm and steered her forward so as to follow the clerk. They entered the court. Hannah took a deep breath and glanced up at Molly who nodded and smiled down to her but Hannah could not return the smile. She had caught sight of George sat in the court and he looked evil. His face was a mask of hatred.

George was called first and answered the questions put before him.

The colour drained away from Hannah's her face as she listened to the reasons that George

Was giving for the failure of his marriage. He had sworn on oath that the things that he was saying about her were true, but most of what he was saying was a pack of lies. She had refused to have sex with him. She had worn knickers in bed always out chasing other men and that she was a hopeless cook. Stay calm Mr Barnett's voice was saying beside her.

Hannah was called to take the stand. Her hand trembled as she read the oath from off the card the clerk of the court had handed to her.

The judge sat there in his robes and that wig terrified her. For a fleeting second a smile crossed his face and then it was gone and his face was a mask of officialdom.

As Hannah stood taking the oath, she was beginning to calm down a little.

"Now Mrs Fleming what have you to say about these accusations? You have applied to this court to end your marriage by divorce. Your Barrister has asked for cruelty both physical and mental to be taken in to consideration also for deserting you and your children of whom I believe there are three.

A Barrister stepped forward and started firing questions at Hannah. Her nerves caused her voice to stammer she looked at Mr Barnett for help.

Mrs Fleming please addresses your answers to the Bench. And speak up Mrs Fleming came a demanding voice of the judge. Hannah felt tears coming into her eyes. Don't you dare start crying, an inner voice was saying? For goodness sake take hold of your self. After answering more and more questions Hannah heard that stern voice saying

"Please address your answers to me and not to the floor there is no one down there to listen to you. Hannah looked up "Yes sir".

"Well you tell me why you wore your knickers in bed?" Said the Barrister.

"Because I was so cold. It was only in the bad weather in the winter there was not a proper roof on the house"

"You took a job instead of staying at home and looking after the children. Tell me why, where they of no importance to you.

"I needed the money to keep them in food and clothes" Hannah was now beginning to feel angry by the questions as if she would have gone out to work otherwise. "

"But your husband has said that you had no need to"

"That's not true" Hannah felt as if all was going against her by the questions that were being asked She glanced at George and saw that he was looking smug and was smiling. The smile on his face made her suddenly feel angry. You bastard thought Hannah You know that I cared about the kids. Mrs Fleming the judge's words broke into her thoughts

"Answer the questions please"

"What was your relationship with a neighbouring farmer?" The Barristers voice boomed out once again.

"What farmer?" Hannah was gob smacked.

"Mr Parker".

"He gave me work when I was hard up for money

"What was the work?"

"Beet hoeing".

"Sugar beet hoeing"

"Were there any other workers in this field that you say that you were hoeing Sugar beet?"

"Yes of course there were about six of us".

"Your husband maintains that you were very friendly with Mr Parker. In fact he would go as far as to say that you were having an affair with this Mr Parker".

"His wife was a friend" What are they driving at; Hannah wondered what were they implying? She had given the cartridges that George used for his twelve bore shot gun to Mabel Parker once when she had confided in her about George's behaviour and that she had threatened to shoot George when she found that she could take no more. "Give me any cartridges that you have Mabel had told her. You do not want to go down for murder.

"Mrs Fleming speak up. The judge brought her back to what was going on around her. Repeat the question the judge ordered the barrister.

""Why did you leave your husband?"

""I found out that He was having an affair with some one else. And that he was a pig to me and up to his eyes in debt"

"But who was he having an affair with?"

"I'm not sure"

"Tell me Mrs Fleming. You only think that he was having an affair with another woman. You are not sure".

"I am sure but have been advised not to name her because of the hurt and embarrassment that it would do to my parents if it were to be put in the press".

The Judge called Mr Barnett forward to have a word with him.

What was being said Hannah did not know and could not hear? She did not care as far as she was concerned she had lost the case? George was sat and still had a smile on his face it had been a great relief that Hannah had not named Sandra. What Hannah did not know was that Probation officers had been working in the background finding out all about her and George they had been to take statements from neighbours and had secretly been following Hannah and how she was coping since leaving. These reports had been presented to the court before the hearing. This was the first time that she had seen George since she had left the night when they went back for some clothes. Was it love or hate that she felt for him now? She was not sure, then she thought of him having sex with Sandra in the woods, she now knew that she hated him He was a disgusting lying Bastard. Even on oath.

"Mrs Fleming are you listening? "The Judges voice brought her back to reality again. She sensed the worst. "Mrs Fleming I find in your favour. You are granted your divorce. I have decided that the custody of your three children will be discussed in chambers at a later date In the meantime your eldest boy Michael may stay with his father.

"What he may stay with his father, you must be joking. Thought Hannah and she was just about to say so, when the Judge said. Mrs Fleming you may leave the court".

Hannah almost dropped to the floor with relief. Mr Barnett came forward and ushered her from the wooden stand. Molly was waiting at the exit door for her.

"Thank god that is over "She announced. "Let's go home and get on with living. That certainly took the smile off George's face. I saw him sitting there smiling like a cat that had swallowed the cream. His face changed when he saw it taken away from him". They left the building and went out into the sunshine. There should be a bus along soon. "It's good that they have ordered the twins to stay with you"

"But what about Michael I don't want him to stay in that hell-hole of a house down the lane"

"Don't you worry things will soon change down there. The court will decide what is best for them. I don't think that they will send the twins to live there especially now. It will be very interesting to see what happens. I don't think that it will be long before that bugger has that evil sister of yours moving in".

"She wouldn't would she. No way would she do that to Mother and Dad "

"She would you know Do you think that she cares a monkeys who she hurts as long as she can get in bed with him".

"Is it true that she is living in a flat near Whit church, some one said that she had left Jim?"

"I have heard that she tried to get him for cruelty, apparently he had slapped her one".

"Well if you ask me it's a stepping stone to the next place and George is behind it"

"I never thought of that. They say that Jim has been running around like a headless chicken in all directions trying to find her. He's been to Helen's and goodness only knows where"

"Too busy thinking about your self and your own problems forget them, Jim will have to get over it so have you. Let that George and Sandra rot together. No good can come of it and you are out of it now"

Sitting at Molly's side on the back seat of the bus going home they were having such a chat. Hannah noticed that Molly was smiling. "Penny for your thoughts?"

"Oh that. What was all the fuss about wearing knickers in bed?"

"Molly it was only to keep warm. I often wore a jumper and socks when it was very cold."

"I would have had to have worn a top coat and a hat if I was expected to sleep in that house".

Hannah started to laugh visualising Molly cuddled up to Terry wearing her hat and coat.

"That's the first time that you have laughed today"

"I know Molly I was simply terrified"

"What of?"

"Oh so many things"

"And you had no need to these people in court are not daft you know. They do their homework. If they were to believe what they were told in court they would not be able to find out the truth. Goodness me I will be glad to get home for a cuppa it has almost gone dinner time"

"We could have stopped for a cup of tea in a café Molly you certainly deserve one"

"What and risk bumping into him in the street No thank you I would have a job to keep my hands off the disgusting pervert. You know Hannah the more I hear about him the more that I could throttle him. A dirty pervert that is what he has been, touching that girl from when she was at school. It does not bear thinking about Terry would be turning in his grave if he had had to witness this carry one. You know that he thought the world of George I could see that when I married him George was his favourite, but it was Thomas that I liked, to me he was far the better of the two boys".

Hannah neither knew whether to feel happy or sad. What would the twins say when she had to tell them that they would not be going back to live with their Dad. She knew that Jennifer secretly hoped that they would. Jennifer was being very difficult. It was the little things that hurt so much she made Hannah feel so guilty for getting out. If only Jennifer had known the times that Hannah had wished George would have come and asked her to go back even with the house only half finished. Hannah had longed to get the family back together. At the time she would have forgiven George any thing.

Suddenly her thoughts came down to earth with a bump. Forgive George now. Never. Not now that she knew about him and Sandra and now that Sandra had left Jim. The thought of her going to live in her house was repugnant.

Judith and Carl called in to see her later.

"Now let him paddle his own canoe" Judith announced" He had this coming I know that he is my brother but you did not have to tolerate that sort of behaviour from any one, I am sure the court will decide what is best for the children"

"My goodness" Said Hannah "I had forgotten about that. I wonder when I will have to go back again Lets hope that they will let Michael join us here I worry about him so much"

"They will decide what is best for them" Judith remarked in her usual assertive voice.

"But but "Hannah started to say, She was cut short.

"You have to stop worrying; you have enough to do to rear the twins. What about maintenance I don't suppose that has been arranged. I expect that it will come at the next hearing. Just think Hannah if he is made to pay for the maintenance for the last eight-teen months think what you will be able to do?" You have paid your way until now so I think that it would be a good idea to treat your self to a carpet for this room "

Hannah had made a wool rug from a rug making kit that was on offer in the sales. She had put it where there should be a hearth but the flats only had a two bar electric fire fitted to the wall in the living room. Hannah looked around and she could see what Judith meant. The room did look a bit sparse. Both Hannah and Judith started to laugh together If George was ordered to pay maintenance for all those months that

Hannah had been on her own My goodness she could certainly go shopping and she certainly do with a bit of extra money.

The two-second hand chairs did look a bit more presentable since Hannah had recovered them from some loose covers that she had been given and she had taken to pieces and put together again. Judith gave her a big hug as she left the flat she whispered". You will survive you know"".

George left the divorce court with a smile still on his face. It was over now even if what Sandra had told him to say had not worked in his favour. He was a free man Sandra could move in with him and bring John. He unlocked the van door sat inside lit a cigarette on which he drew deeply. He had been gasping for one all the time that he had been in court. First things first He must go and collect Sandra from the flat. He needed her now She could share his bed tonight .He had already explained to Michael that he might be a bit late home and that he was to go to his friends house until he returned.

When Sandra opened the door to him and he said that it was over she flung herself into his arms. "It's over its over you are free at last.". He told her what had happened at court omitting a bit of the truth. It was now twelve o'clock. "I could do with something to eat and drink"

"Shall I get some thing for you now Darling"

"No on second thoughts let's get back to my place, I can manage until then. I will bet the nosy buggers in these flats don't miss much".

Sandra had some of their clothes and John's toys already packed Win or lose she was going to stay with George. He took hold of John as Sandra gathered together what things that she wanted she had no intention of coming back to the flat tonight. She closed the door of the flat as they went out so that it locked. As she left she said "I can come and tidy up a bit another day", they made their way down the steps and out to the van parked in the yard below.

"That's got rid of her "Sandra commented as George drove towards Wellington." Now we can plan our lives together. She cuddled John saying." You are going to be with your real Daddy at last and for good" Sandra could not contain her excitement. She had made so many plans, now she had a chance to put them into action. She was with the man she lad loved since she was a girl still in school uniform and now she was free to be his wife. They did not have to worry about being seen together any more. No more secrecy, She did not care what people would say. Sandra knew that she was perfectly capable of giving answers to any inquisitive questions. "We will marry and make little John legally yours "

"Hold your horses Just a minute "George was certainly not ready for marriage so quickly He had only just got rid of Hannah. No way did he want to go rushing off to get wed again".

"Are you listening George? Your Daddy is not listening to your mummy "She cooed too little John".

"I heard you" He replied

"Well you will want us to get married will you not". She said sounding a wee bit alarmed.

"Of course my little love Of course but I think you have forgotten one thing".

"What? Well what is it that I have forgotten?"

"Well I could be wrong but I don't think that you can marry your sister's husband if she is still alive". George had thought a lot about this and had realised that there would be no need for him to marry again probably for many years to come. He would have Sandra for both Mistress and slave.

Sandra had not thought about that.

"You mean to tell me that we may not be able to marry after all that we have been through" .Sandra was gob smacked and astonished, it took her off guard for a moment. "Don't you worry George I will find out if that is true? You know that you could be wrong. Never mind" Her voice changed with softness "We are going to be together are we not and I am prepared to accept that much for the time being" She then directed her voice to John" You could have baby sisters and brothers.

George's stomach churned. More kids. What do I want more kids for? Not if I can help it. He said nothing he just kept his thoughts to him self.

"Wouldn't it be nice if Hannah could fall under a bus or something" Sandra's laughter broke into his thoughts.

"What did you say?

"What if Hannah were to fall under a bus"

"Lord don't let that happen or there will be more kids to look after".

"What do you think that Michael will say"?

"Not much. I don't see much of him. He's always off with his mates He's grown a big lad now."

"I hope he takes to John alright. Glory help him if he doesn't. I will certainly deal with him".

"He'll be aright" Said George not caring what was said next.

They pulled up in the yard at the cottage Sandra looked up at the house in dismay It could be worse I suppose.

"How long will it take do you reckon for us to finish this house" She asked when they were inside"

"Not long I should not think". Not on about the house already was she. He thought that he had had enough of that from Hannah. "Well" Said Sandra as she stood in front of the brick fireplace. "I must think about getting some sort of a job so to get some money moving again"

"What sort of job" George was dumb struck

"I don't know I'll see what I can do". But first I must learn to drive

She saw the look on George's face and she did not like what she saw. She might have her two feet well and truly placed on the hearth but she realised that she had not better start to dictate as she had done with Jim. She moved forwards towards George putting her arms around his middle looking up into his dark brown eyes

"I am sure we have much more important things to do first than worry about the house. Her hand slid down the front of his trousers feeling him re-act to the touch of her fingers.

"Steady on Michael will be in soon. "

"Don't worry we will make up for lost time later. Early night to night darling" She whispered flouncing out to the back kitchen to prepare some food for a meal". Sandra had given George a list of shopping to do the day before. I am not going there to an empty cupboard she had said to her self. She quickly did some scrambled eggs and beans on toast. They ate the meal in silence each deep in their own thoughts.

"Don't worry", she said to her self. Can't get married in deed. I'll get that clarified for a start. So we're not rid of her yet, after all I've been through. Hannah still has a hold over him. It's a pity that she did not crack up, then she would have been locked away and then it would not have mattered so much. I'm sure that it is only a temporary set back. We can get over that hurdle it will only be a matter of time. He is mine now, and mine he is going to stay. There will no more bonking for him in the woods and now that I have got him I will see to that. It is some money that he has to get and finish this house off. If he thinks that I am going to tolerate this, He has another think coming. I am not as daft and naïve as Hannah was with him. She swallowed any thing that he told her. Silly woman. She could have caught us out many a time but she believed all he told her, Stupid woman.

Michael came in from school and saw that they had visitors. He just nodded at Sandra and went up stairs to change from his school uniform. Some time later he went down to see what was going on and if Sandra had cooked any tea for them. It did make a difference when she came for the day the living room always looked a bit cleaner for a dust and polish. He sat at the table and took his time eating what she had put in front of him.

"Come on Michael eat up I will get cleared away and do the washing up. Your father wants to have a few words with you."

"What about?"

"Not much it's just that Sandra and John are going to stay with us. Uncle Jim has been so horrible to them; I'm letting them move in with us. John will share your room Sandra will sleep with me. I need some one to keep me warm now that your mother has gone".

"I'm not bothered" Was Michael's reply. He did not care one way or the other. Why his mother had gone at all was still a mystery to him despite listening to them arguing at night. He had never imagined that she would actually leave them and go. Well he supposed that it did not matter to him one way or the other as long as he could get his washing and ironing done. There was a girl at school who was sweet on him so he spent a lot of his spare time at her house. The most important thing on his mind was how to get some transport of his own. A small motor bike was going to be the answer, but he must get some money together perhaps Aunt Sandra just might be able to help especially if he played his cards right. He and his father had always got on well together. The going of his mother had not bothered him all that much She had always been so busy she was either gardening or at work or busy with this or that. When he had been younger the twins had taken priority for her time. It was David this or David that I was glad that I did not have to be taken to the doctors and hospitals like they were.

Sandra and George waited until they thought that both the boys had settled for the night. Then he teasingly stroked her leg as she sat on the hearth next to his chair. His hand was moving higher. She could not contain her need for him.

"Come my darling, all seems quiet above, come with me, as he got from his chair and followed her to the bedroom. She did not take any persuading to reveal her complete nakedness. She performed to satisfy the needs of the sex hungry man sharing a bed with her. Finally they exhausted them selves and fell asleep,

She awoke next morning and looked around her; this squat little room was now her bedroom. There was no comparison with the large rooms of the farmhouse she had shared with Jim. She felt claustrophobic. I can't stand this for long. This house will have to be finished. George's hands moving around her body interrupted her thoughts.

"Awake Darling" she murmured.

"Just about. God I've waited for this he whispered "As they made love again,

It was gone seven o'clock I had better move she said when he had once again released all his pent up tensions.

"Put the kettle on, I will be with you. No way dared he let Sandra see him lie in bed until she brought him a cup of tea Hannah never had unless he had been unwell. He knew that Sandra would He only had to ask. Infect he was sure that if he said jump over the moon, She would. George felt good having a woman about the house again. He felt no remorse that Hannah had gone Sandra would take a lot more satisfying sexually and this certainly suited him.

"Its not the thing to do, Hannah would quibble if he had suggested five minutes on the bed at lunch time Not the thing to do at all You can wait until bedtime. There was always this to be done or that to be done.

Not with Sandra She did not give a toss about the ironing or the cleaning. He only had to arrive at her flat and she was more than happy to go to bed with him, at any time of the day or night. He reluctantly got out of bed and went down to join her at the table.

Sandra had made a pot of tea and poured it into mugs, mugs were now taking preference to cups and saucers. "Come darling Let us have this together before Michael comes down" She said handing him a mug of hot tea. She asked what he would like for breakfast. Sit here and tell me all about the work that you are doing on that hospital that is being built."

"Well I should be going to work. But do you think that I should stay with you and John in case Jim comes looking for you?"

"Why should he? If I am not at the flat he won't know where I have gone and besides I can handle Jim. You do not have to worry about me. I can take care of my self. That's if he does come looking for me which I very much doubt I've been thinking Darling. I don't think that I will give up the flat immediately".

"And why not?" George's mind was racing forty to the dozen He sounded surprised "You are here with me now"

"If I keep the flat on for a bit longer, the care taker can only tell Jim that I am out not that I have left that is if Jim does go sniffing about.

"But what about the rent?" George was not keen to pay rent on an empty flat No way.

"Well I have been thinking that if I am still officially there, I only need to go and stay one night a week or could be one night a month or some thing like that. And besides what is to stop you staying the night with me"

George was not slow on the uptake where there was money mentioned. Sandra had been drawing an allowance for herself and baby John and for the up keep of the flat.

"I suppose as long as the rent is paid by you. You are still the tenant in the flat and still entitled to your allowance. Good thinking girl Good thinking"

"I'm sure you can now see it my way. The allowance is more than enough to keep myself and John. George I don't like to ask but what is to be done about this house"

"Let's get it finished"

"I'll help you my darling".

"Now that I have the job working on that new hospital the money is good so we will be able to push on with it now that you are here to help with household chores. I can get a few freebies from the hospital. A bag of cement, a few tiles and a bit of wood are not going to be noticed the contract is so big the bosses don't even know what is used for what "

"Well haven't I been doing that for you the last eighteen months"

"Well you know what I mean you will be here all day from now on".

"That is splendid we can talk again tonight".

"We won't have much time for talking once we get to bed "He replied laughing.

After some breakfast George went off to work and Michael to school. Sandra sat down and took stock of the place. I'm not prepared to put with this place as Hannah did. As much as I love George this house has to be finished. I wonder if he has any money worth talking about. After all he has had only Michael to keep for the past eighteen months. Little did she know about the huge amount of debts that he had incurred while he had been spending his time with her and not working. I must tread very carefully and keep on the right side of him. That won't take much doing. I only have to suggest going to bed and I have won him over completely. She sat and thought back to when she had been living with Jim and she was amazed how every thing had fallen into place and every thing had gone in her favour.

I wonder what the family will have to say when they find out that I am here. Please them selves. The phone lines will be red hot. She started to laugh at the thought of all her sisters ringing each other up to pass on the news But don't worry she said to John as she bounced him on her knee. I can think up some story to tell them quicker than what they can swallow a cup of tea. They can please them selves. You and I Johnny are going to be happy here. You'll see" It will soon be time for you to go to school now aren't you going to be a lucky little man. The school bus will pick you up right out side the door. No walking for mummy and it will bring you safely back to me in the afternoon. Sandra was a bit worried about his eyesight. He seemed to be having difficulty. Things did not seem to be right she had been watching him closely of late and noticed that he was very short sighted.

"We must get those eyes of yours checked now that we are with Daddy I can now sort all these little things out perhaps you will be like your mummy and have to wear glasses but that will be no big deal. Come on I had better give this place some cleaning and make it more fit to live in. Show that Daddy of yours that Mummy is not going to sit and watch the telly like we did at the other house No your real Daddy would not like that at all. You are going to be a good boy for Mummy today aren't you? First I have to put something to stop you going onto the road we don't want your Daddy coming home and finding no little John. On with your wellies and let us see what can be done There is such a big garden for you to play in. Oh I forgot that stinking loo in the garden George my man," she said to her self that is going to be top priority. I am not putting up with that, it stinks. She took John by the hand and went outside and she looked around in dismay. What a mess the garden was. It was now quite over grown there had been nothing done since Hannah had left. The yard was littered with this and that; oil tins bits of engines that George had left about. "Come on John lad, let's make a start and secure you in that yard and then I can go in and have a go at the inside. Her father's words came back to her as he had told all his daughters you make your bed and you lie in it".

"This was only going to be a temporary set back between George and her self the house would soon be finished and then it should be worth a thousand or two. I have no longer to worry about paying rent or being tied to a farmhouse. She would rid the house of Hannah's furniture as soon as she could. She would get rid of anything that reminded her of Hannah. She made a start by fixing some large pieces of timber so that John could not run on to the road. She was so absorbed in what she was doing and of what plans that she was going to put into place she had not seen old Tom come out into the road and he was standing watching her.

"Your busy" A voice made her jump. Who the devil "Oh its you" She recognised him as the old boy from the cottage next door.

"Just doing a bit of tidying up. I had better make sure that this little man can not wander on to the road"." I must be pleasant to the old devil she told her self.

"Here for the day are you?

"Could be", She turned to walk away so as to put an end to any further conversation the old man wished to make.

Old Tom went on his way he had taken the hint; his little mongrel dog was getting impatient to be going for his walk. Tom had seen Sandra arrive the previous afternoon from his up stair window. He had listened last night to see if he heard George's van going out to take Sandra back to where she had come from. He had made sure that he was up earlier that morning He saw George go out in the van on his own. Not much went on down the lane that his inquisitive beady little eyes did not notice. He realised that he had swore that he would not talk to either of them but curiosity always got the better of him If there was any gossip worth passing on down the lane. Seeing Sandra had been there over night and was making sure that the little lad could not run onto the road told him all he wanted to know.

Tom stopped to have a chat with Fred Talbot as he passed the farmyard gate.

"So what is going on next door" Fred wanted to, know .He knew by the look on Tom's face that he had some gossip to pass on. They passed the time of day.

"It looks to me as she has moved in already, the bloody cheek of it. That George and Sandra don't think that we notice what goes on. "The times that he has been beggaring off, and left that lad in on his own. Now we know where he has been going to meet that little bitch."

"You could be right, I don't expect for one minute that Hannah knows what has been going on. I'll bet that she doesn't. Well out of it that girl is that is what I reckon".

"That George is a bad UN Never will do any good. I bet you a fiver that he will finish that house what do you reckon" Old Tom chuckled "Your on, I reckon that you could be right. Funny goings on to be sure".

"Well it's not surprising, that wench has got the nerve of the devil I suppose that she has come to live here for good. I wonder if they will marry. Said Fred".

"They can't do that. Hannah's still alive. Oh My God I wouldn't like to be in her shoes I reckon that those two buggers will stop at nothing by what we have seen going on in the past I would put nout passed the evil buggers The pair of them".

"It's a bloody good job that she got out when she did"

"I agree but must get on "Fred had seen his wife come out into the yard and he knew that she did not approve of him standing talking for too long. Wasting time gossiping, although she was anxious to hear any fresh news that old Tom had to pass on.

By the time that Old Tom and his dog had finished their walk to the other end of the lane and back, there was no who lived in the lane who did not have first hand knowledge of what was going on next door him. They could not believe that such goings on could take place. A sister moving into her sister's house was one thing but having the nerve to let her self be seen as if she had come to stay for good it was scandalous

Mean while Jim was absolutely shattered and devastated by Sandra's leaving. He was managing to feed him self only just His Mother was there for him and she came occasionally and brought pies and cakes for him. Jim like Hannah was putting all his energies into work Every thing seemed such a nightmare, He missed little John so much The sound of the child's voice, Always being so pleased to see his daddy when he came in through the door from work. Why oh why. What had gone wrong? His Mother had visited him for the day and she was sitting opposite him at the kitchen table.

"You might not believe me now but I think that you will eventually find that this has all happened for the best That girl never was any damned good". Jim was sat staring out through the kitchen window.

"Are you listening Jim."

"Yes Mother" His gaze returning to the kitchen from looking out across the fields

"No good No good at all I said so before you married her"

"I know that you did but I loved her and then there was little John to think about"

"I would not be surprised if that child is not yours. Your Uncle Robert was sterile so was one or two other male members of the family. I think that you should have some tests done I don't see any point in you paying for a child that is not yours".

Jim looked at his mother in amazement. There was a stony silence.

"Have another cuppa I can't believe what you are saying. Could I have been taken for a ride good and proper I'll have a word with that little bitch I swear I will"

"Now be careful Son make sure that you don't lose your temper because that would play right into her hands. She won't get away with it Time will tell. I thought that it was funny when she wanted you back I wonder who the father is of that child. I made a note on the kitchen calendar the night that you did not come home. That child was not born before its time. It was a full time pregnancy if you ask me, Seven months my foot a baby that size and another thing, she would not have brought a premature baby from the hospital as soon as she did. Any way I reckon that who ever is the father? That is who she has gone running to."

"Jim recalled what the nurse had said about it being a full term baby when John had been born" My god what was Sandra capable of doing. He and her family had all swallowed what she had convinced them of hook line and sinker. Jim was not sure how he felt, relieved or very angry when he said goodbye to his mother and she had driven out of the farm gate.

He went back into the kitchen and sat down in front of the Rayburn putting a bit more wood on it to keep the kitchen warm. He felt cold and chilled right through to his bones, he poured another mug of tea The house was so quiet He hated being on his own Mr Howells had been extremely good to him and given him some over time to keep his mind occupied. His boss's wife Mrs Howells had made him some cakes and pies for which he had been very grateful. Every one was doing their best to rally around him. His love for little John had been profound to say the least; He had never doubted his father hood until now,

She wouldn't have used me. Sandra; the woman he had loved fed and slept with could have not been that cruel. I can't believe it. Mother must be talking through her hat. He knew that she had never liked Sandra He sat contemplating of what he should do. He emptied his mug of tea and put the fruitcake his mother had left on the kitchen table in the cake tin and put it in the larder. He went upstairs he did not know why or what he had gone up for. He was starting to notice things that were not there any more. The evil bitch has been planning this for some time by the look of it taking a bit out of the house bit of a time so that I did not notice. I have been too busy working my guts out to keep her. I just can't believe the amount of money that I owe, now that the bills for this and that were starting to come in. He had given her a signed cheque to pay for a three-piece suit she had wanted leaving it blank to who it had to be made out to.

"You can ask the store manager to fill the details in for you". Sandra took the cheque to the bank telling the cashier such a sob story and had it cashed for ready money for her self. Unknowing to Jim she had torn a second cheque from his cheque -book and forged his signature this she used for the deposit on the suite. She had taken the rest of the amount on hire purchase. She told the manager of the store that her husband was away and unable to come with her but that he had given her a cheque for the deposit. Sandra took the cheque from her hand bag; the eager sales man had no reason to check it out. Poor Jim had the rest to pay that off plus the interest that was charged. She had taken that with her, how he did not know but she had. It was gone that day when he came in for his tea and found the house empty. The telephone bill was over a hundred pounds and the number of reverse calls that were on it absolutely amazed him who had been making the calls he had no idea He tried to have it checked out, but they had been made from different telephone boxes. He did not know but it had been George saving money on his bill.

"You reverse the charges My darling so that I can speak to you every day Jim won't know who it is if you use a call box and he can pay the bill when I am gone" She had chuckled.

Taking a look at him self, in the wardrobe mirror Jim began to realise how he had let himself go. His hair needed cutting and if he shaved his face it would certainly be an improvement. Oh dear, he thought that he had heard some one knocking on the door and some ones voice calling him.

"Any one in?" Called the voice "Coming "Shouted Jim

It was his neighbour Anne "I saw your mother go, Are you all right Jim?

"I'm alright looking a bit of a mess, I reckon"

"It's easy to let your self go. Listen My Mother says come around and joins us for a meal" Will you Jim?"

"I'm alright" He replied"

"All right my foot Jim Beddows. You look awful. Come on, I suggest that you tidy up a bit and join us. No sense in sitting here on your own in this big empty house any more than what you have to. Do you think that Sandra will come back?"

"I don't know I miss them so much"

"I know that you do I know you do".

Jim sat down in his familiar chair and let the tears fall".

"Now Jim things can't be that bad".

"Why Anne. Why has she gone taking little John with her what more could I have done?"

"Not a lot".

"I'm worried about some thing that mother has said

" What's that?"

"That little John may not be mine. I've never thought any different"

"Oh My lord why should she say that?

"Just that there have been problems with other members of our family"

"Well whose could he be?"

"I don't know if he's not mine"

"How can you fine out?

"I'm thinking of going to see her and have it out with her".

"You could do that but would she be honest with you?"

"I don't know Do I"

"Come on Jim if he is not yours you will not have to support him"

"But he is mine I am sure about it I loved them both so very much I've got nothing to live for now".

"Come on now Jim, come on tidy your self up a bit you will feel much better and come and eat a good dinner". Jim reluctantly agreed. Anne waited for him so that he could not get out of it. Her mother had been too busy to have the main meal of the day ready for midday she was now getting it ready for teatime.

Chapter Twenty
The Truth Can Hurt

Hannah gathered her big bag of dirty washing and the amount of washing powder from the box by the sink, she just took what she thought would be enough to do the wash. The washing had to be done. She must go to the launderette and get the bigger items such as the bed sheet towels and pillow slips Etc, washed so that she had the rest of the weekend to dry and iron them. She washed as many of the smaller items in the kitchen sink to save money. The washing machines spun them so much drier getting far more water from them than what she could by trying to wring them out by hand.

It was Friday and the launderette was quite busy. Hannah took the required amount of money from her brown purse. She put the money in the machine and with out thinking placed her purse on the top of the it, while she put the washing in to the drum and powder into in to the slot provided. That done she switched the machine on. She automatically went to pick up her purse but it was not there, She looked and looked around the launderette, but it was gone A whole weeks wages was in that purse. What was she going to do? Panic over took her. She did not know how she was going to cope. It had obviously been taken. But by who? None of the other women in there looked like thieves.

"You can't trust any one these days, "One of the other women said' When Hannah started to ask if they had seen anyone take her purse.

"That will teach you a lesson don't you think "Said another "We are never daft enough to give anyone the chance of taking our money. Take the sugar from your tea if you look around for a second they will. That is a good lesson for you my dear. You had better report it to the police, Not that you will get your money back you can be sure of that. Already spent I expect in that pub across the road".

Hannah reported her stolen purse at the local station but like the women had said the clerk at the station agreed that there would be no hope of getting her money back for her. All they could do was ask around and warn Hannah to be more careful in the future.

Hannah was so angry how come she did not see the person take it. To think how careless that she had been.

She went to tell Molly about it that evening Molly gave her a loan of five pounds to tide her over until she was paid again next week. She also gave Hannah such a lecture about being so careless.

"The trouble with you, you have never had to live where there are so many light fingered people around you. You will learn as time goes on. Believe me you will. You should have lived in Birmingham where I did. It did not do to turn your back for a second".

A policeman returned Hannah's purse to her a week later. It was empty of any money. It had been found in the pub just across from the flats. Hannah was taught a good lesson, one that she would never forget.

She was still feeling so angry with her self, to think that she could have been so thick and stupid not to notice what George and Sandra had been up to all those years. Why had she not noticed that something had been going on? Why had she not checked up on him when he said that he was working late? There were so many questions that could not be answered.

Her own sister. How could they? Hannah had never heard of such a thing. If some one had hinted as to what had been going on she would have dismissed it as being ludicrous. Her husband was touching her little sister.

Why had Sandra not said something when he had tried it on so long ago? Sandra was with him now she was so many years younger than he was. Her little sister that Hannah had gone out of her way to be so nice to and do so much for. She had felt so sorry for Sandra being the last one at home and having to cope with her Mother who was now getting older.

How bitter Hannah felt, she wanted to get revenge but how. Why had they not gone off together and left her to cope with the house and looking after the children .She would have managed some how, she was sure that she would have, but to drive her out as they had. She could not comprehend. If it had not been for the Doctor advising her to get out. Goodness only knows what length that they were prepared to go to. It did not bear thinking about. No matter how Hannah tried to come to terms with it, she could not. She was convincing herself that they should not be allowed to get away with what they had done. They had Michael and that hurt the most. Her precious son taken from her she could never forgive them. In her mind she planned all sorts of ways to get back at them. She would wait until they went to bed and then set fire to the house. This was the one thing that she was certain that she could do. But the fact that there was her son and their child there, she could not take their lives, they were not to blame and their son was going to have to grow up with a father old enough to be his grandfather. He would have enough to cope with.

Charles was a godsend he seemed to be there for her and it was so comforting. He had changed his car and had bought a new one and at the same time his mother had persuaded him to buy one for her. She was of a very greedy disposition. He had given in to her demands as usual to keep the peace and she had her own way. She was a woman of short stature only about five feet tall but what she lacked in height she made up for in width in fact she was grossly over weight. She ate all the wrong foods and fed her self so well there was never any hope of her loosing any of her obesity. She was the complete opposite to her husband who although he too was no more than five foot two he was as thin as a lathe. He had retired from the air force with extremely poor health. He had met Beatrice (Beatie for short) when she had been working as a nanny in London during the war. Beatie had never got over the fact that her father had left her practically nothing and that he had left every thing to her spinster sister Maude. Now that Charles had come into his share of his grandfather's estate she was going to have as much of it as she could. With the help of her solicitor she had managed to have her present bungalow built out of her son's share and unknowing to him the deeds of the property had been put into her name. She had considered that she was entitled to some luxury before she died. Charles was later in life to find out how devious his mother and father had been.

Judith and Carl called to see Hannah and announced that they were leaving the country and that they were immigrating to Australia before Christmas. Carl was to be made redundant again. O. D. Murphy where he was working was closing down and the ground that the factory was built on was sold for a housing development

Carl and Judith were so excited about their plans. Hannah had difficulty taking it all in. They had been there for her and now they were going all the way to Australia. Molly was leaving after Christmas to have the alms bungalow that Cadburys factory had offered her.

But why, were Judith and Carl leaving? Surely there was other employment in this country with out having to go so far away. Carl had planned for his Mother and Father to follow them He said that he and Judith with the children would be going by air and that his Mother and Father would go by sea.

"Hannah we have made our plans I am fed up to the back teeth with this country I am not going to be made redundant again if I can help it.

I have already made enquiries about a job in Australia and there seems to be plenty of work available there for plumbers and another thing we can give Melissa a much better chance with her swimming than we could possibly afford for her in this country. I can see her going on to win medals in time, but we can't give her that sort of hope and training if we stay here. She can have so much better facilities over there. Carl had always wanted to be a professional swimmer but he had never had the opportunity to do so, He had been taking Melissa to the local swimming baths since she was only eighteen months old and he could see that she had great potential if only she could be given the right opportunity.

"You have it all worked out I can see. Heaven forbid I am going to miss you "

Judith was quick to say why they had made such an enormous decision

"Well it's like this. Now that Molly is going back to Birmingham she will be well taken care of there and as far as I am concerned I have no Brothers". "I will never forgive George for what he has put you through for the sake of that over sexed bitch that he has now landed himself with. Good luck to the pair of them No good can come from that lot I am sure. Thomas does not want to know us since he has married that little Emily from across the road. We have decided that it would be the best thing that we should go while we are young enough to start again."

It was Carl who broke into the conversation "We were wondering if you would be interested in buying our washing machine and some of the furniture. There are a few bits and pieces that you can have but we would like to sell as much as we can, if possible. We are going to need every penny that we can get".

"I don't know about that I can not afford to buy much. It is taking me all my time to pay my way as it is but I would like to buy your washing machine it would save me going to the launderette and having to wash as much as I can in the sink. Yes that would be very useful, Can you give me a couple of days to think about the rest. Your three piece would most certainly be better than what I have got. What are you asking for the lot? "

"Fifty pounds how would that suit you? Carl said looking around Hannah's barely furnished room "You could do with a bit extra I am sure".

"I know that I could and it is difficult. But we are coping"

Charles called the next night and Hannah told him about Judith and Carl's decision to go to Australia and that they were offering her some of their furniture.

"Well I for one don't blame them. I agree with Carl there does not seem much to stop in this county for. Can you afford to buy their bits and pieces?"

"Of course not, it is taking all that I earn to keep the three of us and pay the rent and the heating not that I am grumbling it is so good to have proper bathroom and David has his own bedroom. I will be only too glad when they put a maintenance order on George But the courts seem to be so long winded, because he has not bothered to turn up"It had to be put off so many times".

"What would you say if I was to lend you the money and then that would save you having to walk and carry you're washing to the launderette and you would not have to worry about having your purse stolen again? I have been thinking that it would be better for the three of you if you were to get away from here... What would you say if I was to buy a house? You could live in it and then you could pay me the rent just like you do now. We could try and find some thing in the country. What would you say if you were to move to Drayton or even Cosford? Get away from everything around here and then the three of you could start a new life, My grandfather always maintained that it was best to put any money that you could into bricks and mortar. So I have been thinking of doing the same as he did. I was not expecting to come into so much money so soon. If the tenant of the farm that Grandfather left me had not died I would only be having the rent for it. As it is my aunt and my mother have decided that it would be better for me if the farm was sold. They have had the bungalow that we are living in built out of the money.

Dad's health is not good and mother continually complained about that little cottage that they had left them was far too damp a pretty bad chest he has. The remainder of the money for the farm had to pay off the mortgage that had been taken out on the farm by my Grandfather. The rest is invested in shares but I can cash them in any day if I want to. You know that is how he made his money He would buy one property and the rent from that paid for the mortgage he had taken out on it and for a deposit on the next one that he bought.

"Get on with you Charles. You can't possibly do that. Buy a house indeed I can just imagine what your Mother would have to say about that. She would blow her top completely don't you think".

"There is little that she could say I am over twenty one and I can do as I like with my own money. Infact the more that I think about it the better it could be. Property can only rise in price and it would earn me much more than what I am getting at the moment. Why do you think that I joined the RAF? It was just to get away from her she was so possessive and over powering I could not get away quick enough and that sister of mine is a right pain in the ass. If Dad was not in, Mother expected me to sit with her every time he went out. She likes to go to play bridge you know. That sister of mine is a pathetic little thing".

"Charles don't be so unkind towards your sister I think that it is what your Mother has made of her. Spoilt her too much as a child. There was always gossip and comments made in the village about the way your Mother ran the roads taking and fetching her home from school. She would even fetch her back during the day for her lunch. She did not give the girl any incentive to do anything for her self. Every thing was done for her."

"I know she has always been treated as a baby .Not able to think for her self. What is to become of her I do not know? She was adopted and perhaps it's something that she has inherited"

"She will meet some one some day and leave home you see if she does not. Other wise she will stay and look after your parents and that will be a very heavy burden for her to have to undertake. Look at your Aunt She stayed and looked after her parents and now she has had no life of her own at all. She has been nowhere and done very little. She is now a spinster in that big house of hers and only a dog for company".

They went on to discus other events especially Sandra and George and what the latest village gossip was. As Charles left he told Hannah to think about having all Judith's bits and pieces and told her not to worry He would lend her the money and then she could pay him back as and when she could

". What's fifty pounds "

"A hell of a lot when you don't have it".

"You stop worrying "He looked around the practically bare room thinking that what ever was added could only make it look more homely.

"And you think hard about getting out from here it would do you good to get back out in the country again. Have a garden and such. The offer is there if you will agree to it."

Hannah thought about nothing else for days. She was feeling so ill Her Doctor suggested that he thought that she should see a specialist who was a psychiatrist. Hannah was appalled at the suggestion. He went on to explain that he considered that she was suffering from delayed shock from the events that had taken place. It had all gone to contribute to her being in the situation that she was in. It was this that was making her so ill and he considered that she needed help with coming to terms with things. He felt sure that she could not go on any longer as she was and that she must consider her situation other wise she could have a complete break down and then she would stand to lose the twins".

"Lose the twins". Hannah kept repeating to her self time and time again. Not on my life that bitch has Michael and she is not having the twins. Never, I will go and see who ever Doctor Price advises".

An appointment was made for Hannah to see the psychiatrist and she had a long chat with him she told him of Charles's offer and he agreed that it would be best for her to accept it and get as far away as she could and start a new life. He came to the conclusion that she was living in fear of her life and nothing could help her by staying where she was. Hannah went back to the flat more confused than ever. When she told Charles what the psychiatrist had talked about he was more concerned for Hannah's safety than he had been before.

The law was that a woman could not marry her sister's husband as long as the sister was alive. There had been talk in the press where a new divorce law was being considered where the law would allow a sister to marry her sister's husband while she was still alive. If this was to become law then Sandra could marry George and Hannah would have nothing to fear any more. Some times Hannah did wonder if she was imagining the fact that Sandra and George would have the audacity to get married but why should they not Sandra was such a convincing liar that so many who did not know otherwise believed every word that she said.

Hannah walked along the riverbank glancing at the water. The sun shone down making it a lovely warm day, she felt cool by the side of the river. David and Jennifer had run on ahead of Charles and her self. Hannah was suffering from what the doctor had described as delayed reaction but it was unknown to her what was wrong she just felt like a zombie these days.

Life had no meaning, getting up to see to the children going to work and then home again to be in bed early. The doctor had urged her to take the tablets that he had prescribed to help her cope, as she was being so sick all the time. Charles had called this Sunday afternoon and had offered to take them out for an hour. The twins were so fed up with nowhere what they called decent to play that they encouraged Hannah to take up the offer. She had sat silently in the car on the way to Shrewsbury not wanting to make conversation and spoke only now and again. Charles was becoming really concerned for her. He could see that she was not responding to the medication very well. They had parked the car and the children made haste to reach the play area in the quarry they were so eager to go on the swings, slides and things that were there for them to play on having tired of that they were running ahead along the river bank.

Hannah and Charles were following slowly behind them

"Hannah was glancing at the slowly moving water when she was sure that she saw an image just under the surface of the water. Was it an image? Was she seeing things? A kindly gentle face appeared just under the surface of the moving water, was it the face of a woman or that of a man. It was the face of a woman smiling to her from under the water. Hannah looked again She was not seeing things the face was real, the hands reached out to her Long slender hands beckoning her to come closer. The face went deeper into the moving water almost out of sight then it re-appeared again still smiling. Hannah imagined that her name was being called. She was transfixed by the image. I must see what it is about and why she wants me to follow her she needs me I must go a little closer I need to get closer. What is she trying to say to me?

Suddenly she heard Charles's voice "Hannah be careful". A strong hand took hold of her pulling her away from the edge of the riverbank.

As she came to her senses Hannah suddenly realised how close that she was to walking into the river.

"What were you doing? I thought that you were going to walk into the river. Look where you are going." Hannah realised that if she had taken one more step forward she would have been in the water, which now looked to be very dangerous it was moving quickly and looked very dark beneath the surface.

"But the face" she stammered" "What face?" asked Charles "Oh nothing" she replied now realising that she had almost walked into the river and would have been quickly washed away. The shock of which was now beginning to dawn on her.

David and Jennifer had run back fed up with waiting for them to catch up "Come on, keep up with us "Jennifer shouted "You pair are a pair of slow coaches. "We are coming" Replied Hannah. She was still very shocked at what she had nearly done What was I thinking about, but she was calling to me I know that she was, It went round and round in her head as she silently walked to the car. Pull your self together she told herself. Who is going to look after the twins, that little bitch has Michael with them She and George are not having these two. I will see to that. She told herself?

"Are you feeling alright now "Asked Charles breaking into Hannah's train of thoughts?

"You looked as white as a ghost I Thought that for one minute you were going to walk into the river. Where the devil were your thoughts, Hannah?

"I don't know Charles I wasn't thinking where I was walking Sorry to give you a scare".

"Don't do that again. I mean walk so close to the edge of the water. It would have been so easy for you to have slipped. Can you swim?"

"No I can't"

"Well who do you think is going to look after those two? They have only got you"

"I know. I know I will look after them". For the first time in months Hannah realised that she had to take care of David and Jennifer. If it meant a struggle then struggle she would.

"I think that we should make our way back now and get a cup of tea. You look as if you need one and if you don't, I certainly do .You gave me quite a scare. I could see you just walking into the water. We can buy some pop and sweets for that pair".

"You are so kind Charles. It had been a long time since Hannah had any one speak kindly to her and with concern. She could still feel the strength of Charles firm grip on her arm as he had led her away from the river.

The walk along the side of the river had really frightened Hannah. She realised how close she had been to the water and if Charles had not been there she could have stepped into the river and would have drowned. Back at the flat she realised how stupid that it had been to walk so close to the waters edge. She had two children to care for. They needed her if no one else did. They were her responsibility.

Hannah had been so disappointed when she had attended the court hearing to see whether she or George would have the custody of the children. She was on her own George had not turned up and the Judge was not prepared to delay any further he had other work to do. He was a very kindly man Hannah thought that he must be in his late fifties. He was very sympathetic to Hannah but he explained to her why he was making the decision that he had come to. He told her that she was to have the custody of the twins but much to her disappointment he had said that Michael was to stay with his father as he thought that Hannah would have more than enough to cope with. George having failed to turn up as usual which was quite a relief in a way for Hannah she did not have to see his smug smile that she knew he would have on his face. Sandra had told him that it was best for him not to attend so that they could not take Michael away from him. When he received the copy of the hearing he was so happy not to have to send Michael to live with his mother he was prepared to listen to anything that Sandra said in the future.

Sandra had urged George to leave his job for the period of the court hearing regarding Hannah's claim for maintenance.

"You can always go back to work after wards but if you are on the dole they can't award her very much can they you have me and two growing boys to keep."

"Good thinking do you think that we can manage for a couple of months and now that I can afford some stuff for the house. It will give me a bit of time at home to get on with it".

At the court hearing for maintenance Hannah sat on a seat at the end of a row of six seats and George was sat at the other end of the row. There were three magistrates sat in front of them, they studied the paper work that had been put before them. They put various questions to each Hannah and George. Hannah could not believe what she was hearing. He was giving such a sob story how they were struggling to cope on his unemployment money and that he must get his house finished before the winter set in. It's a pity that you did not think of that some years ago. Thought Hannah I suppose that you have to finish it for that little slut that you have got living there.

They discussed Hannah's earnings and went out to decide and to deliberate. Hannah looked at George and all she saw was hate for him. You bastard she hissed at him you are going to have to start and pay from now on."

"I don't think so and in any case if you can't keep them you can always put them in a home I certainly don't want any of you taking any thing from me. The entry of the magistrates interrupted them. The woman who sat in the middle started to speak

"Mrs Fleming. Being as your ex husband is out of work there is very little that we can do. We have to take in to consideration the fact that there is another family. We are going to make an order that he pay you a weekly sum of three pounds One for each of the children and one for your self". Hannah was gob smacked. "

"But what about the arrears that you owe? He has not paid me a penny as yet".

"There are no arrears to be paid as this is the first time that we have been able to bring the matter to court". Hannah saw the smile on George's face. She could not get out of the building quick enough .If she had had a knife with her at that moment of his smiling at her she knew that she could have easily stabbed him The bastard. She could not believe that three pounds was all that he had been ordered to pay. Hannah was still feeling as angry as she made her way back to the flat

"Well there goes the new carpet I certainly will not be having that". When Hannah told Judith she was amazed "The crafty beggars. I will bet you that he is back in full time employment before the end of next week "Sure enough George was back working full time again with in two weeks of the court hearing.

Hannah's health started to deteriorate she was beginning to have bilious turns she was being so sick she needed to take time off from the bread round but this she could not afford to do. She knew that she would have to start looking for a lighter job that would mean that she could be working indoors especially in the bad winter weather. She must start looking for another job.

The day came for Hannah and the twins to say goodbye to Judith and Carl Melissa and Robin. They were waiting on the railway platform to say goodbye and see them board the train, which was to take them to London and then to Heathrow Air port. As they all hugged and kissed good bye the tears were just falling. Hannah made up her mind not to cry but when the time came they were all crying. Hannah was going to miss them so much.

Molly had her date to move to Birmingham in the spring Charles offered to bring one of the RAF Lorries to move her with. They loaded her belongings. The Twins sat in the lorry they enjoyed riding in that. It was some thing different for them. Hannah and Molly followed in Charles's car to bring them back home. The lorry would have to be returned to base camp. It all went well but Hannah was going to miss her. Molly had been more than a mother to Hannah through all her troubles

The little bungalow that Cadbury's had allocated to her was neat and compact it was in a quadrangle of several others and there was a Matron to keep an eye on the residents in case they should need help. The centre of the quadrangle was made up of lawns and flowerbeds it was so nice and pleasant.

"Yes "Said Molly as they left her and all her belongings were safely inside. "I will be quite happy here. Quite happy".

It was late when Hannah and the twins got back she offered Charles a cup of tea, which he accepted so Hannah made some sandwiches to go with it.

"Now you are left on your own" He said "But don't worry if there is any thing that I can do for you don't be afraid to ask. You are going to Miss Molly. My God what a good sport that she is. She will have a go at anything she will. If you like I will take you for a ride one of the Sundays to see her."

"Thank you for your offer I will promise you that I will think about it but yes Charles I am going to miss her. She has been so good. But now that she and Judith have gone I have to stand on my own two feet. I have been thinking about changing my job. There are some days when I feel so ill that I have a job to finish the bread round. I am going to look for something inside and some thing that would fit in better with the school hours I must have a fairly well paid job we need the money".

"See what you can find and don't for get that the offer stands if we could find a cottage in the country, I will buy it and you can rent it. You could do with getting away from this noisy lot."

"I will bear it in mind. I will have to take one step at a time and another thing it has been so good of you to give a hand with the moving of Molly. I have to watch who calls here or there will be more gossip and I certainly can't be doing with that".

Charles started to laugh. What gossip? Folks will soon find some thing to talk about so if it is not you they will certainly have a go at some one else. I will tell you what, will it be all right if I just call from time to time, to see how you are coping. Thanks for paying the loan back but fifty pounds is quite a lot for you to have to find. What I mean is don't get stuck you know that you only have to ask for any help if you need it. My god the three pounds George has to pay is not going to go very far. The rotten bugger. He was clever to get away with that but what can you expect. I guess that she was behind it the scheming little bitch.

The gossip is that they are getting on with the house now. We thought that he might once he got rid of you and got her in with him. They say that she is pregnant but I don't know if there is any truth in that. "Could be I suppose "

"Could be I have to try to shut them out of my mind completely if I can, otherwise I just might crack up altogether"

"Now don't you go doing that they are not worth it and you have the twins to look after. I must be going but remember that I will be calling in now and again just to keep an eye on things and see that you are coping.

Hannah said goodnight and closed the front door to the flat. When the twins were in bed she sat down on what had been Judith and Carl's settee and for the first time since she had left George she felt completely alone. The flat felt empty No Molly living in the flat beneath and she could no longer ring Judith and Carl from the public phone box on the landing outside her front door. The only member of the family who had been in touch with her had been when Lizzy had called but she had not called again.

Hannah studied the vacancy columns in the Wellington journal and one week she saw a job advertised for work in a clothing factory. She decided to go for an interview on her next day off. The pay was good and so were the hours there would be no more week end work so she accepted the position offered. She understood that she would to be working in the sewing room. Hannah had reluctantly given her notice to Brian and Beryl who were so sorry to see her leave but they knew of her circumstances and were very good about her leaving.

When she started her new job on the Monday morning she found that she was put in the pressing room. She had been conned into taking the job. The first day that she reported for work the supervisor was making so many excuses as to why she was not being put to work a sewing machine. She now knew that she would have to make the most of this job there was no going back. Hannah had to leave the flat to be at work for eight in the mornings and she would have to trust the twins to go to the bus stop at eight fifteen to catch their bus to school. Every morning Hannah watched the clock on the factory wall. When it had turned nine o'clock and she had not been called into the office she took a long deep breath. She knew that by now the twins must have got to school OK other wise she would have been informed straight away if any thing had gone wrong

It did help that she finished and was home almost as soon as they were and on a Friday she was able to catch the same bus that they were travelling on. The work was extremely hard but she had no choice. She could not and would not do as George had suggested and have the children put into a home. She was going to keep them with her no matter how hard and rough that it was going to be.

Jim was coping very well considering how lonely that he was feeling. A week had passed since his Mother had last visited. He was still feeling confused about what she had referred to about little John not being his son. His mind had been in turmoil all week. Where had Sandra taken him to This Sunday he was going to do some finding out if he could? He had already rung Helen and her parents but they were as amazed as he was. He decided to get some fish and chips on the Saturday evening. He ordered and paid for what he had wanted and was walking to his car when a voice attracted his concentration.

"How are you mate? I thought you were going to book our big van to move the rest of your stuff". It was Joe who had moved Sandra's things to the flat.

"Don't know what you are talking about Joe"

"Well your missus told me that you would want us to take the rest of your things to Wellington or some where like that"

"She did, Did she And can you tell me where it is that you have taken her things? Because I am not moving any where"

"Oh aye I took her stuff to a flat in a big house over by Wem"

"Over by Wem. You have not by any chance got the address I could do with knowing that".

"Jim you don't mean to tell me what I think that you are about to tell me. That she has buggered off".

"Yes that is right and took the little lad with her. There is more to this and I want to find out what has been going on behind my back".

"Oh dear Jim I am so sorry. Not that a lot of us could take a liking to the woman. Funny kind of woman that she was, She always gave men the impression that she was free and easy. Well if you like I will get my supper and I can call in at the office and give you a ring as to where we have taken her. We have to keep records because the DHHS are paying us to move her"

"Oh are they indeed looks to me as if this has been well and truly planned. Thanks mate I will be glad of that address remind me to repay you the favour one day I will owe you one"

"Aye it's no trouble and if I can be of any help just let me know. Buggered off as she, well you can take it from me that there is some one else behind this you can bet your bottom dollar on it. By the way a fellow came with a grey van for her and some of the small stuff perhaps he can tell you more about it".

"A fellow with a grey van you say about forty with black hair." Joe nodded "That would be her brother-in – law but nothing seems to make much sense if that is the case. How the hell is he involved? Leave it with me Joe I am going to do a bit of finding out what has been going on behind my back".

Joe kept his word and rang with the address of Sandra's flat

On the following Sunday after Jim had fed the animals and had some lunch he took the car and drove to the address near Wem that Joe had given him. He parked the car in the yard and went to the flat but there was no answer. He waited for a while and then tried again. But still no answer. One of the other tenants had been watching and called out to him.

"I don't think Mrs Beddows is at home today. Who are you? You do seem a little lost if you don't mind my saying so. "Not really I believe that Mrs Beddows has taken a flat here .I am her husband and I am looking for her she has not been in touch".

"Well Mr Beddows she is hardly ever here. That nice man usually comes and takes her out some where we don't see much of her at all just lately it looks as if it won't be long before she moves out all together"

"Can you tell me what this fellow who comes for her looks like "

"Of course he is about forty good looking has nice black hair. Sorry Mr Beddows but you look as if you have just seen a ghost do come in and have a cup of tea I am sure that my husband will not mind"

"Every thing was beginning to click into place and Jim felt sick. "Yes thank you I could do with that cup of tea"

"Come in you are welcome. There sit your self down and tell us what has been going on".

Jim told the woman and her husband how he had come home to an empty house and she in turn told Jim of Sandra and of George' and the little boy on the Saturday. Yes that was the last time that we saw them she has only been back for one night last week as we know of."

Jim left the friendly couple thanking them for their hospitality. He was angry very angry, in fact he was seething with rage. How could she? How long had this been going on? His mind went back and back and then it dawned on him that she had set him up to take the blame for John. I'm off to see what she has to say for her self right now the conniving little bitch

He drove towards Wellington and on to the lane; Jim stopped the car outside the house and saw John playing in the yard.

And within seconds he saw Sandra roughly taking hold of him and disappearing into the house. She had seen his car stop and had guessed that there might be a row and she certainly did not want John to see Jim, he might make a fuss.

"Stay where you are "She said to George and keep John inside until he has gone"

"OK I think that it would be better if you went out to him than if I did." George was too scared to face Jim in case Jim hit him. He stayed in and watched from behind the living room curtain. But Jim had not missed seeing him standing there.

"What do you want coming here? You have a nerve". Sandra met Jim when he had got out of his car.

"Not much you evil conniving little bitch so that is what has been going on behind my back"

"So what if it has "Sandra was being so flippant.

"Just answer me one thing, was I used to cover up for that bastard that is standing there hiding behind the curtains".

"So what if you were there is nothing that you can do about it now. I want a divorce so you can just go back and start working on that," She sneered.

"The sooner the better as far as I am concerned. I am already looking to it." Jim said very calmly he did not want to lose his temper. He had now found out what had been going on.

Sandra continued "Yes you did cover up for George but now that he has got rid of Hannah we can now be together and there is nothing that any one can do about it. You are not John's father you never have been" The look that she now saw on Jim's face, she thought that he was about to strike her".

"Go on hit me and see where that will get you, the last time you hit me gave me just what I had wanted. Just get back in that car and bugger off back where you have come from and don't you ever come snooping around looking for me again or you will wish that you hadn't." She turned on her heels and went back inside.

"We won't be seeing him here again "She said to George and started to laugh.

Jim had no choice but to drive away. He called at the Willowmoors and told William all about what had happened. But he could see that neither William nor Sheila wanted to get involved. Oh yes they voiced their concerns for him and what they would like to do for Sandra and George but none of it was with in the law. Jim started to drive back home feeling so angry His Mother had been right She could see right through Sandra from the beginning and he had taken no notice of her advice, he was beginning to feel that he had let her down badly. He could not make up his mind whether to call and see her but then he thought better of it. He did not want to upset her at the moment, she was still very upset by what had happened as it was and she was still trying to come to terms with it. Jim wondered if he would feel any better if he went and got well and truly drunk. Then he decided against that idea his head felt as if he was already drunk. As he drove he was having so much difficulty concentrating on the road as it was. He almost drove in to the wood as he went down towards the Forest Glen. He was trying hard to digest what Sandra had told him and trying to come to terms with the fact that she had been seeing George before and after they had been married. He suddenly recalled the night of his wedding when George had taken her back to their cottage and that they had been so long away. Surely they had not planned that on his wedding night, surely. Yes they had every thing was all beginning to make much more sense. He had been well and truly taken for a mug. How could he make them pay for it he did not know? Tomorrow he would make an appointment to see a solicitor and start the ball rolling he made up his mind there and then to get rid of her as quickly as he could. Jim put his car in the yard at the back of the house and went inside. He switched the electric kettle on to boil so as to make himself a pot of tea. When it was brewed he sat down at the kitchen table to try and gather his wits together. He felt too sick to eat His belly could wait until tomorrow. He just could not comprehend what a fool that he had been or how deceitful that Sandra was capable of being. My God he said to him self, what an evil pair those two were and to think that they were going to get away with it.

Jim took advice and saw a solicitor only to be told that there was nothing that he could do about the debts that Sandra had left him to pay He was told that he must pay them because the bills were in his name. There was nothing at all that he could do about John not being his because he had accepted responsibility at the time of it taking place and had married the mother of the child. He was just advised to watch what was put in his pints of beer in future and to stay wide awake at parties that he went to and not drink him self into complete oblivion or there just might be a very high price to be paid. He went back home and sat and put his head in his hands and he had never in his life before felt such a very lonely and isolated man and oh boy oh boy was he angry at having been taken for such a ride. The wicked pair of buggers and they were getting away with it. The words that his father had said to him and his brothers and sister when they had been young came to his mind. His father believed in the church and had brought his family up to do the same. Jim sat and thought about it now and said to him self. Let's hope that it will be as my father always said. "That you will pay for your sins that you have committed on your fellow beings one way or another before you die, and only then you may enter into heaven.

About the Author

As stated in the two previous novels. She is very tenacious. She had in mind to write this novel some years ago, hopefully to be a benefit to other women and that they would not endure what she went through. After having some one read it with the prospect of publishing she was advised to write another novel to say more about the characters.

She was diagnosed with terminal cancer and was very poorly for quite along time. It was during this long haul back to reasonable health that she learned to use a computer and write the two previous novels. Also the painting with oils was very therapeutic.

Lightning Source UK Ltd.
Milton Keynes UK
21 April 2010

153162UK00001B/2/P

9 781449 044800